Michelle Paver was born in Malawi but has lived for most of her life in Wimbledon. After gaining a First in biochemistry at Oxford she became a lawyer, and was for five years a partner in a large City law firm. She has now given up the law to write full time. Her previous novels, *Without Charity*, *A Place in the Hills* and *The Shadow Catcher*, which is the first book of the Eden trilogy, are also published by Corgi Books.

Fever Hill is the second book of the Eden trilogy and the third book, *The Serpent's Tooth*, is now available in hardback from Bantam Press.

To find out more about Michelle Paver and her novels, visit her website at www.michellepaver.com

Also by Michelle Paver

WITHOUT CHARITY
A PLACE IN THE HILLS
THE SHADOW CATCHER

and published by Corgi Books

FEVER HILL

Michelle Paver

CORGI BOOKS

FEVER HLL
A CORGI BOOK : 0 552 77126 0

Originally published in Great Britain by Bantam Press,
a division of Transworld Publishers

PRINTING HISTORY
Bantam Press edition published 2004
Corgi edition published 2005

1 3 5 7 9 10 8 6 4 2

Set in 11/12pt Sabon by
Falcon Oast Graphic Art Ltd.

Corgi Books are published by Transworld Publishers,
61–63 Uxbridge Road, London W5 5SA,
a division of The Random House Group Ltd,
in Australia by Random House Australia (Pty) Ltd,
20 Alfred Street, Milsons Point, Sydney, NSW 2061, Australia,
in New Zealand by Random House New Zealand Ltd,
18 Poland Road, Glenfield, Auckland 10, New Zealand
and in South Africa by Random House (Pty) Ltd,
Endulini, 5a Jubilee Road, Parktown 2193, South Africa.

Printed and bound in Great Britain by
Cox & Wyman Ltd, Reading, Berkshire

Papers used by Transworld Publishers are natural, recyclable
products made from wood grown in sustainable forests. The
manufacturing processes conform to the environmental
regulations of the country of origin.

FEVER HILL

PART ONE

JAMAICA 1903

CHAPTER ONE

The doctors said she had tuberculosis, and blamed it on invisible creatures called 'bacilli', but Sophie knew better.

She was ill because the duppy tree was trying to kill her. The washerwoman's little girl had told her so, and Evie knew all about things like that, for her mother was a witch.

The following year when Sophie was twelve, she recovered. But she still had bad dreams about duppy trees. So one night her brother-in-law took her up into the hills to meet one. Cameron rode his big bay gelding, and Sophie her new pony Puck, and when they reached the great tree in the glade on Overlook Hill they sat on the folded roots, and ate the fried plantain and johnny cake which Madeleine had packed for them. Sophie felt scared, but safe, because Cameron was with her.

And as she sat beside him in the blue moonlight, she watched the little lizards darting up and down the enormous trunk, and the fireflies blinking in the leaves; she listened to the whirr of the mango-bugs and the ringing pulse of the crickets; and Cameron said, 'Look, Sophie, there's a yellowsnake,' and she glimpsed a tail disappearing behind a root.

She thought about all the small animal lives sheltering in the branches above her head, and realized that she must have been mistaken about the tree wanting to kill her. And after that she wasn't scared of duppy trees any more.

Instead, she became passionately interested in them, and tried to grow one in a pot.

'Sophie's making one of her about-turns,' said Cameron with a laugh. And Maddy smiled at him, and helped her little sister to find a place for the potted duppy tree on the verandah, where it gradually died.

Then Maddy said, what about growing something which grows *on* duppy trees, instead? So they bought a book on Jamaican orchids, and Cameron took Sophie into the forest behind the house to find her first specimens.

Thinking of that now as the train rattled through the hill pastures on its way to Montego Bay, Sophie felt a sudden uprush of love for them both – and a tug of concern. She needed to see for herself that they were happy and well. She needed to dispel the vague impression which she'd gathered from Maddy's last letter that something wasn't quite right.

Pushing the thought aside, she turned her head and watched the pastures slipping past. Acid-green guinea grass rippled in the wind, dotted with ambling white Hindu cattle. On a dusty red track a black woman carried a basket of yams on her head with easy grace.

I'm home, thought Sophie. She still couldn't believe it. For three years she had dreamed of coming back to Jamaica. She'd been dizzy with homesickness every time another letter arrived from Eden. Then suddenly it all seemed to happen in the blink of an eye. School was over, and she was on her way out from Southampton. Now, here she was on the last leg of the journey. Kingston was far behind them, and Spanish Town and Four Paths. Such well-loved names. The hours she had spent as a child, lying on the Turkey rug in her grandfather's study at Fever Hill, gazing up at the great tinted map.

On the opposite seat, Mr van Rieman cleared his throat. 'According to this,' he said, tapping the journal in his hand, 'the Jamaican sugar planter is fast becoming an endangered species. It says that since the slaves were freed, hundreds of plantations have been turned over to cattle, or simply abandoned.' He regarded Sophie over his wire-rimmed spectacles, his small eyes bright with the pleasure of finding fault. 'I take it, Miss Monroe, that such will not be the fate of your brother-in-law's estate?'

She shook her head and smiled. 'Somehow Cameron always manages to keep Eden afloat.'

'Indeed,' said Mr van Rieman, looking slightly put out.

'Eden,' said Mrs van Rieman brightly. 'What a lovely name.'

Sophie threw her a grateful look, and almost forgave the fact that for most of the journey the Americans' small, baleful son Theo had been surreptitiously kicking her leg whenever his mamma wasn't looking.

The train pulled into Appleton for the lunchtime stop, and they stepped stiffly down into the blaze of the November sun. Jamaica broke over them like a wave. Pickneys raced about between people's legs. Higglers crowded the platform, plying their wares. *Butter-dough! Paradise plums! All sort a mango! Paperskin, Christmas, cherry-cheek!*

Sophie breathed in the spicy scent of the red dust, and the familiar rhythms of *patois*. Mrs van Rieman clutched her husband's arm and bemoaned his choice of holiday destination. She'd never seen so many darkies in her life.

Mr van Rieman led the way to the Station Hotel with the air of a missionary tackling darkest Africa. Twice he voiced his astonishment that Jamaica possessed no proper guidebook of its own. Plainly any country which lacked its own Baedeker hadn't yet dragged itself clear of the swamp of barbarism.

Luncheon was awkward, with the van Riemans questioning Sophie in ringing tones, while the rest of the dining-room listened with open ears. Sophie swallowed her pride and answered as best she could, for the Americans had been kind to her when they'd met in the ticket office at Kingston – albeit politely appalled at the notion of a young lady of nineteen travelling alone.

'If I have this right, Miss Monroe,' said Mrs van Rieman, 'you're ten years younger than your sister, who has two darling little children?'

Sophie's mouth was full of pepperpot, so she could only nod.

'And what about you?' said Mrs van Rieman with an arch twinkle. 'Any sweethearts yet?'

Sophie gave her a fixed smile. 'No,' she replied. A woman at the adjacent table threw her a pitying glance.

'Miss Monroe is above such trivial concerns,' put in Mr van Rieman with ponderous wit. 'Miss Monroe is a *bluestocking*! She intends to *study medicine*.'

'I'm only thinking about it,' said Sophie quickly. 'There's a clinic near my brother-in-law's estate, and I thought I'd try to get some experience there, and see if I like it.' She flushed. There was no need to tell them all that. But she always talked too much when she was embarrassed. It was one of her besetting sins.

'I believe you spent your early childhood in London?' said Mrs van Rieman. 'Then you came out to Jamaica, as you had family here?'

Again Sophie nodded. Then, because she was nearly home and feeling a little reckless, she said, 'Also I was ill, and Maddy thought the tropics would do me good. I had TB.'

There was a small silence.

'Tuberculosis,' repeated Mr van Rieman with a ponderous nod. His wife put her hand to her throat. The other diners applied themselves to their food.

'Tuberculosis of the knee,' Sophie explained. 'That's what made me interested in medicine. But I've been free of it for the past seven years. There's no danger of infection.'

'Of course not,' said Mrs van Rieman faintly.

The waiter arrived with a bowl of fruit. Sophie reached for a naseberry, and little Theo made to do the same. His mother snatched his hand away. She gave Sophie a nervous smile. 'Too acid,' she murmured.

Sophie wished she'd pleaded a headache and stayed on the train. Or at least kept quiet.

Beside her, Theo kicked the table leg in a repetitive tattoo. 'Did you have a splint?' he said loudly.

'Theo, hush,' whispered his mother.

'But *did* you?'

'Yes,' said Sophie. 'A big clumpy iron one that I had to wear all the time for two years. I hated it.'

'Were you always falling over?' said Theo with a hint of contempt.

'Not to begin with, because I wasn't allowed to get up. I had to lie on the verandah and read. After that I had crutches. Then I fell over.'

'Do you limp?'

'*Theo!*' said Mrs van Rieman.

'No,' lied Sophie. In fact she did limp a little, when she was tired or self-conscious. But she wasn't going to tell that to the entire Station Hotel. They were already feeling sorry enough for her as it was: the sickly, bookish younger sister without a sweetheart.

'If you never took the splint off,' said Theo, 'how did you wash?'

'That's enough,' snapped Mrs van Rieman, and the subject was dropped.

As they rejoined the train, Sophie considered offering to move to another compartment. But she guessed that that would only embarrass the van Riemans. So instead they all settled back into their seats with self-conscious smiles, and Sophie gazed out of the window and longed for home.

Gradually, the cattle pastures gave way to cane-pieces. They were in sugar country now, and the heavy scent of molasses drifted in through the window.

Someone's starting crop-time early, she thought. She breathed in deeply. The smell of home.

The familiar names flashed past. Ginger Hill, Seven Rivers, Catadupa. And far in the distance, she glimpsed the eerie blue-grey humps of the Cockpits: a harsh wilderness of treacherous sink-holes and oddly conical hills which had fascinated her as a child. Her pulse quickened. On the other side of the Cockpits, with its face to the sea, lay Eden.

The train halted at Montpelier for the final rest-stop, scarcely ten miles from Montego Bay. Mr van Rieman hurried off to the third-class compartment to consult his courier, and Mrs van Rieman went inside the station building to use the facilities, leaving her son – plainly with some misgivings – with Sophie.

They waited at the top of the station steps in the shade of a big silk-cotton tree, and watched the small-town bustle and the ox-wagons trundling past, piled high with sugar cane. Then Theo resumed the attack. 'How *did* you wash?' he said with quiet insolence.

'I didn't,' said Sophie without turning her head.

Theo digested that. 'I bet that's an untruth,' he muttered. Sophie did not reply.

'I don't *like* Jamaica,' said Theo.

'I'm not surprised,' Sophie replied. 'It's a very frightening place for a little boy.'

'I don't mean that I'm scared,' retorted Theo.

'Well, you should be. Jamaica's full of ghosts.'

Theo blinked.

'Some of them live in caves in the hills,' she said calmly, 'but mostly they live in trees like this one behind you.'

Theo jumped. 'You're making that up,' he said belligerently. 'It's just an old tree.'

'Actually it's not, it's a duppy tree. Ask anyone. Duppy is Jamaican for ghost. D'you see the folds in the trunk? That's where they live. They come out at night and make people ill.'

Theo swallowed.

She was beginning to enjoy herself. 'I used to believe that a duppy tree was making *me* ill,' she went on. 'But then a very brave little boy sorted things out for me, and after that I got better.'

Theo looked pale but defiant. '*How* brave?'

'Extremely. He was a street urchin from London, and he swore all the time.'

'What was he called?'

'Ben.'

'What happened to him?'

'Nobody knows. After he dealt with the duppy tree he was never seen again.'

Theo thought about that. 'Did it get him?'

'Quite possibly,' said Sophie.

Theo's shoulders were hunched, and he was staring wide-eyed at the silk-cotton tree. Sophie nearly relented and told him that in fact the urchin had been spotted shortly afterwards, working as a cabin boy on a coastal steamer. But then she remembered those surreptitious kicks, and hardened her heart.

'What did he look like?' mumbled Theo, scarcely moving his lips.

'Who?'

'The street boy who disappeared. Ben.'

She shrugged. 'Like a street boy.'

Across the road, a young groom jumped down from his carriage to check the harness on his horses. Something about the way he moved reminded her of Ben.

Strange the way memory works. She hadn't thought about him in ages, and now suddenly she could almost see him. Thin as an alley cat, with filthy black hair and a grimy, sharp-featured face, and narrow green eyes. The ten-year-old Sophie had been captivated. And desperate to impress him.

'You know an awful lot about Jamaica,' said Theo humbly.

She felt another twinge of remorse. 'Actually,' she said, 'there's one thing I forgot to tell you about duppies and duppy trees. They never attack Americans. It's against the rules.'

Theo looked up at her uncertainly. 'But how will they know that I *am* American?'

'They can always tell.'

He nodded, and some of the colour returned to his lips.

'Come along,' said Sophie, 'let's find your mamma.' But as she took his hand and turned to go, she glanced back over her shoulder at the young groom. His master and mistress were approaching down the street, and he was waiting for them. Suddenly Sophie's heart lifted. The young groom's master and mistress were Madeleine and Cameron.

She forgot the proprieties and yelled her sister's name. '*Maddy!* Cameron! Over here!'

They didn't hear her. And at that moment a wagon laden with sugar cane trundled down the street and hid them from view.

She let go of Theo and picked up her skirts and ran down the station steps to the edge of the street. Impatiently she waited while the oxen plodded past. And as the red dust slowly cleared, she saw them across the street: beautiful, unmistakable Maddy, with her luxuriant black hair piled beneath a wide straw hat, and her magnificent figure swathed in her favourite bronze silk dust-coat. She was leaning on Cameron's arm, and he was bending over her, and she was wiping her eyes and nodding, and trying to smile.

Sophie opened her mouth to call again – then shut it. Something was wrong. Maddy looked upset.

At that moment Cameron turned to speak to the groom, and Sophie saw with a jolt that it wasn't Cameron at all. Cameron was tall and broad-shouldered and in his early forties, with unruly fair hair and features that could never be called refined, but that possessed great strength and undeniable charm. The man to whom her sister was clinging – *clinging* – was also fair-haired, but much slighter and more delicate, and only in his late twenties, like Maddy herself. Sophie had never seen him before in her life.

Her thoughts darted. Something must have happened to Cameron. Something was terribly wrong.

'Miss Monroe?' said Mrs van Rieman, coming up behind her. 'The train is about to leave . . . Is something wrong?'

Sophie turned and tried to say something, but her words were drowned out by another ox-wagon. And when she looked back, and the dust had settled again, the carriage and groom and the fair-haired young gentleman and her sister had gone.

Suddenly she was desperate to get to Montego Bay. But as Mr van Rieman informed her with grim pleasure, the train was delayed. A wagon had overturned just outside Montpelier, spilling its load of logwood across the tracks. It would take at least half an hour to clear.

As Sophie paced up and down outside the train, she talked herself out of panic. After all, there couldn't be anything seriously wrong, or Maddy would have sent her a wire. Wouldn't she?

At last, after nearly forty-five minutes, they got under way again, and the train began its lumbering descent towards the plains of the north coast. They trundled through acre on acre of green cane-fields shimmering in the breeze. Sophie counted the minutes till they would reach their destination.

Mrs van Rieman exclaimed with pleasure at the view of Montego Bay spread out below them – at the tidy red-roofed houses and the royal palms, and the glittering turquoise sea. Sophie hardly saw it. Surely, *surely* Maddy and Cameron would be waiting at the station, just as they'd promised? And perhaps the delicate-featured young man would be with them too, and it would all be cleared up. Surely it would be cleared up.

They drew into the station in a cloud of dust and steam. The platform was thronged with higglers of every shade of black and brown, and poor Mrs van Rieman softly shrieked at Theo to *stay close*, and barely registered Sophie's muttered thanks and hasty leavetaking.

Then suddenly there they were – *both* of them. Her knees nearly buckled with relief. There was Maddy in her bronze silk dust-coat, pushing her way up the platform steps with a brilliant smile on her lovely face – and here was Cameron coming forward and sweeping Sophie off the ground in a hug. The delicate-featured young gentleman was nowhere to be seen.

'*What* a relief!' cried Sophie, when Cameron had set her down and she could breathe again. She turned to Maddy. 'I saw you at Montpelier. I shouted, but you were gone before I could catch your eye.'

'Montpelier?' said Maddy, laughing as she stooped to free her dust-coat from the wheels of a passing trolley.

'Sorry, but it wasn't me. Cameron, would you tell the porter to be careful with that? If I know Sophie, it'll be stuffed full of books, and weigh a ton.'

'But Maddy,' said Sophie, astonished, 'I saw you.'

Madeleine straightened up and looked at her in amusement. 'So now I've got a double up at Montpelier, have I? How very exciting.'

'But—'

'Sophie, I've been shopping in Montego Bay all afternoon. Now come along. You must be exhausted. And there's so much to talk about. I can't believe it – *three years*! We've planned it all out. Cameron's riding behind, so we'll have the dog cart to ourselves. And Braverly's making a special dinner, and the children are staying up for a treat. They're absolutely wild with excitement. Come *along*!'

CHAPTER TWO

She awoke at daybreak with a dragging tiredness, and a sense of unease that wouldn't be reasoned away.

She opened her eyes and drew back the mosquito curtain, and lay watching the sunlight warming the terracotta floor tiles. She listened to the soft slap of the servants' canvas slippers, and the chatter of the grassquits beneath the eaves. She breathed in the mingled scents of beeswax, jasmine and woodsmoke. It was the smell of Eden: reassuring, but now obscurely threatened.

Stop worrying, she told herself. Just enjoy being home.

She remembered when she used to wake up in this same room at dawn, and slip down to the river to meet her best friend Evie, who had run up through the cane-pieces from Fever Hill. They would go off to one of their secret places in the woods, and ask the spirits to get rid of Evie's freckles, and keep the bacilli out of Sophie's knee, and watch over Ben Kelly, wherever he was.

She turned and pressed her face into the pillow. Why think of him now? It was as if her thoughts were determined to revert to the unresolved and the unexplained. The boy who'd briefly been her friend, and then left without saying goodbye. The sister who was behaving so inexplicably.

She got out of bed and went to the window, flexing the stiffness out of her knee. Her room looked east, over a jungle of huge-leaved philodendron and wild almond trees, towards the stables at the bottom of the slope. Through the green-gold fronds of a tree-fern beneath the eaves, she saw Cameron mount his horse and give a last word to Moses the groom. He wore his usual riding-breeches, shooting-jacket and topboots, and looked as he always did: hurried and untidy, but utterly capable. Surely, she thought, he'd show it if something were wrong?

Turning back to the room, she saw with what care her sister had prepared it for her return. There were new curtains of blue and white dimity, and a desk amply stocked with paper and ink; a wash-hand stand with eau de Cologne and rosewater, and, on a shelf, a substantial pile of books.

It was a motley collection, assembled with respectful incomprehension by someone who'd never acquired a taste for reading herself. A Thomas Hardy; Carlyle's history, *The French Revolution*; a volume on Florence Nightingale. Madeleine must have raided their grand-father's collection at Fever Hill. Surely such thoughtfulness could not have been motivated by guilt?

And touchingly, Madeleine had brought up the great map of the Northside from Jocelyn's study, and hung it where it could be seen from the bed. As Sophie climbed back under the covers, she could almost hear her grand-father's sharp, no-nonsense voice telling her tales of the family history. How Benneit Monroe and his friend Nathaniel Lawe had come out to Jamaica to fight the Spanish in 1655, and then carved up the Northside between them. Benneit Monroe had taken the land to the west of Falmouth, and Nat Lawe – Cameron's ancestor – that to the east. And, as Jocelyn never tired of telling her, they had always retained their properties back 'home': the Lawes' estate in Dumfriesshire, and the Monroes' great staring barracks at Strathnaw – which Sophie knew only from the grim yet fascinating oil painting behind Jocelyn's desk.

As a child she'd wanted a happy ending to the fairytale: an assurance that everything remained unchanged 'to this very day'. She'd been dismayed to learn that after the great slave rebellion of 1832 the fortunes of the Lawes had dwindled, until they'd been forced to sell first Burntwood, then Arethusa, and finally the estate back 'home'.

'But Cameron has stopped the rot,' Jocelyn would say, with a gleam of pride in his fierce, sun-bleached eyes.

'But what about us?' Sophie would say with a frown. 'There aren't any boy Monroes left, are there? Only Maddy and me, so—'

'So what?' snapped Jocelyn. 'When I'm gone, you shall have Fever Hill, and Madeleine shall have Strathnaw. That's what counts.'

'But—'

'Sophie, at the best one doesn't get to see further than the next couple of generations. The land remains in the family. That's good enough for me.'

Perhaps for him, but not for her. She'd wanted permanence. But it seemed that, even with land, permanence could never be guaranteed.

She thought about that now as she lay in bed, trying to summon up the sound of her grandfather's voice. It didn't seem possible that there was no Jocelyn Monroe waiting for her at Fever Hill.

And it didn't seem possible that Madeleine was deceiving Cameron. She loved him, and he loved her. There must be some other, quite innocent explanation. Maddy had gone to Montpelier to buy him a secret birthday present. Or – or something.

She turned on her side, and met the eyes of her mother, gazing at her from the faded daguerreotype in its leather travelling frame.

Rose Durrant had been darkly beautiful, like Maddy, and had died when Sophie was born. Sophie knew her only through gossip and family legend. Permanence? Stability? Rose Durrant had snapped her fingers at all that. She had flouted convention and ruined lives – including her own – by running off to Scotland with Jocelyn's married son and heir.

Sophie gazed into her mother's wilful, long-dead eyes.

The trouble with the Durrants, a family friend had once told her, *is that they always went too far*.

Had Maddy inherited more from her mother than her striking good looks and her talent for photography? Had she also gone too far?

Turning that over in her mind, she fell asleep. But in her dreams it wasn't her harsh, loving, utterly dependable grandfather who visited her, but reckless, secretive Rose Durrant.

When she awoke again it was nearly noon, and the dawn freshness had given way to heat. The house felt empty and quiet, but she could hear Madeleine calling to the children in the garden.

She dressed hurriedly and went out into the big raftered hall which served as sitting-room, dining-room and general dumping-ground.

In the flurry of last night's arrival she'd hardly noticed her surroundings, but now she saw with dismay how much shabbier everything had become. The huge old mahogany table still showed the water-stains from when Cameron had first lived here as a bachelor beneath a leaky roof. And along with the usual clutter on the sideboard – a hurricane lamp with a chipped glass shade, a child's velveteen zebra (missing one ear) – was a pile of sheets awaiting turning. Clearly money at Eden remained as scarce as ever.

That was partly her fault. Madeleine and Cameron had sacrificed a lot when they'd sent her to the college at Cheltenham, although they'd never said a word about it. The only thanks she'd been able to give was to invent pre-texts for staying in England over the holidays, in order to save the passage back to Jamaica.

She looked about her at the great, shabby, golden room. Her Goldilocks house, she used to call it, for everything at Eden had always seemed just right.

Compared with many a Jamaican great house, it was small, with only a single storey of living quarters over an undercroft of storerooms and Madeleine's darkroom. Bedrooms, the nursery, and Cameron's study were arranged around the central sitting-room, while a loggia on the south-east side led out to the bath-house and the cookhouse beyond.

As a child, Sophie had thought it the very pattern of what a house should be. It was never too hot and never too cold, for it stood seven hundred feet above the plains, and caught the sea breezes during the day, and the land breezes off the hills at night. Her Goldilocks house.

She frowned. Maybe it was the dream still clinging to her, but this morning she could see only the shabbiness and decay.

And there was something else, too. Eden had been built by a Durrant. One drunken night in 1817, Rose's great-grandfather had ridden up into the virgin forest, and vowed to build a mansion here.

Who else but a Durrant would have carved out an estate at the edge of the Cockpits? Who else but a Durrant would have failed so dismally at being a planter that he'd been forced to abandon it again to the forest?

By the time Cameron had bought the estate in 1886, Eden had been a ruin for over twenty years. As a child, Sophie had often tried to picture it as it must have been then: beautiful, mysterious and other-worldly as it slipped gently back into the past, its fretwork window shades crumbling like tattered lace, its high panelled rooms silently overtaken by creepers and strangler fig.

To a child it had been a fairytale image, but now she perceived the latent threat. Was Madeleine more of a Durrant than a Monroe? Was that where she got her flair for secrecy?

She went out onto the verandah, and found her sister sitting on one of the big cane sofas, mending a cushion cover.

Madeleine looked up at her and smiled. Then she caught her expression, and the smile wavered. She glanced down at the cushion cover, and smoothed it out over her knee. 'Braverly saved you some breakfast,' she said. 'But it'll be time for lunch soon, so I expect you'd rather wait?'

Sophie nodded and said that would be fine.

'And you're not going to like this,' said Madeleine, biting off a thread, 'but I've accepted an invitation to a tea party at the Trahernes'. I know it's a bore on your first day, but Sibella wanted to welcome you home. Well, that's what she said. Actually I think she wants to ask you to be her bridesmaid. I hope you don't mind?'

I hope you don't mind? Since when had Maddy been so polite with her? 'Not at all,' she said, hearing her own false politeness with disbelief. 'It'll be nice to see her again.'

She looked about her at the wide verandah with its simple roof of cedar shingles. At least out here nothing had changed. There was the bird-feeder hanging in the doorway to Madeleine and Cameron's room. He'd put it up in the early days of their marriage, so that Maddy could watch the hummingbirds as she lay in bed. There were the tartan cushions which she herself had helped to sew: red and green for the Monroes, and blue and yellow for the Lawes. She remembered furious cushion-fights with the dogs, with Madeleine and Cameron both laughing too hard to protest.

It's all just the same, she thought, and inside her the knot of worry fractionally loosened. There can't be anything truly wrong. There must be some explanation that you've simply missed.

She turned and looked out over the garden. From where she stood, a graceful double curve of white marble steps swept down to the rough green lawn. The grass at the foot of the steps was trampled and brown, for although the front door was at the other side of the house, everyone always rode round to the steps to tether their horses.

All just the same.

Down in the garden, hummingbirds flashed and hovered in a jungle of tree-ferns and hibiscus. She caught the brilliant orange and cobalt of strelitzia, and the cloudy blue of plumbago. At the bottom of the lawn, the Martha Brae slid by between banks overhung with scarlet heliconia and giant bamboo. Beyond it, past the shimmering green of the cane-pieces and the red slash of the Eden road winding towards Falmouth, she glimpsed the far-off glitter of the sea.

With both hands she gripped the sun-hot balustrade. 'Cameron was out early,' she said.

Madeleine sighed. 'Actually, that was late for him. These days I hardly see him. I hate to think what it'll be like at crop-time.'

'But I thought he'd got a manager for Fever Hill.'

'He has, Oserius Parker. But you know Cameron. He has to see things done for himself, or he can't relax.'

'But that isn't his fault, is it?' Sophie said over her shoulder.

Madeleine threw her a surprised glance. 'Of course not. I wasn't criticizing him.'

Sophie nodded. Below her on a banana leaf, a small green lizard regarded her with a swivelled and ancient eye.

'Sophie,' Madeleine said quietly, 'you don't need to worry.'

Sophie turned and met her sister's eyes. 'Then why won't you tell me what you were doing in Montpelier?'

Madeleine sighed. 'Because I wasn't in Montpelier.'

'But—'

'Sophie. Enough.' They locked gazes. Then Madeleine shook her head, as if to dispel a disagreeable thought, and went back to her sewing. 'As I said,' she muttered, 'you don't need to worry.'

Angrily, Sophie turned back to the garden.

Down by the river she caught a flash of red. Belle – small, determined, and dark as her mother – emerged from the bamboo, sneezing and rubbing dust from her eyes. She wore a pinafore dress of scarlet twill which her mother said was indestructible, and easy to spot. A flash of blue sailor suit, and six-year-old Fraser, tall and fair like his father, exploded after his little sister, closely followed by a mastiff puppy with flapping caramel-coloured ears. They were happy children growing up in a happy, secure home. If Madeleine was doing anything to threaten that, Sophie would never forgive her.

The next instant she felt mean and disloyal for even

thinking such a thing. 'You've got a new dog,' she remarked, to make amends.

'That's Scout,' said Madeleine, sounding relieved that they'd moved onto neutral ground. 'He's a pest, but the children adore him.'

'Where's Abigail?'

'Fast asleep in the undercroft. She's never quite forgiven Cameron for exiling her from our bedroom.'

Sophie drew a circle on the balustrade. 'Yesterday at Montpelier—'

'Oh, Sophie, do stop.'

'– I saw someone who looked like Ben.'

Madeleine blinked. 'Which Ben?'

'Our Ben. Ben Kelly. From years ago.'

Madeleine looked down at her sewing. 'Good heavens. Well, don't mention that to Cameron, will you?'

'Why not?' said Sophie sharply.

'Surely you remember? He never did understand how we could've been friends with a boy of that – sort.'

'Is that the real reason you don't want me to mention it?'

'Of course,' snapped Madeleine. 'What's the *matter* with you?'

There was an edgy silence.

Down in the garden, Belle erupted shrieking from the croton bushes, her sunhat flapping as she raced across the lawn with Scout at her heels. Still shrieking, she launched herself at a rope swing which hung between two wild lime trees.

Sophie watched Madeleine's needle flashing in and out, and thought how strange it was that they never talked of Ben, or of the old days in London; or of Cousin Lettice, the grim little martinet who had brought them up. Nor did Madeleine speak of her childhood in Scotland, or their parents or their early days at Fever Hill, or the two fine scars which encircled her wrists, and which she always concealed with a pair of narrow silver bracelets.

Sophie had always supposed that it was because she talked to Cameron about such things. Now she wondered if Madeleine talked – really talked – to anyone. She'd always had a talent for secrecy. That was how she'd survived.

In the pony-trap the night before, they had chattered without drawing breath all the way home, while Cameron rode beside them, listening and smiling the almost-smile which was habitual with him. But looking back on it now, Sophie realized that in fact it was she who had done most of the talking, while Madeleine herself had said very little.

Down on the lawn, Belle had fallen off the swing and bumped her knee. She sat hunched on the ground, peering at her leg for signs of blood. Her brother bent over and told her not to be such a muff, and Scout pushed in his nose and got in the way.

Sophie watched Madeleine imperturbably biting off another thread, and felt a pang of unease. She was so very like their mother. That glossy black hair, those beautiful dark eyes; the extravagantly curved red mouth. *A secretive lot, the Durrants. And they always went too far.*

For lunch, Braverly had surpassed himself in Sophie's honour. Baked black land-crabs with rice and peas; puréed sweet potatoes and an avocado salad; and to follow, his famous coconut pudding, flecked with flakes of pounded vanilla and laced with golden rum from Eden's own distillery at the Maputah works.

Somewhat to her relief, she didn't get a chance to ask any more questions. Cameron was back, and the children had pestered Madeleine until they were allowed to eat with their aunt Sophie.

'When you were in England,' said Belle, 'did you see the King?'

'Can one really eat snow?' asked Fraser.

'How big *is* the Koh-i-noor diamond?'

It wasn't until Poppy the nursemaid had taken them off for their nap and the coffee had been brought out onto the verandah that conversation became possible. But even then, a state of armed peace prevailed between Sophie and her sister.

And yet whose fault is that? she thought with exasperated affection, as she took her cup from Madeleine's hand and watched her valiantly trying to paper over the cracks.

'I meant to ask you,' said Madeleine, raising her eyebrows in the way that people do to signify interest in something utterly trivial, 'did you remember to order your calling cards?'

'Ah,' said Sophie, raising her eyebrows in her turn. 'I'm afraid I forgot.'

Cameron lit a cigar and leaned back in his chair, and glanced from one to the other.

'Oh well,' said Madeleine brightly, 'you can borrow some of mine. We can send a wire to Gardner's, and ask them to make you a priority.'

'Yes,' said Sophie, 'let's.' My God, she thought, we sound like characters in a play. This is Maddy. *Maddy*. What's happening?

'I know it's a bore,' said Madeleine, not meeting her eyes, 'but there are all sorts of duty calls that you'll simply have to make.'

Obediently, Sophie nodded.

'The Mordenners and the Palairets,' said Madeleine, 'and old Mrs Pitcaithley and Olivia Herapath. And Great-Aunt May. That'll be a trial, I know, but you can't possibly not.'

'No, no, of course.'

'And then there's Clemency. Though she can hardly be called a duty.'

'How is she?' said Sophie.

'Much worse, I'm afraid. Not even Cameron can do anything with her. Perhaps you can work a miracle.'

'Mm,' said Sophie. 'Or perhaps,' she added, on the spur of the moment, 'she could move out of Fever Hill and come and live with us? I mean, she can't go on in that great barracks all alone.'

'Of course she can't,' said Cameron, 'but you try getting her out.'

Sophie set down her spoon. 'What if I sold it?' she said suddenly. 'Then she'd have to move.'

There was a silence. Madeleine looked at her in horror. Cameron merely looked.

Until she'd said it, she hadn't even known that it was in her mind. And she didn't know why it occurred to her now – except perhaps that if Clemency moved in with them, there'd be one more person to distract Maddy, and keep her away from that delicate-featured young gentleman in Montpelier.

'But you're not going to sell it,' Cameron said calmly.

'No,' said Sophie, 'but I could. I mean, it's just an idea. And Eden needs the money—'

'No we don't,' he said.

'– and then – then you wouldn't have to work so hard. And Maddy,' she took a breath that was almost a gulp, 'well, she wouldn't be on her own all the time.'

'What on earth are you talking about?' said Madeleine sharply.

'It was just an idea,' muttered Sophie.

'But Sophie,' said Cameron, coming to her rescue, 'even if you wanted to sell, what sort of guardian would I be if I let you squander your inheritance before you came of age?'

Sophie smiled. 'Isn't that rather Victorian?'

He laughed. 'Of course it is. But then, I am a Victorian.'

'Can we please talk of something else?' snapped Madeleine.

There was another awkward silence.

Madeleine put the little beaded cover over the milk jug to keep off the flies, and shooed Scout away from the coffee tray, and told Belle, who was just creeping down the steps at the far end of the verandah, to go back to bed at once and take her nap. Then she took up her cup and stirred her coffee rather fast.

Cameron flicked a sugar-ant off his knee, leaned back in his chair and studied the horizon with a distant frown which said that he was well aware that there was some kind of tension between the sisters, but that he wasn't fool enough to get caught in the crossfire.

When the silence had gone on long enough, Madeleine smoothed her skirts over her knees, and got to her feet. 'Well,' she said briskly. 'I must go and dress. The Trahernes expect us at four.'

Half an hour later, Sophie was battling with the bodice of her afternoon gown when a button popped off and shot across the room.

God, why was everything going wrong? She couldn't even fasten a wretched dress.

She threw herself onto the bed, feeling hot and disgruntled and angry with herself. She and Maddy never fought. And they never, ever had these arms'-length silences, these evasions and coverings-up.

In the looking-glass, her reflection glared back at her. An untidy cloud of light brown hair – the colour of dust, she thought in disgust – and dust-coloured eyes, and mannish dark brows, and a too-wide mouth that was prone to turn sulky when she was tired.

And now, to add insult to injury, this wretched, wretched dress. It had been a mistake not to have ordered a new gown in England while she had the chance. This pale green foulard would not, as she had blithely told herself, do for another year. It wouldn't do at all. It made her look sallow and bony, and the bodice pulled at the neck.

'*God!*' she cried, giving it another tug.

There was a knock at the door, and Maddy put her head round. 'May I come in?'

Sophie stood up and turned to face her, and flapped her arms at her sides. 'It's awful, isn't it?'

Madeleine tilted her head and looked her up and down. 'You always exaggerate.'

'Not this time,' said Sophie.

'Yes, this time. You've buttoned it wrong at the back. That's why it's pulling.'

Sophie blew out a long breath.

Madeleine turned her round and started adjusting the buttons. 'You're missing one, too.'

'I know. It went under the wardrobe.'

'Ah. Well, in a minute you can fetch it and I'll sew it back on.'

As Sophie stood waiting for her to finish, she thought of all the times in the past when her sister had fixed things for her. The broken reins for the beloved toy donkey. The ripped cover of the birthday journal. The over-large nose-band which she'd knitted with scowling incompetence for her pony, and Maddy had somehow made to fit. Years and years of making things better.

What did it matter if she'd lied about Montpelier? What did it matter?

'There,' said Madeleine, giving her a little pat. 'Now all we've got to do is sew on that button.'

CHAPTER THREE

'If I know Rebecca Traherne,' whispered Madeleine as they followed the butler across the echoing marble ball-room, 'it'll be irreproachably English. You'll see. We could be at a tea party in Kent.'

'Except for the servants,' murmured Sophie, as they passed a tall black footman in the house livery of azure and silver.

To her surprise, she found herself battling nerves. She'd forgotten how grand the great house at Parnassus actually was. An enormous three-storeyed pile of golden cut-stone, it dominated the Coast Road into Falmouth, staring down from acres of Italian gardens and French parterres. The contrast with Eden couldn't have been starker. But if Madeleine or Cameron was aware of that, they gave no sign.

Just before they reached the gallery, Madeleine stopped and gave Sophie a quick, searching glance. 'I know you hate these sorts of things. Are you going to be all right?'

Sophie was touched. 'I'll be fine.'

'Just remember that everyone's in awe of you because you're so clever, and went to school in England.'

Sophie glanced at her in surprise. It had come out so readily that she wondered if Madeleine herself felt something of the same. 'Well I'm in awe of them too,' she replied, 'because they're all so beautiful and well-dressed.'

Madeleine gave a wry snort.

It was too hot for tea in the grounds, so the little gilt tables had been set out in the great south gallery, which had been transformed into an artificial garden of potted orange trees and ferns. It was cool, civilized and, as Madeleine had predicted, quintessentially English. Rebecca Traherne had a horror of appearing vulgar, and eschewed anything Jamaican in favour of importations from 'home'.

Thus the china was Wedgwood, the tea had been shipped out from Fortnum's, and the shortbread had been made to a traditional receipt belonging to Mrs Herapath's Scottish cousins – and so was doubly sanctioned, by time and Mrs Herapath's aristocratic connections. Only the lobster salad carried a taint of Jamaica, but it was rendered respectable by being the tea-time favourite of His Majesty the King.

None of it, thought Sophie with a pang, would have fooled her grandfather for a second. Jocelyn Monroe had detested the Trahernes – whom, with the exception of his daughter-in-law Clemency, he'd always regarded as insufferable *parvenus*. And so they were; at least, to a Monroe who could trace his ancestry back seven hundred years.

Owen Traherne had been a blacksmith, who'd come out from Cardiff in 1704, bought a swath of cheap land west of Falmouth, and set about becoming a gentleman. Successive Trahernes had made fortunes in sugar, while working their way through tens of thousands of slaves. And when the government freed the slaves in 1834, Addison Traherne had swiftly perceived that the old plantocracy was going to the wall and had become a money-lender instead. He'd prospered, and risen to the top of Northside society through a succession of strategic marriages.

His son Cornelius had done the same, and was now the richest man in Trelawny: an astute financier and a gentleman planter, who still maintained vast stretches of cane at Millfield and Waytes Valley, and an extensive cattle farm at Fletcher Pen.

He also kept a string of very young mistresses, which Society discreetly ignored – just as it chose not to mention (at least, not out loud) the fact that Cornelius's wealthy third wife, Rebecca, had had a grandfather who'd changed his name to Sammond – from Salomon.

'Remember what Jocelyn used to say?' Madeleine murmured as they paused at the entrance to the gallery and surveyed the throng.

Sophie leaned towards her, and together they mimicked their grandfather under their breath: '*Parnassus? Ridiculous name! Why not just call it Olympus, and have done with it?*'

They laughed – a little self-consciously, perhaps, but Sophie felt happier than she'd done since Montpelier.

Everyone who was anyone was attending the tea party, and she knew them all. And because she was a Monroe, albeit an illegitimate one, they accepted her with open arms. She found that hugely reassuring.

She talked to Rebecca's beautiful house guest, a Mrs Dampiere from Spanish Town, and exchanged polite nods with Amelia Mordenner, her childhood foe. She sat with Olivia Herapath (née the Honourable Olivia Fortescue of Fortescue Hall), and fielded a flood of scurrilous gossip and a barrage of loud, well-meaning questions about 'that dratted knee'. 'What, no tennis? Why ever not? You ain't a cripple, I suppose?'

She took refuge with old Mrs Pitcaithley and plied her with scones, for the gentle old lady's income shrank yearly, and she had strict notions of *noblesse oblige*, choosing to go hungry herself rather than see her staff less than amply fed. 'So many changes,' she moaned, when Sophie told her about London. 'And do stay away from those horrid underground railways! Nasty, airless things. And quite improper for a young lady.'

Finally, Madeleine introduced her to a succession of eligible young men. Sophie was relieved when they lost interest after she politely declined the pleasure of watching them play billiards.

'Don't be such a *blue*,' whispered Sibella as she

descended on her in a flurry of primrose spotted muslin.

'I'm not,' protested Sophie, 'I just—'

'Come along, I've got something to show you.' And she dragged her into an ante-room where they could hear themselves speak. 'That's better,' she said, fanning herself with her hand. 'I've been dying to get you on your own.'

'How was finishing school?' said Sophie.

'A bore,' said Sibella.

'You're looking awfully pretty. Being engaged agrees with you. Congratulations.'

Sibella rolled her eyes. 'If I'd known how much work it was going to be I'd never have done it.' But she accepted the compliment as a matter of course.

And she did look enchanting. Plump and fair-haired, she had her father's slightly protuberant blue eyes, and a pert little nose of which she was extremely proud, since it bore no resemblance to her mother's. Rebecca Traherne was sallow and dark, and her nose betrayed her Salomon origins. Sibella made no secret of the fact that she despised her.

Now she fixed Sophie with her blue eyes and squeezed her hand. 'You will be my bridesmaid, won't you?'

'Of course, if you want—'

'But first I must ask. You didn't become a suffragist, did you?'

'What?' said Sophie, startled.

'A suffragist! You know, votes for women. You didn't join them, did you?'

'I didn't join anything,' said Sophie with perfect truth. In fact she'd attended several suffragist meetings, but it seemed pointless to mention that now.

Sibella breathed a sigh of relief. 'Thank heavens! I hate them. Nasty, ugly women who can't get husbands. And Mrs Palairet would never have stood for it.' Mrs Palairet was her future mother-in-law, and the matriarch of one of the oldest families in Trelawny.

Sophie was nettled. 'Why should it matter to Mrs Palairet what I do?'

'Oh, Sophie, what a question! You're going to be my bridesmaid. Think how it would reflect upon me.'

Then Sophie knew that she had not been chosen as a bridesmaid out of friendship, but because she was a Monroe, and would add *cachet* to the wedding, while not being pretty enough to outshine the bride. Oddly, she didn't resent that. Sibella probably wasn't even aware of it herself, for she never stopped to examine her own feelings. And it was hardly her fault if she'd grown up in a family which saw other people in terms of how they could be used.

Now she pulled Sophie over to a side table on which lay two large gilt-edged volumes sumptuously bound in pale blue morocco. 'Look, this one's my Gift Book. Isn't it heavenly?'

'What's a Gift Book?' said Sophie.

'For the *wedding*! It has columns for Sender, Description and Category of Gift, and Date of Thank-you Note. And that,' she indicated the companion volume, 'is the Trousseau Register.'

Idly, Sophie opened the Register and scanned the first page. She blinked. 'Good heavens, Sib, twelve dozen pocket handkerchiefs? What are you going to do with those?'

'Oh, Sophie, where have you been? Any fewer would be impossible! And Mrs Palairet quite approves. She—'

'Ah, then it must be correct.'

Two spots of colour appeared on Sibella's plump cheeks. 'Presumably laughing at one's friends is the newest style of London wit. But I confess I don't find it the least bit amusing.'

'I wasn't laughing at you,' Sophie said insincerely.

Sibella stroked the Register and frowned. 'It's just that I want everything to be perfect,' she muttered. 'It's such a lot to live up to, marrying a Palairet. You can't imagine what a worry.' And for a moment Sophie caught a glimpse of the fat, frightened little schoolgirl who'd clung to her in their first term together at Cheltenham.

'Well just remember,' she said, 'that you're not marrying Mrs Palairet, you're marrying Eugene.'

'What's that got to do with it?' said Sibella irritably.

Sophie looked at her. 'But Sib – you do love him, don't you?'

'Of course I do,' she snapped. 'But I don't see the use in going on about it.'

Sophie did not reply.

'You're such a romantic,' said Sibella. 'This is real life, Sophie, not some novel. And it's jolly hard work.'

Sophie thought about that. On the drive over, she had asked Madeleine about Sibella's fiancé. 'Fat, self-satisfied, and a little too fond of the tote,' her sister had said with her usual shrewdness, 'but he'll probably run the right side of the post in the end.'

Out loud Sophie said, 'Where *is* Eugene? I haven't had a chance to congratulate him yet.'

'Over there,' said Sibella without noticeable affection, 'talking to your brother-in-law.'

Sophie followed her glance and saw a fat, self-satisfied young man in a white linen suit – Madeleine's description was cruelly accurate – expounding something to Cameron, who was swallowing a yawn. 'He looks very agreeable,' she said weakly.

Sibella fingered the Register and nodded.

Just then, Cameron turned his head and searched discreetly for his wife. At the same moment Madeleine, on the other side of the gallery, raised her head and looked for him, too. Their eyes met, and for an instant they exchanged slight smiles. It was clear that for both of them, the other guests had ceased to exist.

Oh, thank God, thought Sophie in a wave of relief. It's all right between them.

Beside her, Sibella shut the Trousseau Register with a thud. Her face was stony. Perhaps she too had witnessed that look.

'Sib, what's the matter?' said Sophie.

'Nothing,' said Sibella, opening her eyes very wide. 'Go back to the others, and leave me to put these away.'

Sophie looked at her in exasperation. Sibella was the same age as herself, and an heiress at the top of the social tree. She had no need to marry anyone she didn't love, not even a Palairet. So why on earth was she doing it?

But I do *love him*, she would doubtless snap if Sophie was fool enough to raise it again. *This isn't the novels, Sophie. It's real life, and jolly hard work.*

Can that be true? wondered Sophie. Does one really have to leave it all behind in novels?

Thinking about that, she went out into the gallery, and found a cup of tea, and turned to look for a seat, and came face to face with the delicate-featured young gentleman from Montpelier.

The sounds of the tea party fell away, and she nearly dropped her cup and saucer.

He was startlingly good-looking, with pale blue eyes and chiselled features and fine, silky golden curls. And he was looking down at her with a slight smile, as if he knew her. 'I'm afraid you don't know who I am, do you?' he said gently.

She opened her mouth, but couldn't think of anything to say.

He held out his hand. 'Alexander Traherne.'

Awkwardly fielding cup and saucer, she took it. 'Not – Sibella's older brother?'

He bowed. 'Guilty as charged.'

She swallowed. 'You've been away, I suppose?'

'Eton. Oxford. The usual round. What about you?'

'Cheltenham Ladies' College.'

'Does that mean you're a frightful blue?'

'Frightful, I'm afraid.'

'Dear me, what a pity. But how odd that we've never met. Or did we? Yes, on reflection I believe we did, years ago, when I was back for the holidays. No doubt I was the most insufferable prig.'

He was talking too much, and she wondered if he was trying to distract her. 'As it happens,' she said smoothly, 'I saw you yesterday in Montpelier.'

For a moment his smile faltered, but he recovered fast. 'But how fascinating,' he said, 'particularly since I spent the entire day being horribly bored at the races at Mandeville.'

'Are you sure?'

He laughed. 'Regrettably, yes. I dropped five hundred guineas in the Subscription Plate.'

'Then I wonder who it was that I saw at Montpelier.'

'So do I. I must have a doppelgänger. How wildly intriguing.'

She made herself smile. 'As you say. I must be mistaken.'

'Ordinarily I should be loath to suggest that a lady could ever be mistaken. But in this case, I rather fear that you are.' He met her gaze without blinking, and his light blue eyes were clear. But she knew that he was lying, and he knew that she knew it, too. 'Oh, look,' he said, with a hint of relief, 'here's Davina, coming to bear you away. If you ever solve the mystery, do let me know.'

'I shall make a point of it,' she said.

That earned her a startled glance as he walked away.

She made her excuses to his sister, and passed swiftly through the gallery, and out into the grounds. There were people strolling beneath the pergola, so she walked quickly round to the front of the house, and down a flight of shallow stone steps into the great formal parterre to the right of the carriageway. As she left the shade of the royal palms, the heat hit her like a wall. She didn't care. She needed to be alone. She found a bench and sat down, clenching her fists.

She was beginning to be genuinely angry with her sister. What on earth was she playing at? *Alexander Traherne?*

After the look which had passed between Madeleine and Cameron, it could hardly be an affair, but there was definitely something going on. Some kind of intrigue which was so important that it had to be kept from her own husband and sister.

God, Maddy, what are you doing? Do you have any idea of the risks you're running? Don't you realize that if word gets out, people will only jump to the worst possible conclusion?

She shut her eyes and forced herself to be calm, while

the sun beat down on her shoulders, and the crickets' rasp rang loud in her ears.

When she opened her eyes again, she was still just as angry as before. The sunlight was so stark that it hurt her eyes, and everything about her was blindingly bright. The parterre lay stunned beneath the sun: a joyless formal arrangement of dry grey lavender and small clipped lime trees. To her left, a stiff parade of royal palms cast harsh black shadows on the glaring white marl of the carriage-drive. In the distance she could just make out the blind stone lodges which marked the Coast Road, and beyond it the hard glitter of the Caribbean Sea.

No shade and no respite. Well it's your own fault for forgetting your sun-umbrella, she told herself angrily.

She got to her feet and walked the length of the parterre, then stopped. She couldn't face going back inside.

To her right, beyond the low stone wall of the parterre, an avenue of copperwoods demarcated the formal gardens from the stables beyond. In front of the stables, in a broad, sunlit expanse of hard brown grass, a groom was walking a pretty little bay mare up and down, presumably to cool her down, while a clutch of stable boys looked on from their perches on bales of straw.

Sophie climbed the steps and leaned against the parterre wall to watch. Then she shaded her eyes with her hand and frowned. The groom walking the mare was the same one she'd seen in Montpelier. She recognized the way he moved: that graceful, straight-backed wariness which reminded her of Ben Kelly. Grimly, she wondered how Alexander would try to wriggle out of this.

The groom took off his cap and wiped his forehead on his wrist, and she realized that he didn't just remind her of Ben Kelly. He *was* Ben Kelly.

She wasn't even all that surprised. In some way, she had known it was him from that first moment in Montpelier.

It was Ben Kelly – and yet it wasn't. The Ben Kelly she remembered – the image she'd carried around with her – had been a whip-thin street urchin of fourteen or so: more than a boy, but not yet a man, his face hardened by a childhood spent in the slums. The young man she was looking at now must be – what, about twenty-two? Still thin, but with nothing of the child about him. He was clean-shaven, with straight black hair and a sharply hand-some but resolutely unsmiling face.

She remembered what Madeleine had said on the verandah when she'd taxed her with seeing him in Montpelier. *Which Ben? Good heavens. Don't mention that to Cameron, will you?* Madeleine had known it was him all along. And she'd never said a word.

Well, my God, Maddy, thought Sophie angrily, you shan't wriggle out of it this time. And neither shall that simpering Alexander Traherne.

She pushed herself off the wall and took a step forward. 'So it *was* you at Montpelier,' she said loudly, and her voice echoed across the dead grass.

He spun round, saw her, and stopped dead. He was only about five yards away. She was close enough to see how his face went still, and his eyes widened slightly with shock.

'Hello, Ben,' she said. 'Remember me? Sophie Monroe.'

He did not reply. He just stood there in the blazing sun-light, staring at her. Beside him the little mare shook out her mane, then playfully nuzzled his shoulder.

'I saw you yesterday,' said Sophie, 'in Montpelier. But you'd gone before I could come across and say hello.'

Still he did not reply. Instead he gave her a slight bow – the perfect groom – and then, to her astonishment, put his cap back on and turned and started leading the mare towards the stables.

'Ben!' she called out sharply. 'Come back here.'

The stable boys stopped talking and turned to look. Sophie ignored them. 'Come back here. I need to talk to you.'

But he threw her a glance over his shoulder, and shook his head. Then he walked away.

She moved to follow him, but her knee buckled and she had to steady herself on the parterre wall.

Somewhere behind her, a woman tittered. Sophie glanced round and saw Amelia Mordenner and the lovely Mrs Dampiere standing on the steps by the house, watching her. She glared at them.

And when she turned back to the stables, Ben Kelly had gone.

CHAPTER FOUR

He thought he was doing all right until he saw Sophie.

Second groom at Parnassus, and it's only a matter of time till they put old Danny out to pasture and make him head. Ben Kelly, head groom. That's not bad for starters.

Then yesterday he was walking Trouble round to cool her off, and suddenly there she was: Sophie Monroe, but all grown up.

He hasn't thought of her in years. Not once. It's an easy trick to master when you get the hang of it. You just slam the lid down and put your thoughts to something else. Just slam the lid down hard.

At least, he thought that was how it worked. But then yesterday, just for a moment, everything blew wide open, and he was back where it started. Nine years ago, in that photo shop in the Portland Road, with this posh kid in the stripy red pinafore trying to give him a sodding book.

'I thought you might care to have it,' she said, as if it was the most natural thing in the world. 'And then you'll be able to read too.'

For the life of him he couldn't work out what she was after. *Giving* him things? What for? It made him go hot and prickly in his chest. It made him want to hurt her, so that she'd know better than to give things to people.

And yesterday, as she'd stood there in the glare, telling him to come back and talk to her, he'd got it again: that hot prickly tightness in his chest.

Ah, sod it. She'll get over it. What's she expect?

It's still dark, and in the bunk-house everyone else is fast asleep. He can't stand it no more, so he pulls on his togs, and puts Sophie out of his mind, and goes out to see to his horses. It's been a bloody long night.

After he's done his horses, he fetches a bit of sweet hay for Trouble, his favourite, to get her appetite going. What a daft name, Trouble. Whoever called her that didn't know shit about horses, cos this one wouldn't hurt a fly. She wouldn't know how. She's too busy puzzling out what people want of her, so she can obey them, and not get thrashed. Only that's easier said than done, seeing as she's a horse, and dumb as a post.

So now she's happily snuffling up the hay, and he's scratching her ears, when all of a sudden she jerks up her head, all startled and worried.

It's Master Alex, come for an early ride. Trouble's scared of him. Maybe it's his yellow riding-gloves. Maybe in the past she got thrashed by a groom in a yellow coat, or kicked by a horse with a yellow saddlecloth. Or then again, maybe it's just Master Alex.

'Now then, my lad,' he goes, with that false jauntiness that sets Ben's teeth on edge. 'Saddle her up, there's a good fellow.'

'What, sir?' goes Ben, playing for time.

Master Alex gives an irritated little laugh. 'The mare. Saddle her up. That is, if you have no objection.'

As it happens, Ben does. The thing about Trouble is that somewhere down the line, she had a bad time of it. She was in a right state when she come here: running with lice, scared of her own shadow, and all sorts of bad habits. Ben worked on her for months. He oiled her for lice and washed her out for worms; he talked to her all the time, so she'd know he wasn't going to hurt her. And as for them bad habits, she was just bored. So he put her in a loose-box where she could see into the yard, and gave her a turnip on a bit of twine to play with, and now she's happy as a lark. She even looks like a horse again. Nice glossy coat, and the free step of a really good mover.

Not that Master Alex would know about that, as he hasn't been allowed to ride her yet. Ben's seen to that. The last thing she needs is a heavy-handed idiot like him yanking her about.

'When you're ready, my lad?' goes Master Alex, all sarky. Funny how Ben's always 'my lad', even though they're pretty much of an age.

'Yessir,' goes Ben, tipping his cap. 'It won't take a moment to give her the once-over with a bit of soft soap.'

Master Alex frowns. 'Whatever for?'

'On account of the lice, sir. She's nigh on free of them. But it's always them last little few that do like to hang on.'

Master Alex shoots him a look, like he *thinks* he's being played, but he's not quite sure. At least, not sure enough to risk the lice.

So in the end he gets up on Eagle, a big flashy chestnut with no staying power. They're made for each other, them two. Ben bites back a grin as he watches them go.

'Watch youself, bwoy,' says Danny Tulloch on his way to the tackroom.

'Why's that, then?' goes Ben.

Danny crinkles up his sour old face and spits. 'You know what I referring to, bwoy. That likkle mare belong to Master Alex, not you. You run you mouth with him, he put you out the door quick-time.'

Ben shrugs. 'Well then I'll watch myself, won't I?'

Danny gives a sour grin and shakes his head.

He's all right, is Danny. Him and Ben have an understanding. Danny's a cousin of Grace McFarlane, Evie's ma, and years ago she done Ben a favour, and he done her one back. So any cousin of hers is all right by him, and that's how old Danny sees it too.

By now Master Alex is well gone, so Ben slips a head-collar on Trouble and gets up on her bareback, and takes her down the beach, for the iodine.

It's all right, the beach. Willow trees and white sand, and that clear water: as clear as gin. When he first come to Jamaica, he used to sleep out here. It was the only place where he could find a bit of peace. Everywhere else got him all twisted up inside.

The trouble was, there was too *much* of everything. Every kind of fruit you could think of, just growing wild by the side of the road. All the flowers and the coloured parrots, and the warm, clean, spicy-smelling air. It made him think about Kate and Robbie and the others back in London, rotting away in their freezing, muddy graves. It made him feel so bad. That's when he learned to slam the lid down hard.

But Trouble likes the beach, and all. So they have a bit of a gallop, with Ben down low against her neck, muttering, 'Go on, sweetheart, let's see what you can do.' She's got a lovely action. Proper little Jamaican thoroughbred: goes fast, stays well, and runs small and light.

After a bit he slips off her back and they take a walk in the sea. He lets go of the reins and she follows him like a dog, giving little snorty blows to tell him she's enjoying herself. And when he jumps back on, she twists round and nibbles his knee. That's horse-talk for 'We're mates, you and me', so he returns the favour by finger-nibbling her neck. More snorty little blows.

The last time he saw Sophie – before she went to England, that is – she was scratching her pony's neck, too. She was out riding with her grandpa, a little ways past Salt Wash. The old man was up on a big clean-limbed grey, and Sophie on a fat little Welsh Mountain cross. She must of been about fourteen, riding astride in one of them divided skirts, maybe because a side-saddle would of buggered up her knee. And she was chattering, of course, and scratching her pony's neck.

She didn't see Ben. He was in a weeding gang in the cane-piece by the side of the road, and she never noticed. Well, why should she? He could of called out to her, but he didn't. What's the point? She's quality and he's not. It's all very well when you're kids, but you don't want to go mixing things up later on.

Madeleine understands that. The other day at Montpelier, they'd glanced at each other, and she'd smiled and said *Hello, Ben, you're looking well*, but after that she'd hardly said a word. And she was right. They might of been mates in London, but that was years ago. You can't go mixing things up.

That's what Sophie needs to understand. The way she'd looked at him yesterday. Sort of puzzled, and maybe a bit hurt that he wouldn't stop for a word.

But then – oh, how she'd glared at that Mrs Dampiere, when her knee went, and they laughed at her! So she's still got a temper on her, just like the old days.

One time back in London, they were in the kitchen of that Cousin Lettice's, and he was standing by the door, ready to cut the lucky at the first sign of trouble, while Madeleine and Sophie and Robbie were sitting at the table, eating soup. And all of a sudden Sophie twisted round in her chair and hiked up her pinafore dress a few inches, and peeled back her stocking. 'Look, Ben, I've got a bruise.' And she pointed to a tiny pink swelling on the cleanest knee he'd ever seen.

'That's no bruise,' he'd snarled.

'Yes it jolly well is,' she'd flashed back.

Oh, she had a temper all right. But the rum thing was, she was also easy to hurt. Like when she give him the picture-book and he snapped at her, and for a moment her honey-coloured eyes filled with tears.

So had he hurt her yesterday, when he walked away? Had he? Ah, sod it. Who cares?

Once there was this old bloke in London, Mr McCluskie, and he said, 'You know, Ben Kelly, you're better than you think you are. Why not give yourself a chance?' But that's just bollocks. And the sooner Sophie works that out, the better.

He puts Trouble into a canter, and they cross the Coast Road and go up through the gates of Parnassus. The lodges are big stone affairs with blind windows and a Latin motto on the front. *Deus mihi providebit*. Danny's brother Reuben, who's a preacher at Coral Springs, says that means 'God will provide for me'.

Well, that might be true if you're Alexander Traherne or

Madeleine Lawe or Sophie Monroe, but it don't mean a sodding thing if you're Ben Kelly. God leaves the Kellys to shift for themselves.

So what? It's the way of the world. But the point is, you don't want to go mixing things up.

It's midday when he gets back, and the stableyard's silent and still beneath a hammering sun. Nothing but the red dust shimmering, and the crickets loud in your ears.

He gives Trouble a rub-down, and now she's leaning over the door of her loose-box, all happy and relaxed.

She's all right, is Trouble. In the morning when he brings her her feed she nickers at him. The first horse he ever met, actually met, so to speak, it nickered at him too. Till he got the job in Berner's Mews he'd never given much thought to horses. But on his second day there, this ratty old bay nickered at him. He asked Mr McCluskie why it did that, and he said, 'It's because you fed him last night, lad.'

'So?' said Ben. 'That don't mean I'll do it again.'

'Yes, but he don't know that, do he, lad?'

That's horses for you. Not much in the upper storey, but they never forget. Not ever. What a way to live. To remember *everything*. Everything about Madeleine and Sophie, and about Robbie and the others, and – and Kate. Bloody hell. He'd sooner top himself.

So now it's the afternoon, and the ladies are going out calling. They always like Ben to drive, as it adds a bit of class to have a white groom instead of a darkie, so he's got to get all poshed up in his buckskin breeches and top-boots, and the tight blue tunic with the high collar. All to drive the quality about, so they can leave their little bits of pasteboard on each other.

This afternoon it's just Madam doing the rounds, so he's back in time for tea. Only there's a riding party going out, and four horses wanting tacking up, so no tea.

Master Alex and Master Cornelius are taking that Mrs Dampiere up to see Waytes Lake. They've both got the hots for her, and they're dragging Miss Sib along to keep

48

it respectable. So off they go. But an hour later Master Cornelius is back again, all hot and cross. Miss Sib's mare's gone lame. Ben's to take her a fresh horse, and then walk the lame one back.

So off he goes on Samson, heading south-west through the cane-pieces of Waytes Valley. It's good being on his own. Nothing but the creak of the tack and the wind in the cane. To his right he can see the vast flat acres of the Queen of Spain's Valley, that Master Traherne bought from Sophie's grandpa; to his left, far in the distance, the giant bamboo along the Fever Hill Road.

He finds them up the southern end of Waytes Valley, and swaps round the saddles, and helps Miss Sib up onto Samson. The mare's lame, all right. It'll be a long walk back.

But now the quality are having a squabble. Miss Sib's got a headache and wants to go home, but she don't want 'the groom' taking her, as that'd be too slow; she wants her brother and Mrs Dampiere. Master Alex isn't having any of that, he wants to take Mrs Dampiere to the lake by hisself. Well he would, wouldn't he?

In the end, of course, Miss Sib wins, and Master Alex has to do the gentlemanly thing and take her back. That's when Mrs Dampiere puts in her oar. 'I'd so set my heart on seeing the lake,' she goes, all apologetic. 'I wonder, Alex dear, would it be too much trouble – could the groom possibly show me the way?'

She's a pretty bit of muslin. Very young and very meek, with pale gold hair and surprised grey eyes, and a little soft pink mouth. The sort that always gets their way.

And Master Alex grits his teeth and smiles at her, and says, 'Why, of course.' Then he tells Ben to walk the lame mare up to the house at Waytes Point, pick up a fresh horse, then take the lady on to the lake.

'Yessir,' goes Ben. Like he hasn't thought of that already.

Master Alex shoots him a look. He's got the Traherne eyes: pale blue, with the centres black and bottomless, like a goat's. 'Make sure you're back before dark,' he goes, with a hint of a warning in his voice. 'There's a good lad.'

So now they're off to Waytes Point, him and Mrs Dampiere. And pretty soon they've left the lame mare grazing in the paddock, and Ben's up on Gambler, who's fifteen if he's a day, but only too glad of an outing. Mrs Dampiere rides behind and don't say a word, which is fine by Ben. He's not sure about her. Why did she have to go and laugh when Sophie nearly took a tumble?

He slams the lid on that, and in half an hour they get to the lake. It's not much of a lake. Just a cut-stone dam to catch the runoff from the hills, with a sheet of slimy green water behind. Not Ben's favourite place, neither. That dead water, smothered in waterlilies. The big flat sickly yellow leaves. The whole place stinks of rottenness and graves.

But Mrs Dampiere don't seem to notice. They stop beneath a clump of trees by the dam, and she tells him to help her down. It's the first thing she's said to him all afternoon.

While he's seeing to the horses, she walks out onto the dam wall. It's smooth underfoot and over a yard wide, but on one side there's a nasty drop into some thorn bushes, and on the other that swampy green water; so he goes after her, to see her all right. Master Cornelius would have his hide if she took a tumble.

Halfway along she nearly does, and he offers her his arm, and she takes it without a word.

She's wearing a dark blue riding-habit, very nipped in at the waist, and long black gloves with black pearl buttons, and a glossy top hat with a dark blue spotted veil. He can see a wisp of pale gold hair escaping at the nape.

For some reason, that puts him in mind of Sophie when she was a kid. Her hair wasn't fine like Mrs Dampiere's, but thick and coarse like a horse's mane, and strawberry blonde. Only now that she's grown up it's darker, sort of light brown.

Apart from that, she hasn't changed much. She never was a beauty, not like Madeleine. She's too skinny, and she looks like trouble. Them straight dark eyebrows, and that mouth of hers. Little shadowy dents at the corners, that get deeper when she's in a sulk. No, she's not a beauty. But she's grown up into the kind of girl that you'd give a second look.

Shut it, he tells himself angrily. You just shut it about Sophie Monroe. She's not your mate, she never was. She's sodding quality.

'So this is where you go swimming,' says Mrs Dampiere, cutting across his thoughts.

He shoots her a look. 'I spose some people do, ma'am.'

'But not you?'

'Ma'am?'

'You do not care to swim here?'

'No, ma'am.'

She leans over the edge and studies the waterlilies. 'What is your name?' she says, without looking round.

'Kelly, ma'am.'

'Kelly. So you're Irish?'

'No, ma'am.'

'But your colouring is Irish – or I should say Celtic. Although I don't suppose you know what that means. But Kelly is an Irish name.'

'My pa was Irish, ma'am.' And may the bastard burn in hell for eternity.

'Ah. So you take after your father?'

'No,' he goes quickly, before he can stop himself.

But she can see that she's got to him, and her little soft mouth twists in a smile.

That's when he understands what she's about. It's simple. She's a flirt.

Lots of the ladies are. It's just a game they like to play. They give you orders, and you obey, and it's all very right and proper; but now and then, they give a little hint that they know you're also a man. They only do it because they're bored, and nine times out of ten they leave it at that, so there's no harm done.

Across the pond, a big blue heron hitches itself off a log and flies away. Mrs Dampiere watches till it's just a speck in the sky. 'They beat their women,' she says, without turning round.

'Ma'am?' he goes. It give him a bit of a start.

'The Irish. They beat their women. Or so I understand.' She turns and looks up at him. 'I wonder, Kelly, do you beat yours?'

He stoops and flicks a grass seed off his boot. 'It's time we were starting back, ma'am,' he says. The perfect groom.

She gives him a wry smile. 'Just so, Kelly. Just so.'

So they start back towards the horses, and he's well relieved, because she's acting like nothing's happened. She's pointing out the trees with her riding-crop and asking him the names. She says she's new to Jamaica, and it's all a bit unfamiliar.

So of course he goes along with it. 'That's a guango, ma'am.'

'And the one with the feathery leaves?'

'Poinciana. And the one beside it,' he adds on the spur, as he's still narked at her for taking advantage, 'that's a mimosa, ma'am. What the darkies call shame o' lady.'

That makes her laugh. She's got some brass, all right.

When she gets to the shade of the poinciana tree, she stops. He thinks she's waiting for him to fetch her horse, but then she unhooks the little pearl buttons on her glove, and starts drawing it off.

Oh, shit. *Shit.* She means it. Not here. Not now. Not with Sophie still in his head.

'You know, Kelly,' she says, as she gives each narrow finger a sharp little tug, 'you're something of a favourite with Master Cornelius. Are you aware of that?'

He don't say nothing. Why should he? Why the sodding hell should he?

Tug, tug, tug. Off comes the first glove. She drops it in the grass.

'In fact,' she says, starting on the second glove, 'he tells me that you can ride anything. Is that true?'

Still he don't reply. But then, she's not expecting him to. She drops the second glove, then puts up her veil, and unpins her hat, and lays it on the ground. 'I should perhaps explain that Master Cornelius was paying you a compliment.'

He gives her one of his blank stares. 'I wouldn't know about that, ma'am.'

She puts her head on one side and looks at him. 'You don't like to show your feelings, do you, Kelly?'

'I don't have any, ma'am. I'm a groom.'

'Oh, indeed?' She puts out her hand and runs her finger slowly across his bottom lip. 'No feelings? I don't believe you. Not with a mouth like that.'

He clears his throat. 'I'll fetch your horse, ma'am. It'll be dark soon. We should—'

'If you don't do as I say,' she cuts in, 'I shall tell Master Cornelius that you were impertinent. I shall have you dismissed.'

For two pins he'd say to her, Well go on then, you slimy little bitch. But why should he let her get him sacked? Besides, if he left Parnassus, who'd look after Trouble?

Anyway, why is he even hesitating? She's beautiful. And it's not as if he don't know how.

She comes up close to him, and tilts back her head to study his face. Her eyes are shining, her lips parted so that he can see her little pink tongue. He wants to take her by the shoulders and shake her till her teeth rattle; till she knows what it's like to be used.

She puts up her hand and unfastens the top button of his tunic. Her nails scratch his throat, and he flinches. 'Headshy,' she says with a smile. Headshy, like a horse. Like he's a sodding animal instead of a man. Anger thickens in his gut.

She unfastens the next button, and the next. Then the buttons on his shirt, and then his undershirt. Then she puts her manicured hand flat on his belly. He tenses as the little cold half-moons of her nails dig into his skin.

Her smile widens. 'Don't worry. I'm not going to hurt you. Although I'm very much hoping that you'll hurt me.'

* * *

53

It's long past midnight and he's down at the beach, washing off the smell of her in the sea. The night wind's sharp and the water's cold, but it's clean and salty, and it's what he needs.

They were late getting back to Parnassus, and of course she blamed it on him. She said he lost his way. Master Alex made fun of him in front of the others, and Master Cornelius tore him off a strip, then docked him a week's wages.

She stood there watching until she got bored, then tossed him her reins and walked away. The same woman who'd lain beneath him in the grass, moaning and clawing at his back, and screaming for more.

She got him into trouble because she could, and because she knew she'd get away with it, and he can't pay her back. Well, so what? That's people for you. They'll do anything if they know they can get away with it; if they know you can't ever pay them back.

For a moment he shuts his eyes and fancies himself a millionaire, paying back the quality. But the trouble with that is, Sophie's quality, too. And he can't pay her back, can he? Because she's never done him any wrong.

Thinking on that gives him that hot, prickly tightness in his chest. He snarls and grinds his knuckles into his eyes.

So don't think about it, you daft bugger. Don't think about Sophie or Madeleine, or any of it. Just walk away. Walk away and slam the lid down hard.

CHAPTER FIVE

The thing about Ben Kelly was that he'd never lied to her.

He'd been scornful and harsh, and once he'd nearly made her cry. But he'd never lied. 'What's the bloody point?' he'd have said if she'd asked. 'If you can't take the truth, that's your lookout.'

The first time they met was in London in 1894, at the photography studio in the Portland Road where Maddy did a little ladylike helping out. Early one foggy March morning she took Sophie along with her for a tenth-birthday treat, and they stumbled upon two unbelievably filthy urchins looking for something to steal.

Neither Sophie nor Madeleine had ever met an urchin before. So instead of shooing them out of the studio or summoning a policeman, Maddy grabbed a wooden rifle from the props shelf and cried, 'Stop, thief!', with what Sophie thought was incredible presence of mind. And as neither boy could tell a real gun from a fake, they froze like cornered animals.

'What have you got in your pockets?' snapped Maddy, trying to look fierce.

With grim obedience the urchins emptied their pockets, and several rotten apples and a pear thudded wetly onto the counter.

The girls were astonished. Every week Mr Rennard, the studio proprietor, bought a bowl of fruit in case any of his sitters needed livening up with what he called 'a bit of background'. But this week he hadn't got round to replacing it.

'What were you going to do with those?' said Maddy, voicing the question in Sophie's mind.

'Eat them,' snapped the older boy, as if she'd said something idiotic. 'Wha'd'ya think?'

'But they're rotten,' said Maddy. 'We were going to throw them away.'

'Shows how much you know,' he muttered.

Sophie was captivated. She'd never met anyone like him. In fact, she hadn't met too many people at all, because Cousin Lettice didn't allow them to mix with company. And of course the Poor were doubly out of bounds, since they lacked moral fibre and harboured disease.

He said his name was Ben Kelly, and his brother's name was Robbie, and he spat out his answers in a voice sharp with scorn, for he knew that he'd seen more of the world than they.

Sophie caught her breath and tried not to stare. He was grey with dirt and he smelt like a sewer rat, but for her that only heightened his glamour. He was like an imp from another world; like some kind of exotic and perilous birthday present.

His brother Robbie was a hunchback, with matted orange hair and a dull but trusting little face. One scabby bare foot was clumsily bandaged with a scrap of newspaper, so he had to stand on one leg as he stared open-mouthed at Maddy, dribbling bits of half-chewed apple down his front.

Ben was tall and thin, and beneath the ground-in dirt his face had a sharp-boned purity which reminded Sophie of an effigy in a church. Then she noticed his eyes, and felt a faint, cold settling of awe. She'd never seen anyone with green eyes. She decided that he must be a changeling, with a lineage tracing back to a race of mermen, or possibly King Arthur.

She could tell that he was older than her, but to her amazement he didn't know *how* old, and he didn't seem to care. 'I dunno,' he said with a shrug. 'Thirteen? What's it to you?'

But what does he do about birthdays? she wondered.

She felt sorry for Robbie, but she never felt sorry for Ben. Right from the start she just wanted to be his friend.

So to get his attention, she plucked up her courage and decided to show him her new book. 'It was my birthday last week,' she said, speaking quickly, as she always did when she was nervous. 'I didn't have a party, as we don't really know anyone. That's why it's so nice to meet you—'

'Sophie—' muttered Maddy with an admonitory glance.

'– but Maddy gave me *Black Beauty*,' she went on, throwing her sister a beseeching look, 'and it's absolutely *brilliant*, I've read it twice already.' She put it on the counter and pushed it over to where he could see it.

He glanced at the calfskin binding. Then his eyes returned for a closer look. She felt a thrill of triumph as she watched him put out one grimy forefinger and trace the gilded curve of the horse's neck. Then he glanced up and caught her watching him, and his face closed. 'They got the bridle wrong,' he snapped.

She was impressed. 'Do you know about horses?'

'Ben had this job once,' said Robbie, talking in a sing-song voice as if he'd learnt it by heart. 'It was at Berner's Mews, and he—'

'Shut it,' snarled his brother. Then to Sophie, 'So you can read. So what?'

She blinked. 'But – everyone can read.'

Then she noticed that Maddy was shaking her head and giving her that lopsided grin which meant *Oh, Sophie, really!* and she suddenly perceived her mistake. She was appalled. She herself spent every available moment buried in a book; it was her favourite thing. It had never occurred to her that there might be people who couldn't read.

But what must that be like, she wondered. If you couldn't ever get into a book, you'd be shut out. The whole world would be grey. Surely, surely it wasn't like that for him? 'I'm most awfully sorry,' she said earnestly. 'I didn't mean – um – can't you read?'

'I know my letters,' he snapped.

It was the closest that he ever got to telling her a lie. She found out later that he'd only gone to school once, for a couple of weeks, when they were giving out soup tickets. And because he was clever, he'd picked up most of the letters, although he hadn't yet learned how to string them together into words.

At the time, though, she didn't know any of that. She was still grappling with the notion of not being able to read. Then she had her idea. 'Maddy keeps a few books for the clients' children,' she said, running to the drawer behind the counter and giving her sister a questioning look.

Maddy nodded, hefting the gun on her hip.

'It's to keep them amused,' Sophie went on breathlessly. She glanced at him over her shoulder, and met his narrow unsmiling gaze, and turned back to the drawer in confusion. 'I thought you might care to have one,' she went on, 'and then you'll be able to read too. It's about a cavalry horse in the Crimean War. I thought you might enjoy it, as you like horses.'

She thought he'd be pleased, or perhaps even a little grateful. Instead he glanced from her to the picture-book with scowling incomprehension. His face worked as if she'd flung him a deadly insult. 'Not going to read it, am I?' he snarled as he snatched it from her hand. 'Going to sell it, that's what.'

She thought she must have misunderstood. She tried to smile, and told him that when he'd finished this book, he could come back and she'd give him another. But to her horror, that only made things worse. 'You cracked or what? Why would I come back?'

By this time she was blinking back tears. I will *not* cry, she told herself fiercely. I jolly well will *not*.

Luckily that was when Maddy stepped in and glared at him, and he backed down, and Sophie's self-respect was saved. A moment later he muttered, 'Come on,

Robbie, time we was off,' and shortly afterwards they left.

Sophie stood at the door swallowing tears as she watched them disappear into the bitter yellow fog. She didn't understand what she'd done wrong.

It was only later that she realized that he simply hadn't known how else to react. He was like a dog who has experienced nothing but beatings, and can only snarl when someone offers it a bone.

She thought that she would never see him again, but a few months later he came back.

It was just after Cousin Lettice's husband had died and left them bankrupt. Madeleine had explained that bankrupt meant extremely poor – at least, it meant poor by Cousin Lettice's standards, for they had to dismiss Cook and Susan, and have their clothes dyed black, instead of simply buying new ones from the Mourning Department at Peter Robinson's. But it didn't mean poor like Ben and Robbie. Even Sophie understood that.

It was a hot, sticky day in August. Cousin Lettice had taken a sleeping powder and gone to lie down, and Sophie and Madeleine were in the kitchen making lunch. Sophie was sitting on the table swinging her legs, and Madeleine was stirring the soup and reading aloud from Mrs Beeton in a funny voice. Suddenly the basement door opened, and there they were.

Sophie's heart swelled painfully. 'Maddy, *look*! It's Ben and Robbie!'

It turned out that Ben had heard about Cousin Septimus 'popping his clogs and going all to smash', and found out where they lived by 'asking around', and just dropped by 'to see what was what'.

Maddy darted him a cool look and told him to shut the door, so it fell to Sophie to make them welcome. 'Can I show them the morning-room?' she begged her sister. Then, to Ben, 'There's a stained-glass window which Maddy detests but I think is absolutely stupendous, like in a church.' He threw her his wary, shut-in look, and she realized with a sinking feeling that she was talking too much. Again.

Maddy vetoed the idea of the morning-room on the grounds that they'd only steal things. Sophie thought that shockingly rude, but Ben didn't seem to mind at all. In fact, he shot Maddy a sharp, feral grin and said with approval, 'Now you're learning.'

After that he and Maddy fell to talking about bankruptcy, while Sophie chatted self-consciously to Robbie, and wondered what she had to do to get Ben to grin at *her* like that. She was determined that this time she wouldn't offend him. There was to be no repeat of the picture-book fiasco.

So when Maddy asked her to lay the table, she didn't even look at him as she went to the dresser and fetched four of everything and set it on the table. Yes, he could have some soup if he wanted – but it was entirely up to him, and nobody would say a word about it either way. She reflected that it was a bit like trying to lure a squirrel with a trail of bread, and that made her feel more hopeful, because she'd always been rather good at that.

Maddy poured out four bowls of soup and set them on the table, but when she, Robbie and Sophie sat down, Ben remained edgily by the door.

To avoid any awkwardness, Sophie kept up a flow of chatter, while observing him out of the corner of her eye. To begin with he watched them eating, but then he gave himself a little shake, and started gazing about him at the pots and the china on the dresser. He didn't look bitter or envious. He just looked at it all with a flat-on acceptance, as if he understood that what Madeleine called 'poor' bore no relation to himself.

Ten minutes later he was still leaning against the door, so Sophie decided to take matters into her own hands. 'Look, Ben,' she said, 'I've got a bruise. I fell down the steps and banged my knee.'

'Sophie . . .' mumbled Madeleine through a mouthful of soup.

Sophie ignored her. Greatly daring, she twisted round

in her chair and peeled back her stocking to show him.

He snorted. 'That's no bruise.'

'Yes it jolly well is,' she snapped, 'and it hurts, too.'

She was furious with herself for flaring up, but to her astonishment he merely gave a harsh bark of laughter. Then he sidled over and sat down, and worked his way with frowning concentration through three bowls of soup.

She felt a glow of triumph. She only had a vague idea of how she had achieved it, but she'd got him to the table, and that was the important thing.

They talked a little about their respective parents, and established that both sets of fathers and mothers were dead. Well, that's a point in common, thought Sophie happily.

Then Robbie lifted his head from his bowl long enough to recite one of his by-rote narratives. 'Ma had red hair like me, but Pa's was black like Ben's, and Pa knocked her about so she died. Then Ben took me away and Pa died too and Ben said good riddance. Ma used to send us hop-picking, that's why Ben's so strong, but I had to stop home on account of I was too little. And we had *two whole rooms* in East Street and a separate bed for the kids, and every Sunday Ben had to fetch the dinner from the bake-house, brisket and batter pudding and spuds.'

Sophie was fascinated. Only two rooms? And from the sound of it, they hadn't had a kitchen of their own. No wonder he'd stared at theirs.

She wanted to ask questions, but Ben cuffed Robbie around the head and told him to belt up, and Robbie grinned and did as he was told. That fascinated her, too. Ben was like a sheepdog with his brother: making him do what he wanted and snapping at him if he didn't, but also fiercely protective.

Maddy was a little like that with her, although without the cuffing. So when they finished the soup and Maddy told Sophie to take Robbie out and show him the garden, she didn't hesitate, although she desperately wanted to stay behind with Ben.

How was she to know that Maddy was going to mess

things up, and give him the book, *The Downfall of the Dervishes*, which Sophie herself had picked out weeks ago and bought with her own personal money, in case he ever came back?

She was outside with Robbie, showing him Cousin Lettice's potted ferns, when they heard Ben yelling angrily for his brother. 'Here, Rob, look sharp! We're off!'

Robbie jammed on his cap and scuttled down the stairs, and by the time Sophie reached the kitchen they were both on their way out – Ben with a face like thunder, and *The Downfall of the Dervishes* tucked under his arm.

Sophie was incandescent. '*I* was going to give it to him!' she shouted at her sister when they'd gone. '*I* bought it, it was *my* present!'

'I'm sorry,' said Maddy, 'I forgot.'

'What did you *say* to him to make him go off like that?'

'Nothing,' said Maddy unconvincingly. 'We were just talking about how to make money. And – things like that.' She didn't elaborate, but Sophie could tell that there was more. At times, Maddy could be infuriatingly secretive.

For weeks afterwards, Sophie loitered in the kitchen, on the off chance that Ben would come back. She daydreamed about swapping books with him, and impressing him with her knowledge of Dervishes. But he never returned.

Then, suddenly, she fell ill. The small pink bump on her knee turned into a painful swelling. She became feverish at night, and floppy and tired in the mornings. Finally the doctor was called, and he prodded her knee, and pronounced the dreaded word. She lay in bed looking up at the grim faces leaning over her, and felt truly scared for the first time in her life.

The condition first makes its appearance, said the medical book which Maddy borrowed from Mudie's library, *with a slight lesion such as a knock or contusion, into which the tuberculosis bacilli are thought to gain entry to the organism*. The organism. That meant her.

Her world shrank to her bedroom.

Cousin Lettice was outraged that any 'charge' of hers

should have fallen so shamefully ill. Maddy became secretive and anxious. She saw Ben Kelly a couple of times more – without Sophie, of course – and, under questioning, she admitted that she'd told him about the TB.

Sophie was furious. Then appalled. Then – when he failed to come and see her – in despair. She knew why he was staying away. It was because of the TB. And now he was never coming back.

But she never stopped hoping that he might.

She wrote about him in a secret code in her journal. She debated how she would behave if she saw him again: whether she would be angry and aloof, or just pretend not to have noticed that he'd ever been away.

Of course when it finally happened, she was neither.

It was July 1895, and they'd been living at Fever Hill for just over eight months, when one day Maddy suggested – in a voice which brooked no opposition – that Sophie should take a little drive with Jocelyn to Falmouth, 'for a change of air'.

The truth was that Maddy was worried about her. They all were. Although her health had improved when they'd first arrived in Jamaica, over the past few weeks she'd been getting steadily worse. And no-one knew that better than herself. She'd become horribly thin and yellow, and so weak that when she practised walking with the hated splint and the calliper on the other leg to even up the lengths, she hardly had the strength to manipulate her crutches.

It was market day in Falmouth, and the square was heaving with people as she sat on the bench on the courthouse verandah and waited for Jocelyn to come and collect her. It was a noisy, colourful sight: the cassia trees dripping with great festoons of yellow blossom, the Negro ladies raucous and brilliant in their green and mauve and orange print gowns. Sophie hardly saw any of it. She felt more anxious and alone than ever before in her life.

Things at Fever Hill were going from bad to worse. Maddy had become unhappy and withdrawn, and wouldn't tell her why. The house was full of whispers; they were surrounded by illness and death. A duppy tree had stolen her shadow and she was going to die.

There was no-one she could talk to. She couldn't tell the old people like Jocelyn and Great-Aunt May, and Clemency was nice, but not yet familiar enough to confide in. And worst of all, Maddy – *Maddy* – had become unapproachable; she seemed to have too many dark secrets of her own to be able to spare time for Sophie's.

There was nobody, absolutely nobody to help.

Then suddenly, through a haze of red dust at the other end of the square, there was Ben. *Her* Ben, from London. It wasn't possible. Not possible that he could be here in Jamaica, when she needed him most. But there he was.

After the initial shock she struggled to her feet and yelled his name at the top of her voice. '*Ben! Ben! Over here!*' She waved her sunhat so wildly that she nearly overbalanced on her crutches.

What seemed like an age – an age of terror lest he miss her and disappear for ever – passed before he finally heard her, and stopped dead. No smile. Just a sudden wary stillness as he spotted her.

She scarcely noticed. She was too busy laughing and crying and shouting his name. And as she watched him shoulder his way through the crowd towards her, she saw how he'd changed. He was taller and stronger – she later learned that he'd worked his passage to Jamaica on a sugar boat – and most noticeable of all, he was *clean*. His black hair was glossy, his skin wasn't grey any more, but lightly tanned, and he wore clean blue dungarees and a calico shirt. And someone must have told him about cleaning one's teeth with a chewstick cut from a roadside bush, for when he spoke to her his teeth were no longer grey, but white.

'What's up, Sophie?' he said as he jumped up onto the verandah. He took off his frayed straw hat and sat down at the other end of the bench. Then he threw her a questioning look, as if he'd only seen her the day before.

She sat down clumsily, scattering her crutches, and

hardly able to breathe. 'You've grown so tall,' she gabbled, 'and brown! And you've got new clothes, and – and everything.'

'And I don't pong no more,' he said, flashing his feral grin and rescuing the crutches.

She gave a self-conscious laugh.

'And look at you,' he said. Then his grin faded. She could tell that he was trying to think up something else to say, but couldn't, because she looked so awful, and he wouldn't lie to her.

It flashed across her mind that although he knew about her TB, he'd never seen her splint, or the calliper. And he'd never seen her so thin and yellow. She smoothed her skirt over her knees. Her hands were bony and horrible. Her spirits plunged. 'I thought I'd never see you again,' she said. 'You never came to say goodbye.'

'Couldn't,' he said. 'Got into chancery, didn't I?'

'What's chancery?'

'Trouble. Bluebottles after me.'

'Bluebott— Oh, you mean policemen.' She nodded, sucking in her lips. 'I guessed it must have been something like that.' In fact she hadn't guessed anything of the sort. In her imagination she'd invested him with some kind of interesting but curable illness which prevented him from seeing her, while at the same time making him extremely sympathetic about tuberculosis.

She decided not to ask what kind of trouble he'd been in. It was enough to know that he hadn't kept away because of her illness. But it seemed impolite not to acknowledge it at all.

'Um,' she ventured, 'the trouble you were in – is it all right now?'

He turned away and looked out over the square, and the slight contraction of his features told her that it wasn't.

Anxiety seized her. 'Where's Robbie?'

He drew in his breath like a wince. 'He's not here,' he muttered.

Then she knew. Dead, she thought. Poor Robbie. Poor Ben.

She resolved not to say another word about it. If he wanted to tell her, he would. If not, there was no point in asking. So instead she asked him how he'd got to Jamaica.

He thought for a moment, then told her that he'd worked on a boat.

'Gosh, how exciting,' she said as brightly as she could, for she could see that he was still thinking about Robbie. 'Did you get seasick?'

He shook his head.

'I didn't either. Or Maddy.' She twisted her hands in her lap. It was hard not to think about Robbie. She wondered how he had died, and if she would meet him when she went to heaven herself. These days, she thought about dying a lot. She had to. There was a distinct possibility that the duppy tree would get its way, and she would die very soon.

To push the thought aside, she took out her purse and tried to offer Ben some of her pocket money. She should have known better. He pushed it angrily away. She shut her purse and put it in her lap, clutching it in her bony fingers. 'Oh, B-Ben,' she stammered, 'I'm so glad you're here.' Then she burst into tears.

She cried for what seemed like ages: great noisy hiccupy sobs. Through the sobs she felt him briefly touch her arm, then brush off her sleeve as if he'd made her dusty. 'What's up, Sophie?' he said brusquely.

Then out it all came. The tension at Fever Hill. The terror of the duppy trees. Her dragging conviction that she was going to die.

To her relief he didn't tell her to stop being an idiot. Nor did he try to cheer her up. He simply listened without interrupting. Then he asked one or two questions, and told her not to talk about it to anyone. Then he sat for a moment in silence, gazing at the higglers in the square without really seeing them. 'Right,' he said flatly. 'You leave it to me. I'll sort it out. But you got to do your bit. All right?'

She nodded, and shakily blew her nose. 'What – what do I do?'

'You don't say nothing to nobody, you stop fretting, and you start getting better.'

And somehow, knowing that he was in Jamaica, she had. From that day her appetite came back, and she slept peacefully for the first time in weeks. But she never saw him again. Once more he had dropped out of sight as noiselessly as a cat.

At least, he had until now.

CHAPTER SIX

'Sophie, what do you think you're doing?' said Madeleine as she watched her sister drawing on her gloves.

'I'd have thought that was obvious,' replied Sophie. 'I'm going out to make a call.' She put on her hat and jammed a hatpin into the crown.

'But you hate making calls. And yet suddenly you can't stay away from Parnassus.'

'I'm not going to Parnassus.'

'You know what I mean. The only reason you're going to Fever Hill is because it's Sibella's day to call on Clemency, and—'

'And I can see Sibella as well as Clemmy,' put in Sophie. 'Precisely. Two birds with one stone.'

'Don't you mean three?'

Sophie did not reply. Since the Trahernes' tea party she had veered between anger at the risks Madeleine was running, and frustration that she was being kept in the dark. But she hadn't confronted her sister over Alexander Traherne. What was the point? She'd only deny everything.

No, the only way to get at the truth was to corner Ben and make *him* tell. He'd never lied to her in the past, and she was fairly sure that he wouldn't now.

The day after the tea party, she had tried to put her plan into effect. She'd borrowed the dog cart and driven to Parnassus, 'to call on Sibella'. But to her dismay, Ben hadn't been there, and she'd learned from old Danny Tulloch that he'd been sent up to Waytes Valley on an errand. The following day, Sibella had driven up to Eden to call on her – but *she* had been out. It felt as if Fate were trying to stop her from seeing him.

'You don't need to go to Fever Hill to see Sibella,' said Madeleine relentlessly. 'You'll be seeing her in a few days at the Historical Society picnic.'

'But Clemency won't be there, will she?' Sophie said sweetly. 'And I really ought to see her, oughtn't I?'

Madeleine sighed. 'Well, whatever you do,' she said quietly, 'don't make trouble for Ben. It wouldn't be fair.'

Sophie paused with another hatpin in her hand and looked at her in surprise. 'So you admit that he's at Parnassus?'

'Well of course. He's been there for nearly two years.'

'But – Maddy. Why did you never tell me before?'

'Sophie—'

'He was my friend.'

'That's precisely why I didn't tell you.' Frowning, she picked at the lacquer on the looking-glass frame. 'Listen, Sophie. You had a schoolgirl crush when you were little—'

'I did not,' said Sophie indignantly.

'– but things are different now. You're no longer a child. You can't go around making a spectacle of yourself like you did at Parnassus.'

'I didn't,' muttered Sophie without much conviction.

'Yes you did. Sibella saw you, and so did that house guest of Rebecca's, and half the staff.'

Clever Madeleine, thought Sophie. Diverting attention from her own goings-on by focusing on me. 'I wouldn't have needed to "make a spectacle of myself",' she replied, 'if you'd been more open with me.'

They met each other's eyes in the glass. 'Why can't you have a little faith in me?' said Madeleine. 'Why can't you just let things be?'

'How can I? If I see something going wrong, how can I just stand by and "let it be"?'

Madeleine opened her mouth to reply, then shook her

head. 'You always do this. You get hold of something and you just will not let go.'

She's treating you like a child, Sophie told herself angrily as she crossed the bridge at Romilly and drove north along the Eden Road. Keeping you in the dark as if you're not ready to handle the truth. Who does she think she is?

It was horrible to feel like this about her own sister; horrible to be so angry with her. But she couldn't help it.

In the dog cart beside her, Fraser whistled tunelessly through his teeth, happily unaware that he'd been brought along as a pretext. Once they reached the house and found Sibella safely ensconced with Clemency, Sophie intended to take him down to the stables 'to see the horses'.

At the big guango tree she turned left onto Fever Hill land and headed west through the cane-pieces of Bellevue. Two miles in, the track veered north, and followed the trickle of the Green River, until presently the great house loomed up ahead: huge, shuttered and lonely on its bare brown hill.

She felt a twinge of guilt about Clemency. It was hardly fair to call on her simply as an excuse for questioning Ben. Clemency deserved better than that. And she needed help. 'She hasn't been off the estate in years,' Cameron had told her the night before. 'Scarcely eats a thing – except for laudanum, of course. She mixes it with pimento dram to hide the taste. Try to make her see sense and come and live with us.' As a sop to her conscience, Sophie had resolved to do just that.

But to her frustration there was no-one about when they drew up at the steps. No sign of Sibella's pretty little buggy, or of Clemency and her niece taking tea in the gallery.

Fraser sucked in his lips importantly, and jumped down and ran to the horse's head. 'Shall I take the carriage down to the stables?'

'Just tie it up here,' murmured Sophie, gazing up at the blank, shuttered façade. Her anger had drained away, leaving only self-doubt. Perhaps Maddy was right. Perhaps she shouldn't interfere.

Dead leaves rattled sadly across the steps as they climbed to the gallery. It was empty and dim, and smelt of desolation and decay. The floor was soft with dust, the cane furniture mildewed and broken. But someone had replaced a leg of the sofa with a pile of books, and made a nest for themselves with a tattered tartan throw. On the floor beside it lay a stack of *Gleaner* Saturday supplements, and Clemency's silver scissors and cuttings book. On a side table, next to a battered kerosene lamp, stood a gleaming silver frame containing the familiar funeral photograph.

'Clemency?' called Sophie. Her voice echoed through the shadowy house. 'Clemmy?'

No answer. She felt a curious reluctance to go inside. It had always been a strange house: a place of shadows and whispers, turned in upon itself. In his last years Jocelyn had hardly moved from his library, while his ancient aunt, known to all the family as Great-Aunt May, had lived in implacable isolation in the upper gallery, and Clemency flitted between her rooms and the family Burying-place.

But now Jocelyn was dead, and Great-Aunt May was living in a townhouse in Falmouth. Only Clemency remained, attended by Grace McFarlane, who made the daily climb from her home in the old ruined slave village at the bottom of the hill.

This afternoon, however, not even Clemency was to be found. Impatiently, Sophie drew out her watch. She sighed. Five o'clock. According to Madeleine, Sibella usually called at four.

With the toe of his boot, Fraser drew an arrow in the dust. 'Aunt Clemmy will probably be at the Burying-place. That's where she has her tea.'

'But I cannot possibly leave,' whispered Clemency, handing Sophie her cup and fluttering her pale, dry hands at the dead. 'How could I leave all this?'

Once again Sophie bit back her frustration. They'd found Clemency alone, sitting on the bench beneath the poinciana tree which shaded the graves. There was no sign of Sibella. When Sophie asked if she was expected, the older woman simply looked blank.

'Sometimes Miss Traherne comes later,' offered Fraser, sensing Sophie's disappointment. Then he ran off to set out his toy soldiers on a tombstone.

Sophie hoped he was right. But she couldn't help reflecting that as they were on the other side of the hill from the house, she wouldn't hear the carriage even if Sibella did turn up. For all she knew, Sibella might come, find no-one at home, and go away again. And here she was, trapped in this dismal place: an overgrown clearing hemmed in by coconut palms and wild lime trees, where seven generations of Monroes dreamed away the decades in a tangle of asparagus ferns and long silver grass.

Stifling her impatience, she turned back to Clemency, and grimly resolved to do her duty. 'You'd love it at Eden,' she said as persuasively as she could, 'and the children would adore to have you with them.'

But to her astonishment, Clemency's china-blue eyes widened with alarm. 'Oh, *hush*! You'll make Elliot feel left out!'

Sophie hesitated. 'Clemmy, darling. Elliot has been dead for twenty-nine years.'

Fraser raised his head from his hussars, and scanned the Burying-place with interest. According to Madeleine, he regarded his deceased relation as some kind of shadowy friend who liked to hide in the grass.

'*Hush!*' whispered Clemency again, as if the inhabitant of the little white marble tomb might hear and be offended. 'I am very well aware of that, Sophie. But I fail to see that it signifies.'

Her son had died in 1873, two days after he was born. Through a chain of mishaps he had not been baptized, and for a decade afterwards she had tormented herself with the conviction that he was in hell. Then Cameron had persuaded her that Elliot was in fact in heaven, and she had blossomed. For the first time in years she had ventured out in daylight. She'd even gone to church. But it had been a false dawn. Gradually, the notion of her son looking down from heaven had seized hold of her mind, until he'd become an all-seeing, admonitory, God-like presence from whom she could never escape.

Sophie put Clemency's teacup back on the tray and tried again. 'You'd only be an hour's ride away. You could come here every day if you wished.'

'It wouldn't be the same,' said Clemency. She took a little flask of pimento dram from her pocket, poured a measure into her cup and drank it down, giving Sophie her wincing, apologetic smile.

Sophie forced herself to smile back. As always with Clemency, she felt a twinge of vicarious guilt. This submissive yet curiously stubborn woman had once been married to her father. Married, and then deserted for Rose Durrant.

Clemency had never uttered a word of reproach. Indeed it was doubtful if she even remembered that she'd had a husband, for she'd only married him because her brother Cornelius had told her to. The defining event of her life had not been her husband's desertion but the death of her child. She had pulled her loss around her like a shawl, and devoted herself to grief. For nearly thirty years she had worn nothing but dull white mourning, and papered her rooms with funeral photographs of the dead infant. And when her hair had failed to turn white from grief, she'd simply dyed it grey.

She was now fifty-one, but looked nearer thirty, her extraordinary young-old features still delicately pretty, her blue eyes wide with perpetual apology. Except when it came to the question of leaving Fever Hill.

Sophie stirred her tea and fought the downturn in her spirits which this place always brought about. Her terrible old ancestor Alasdair lay over in the far corner. Her grandfather Jocelyn lay close by, reunited after five lonely decades with his adored young wife Kitty. And her father Ainsley lay beneath the low slate slab on which Fraser now paraded his lead hussars. Her father, who had left a trail of ruined lives: an unwelcome reminder of the risks which Madeleine was running.

'Oh look,' said Fraser, glancing up from his battle, 'here's Miss Traherne.'

Oh, thank God, thought Sophie. She got to her feet, took up her sun-umbrella, and gave Clemency a brisk smile. 'I've just remembered, I promised Fraser I'd take him to see the horses. Do you mind? I'll be back very soon.'

Her heart was beating uncomfortably fast as they crossed the hard brown lawns and started down the croton walk towards the stables. Fraser raced ahead like a puppy, doubling back every so often to make sure that she was following. She felt slightly bad about using him like this, especially as he'd fallen in with her plan with a six-year-old's unquestioning trust.

'You'll never guess who's in the stableyard,' he told her breathlessly as he tugged at her hand to make her go faster. '*Evie!* She can make animals out of cane-trash. She made a giraffe for my birthday and it's absolutely *brilliant!*'

Oh no, thought Sophie. She wanted to see Evie again, but not here. Not now, when she needed to talk to Ben.

Apprehensively, she emerged from the croton walk into the glare of the stableyard. At the far side she could see Sibella's little buggy. Beside it Ben, hatless and in shirt-sleeves, was setting down a pail of water for the horse. On the seat of the buggy sat a coloured girl in a pink print dress, chatting to him and swinging her legs.

Fraser raced across the yard, and Evie turned and smiled down at him. Then she saw Sophie, and said a word to Ben. He straightened up, wiping his hands down his breeches and throwing Sophie a wary, unsmiling look.

She felt horribly self-conscious as she walked towards them across the yard. It was a struggle not to limp. 'Hello, Ben,' she said with as much ease as she could muster. 'Hello, Evie, how are you? It's good to see you again.'

Out of the corner of her eye, she saw Ben roll down his shirtsleeves and reach for his tunic and cap. He did not respond to her greeting.

'Hello, Sophie,' murmured Evie with a shy smile. 'It's good to see you, too.'

As a child, Sophie had always been a little in awe of Evie, who, apart from being a year older, had been prettier and healthier, and had a secret born-day name, and a mother who was a witch. Now Sophie saw that the child had grown into a breathtakingly beautiful young woman. Dark almond-shaped eyes with an almost oriental slant; chiselled features of unnerving perfection; flawless coffee-coloured skin. Sophie felt overdressed in her fussy, unflattering afternoon gown, with her frilled sun-umbrella and gloves.

She turned her head and nodded at Ben in what she hoped was a friendly manner. He nodded back, but didn't meet her eyes. Fraser sidled over and stared up at him with the wary respect which small boys show for the mysterious brotherhood of grooms.

Awkwardly, Sophie furled her sun-umbrella and dug the point into the dust, wondering how to begin. In the old days, Ben would have flashed her his feral grin and said, 'What's up, Sophie?' But this wasn't the old days.

Hating herself for her cowardice, she turned back to Evie. 'I was wondering when we'd bump into each other,' she said brightly. 'I didn't know that you'd taken a position at Fever Hill.'

'I haven't,' replied Evie in her soft Creole accent. 'I teach school over at Coral Springs.'

She was too polite to show offence at being mistaken for a maid, but Sophie's cheeks burned. Evie had always been bright and ambitious. How could she have made such a blunder?

But Evie goodnaturedly smoothed things over by telling her about the teacher's dissertation on local history which she was writing at weekends.

'My grandfather had lots of old estate papers,' Sophie said quickly, to make amends. 'You must make use of the library whenever you like. Really. Do.'

Evie smiled and thanked her, but they both knew that she never would.

How pompous I sound, thought Sophie. The white Lady Bountiful patronizing the coloured girl. She summoned what remained of her courage and turned to Ben. 'Hello, Ben,' she said. Then she remembered that she'd already greeted him.

He tipped his cap to her with wary respect. 'Is it about the horse, miss?' he muttered, looking at the ground.

'The horse?'

'Your horse, miss. He's still out front. I took him a pail of water, but were you wanting me to bring him down here?' He still wasn't meeting her eyes, and his face wore a determined look, as if he'd worked out beforehand how he would behave.

'Um – no. No, thank you, that's quite all right.' She bit her lip. 'Ben – I'm sorry if I embarrassed you the other day. I mean, at Parnassus.'

'You didn't, miss,' he muttered. 'And – it's Kelly, miss. Not Ben. Better like that, if you understand.'

Again she felt herself colouring. So that's how it's to be, she thought. Madeleine was right after all. *Things are different now. You're no longer a child.*

She glanced down at the sun-umbrella, and traced a line in the dust. 'Just as you wish,' she said. 'Well, I won't take up too much of your time, I just needed to ask you something. I think I saw you in Montpelier? On Monday?'

He frowned at his boots. 'I don't remember, miss.'

Oh, no, she thought with a sinking heart. Not you too. 'Are you sure?' she asked.

He nodded.

There was another awkward silence. Evie sat in the buggy, studying her shoes. Ben turned his cap in his hands and frowned.

Sophie wondered why she'd come. What was she doing here? What could she possibly achieve, except to make everyone, including herself, supremely uncomfortable?

She looked at the young man standing before her with his head bowed and his black hair falling into his eyes, and she realized that she had been wrong about him. She'd built him up in her mind into something that he could never be. He was just a groom. His skin was tanned from the wind and the sun, and his hands calloused from stable work. He was just a rough young man who'd pulled himself out of the slums – who'd made good, according to his lights – but who would never be anything other than a rough young man. He wasn't some kind of special friend, as she'd believed when she was a child. He didn't think as she did.

It was a bleak thought, and it made her feel bereft. She had lost something which had never really existed. And she hadn't realized how much she'd valued it until now.

It was Fraser who came to her rescue. Perhaps sensing that something was wrong, he moved across and took her hand and looked up at her and smiled: a small tow-headed ally in a sailor suit.

She felt a rush of gratitude. 'Well,' she said, looking down into his big grey eyes, 'Fraser and I must be getting back. Goodbye, Evie, I'm sure I shall see you again soon. And good luck with your dissertation. Goodbye – Kelly.'

'Goodbye, Sophie,' said Evie with her shy smile.

'Miss,' said Ben with a nod.

The croton walk seemed endless, and she knew that she limped. She could feel their eyes on her all the way.

But when she glanced back, she saw with a pang that Ben wasn't even watching. He was bending down under the horse's belly to adjust its harness. Only Evie was looking after them, with a curiously intent expression on her lovely face.

At Sophie's side, Fraser held fast to her hand and took slow, giant strides. 'Aunt Sophie?' he said with a frown.

'Yes?'

'Did you notice that Miss Traherne's groom has green eyes?'

She did not reply.

'Does that mean he's a changeling? Mamma read us a story about that once. It means that he was snatched as a baby and swapped, and is really a prince.'

'Nonsense,' muttered Sophie. 'He's not a changeling. He's just a groom.'

*　*　*

She found Clemency with Sibella in the library. Clemency was struggling to explain her system for reorganizing the books, and Sibella was fast losing patience. '*Bonne chance*,' she murmured, pressing her cheek to Sophie's in farewell. 'If I stay an instant longer I shall forget myself. Come along, Fraser darling, you can show me out.'

'But the *principle* isn't difficult,' said Clemency, running a hand through her dyed grey hair and scattering hairpins over the parquet. 'I simply *feel* that for the sake of propriety, the gentleman writers ought to be kept separate from the ladies.'

Sophie stooped to retrieve the hairpins. She envied Sibella. She wanted to leave too. She felt lonely and forlorn, and she couldn't take much more of Clemency's nonsense, especially in this great book-lined room which echoed with memories. On the wall hung the grim old oil painting of Strathnaw; below it the daguerreotype of Kitty. She missed Jocelyn savagely. *Things are different now. You're no longer a child.*

'– unless of course they're married to each other,' continued Clemency, 'in which case they get a shelf to themselves.'

Sophie took a deep breath and pressed her fingers to her eyes. 'Is that why the Brownings are on the floor?'

'Precisely,' said Clemency. 'You see, I haven't yet found them a shelf. Poor dear Jocelyn had such a huge collection.'

Sophie picked up an old estate book and flicked through it. It seemed to be some sort of overseer's journal. Perhaps she should take it to Evie as a peace offering.

'Oh my dear,' cried Clemency in one of her startling changes of mood, 'I am so *frightfully* sorry.'

Sophie stared at her. 'What ever for?'

'I've just remembered. You *own* all this! And here I am rummaging about as if it belongs to me!'

'Clemmy—'

'I had quite forgot! Dear Cameron explained it all to me when Jocelyn died, but I forgot. How wicked it was of me to refuse to leave when you asked! I shall go at once. At once.'

'Oh, Clemmy, stop! Stop.'

Obediently, the older woman shut her mouth, sucking in her lips like a child.

Sophie glanced about her at the well-loved volumes, and at Clemency's pretty young-old face, so fraught with tension.

She had mishandled everything. She'd patronized Evie, and embarrassed Ben, and now she'd upset this poor woman, whom she ought to have helped. Madeleine was right. She shouldn't interfere. She would only make things worse.

She took Clemency's hot, dry hands in hers. 'You must stay here for as long as you wish. For ever, if you care to. Do you understand?'

Clemency watched her lips and nodded.

'Good. That's settled, then.' She kneaded her temple. 'Now. Where shall we put the Brownings?'

Night's coming down quick at the old slave village, and Evie's sitting out on the step, eating fufu with her mother, and trying to keep the black uneasiness from creeping into her heart.

Mosquitoes are humming a hive roundabout, the crickets and the whistling frogs are starting up their night song, and Patoo's going hoo-hoo up in the calabash tree.

Evie shivers. Sophie's in trouble, or she will be soon. What that trouble is, or when it will come, Evie doesn't know. But trouble will come for sure. She's seen the sign.

'Eh, Patoo!' shouts Grace. 'Get outta me yard!' And the owl hitches up his wings and flies away. Satisfied, Grace takes another pull on her pipe. Then she throws Evie a narrow-eye glance. 'Looks like you got some worry-head, girl. Make a try and tell me.'

Evie shakes her head. 'From this I can take care I self.'

Damn. Why is she always talking *patois* when she comes home? Soon as she's here, it seems like she just slips off her education like a pair of old board sandals, and leaves it at the door.

That's one of the things she hates about living here. Talking *patois* and eating out in the yard, like some low-class mountain nigger. That and the obeah-stick by the door, and her mother's broad bare feet and country nigger headkerchief. And her insistence on living in this rundown ruin of a place.

Merciful peace, her mother's only forty-five! She's still a fine, limber, beautiful woman. Why should she choose to live like this? Doesn't Evie make good money as a teacheress? Wouldn't she gladly pay for shoes and a store-bought dress? Why can't they go and live at Coral Springs, and forget about slave time and duppies?

But no. Not Grace McFarlane. *I not about to forget who I am and where I from,* she always says, *and you take care not to forget too. You one of the four-eyed people, Evie. You born with a caul. You wearing a little piece of it right now, in that guard you got at you neck, to stop the spirits troubling you.*

But Evie never did *want* to be four-eyed. Who asked her? Who gave her the choice? And her mother is wrong. Wearing a little piece of the caul is *no good at all* for keeping away spirits.

It always starts the same way. A sudden rush of sweet-sweet smell, then the cold fear creeping down the back of her neck. A spirit looks just like a regular person, but still there's something wrong about it. You always know that it's dead. It's got no sound to it, and the wind never lifts a hair of its head. It's in the wrong time and the wrong world. And for a while, when she sees it, Evie's in that world too.

Once when she was little, her mother warned her about spirits. *They're trickified things*, she told her. *Sometimes they mean good, and sometimes bad. And four-eyed people like you, Evie, you got to learn which is which,* or *you'll get things wrong-side and tangle-up.*

But Grace never did say *how* Evie was to learn that. And long ago Evie learned that since she can't tell if they mean good or bad, it's best to swallow her spit and say nothing at all.

Like the time when she was twelve, and saw blind old grandmother Semanthe, who'd died when she was little, sitting by the hearth, as sharp as sin. Two weeks after that, Evie's brother died. For years she blamed herself. Maybe if she'd told, he would have lived. But how was she to know that nana Semanthe had meant it for a warning?

And last month she'd seen a spirit-girl standing behind Ben. A thin, sad spirit-girl with red hair and blue shadows under her eyes, just standing there. Evie hasn't told Ben yet. What good would it do, since she doesn't know what it means?

Thinking on that, she gets up quickly and brushes the dust from her skirt. 'I'm going for a walk.'

Grace chews on her pipe and blows a smoke ring. 'Watch youself out there, girl.'

'I always do.'

She leaves the yard and starts off into the dark, moving noiselessly between the tumbledown slave houses mounded over with creepers, and the big black pawpaw trees standing guard. All the houses are ruined, except for theirs. They're the only ones who live here. Apart from the duppies.

Ratbats and moonshine, she thinks with disgust, that's my home. Halfway between the gates to the Fever Hill Road and the busha house up on the hill. A halfway place for a halfway girl who's neither black nor white.

She reaches the old aqueduct at the edge of the village, and curls up on the ancient cut-stone wall. The frogs are loud roundabout, and the scummy smell of the stagnant water fills her nostrils.

When they were children, she and Sophie used to come down here looking for treasure: for one of the big jars of Spanish gold that the nanas say got lost from ages back. Of course they never found one. But once they found a little calabash baby rattle from slave time, still with a couple of john-crow beans inside. They tossed for who should keep it, and Sophie won. She was always the lucky one. It's no different now.

Evie stretches out her legs and studies her brown canvas shoes with dislike. This afternoon at the stables, Sophie looked so pretty and fine in that beautiful flounced dress, with the white lace gloves, and those lovely high-heeled shoes with the little pearl buttons on the straps.

Jealousy curdles within her. *How are you, Evie? I didn't know that you'd taken a position here.* As if Evie's some kind of maid!

A ratbat flits across the moon. A forty-leg ripples up the trunk of the ackee tree. Evie clasps her knees and scowls at it.

The truth is, it wasn't Sophie's fault. She meant no harm, and she was mortified by her mistake. It's Evie McFarlane who's got this black, uneasy confusion in her heart. There's trouble coming for Ben because of that red-haired spirit-girl. And some kind of trouble for Sophie, too. But how bad? And when? And what should she do?

Maybe she should talk to Ben. She can tell him most things, for he's like a brother to her; sometimes she even calls him her 'buckra brother'. His skin may be white and hers brown, but underneath they're the same; they've both lost loved ones and done bad things, and they've both got no place where they can fit in.

Thinking of that, she brings out the little bag on the cord at her neck. Not the guard with the piece of her caul inside, but the other one: the tiny green silk bag that she calls her 'buckra charm', for it contains the fine gold chain that she can never openly wear. If she did, her mother would ask questions, and the man who gave it her would know that he can have her for true. The sweet-mouth man with the cut-crystal eyes and the up-class buckra ways.

But she's no fool, is Evie McFarlane. He's had no kisses from her, and no hand's play, either. She's a decent girl and she knows her worth.

And yet – sometimes it feels good just to take out the fine gold chain and pour it from palm to palm, and remember that she only has to crook her finger at him, and everything will change. No more slave village. No more fufu out in the yard. And best of all, no more four-eyed nonsense. No more dead-bury spirits walking about under the sun.

Because all that four-eyed talk is just so much cane-trash, Evie, it's just so much trash. You're *not* four-eyed. You've got *no* spirit-sight. You never saw nana Semanthe sitting by the hearth, or the red-haired spirit-girl standing behind Ben.

And you did *not*, this afternoon at the stables, see old Master Jocelyn following Sophie up the croton walk; stooping a little and leaning on his silver-topped cane, like he always did before he died.

CHAPTER SEVEN

Sophie always was pretty bad at hiding her feelings. So when she ran into a spot of bother it wasn't long before all Trelawny knew. Including Ben.

He did his best to steer clear of it, but he couldn't help picking up talk. Moses Parker and his niece Poppy heard it first, up at Eden. Then they told their cousins the McFarlanes down at Fever Hill, and they told *their* cousins, Danny and Hannibal Tulloch at Parnassus. And on to Ben.

It turns out that Miss Sibella saw Sophie chatting to Evie in the stableyard, and then 'had a quiet word' with her about getting too familiar with the coloureds. Sophie didn't take too kindly to that. In fact, the very same afternoon she rode over to see that Dr Mallory at his darkie clinic at Bethlehem, and started helping out. She made out that she'd meant to do it all along, but Ben's not fooled. She's just doing it because Miss Sibella had that 'quiet word' with her.

And according to Moses and Poppy, the quality up at Eden were none too pleased about it, neither. Madeleine was worried that it'd keep the young men away. 'How are you going to meet anyone if you're always at Bethlehem?' As for Master Cameron, he couldn't see the point. 'I'm not sure where you'll find the patients, Sophie. I mean, people of our sort are hardly going to desert their own doctors for a bush hospital in the woods. And as for the

84

blacks, I'd have thought they'll see it as undercutting their own people – the myal-men and the obeah-women. They may even be offended.'

He had a point, but Sophie wouldn't see it. She'd got the bit between her teeth, all right.

That was a week ago, and since then things have been limping along quietly enough. But today it's the Historical Society picnic, and it looks like the ladies are ganging up on her again.

The picnic's a big posh charity affair with a lecture and a lunch and tea after. This year, Master Cornelius is the host, so it's no expense spared. Huge stripy marquee and a band, and all sorts of fancy nosh. The only thing is, it's up at Waytes Lake. Not Ben's favourite place.

The last time he was here was with Mrs Dampiere. He can see her now, talking to Master Cornelius under the poinciana tree. She catches his eye and tries not to smile. She thinks it's funny. Ben don't. He feels like everybody's watching him, like everybody knows. And it only makes it worse that Madeleine and Sophie are here, too.

So now it's tea-time, and Madeleine's off by the lake talking to Master Alex, and Sophie's sitting in the marquee with Miss Sibella and old Mrs Pitcaithley and Mrs Herapath, and that's when they start in on her about the clinic. All very ladylike and polite and 'for her own good', but still having a go. Hannibal Tulloch's on serving duty, and hears it all. Though why he thinks Ben cares one way or the other is anybody's guess.

What's it to Ben if some posh bint's got in over her head? Besides, just because he give her a hard time in the stableyard the other afternoon, that's no reason why he should worry about her now.

But still. He takes a little walk past the doorway, to see what's what. And when he does, he gets a surprise. He'd expected her just to be a bit narked. After all, she's not the sort to be fazed by a telling off. But when he sees her she's sitting by the tea urn, all alone, and with that look on her face that she gets when she's trying not to show she's upset. It puts him in mind of when she was a kid, and she give him the picture-book and he went for her. It puts him in mind of the other day at Fever Hill.

A while later, he's standing by the carriage with Trouble when he sees her again. Master Alex and Madeleine are still by the lake, and she's making straight for them, very determined. Up she goes to Master Alex – not a glance at her sister – and draws him aside and starts talking to him, all sweetness, but very, very firm. That's Sophie for you. One minute she's down in the dumps, and the next she's doing something about it.

To begin with, Master Alex is looking down at her and smiling, the perfect gentleman; then his smile fades, like he's just had a nasty surprise. Then he looks over at Ben.

Shit, thinks Ben, as he watches them coming towards him. What's she gone and said to him?

'It seems that Miss Monroe has hurt her wrist,' goes Master Alex, looking a bit pink about the cheeks. 'You're to drive her home at once.'

Ben shoots Sophie a look, but she's turned away, very composed. What's her game? Her wrist was fine ten minutes ago when she was pouring the tea.

He scratches round for an excuse. 'Trouble didn't ought to be pulling a carriage in the first place,' he tells Master Alex, 'let alone traipsing all the way up to Eden and back.'

Master Alex raises an eyebrow. 'I think, my lad, that you may safely leave me to make the decisions.'

'But sir—'

'Look to it, Kelly. And no more talk.'

For a moment, Ben meets the pale blue eyes. He can tell that Master Alex isn't best pleased about it neither, but for some reason he's going along with it. Maybe Sophie said a word to him about what she saw at Montpelier, to persuade him to toe the line. She's not stupid, is Sophie.

So Ben heaves a sigh and tips his cap at Master Alex, and jumps up into the driver's seat and stares stonily ahead.

'Is anything wrong?' goes Sophie to Master Alex, as cool as mint.

Out of the corner of his eye Ben sees Master Alex pull

a wry face and shake his head. 'Just a typical groom. Overprotective of the horses to the point of insolence.' Then he hands Sophie into the phaeton, and turns to Ben. 'Up to Eden, and look sharp. I want you back by seven.'

So now it's been twenty minutes since they set off, and she still hasn't said a word, but he's buggered if he'll be the first to speak. He didn't ask to drive her home. And if she thinks she can make him talk just because he's a servant, she's got another think coming.

They turn a corner and come on a john crow in the middle of the track, gobbling up the last of a cane-rat. Trouble snorts and tosses her head, and the john crow twists its ugly red neck and hitches its wings and buggers off. Ben tells Trouble not to make a fuss, and she shakes her mane tetchily in reply.

And still Sophie don't say a word.

They come out of Waytes Valley onto the Fever Hill Road, and that's when he realizes that he'll *have* to speak first, to ask her which way she wants to go. Oh, bugger. *Bugger.*

He tips his cap and turns his head sideways. 'D'you want to go by town, miss, or cut through Fever Hill?'

'Fever Hill,' she replies. 'That is, if you think you can find your way through the cane-pieces.'

He sets his teeth. He can find his way blindfold, as she must know. What's her game? Is she needling him because he give her a time of it at Fever Hill? Well, what's she expect? She's grown up now, and a lady. It's not her place to talk to grooms.

So after a quarter of a mile they turn right into the Fever Hill carriageway. They go up through the cane-pieces of Alice Grove, and past the Pond, and the old ruined sugar works that got burnt in the Rebellion; past the slave village where Evie lives, and the tumbledown aqueduct. They skirt the bottom of the hill and go past the great house stables, then across the trickle of the Green River and out into the cane-pieces of Bellevue. It's a hot after-noon for the beginning of December, and everything's breathless and still. Even the crickets are half asleep. All he can hear is the clip-clopping hooves and the creak of the carriage, and the blood thumping in his ears.

They reach the guango tree that marks the end of the estate, and he turns right onto the Eden Road. The land starts to climb, so he slows Trouble to a walk. Wild almond trees overhang the road, their big dark leaves casting stripy shadows in the dust. The noise of the carriage is loud. Sophie's silence is getting on his nerves. Why don't she say something?

They start down the slope towards the bridge over the Martha Brae, and he catches the familiar smell of greenstuff and rottenness. This time of year the river's a sluggish, muddy green, its banks choked by creepers and those big red claw-flowers. The bridge is soft with moss, and over on the other side he can see the ruins at the edge of Eden. Only a couple more miles, he thinks with relief.

It's a rum old place, the ruins at Romilly. Tumbledown walls tangled over with hogmeat and strangler fig. Ironwood trees and giant bamboo shutting out the light. And in among the creepers, these strange little twisted mauvy-white flowers. Evie says they're orchids. All Ben knows is that they've got a thick, sweet scent that makes him think of graves.

The darkies say that years back, Romilly was some kind of slave village like the one at Fever Hill. That's why they don't come here, on account of all the duppies. But Ben don't give a tinker's cuss about duppies. When he was a lad he used to come here all the time. He used to sleep out here. Darkie ghosts? What are they to him? He's got a packload of ghosts of his own.

'When you get across the bridge,' says Sophie, making him jump, 'just pull up on the other side.'

What? Christ. What's she up to now?

He gives the reins a flick. 'Very good, miss,' he mutters.

'After that, you may help me down.'

'Yes, miss.'

'And stop calling me miss.'

'All right.'

When they're over the bridge he pulls up. Then he jumps down to help her out. As she puts her foot on the step she stumbles, and has to steady herself on his arm. She don't look at him, but he can tell that she's angry with herself. She always hated that knee of hers. He wonders if it's still giving her trouble. She don't limp or nothing, but it looks like it buckles now and then.

He ties Trouble to a clump of giant bamboo, then stands by her head with his hand on her coarse black mane. It's stuffy under the bamboo, and sort of muffled. Just the slow creak of the canes, and the rise and fall of the crickets, and the whisper of the river. He takes a deep breath, but still feels breathless. Where's all the air gone?

He watches Sophie walk to the riverbank and pace up and down, her arms crossed about her waist. She's in pale green. Floaty pale green frock, lace gloves, and a big straw hat with a pale green ribbon down her back. It's pretty, but it don't look right on her. Funny, that. Madeleine was born for nipped-in waists and leg-of-mutton sleeves. She's made of curves, just like that Lillie Langtry on a postcard. But when Sophie's all poshed up, she don't look right. And she knows it, too. She's too skinny and she moves too fast, like she keeps forgetting that she's in long skirts. She can't seem to stay still long enough to play the grand lady.

He tells hisself that she's just some bint like all the others; just some posh bint like that slimy Mrs Dampiere. But it don't work. It never did with Sophie.

'I used to come here with Evie,' she says, looking down at the river. 'We used to give offerings of rum to the River Mistress, and make a wish. I always made the same wish. I asked the River Mistress to make sure that wherever you were, you'd be all right.'

Christ, she can talk straight when she wants to. He'd forgotten that. It gives him that hot, prickly tightness in his chest. It makes him feel trapped.

'It looks as if the River Mistress heard me,' she goes on, 'although it did take rather a long time to find out.' She turns and shoots him a look. Her face is stubborn and set. Straight dark brows drawn together in a frown; little shadowy dents at the corners of her mouth deeper than usual. He's in for trouble, all right. 'I know you don't want me to talk to you,' she says, 'but I don't care. I'm fed up with being told what to do. So just this once I shall do as I please, and you can't stop me.'

She's right about that. He can hardly put her in the dog cart if she don't want to go, can he? And he can't just leave her here to walk the rest of the way home – although that's what she deserves for putting him on the spot like this.

'Ever since I got back,' she says, 'everything's been different. Eden. Maddy. My friends. You. I've tried to pretend it isn't so, but what's the use?'

So what d'you want me to do about it? he tells her silently. If you're asking me to make you feel better, you've come to the wrong bloke.

She takes a couple of steps towards him, and lifts her chin. 'Eight years ago, you disappeared. You just disappeared. Where did you go?'

He don't reply. Why the hell should he? Why the sodding hell should he?

'Come on, Ben, answer me.'

He turns his head to the river, then back to her. In the dappled green shade she looks like something under water. She's got that pale, pale skin: the sort that never even gets a flush from the sun. 'I went to Kingston,' he says between his teeth. 'I went to Kingston and Port Antonio and Savanna la Mar, and half a dozen other places in between. There. Now you know.'

'But what did you do?'

'What d'you mean?'

'How did you live? How did you survive?'

'What d'you think? I worked.'

'Yes, but at what?'

'What's it to you?'

'I want to know.'

'Well that's a shame, because I'm not going to tell you. It's high time we was going—'

'No!' she cries, stamping her foot.

A couple of ground-doves shoot up into the trees in a startled flurry. Trouble puts back her ears and looks worried.

Sophie ignores them. She's pressing her lips together to keep them steady, and suddenly she looks very young. He almost feels sorry for her. She's still the same old Sophie. Easily hurt, but always putting herself in the way of more hurt. Why else would she be talking to him?

'When I was little,' she says, 'you helped me get better.' She says it almost angrily: like an accusation. 'I don't know what you did. Perhaps it was just seeing you, and knowing I had a friend – or – or merely thinking that I did. You can pretend all you like that none of that happened, Ben Kelly, but I don't believe that you can have forgotten everything.'

'Well of course I haven't forgotten,' he snaps. 'Forgotten? How could I sodding well forget?' Suddenly he's so angry that he wants to shake her. He pulls off his cap and wipes his forehead on his wrist, and takes a few paces in a circle. Then he comes back to face her and stands with his hands on his hips, glaring down at her. 'Do you think that when I was a kid, people used to just give me things? Me? A fucking little sewer rat? Well do you?'

She blinks as if he's hit her.

'*Blackie the Charger* and *The Downfall of the Dervishes*,' he goes, counting them off on his fingers. 'Plus a whole load of soup, and that fruit on the first day, and that bag of cherries that Madeleine give Robbie one time. Of course I haven't sodding well forgotten.'

She chews her lip, and looks down at her feet, then back to him.

'Just because somebody don't talk about it, it don't mean they don't remember. But what's the good in raking it up? What's the point?'

She starts to say something, but he cuts the air with his palm. 'No. Don't start. I know what you're going to say.'

The dents at the corners of her mouth deepen, but this time it's a bit of a smile. 'No you don't.'

'Yes I do. You're going to have another go at me about

Montpelier. Well I'll save you the trouble, shall I? You're right, I was there, just like you said. So was Master Alex, and so was your sister.'

Her mouth falls open. The light brown eyes are very wide. 'But – *why*?'

'Why what?'

'Why were you there? What were they—'

'That's enough!' he shouts. 'I'm not telling you no more.'

'But—'

'No! It don't matter how long you go on at me, I'm not telling. I promised Madeleine I wouldn't, and I'm not going back on that now. Not for you, not for nobody.'

There's a silence while she takes that in. Then she turns away from him, crossing her arms about her waist. Her arms tighten. He sees her shoulder-blades jutting beneath her frock.

She turns back and looks up into his face. She's very intent, but for once he hasn't a clue what she's feeling. He can see the little flakes of gold in her eyes, and the way her eyelashes are tipped with gold, so that you can't tell how long they really are till you're right close up. Again he gets that prickly tightness in his chest. He can't hardly breathe.

Trouble nudges his back with her nose, and he puts a hand on her neck to tell her to give over. 'Why can't you just trust Madeleine?' he says. 'She's only looking out for you.'

'She's treating me like a child.'

'No she's not. She's your big sister, she's looking out for you. You're bloody lucky to have her.'

That makes him think of his own big sister Kate, and for a moment a horrible feeling wells up inside of him. It's frightening. Like everything's about to crack wide open. He has to slam the lid down hard.

Oh, he should of never let this happen. What was he thinking of? Talking to Sophie like this? It makes him angry all over again – although whether with himself or with her, he couldn't say.

He gives himself a shake, and turns on his heel and goes

over to the giant bamboo and unties the reins with a snap.
'You said we was friends,' he tells her over his shoulder,
'but that's in the past. We're not kids no more, and we're
not friends, neither.'

'But—'

'Look. The only reason you can make me talk to you is
because I'm a servant, and you can order me about. That's
not being friends.'

She opens her mouth to reply but he talks her down.

'You didn't ought to of done this,' he says, yanking
down the carriage step and jerking his head at her to
climb up. 'And don't you ever do it again.'

'Ben, I didn't mean—'

'It's not fair, and I won't have it. I don't care how posh
you are.'

'I'm sorry.'

'I don't want sorry. I just want you to promise –
promise – that you won't pull a trick like this again.'

She catches her lip between her teeth, and those eyebrows of hers draw together in a frown. Then she gives a
curt nod. 'Very well. I promise.'

CHAPTER EIGHT

They made the rest of the journey in awkward silence. Sophie watched Ben's rigid back, and wondered what he was thinking. But not once did he turn round or say a word to her. He didn't seem angry any more, but neither did he appear to think that there was anything left to say.

She wasn't sure what had been in her mind when she'd arranged for him to drive her home – or what she'd been hoping to achieve. She felt confused and upset, but oddly elated. And she was already beginning to regret having given him that promise.

They reached the house, and she was startled to see Moses waiting by the door, looking scared. 'Jesum *Peace*, but I glad to see you, Missy Sophie!' he cried, wringing his hands and getting in the way as Ben was letting down the carriage steps. 'Master Camron into a *rage*, missy! Swearing like half past midnight, and blazing at Mistress—'

'At Mistress?' said Sophie as she stepped down. 'But Mistress isn't home yet, I left her at Waytes Lake.'

Moses tried to swallow and shake his head and talk, all at the same time. 'No, missy. Master Camron sent for her to come *straight* home, and now they on the verandah, and he *blazing* into her, lip-lashing and throwing black words! True to the fact, Missy Sophie! I about ready to take foot and *run*!'

Sophie threw an anxious glance at Ben, but he didn't

even look at her. The perfect groom, she thought in exasperation. She watched in disbelief as he jumped back into the driver's seat and turned the phaeton round, and headed off down the road without a backward glance.

Moses's hovering presence dragged her back to the problem in hand. Clearly he was relieved to see her, but anxious for her to go inside and sort it out.

Pushing thoughts of Ben to the back of her mind, she glanced apprehensively at the house. Something must be very wrong. Cameron was the last man to lose his temper with his wife, let alone send her a peremptory summons and then swear at her when she arrived.

And Madeleine's own route home proved that she wasn't herself. To have missed out Romilly altogether, she must have taken the most direct route from Waytes Lake, due south through the cane-pieces of Glen Marnoch, then across the river at Stony Gap. That would have taken her very close to the Cockpits, and she hated the Cockpits. She would never have gone that way if it hadn't been an emergency.

Squaring her shoulders and dreading what she might find, Sophie went inside.

The very air of the hall crackled with tension. 'What on earth is the matter?' she whispered to a terrified Poppy. But the black girl only shook her head and hustled the children into the nursery.

'How could you do it?' came Cameron's voice from the verandah. 'How could you bring yourself to do such a thing?'

Madeleine's reply was low and indistinct.

'*What?*' roared Cameron. 'Is that supposed to make it all right?'

Sophie's heart sank. In all the years that she'd known him, he'd hardly ever lost his temper. It could mean only one thing. He'd found out about Montpelier. And God knew what else besides.

Without pausing to take off her hat, she crept across the hall towards her room. But she was only halfway there when Cameron spotted her. 'Sophie, is that you?' he called brusquely from the doorway. 'Could I trouble you to come out here for a moment?'

She floundered for an excuse, and came up with nothing. 'Er – of course. Just give me a minute to take off my hat.'

In her room she yanked out the hatpins and threw her hat on the bed. Then she went to the looking-glass and tidied her hair. Her hands were shaking. Her reflection looked guilty and wan. What could she say if he asked? Tell him a direct lie? Or betray her own sister? It wasn't much of a choice.

When she reached the verandah he was prowling up and down, his fists jammed into the pockets of his shooting-jacket, his light grey eyes glassy with anger.

Madeleine sat very straight on the sofa, her face rigid and defiant. Scout the puppy was pressed against her skirts. He was trembling, his ears flat against his skull, his blunt black muzzle twitching back and forth as he watched his master pacing up and down.

Sophie halted in the doorway and put on what she hoped was a non-committal smile.

Cameron shot her a look and continued to pace. 'I dare say you know all about this,' he said between his teeth.

She glanced at her sister. But Madeleine's eyes were fixed on some point in the middle distance, and her face gave nothing away. 'Know about what?' said Sophie.

Cameron threw up his hands. 'Why, the simple matter of my wife selling her inheritance behind my back.'

Sophie's mouth fell open. 'Wha-t?'

'You mean to say you didn't know? It's true. Strathnaw. The Monroe family seat. Sold. Behind my back.' Again he began to pace. 'My God, how people will laugh when they find out—'

'Nonsense,' put in Madeleine robustly. 'No-one can laugh if they don't know anything about it, and I went to enormous trouble to keep it secret.'

'Yes,' said Cameron, 'secret from your own husband.'

'If you'd known beforehand you'd have stopped me.'

'Well of course I'd have stopped you!' he roared. 'What kind of logic is that?'

This was too much for Scout. He gave a yelp and hurtled down the steps with his tail between his legs. A flock of pea-doves shot off the lawn in an outraged flurry.

There was an echoing silence on the verandah. Madeleine's bird-feeder swung gently in the breeze. A doctorbird hovered over it, its wings an iridescent blur.

Cameron rubbed a hand across his face, and went to the balustrade and stood looking over at the garden. Sophie could see the tension in his shoulders: the effort it cost him to bring himself under control. He hated losing his temper. And he would not easily forgive himself for raising his voice to his wife.

Quietly, Sophie made her way to the sofa and sat down beside her sister. Madeleine turned her head and made a valiant attempt at a smile. Sophie couldn't smile back. She felt too ashamed. Some idea of what she had witnessed at Montpelier was breaking over her like a wave.

To have been *such* a fool. Worse than a fool. To have suspected her own sister of infidelity – infidelity with a thoughtless young cub like Alexander Traherne – while all the time she'd only been trying to sell that grim old Scottish barrack to save the home she loved. And who better to help her make a secret sale than the Trahernes, the premier mercantile family in Trelawny?

How could you have been so blind? Sophie berated herself. To have harboured such suspicions! And to have failed utterly to perceive that Eden wasn't just hitting a rough patch, but was in danger of going under.

Yet all the signs had been there. The long hours Cameron worked. Madeleine's constant sewing: turning her own gowns instead of ordering new ones; making the children's clothes herself. And what made Sophie go hot and cold with shame was that through it all they had financed her without complaint. The Ladies' College at Cheltenham, the first-class passage home; even the little second-hand pony-trap for taking her to that wretched clinic.

She watched her sister put her hands to her temples and smooth back her hair. Ever since Sophie could remember, Madeleine had done that when she was under pressure. She'd always been the strong one. Brave, resolute, and sure of herself, even when she was in the wrong. Suddenly Sophie felt weak, and very much the younger sister.

'Surely you can understand why I did it?' said Madeleine to Cameron's back. 'Eden is our home. For sixteen years you've put your heart and soul into this place. I will not stand by and watch it taken away by the bank.'

Still with his hands on the balustrade, he glanced at her over his shoulder. 'Even if it means going behind my back?'

Madeleine's lips trembled. 'I told you why I did that. I explained—'

'When we got married we made a promise to each other. No secrets. No more secrets. Have you forgotten that?'

She looked down at her lap, and her hands curled into fists. 'Of course not,' she said. 'But Eden is our home. It's more important than Strathnaw—'

'Strathnaw was your inheritance. My God, Madeleine! There have been Monroes on that land for over four hundred years. How could you sell it? How would Jocelyn have felt if he'd lived to see this?'

'Oh, that's a low shot—'

'It would have broken his heart. Did you ever think of that?'

'Of course I thought of it! I thought of very little else!'

Sophie reached out and took her hand, and gave it a squeeze. 'I think you were immensely brave,' she said. 'Whom did you find to buy it?'

Madeleine gave her a wan smile. 'I don't even know. I didn't want to. The Trahernes handled all that.'

'*The Trahernes?*' said Cameron in disbelief. He raised his eyes to the ceiling. 'Oh, God in heaven.'

Madeleine looked perplexed. 'But – they were wonderful. Both Cornelius and Alexander.'

Cameron snorted. 'I'm sure they were. I'm sure they were delighted to carry on an intrigue with a beautiful woman behind her husband's back.'

Madeleine's chin went up. 'What's that supposed to mean?'

'A young rake like Alexander and an old lecher like Cornelius? Superlative choice of conspirators, my darling. Now you'll be the talk of every club from here to Kingston. What were you thinking?'

'I was thinking of saving Eden,' she retorted. 'Which clearly was horribly wrong of me. I do apologize.'

'But the Trahernes, Madeleine? Have you ever known Alexander to keep a secret?'

'Cameron, lower your voice, or the servants will hear.'

'They already know! By now I should imagine half Trelawny knows!'

'Oh, how you exaggerate!'

Sophie drew a deep breath, and struggled to take it in. 'So that's what you were doing in Montpelier,' she said.

'What?' said Madeleine.

'You went there about the sale. That's it, isn't it? And you were upset, and Alexander was comforting you.'

'Of course,' said Madeleine distractedly. 'What did you think?' Plainly the nature of Sophie's suspicions hadn't yet occurred to her.

Cameron turned to Sophie. 'What do you mean, you saw her in Montpelier? Are you telling me that you did know about this?'

'No,' said Sophie. 'It's just that—'

'But you said you saw her in Montpelier.'

'Well – yes. With Alexander Traherne and—' She was going to say 'Ben Kelly' but stopped herself just in time. This was not the occasion for Cameron to learn that the 'street-Arab' he'd always mistrusted had been in on his wife's little scheme.

'Yes?' demanded Cameron. 'And who else?'

'And I was puzzled,' said Sophie, looking up at him with a tight-lipped smile. 'I saw her with Alexander and I was puzzled.'

He gave her a narrow look.

'Cameron, do come and sit down,' said Madeleine. 'All this looming is giving me a headache.'

He glanced from Sophie to his wife, and back again. Then he rubbed the back of his neck, and sighed, and went to a chair and threw himself down. He put his elbows on his knees and shook his head. 'We would have found a way,' he muttered. 'We would have found some way to dig ourselves out of this mess without selling an acre.'

'How?' said Madeleine quietly.

'I don't know. I'd have found a way.'

Madeleine looked at him for a moment. Then she rose and went to sit on the arm of his chair, and put her hands on his shoulders. 'And what was I supposed to do in the meantime? Watch you work yourself into an early grave?'

'Madeleine—'

'I did it for us,' she said firmly. 'And I would do it again. Tomorrow.'

He opened his mouth to protest but she gave his shoulders a little shake. 'I would do it again,' she repeated. 'You'd better just accept that.'

He heaved a sigh.

She smoothed a lock of his hair back from his temple. 'I know it's a blow to your pride. I know that. But really, what of it? You've suffered worse in the past, and lived.'

He gave a snort of laughter.

'And you'll live with this,' she went on. 'But I will not let us be forced out of Eden. And there's an end of it.'

When Sophie left them, Madeleine was leaning against him with her head close to his, talking in her low, firm voice. And he was listening.

'Maddy, why didn't you tell me?' said Sophie the following afternoon when she'd finally caught up with her sister alone. It was Poppy's half-day off, and they were walking together in the garden, and watching the children chasing an exuberant Scout around the lawn.

'How could I tell you?' said Madeleine. 'That would

have been asking you to lie for me. To lie to Cameron. How could I do that?' She turned sharply away, and for the first time Sophie realized what the weeks of deception must have cost her.

'Oh God, Maddy. I'm so sorry.'

Madeleine laughed and wiped her eyes with her fingers. 'Whatever for?'

'For being such an idiot. For pestering you all the time.'

'Good heavens, in your place I'd have done far worse. No, I'm the one who's sorry. What a homecoming for you! I couldn't believe it when Alexander told me we had to go to Montpelier on the very day you were arriving. I didn't sleep all night.'

'But – why did you have to go on that particular day?'

'It was the only time the attorney could come. He was bringing the papers for me to sign from Spanish Town.' She paused. 'Cornelius thought the Montpelier Hotel would be a quiet, unobtrusive place to meet. And look how that turned out.' She shuddered. 'I was terrified that we wouldn't get back to Montego Bay in time to meet you. That was our one piece of luck, when the train got delayed.'

Sophie frowned. 'I still don't quite understand. When you met me at Montego Bay, you were with Cameron. How—'

'I told him I was going in early, to do some shopping, and I'd meet him there. Another lie, I'm afraid.'

Sophie paused. 'All that was three weeks ago. Once it was done, why didn't you just tell us?'

'Because it wasn't done. The attorney had to perfect the title, or some such thing. I don't understand all the details, but I did know that I had to wait until it was absolutely irrevocable before I told Cameron, or he'd put a stop to it.' Suddenly she looked as if she were about to cry. 'You know how he felt about Jocelyn. The old man was like a father to him. He'd never have consented to Strathnaw's going out of the family, even though it's been nothing but a drain on us for years.'

'How did he find out?'

Madeleine gave a hollow laugh. 'Oh, that was the most wonderful mix-up you could imagine! The letter from the attorney came through yesterday, confirming that it had all gone through. But the clerk addressed it to Cameron by mistake. He picked it up when he went to town to collect the post.'

'Oh, Lord,' said Sophie.

'Quite,' said Madeleine. 'Oh well. I brought it on myself. I usually do. But we'll get over it.'

Sophie was silent for a moment. 'I had no idea that things were this bad. I mean, with Eden. Somehow I always thought that Cameron would pull through.'

Madeleine smiled. 'He can't work miracles, Sophie.'

'You do know that you can have Fever Hill, don't you? Just say the word and I'll sell it tomorrow, and you can have the money.'

'My goodness, what an offer! Whatever would Clemency say?'

'It's not a joke, Maddy. I mean it.'

Madeleine put a hand on her arm and tried to smile. 'I know you do. And it's wonderful of you. But there's no need to sacrifice your inheritance just yet. Strathnaw will see us through for a good many years. And who knows, the price of sugar may soar, and we'll all become millionaires!'

Sophie saw that she was determined to make light of it. And perhaps that was the best way of dealing with it.

For a while they walked in silence beneath the tree-ferns. Scout rooted about under the plumbago, and emerged with his muzzle neatly encrusted with a ring of red earth. Among the lime trees, Belle jumped up and down and shouted at Fraser to give her a turn on the swing or she'd tell on him.

Madeleine called to Fraser to let his sister have a go, and not to push her too hard. Then she turned to Sophie as if to say something more, but thought better of it, and moved on.

Walking beside her, Sophie thought about her own behaviour over the past few weeks, and winced. She'd antagonized Madeleine at every opportunity, practically called Alexander a liar to his face, and persecuted Ben – all in an ill-conceived crusade to get at 'the truth'. And she was supposed to be the clever one of the family.

Thinking of Ben, she felt a twinge of unease. What if that trick she'd pulled yesterday had consequences for him? Or indeed for her? No-one had said a word about it, but it couldn't have gone unnoticed. And if Sibella had felt constrained to have a 'quiet word' about Evie McFarlane, how much more strongly would she feel about a servant?

There was a wail from the lime trees. Belle had fallen off the swing. Then, when nobody came to see what the matter was, she sat up in the grass, grinning at them to show that she was all right.

Madeleine watched her daughter for a moment, then put her arm through Sophie's and started back across the lawn. 'There's something else I need to talk to you about,' she said in a low voice.

Sophie glanced at her in surprise. 'Something else?' She made a face. 'My goodness, you mean there's more?'

She'd meant it as a joke, but Madeleine didn't smile. 'I'm afraid there is,' she said. 'It's about Ben.'

Sophie braced herself. 'If it's about yesterday—'

'Not exactly. At least, I don't think it is.'

'What does that mean?'

Madeleine looked down at her feet and frowned. 'Susan told me just now. She heard it from Moses.'

'What did she hear? Is anything wrong?'

'I'm afraid they sacked him, Sophie.'

Sophie stopped and stared at her.

'Apparently, Cornelius gave him his notice last night.'

'But – why?'

'I don't know. Something about insolence. But I get the impression that that was just an excuse.'

Sophie cast about in dismay. 'Of course it's an excuse! It's because of us, isn't it? It's because I got him to tell me about Montpelier, and somehow Alexander found out, and—'

'No, that's just jumping to conclusions.'

'Well, then, maybe it's because I kept him talking at Romilly and he was late getting back. Either way, it's our fault.'

'Sophie—'

'Well it is, isn't it? It's got to be.'

Madeleine did not reply. But Sophie could see from her face that she thought so too.

'It's so unfair,' said Sophie, nearly in tears. 'He didn't want to have anything to do with us, he kept telling me. And he wouldn't have, if we hadn't forced things.' In her anger she included Madeleine as a guilty party, but they both knew who was mostly to blame. 'He was doing so well at Parnassus. And now we've spoilt it for him.'

'We don't know that for sure, Sophie.'

'Yes we do. He's lost his job, and he's got nowhere to go. And it's all our fault.'

CHAPTER NINE

It takes him a while to work out why he's got the sack, on account of it all came a bit out of the blue. One minute he was in the tackroom cleaning stirrup irons, and the next thing there was Master Cornelius giving him two weeks' notice without a character. 'I'm disappointed in you, Kelly. Disappointed and severely displeased.'

Me too, thought Ben, putting down the stirrup iron on a bale of hay. Sacked? What for? That bit of backchat with Master Alex at the picnic? Coming home late? What?

He watched Master Cornelius walking up and down the tackroom. He's a short, meaty, good-looking man in his late fifties; the sort of man you take to at first, but never quite trust. There's too much of the lizard in him for that. Bulgy pale blue eyes, always swivelling about for the next bit of skirt. Red lips that never look dry. Scaly lizard hands.

'You know, Kelly,' he said, picking up a jar of paraffin wax and frowning at the label, 'you brought this on yourself. Perhaps in future you'll keep a civil tongue in your head. Especially when there's a lady present.'

A lady? What lady? What's this about?

Two years down the plughole – that's what it's about. And without a character there's precious little chance of another situation, at least not around here. Which means no more accidentally-on-purpose drives up to Eden, and no more bickering with Sophie.

And that's a *good* thing, he tells himself the next day. You were right when you said it had to stop. You were right when you made her promise. It's all for the best.

He's in the loose-box with Trouble, showing Lucius the ropes. He's still got two weeks' notice to work, but he wants to make sure that Lucius gets the hang of it. 'She don't like being tied up when you're grooming her,' he tells him.

As if to make the point, Trouble twists round and nuzzles his neck, to get his attention. It's like she knows there's something up.

Lucius nods. He already knows what Ben just told him, but he also knows that Ben needs to say it. He's all right, is Lucius. Big as a shed and black as pitch, and the lightest hands with a horse you ever saw.

'And sometimes,' goes Ben, 'she gets a bit of a swelling in the off hind pastern. Bran poultice'll sort that out. And don't work her too hard when it's hot, or she gets the megrims.'

'I hear you, Ben.'

Ben strokes her nose for a bit. Then he gives her a slap on the neck, and gets the hell out of the loose-box. All this fuss over a sodding horse.

Just then there's a clatter of hooves, and in come Miss Sib, Mrs Dampiere and Master Alex back from their ride. Master Cornelius is out in the yard too, smoking a cigar and watching Mrs Dampiere sitting her mare in her tight little habit. As she rides past Ben she glances down and throws him a cool look. He's used to that. Since the first time up at the lake she's taken a couple more tumbles with him, and she's always been specially cool to him after.

But today there's something more to it, too. She looks – satisfied. Ben glances from her to Master Alex, then to Master Cornelius, and back to her. And suddenly he knows why he got the sack.

Why did it take him so long? It's obvious. Master Cornelius and Master Alex are both panting for her, but they haven't been getting any, and recently they've worked out why. And maybe she put in a word too, like she said she might. *I shall say you were impertinent, and have you dismissed*.

Two years down the plughole, he thinks. And all for a bit of snug that you never even wanted.

Just then, Master Alex jumps down from the saddle and chucks him the reins, and tells him to clean the tack *properly* for a change. And Ben looks down at the reins trailing on the ground, and something inside him just gives, like a worn-out stirrup leather. 'You know what?' he goes. 'Why don't you do it yourself?'

It's quite funny, really. Suddenly you can hear a pin drop in that yard.

Master Cornelius takes his cigar out of his mouth, and Master Alex gapes, like he can't credit what he's just heard. Miss Sibella's mouth is open too, but you can tell she's enjoying it. This'll give her something to tell the ladies over tea.

Mrs Dampiere is still in the saddle, carefully rearranging her habit and not looking at nobody. In the hayloft, Reeve and Thomas are stopped dead with bales in their arms. Danny's standing in front of the carriage-house looking grim, and Lucius is leaning over the loose-box door, biting back a grin.

Ben stoops for a bit of straw to wipe off his hands. No time now to go back to the bunk-house for his kit. He'll have to leave his spare shirt and breeches and that special curry comb he saved up for. Shame about that. And now he definitely won't be seeing Sophie no more, and it's a shame about that too. Oh well. Way of the world. 'So I reckon I'll be off, then,' he says.

Master Alex blinks. 'What?'

'Leaving. Cutting the lucky. Out of here.'

'Not so fast, my lad—'

'You still have two weeks to work,' says Master Cornelius at the same time.

Ben snorts. 'Two weeks? You can shove that. Both of you.'

'*What* did you say?' says Master Alex.

'You heard me,' snaps Ben. 'Or don't you got an arse, like everybody else?'

A horrified gasp from Miss Sibella. A choky splutter from Lucius. Poor old Danny rolls his eyes up to heaven, like he always knew it'd come to this.

Why do people always pretend? thinks Ben. Look at them all, pretending to be outraged when they're loving it, really.

He sweeps off his cap and gives them all a mock bow. Then the devil in him remembers Mrs Dampiere. 'You know what?' he goes to Master Alex and Master Cornelius. 'The funny thing is, I never even wanted her.' He jerks his head to make sure they know who he means. 'She made all the running. You can have her and welcome. Besides, she isn't even that good.'

And that, he tells himself as he shoves his hands in his pockets and starts off down the carriageway, is what you might call burning your boats.

To Sophie's consternation, Madeleine flatly refused to give Ben a job at Eden. 'It's out of the question,' she said as they drove to Falmouth the following morning. 'We can't possibly afford another groom.'

'But why won't you even *ask* Cameron to consider it?' said Sophie.

Madeleine's nose turned pink. 'Don't say a word to him about Ben.'

'Isn't it time he got over that? They only met once, and that was years ago when Ben was just a boy.'

'That's not the point. No man likes to be reminded that his wife was once acquainted with – with a . . .'

'A street-Arab,' Sophie put in. 'A street-Arab who was a friend to us, and now needs our help. Maddy, these are just excuses. What's the real reason?'

Madeleine's lips tightened. 'I should've thought that was obvious. He's far too good-looking, and he's a *groom*. The less you see of him the better.'

Sophie felt herself colouring. 'That's absolute nonsense.'

'Then suppose you tell me why you're so keen to help him?'

'Because it's my fault that he got dismissed!'

But even to her, it didn't sound wholly convincing.

She turned her head and watched the countryside slipping by. They were about three miles north of Romilly. To her left, the cane-pieces of Fever Hill shimmered in the sun; to her right, nightingales and cling-clings chattered in the tall cedars of Greendale Wood. She thought of Ben at Romilly, pacing up and down beneath the giant bamboo. *Forgotten? How could I sodding well forget?*

He'd been angry with her, and yet he'd made her feel better. Because he was still the same Ben. But her sister wouldn't understand about that.

She turned back to Madeleine. 'Very well,' she said, 'if not Eden, then Fever Hill. Clemency would give him a job if we asked her.'

'You never give up, do you? Clemmy doesn't need a groom. She doesn't even own a horse.'

'But Maddy, we can't just do nothing.'

'Yes, Sophie, we can.' Madeleine gave the reins a flick. 'Besides, you don't even know where he is. For all you know he could have left the parish by now.'

'That's not an argument,' said Sophie. 'I can ask Evie. She's bound to know.'

'Stay out of it, Sophie,' said her sister. 'There's nothing you can do. And even if there were, you wouldn't help him by meddling. You'd only make things worse.'

Sophie did not reply. Madeleine was wrong. There was still something she could do. And she intended to do it, too. Why else would she be going to Falmouth?

Her terrible old ancestor, Great-Aunt May, had lived at Fever Hill all her life, but on the death of her nephew Jocelyn she'd astonished everyone by moving to a townhouse in Falmouth.

Here she continued her life of implacable seclusion. Except for a weekly carriage-ride to church, she never left the house. She never made calls, although all Trelawny left their cards on her out of pure fear. She never opened a novel, and periodicals were beneath her contempt – as were gramophone apparatuses, gas lighting, and easy chairs.

Not even her own servants knew how she passed her time, but the pickneys of Duke Street had their ideas. 'She Ole Higue,' they would whisper as they darted frightened glances at the blind mahogany louvres of her first-floor gallery. 'She got raw eyes, and always wear gloves to hide her skinny-bone fingers, and she ride out at night for to suck newborns dead.' Whenever Sophie heard that story she felt a twinge of guilt. The notion that Great-Aunt May was the old hag of local legend had originated with herself and Evie when they were girls.

Now, as she followed the silent butler Kean to the upstairs drawing-room, she felt oddly apprehensive. She told herself that she had nothing to fear from an old lady of eighty-four, but it wasn't entirely true. Great-Aunt May possessed a grim talent for exposing weaknesses. She could sniff out vulnerabilities that one didn't even know one had.

After the glare of Duke Street, it took a moment for Sophie's eyes to adjust to the gloom. The louvres were shut, and the mahogany wall panelling swallowed most of the light that filtered through. No outside sounds penetrated. No clock ticked. The drawing-room was deathly still.

Great-Aunt May sat very straight on a hard mahogany chair, with her gloved hands crossed atop her ivory-headed cane. Great-Aunt May always wore gloves. She hadn't touched another living being for sixty-six years.

She was just as narrow and rigidly upright as Sophie remembered: encased in a tight, high-collared gown of stiff grey moiré which made no concession to the heat. Great-Aunt May despised concessions, just as she despised sickness, pleasure and enthusiasm.

Behind her hung the famous Winterhalter portrait of herself in presentation dress. At the age of eighteen she'd been imperiously lovely: golden-haired and statuesque, with ice-blue eyes and a porcelain complexion which had never seen the sun. *Look at me and despair*, the portrait seemed to say. Sophie felt its gaze on her as she made her way across the parquet and tried not to limp.

'Well, miss,' said Great-Aunt May in her hard, dry voice. 'I had not expected that you would be so *prompt* to call. It can scarcely be more than three weeks since your ship docked at Kingston.'

Despite her age, the old lady still retained traces of her former beauty. Her complexion had a powdery delicacy, and the famous eyes were still blue, although now rimmed with angry red. She watched in grim amusement as Sophie perched on the edge of a chair, and her gloved talons rearranged themselves on her cane.

'You're very well-informed, Great-Aunt May,' said Sophie, ignoring the jibe.

'Why have you come? You have never had the slightest regard for me, and you must be aware that I have never entertained any liking for you.'

'I know that. But—'

'I must have things about me which are beautiful. You are not beautiful. Moreover you are ill.'

'Actually, I've been better for years.'

The old lady rapped the floor with her cane. 'You are ill, I say! Why, you are practically a cripple. I saw you limp. Now answer my question. Why have you come?'

Sophie paused for a moment, to bring herself under control. 'I've heard that you're in need of a coachman,' she said evenly.

'Upon my word, miss, you surprise me! What conceivable interest can you have in my household arrangements?'

'Well, I know of someone who was recently dismissed from another establishment, and might suit.'

'Dismissed, you say. For what infraction?'

'For insolence. But that was—'

'Indeed. A pretty notion you have of the quality of manservant I might care to retain.'

'I think it may have been a misunderstanding. Mr Traherne . . .' she paused to give weight to the name, 'has always had the highest regard for the servant in question.'

Something flickered in the inflamed blue gaze.

Sophie kept very still. If the old lady sensed that she was being manipulated, she would be intractable. And yet – if there was any possibility of vexing the Trahernes . . .

It was common knowledge on the Northside that Great-Aunt May hated the entire clan with a deep, corrosive hatred which had no end. Six decades before, she'd suffered the ignominy of an offer of marriage from Cornelius's father, and had never got over the humiliation. The great-grandson of a *blacksmith* – and he had the effrontery to aspire to the hand of Miss May Monroe! Sixty-six years later, her rancour remained undimmed. It was probably the only thing keeping her alive.

Again she rapped her cane on the floor. 'I will *not* be influenced.'

'I know that, Great-Aunt May.'

'Should anyone apply for the post, I shall consider him, *if* I see fit. But I will not be influenced. Now tell me the truth. What possible interest can you have in a man-servant of Mr Traherne?'

Sophie hesitated. 'None.'

The old lady pounced on the hesitation. 'Then why are you here?'

Sophie felt herself colouring.

'Shall I tell you, miss? Shall I tell you why you show such inappropriate interest in your inferiors?'

'I don't,' said Sophie between her teeth. 'It's just that in this case there are reasons—'

'Do not attempt to exonerate yourself! I have heard reports of your behaviour. Your friendships with mulattos. Your involvement in that – clinic, do they call it?' She leaned forwards, and her hot blue eyes bored into Sophie's. 'You are drawn to your inferiors because you know that you are unfit for anyone else.'

Sophie got to her feet. She didn't have to take this. Not even for Ben.

But Great-Aunt May had her prey in her talons, and she wasn't about to let go. 'You have no breeding,' she continued. 'No manner. No health. No beauty.'

'I don't have to listen to this—'

'You *may* find yourself a husband, of course, but he will only be after your property.'

'Why should you imagine that you can say such things to me? Is it because you're old? Is that it?'

The blue eyes glittered with grim relish. 'Since impertinence is your only response, I must assume that you accept the truth of what I say—'

'Nonsense!'

'Ah, and now you insult me in my own drawing-room! If it is nonsense, miss, then tell me this: have you ever had a sweetheart? Has one single young man of good family ever made himself attentive to you? No. And shall I tell you why? Look behind me at that portrait on the wall. That is beauty. That is breeding. You have none of it. You never shall. You are not a true Monroe.'

'I'm as much a Monroe as you—'

'You are a Durrant. Your mother had the instincts of a guttersnipe, and so have you.'

Sophie turned on her heel and ran. She slammed the drawing-room doors behind her, pushed past a startled Kean, and ran down into the street.

She stood there panting, blinded by the glare.

After the darkness of the drawing-room, Duke Street was absurdly sunny and peaceful. A Chinese man cycled past, raising a little plume of dust. An East Indian girl in a brilliant purple sari crossed the road with stately grace, her bangles clinking on her ankles. She carried a wide, shallow basket of mangoes on her head, and only her dark eyes moved as she glanced at Sophie with polite curiosity.

Sophie breathed in the reassuring smells of dust and mangoes, and felt her heartbeat slowly returning to normal.

You are drawn to your inferiors because you know that you are unfit for anyone else.

Your mother had the instincts of a guttersnipe, and so have you.

It wasn't true. None of it was true. She felt angry with herself for allowing Great-Aunt May to upset her – and, which was worse, for showing it. Why should she be troubled by the rantings of an evil old witch who fed on other people's fears and twisted them into lies?

She started slowly up the street, and as she walked, the sunny peace of the little town had its effect. She began to feel better.

After all, what did it matter what Great-Aunt May had said to her? She'd achieved what she'd set out to do. She'd shown the old witch a way to discountenance the Trahernes; now it was up to Ben to apply for the position.

Although of course, she remembered suddenly, he doesn't know about it yet. So now you've got to find him.

CHAPTER TEN

From the Journal of Cyrus Wright Esquire, Overseer, Fever Hill Plantation

May 1st, 1817
On this day I began my duties at Fever Hill Plantation. Mr Alasdair Monroe shewed me over the Property: a vast of cane-pieces, a cattle Pen, citrus & pimento walks, dye-wood, & much livestock & Negroes, including two dozen newly purchas'd at auction. Mr Monroe is sixty-seven years old, but still hale. He counsell'd me to take a wife or at least to keep a Negro girl.

May 10th Heat very dreadful. The land all scorch'd up, & in places over-run by fire. My new house on Clairmont Hill is very well, but lonely. Have put a Chamboy woman-girl, Sukey, to weeding the garden, but she is impudent. Catch'd her eating sugar cane, & broke my stick over her. This night I dined at the Great House with Mr Monroe, his eldest son Mr Lindsay & Mr Duncan Lawe. Broiled crabs, stewed duck, honey-melon & a cheese. The talk was of Mad Durrant, who is building his Great House at Eden amid the tree-ferns. Much claret & brandy. On returning to my house, cum Sukey in the store room, stans, backwards.

May 18th This day I am forty-eight years old. Still no rains. Parroquets have made sad havoc with my garden,

& in the night a cattle has been at the corn, though I had set old Sybil to watch. Had her flogged & rubbed in salt pickle. She made loud commotion. Cum Accubah, supra terram, in Cotton Tree Piece.

May 31st Heat excessive, & still no rains. Put two Negro gangs to weeding, & the pickney gang to loading manure at Glen Marnoch Cane-Pieces. Much idleness. These Negroes would loiter away the time if I let them. To my supper had mangrove oysters, cold tongue & ale mixt with sugar. Cum Sukey in dom., bis.

An ackee leaf drops onto the page. Evie stares at it for a moment, then brushes it away.

She gazes at the neat copperplate handwriting crawling across the page, and there's a sour taste in her mouth. She knows enough Latin to work out the meanings. *Cum* Sukey in the store room, *stans*, backwards. That means, 'With Sukey in the store room, standing, backwards.' *Cum* Accubah *supra terram*, in Cotton Tree Piece. 'With Accubah on the ground in Cotton Tree Piece.' *Cum* Sukey *in dom., bis.* 'With Sukey in the house, twice.'

She shifts position on the aqueduct wall, but can't make herself easy. Is it just her fancy, or is there a sense of watchfulness roundabout? A secret whisper of leaves in the ackee tree, a stealthy creak in the giant bamboo?

Why, she wonders, did Cyrus Wright feel compelled to record every one of his forced and furtive couplings? And why in Latin? Was he ashamed? But then why not keep silent altogether? No, he had *wanted* to remember. That makes her feel sick.

A ground-dove waddles along the track towards her, and she flaps her hand to shoo it away. 'Out! Outta here, you duppy bird!'

The ground-dove flies off a few yards. But a minute later it's back, tilting its head and fixing her with its impassive red eye.

'Go *way*,' she whispers. She reaches inside her bodice and grasps the little green silk bag which contains the buckra gentleman's gold chain. She holds it tight, like a talisman.

On her lap the book is a dead weight. Why does it trouble her so? She knows what went on in slave time. Since she was little, her mother's told her the stories. Why is it so much worse to read about it? To see the details and the names in that spidery hand, along with what Cyrus Wright *had to his dinner*?

Everywhere she turns it seems like the past is seeping in through the cracks. That day at the busha house, when she saw old Master Jocelyn following Sophie up the croton walk. What's happening? What's *about* to happen?

And why did Sophie send this book to her? *Dear Evie*, said the note in Sophie's big, untidy hand, *I found this book in my grandfather's library, and thought it might help with your dissertation. With best wishes, Sophie Monroe.*

The dissertation? That's just an excuse. Is Sophie trying to say sorry for the other day? Or is she after something?

But in the end, it doesn't matter. What matters – what makes Evie feel breathless and trapped – is that Fate has sent this book to *her*: the four-eyed daughter of the local witch.

The book is heavy and alive in her lap. She's afraid of it, but she can't escape. She turns the page, and begins again to read.

September 13th, 1817 *Excessive hard rain. The Negroes had planted yams & plantain suckers at their provision grounds, but all were washed away. I told them they must plant deeper next year, & in the meantime must content with salt fish. In the forenoon, went to Falmouth for the auction. Purchas'd:*

> *1) A great boy, an Ebo, 5ft 8ins & about 16 yrs. Face & belly much cut about with country marks. Country name Oworia. I have named him Strap. £45.*

2) A Coromantee boy, 4ft 5ins, about 9 yrs, country name Abasse. Have named him Job. £25.
3) A small Coromantee girl, 3ft 5ins, about 6 yrs. Leah. *Sister to the above.* £15.
4) A Coromantee woman-girl, 5ft 4ins, about 14 yrs, name of Quashiba. *Sister to Job and Leah, & very comely. No country marks on belly or back, small taper fingers, teeth not filed, clear complexion. Somewhat majestic look.* £40.

I was about to have them branded when Mr McFarlane's bookkeeper Mr Sudeley offered me to buy the small girl Leah. He said that Mr McFarlane is seeking a wedding present for his bride Miss Elizabeth Palairet, & that the girl will suit. I concluded the sale right readily, & at a guinea profit. However as the girl Leah was led away, a strange commotion. Quashiba & Job seem'd much attached to their sister, & begged not to be separated. Indeed they protested so violently that they had to be beaten back with sticks. Had them branded & led away, whereupon the boy Strap, who seems their friend, comforted Quashiba in their own tongue. I remark'd to Mr Sudeley that the woman-girl will soon forget her sister, for all the world knows that Negroes are incapable of forming close attachments.

September 14th *Have put Job in the Negro village, in Pompey's hut by the aqueduct, & mated Strap to Mulatto Hanah, though they protested against it. Have taken Quashiba to my house, intending her for an housekeeper. She persists in lamenting the loss of her sister, & had to be restrained from visiting Job & Strap down in the village. Had stewed guinea fowl to my supper. Cum Quashiba in dom., but she would fight. Strange impudence. I have named her Eve.*

Evie shuts the book with a thud. A cold sweat breaks out on her forehead. Her heart starts to pound. She wants to throw the book in the aqueduct – to consign Mr Cyrus

Wright to the scummy green water, where he belongs.

I have named her Eve.

No. No. This has nothing to *do* with her. She's not some long-ago nigger from the Guinea country. They just happen to have the same name.

Besides, what does she care about slave time? It's nearly seventy years since the slaves were freed. They're nothing to her. She's Evie McFarlane, teacheress at Coral Springs. She's half white.

A breeze stirs the bamboo leaves to a hot, dry rustle. Evie reaches out to a nearby bush and snaps off a ginger lily, and crushes the waxy white petals in her hand. The scent is so sharp that it stings her eyes – but that's good, for it washes her thoughts clean.

What you've got to remember, she tells herself, is that this is not who you are. Any time you want to, you can get away from here. *Any time.* You've only to say the word to that buckra gentleman, and he'll help you. *You name the place and the time*, he said. *Just to talk, of course. I only want to talk.*

And he promised to treat you respectful, and to never get fresh. Not unless you want him to.

'Hello, Evie,' says Sophie at her shoulder.

Evie jumps, and the book nearly topples into the aqueduct.

'I'm sorry,' says Sophie, 'I startled you.'

Evie tosses away the crushed petals and swings her legs off the wall, and searches for her shoes. 'Hello, Sophie,' she mutters.

'I'm sorry,' Sophie says again. She's nervous, twisting her riding-crop in her hands. She's much less elegant than when Evie saw her up at the busha house, in a calf-length divided riding-skirt, and a short brown jacket and bowler hat. Does she think that by dressing like this she can make it seem that there's less of a gulf between them? Well, she can't. Her boots are calfskin, and at the collar of her blouse there's a little silver brooch.

Looking at her, Evie feels the familiar confusion of jealousy and liking and self-loathing. She hates that she's been found in her old print dress and her canvas shoes, in this rundown ruin of a place. She hates that she's pleased to see Sophie.

Sophie glances at the book. 'Is that any use?'

Evie shrugs. 'Why did you send it?'

'I thought it might help for your dissertation.' She hesitates. 'And I felt bad about the other day. I mean, just assuming that you were in service, like that.'

Evie ignores that. 'Did you read it?' she asks.

'No. Why?'

She snorts. 'It's all about slaves.'

Sophie sighs. 'Oh, I'm sorry, Evie. I genuinely didn't realize.'

'I know you didn't.'

Sophie turns and gazes out over the scummy green water, then back to Evie. 'The thing is, I need to see Ben. Can you tell me where he is?'

So that's it, thinks Evie. I should have guessed. Sophie always did have a peculiar deep regard for Ben. 'Ben's gone,' she says.

'Where?'

'I don't know.'

Sophie doesn't believe her. 'You see, I've found him a position, and I need to tell him, or it'll get filled. It's in Duke Street, at Great-Aunt May's.'

'Miss May?' Evie's surprised. 'Cho! Ole Higue herself!' Then she remembers who she's talking to, and puts a hand to her mouth.

Sophie grins. 'Ole Higue indeed! I saw her yesterday, and she still frightens the life out of me. But you see, she really does need a coachman. It's ridiculous, she only ever drives eight hundred yards to church, but I thought that if Ben were to apply, she'd probably take him. It would appeal to her, to cock a snook at the Trahernes.'

Clever Miss Sophie. Clever, unwise Miss Sophie, walking into trouble with her eyes wide open and blind.

And now Evie really doesn't know what to do. Of course she knows where Ben is. He's over east in the hills back of Simonstown; Daniel Tulloch found him a bed at his cousin Lily's who teaches school in the village. But always at the back of Evie's mind is that vision of old Master Jocelyn following Sophie up the croton walk. Maybe it means trouble for Sophie, or maybe for Ben. Or maybe for both of them.

With the toe of her shoe she draws a pattern in the dust. 'Better stay away from him, Sophie.'

'Everyone keeps telling me that.'

'Everyone?'

She taps her riding-crop against her boot. 'I'm just trying to put things right. That's all.'

Evie wonders if Sophie truly believes that.

'Will you at least see that he gets the message?' says Sophie.

Evie shakes her head.

'Why not? Don't you want to help him? He's your friend too.'

Evie does not reply.

'Just take him the message,' urges Sophie.

Well, and why not? thinks Evie. After all, you're not really friends with Sophie any more, so why worry about keeping her out of trouble? And why worry about Ben? Ben can look after himself. He always has.

'Evie – please.'

She sighs. 'All right.'

'*Thank* you.'

After that Sophie doesn't stay long, and Evie doesn't try to keep her. But still she's sorry when she's gone. It's lonely by the aqueduct, with the ackee tree whispering overhead and the wild bamboo creaking to itself, and the journal of Cyrus Wright calling to her from the wall.

She half expects it to have moved by itself, but when she turns round it's still there, waiting for her. With a sense of foreboding, she curls up on the wall and opens it.

But to her frustration she can find no further mention of Eve. With mounting apprehension she flicks through pages of crop-times and how many hogsheads per acre, and terse Latin accounts of forced couplings in cane-pieces. What happened? Was there an illness? A beating that went too far?

Just when she's beginning to lose hope, she finds it.

December 3rd, 1817 Yesterday I gave Eve my old blue Holland coat, but by nightfall she had lost it, or so she said. Old Sybil says that Eve gave it to Strap. I was vex'd, and sent Eve to the field gang for a punishment. Had a search made of Strap's hut, but found no coat. (NB: Old Sybil says the Negroes have taken to calling Eve 'Congo Eve', to tell her apart from Mr Durrant's Chamboy Eve, up at Romilly. But this is without my leave.)

December 15th Congo Eve has gone runaway. Have sent men to make search, and am too vex'd to take more than ham & a cheese to my supper. Cum Accubah in dom.

December 17th Congo Eve has been catch'd & brought back by Mr McFarlane's overseer. She went runaway to Caledon to see her sister Leah. Had her flogged & rubbed with brine. In the evening, noticed that she wears an anklet of john-crow beads. She told me that her brother Job made it for a present. Suspecting it to be some vile Obiah practice (i.e. Black Magick), I made her throw it on the midden.

December 18th Had a strange complaining visit from a Mr Drummond, overseer at Waytes Valley. He told how yesterday he was on his way to Pinchgut when he met a well-made Negro wench on the road. She agreed to go with him among the bushes, but when they got there she desired payment first, upon which he pulled out his purse of knitted blue silk. As he was holding it rather carelessly, the girl snatched it out of his hand and ran away, and he has not seen her or the purse since. Nor would he know the girl again, for she wore a kerchief pulled down low on her head. He said he lost five shillings, and sought compensation from me, saying that the girl must be mine. I denied this with all vehemence, & he went away. I then questioned Congo Eve, but she said she knew nothing about it, though she looked at me with excessive impudence.

December 19th *This past sennight I have put my Field Negroes to cutting copper wood on Pinchgut Hill, & now have one hundred & 16 cart-loads stacked ready beside the boiling-house. I was walking back from the works just after shell-blow, well satisfied, when I saw Congo Eve talking to Strap by the Pond. She was smiling & touching his cheek with her hand. Had him flogged, & both nostrils slit. Cum Congo Eve in dom., sed non bene. Illa habet mensam.*

'Evie! Evie!'

She raises her head blearily, as if from a dream.

It's her mother, calling her to supper. She gets up and shuts the book, and brushes off her skirts. She's not sorry to go. It's getting dark, and there's a swampy, destroyful feel of duppies about the place.

With Congo Eve in the house, but it was not good. She had her courses. Just reading it makes her feel dirty; as if Cyrus Wright has left little spidery stains in her memory.

When she reaches the yard, her mother glances up from the hearth, sees the book in her daughter's hand and gives her a small, proud smile. Grace McFarlane never did herself learn to read, but she dearly loves to see Evie with a book. 'What did Miss Sophie want?' she asks as she hands her daughter a bowl of steaming fufu.

Evie shrugs. 'Nothing. Just to visit.'

For a while they eat in silence. Then Grace says, 'You know, you're better not spending time with her, girl.'

Evie blows on her fufu and frowns. 'Why not?'

'You know why. She's from a different class of ideas and life.'

'Mother, I'm a teacheress, not a maid. I can spend time with who I like.'

'That all very well. But it does no good to go meddling with carriage folk. You know that.'

Evie sets her teeth. All her life she's been hearing this. And it's specially hard coming from her mother. 'Meddling with carriage folk?' she says quietly. 'But Mother, you're the one who did that. Not so? You "meddled" with a buckra gentleman, and—'

'Evie—'

'— and I'm the result. Not so, Mother? You went with a buckra gentleman, though you never would tell me his name.'

Grace gives her a black hard look, but Evie's blood is rising and she don't care. 'So please don't tell me who I can't spend time with, Mother. I'm half white. I can—'

'Half white is no white,' snaps Grace. 'Don't you know that yet?'

Evie can't take any more. She throws down her bowl and quits the yard, slamming the bamboo gate behind her. She gets all the way to the aqueduct before she even realizes where she is – or that she's got the journal of Cyrus Wright clutched under her arm. Her heart is pounding.

Now what to do? It's getting dark. Mosquitoes are humming roundabout, and swallows flitting down to drink. Should she catch some peenywallies and put them in a jar, and read some more by the light?

Reading some more is the last thing she wants to do. But because she's so angry, it's exactly what she *will* do.

And once again, she can find nothing about her namesake for several pages. It's as if Cyrus Wright became disenchanted with everything but sugar planting and coffee growing. Or maybe he was ashamed. Whatever the reason, it's two years before there's another mention of Congo Eve.

September 13th, 1819 *Still no rains; heat excessive strong. Had set my Field Negroes to collecting mahoe bark for rope-making, when Job cut his leg. It swell'd with the guinea worm, so I sent him to the hot house. Congo Eve troublesome in running to visit him & supper him, so I had to restrain her yet again with a collar & chain about her neck. She is perverse & will not help herself, but always must defy me.*

September 15th Mr Monroe's wife brought to bed of a daughter. He has named her May. It is his seventh child by his wife, though of course he has very many Mulattos borne for him by his Negro females. Job still in the hot house, very fever'd & troublesome in calling for his sister. I myself have a scalding urine, & fear it is a dose of the clap. Took 4 mercurial purging pills & a cooling powder on advice of Dr Prattin. He suggested that I physick myself at the hot house like my Negroes, he thought it a good jest. I did not. Cum Congo Eve, stans, in the curing-house. To my supper had a stewed turtle with a pint of porter.

September 17th Job dead of a locking on the jaws. Congo Eve almost out of her senses, & would hear no reason. Had to collar her again. Gave the Negroes leave to bury the body behind the bee houses.

September 26th Much havoc in the night. Against my orders, Strap held a Negro nine-night for Job down at the village, & Congo Eve slip'd from my house & went to it. I follow'd her in the dark, & there espied a vast many people with drumming & strange music, & Strap playing on a Banjar. Saw Congo Eve at work with her Obiah. Then she & Strap danc'd the Negro Motion they call the shay-shay, a most revolting sight: much slow winding of the hips, but with the upper body still. I broke in on them, brandishing my musket & greatly vex'd. Had Congo Eve flogged, 29 lashes, and have this afternoon sold Strap to Mr Traherne at Parnassus for £43, a loss of £2. Then I took Strap's Banjar & shewed it to Congo Eve, & chopped it all to pieces in front of her with my cutlass. She threatened to make away with herself, & since then has said no more to me. Mr Monroe is right when he says that the Negro's lack of moral faculties keeps him in subjection to his passions. To my supper had two broiled pigeons, very fat & sweet. Cum *Congo Eve* supra terram *in Pimento Walk,* bis.

Evie puts her hand inside her dress and grips the little bag of warm green silk like a talisman.

Day has just commenced to light, and the peenywallies in the jar are dead. Soon her mother will come out of the house and start waking up the fire, and wonder why her daughter is up so early.

She can't read any more. Her heart is beating so hard that she feels sick. Reading the close-written pages has made her head ache.

The Negro's lack of moral faculties keeps him in subjection to his passions. What lies people tell to excuse the wrong they do.

Around her the birds are waking up. A flock of jabbering crows settles in the ackee tree. Ground-doves peck the dust. She looks about her at the tumbled cut-stone, still streaked with black from slave time, when old Master Alasdair burnt the village after the great Rebellion.

In this place where she is now, Strap lived, and Job, and hundreds, perhaps thousands, of others. Here Congo Eve danced the shay-shay in defiance of Cyrus Wright. Are their spirits still here? Are they watching her now?

Quickly she swings her legs off the wall and jumps to her feet. They're nothing to do with her. Congo Eve is nothing to her. Any time she wants to get away from this, she can. *Any time.* All she has to do is say the word.

Quickly, so she can't change her mind, she runs up the path to her mother's place, hugging the book to her breast. She creeps up the steps – quietly so as not to wake her mother – and fetches her little wooden writing-box from under the bed. Then she makes her way out to the end of the yard, and seats herself on her grandmother's tomb under the garden cherry tree. She takes out her pen and ink and a sheet of her special notepaper, and swiftly writes: *I shall be taking the air in Bamboo Walk tomorrow, at four o'clock. EM.* Then she seals it with a little stump of sealing-wax.

This has nothing to do with Congo Eve, she tells herself. In fact this only proves how *different* things are now: that these days a mulatto girl can receive admiration and *respect* from a buckra gentleman.

Without returning for hat or shoes she runs out of the yard, and takes the path round the old Pond, and heads due west through the cane-pieces of Alice Grove. She runs all the way to Pinchgut Hill.

When she reaches it, the settlement is just waking up. Dogs and goats are nosing around in the dust. Cooking-fires are smoking. There's a good fat smell of coconut oil and fried breadfruit and cerassee tea.

Nobody is surprised to see her dropping by, and nobody wonders when she collars little Jericho Fletcher and draws him behind a jackfruit tree for a private talk. She can trust Jericho. He's clever and quiet, and he has a shy little-boy admiration for her.

'Here's a quattie for you,' she tells him. 'You'll get another if you run as quick as a black ant and give this note to who I say. To who I *say*, mind, and nobody else. Understand?'

Jericho gazes up at her with his shiny black ackee-seed eyes, and solemnly nods. For a moment Evie feels a twinge of guilt at using a child. But then she reminds herself that he'll get his two quatties, and with them he can achieve that impossible dream of buying the longed-for hobby-horse.

She gives him the first quattie and the note, and closes his hand over both. 'Run quick,' she whispers, 'quick now. And give this to Master Cornelius Traherne.'

CHAPTER ELEVEN

A slumbrous afternoon at the clinic, and not a patient in sight. Dr Mallory had gone off in disgust, leaving Sophie on her own. She sat by the open door at the rickety little table, struggling to concentrate on *Diseases of the Lungs*.

But the words conveyed nothing to her. It had been five days since her conversation with Evie by the aqueduct, and still there had been no word of Ben. Perhaps Evie had changed her mind about passing on the message. Perhaps he'd left Trelawny, or taken ship back to England, or Barbados or Panama or America.

She had no means of finding out, except to ask Evie again, and she was too proud to do that.

She rested her chin on her hands and heaved a sigh. What was she doing here? What did she want? These days she couldn't concentrate on anything. She felt constantly dissatisfied: edgy and tearful, and full of vague yet insistent longings. At times she found herself envying Madeleine – for being beautiful, for having a husband who adored her – even though she'd never envied her before. What was wrong with her? What did she *want*?

One thing, though, was painfully clear. She didn't want the clinic. It had been a huge, humiliating mistake.

Bethlehem itself was a pleasant little place. A typical smallholder's settlement, it lay about three miles east of Eden great house, and a mile south of the Martha Brae. A cluster of wattle-and-daub houses thatched with cane-trash enclosed a dusty clearing containing a white-washed Baptist chapel, a breadfruit tree, and the small tin-roofed barrack which Dr Mallory had commandeered for his clinic. Surrounding the village was a tidy patch-work of banana walks, coffee plots and provision grounds, reaching east to the cane-pieces of Arethusa, and north to the river and the edge of Greendale Wood.

The people were friendly but stubborn, and, as Cameron had predicted, reluctant to betray their own bush-doctors for a 'doctor-shop' where they couldn't buy Calvary powder or dead-man oil. Most days, Sophie had little to do except dole out cough linctus, and dig the occasional jigger out of a pickney's foot.

She wouldn't have minded if it hadn't been for Dr Mallory. A clever, bitter, distressingly fat widower, he detested the practice of medicine, and had only become a doctor because God had told him to. He made no secret of resenting Sophie's presence, even though it had been his own idea that she should help him. His chief delight seemed to be in criticizing her – in the guise of giving 'friendly advice' – and covertly ridiculing her lack of medical experience.

'I fear, Miss Monroe, that for you our little clinic is beginning to pall? No, no, I *quite understand*. How in-adequate we must seem after your London hospitals!' He knew very well that her only experience of hospitals was three days as a volunteer at the Cheltenham Working Woman's clinic. But when she reminded him of that, he always pretended to have forgotten.

The clinic had become a battle of wills between them. Dr Mallory clearly expected her to throw in the towel, while she was just as determined to deny him the satis-faction. So every afternoon she grimly drove east past the Maputah works, then turned north down a cane track and crossed the trickle of Tom Gully, which marked the boundary between Eden estate and Bethlehem village.

There Dr Mallory would greet her with an ill-tempered grimace, she would throw him a determined smile, and they would settle down to wait for the patients who rarely came. After an hour or so, Dr Mallory would take himself off to his little house for a rum and water and a nap, and Sophie would get out a book.

This afternoon, the village was more than usually quiet, for it was market day, and most people were away. Through the open door Sophie could see an old man sitting under a pawpaw tree at the far side of the clearing, polishing his Sunday shoes with a handful of shoeblack hibiscus petals. A couple of pickneys cantered past, playing pony and driver. Cling-clings chattered on the bamboo fences. Chickens pecked the dust. Beneath the breadfruit tree, Belle squatted on her haunches and admonished her toy zebra, Spot. She had conceived a passionate devotion for Sophie, and had badgered her mother until she was allowed to accompany her aunt.

With a tact which Sophie appreciated, Madeleine rarely enquired about the clinic. Cameron, however, was more outspoken. 'Sophie, it's been what, two weeks?' he'd said after dinner the night before. 'Isn't it time to call it a day? After all, old Mallory doesn't need you, and you don't need him, and heaven knows the blacks don't need either of you.'

He was right, of course. But how could she back down now, after making a stand about it? Was this to be yet another of her famous 'about-turns'?

Belle's voice outside the door cut across her thoughts. She was asking someone just beyond Sophie's line of vision to take a look at Spot's hoof. 'It's wobbly because Fraser pulled it,' she said. 'Aunt Sophie gave me some carbolized dressing.'

'Dressing's not much use for a broken cannon bone,' said Ben.

Sophie's heart jerked.

'What's a cannon bone?' said Belle.

'The bit above the fetlock,' said Ben. 'It's broken all right. Flopping about all over the place.'

Very quietly, Sophie got to her feet and backed away from the door. She moved to the high louvred window, and stood on tiptoe to peer out.

He was squatting down to Belle's level in the shade of the breadfruit tree. He wore his usual breeches and top-boots and a collarless blue shirt, but instead of his groom's cap a battered straw hat lay beside him in the dust. He was frowning and turning the zebra in his hands.

'Will he get better?' asked Belle, standing before him with her hands clasped behind her back.

He shook his head. 'Best make an end of him.'

'Oh. What does that mean?'

'Put a bullet in him.'

Belle blinked. 'You mean I ought to shoot him?'

He handed the toy back to her. 'Best thing for him. He'll never walk on four legs again.'

'But if I carry him.'

He shrugged. 'Suit yourself. If you want to carry a stripy horse all day, that's your lookout.'

She nodded, and hugged Spot under her chin. 'Actually he's not a stripy horse. He's a zebra.'

'What's a zebra?'

'Um. A sort of stripy horse.'

Ben smiled.

It was the first time that Sophie had seen him smile – really smile – since he was a boy. It made her want to cry.

Standing there with her hands on the window sill, she felt a sudden shattering rush of feeling for him. It took her breath away. It made everything clear.

He *mattered* to her. He always had. Ever since that first day in the photographer's studio, when he'd stood at bay before Madeleine's imitation gun: a whip-thin alley cat of a boy who'd snapped and snarled, and then been reduced to captivated silence by a gilded horse on the binding of a book. He mattered to her because his mind worked the same way as hers, and because he could sense what she was feeling, and because – because he just did.

And now at last she understood why she'd never been attracted to any of the young men she'd ever met; why she'd simply felt that it wasn't possible to develop a regard for them. It was because they weren't Ben.

The window sill was rough beneath her hands, and she

clung to it. This was what Madeleine had warned her about. She felt dizzy and shaken. And hopelessly sad.

She couldn't tell him what she felt. She couldn't tell any-one. No-one must know, because it was impossible. Even she could see that.

There is nothing you can do about this, she told herself, and the truth of the words settled inside her like a stone. There is nothing that can be done.

Holding her breath, she watched him reach for his hat and look about him, then make for the door.

Quickly, before he spotted her, she drew back from the window and sat down, and bent over her book.

When his shadow cut across the doorway, she glanced up, and made what she thought was a creditable job of appearing surprised. She was on the verge of tears, and she was sure that it showed in her face – but if he noticed, he made no sign. He just stood in the doorway and gave her his unsmiling nod. 'Can I come in?'

She clasped her hands together on the book, and nodded.

He tossed his hat on the medicine trolley, and went to lean against the opposite wall, glancing about him at the bottles and jars on the shelves. He moved with his usual wary grace, and for an instant she felt a flicker of sympathy for poor fat Dr Mallory, who'd probably never had a graceful moment in his life. 'So this is the clinic,' he said.

She cleared her throat. 'Yes. This is it.'

He picked up a jar of carbolic and turned it in his fingers, then put it back again. 'I worked for a hospital once. Runner for St Thomas's. Learned all the names of the medicines.'

'Was that before you knew me and Madeleine?'

He nodded.

She wondered where he'd been for the past five days. His clothes were dusty but clean, and he didn't look as if he'd been sleeping rough. He'd even managed to shave, and given himself a scrape along the jawbone.

As she looked at the hard, clean planes of his face, she

wished savagely that her childhood fantasy could come true – that he would turn out to be a changeling prince, so that everything would end up all right.

She looked down at her hands, and saw that they'd tightened into fists. 'So what happened to that promise you made me give you,' she said, 'about not seeing you again?'

He crossed his arms on his chest. 'Yes, but *I* never promised nothing, did I? Anyway. I just come to say thanks. That's all.'

'For what?'

'For putting in a word for me at your aunt's. Great-aunt. Whatever she is.'

'I take it that this means you've got the position?'

He nodded. 'Scary old cat, isn't she? But I think we'll muddle along all right.'

She remembered Great-Aunt May's imperious declaration: *I must have things about me which are beautiful.* 'I imagine,' she said, 'that you'll do very well.'

'So why'd you do it then?'

'Why did I do what?'

'Put in a word for me with Miss Monroe.'

'It was the least I could do, since I got you dismissed.'

'You didn't.'

'Yes I did. That day when you drove me home, you had words with Alex – Master Alex – I mean, with Alexander Traherne.'

'That's not why I got the sack.'

'Then why did you?'

He did not reply. A faint redness stole across his cheekbones.

'Sibella said you were insolent.'

He laughed. 'You could say that.'

'She mentioned some incident at the stables, but she didn't say what. Just that Cornelius and Alexander were both incandescent.'

'Does that mean angry?'

'You know it does.'

'Well. They had it coming.'

133

'But why did you do it? Why antagonize the most powerful family in Trelawny?'

He turned his head and studied the jars on the shelf. Then he shrugged. 'I don't know. I suppose because I knew it wouldn't last.'

'What wouldn't last?'

'The job. It was too good. So I made it end. That's what I do.' He turned back to her, and they regarded one another in silence.

She was still sitting behind the table, and he still stood by the shelves against the opposite wall. There was about six feet between them.

Only six feet, she thought. All you've got to do is get up and cross that little distance. But you can't do it, can you? It's just as impossible as if you were standing at the top of a cliff, and all you had to do was take one step to go over the edge, but you still couldn't do it. Because you're not brave enough.

There was no sound in the clinic, but outside she could hear the rasp of the crickets, and the distant humming of the old man under the pawpaw tree. She could feel the afternoon heat against her skin, and the warm leather-bound book beneath her fingers. She could see the shaft of sunlight cutting across Ben's face. His arms were still crossed on his chest, and she could see a streak of dust on his wrist, and the cord-like veins on the backs of his hands.

Until now, she'd never felt the urge to touch a man. And she'd never wanted a man to touch her.

But you're not going to do it, are you? she told herself in disgust. Because you're not brave enough. Because what if he doesn't feel as you do? What if he doesn't want to touch you?

Belle appeared in the doorway. She was carrying the injured Spot – who now sported a handkerchief bandage – and she was scowling as she held it up for Ben's inspection. 'Will this help?'

Ben shook himself, and glanced down at her and blinked. 'Um – a bit. Just don't let him put any weight on that hoof.'

Belle nodded. 'Can I have some cyanide ointment?'

'No,' said Ben and Sophie together.

Belle thrust out her lower lip, and threw them a look, and stalked out of the clinic.

When she'd gone, there was another silence. Then Ben shook himself again, and reached for his hat. 'I'd better be off,' he muttered. 'I start work tomorrow, and I've still got to get down to town.'

'Will you come again?' she said quickly.

'No.'

'Why not?'

'Because it's not a good idea.'

'Why?' Now that they were talking again, she felt stronger. She might lack the courage to go to him, but she always had the courage to argue. 'You're friends with Evie,' she pointed out. 'Why can't you be friends with me?'

'Because I can't, that's all.'

'Why?'

She watched him walk the length of the room, then back again. 'You can't go saying things like that,' he told her angrily. 'Not to me.'

'Why not to you?'

'Because I'm common. Because I grew up in a slum.'

'I know that, but—'

'That's just it, you don't know.' He shook his head. 'You don't know.'

'Perhaps not. But that's all in the past. What does it matter?'

'Of course it sodding well matters.' He looked down at his hat, then tossed it back on the trolley. 'Look. When I was the same age as that little girl out there, we lived in two rooms on East Street, for the eight of us. We used to sleep six kids to a bed. D'you know what that's like?'

She shook her head.

'Bedbugs and lice, and all the girls and boys mixed up together. So not much sodding chastity, if you take my meaning.'

She felt her face growing hot.

'So one night,' he went on, 'when my sister Lil's about twelve, our Jack – he was our big brother – he gets into her. You know what that means?'

She swallowed. 'Yes. I think so.'

'So the next day she finds herself a fancy man, and she's off on the streets, doing tricks for a tanner. And that's *good*. Because now it means she's earning her keep.'

She dug her fingernail into a crack in the binding. 'Did Jack get punished?'

'Course not! Why would he get punished? He only done – did – what everyone else did.'

'Why are you telling me this?'

'To make you see the difference between you and me. I'm just the same as Jack, and Pa, and any of them. Christ, I was getting into girls when I was eleven.'

She raised her head and looked at him steadily. 'You're right,' she said between her teeth, 'it does make a difference. It makes me feel horrified, and sorry for you. There. Are you satisfied?'

He met her eyes, then glanced away.

'What happened to Lil?' she said suddenly.

'What d'you mean?'

'Well, something must have happened to her. Did she get – some disease? Did she get pregnant? What? Did she have to go to a – an angel-maker? That's what they call them, isn't it? When they get rid of unwanted babies?'

He flinched as if she'd hit him.

'Why do you always do this?' she demanded, angrily blinking back tears. 'Always pushing me away when I get too close.'

'Well I've got to, haven't I? Otherwise you'd just blunder in and get hurt.'

'You wouldn't hurt me. Not really.'

'Oh, yes I would! I'm like my pa that way. Anyone gets too close, and they get hurt. You take my word for it.'

'No. No, I don't believe that.'

'That's because you don't know nothing. And the worst of it is, you don't even know that you don't know.'

'Well then, tell me!' Without thinking, she got up and

went round to his side of the table. 'You say that I don't know anything, but whenever I ask, you won't answer my questions.'

'You're twisting things round,' he muttered.

'No I'm not.'

He drew a deep breath. 'Look. I didn't tell you those things to make you feel sorry for me.'

'I know that.'

'I told you to make you understand. To show you what I am, so you'll stay away.'

She did not reply. She stood with her hands by her sides, looking up into his face. There was only a yard between them. She had reached the edge of the cliff.

She was close enough to see that the green of his eyes was ringed with turquoise, and split by little spokes of russet.

Green eyes, she thought, aren't as noticeable as blue; you don't remark on them straight away, but when you do, it's like sharing a secret.

'Christ, Sophie,' he muttered. Then he closed the distance between them and laid his warm hand on her cheek, and bent and kissed her quickly on the mouth.

It only lasted a moment. She just had time to feel the warmth of his lips on hers, and to catch his dry spicy smell, and then he'd twisted away and was making for the door.

In a daze she heard the jingle of a bridle and a horse trotting, and a man's voice, suddenly nearer. She turned, blinking in the glare, and saw Cameron standing in the doorway.

When he saw her, his face lit up with a smile. Then he recognized Ben, and froze.

Dawn. The glade of the great duppy tree on Overlook Hill.

It was only an hour's ride from the house, and yet it seemed a world away, for this was the start of the Cockpits. Vapour rose from the great tattered leaves of philodendrons, and beaded the spokes of spiders' webs strung from tree to tree. Curtains of strangler fig and clots of Spanish moss hung down from the outstretched arms of the oldest silk-cotton in Trelawny.

Sophie sat on one of its great folded roots, and watched her horse cropping the ferns. Her eyes felt scratchy with fatigue. She hadn't slept all night.

Cameron hadn't said a word at the clinic. He'd simply glanced at Sophie, and given Ben a long, unreadable look, and then gone back outside and scooped up Belle, and ridden out of Bethlehem. Ben had stood in the doorway watching him go, then shaken his head, and walked out of the village without a backwards glance.

Dinner that night had been a fraught affair, with Sophie braced for an attack that didn't come. Cameron was courteous as always, but silent and withdrawn. It was clear from Madeleine's constrained attempts at conversation that he'd told her everything.

But after all, Sophie kept telling herself, what could he have seen? By the time he'd reached the doorway they'd already drawn apart. He hadn't seen them kiss. All he'd seen was their taut faces. Which would have fooled no-one. Least of all a man as perceptive as Cameron.

Somehow Sophie had got through dinner, and then pleaded a headache, and gone early to bed. She'd half expected Madeleine to come to her room and have it out, but she hadn't. And that made it worse.

All night she'd lain awake, staring up at the mosquito net, her feelings in turmoil. Exasperation at Cameron for making her feel guilty; anger at herself for getting Ben into trouble again; a welter of emotion when she remembered that kiss.

The sun climbed higher. The heat grew. High above the canopy came the lonely cry of a red-tailed hawk. She breathed in the heavy sweetness of growth and decay, and listened to the secret rustle and hum of the forest, and the crickets' rasping song.

If she shut her eyes, she could summon up the exact feel of him against her mouth. His lips had been hot and dry and surprisingly gentle, his hand warm on her cheek. She could still smell his sharp, indefinable scent.

It had happened so quickly that she hadn't had time to respond. But how, she wondered, how *does* one respond? What does one actually do?

She had never kissed a man before. But once, when she and Evie were fourteen, they'd tried to kiss each other for a dare. They had leaned towards one another with their eyes tightly shut, and stuck out their tongues until the tips just touched – then leaped apart with squeals of horrified laughter at the alien feel of warm, wet flesh.

She put her hand on the tree's rough bark, and by her thumb a big green cotton-cutter beetle tasted the air with delicate antennae. She raised her head and gazed up at the great spreading canopy, laden with tiny scarlet orchids and spiky wild pines.

Years ago, Cameron had brought her up here to help overcome her terror of duppy trees. And under this same tree, nearly three decades before, her sister had been conceived. Rose Durrant had called it the Tree of Life. She had told Madeleine stories of how she and her lover Ainsley Monroe had met in secret in the forest at midnight, when the fireflies spangled the creepers, and the pale moonflowers were open to the night.

Rose Durrant had been almost as young as Sophie was now: blinded by love, and utterly reckless. *Oh, the Durrants were an impossible lot*, Olivia Herapath had once remarked. *They always went too far.*

Like mother like daughter? wondered Sophie, looking up at the tree. It had not escaped her notice that a few weeks ago she'd been suspecting Madeleine of the Durrant taint of recklessness, when it turned out to be she herself who most resembled their improvident mother.

Falling in love with a *groom*?

Something Great-Aunt May had said came back to her. *Your mother had the instincts of a guttersnipe, and so have you.*

'It isn't true,' she said. Beside her hand, the cotton-cutter opened its wings and buzzed away.

*You are drawn to your inferiors because you know that
you are unfit for anyone else.*

That wasn't true either. She knew that. It was merely
the vicious, twisted lie of an angry old woman.

And yet she couldn't repress a flash of bitterness.
Others had found love safely within their own class.
Sibella. Madeleine. Why couldn't she?

And what was she going to do about it now?

CHAPTER TWELVE

When she got back to Eden, there was a letter waiting for her from Sibella. Sensing trouble, she took it to her room to read.

Parnassus
15th December 1903

Dear Sophie,
   I called on you yesterday at that beastly 'clinic' of yours, but you weren't there, and a horrid old man told me that Cameron had sent you home. I shudder to think why.
   Sophie, how <u>could</u> you disgrace me so? You positively <u>engineer</u> an assignation with one of <u>my own father's servants</u> at the Historical Society picnic, and then your brother-in-law is forced to drag you away from yet <u>another</u> assignation in some ghastly slum. Are you deaf to all reason? To all sense of propriety? Most of all, are you deaf to your obligation to me in this most trying time of my life?
   What would happen if everyone felt at liberty to associate with inferiors? Why, every schoolchild knows that God Himself created the different ranks, and that we as Christians must do our duty in whichever degree it has pleased Him to place us.

What would happen if people simply ignored this? Everything would get horribly mixed up, and soon there would be no difference at all, and then where should we be?

It pains me to say this, but I feel it my duty to tell you that you have utterly degraded yourself by this unnatural partiality. Moreover you have, by association, degraded me. I had thought that I was bestowing a favour upon you by asking you to walk up the aisle behind me as my chief bridesmaid. Indeed, I positively <u>set</u> upon Amelia Mordenner when she suggested that you might be too self-conscious, because of your limp. And this is the thanks I get.

It grieves me unutterably to say this, but you have left me no choice. I must absolutely rescind my offer, and make Amelia chief bridesmaid. Perhaps this will teach you the folly of . . .

There was more. Four close-written pages of it. Sophie read it to the end, then tore it up and burnt the pieces in the wash-hand stand.

She was surprised to find that Sibella's arguments left her completely unmoved. The only thing which angered her was that reference to her limp.

She sat on her bed for several minutes, thinking. Then she went to her desk and dashed off two short notes. One was to Sibella, wishing her luck with Amelia Mordenner. The other was to Ben, asking him to meet her at Romilly Bridge on the day after tomorrow.

Quickly, before she could change her mind, she sealed the notes and took them to the stables, where she gave Quaco the stable boy a shilling to deliver them at once and in secret. Then she went back inside and sat down at the breakfast table. She was fairly certain that she'd made a mistake in writing to Ben, but she didn't care. She needed to see him again, to sort things out. She wasn't at all clear what that might entail, but she knew that it would be quite impossible to leave things as they were.

To her relief, Cameron had already left for the works, and she only had to face Madeleine and the children. 'What did Sibella want?' asked Madeleine, pouring the tea.

'To excommunicate me,' she replied.

Fraser looked up from his milk. 'What does ex—'

'I'll tell you later,' said his mother, putting a slice of toasted johnny cake on his plate and starting to butter it. She threw her sister an enquiring glance. 'Does that mean you won't be coming with us on Boxing Day?'

'What?' said Sophie.

'The Boxing Day Masquerade. At Parnassus?'

'Oh, God,' said Sophie, 'I'd forgotten all about that.' It was *the* Christmas event on the Northside, and everyone would be there. Even Great-Aunt May always sent her carriage as a mark of recognition, along with her butler Kean. And this year, of course, it would be driven by her new coachman.

Sophie put her hands to her temples and stared down at her plate. Sibella would be watching her like a hawk. And by then, too, she would have met Ben at Romilly, and had it out with him. Whatever that meant.

Madeleine got up and came and sat beside her, and put an arm round her shoulders. 'Personally, I've always detested masquerades. The drumming gives me a headache, and the masks give me nightmares. Don't go if you don't want to.'

Sophie kneaded her temples. 'But what about Sibella?'

'Bother Sibella,' said Madeleine robustly. 'Listen. Cameron and I will go because we must, but there's no reason why you should be martyred, too. Send a line on the day, to say you're unwell. Say you've eaten too much plum pudding, or something.'

Sophie looked at her in bemusement. So far, Madeleine hadn't said a single word to her about Ben, and what Cameron had or hadn't witnessed at the clinic. And now she was being so understanding about Sibella. Why?

It crossed her mind that this might be some sort of war of attrition. But the next moment she dismissed that as unworthy of her sister. If something was wrong, Madeleine usually just spoke her mind.

Nevertheless, she began to wish that they could have it out, and clear the air. Anything would be better than this looming suspense. But Madeleine was busy with the children all morning, and when Cameron returned for lunch the conversation was general. Then after lunch, Madeleine went out to make some calls.

Sophie skipped the clinic and stayed at home. But as the afternoon wore on, her temper worsened. She snapped at Poppy and at Scout, and finally at the children. Then she felt guilty, and read them two whole stories from their favourite book of folktales: *The Treasure of the Spanish Jar* and *How the Doctorbird got his Tail*.

'Above and beyond the call of duty,' murmured Madeleine with a wry smile, after Poppy had put them to bed. 'Even for the favourite aunt.'

'Hardly that,' replied Sophie. 'The favourite aunt's been ignoring them for days.'

'It does them good. They get enough attention as it is.'

Sophie did not reply. She was standing at the edge of the verandah, looking out over the garden. Dusk was coming on. Cameron had just returned from the works, and was dressing for dinner. A low murmur of voices drifted up from the cookhouse, along with the scent of woodsmoke. Below her the garden was settling down for the night. The rasp of the crickets had sunk to a low, throbbing ring, and the whistling frogs were taking over. An early ratbat flitted about among the tree-ferns.

Madeleine came to stand beside her. 'Sophie,' she began with a slight frown.

Sophie braced herself. Here it came. A lecture about Ben.

'I know it sometimes seems as if I'm – rather too conventional,' Madeleine said quietly. 'I mean, too keen on making calls and leaving one's card, and that sort of thing.'

Sophie glanced at her in surprise. It was the last thing she'd expected.

'But you see,' Madeleine went on, worrying at a flake of paint on the baluster with her fingernail, 'I know what it's like to be on the outside.' She bit her lip. 'You were too young to remember, but for me it's as if it were yesterday. That dreadful sense of being inferior. Never being allowed to mention one's parents. Never being allowed to make friends. Always shut out.'

'I remember,' said Sophie.

Madeleine turned and looked into her eyes. 'But do you? I wonder.'

Sophie sighed. 'But Maddy, we're not in London now. This is Trelawny. Things are different out here.'

'No, they're not. That's just it. It may seem as if they are – as if they're more relaxed. Certainly, people will turn a blind eye to matters of birth if one's a Monroe of Fever Hill, or a Lawe of Eden. But that doesn't mean they'll overlook – well, indiscretion. Not when one makes it impossible to ignore.' She softened that with an anxious smile. 'People can turn on you, Sophie. It can happen in a moment. And it's a cold place to be: on the outside, looking in. I don't want that for you.'

Sophie did not reply. She'd been expecting a row. But this was far more devastating. She thought of the note she had sent to Ben. What would Madeleine feel if she knew about it? It would be like the worst kind of betrayal.

'Well,' said Madeleine, giving her hand a little pat. 'Just think about what I've said. That's all I ask.'

For a moment, Sophie did not reply. Then she leaned over and kissed her sister's cheek.

Madeleine tried not to look too pleased. 'What's that for?'

'Nothing. Just for being you.'

'Well,' said Madeleine, colouring, 'I'd better go and dress.'

'I'll be along in a minute.'

'And Sophie . . .' she paused in the doorway, 'don't worry about Sibella. She'll come round. And if she doesn't, we'll tackle her together.'

Sophie nodded and tried to smile. When Madeleine had gone, she turned back to the darkening garden.

Now she was certain that she'd made a mistake in writing to Ben. And yet – and this frightened her more than anything – she didn't care.

It's been five days since Evie met Master Cornelius in Bamboo Walk, but she can still feel the throb of the bite-mark on her breast, and the scratches on her arms and belly and thighs. He'd very nearly got what he wanted.

It's been five days since it happened, and she still can't get her balance. One moment she's close to tears, and the next she's into a rage. She wants to shout and scream and cry. She wants to holler like a pickney.

He'd been strong, but she'd fought like a cat. She dreams of it every night. She thinks of it all day. Even now, as she's coming out of Dr Mallory's clinic with a little bottle of iodine for the scratches, she can't get it out of her mind. His rough wet tongue. The yellow ridges on his fingernails. The oniony smell of his sweat. Thinking of him makes her feel dirty. It's like he's leaving slimy snail-trails in her mind.

With a flush of shame she remembers her pitiful self-deception: that he *respected* her; that he wanted to further her career. She remembers her contempt for her mother's place, and her pride in her education. What education? She's as thick-witted as any mocho nigger from the hills.

Luckily for her, Sophie had been away both times that she'd stopped at the clinic. Luckily for her, Dr Mallory had accepted without question her muttered explanation of a fall from a verandah. But then, he'd been so overcome at dealing with a young female patient that he'd have accepted anything. His collar had become dark with sweat, and he'd kept glancing at her breasts as he was putting the sticking-plaster on the scratches on her arms. He hadn't noticed that she was shaking with anger and self-loathing and disgust. And she'd wanted him dead. She'd wanted her mother to get out her obeah-stick and make him die away of the spirit-sickness before her eyes.

No. No. She doesn't want that. Dr Mallory is just a lonely, well-meaning, unattractive man whom nobody likes. Besides, it's not his fault. It's nobody's fault but her own.

How could she have been such a fool? How many times has her mother warned her that when a buckra gentleman starts sniffing around a coloured girl he's only after one thing? Well, Grace McFarlane was right, and her daughter was wrong, wrong, wrong. *Sweet tongue hide bad heart*, as the saying goes. Or as they chant in infant school: *B is for buckra, very bad man.*

She crosses the clearing and starts for home, heading north between the coffee walks and the little plots of cane.

She's approaching the edge of Greendale Wood when she bumps into Ben. He's leading a big chestnut gelding and wearing his new coachman's uniform, a dark green tunic and breeches which suit him wonderfully. He looks handsome-to-pieces, as her mother would say, and un-usually carefree and at ease. Evie doesn't want to see him right now. She doesn't want to see anyone so carefree and at ease.

'What you doing up here?' she says tartly. 'What about that new job of yours?'

He grins. 'This job! I got nothing to do all day except exercise the horse. So I thought I'd nip along and see Sophie.'

'She didn't come today.'

He frowns. 'Why not? She in trouble?'

'How should I know? I'm not her sister.'

He gives her a considering look, then falls into step beside her, with his hands in his pockets. His horse ambles behind him like a dog, with the reins slung over the saddle.

They reach the trees and take the westward path towards the river. Evie watches Ben break off a switch and start slashing at the ferns. Something's different about him, but she can't work out what. 'You won't keep your job long', she tells him, 'if you go gadding about like this.'

Another grin. 'Ah, that's where you're wrong. This *is*

the job. Turns out the old witch likes me to go out and pick up the odd bit of news. It's called "exercising the horse".'

'What kind of news?'

He shrugs. 'Gossip. And the grimmer the better. Who's just dropped dead. Who's just gone all to smash and blown out his brains and left his kids to take their chances on the parish.'

Who's just escaped being raped in a cane-piece, thinks Evie.

'The way it goes,' he explains, 'is that I mention it to Kean, sort of in passing, and it filters through to her. Not sure how, but it always does.'

'And you think that's a good thing, do you?' she says between her teeth. 'Passing on bad news?'

He blows out a long breath. 'So she likes to find out the worst of people. So what? She's paying.' He gives her a narrow-eye look. 'What's up with you, then?'

'Nothing.'

'Oh, yeah? So how'd you get them bruises on your arms?'

'I fell off a verandah.'

He snorts. 'Since when did that get you a set of finger-marks on your neck?'

She turns away. Damn him for being so sharp.

'Tell me who he is,' he says calmly, 'and I'll give him a going over. Next time he claps eyes on you he'll run a mile.'

His tone is utterly without swagger, but she knows that he'll do it. And for a second she feels a flash of gratitude. But she shakes her head. 'You'd only get into trouble.'

He laughs. 'Me? Never.' Then his smile fades. 'So this bloke who give you the bruises. Did he get what he wanted?'

'No.'

'You sure about that?'

'Yes! Now leave me be!'

He gives another shrug, and goes back to slashing the ferns. They walk on in silence. As they near the river, the trees become taller, the undergrowth thicker. They push through great waxy leaves, and Evie blunders into a spider's web. It's only after she's brushed it away and walked on fifty yards that she realizes what she's done. Every pickney knows that you've got to be polite to Master Anancy spider-man, or he'll bring you bad luck. And if you tear up his place, you need to say sorry fast. But it's too late to say sorry now.

Automatically her hand goes to her neck to find her charm-bag, but of course it isn't there. It got torn off in the struggle in Bamboo Walk, along with the little green silk bag that contained his golden chain.

Strange. Since she became a woman, she's looked down on ignorant superstitions like charm-bags. But without its weight against her heart, she feels vulnerable and afraid.

'So,' says Ben, startling her, 'have you seen Sophie, then?'

'No. I told you.'

He rubs the back of his neck. 'Oh, well. I spose I'll see her soon enough.'

'What do you mean?'

'I'm sposed to be meeting her, day after tomorrow.'

'Where?'

But he just shakes his head. He's trying to keep from smiling, but he can't, and suddenly she knows what's different about him. He's happy. She didn't realize it before because it's so rare with him, but now she sees it in his eyes and his mouth, and the way he moves.

It puts her into a rage. Here is this buckra man, this handsome carefree *buckra* man, walking beside her and just about boiling over with happiness. Why should he be in love when she's so wretched? Why is everything so black-feelinged and tangle-up? 'Ben,' she says in a hard voice, 'I got to tell you a thing. You got to stay away from Sophie Monroe.'

He stoops for a stone and sends it whizzing low over the ferns. 'Now tell me something I don't know.'

'No, *listen* to me. Do you know what I see sometimes when I look at you?'

'What?'

'I see a red-haired girl standing at your shoulder.'

Oh, Jesum Peace, but he's not expecting that. He stops in his tracks and stares at her. His face has gone blank with shock.

She'd not thought it'd have this strong an effect on him, and it frightens her. But she can't stop now. 'Long red hair,' she says, 'and a white face. Like she's sickening for something.'

'No,' he whispers. 'No.'

'She died in pain, didn't she, Ben? Blue shadows under her eyes. Fever-sweat on her skin. And one side of her face turned all to pulp.'

The blood's gone from his cheeks. His lips are grey. 'How d'you know?' he says in a cracked voice. 'How can you know? I never told you about her. Did I?'

'She came for a reason, Ben. They always do. She's warning you. Telling you to keep away.'

He's shaking his head. A fine sheen of sweat has broken out on his forehead.

Now she's frightened bad. She'd expected him to laugh, and shrug it off. She'd *wanted* him to. After all, he's buckra. He's not supposed to be scared of spirits.

'You can't of seen her,' he says dully. 'She's dead. Kate's dead.'

'Oh, I know it,' she says. 'I always know when I see a dead one.'

But he's not hearing her. He's staring past her into nothingness.

'It's a warning, Ben. You got to heed what she's telling you.'

'A warning?' His gaze swings round to her, and he looks at her from a great distance. 'Why would Kate want to warn me? I'm the one that got her killed.'

CHAPTER THIRTEEN

It's twenty-four hours since Evie told him, but it feels like a month.

He can't sleep. Can't eat. Can't even ride like he used to. When he takes out Viking – a big clean-limbed chestnut that he ought to be itching to put through his paces – he just lets the horse wander wherever he likes.

He hasn't felt this bad since Robbie died. He didn't think he could, not with all of them gone. But now things long buried are pushing their way to the surface.

Kate's back. She's back.

Is she here now, as he's riding down the Eden Road? Is she walking beside him? Gliding in and out of the shadows and the sunlight, and trailing her dead hand over the grass? Would he know it if she was?

A cane-rat darts across the road, startling him. A john crow casts a wheeling shadow. The only noises are the creak of the saddle and the stony clink of Viking's hooves.

He keeps thinking of Kate as she was that last summer. He was only about ten, but the memory's so sharp that he can almost see her. That coppery hair that used to crackle and spark when she brushed it. The warm, clever blue eyes.

He read once in a penny newspaper that each man kills the thing he loves. Well, it's true for him. When he was a kid he loved his big sister, though he didn't know it at the time. She was more of a mother than his ma. She walloped him when he nicked things, and she walloped the big boys when they beat him up. He loved her, and he killed her.

So maybe that's why sometimes when he's thinking of her, he gets a picture of Sophie. Because it's a warning, only Evie got it the wrong way round. It's not Sophie who's going to hurt *him*. It's him who's going to hurt Sophie.

So all in all, it's the right thing to do, not turning up at Romilly tomorrow. It's for the best.

But ah God, she'll be so hurt. She'll think it's because there's something wrong with her – that she's not pretty enough, or some bollocks about her knee. She won't understand. And he can't tell her. But it's the only thing to do. It's for the best.

He just wishes he could get her out of his head. That moment before he kissed her. Her clever, wilful face looking up at him: grave and curious and not scared, but a bit nervous, as if she was wondering how far he'd go. He'd never felt so close to another person. And the strange thing was that he didn't mind. He didn't get that prickly tightness in his chest. He was just falling, falling into those honey-coloured eyes.

A distant pounding of hooves jolts him back to the present. It's some horse in a flat-out gallop over to his left, only he can't see, on account of the trees.

Viking skitters about a bit, and Ben tells him to pack it in. 'Listen,' he says, 'if some crazy planter wants to take a gallop in this heat, that's his lookout. You just thank your stars I got more sense.'

Viking snorts, and tosses his head in agreement.

They leave the trees behind and the cane-pieces open out around, and that's when he catches sight of the crazy planter. The silly sod's just come a cropper on a cane-track, and broken his horse's knees.

Ben turns Viking's head and puts him forward through the cane. 'You all right?' he shouts. Not that he cares much one way or the other.

The planter struggles to his feet and gives a rueful laugh. 'Does it look as if I am?'

Ben ignores him. He jumps down and tethers Viking to a stand of cane, and walks past him to check on the horse.

It's a nice little mare, or it was once, but now she's only fit for the knacker's. She's got her head down, and she's shaking like a leaf: foam all over her, blood streaming from her shattered knees, and the left front cannon bone's snapped clean through. Ben can see the white bone jutting from a pulpy mess of muscle. What a sodding waste.

She smells him coming and manages a welcoming nicker, and – oh, no. No. It's Trouble.

'Christ Almighty,' he snarls over his shoulder. 'You bloody fool. Look what you done.'

Behind him the man gives an astonished laugh. 'Steady on, old fellow. It was an accident.'

That's when Ben turns and recognizes Master Alexander Traherne.

Master Alex recognizes him at the same moment, and goes still. The pale blue eyes flicker over him, sizing him up. Maybe he's thinking how Ben made a fool of him over Mrs Dampiere, and what about getting his own back? But then he takes in the empty cane-pieces, with nobody to lend a hand if things get rough. So instead he just gives himself a shake and straightens his necktie.

He's a coward, thinks Ben. That's what it is. He's a sodding coward. Only good for ruining horses.

'Lend me your mount,' says Master Alex calmly, 'there's a good fellow.'

Ben snorts. 'As if I would.'

Master Alex studies him for a moment, then brushes off his hands. 'Watch yourself, my lad. No sense in talking back to your betters. Now lend me your mount and we'll call it quits.'

'I'm not your lad,' snarls Ben. 'I never was.'

Beside him, Trouble keeps looking from one to the other, twitching her ears and trying to follow, in case they're giving her an order.

That makes Ben feel sick. Sick and ashamed. Because this is his fault. If he hadn't spent so much time schooling her, Master Alex would of never ridden her in the first place. She'd be just another fair-to-middling little carriage horse trotting happily along in front of Miss Sibella's dog cart, and looking forward to a snooze and a bit of sweet hay for her supper. He done this to her. Each man kills the thing he loves.

A movement at his shoulder, and he turns to see Master Alex walking off down the track. It seems he's given up on getting a ride home, and decided to hoof it. 'Oi!' shouts Ben. 'Where d'you think you're going?'

'Home,' calls Master Alex without turning round. 'Not that it's any business of yours.'

'What about Trouble?'

'What about her?'

'You can't just leave her. You got to finish her off.'

'I'll send a boy to do that.'

'But that'll take hours! Look at her. You can't leave her in this state.'

But Master Alex just waves an irritable hand and keeps going.

Ben thinks about fetching him back, then gives it up as a bad job. It's Trouble he's got to think of now.

She tries to move towards him, but of course she can't. She just lies there trembling. Watching him. Please don't leave me, she's asking him.

'Don't worry, sweetheart,' he tells her. 'I'm not going nowhere.'

He takes out his knife and keeps it behind his back as he walks over to her, talking all the time so as not to frighten her. When he gets up close, he puts his free hand on her wet, shivering withers, and moves it gently up her neck, under her mane. She's boiling hot and running sweat. That idiot must of ridden her like a madman. 'All right, sweetheart,' he murmurs. 'Soon be over now.' His eyes are stinging, and there's a lump like a bit of meat in his throat, but somehow he manages to keep his voice steady. More or less.

She's got her ears down, looking at him with her great, dark, velvety eyes. She's trying to tell him how much it hurts. She's telling her friend. The one she trusts to make it better.

He moves his free hand up to her forelock, then down to cover her eye. For a moment that he'll never forget he feels the long, bristly lashes trembling under his palm. Then he raises his other hand and brings the knife up under her ear, and with a single thrust he drives it deep into her brain.

For a moment, she stiffens, then a shudder goes through her. He kneels beside her, stroking her cheek and watching the great velvet eye glazing over, and murmuring, 'All right now,' over and over again. The hot blood bubbles over his thighs. Black spots dart before his eyes. He feels dizzy and sick, and suddenly very, very tired.

'What the devil d'you think you're doing?' says a voice.

Ben blinks. Who's that? It's like it's coming from a very long way away.

'Who gave you permission to kill my horse?' says Master Alex, behind him.

In a daze, Ben turns and squints up at him.

Master Alex has retraced his steps, and is standing about a yard away: hands on hips, sun at his back, face dark against the glare.

'I – I done you a favour,' mutters Ben. 'You left her—'

'That's my property. Who gave you permission?'

Wearily, Ben stands up. He glances down at the knife in his hand. How did that get there? He drops it in the dust. He's so tired. So sodding tired. Why can't Master Alex stop yapping?

'I said, who gave you permission?'

'Shut up,' mutters Ben. His hand is sticky with blood. It's already turning black under his fingernails. Clumsily he wipes it off on his thigh.

'You think you're special, don't you?' says Master Alex. 'For some reason which entirely eludes me, you actually think you're entitled to speak to your betters as if . . .'

There's more, but Ben's not listening. He squints into the sun, and takes a swing, and lands Master Alex a short, hard punch on the jaw.

Master Alex grunts, and goes down hard in a cloud of dust.

Ben stands over him, blinking and shaking the feeling back into his hand. 'I told you to shut up,' he mutters. Then he walks over to Viking and unties him, and swings up into the saddle and rides away.

'Are you sickening for something, girl?' says Grace McFarlane with her hands on her hips.

Evie shakes her head.

'Cho! You working too hard. Always got your nose in that damn book.'

'I want to find out what happens,' mutters Evie.

Grace gives a small proud smile, and shakes her head, and squats down to poke the fire. 'You and your damn books.'

If only she knew, thinks Evie, shifting position on the step. If only she knew what her teacheress daughter is reading.

It's nearly supper-time, and dark in the yard. But it's not total dark, for beyond the village Master Cameron's burning off the cane.

They always burn off the cane at night, so that they can spot the stray sparks and stamp them out. Then, early in the morning, they start taking off the crop. It's much easier with the trash all burnt off, but you got to work quickly, before it spoils.

Lying in bed listening to them burning off the cane is one of her best memories of when she was a pickney. The sound of the men calling to each other; the crackle and roar of the flames. She used to lie in bed and picture the men bringing to life this great hungry fire-animal – but always hemming it in, never letting it escape. She used to find cane-fires oddly reassuring.

She doesn't tonight. Tonight everything's wrong-side and tangle-up. She's full of worry-head about Ben. Why did she tell him about the red-haired girl? And why did she tell him *then*, on that particular day, when she'd been keeping silent for months? Was it chance? Or was she being used by some spirit of darkness?

Everything she touches seems to go wrong. Maybe she should get right away: out of Trelawny, and all the way to foreign. To Kingston, even. Get right away and start again.

'Evie,' says her mother.

'In a minute,' she mutters. With a sense of weary compulsion she looks down at the journal.

Six years have passed since Congo Eve lost her little brother Job, and near went out of her mind with grief. Six years since Cyrus Wright caught her dancing the shay-shay with Strap, and sold him to Mr Traherne. Since then the rains have failed once, and old Master Alasdair has sent his younger son Allan to Scotland to manage the Strathnaw estate. And Master Alasdair's oldest son, Master Lindsay, has himself fathered a son, and named him Jocelyn.

Evie has lost count of the times that her namesake has 'gone runaway', and been brought back and flogged. Once Congo Eve went runaway to Caledon, to see her little sister Leah matched with a Coromantee field-slave. Twice she's fallen pregnant. Both times she has miscarried, *'or so she said,'* wrote Cyrus Wright, *'though I suspect her of using foul Negro potions to purge herself.'*

Now it is 1824, and there has been a small revolt at Golden Grove in the neighbouring parish, savagely suppressed. *'Several hangings & slow burnings,'* noted Cyrus Wright, who made a point of witnessing them. *'Cum Congo Eve behind the trash house, stans, backward.'*

September 26th, 1824 *Last night a hurrycane blew the thatch off the cooperage & the shingles off the Necessary House. The woods on Clairmont Hill look bare & like to the trees in England after the fall of the leaf. Congo Eve said it is an omen, but I replied that as my own house was spared, it must be a good one.*

September 29th *Found her with Strap in the curing-house. He was wearing my blue Holland coat that I gave her years back, & she said was lost. I shouted at Strap & he knocked me down & fled, but I sent my Negroes & they catch'd him. If propriety had not prevented me whipping another man's Negro, I would have done it. As they led him back to Parnassus he shouted that I would not live much longer in a whole skin. I was much put about, & had to take brandy. Congo Eve said not a word, but would only look at me.*

September 30th I have heard that Mr Traherne only had Strap flogged. Am much vex'd, for it is far too lenient. That Negro should be hanged.

November 12th Congo Eve runaway again, to Caledon. When she was brought back, she told me with all impudence that her sister Leah has been brought to bed of a girl, named Semanthe. What of that, said I, when the whelp will be dead within the week? Not so, cried she, for this is a full Coromantee child, & not got on Leah with force by a buckra man. I said I would hear no more, but she would not be silenced, & taunted me that the child will grow powerful & strong, & will know all the arts that she & her sister can teach it.

'Come, Evie,' her mother says again. 'It's getting cold.'

Evie closes the book and stares down at the mildewed calfskin. There's a roaring in her ears. *Semanthe, Semanthe, Semanthe.*

Semanthe, the daughter of Leah. Semanthe, the blind, raggity old obeah-woman who'd appeared to Evie beneath the calabash tree when she was ten. Semanthe. Her grandmother.

Congo Eve and Evie McFarlane. They're one and the same family.

She turns and stares up at the house where she was born and raised. It's a two-roomed house of cut-stone, and built to last. It should be. Her great-grandmother Leah put it up when she came to Fever Hill with Master Jocelyn's young bride Miss Kitty, in 1848.

Great-grandmother Leah had been a widow by then, but she'd mortared that house herself, with red clay and molasses and powdered bones, and some special ash that she'd been keeping in a yabba for seventeen years. Ash from the ruins of Fever Hill great house, that got burnt in the Black Family Rebellion which killed her man. And when the house was built, her blind daughter Semanthe wove the roof: of good strong thatchpalm, and a spell or two, besides.

Congo Eve and Evie McFarlane. Family.

What does it mean? wonders Evie. Is it some sort of sign? Some trickified message from the spirits?

She doesn't know. All she knows is that everything's coming together in a wrong kind of pattern.

Her mother comes and sits beside her on the step, and stretches out her legs. Her shins are a glossy dark mahogany next to Evie's smooth coffee-coloured skin. 'I got something will cheer you right up,' she says, putting up a hand and smoothing back a lock of Evie's hair from her temple. And in the middle of her confusion, Evie is touched, for Grace McFarlane is not a caressing kind of mother.

'That buckra boy,' says Grace, 'Ben Kelly, with the green puss-eye?'

Evie looks at her in alarm.

Grace cracks a smile. 'Yesterday he punched Master Alex smack on the jaw!'

Evie's horrified. Merciful Peace, Ben, what were you thinking?

But her mother's slapping her thigh and chuckling, for she always did detest the Trahernes. 'Jesum *Peace*, but they say Master Alex is *bad* vexed! He's got a bruise the size of a john crow egg on that pretty-pretty jaw of his. And just in time for the Christmas Masquerade!'

Evie's thoughts are teeming like black ants. Everything's tangling together like strangler fig. She can't see the pattern, but she can feel that it's bad.

If she hadn't met Master Cornelius in Bamboo Walk, she wouldn't have gone to the clinic; and then she wouldn't have bumped into Ben and told him about the red-haired girl; and then *he* wouldn't have been shaken off balance and lost his temper and hit Master Alex.

And now this link with Congo Eve. This link which she can never escape.

What does it mean? And how does she stop the bad from coming?

With Christmas only a week away, the dawn air was cool, and Sophie's breath steamed as she waited at Romilly Bridge.

It would be hot by midday, but now everything was deliciously fresh, and the colours sharp and clean. Black swallows dipped to drink at the turquoise river. She caught the saffron flash of a wild canary; the iridescent green of a doctorbird. Mauve thunbergia trailed from the trees at the edge of the clearing. A white egret flew past the emerald plumes of the giant bamboo.

Putting her hands on the parapet, she took a deep breath of the fresh, green-smelling air, and watched her horse cropping the ferns, and nearly laughed aloud. She felt scared and exhilarated, and appalled at what she was doing. Now and then a surge of elation made her heart swell till it hurt.

She'd hoped to find him waiting when she arrived. But of course, she reminded herself, it was a good six miles from Falmouth, and he wouldn't find it easy to get away.

A noise behind her. She spun round; then gave a disappointed sigh. Only a ground-dove. She smiled, but the smile felt forced. Where was Ben?

She walked down to the riverbank and snapped off a stem of scarlet heliconia. She tossed one of the big gold-tipped claws into the sliding current. By the time you've thrown them all in, she told herself, he'll be here.

He wasn't.

Perhaps he hadn't received her note. Perhaps Great-Aunt May had taken it into her head to change the habit of a lifetime, and go for an early morning drive.

Or perhaps, she thought with a sudden sense of falling,

perhaps you've made a mistake. Perhaps when he kissed you it was just the impulse of the moment. After all, why should he want to see you again? He's so good-looking, and you're not nearly pretty enough. And you limp.

'How do you know he isn't after your money?' Cameron had said with his customary bluntness the night before, when he'd asked her to take a turn with him in the garden after dinner.

'You only say that,' she'd retorted, 'because you don't know him.'

'And you do?'

'Yes.'

'Are you sure?'

She did not reply. Until he'd said it, the thought of money hadn't occurred to her. She knew that that was naive, but she also knew that it hadn't occurred to Ben, either. They didn't think of anything but each other. And especially, they didn't think about the future. How could they? They didn't have one.

She and Cameron had walked on in the blue moonlight, while Scout crashed around in the bushes, and the ratbats flitted across the stars. She glanced at Cameron smoking his cigar, but couldn't read his mood. When he chose, he could be inscrutable.

Suddenly he stopped and ground out the cigar under his heel. 'The thing is, Sophie,' he said evenly, 'I won't have Madeleine hurt. I won't let anyone do that. Not even you.'

She caught her breath. 'I wouldn't hurt Madeleine,' she said. 'I wouldn't ever do that.'

'But that's precisely what you will do if you persist in this.'

'Cameron—'

'You'll cause a scandal, and that inevitably will—'

'Why must there be a scandal?' she said.

'Sophie, be practical! We live in a real, imperfect world. Not the world as you might wish it to be.'

'But if we're ever to make it better, surely—'

'I won't have Madeleine hurt for a theory,' he cut in with a firmness that made her blink.

And suddenly, as she stood there looking up into his face, she felt an overwhelming loneliness. This man before her loved her sister so much that he would do anything to keep her from harm. He would die for her if he had to. Did Ben feel like that about her? Did she feel like that about Ben? Did she really love him? Was this how love felt? How would she know? How would she *know*?

At the edge of the clearing, someone was coming. Sophie froze.

This time it wasn't a ground-dove. It was a small boy pickney on his way to school. Barefoot, in patched but scrupulously clean calico shirt and shorts, he was kicking an unripe mango before him like a football, and whistling between his teeth.

He caught sight of Sophie and gave her a brilliant smile. 'Morning, Missy Sophie,' he called politely.

She forced an answering smile and returned the greeting.

When he'd gone, she watched the dust settling softly back to earth.

It was getting warmer. The rasp of the crickets was gathering strength. A mongoose emerged from a tangle of hogmeat and gave her a sharp, indifferent stare. As she watched it slip away into the ferns, something tightened in her chest.

He isn't coming, she told herself, and the words thudded in her heart.

He isn't coming.

One of the darkies stamps on Ben's knee, and pain unfolds like a black flower.

Pain like that probably means it's broken, he tells himself. So if it's broken anyway, and if they just keep hitting you there, you'll be all right.

But of course they don't.

They came on him on the Arethusa Road as he was heading back from a ride: three big, silent darkies he's never seen before. Which stands to reason. Master Alex couldn't get the lads from Parnassus to beat up one of their own.

They came up behind him and yanked him off Viking and dragged him into a cane-piece. He managed to give one of them a good bash in the ribs and another a broken cheekbone before they brought him down. But they know what they're about. Measured. Precise. Nothing too visible – that bash in the face was a mistake – and they don't got coshes, which is something, as it probably means they're not out to kill.

The blood's salty-sweet and gritty in his mouth. He can smell their sweat and hear them grunt, but he can't see much on account of all the blood. Still, he can see *something* – red flashes and a bit of guinea grass – and that's good, because it means his eyes aren't burst.

Another kick in the ribs, and this time a groan which might of been him, and another black flower flares in his side.

Happy Christmas, he thinks. He starts to laugh. Once he's started he can't stop. He's heaving and gasping as they're hitting him. He's blowing blood-bubbles through his mouth. Happy sodding Christmas.

Did one of them mutter 'enough', or did he only hope they did? It's hard to tell, as things are getting a bit floaty. Sorry, Sophie, he mumbles. It comes out as a choking moan.

Very small and clear, he gets a picture of her inside his head. Only it's not Sophie as she is now, but when she was a kid, the first time he seen her in the Portland Road.

He grabs hold of the picture and clings on to it. Sophie in her stripy red pinafore and her black stockings, with a black velvet ribbon in her hair, and her gold-tipped eyelashes shadowing her cheek as she shows him her book. 'It's *Black Beauty*,' she tells him breathlessly, 'Maddy gave it to me for my birthday and it's *brilliant*, I've read it twice already.'

Sorry, Sophie, he tells her inside his head. Sorry, love.

That's his last thought before it goes black.

CHAPTER FOURTEEN

'Apparently he had some kind of accident,' said Madeleine as they were coming out of church on Christmas Day.

'What do you mean, an accident?' demanded Sophie. 'When?'

Madeleine paused in the aisle to make way for a trio of old ladies who, like the church decorations, were wilting in the heat. It had been a long service, and everyone was eager for luncheon. There was a pervasive smell of Florida water and eau de Cologne, with an undertow of perspiration.

'*When?*' Sophie said again as they moved out onto the porch.

Madeleine opened her sun-umbrella with a snap, and scanned the throng of carriages for Cameron. He never attended services, but sometimes for her sake he collected them from St Peter's and said a word to the rector, thereby quashing suspicions of outright heathenism. 'Some time last week,' said Madeleine, spotting Cameron waiting for them further up the street.

'Last *week*? Maddy, how could you not tell me?'

'Because it isn't serious. He's *fine*.'

'Then why isn't he here? Why did Great-Aunt May have to get someone else to drive her to church?'

'Oh look,' said Madeleine, 'there's Rebecca Traherne. Now remember, you're going to be ill tomorrow, so don't appear too healthy.'

They dealt with Rebecca, then Sophie resumed the attack. 'How did you find out?' she said as they waited beneath a cassia tree for the crowd on the pavement to thin.

'How does one find out anything?' said Madeleine. 'From the servants, of course.'

Sophie chewed her lip. 'Just how bad is it?'

'I told you, he's fine.'

'Then why didn't you tell me sooner?'

Madeleine made no reply.

'Maddy, if you don't tell me everything, I shall force it out of Poppy, or Braverly, or—'

'Oh, very well.' She cast a quick glance about her, then said in a low voice, 'He was found by a weeding gang a couple of miles out of town, just off the Arethusa Road. He must have fallen from his horse—'

'Ben? He's the best rider in Trelawny.'

'– *anyway*,' said Madeleine with a quelling glance, 'they took him to Prospect because it's nearest, and one of Grace's cousins patched him up. Cuts and bruises, a chipped knee bone, and some bruised ribs. So you see, I do care enough to have made enquiries. But that's all I know.'

Sophie took that in silence. Around them churchgoers chatted in little groups, and carriages departed in a haze of dust. Negro families walked by in starched Sunday best with their shoes in their hands.

Madeleine fiddled with the clasp of her reticule. Plainly she was also worried about Ben; and Sophie guessed that she hadn't told everything she knew. But there was a stubborn set to her mouth which warned that she could only be pushed so far.

'Is he still at Prospect?' Sophie asked.

Madeleine shook her head. 'I think – I think they took him to Bethlehem.'

Sophie tossed her head in frustration. It would have to be Bethlehem, just when Dr Mallory had closed the clinic for what he grimly called 'the festivities'.

In silence they started making their way up the street to

where Cameron was waiting with the carriage. Fraser sat beside his father, clutching his presents on his lap. When he caught sight of Sophie he leaped to his feet, waving so hard that he would have tumbled out of the carriage if Cameron hadn't transferred the reins to one hand and gripped a handful of sailor suit with the other.

Just before they got within earshot, Madeleine turned to Sophie and said quickly, 'Sophie, you *can't* go to see him. I need you to promise me that you won't.'

It was Sophie's turn to look stubborn.

'What possible good could it do?' said Madeleine. 'Grace and her people can look after him just as well as you could.'

'But—'

'Leave him alone, Sophie. Don't make things worse for him than they already are.'

Sophie stared at her. 'What do you mean by that?'

Madeleine looked unhappy.

'Maddy – it was an accident, wasn't it?'

But by then they were at the carriage, and Fraser was jumping down, brandishing his new red kite, and there was no more time to talk.

On the drive back to Eden, she debated what to do. Ben was in some sort of trouble, and he was hurt. That much she knew. And she was pretty sure that Madeleine wouldn't tell her any more.

The question was, did he want to see her? After all, he hadn't met her at Romilly Bridge, nor had she heard from him since. And after his accident – or whatever it was – he hadn't sent her any kind of message.

In the end, she decided not to do anything – at least, not today. After all, she could hardly saddle her horse and ride off to Bethlehem in the middle of Christmas lunch.

Fortunately, Cameron was preoccupied with crop-time, and Madeleine had her hands full with the children, so neither of them noticed that Sophie hardly said a word. After lunch Cameron rode over to Maputah, and Madeleine calmed the children down with a game of Answerit. Sophie wrote to Rebecca Traherne, excusing herself from tomorrow's Masquerade, then read the children stories. Then she pleaded a sick headache and went early to bed.

Boxing Day dawned cloudy and cool – 'bleaky', as the servants called it – and everyone was subdued and slightly cross. After breakfast Madeleine took the dog cart to fetch Clemency from Fever Hill. Clemency had flatly refused to desert her dead child on Christmas Day, but after much persuasion had consented to come for Boxing Day and stay the night, to help Sophie look after the children while Madeleine and Cameron were at Parnassus. Predictably, Clemency was now repenting her weakness and desperate to cancel the visit, which was why Madeleine asked Sophie to accompany her.

She would have gone anyway, as she needed to question Evie about Ben. But to her dismay, the McFarlanes weren't at the old slave village. According to Clemency, they were spending Christmas with relations – 'some-where'. Clemency couldn't remember where.

Back at Eden, they ate an elaborate lunch in Clemency's honour. Then Cameron rode over to the western cane-pieces at Orange Grove, while Madeleine withdrew to bathe and dress for the Masquerade, and Clemency and Sophie kept the children amused. At least Clemency did, by drawing an enormous Christmas tree and helping them colour in the decorations. Sophie pretended to watch, and had second thoughts.

Ben was all alone in the world. She'd never known any-one so alone. He had no family, and no friends except for Evie, who hardly saw him. Grace and her relations looked after him because in the past he'd done them a good turn; but they were motivated by obligation, not affection. He wasn't one of them. In a country where a man was either a planter or a banana farmer, a Negro or a coloured or a coolie or a Chinaman, Ben was just a poor white. He didn't fit in. How would he feel if she didn't come and see him when he was hurt?

The answer, she reminded herself sternly, was that he probably wouldn't care one way or the other. After all, he'd been quite happy to let her wait on Romilly Bridge with neither explanation nor apology. Why should he want to see her?

But what if he did?

At five o'clock, Madeleine and Cameron left for Parnassus. They were starting early, as Cameron needed to stop off at the Fever Hill works to talk to the manager.

'We'll be back at some unearthly hour around dawn,' said Madeleine, rolling her eyes. 'Rebecca always lays on an enormous breakfast, and by then everyone's so exhausted, they fall on it.'

Already Poppy was getting the children ready for an early bed. Belle was still a little frail after shaking off a slight fever the week before, while Fraser had simply eaten too many sweets. 'I've hidden the rest,' said Madeleine, drawing Sophie aside, 'but he'll work on Clemency, he always does, so I'm *counting* on you to be strong.'

Did Sophie imagine it, or did her sister give special emphasis to that 'I'm counting on you'? *You can't go to see him. I need you to promise me that you won't. Don't make things worse for him than they already are.*

At last the carriage departed in a cloud of dust, and the house settled into peace. It was twenty past five. It would be light for about another two or three hours, and after that there would be a nearly full moon. Plenty of time to ride to Bethlehem and see him. She'd be home by eight. Nine at the latest. And Clemency and Poppy could look after the children.

But would that be fair on Clemency? To leave her alone, and in charge of the house?

And think of the humiliation if she rode all the way there, only to find that he'd already left. Everyone would know why she'd come. She'd be a laughing stock. The love-sick buckra miss, forlornly dogging the footsteps of her reluctant swain.

Clemency came out onto the verandah and perched on the sofa, and gave Sophie one of her wincing smiles. 'They're fast asleep,' she whispered. 'Exhausted, poor little dears. I must say, I am too.'

Sophie forced a smile. A whole evening with Clemency. She couldn't do it. She needed to know that Ben was all right. She needed to see for herself.

Quickly, she stood up. 'D'you know, I think I need some air. Should you mind dreadfully if I take myself off for a ride?'

Clemency's pretty young-old face lit up with relief. 'Darling, not at *all*! In fact, I was just going to ask if you'd mind if I went to my room for a little lie-down, and perhaps a short prayer?'

Sophie felt a twinge of sadness. A *short prayer* probably meant several hours on her knees, apologizing to Elliot for having deserted him. 'Of course I don't mind,' she said. 'You do whatever you like, Clemmie. I shall be back in a couple of hours, but don't worry if I'm late. And don't wait supper for me.'

Enough agonizing, she told herself briskly as she changed into her riding-skirt and pulled on her boots. For once, stop debating things from every angle, and simply *act*.

In the looking-glass she gave herself a small, determined smile. She felt better already.

In old times, the slaves had had three days' holiday a year: Christmas Day, Boxing Day, and New Year's Day. They'd made good use of them.

They'd shed their drab osnaburg clothing and dressed up in the brightest prints they could find, with anklets of scarlet john-crow berries and necklaces of blue clay beads, and fearsome cow-horned masks. Then, for those three days, they'd yelled and danced and drummed their way through towns, villages and estates, in a make-believe return to the African homeland they had lost.

The Masquerade at Parnassus was a tidy Anglicized version of the old parade. A sedate Britannia headed the procession, followed by the Montego Bay Coloured Troupe playing patriotic songs. Then came a carnival king and queen in flowing robes and gilt paper crowns, and an entourage of servants in fancy dress and papier mâché masks: the Sailor, the Jockey, the Messenger Boy; and finally a civilized version (in nautical dress) of the traditional ring-leader, 'Johnny Canoe'.

After the procession came a supper, a *tableau vivant* staged by the Falmouth Horticultural Society, dancing, and finally a breakfast. Such was the Trahernes' Boxing Day Masquerade. It carried not the faintest echo of that darkest of all Christmases seventy-two years before, when the slaves had begun a rebellion that lasted for months, and destroyed over fifty Northside great houses.

But at Bethlehem, on the edge of the Cockpits, the echoes remained. And the parade was the real thing: a throwback to a darker, wilder past. No-one mentioned 'Johnny Canoe'. *Jonkunoo* was king. Jockeys and sailors were nowhere to be seen; in their place were half-naked men in grotesquely horned masks: Devil, Horsehead, Pitchy-Patchy, the Bull – leaping, dancing and yelling to the harsh rhythms of pipe and drum. Europe had given way to Africa; English to half-forgotten snatches of Eboe and Koromantyn; pantomime royalty to witch-doctors and the Mothers of Darkness.

As a child, Sophie had watched Jonkunoo parades with a mixture of excitement and terror, but she'd always had Cameron to huddle against when it got too frightening. Now, as she tied her horse to a tree at the edge of the village, she was sharply aware that she was the only white person there.

A shouting, drumming, dancing crowd thronged the torchlit clearing. She saw faces she recognized, but they looked unfamiliar in the leaping shadows. The drums were loud in her ears. The air was thick with the smell of pimento-wood fires, and jerked hog, and pepperpot and rum. It had been a mistake to come. Ben couldn't possibly be here.

As she stood uncertainly at the edge of the crowd, the Bull – the Jonkunoo himself – leaped out in front of her. The cow-horned mask thrust into her face, and she caught an alarming glimpse of dark eyes through painted slits, their whites stained yellow with ganja. '*Jonkunoo!*' he bellowed, then leaped away.

She drew a shaky breath. Ridiculous to be frightened. She *knew* these people.

As she was pushing her way through the crowd, she saw a pickney she recognized: the schoolboy from Romilly Bridge. 'No, Missy Sophie,' he said when she asked if he'd seen the injured buckra man. 'He went away.' Where did he go? He shrugged and gave her an encouraging smile. 'Not far.' But she could see that he didn't really know, and was only being polite.

It was as she'd feared. Ben was gone, and all she'd achieved was to make a fool of herself.

Then she caught sight of Evie, and relief washed over her.

The coloured girl was sitting with her mother and the village nanas beneath the breadfruit tree. She was hunched on the ground, and gazing at the procession with unseeing eyes. When she saw Sophie, her lips parted in a little 'O' of surprise. She glanced about her, signalled to Sophie to stay where she was, and got up and ran over to her. 'What are you doing here?' she said in a hoarse whisper. She looked tired and troubled, and her hand on Sophie's arm was feverishly hot.

'Where's Ben?' said Sophie.

Evie bit her lip. Then she drew Sophie aside into the comparative privacy of a coffee walk behind the houses.

'Evie, you've *got* to tell me. He's not at Great-Aunt May's, I checked. She sacked him. So—'

'He's all right,' said Evie. 'Not to fret, Sophie. He's all right.'

Sophie crossed her arms about her waist and took a few paces between the coffee trees. Suddenly she was alarmingly close to tears. She hadn't realized until now how worried she'd been. 'What *happened*?'

Evie put her hand on Sophie's back and rubbed it gently up and down. 'I don't know.'

'Well, you must know more than me. Maddy said it was an accident, but—'

'An accident?' Evie snorted. 'No, he had a fight with Master Alex, and then—'

'Master Alex?' Sophie looked at her in bemusement. 'But – you can't mean that Alexander Traherne managed to beat him up?'

Evie burst out laughing. 'Course not!' She wiped her eyes, suddenly much more her usual self. 'No, they met on the road, and got to argifying – I mean, arguing. Why they were arguing, I don't know, but then Ben hit him. And the next day, he got set on by some men, and beaten up.'

'What men?'

Evie shook her head. 'Strangers from foreign.'

'Strangers,' Sophie repeated. Presumably 'Master Alex's' hired thugs. 'And where is he now?'

'I don't know, Sophie. He left yesterday. Got a lift part-way with Uncle Eliphalet on his mule, but I don't know to where.'

'What direction? North? South?'

'North-west.'

'Towards the river?'

'I think so. But truly, I don't know.'

I do, thought Sophie.

It was nearly eight o'clock by the time she reached Romilly, and the light was fading. The most direct route from Bethlehem would have been by the river path which followed the Martha Brae all the way to the ruins. But that went straight past the house, and she didn't want to bump into Clemency or one of the servants. So instead she took the main road that went past Maputah and skirted the edge of the Cockpits, then turned right at the cross-roads, and headed down the Eden Road to Romilly. She was lucky. Everyone was either at a Jonkunoo parade, or sleeping it off. The countryside was strangely hushed, for the sea breeze had long since dropped, and the land breeze was only blowing faintly from the hills.

When she reached Romilly it appeared deserted, but she'd been expecting that. She tethered her horse to an ironwood tree and made her way on foot along the river path which led to the innermost ruins of the old slave compound. Giant bamboo turned the path into an airless, shadowy tunnel. A thick carpet of leaves muffled her footsteps.

Ben had set up camp in a roofless, three-walled ruin a few yards from the river. He hadn't heard her approach. He was in shirtsleeves, sitting on a block of cut-stone beside a small fire, with one leg stuck out in front of him, and a pair of bamboo crutches laid on a blanket on the ground.

The side of his face that was turned towards her was unmarked, but she saw the patchwork of purplish-yellow bruises on both forearms, and the bandage round his knee. His shirt was open to the waist, revealing lower ribs strapped with tape, and more cuts and bruises above. By the crutches lay a small calabash, probably containing one of Grace's special salves, with a roll of tape beside it, a pair of rusty scissors, and a can of water that he'd obviously been heating on the fire. It looked as if he'd started to change the dressings, and then lost interest.

As he turned to poke the fire, she saw the dark bruising down his right cheekbone and around the eye; the crusted blood on a deep vertical cut bisecting his eyebrow. The contrast with the unmarked side of his face was startling.

She stepped out from under the giant bamboo, and he saw her and went still. 'I thought I'd find you here,' she said.

CHAPTER FIFTEEN

He did not reply. But plainly he was horrified to see her.

Suddenly she saw herself as she must appear to him: her hair coming loose, her jacket and riding-skirt covered in dust. The bedraggled bluestocking, trailing after her unwilling prey.

What was she doing here? He didn't want her. And why should he? Look at him. After that one long stare he had turned back to the fire, and, in profile, the unmarked side of his face was forbiddingly beautiful.

But still she floundered on. 'Why didn't you stay at Bethlehem? I mean, they were looking after you there, so why—'

'Because I wanted to come here,' he cut in. In the leaping firelight his cheeks were dark with stubble. It made him look older, rougher, and startlingly unfamiliar. 'I wanted to be on my own. All right?'

'Does that mean you want me to go?'

'Yes,' he said without looking at her, 'I want you to go. You shouldn't of come.'

'But I couldn't just—'

'I thought you'd be down at Parnassus. At that party.'

'I sent them a note to say I was ill.'

'Why'd you do that?'

'Why d'you think? I was worried about you.'

'That's daft,' he snapped. 'You shouldn't of come.' He reached for one of the crutches to poke the fire, but dropped it with a clatter, and swore under his breath. His movements were awkward, and without his usual grace. Somehow that gave her the courage to take a step forward, and remove her hat, and sit down on a corner of the blanket, a safe distance from him. 'What happened to your leg?' she asked.

'What's it to you?'

'Oh, absolutely nothing,' she retorted. 'That's why I'm here.'

He drew a breath. 'Grace says I've bruised the knee bone. Or something.'

She considered that. 'Your ribs – do they hurt?'

'No.' He shrugged. 'A bit.' He reached for the can of hot water and knocked it over. '*Bugger.*'

She felt herself reddening. She leaned forward and righted the can, then took her handkerchief from her pocket and held it out. 'Here. Use this.'

He looked at it for a moment, then took it with a scowl. She remembered a thirteen-year-old boy being offered a book, and snarling like a fox-cub because he didn't know how to accept a kindness.

She watched him dip the handkerchief in what remained of the water, and make a clumsy job of cleaning a long, bloody bruise on his side. Then she had to look away. He was finely muscled, and below the sunburn which ended at the base of his throat his skin was pale and smooth. He looked both familiar and unfamiliar: boy and man, known and unknown. It made her want to cry. She was glad of the shadows beyond the circle of the fire, and of the cool, blue, concealing moonlight.

Around them, night settled on the river. Fireflies spangled the creepers that choked the low ruined walls. Tall spikes of ginger lilies glowed white in the moonlight. The crickets' rasp had given way to the clear pulse of the whistling frogs, and on the breeze Sophie caught a drifting sweetness.

Glancing about her, she saw a cluster of cockleshell orchids clinging to a block of cut-stone to her left. The pale, twisted petals seemed to catch and hold the moonlight. Their scent was heavy and sweet. Perhaps decades before, she thought, some slave sat where I am now, beside this same stretch of black river, breathing in this sweet, slightly funereal scent.

Raising her head, she saw with a shock that Ben was watching her, his expression unreadable in the moonlight. She said quietly, 'Why didn't you meet me at the bridge?'

'I couldn't.'

'Why not?'

He turned back to the fire. 'Look. I know I hurt you. And I'm sorry. I really am. But I had to stay away. If I'd met you on the bridge, I'd of hurt you more.'

'I don't understand.'

'You don't have to.' He sighed. 'It's nothing to do with you. It's nothing to do with you, or your knee.'

Nothing to do with your knee. Was she so easy to read? So transparent and pitiful? She tugged at a snag in the blanket.

'Sophie,' he said quietly.

She raised her head and glowered at him.

'Christ, Sophie,' he said, 'when are you going to forget about that bloody knee?'

'That's easy for you to say. You don't limp.'

He nodded at his bandaged leg. 'I do now.'

'Not permanently.'

'What would you know? You don't either.'

'I do when I'm tired.'

'So what? Sophie – look at me.'

She met his eyes. He was close enough for her to see the black blood crusting his eyebrow, and the bruises down the side of his face, and the gleam of his teeth between his lips. And as she looked at him, she realized that he did want her to stay, after all.

'Let me see it,' he said, startling her.

'What?'

'Your knee. Let me see it.'

'No!' She drew in her riding-skirt and tucked it under her.

He studied her face for a moment, then nodded. 'All right.'

She rubbed her palm up and down her thigh. 'It's just that I don't like anyone touching it.'

'Why, does it still hurt?'

'Of course not.'

'Then why?'

'I don't know, I just don't.'

Again there was silence between them. In the river a fish splashed. In the trees an owl hooted. A small secret rustling announced the passage of a lizard, or perhaps a snake on a nocturnal hunt.

Without looking at Ben, Sophie pulled her riding-skirt a fraction above her knee. 'Promise you *won't* touch.'

'All right. I promise.'

Catching her lower lip in her teeth, she reached under her skirt and unclipped the stocking from the suspenders, then started rolling the thin black silk down her thigh.

'Let me do that,' he said.

'No!'

'Yes.'

'No.'

Suddenly she was breathless and shaking. She was shaking so hard that when she put her hands on either side of her and leaned back to let him approach, her elbows nearly buckled.

She watched him take his crutch and lever himself painfully off the block of cut-stone and onto the blanket beside her. His face was tense and serious as he put out his hand and gently rolled the stocking down over her knee. His fingers were trembling. She hissed as they brushed her shin.

He stopped. 'You all right?'

She nodded. She wanted to tell him to stop, but she couldn't. She couldn't breathe.

He looked down, and his dark brows drew together in a frown. 'D'you remember when we was kids, in that kitchen of yours, and you showed me your knee?'

Again she nodded.

177

'You said, "Look, Ben, I got a bruise." Only I couldn't see nothing.' He paused. 'You were the cleanest person I'd ever seen.'

She wanted to touch his cheek, but she couldn't. She couldn't move.

He peeled back the stocking to just above her riding-boot, and put his warm hand on her shin, and lowered his head and softly blew on her knee. She felt his hair brushing her skin, then the gentle caress of his hand.

'You said you wouldn't touch,' she whispered.

He raised his head and met her eyes. Then his gaze dropped to her mouth. 'I lied.'

He moved closer to her, and she caught the aromatic tang of Grace's salve on his skin, and beneath it his own smell: the sharp clean scent of red dust and wind-blown grass. He bent and kissed her lightly on the mouth.

Then he kissed her again, and this time he pressed harder, opening her mouth with his. For the first time she felt the heat and strength of his tongue. She was frightened and curious and excited. She didn't know how to respond. She tried to do what he was doing, and put her arm round his neck and kissed him back.

With that first real kiss she left everything behind; she struck out into unknown territory. And she knew that it was the same for him, because although he'd done this before, he'd never done it with her. With that first deep kiss they abandoned their old selves and crossed over for ever from being friends to being lovers. And as she felt the roughness of his cheek against hers, and the softness of his hair beneath her wrist, she experienced not only the first deep stab of desire, but also a new tenderness for him, because he was in this with her, taking in the strangeness and the unbelievable closeness, and trembling against her. She buried her face in his throat and clutched his shoulder – and heard him wince. 'Sorry,' she mumbled, and against her neck he gave a crooked smile; then she felt him shake, and the warmth of his laughter on her skin. Then he raised his head to hers and looked at her for a moment, and his smile slowly faded, and he kissed her again, harder and deeper.

They moved closer against one another – carefully, because of his ribs – and he ran his hand down her flank and her thigh and under her hips, and she slid her hands beneath his shirt and grasped the hot, hard muscles of his back.

Suddenly, he broke away with a cry.

'What's wrong?' she whispered. 'Oh God, did I hurt you?'

He shook his head. He was sitting hunched over, breathing painfully through his teeth.

'Ben?'

'We can't do this,' he muttered, still shaking his head.

She put her hand on his shoulder but he shook it off. 'Yes we can,' she said. 'I want to.'

'No. No.'

'Why?'

'I don't – I don't want to hurt you.'

'Ben—'

'The first time it hurts, Sophie. It hurts.'

'I know that.' She tried to make light of it. 'I managed to pick up something in my medical studies. But I – I don't expect it'll hurt too much. I mean, I've done lots of riding, and always astride, and that's supposed to—'

'Sophie, shut up,' he said softly.

She bit her lip. He was right, she was talking too much. But she was so nervous.

She couldn't believe she was doing this. Sitting in a ruin, trying to seduce a man. And suddenly an image popped into her head of the sampler which used to hang above her bed in Cousin Lettice's house in London, when she was small. *Fornication Leads to Misery and Hell. Marriage Leads to Happiness and Heaven.*

What's fornication? she used to ask her big sister. *I don't know*, Madeleine would always reply. *Something bad, I think*. But years later, Madeleine had taken her aside and calmly told her the truth. She said she'd suffered from not knowing about it, and she didn't want that for Sophie.

Now Sophie looked about her at the pale clustered orchids and the thick cords of the strangler fig, and finally at Ben, scowling down at his hands with a strange, angry expression which made him seem very young. 'Do you love me?' she said in a low voice.

He did not reply. She watched him run his hand through his hair, then grind the heel of his hand into his good eye.

'Do you love me?' she said again.

He drew a raw breath. Then he nodded.

'Then it'll be all right.'

'You don't know that. You don't know nothing about it.'

'Then tell me. Show me.'

He was shaking his head. 'You don't know how ugly it can be. All twisted and dirty . . .'

'But not between us.'

Again he did not reply. But this time when she put her hand on his shoulder, he didn't pull away.

'Not between us,' she said again, and lay back on the blanket, and drew him down towards her.

It was past midnight when she got back to Eden.

To her relief, Madeleine and Cameron weren't yet back from Parnassus, and everyone else had gone to bed. Someone had put a lighted hurricane lamp on the sideboard, for her return.

She led her horse down to the stables, untacked her, gave her a drink and checked her manger for hay. Then she walked round the side of the house to the garden.

Abigail and Scout clattered down the steps to greet her. The older dog gave her a sleepy drop-eared welcome, then trotted back up to the verandah and slumped down to sleep. Scout settled himself beside Sophie on the bottom step, and shoved his cold nose under her hand.

She stroked his silky ear, and breathed in the fresh scents of the moonlit garden: the green smell of the tree-ferns, and the perfume of star jasmine.

She felt exhausted, but incredibly alive. She could still

feel the faint throbbing ache inside her, and the tenderness on her inner thighs. She could still feel the weight of his body on hers, she could still smell him on her skin. And if she shut her eyes she could almost summon up the closeness, the unbelievable closeness. She wanted to stay awake all night and not lose a moment of it.

'Meet me tomorrow,' he'd whispered as they lay together, watching the fireflies and feeling the sweat cooling their skin.

'Where?'

'Here.'

'Yes, here. Yes.'

Of course it had to be Romilly. It was right for them because in a way it wasn't a real place at all, just a ruin left over from another time.

But she didn't want to think about that now. She didn't want to think about consequences, and what would happen next.

'Aunt Sophie?' said a small voice at the top of the stairs.

She turned to see Fraser standing in his nightshirt, squinting down at her. She got to her feet. 'Darling, you should be in bed,' she said quietly. 'It's horribly late.'

'My tummy hurts.'

Behind him on the verandah, Abigail lumbered to her feet and tried to nose him back inside like an errant puppy. Peevishly he batted her away.

Sophie sighed, and climbed the steps and took his hand. It was warm but not feverishly hot. She bent and planted a kiss on his sleep-creased cheek. 'You'll live,' she said.

'But it *hurts*,' he insisted crossly.

'Come along then, and I'll take a look at you.'

Together they went inside, and when they reached the pool of light from the hurricane lamp Sophie knelt and put the back of her hand to his forehead. 'You haven't got a fever,' she told him, 'and no swollen glands. That's good; it means you haven't got mumps. You've just had too many sweets, darling.'

'I didn't have a single one after Mamma left,' he grumbled, 'except what Clemency gave me.'

The qualification made her smile. 'Then I'm sure you'll feel better very soon. Come along. I'll make you some rhubarb powder in milk. Then it's back to bed.'

A quarter of an hour later she was curled up in her own bed, wide awake, watching the slatted moonlight on the tiles.

Making love to her, he'd been so careful and so serious: as if she were the one with the bruises, not he. But when she'd tried to tell him so, he'd put his hand gently across her mouth. 'Shh. No more talking.' And after that they'd done the talking with their bodies.

She pressed her face into the pillow and took a hungry breath, and thought about tomorrow at Romilly.

Outside the window, a tree-fern nodded against the louvres. In the distance an owl hooted. Drifting in on the night air came the faint, cloying sweetness of stephanotis.

She buried her face in the pillow and slept.

At Bethlehem, the scent of stephanotis told Evie that something was wrong. She asked if her mother could smell it too, but Grace only gave her a narrow-eye look and shook her head.

It was about four in the morning, and the Jonkunoo parade had broken off for food. The air was heavy with the smells of fried breadfruit and curried goat. Pickneys huddled together over plantain tarts and slabs of chocho pie. Nanas got merry and girlish on rum punch and ginger wine.

Grace brought Evie a slice of her favourite dish: sweet potato pudding made with plenty of coconut milk and vanilla, and drenched in molasses. She couldn't eat a bite. Something was bad wrong.

The feeling had been creeping up on her all day. She couldn't lose it out of her mind; and yet every time she tried to grab hold of it, it flickered away like a yellow-snake down a hole.

'Here,' said her mother, sitting down beside her and handing her a tumbler of cold sorrel. 'Little cool-drink to settle your head. And I added a drop of oil of Calvary to help smooth out your thoughts.'

Evie shot her a questioning glance.

'Well I not stupid,' said Grace with a snort. 'You got some worry-head in you, so you need a little inspiration.'

You never could get round her mother. Just when you dismissed her as some raggity mountain woman with no education, she went and saw right through you.

Evie looked down at the heady red infusion of rum and hibiscus petals. She took a long pull, and its gingery heat coiled down into her insides. It was more than half rum. At Bethlehem they liked their drinks powerful.

Around her the crowd was milling about like ants in a nest. It was like one big birth-night party for the whole village. But still she could feel the darkness closing in. Why couldn't they?

At the edge of the village she glimpsed the velvet blackness of Patoo flitting by, and heard his soft *hoo-hoo*. Several people looked round fearfully and made the cross sign, but Grace just tossed her head and yelled at him to get outta their parade. 'Go way, Patoo! Go trouble someone else's damn place with your bad news!' There was a ripple of laughter.

And once again, Evie smelled stephanotis. Heavy and sweet, like at a burying. What was wrong?

A couple of days before, Ben had told her that she'd made a mistake about that red-haired girl; that it wasn't meant as a warning for him, but for Sophie.

If she'd been wrong about that, then what else had she got wrong-side and tangle-up? Had she been wrong about old Master Jocelyn, too?

She thought back to that day at Fever Hill, when she'd sat in Miss Sibella's dog cart and watched old Master Jocelyn following Sophie up the croton walk. Sophie and little Master Fraser.

She felt a faint tickling on her bare ankle, and looked down to see a small green devil-horse – a praying mantis – crawling up her leg. Thoughtfully, she brushed it off with her hand.

And suddenly she knew what was wrong, and the knowledge was a cold certainty in her belly. Old Master Jocelyn hadn't been following Sophie. Not Sophie.

She grabbed her mother's arm. 'Something's wrong. We've got to get to Eden, quick-time.'

Sophie was shaken awake by a frightened Clemency. Fraser was ill. She didn't know what to do.

'How ill?' mumbled Sophie, still heavy with sleep.

'I'm afraid I don't know, dear.'

'Clemency—'

'But I don't.' She stood by the bed like an ineffectual ghost, twisting her waxy hands and shaking her head so violently that her dyed grey braids brushed against Sophie's face.

But she was right about Fraser. When they reached the nursery he was thrashing about in the bedclothes, and battling against a terrified Poppy, who was trying to hold him down. Belle was curled up on the other bed, sucking her toy zebra's ear and staring at them with great dark eyes.

As Sophie leaned over Fraser, a cold kernel of fear settled inside her.

He lay in a strange, stiff curve, as if he wanted to curl into a ball, but couldn't. His eyes were screwed shut against the light, and his breathing was fast and shallow. 'It *hurts*!' he moaned, pummelling Poppy with his fists.

'Where, darling?' said Sophie. 'Tell me where.'

'All over! My head and my tummy and all *over*! Aunt Sophie, make the hurts go *away*!'

Sophie took his small fist in hers. It felt cold. What did that mean?

She glanced at the nursery clock. A quarter to two. Two hours before, he'd had nothing worse than a tummy-ache.

'I knew something like this would happen,' whispered Clemency, wringing her hands. 'I knew that if I left Elliot on his own he'd be angry—'

'Not now,' snapped Sophie.

'It *hurts*!' screamed Fraser. He threw off the bedclothes

and would have fallen out of bed if Sophie hadn't caught him. In the glow of the lamplight she saw a bright pink rash splashed across the smooth, poreless skin of his calves.

God, she thought. What's that? 'Clemency,' she said without turning round, 'take Belle and go and sleep in the servants' quarters.'

'What, darling?'

'I said take Belle right now, and go and sleep in the servants' quarters, and don't come back till I tell you. D'you understand? Tell Braverly and Susan to stay with you, and *not* to come inside.'

'But darling—'

'For God's sake, Clemmie, whatever this is, it could be catching!'

Clemency's hands crept to her throat.

'Poppy,' said Sophie over her shoulder. 'You run and wake Moses and tell him to saddle Master Cameron's horse and ride as fast as he can and fetch Dr Mallory. As fast as he can, d'you hear? And he's to tell Dr Mallory it's an emergency, and to come at once. And he's to send a man for Dr Pritchard, too, and another down to Parnassus to fetch Master and Mistress. Now go!'

Poppy fled.

Please God make it the measles, Sophie said to herself over and over, when they'd left her alone with Fraser. Let it be the measles or mumps, or something else that we know how to fight.

He was still thrashing and moaning, but slightly quieter now, since she'd moved the lamp to the other side of the room. He had no fever, and he was not delirious. As she tried to raise his head to help him take a little water, he gave an involuntary twitch and kicked her thigh. 'Sorry, Aunt Sophie,' he mumbled.

'Doesn't matter, darling,' she told him, smoothing back his hair from his forehead.

'When will the hurts go away?'

'Soon. Soon. When the doctor comes.' She felt a pang of guilt at deceiving him. It would be at least two hours before Dr Mallory got here; and Dr Pritchard, in whom she had greater faith, would arrive some time after that. Two hours, and she was useless to help him. All she could do was try to reassure him, and get him to sip a little water, while she rifled through her *Introductory Primer on Diagnostic Medicine* with mounting desperation.

And always at the back of her mind was the gnawing dread that this might in some way be her fault. What if she'd been here all the time, and could have spotted some subtle sign of impending illness, and sent for the doctor straight away? What if she'd stayed at home and looked after him, as Madeleine had begged her to?

The wide grey eyes gazed up at her with total faith. When she set down the book on the bedside table, they followed her every move. She tried to smile.

His face contorted. 'It *hurts*!'

'I know, darling,' she murmured, sitting on the edge of the bed and taking him in her arms and stroking his hair. 'I know, I know, and I'm so sorry.'

He twisted away from her and punched the pillow.

The rash was worse. It had spread all over his legs and arms, and when she raised his nightshirt she saw with horror that it now covered his whole body. How could anything spread so quickly?

A terrible thought gripped her. She reached for the book, and turned to the index at the back. The words blurred and shifted, and she couldn't find what she was looking for. Then she had it. *Brain fever . . . see Meningococcal Disease; also Meningitis.*

Dawn was commencing to light when Evie and her mother reached Eden. By the look of things, Master Cameron and Miss Madeleine had just gone inside, for the carriage was still at the door, and the horse had its head down, blowing hard.

In an instant, Evie took in all the wrongness of the house. Miss Madeleine's bronze satin evening mantle dropped in the dust and trampled under the horse's hooves like a body. Miss Clemmie and little Missy Belle standing in the carriageway in their nightgowns, wide-eyed and frightened. Moses hanging on to the horse's bridle like he couldn't let go, and old Braverly swaying and muttering psalms, and Poppy and Susan keeping up a wake-dead moaning in each other's arms.

And there in the doormouth sat Sophie, rigid on the threshold in her dressing-gown, her lips bluish-grey, her eyes staring into darkness.

'Sophie?' said Grace.

Sophie raised her head and tried to find the source of the sound, as if she was having trouble focusing.

'Sophie,' said Evie, going to sit beside her and putting her arm round her shoulders.

'It was brain fever,' said Sophie. Her voice sounded flat, as if she had nothing left inside. 'Dr Mallory came, and Dr Pritchard, and they said—'

At that moment from inside the darkened house came a terrible, wrenching scream. Evie had never heard such a sound in her life. It was like some animal having its innards ripped out.

Sophie's face crumpled. 'I was holding him,' she said. 'I was holding him. And he died.'

CHAPTER SIXTEEN

Sophie was busy in her room when there was a knock at the door, and Cameron asked if he might come in.

She was surprised to see him, for it was the middle of the afternoon, and he'd left for the works straight after luncheon. 'I thought you were at Maputah,' she said.

'I was,' he replied from the doorway. His eyes went to the packing-cases around her, but he made no comment. 'I wonder, do you have a moment?'

She glanced at the folded blouses in her arms, and put them on the bed. 'Of course. Shall we go out onto the verandah?'

He nodded, and stood aside to let her pass.

She wondered if he too was aware of the new formality between them. They even moved differently. Her mourning gown of dull black parramatta seemed to impose on her a rigidity of which even Great-Aunt May would have approved, while Cameron had developed an unconscious habit of touching the black armband on his sleeve, as if it were a bruise.

Apart from Scout, they had the verandah to themselves. Madeleine was lying down in her room, and Clemency was reading to Belle in the nursery.

Cameron took one end of the old cane sofa, and Sophie the armchair opposite. Scout heaved himself up and trotted over to his master, and then slumped down again at his feet.

Cameron ran his hand over his armband, and tried not to look at the gap between the lime trees where Fraser's swing used to hang. He'd lost weight, and his eyes were bloodshot. He looked exhausted. January was the busiest time of the year, when the works at Maputah and Fever Hill had to run twenty-four hours a day or the cane would spoil, and bankruptcy would follow hard on bereavement. Sophie wondered when he found time to grieve, and where he went to cry. She herself had done with crying. She had cried until she couldn't cry any more, and now she was too hollowed out by grief and guilt to feel anything but a desperate fatigue and a longing for peace.

Cameron caught her watching him, and they exchanged tight, meaningless smiles.

'You wanted to talk to me?' she said.

'I – yes.'

'Is anything wrong?'

There was silence while they both considered that. *Is anything wrong?* Everything was wrong. Fraser Jocelyn Lawe had been lying out on the wooded slope behind the house for three weeks now: the first inhabitant of Eden's new Burying-place. Clemency had said that his white marble tomb was almost as beautiful as Elliot's, but Sophie hadn't seen it for herself. She couldn't bear to.

Nor had she attended the funeral. Instead she had stayed at the house, while Cameron had followed the hearse to Falmouth, and stood in the churchyard surrounded by his workers, and finally ridden back for the burying.

Clemency had been one of the few ladies to attend, along with Olivia Herapath and, surprisingly, Rebecca Traherne. The sole female representative of the Monroes had been Great-Aunt May, glacially correct in strict half-mourning. 'Full mourning would be inappropriate,' she had declared in response to a dauntless enquiry from Mrs Herapath. 'The child was four generations removed from my own.'

Madeleine herself had not attended. She'd simply

announced that she wouldn't be going to church any more; that she was finished with God.

Cameron studied Sophie for a moment before he spoke. 'Moses tells me that you've ordered the carriage for Monday. For Montego Bay.'

Sophie put her hands together in her lap. 'I hope that's all right,' she said carefully. 'I shall be catching the eight forty-five to Kingston. I'll be booking a passage on Tuesday's packet to Southampton.'

'Don't go,' he said.

'I think I must.'

He ran his thumb across his lower lip, and gave her a considering look. 'What if you do one of your about-turns halfway there, and want to come home?'

She gave him a faint smile. 'I don't think I shall.'

But she sounded more certain than she felt. Half of her thought she was wrong – that she was running away when Madeleine needed her most. The other half told her that it was the only thing to do. Madeleine didn't want her here any more. They hadn't talked about it – they hadn't talked at all. But Sophie could feel it. Perhaps Madeleine blamed her for Fraser's death. Or perhaps she simply couldn't forgive the fact that Sophie had been with him in his final hours, while she, his mother, had not.

And always at the back of Sophie's mind was the thought of how much worse Madeleine would feel if she ever found out that on the night when her son was dying, her sister had been with Ben.

Sophie had agonized over whether to tell them, but had decided against it. Why make things worse than they already were? So instead, she'd told them only what she thought they could take: that she'd gone for a moonlit ride, and returned to the house around midnight, to find Fraser with a slight stomach ache; that she had sent for the doctors when it worsened, and stayed with him until he died. Cameron had looked at her in puzzlement, as if wondering why she thought it necessary to tell them all that. Madeleine had studied her woodenly, as if waiting for something more. Then she'd nodded once, and got up and left the room.

'Sophie,' said Cameron, dragging her back to the present. 'If you go back to England now, you'll be running away.'

'No. No, I'll be making it easier for everyone.'

'Not for me,' he said quietly. 'Not for Madeleine.'

She shook her head. 'She'll be better without me. Besides, she has Clemency. And Grace.' She didn't need to explain why Madeleine found it easier to tolerate them. Clemency and Grace had both lost children.

'You're running away,' he said again.

'Cameron—'

'It doesn't work, Sophie. I know. I tried it once.'

She did not reply. Perhaps he was right, but surely she had no choice. How could she stay at Eden? She didn't deserve it. She didn't deserve any of it.

And yet, she wanted to be persuaded to stay. Perhaps that was why she hadn't yet booked her passage to England.

Inside the house a door opened and closed, and they both turned to see Madeleine in her long, rust-coloured Japanese dressing-gown walking across the hall on her way to the bath-house. Cameron watched her until she'd gone.

'How is she?' asked Sophie. 'I mean, really?'

Cameron shook his head. 'I don't know. She won't talk to me. That is, she talks to me, but she isn't there.'

It was true. Madeleine sleep-walked through the days. She had bouts of activity when she would sew mourning gowns and run the household, but then she would abruptly wilt, and go to her room and sleep for hours. To Sophie she was kind, if a little distant, but she rarely met her eyes.

To everyone's surprise, it was Clemency who'd kept the household from falling apart. Hopelessly ineffectual when Fraser was ill, she knew exactly what to do now that he was dead. She didn't even seem perturbed at leaving Elliot for so long. She simply handled everything with a brisk, unflinching pragmatism which never faltered. After all, she was used to dead children. She'd been living with one for thirty years.

So while Cameron struggled to bring in the cane, and Madeleine sleep-walked through the days, Clemency took everything in hand. She gently persuaded Cameron to halt all estate work on the day of the funeral, so that the men could pay their respects. 'They'll expect it, Cameron dear. Tradition *matters* at times like these.' She deftly settled the funeral arrangements. 'It'll have to be a mahogany coffin; after they turn five it isn't done to bury them in white.' She ordered yards of black parramatta, bombazine and crêpe, and set Grace to making aprons and armbands for the staff. She sent Sophie to Falmouth to buy visiting-cards and writing-paper with precisely the correct depth of black edging. And she wrote dozens of beautiful little thank-you notes for the flowers which poured in. 'Flowers to Eden,' Madeleine remarked with a wan smile. 'I never imagined that would be necessary.'

Most important of all, on that first appalled and dis-believing morning, Clemency had sent for Olivia Herapath to take the mourning photograph. They took it without Madeleine's knowing. 'But it'll be *such* a comfort to her later,' Clemency told Sophie in her breathless whisper. 'Are you sure you don't want to see it, dear? So beautiful and so very *like*. In his sailor suit, with his favourite lead soldiers, and that new kite that you gave him. Are you sure you won't see it? Well then, at least take a lock of his hair. I nearly forgot about that, but clever Grace reminded me just as they were closing the coffin.'

But Sophie had recoiled in horror from the little ivory envelope containing the carefully folded blue tissue paper. She didn't want mementoes. She didn't need them. She saw him all the time.

She saw him in her dreams, and as soon as she woke up. She saw him when she opened the *Introductory Primer* and read the passage which she'd first turned up in the glow of the nursery lamp. *No microbe can kill more quickly . . . we are wholly at a loss to explain why some patients suffer only mild infections, while others succumb to the acute fulminating form in a matter of hours.* In other words, Belle had caught only a slight fever, while Fraser had died.

Across the verandah, Cameron watched a croaker lizard scuttle along the baluster. Sophie wondered if he was angry with her; if he blamed her for his son's death. But he didn't look angry. Just exhausted and quietly devastated.

The lizard dropped from the baluster and moved towards the mouth of a drain. Scout gave a grunt and shot after it, his claws scrabbling on the tiles. The lizard disappeared down the drain. Scout grunted in disgust, and trotted back to his master.

'Cameron,' said Sophie quietly.

He turned to her, and tried to compose his features into a smile.

'You do understand why I have to go?'

He hesitated. 'Sophie – it wasn't your fault.'

'How do you know that?'

'Because,' he said evenly, 'you sent for the doctor as soon as he became ill. Sooner than anyone else would have done. And you did everything for him – everything that could be done.'

Sophie sat in silence, and her eyes grew hot. She wanted to believe him. If she could believe him, she could remain at Eden. Perhaps she could even see Ben again.

'I don't say this to make you feel better,' Cameron said with an edge to his voice. 'I say it because it's true.'

'And if I'd been with him all the time? If I hadn't gone out and left him—'

'He'd still have died.'

'How do you know? How do you know?'

He gave her a long, steady look. 'Because I asked Dr Pritchard. And Dr Mallory. And they both told me, quite categorically, that it wouldn't have made the slightest difference if you'd been there or not.'

Sophie sat in stunned silence. So it had occurred to him to blame her. He had considered it. And then, being

Cameron, he had found out the facts. And he had asked *both* doctors. There was something about that which frightened her. It showed such a need for confirmation.

She wondered what he would have done if the doctors' answers had been different. *I won't have Madeleine hurt*, he had told her once. *I won't let anyone do that. Not even you.* She looked at his strong, uncompromising features, and wondered if he truly believed – not in his head, but in his heart – that she was wholly without blame.

For herself, she couldn't do it. The events of that night had taken on an unreal quality, and she couldn't untangle them in her mind. She'd been with Ben, and then Fraser had died. She couldn't think of Ben without seeing Fraser's wide grey eyes. *Fornication Leads to Misery and Hell*.

A small noise from inside the house, and they turned to see Belle standing in the doorway.

She wore a black frock with a wide black sash around her hips, and black stockings, and short black buttoned boots. A big black bow was sliding off her hair, and she was scowling and clutching the ever-present Spot by one ear.

She'd been impossible ever since her brother died, whining and clingy one moment, and the next throwing a screaming tantrum. It wasn't until Clemency had put her into full mourning dress that she'd become a little better. 'It's only proper,' Clemency had murmured when Sophie protested. 'And it'll make her feel part of things, which is what she needs.'

Scout jumped up and trotted over to the five-year-old, and nudged her in the chest. She gave him a smack on the nose. Scout shook his head with a soft flapping of dewlaps, and padded back to Cameron.

'Papa,' said Belle, 'Clemency says I've got to stay indoors, and it's *boring*. Why can't I play outside? We've only just had Christmas.'

Cameron blinked as if he was having trouble recognizing her. 'Just do as Clemency says,' he said quietly.

'But can't I—'

194

'No. Not yet.'

Sulkily, Belle thrust out her lower lip. She stalked across to the sofa and leaned against her father's calf, and put one small hand on his knee. 'But it isn't *fair*. Somebody's taken down the swing. Please, *please* make them put it up again?'

Cameron met Sophie's eyes above his daughter's head, and lifted his shoulders in a helpless shrug. The children had always been Madeleine's responsibility. He was too busy around the estate to see much of them, except on Sundays, when he was usually too tired.

'We'll see,' Sophie told her niece.

'Who took it down?' said Belle crossly. 'I bet Fraser will thump them when he finds out. And so will I.'

Again Cameron met Sophie's eyes. '*Qu'est-ce que je peux lui dire?*' he said. '*Elle ne comprend rien.*'

'*Mais bien sûr,*' she replied. '*Elle est beaucoup trop jeune.*' Of course Belle didn't understand. How could a five-year-old understand that her brother was never coming back?

Fraser, too, had been too young. He had died before he understood what death was.

Still in French, Cameron asked Sophie if she would mind summoning Poppy, or Clemency, or – or anyone to take his daughter off his hands.

Sophie considered that for a moment, and then got to her feet. 'I don't think she needs Poppy,' she told him in English. 'Or Clemency. She needs you.'

Belle was still leaning against his calf, scowling and chewing the zebra's ear as she struggled to follow what they were saying. There was a determined set to her chin that was very like her mother.

Cameron looked down at her for a moment, and his face tightened. Sophie wondered if he was remembering all the afternoons when he'd gone off alone to the works, or to some cane-piece, or to town, without taking his son along with him.

He rubbed a hand over his face, and cleared his throat. Then he leaned forward and picked up his daughter beneath the arms, and swung her onto the sofa beside him.

Sophie left them sitting side by side: Belle quietly scolding the zebra for some imaginary transgression, Cameron with one arm on the back of the sofa behind her, absently stroking her glossy dark hair as he gazed out at the lime trees to where Fraser's swing used to hang.

CHAPTER SEVENTEEN

'So that's where you were that night,' said Madeleine between her teeth, as she paced up and down the verandah the following afternoon. 'You were with Ben Kelly.'

Sophie sat on the sofa and watched her sister twisting her hands together, and held her breath.

It had happened without warning, like a thunderclap. She'd come out to join Madeleine for tea, and found her alone and tautly waiting. Apparently the previous evening, Ben had sent word by Moses, asking Sophie to meet him on Overlook Hill – and somehow Madeleine had intercepted the message.

The previous evening. Which meant that Madeleine's anger hadn't sprung from the impulse of the moment.

'I *asked* you not to go to him,' Madeleine said accusingly. Her face was pale, except for a dark red streak on either cheek. 'You promised that you wouldn't.'

Sophie opened her mouth to say that she'd never promised. Then she shut it again. What was the use?

'Did you sleep with him?' Madeleine said suddenly.

Sophie looked down at her fists, clenched in her lap.

'My God,' said Madeleine, 'you did, didn't you? He summoned you – so you left Fraser to go to him. And then he—'

'It wasn't like that.'

'Did he hurt you?'

'No!'

'My God. My God.' She put both hands to her temples. Then she looked at Sophie. Her eyes were hard. Her face had a rigidity that Sophie had never seen before. 'I'll never forgive him,' she said in a low voice.

Sophie stared at her. They both knew that she didn't just mean Ben. She meant her sister, too.

Sophie spread her cold hands on her knees. 'Madeleine . . .' she began. 'It wasn't his fault. It wasn't—'

Madeleine turned on her. 'Don't you ever speak of this again. D'you understand? I'll never forgive him. I hope he rots in hell.'

Vapour misted the tree-ferns as Sophie rode her mare up the overgrown forest track on Overlook Hill. The woods echoed with early morning birdcalls: the harsh rattle of the jabbering crows, the purring *cru-cru-cruuu* of the baldpates, and the lonely, explosive cry of the red-tailed hawk.

It had been shamefully easy to get away. Cameron had left for the works at daybreak, and Clemency was still asleep. Belle was in the nursery, cutting out pictures of ponies from back numbers of *The Equestrian Journal*. Madeleine hadn't yet woken up. After the scene on the verandah the day before, she'd gone to her room. She hadn't emerged for dinner, and Cameron had told Sophie that she'd taken a Dover's powder and gone to bed. He'd given Sophie a thoughtful look, and she'd wondered how much he knew. She hadn't had the courage to ask.

She kept seeing that look in Madeleine's eyes. That hard, accusing stare which told her what her sister couldn't bring herself to say out loud. *I'll never forgive you.*

And who could blame her? She'd begged Sophie not to go to Ben, but she had, and then Fraser had died. The two events were unrelated, but not in her heart.

Sophie understood that, because she felt it herself. And now more than ever she knew that she had to get away.

Away from Madeleine and Cameron, and Eden and Ben. She felt exhausted and fragile, as if the slightest touch would break her into pieces. She longed for the grey anonymity of London.

With her riding-crop she swept aside spiders' webs strung across the path. Dewdrops pattered onto great waxy leaves. Lizards darted up tree trunks netted with creepers. She smelt the sharp green scent of new growth, and the heavy sweetness of decay. The smell of Eden.

Tomorrow it would be nothing more than a memory. And that was the way it *should* be. She couldn't face it any more. Eden had become terrible to her.

She reached a point in the path where the way was blocked by the tilting trunk of a fallen breadnut tree. Dismounting to lead her horse, she came face to face with a tangle of cockleshell orchids on the mossy bark. She blinked at the twisted pale green petals, and breathed in their funereal sweetness. With a dull ache she remembered how they'd glowed in the moonlight, just before he'd kissed her.

Thank God he hadn't suggested meeting at Romilly. She couldn't have taken that.

Half an hour later she reached the glade of the great duppy tree. He was waiting beneath it. His face lit up when he saw her. He came towards her, took the reins and tethered her horse, then helped her down.

He'd dispensed with the crutches, and his bruises had faded. In the forest light his eyes were very green, the lashes long and black. They made him look young, and easy to hurt. 'I missed you so much,' he said, putting his hand against her cheek.

'I missed you too,' she muttered. But when he bent to kiss her she twisted her head away. She felt sick at the thought of what she was about to do. Sick and empty inside.

'You all right?' he said.

'No. I'm not.' She looked down and saw that she was gripping her riding-crop with both hands, her knuckles straining her gloves. *Why* had he asked her to meet him?

This was only making it worse. Didn't he realize everything was over?

She heard him move closer, then felt his arms about her as he drew her to him. For a moment she shut her eyes and relaxed against him, and listened to his heart beat. Then she breathed in, and put her hands on his shoulders and gently pushed him away. 'What about you?' she said without meeting his eyes. 'How's your leg? And – and your ribs? Are *you* all right?'

'Me?' His lip curled. 'I'm always all right.'

Oh, God, I hope that's true, she thought. Close up, she saw that the cut on his eyebrow had nearly healed, and was already acquiring the sheen of a new scar. He's tough, she told herself, he heals quickly. It'll be the same with this.

'I'm sorry about the little lad,' he said, running his hands up and down her arms, as if to warm her. 'I was going to write Madeleine a note, only I didn't have no paper. Tell her I'm sorry.'

'That's not a good idea.'

There was a silence. Then his arms dropped to his sides. 'You told her about us.'

'She found out when you sent the message to Moses. I had to tell her the rest.'

'Oh, Sophie.' He turned and walked away a few paces, and then back to her. 'What did she say?'

She hesitated.

'She blames me,' said Ben. 'That's it, isn't it?'

'Why do you say that?'

He snorted. 'Because it happens.' He rubbed a hand over his face, then shook his head. 'Christ, Sophie. Christ.'

She felt a spark of anger at him. Why was he thinking only of them, when Fraser lay dead in the little marble tomb behind the house? Why couldn't he let her go, without putting them through this?

Suddenly she wondered if she'd ever really known him. Looking at him standing there, he seemed rough and unfamiliar. His blue cotton shirt had lost a couple of buttons, and there was a rip in the knee of his breeches.

Shirt and breeches were crumpled, as if he'd washed them in the river and not bothered to dry them properly.

She wondered how he'd survived over the past three weeks. Perhaps a few days' casual labour in the canefields, or on a fishing smack or a coffee plantation; sleeping rough and living on his wits. Perhaps he simply stole. As a boy he'd been a thief; it was how he'd survived. And in Trelawny, where people never locked their doors, it must be easy pickings.

How was it possible that three weeks ago they'd been lovers? Three weeks. She was a different person now.

She lifted her chin and forced herself to meet his eyes. 'I came to see you – because I need to tell you something.' She moistened her lips. 'I'm leaving. I'm starting for England tomorrow. I won't be coming back.'

To her surprise, he only looked startled. 'That's a bit sudden.'

'I can't stay here any longer.'

He scratched his head, then nodded. 'Fair enough. But it'll take me a while to follow you. I got to get up the fare, and—'

'No. You can't.'

'What?'

'You can't follow me. It's over, Ben. That's what I came to tell you. We can't see each other any more.'

She watched the understanding dawn; the stillness come down over his features. 'No,' he said flatly. 'You can't – no.'

'I have to.'

'No, listen. Don't go to London. Come with me. I been thinking about it, I got it all worked out. We can go to Panama. Or America. We'll do all right there. Nobody'll know us. We can be together.'

'Ben. I can't be with you. Not anywhere. Not after this.'

He stood with his hands by his sides, watching her. 'Don't do this,' he said at last.

'I have to.'

'It's wrong. It's—'

'Why did you have to send for me?' she burst out at him. 'Why make me come? What good does it do?'

'I had to see you. I missed you.'

'Don't you understand? We can't do this. It's over.'

'No, Sophie. No.'

She pushed past him and ran to her horse. 'I've got to go. I can't stay here any more.' She was amazed at how calm she sounded, when inside she was breaking. She was amazed at the steadiness of her hands as she threw the reins over the mare's head, and put her foot in the stirrup and swung herself into the saddle.

'If you do this,' he said, 'it's for ever. Don't you know that?'

'Of course I do,' she flung back at him, 'but what choice do I have? How can I be with you after what happened?'

After what's happened, Evie just wants to get away.

Away from Fever Hill and her mother; away from Sophie and Ben and that poor dead child. And most of all, away from her own self. Away from Evie Quashiba McFarlane, the four-eyed daughter of the local obeah-woman.

So here she is, sitting on the train in an empty third-class compartment, craning out the window as the whistle goes, and Montego Bay drops away behind her. In her whole life she's never been further than Montpelier, ten miles down the line, but now she's clutching a ticket all the way to Kingston. Even as the john crow flies, that's more than a hundred miles.

But she's glad. She is, true to the fact. She's been so full of black feeling that it's a fat relief to be on her way. Home, family, friends. Leave it all behind. Including that damn journal of Cyrus Wright.

Last night, after she'd finished packing her tin case, she'd sat down under the ackee tree to finish it. Only a couple more pages to go. Finish it and then leave it behind with everything else.

It's 1825, a full year since Cyrus Wright caught Congo Eve with her lover Strap, and sent him back to Parnassus. A year since Congo Eve went runaway to see her younger sister and her newborn daughter Semanthe.

October 4th, 1825 *This past sennight, I have had another attack of the clap, but have taken a vast number of mercurial pills, & am now fully restored, by the grace of Providence & my own industry and forbearance. Cum Mulatto Hanah behind the trash house.*

October 7th *Last night found Congo Eve dancing the shay-shay, all on her own, by the aqueduct. On her ankle she wore a band of john-crow beads very like to that which her brother Job had given her, and which I had made her throw on the midden. I was greatly vex'd & shouted at her to stop, but she would not. Whereupon I struck at her & tore away the anklet, & had her flogged & put in the collar for the night.*

October 8th *In the morning I went to the stable & had her releas'd, & bade her come inside. She looked at me most strangely, & said that if this is living, then she wants no more of it. I told her that if she will not help herself but persists in defying me, then misfortune will surely be her lot. After that she would say no more. Had stewed mudfish to my supper, & a bottle of French brandy sent by Mr Traherne's Penkeeper. I have drunk too deep, & am now much put beside myself & disturb'd in spirit.*

And there, abruptly, the journal cut off.

There was plenty of room for further entries – two whole pages – but they'd been left blank. Not even a final line in someone else's hand, to tell what had become of Cyrus Wright. So now Evie would never find out if her namesake ancestor ever went runaway for good, or found Strap again, or a measure of peace.

She'd been so into a rage that she'd wanted to throw the book in the aqueduct. But instead, she'd run back to her mother's place, and penned a quick note to Sophie, and wrapped the book up in brown paper, and given it to her mother to take up to Eden the next time she went.

Eden.

That poor, dead child. If only she hadn't wasted her

time on that damned book, and had spent it instead trying to untangle the signs – then maybe he'd still be alive.

At one point, a few hours before she caught the mail coach, she'd thought about going to see Miss Madeleine and telling her about it. Perhaps it might ease her heart to know that old Master Jocelyn had been waiting to take her little one's hand and help him over to the other side. But then she'd thought better of it. How could she tell Miss Madeleine, when it was through her own self mistake that the warning got missed?

No. Just leave it. Leave it all behind.

The train's whistle sounds. She turns her head and watches the cane whipping past beneath a wide, bleaky sky. Montpelier is long gone, and Cambridge, and Catadupa. Everything looks different here. The cattle picking over the stubble are grey instead of white. On a dusty track two women carry big stacks of cane on their heads, but Evie doesn't know them. She would if she was home.

With an effort of will she puts all thoughts of home from her mind, and leans back and shuts her eyes. Soon she begins to doze asleep.

She's woken by the door slamming shut and a man sitting down across of her. He's young, maybe twenty or so, and his skin is very dark, and his clothes raggity.

Country nigger, she thinks, watching him beneath her eyelids. He's meagre, but his arms are muscle-strong and netted with standing-out veins from years of cutting copperwood and taking off the crops.

The whistle goes and the train pulls out of the station. She catches a look at the sign. *Siloah*. It means nothing to her. It's from foreign. She's in another country now.

The young man from Siloah is shy of her. Still with her eyes half closed, she watches him watching her. There's a lot of fidgeting going on, and little admiring looks. God, she thinks wearily, why did You make me pretty? What in hell is the damned point?

Finally the young man screws up his courage and catches her eye, and cracks a shy smile. 'It look weathery out there, ma'am,' he says, jerking his head at the window. 'You consider the rain go come?'

At least he calls her ma'am, and not 'sister'. That saves him from the worst of her scorn. 'Well, sir,' she replies, giving him a cool but not unkindly eye, 'I do believe that to be in the hands of God.'

He nods vigorously. 'True word, ma'am. Most true word.'

She turns her head and shuts her eyes. He's a big, gentle farmhand who would never talk no rudeness to a woman. But she can't find it in her heart to be civil for long. Not to him, not to anybody.

Far as she's concerned, Kingston can't come soon enough. She wants no more admiring country niggers. No more sweet-tongue buckra gentlemen. No more obeah, no more four-eyed nonsense, no more reading the spirit signs wrong-side out.

Jesum Peace, what a relief to be removing from Trelawny! You should be celebrating, girl! Now you can find yourself a nice quiet position in a nice quiet school, and marry yourself with a nice quiet coloured man. Maybe a parson or a storekeeper, it doesn't matter what. Just so long as he's got a light skin and a starched collar, and has civilized English ways. Just so long as he's never set foot in Trelawny.

Yes. You should be celebrating.

When she opens her eyes again, they've reached the high pastures, and all she can see is guinea grass. For the first time, the hugeness of what she's done begins to bite.

She glances at the farmhand, but he's dropped asleep. She puts her face out the window, and the tears are cold on her cheeks. And all she can see is miles of guinea grass, shivering under the bleaky sky.

Faint on the wind came the far-off whistle of the train, and Sophie glanced up from her packing.

The railway track was miles away. Perhaps she'd only fancied that she'd heard the whistle, because she wanted to. Because tomorrow she'd be on that train, too.

She longed for it to be over. She longed for Jamaica to be far behind her; for the rainy streets of London; for hard, mind-numbing work and forgetfulness.

She glanced about her at the room which Madeleine had prepared for her with such care three months before. Only three months. How was it possible? She remembered sitting on the train with those American tourists – what was their name? – and counting the hours until she would see her sister.

Now look at them all. Look at the trail of desolation she was leaving behind. Fraser. Madeleine. Cameron.

Ben.

Every time she thought of him, she felt cold. She felt as if she were falling from a great height through a frozen nothingness. She kept seeing his face as he'd stood there watching her ride away. For once he hadn't been able to hide his feelings. He'd been devastated.

But he's tough, she told herself, again and again. He's been through so much already, he recovers fast. He'll get over it. Perhaps he's getting over it already.

It's early evening when Ben reaches the sea, and by then he's drunk.

He stumbles onto the beach somewhere east of Salt Wash, peers at the remains of the rum in the bottle, and takes another long, blistering pull.

He's been walking all day. At first he didn't know or care where he was headed, just so long as it was away from Eden. He went west through the forest and out onto the bare, blinding rocks on the other side of the hill. From there he stumbled down the slope, slipping and sliding on the pebbles, and crossed the river at Stony Gap, and followed it north.

After an hour or so he stopped and looked about him. From here the Martha Brae made a great turn east, looping around the cane-pieces of Orange Grove. Orange Grove: the westernmost part of Eden estate. Sophie's out there somewhere, he told himself. Somewhere on the other side of the river, beyond those rippling acres of cane.

He set his teeth and turned his back on her, and headed north through the cattle pastures of Stony Hill.

In the afternoon he reached Pinchgut, where he stopped to buy a bottle of proof rum. Then he kept walking till he couldn't go no further – till he reached the sea.

The hooting of the coastal steamer brings him back to himself, and he looks round blearily, but he can't see nothing. Sodding trees in the way. Somehow he's wandered behind the beach and fetched up at the edge of the Morass.

He's standing by a lagoon in a thicket of mangroves. An ugly, stinking midden of a place. Long black spider-roots streaming down into water as foul and brown as a sewer. 'Welcome to Jamaica,' he mutters. He gives a snort of laughter.

Behind him, beyond the mangroves, he can just see the tops of the coconut palms fringing the beach. That's this country all over. Fifty yards away and you're on the prettiest little beach you ever saw. But slip a few paces behind it, and it's like scraping the paint off an old tart's cheeks. Everything ugly and rotten underneath.

Welcome to Jamaica.

Well, you can shove it.

First thing tomorrow, he'll be down at the quay – beg pardon, the old *Monroe* quay – and get the first job going: on a banana boat or whatever it sodding takes to get out of here.

A shiver runs through him. He's lost his hat, and the sun's sickeningly hot, but the odd thing is, he can't stop shivering. It's been hours since he watched Sophie ride away, but he still can't get warm. And he's got this pain in his chest. Worse than his cracked ribs. Deeper than any bruise.

He's had it before, years ago when Kate died, and then again when Robbie went. It feels like someone's taken a chopper to his breastbone and split him down the middle.

But how can he be feeling that now, when he swore then that he'd never feel it again?

'Because, you sodding idiot,' he mutters, as he squats

down on his haunches and sneers at his reflection in the foul brown water, 'you let it happen. Didn't you? You went and let her in.'

What a fool he's been. Yapping to her like that. *I got it all worked out. We can go to Panama or America. We can be together.* Shameful. Shameful. Why on earth would she want to be with him?

He takes another pull at the bottle, and the overproof burns all the way to his guts.

Forget about it, Ben Kelly. Slam down the lid on the whole rotten, stinking mess. Slam it down hard.

Then a thought occurs to him. Scowling, he fumbles in his pocket and yanks out Sophie's handkerchief that she gave him at Romilly. It's filthy with dried blood, but he can still make out the neat little 'S' embroidered in the corner. Why has he kept it? It's poisoned: a poisoned handkerchief. When he used it to clean that cut, something of her got inside of him like a putrid fever.

'Well not for long,' he snarls. He stands up, cracking his head on a mangrove branch and swearing viciously.

A new cut opens up on his temple. Pain flares. But it feels good. It's clean and harsh, and on the *out*side: not like the pain in his chest.

He stumbles over to the tree and puts his hands on the rough black trunk, and positions himself like a boxer. Then bashes his head against it. Again pain flares. Blood pours into his eyes. Another cut opens up on his cheek. Yes. Better now.

Hot stickiness streams down his face, clogging his mouth and turning the sun red. And as the throbbing in his head flares, that other pain in his chest sinks down deeper, and slowly goes under, like a stone disappearing into a mangrove swamp.

He pushes himself away from the tree and stumbles back to the edge of the water. Across the lagoon a big blue heron twists its graceful neck to regard him. '*Fuck off!*' he yells at it.

The heron spreads its wings and lifts into the sky.

He jams Sophie's handkerchief down the neck of the

bottle, then swings back his arm and lobs it as hard as he can at the bird. 'Get out of here!' he yells. 'Get out of here and never come back!' And the blood runs into his eyes, and the hot tears cauterize the cut on his cheek.

The bottle splashes harmlessly into the swamp. The heron turns inland and rows serenely across the evening sky.

PART TWO

LONDON 1903

CHAPTER EIGHTEEN

A cold, wet afternoon in early April.

Rain rattled the windows of the dingy little office. In the street, a pair of sodden dray-horses hauled a wagon piled with coal from Lambeth Pier. The rumble of Waterloo Station grew to a roar as a train thundered across the bridge at the end of Centaur Street.

Sophie put the box file on her desk in a puff of dust, and looked about her with satisfaction. This was the sort of work she liked: peaceful, predictable and solitary. The Reverend Agate was upstairs in his study working on his History, and the rain was keeping the applicants away, so she had the office of St Cuthbert's Charitable Society to herself.

Nothing to do but sort through old records and shovel most of them into the waste-paper basket. And absolutely no need to deal with that other matter, the unposted letter in her bag.

Pushing the thought away, she opened the box file and gave the contents a cursory glance. Twenty-year-old receipts from the Poor Law Guardians; reports from the Charity Organisation Society. Oh, good: another volume of the daily Register of the Reverend Agate's predecessor, the Reverend Chamberlaine. She was developing a strange fascination for his granite cynicism.

'January 3rd, 1888,' he had written in his tiny backward-sloping hand. *Mrs Eliza Green, aged 27, 10*

Old Paradise Street. She may be 'Green' by name, but looks anything but verdant, & her complexion is unappealingly yellow. Works as a scrubber at St Thomas's. Has borne 10 children, 4 living. Husband in the Madhouse – and yet she has the temerity to seek a Maternity Certificate to finance her next confinement! Told her that if she chooses to indulge in impropriety, she must face the consequences alone. Application refused.

Widow Jane Bailey, aged 45, 8 Orient Street. Exceedingly plain physiognomy. A machinist for 30 yrs, but now arthritic & out of a situation. Seeks a loan for food & firing. Appears decently ashamed of being a burden on the parish. Informed her that we never lend money. Referred her to the COS.

'Still on the same box?' said the Reverend Agate, making her jump.

He was standing in the doorway, rubbing his red hands together and forcing his lipless mouth into an uneasy smile. 'You do remember that it's only the important items we wish to retain? No need to trouble yourself with old Chamberlaine's Registers.'

Serenely she returned the smile. 'Yes, of course.'

His eyes went to the Register before her, but he was too much of a coward to mention it. 'Capital. Capital. Any applicants while I was upstairs?'

'Only two. I gave one a certificate for the infirmary, and the other some oil of turpentine.'

His mouth tightened. 'You know, you must feel free to summon me if—'

'You're most kind. But I didn't think it necessary to trouble you. It was only an abscess and a case of croup.'

'Ah. To be sure.'

They both knew that if he'd been there, there would have been no certificate and no free medicine. It was a little game they played. Sophie would let through as many applications as she could, while he did his best to prevent her.

It wasn't that he was ill-natured; just ferociously mean. And he could conjure up almost as many reasons for refusing an applicant as the Reverend Chamberlaine. The unemployed were lazy; unmarried women were no better than they should be; blacks, orientals, Jews and Catholics were all liars. Sometimes Sophie envied him his narrow certainties.

'Capital!' he said again, rubbing his hands. 'Well, well. I shall be upstairs at my desk, should you need me.'

'Thank you,' she said, and turned back to the Register before he was out of the room.

But to her irritation, she could no longer concentrate. The Reverend Agate had broken the spell of peaceful tedium, and let in the outside world. The rain was showing no signs of easing off, and she'd forgotten her umbrella, so she was going to get soaked going home. And she remembered that she had to be back by four, as she'd rashly promised Sibella that they'd go for a cup of chocolate at Charbonnel's. And of course she must decide what to do about the letter.

For the past fortnight she'd been carrying it around in her bag. It had accompanied her on her daily Tube journey from Baker Street to Lambeth North, on her lunchtime walks to the street market in The Cut, and during her solitary evenings in Mrs Vaughan-Pargeter's drawing-room in New Cavendish Street. It was becoming ridiculous. After all, she had only to stick on a stamp and post it, and then the thing would be done. The following morning her attorney would receive her instructions, and within a day she would be free. So why couldn't she do it?

The answer was simple. She'd forgotten how to make decisions. She had so constructed her life that she didn't need to. She'd freed herself from doubt, and – apart from Madeleine's stilted little bi-monthly letters – she'd freed herself from the past.

But *was* she doing the right thing? What would Madeleine think? And Cameron? And Clemency?

If only I could be sure, she thought. If only I could have some indication that I'm right.

The bell above the door tinkled, and a man entered, hunched under a streaming umbrella, and letting in a blast of cold air.

Anticipating another applicant, Sophie raised her head, and found herself looking at a well-dressed black man standing politely on the doormat with his hat in his hand. He was in his mid-thirties, stockily built and very dark, and his bony, appealing face reminded her powerfully of Daniel Tulloch.

It gave her such a jolt that for a moment she could only stare at him, and wonder what a younger version of Cornelius Traherne's head groom was doing in Lambeth.

'I'm sorry, am I disturbing you?' he said in a pleasant, uneducated voice.

A Cockney accent; not a Jamaican one. She was shaken by the depth of her disappointment. 'Um – not at all,' she said.

'I don't want to intrude.'

'You're not.'

They exchanged slight, awkward smiles.

She wished she could shrug off the feeling that his arrival was not mere chance. But his resemblance to Danny Tulloch had knocked her off balance.

She watched him carefully shaking out his umbrella so that no droplets scattered in her direction. 'It's just that I was in London for a bit,' he said, 'looking up my old stamping-grounds. Didn't this use to be the COS?'

'They moved,' she told him. 'New premises, round the corner.'

'Ah. But St Cuthbert's is still going strong?'

She nodded. 'As you can see.'

'And you're running it?'

'Oh no, I'm just a volunteer.'

He glanced at the little shelf of patent medicines behind her. 'A medical lady?'

She glanced down and rearranged the papers on her desk. 'Not a doctor or a nurse or anything. I just dispense a few simple medicines, and give referrals to the Poor Law Infirmary.'

From anyone else she would have resented the questions, but he was so courteous and unassuming that she didn't mind. And yet it annoyed her to be defining herself in negatives. *Not running it. Not a doctor or a nurse. Or anything.* Why stop there? Not married. Not engaged – although if Alexander remained in London, perhaps that might change. No friends, unless one counted Sibella. No real occupation. Just a twenty-six-year-old lady volunteer who shared a house with old Mrs Pitcaithley's widowed sister.

It was unpleasant to be reminded of how her life had shrunk. A pile of books from Mudie's library, and the odd lecture at the British Museum. Sunday lunch with Mrs Vaughan-Pargeter, because on Sundays there wasn't any whist.

The black man was perceptive. He caught her altered expression, thanked her politely, and turned to go.

She felt compelled to make amends. 'You mentioned that you were looking up old haunts. Did you use to live around here?'

He turned. 'Number nine, Wynyard Terrace.'

Wynyard Terrace was one of the poorer streets, and had as yet escaped the attentions of those in charge of the slum clearances.

Again he caught the current of her thoughts, and gave a slight smile. 'My ma was too proud to be a burden on the parish, so Pa use to send us instead. We weren't sposed to tell her.' He paused. 'The name's Walker. Isaac Walker.'

'Sophie Monroe.' She stood up and held out her hand, and after a moment's hesitation he took it. 'I'm going through old records,' she said, indicating the Register. 'I'll look out for your name.'

'I don't think you'll find it,' he said gently.

She knew what he meant. To the Reverend Chamberlaine, the young Isaac Walker would have been an *'application dismissed'* before he'd even got in the door.

'Well,' he said, 'I'll be off. Thanks for sparing the time.'

'Come again,' she said, and surprised herself by meaning it.

'Thanks. Maybe I will.'

* * *

The day had turned sour.

She stood in the packed, damp-smelling compartment as the Tube rattled through the darkness, and struggled to regain her peace of mind. She told herself severely that Isaac Walker was simply a polite and pleasant Cockney who had made good. All right, a *black* Cockney who'd made good, which was rather more unusual. But still, it was merely a coincidence that he'd arrived just when she was hoping for some sort of sign. A coincidence that he reminded her of someone she'd known in Jamaica.

She was angry with herself. Was this all it took to disturb her hard-won peace? Was this all it took to make her homesick?

Emerging from Baker Street station, she went to the first slot-machine she could find, and bought a penny stamp with a defiant flourish. She didn't need co-incidences to help her make up her mind. She could take charge of her own destiny.

But when she had found a pillar box, she still couldn't bring herself to post the letter. You are weak, she told herself in disgust. Weak, weak, *weak*.

Sibella's brougham was outside the house in New Cavendish Street, and Sibella herself was waiting impatiently in the drawing-room.

'Did you order tea?' Sophie asked as she drew off her gloves.

'I thought we were going out,' said Sibella with a frown. 'You don't mean to say that you've forgotten?'

Sophie repressed a flicker of irritation. She was tired, and she needed to be alone. But clearly, chocolate at Charbonnel's was immovable. Thank heavens that Sibella was going home next week.

She tried a change of subject. 'What did you do today?'

'Mrs Vaughan-Pargeter took me about,' said Sibella in an accusatory tone which Sophie ignored. 'We went to that new department store.'

'Selfridge's? Oh, isn't it grand?'

'Personally, I think it far too large and rather vulgar. And the clothes! "Hobble skirts"? And something ghastly called a "tube frock". They're all very well for you, but if one has any sort of figure, they're absolutely the end.' It was her most frequent complaint. She'd put on flesh since her marriage, and even now, in widow's black, she looked very nearly fat.

Sophie sat on the sofa and kneaded her temples, and wondered how she'd got herself into this position: an unwilling courier to a woman she no longer even liked.

She'd been astonished when Sibella's letter had arrived the previous month, for they hadn't corresponded since Sophie had left Jamaica.

As no doubt you already know, Sibella had written after a brisk introduction, *I recently lost my darling Eugene.* Of course Sophie had heard. Madeleine's letters, while short, were informative on factual matters; and Alexander in his desultory way sometimes remembered to mention his sister.

It was from him that Sophie had learned that the marriage had not been a success. As soon as the honeymoon was over, 'darling Eugene' had taken to spending all his time in Kingston, where he'd gambled relentlessly until felled by malaria. He and Sibella had lived largely apart, and she had not been overwhelmed by grief. She'd simply given up her small house on the Palairet estate, shaken off the stultifying influence of her mother-in-law, and returned to Parnassus. The Palairets had let her go without a struggle, for she had expensive tastes, and her only child had died at birth.

I have of course been inconsolable, Sibella wrote crisply, *so Papa is sending me to London for a change of air. I would have come years ago if it hadn't been for the beastly price of sugar and the beastly earthquake in '07. Such a trial. Dear Eugene's townhouse quite went up in smoke, and even Papa's interests were damaged. The insurers have been absolutely vile. Of course I don't understand it at all. Besides, worrying about money is vulgar and makes one ugly, so I've decided that I shan't.*

I shall be in London for a month, and I shall want you to show me about, as I'm sure that Alexander will be perfectly useless. But I'm afraid that I shall be staying at an hotel, as Papa had to sell our place in St James's Square. Isn't it frightful? So many changes. It's too unfair.

So many changes. For the past three weeks that had been her constant refrain.

Now she fiddled idly with a tassel on one of Mrs Vaughan-Pargeter's cushions, and studied Sophie's plain grey costume with disapproval. 'Everything is different from when I was here last,' she muttered.

'That's life,' said Sophie unsympathetically.

'And it's not just London. Trelawny is absolutely going to the dogs. You ought to come back and see for yourself.' Her tone implied that Sophie had been getting off scot free for years, and should jolly well mend her ways. 'It's dreadful,' she went on. 'Estates going to smash every day. Why, old Mowat absolutely shot himself.'

'You already mentioned that.'

'And I was counting on London to cheer me up.' She sounded aggrieved, as if London were somehow in breach of contract. 'All these horrid motor-omnibuses. And "underground railways". What a ridiculous idea. Who wants to go on a beastly train under the ground?'

Sophie sighed. The Tube had been an unmitigated disaster. On Sibella's one attempt to make her own way from her hotel in Berner's Street to the Kensington shops, she'd contrived to miss the new station at the Oxford Circus, and end up at Baker Street. There she'd found her way onto the Bakerloo instead of the Inner Circle line, and when South Kensington failed to appear she'd become so flustered that a station porter had had to help her outside. After that she'd pronounced the whole system unworkable, and hired a brougham from the hotel for the rest of her stay.

She had, quite simply, lost her nerve. She hadn't been to London for a decade, and it frightened her out of her wits. The traffic; the new telephone boxes; even the meekest lady suffragist with a collection tin. They all inspired in her a terrified loathing – which was why she needed Sophie.

Watching her fiddling with the tassel, Sophie felt a flash

of sympathy. After all, were they so very different? In a way, she too had lost her nerve.

It was a shaming thought, and it lent her the resolve she needed. She jumped to her feet and went to the bell-pull and rang for the parlourmaid. To Sibella she said, 'I just need to give something to Daphne, and then we can go.' Then she opened her bag and unearthed the letter.

'Daphne,' she said quickly, as soon as the maid appeared, 'would you take this and see that it's posted at once? It slipped my mind on my way home, but it has to go now.'

'Yes, 'm,' murmured the girl, looking less than delighted at the prospect of running to the post-box in the rain. But as she took the letter her hand touched Sophie's icy fingers, and she glanced up in alarm. 'You all right, 'm?'

'I'm fine,' said Sophie with a brief smile. 'Just do as I say, will you? Straight away?'

Sibella had seen none of this. She was standing by the chimneypiece, inspecting her new mourning-bonnet in the looking-glass. 'I do think it's amazing', she remarked, 'that they found anyone to buy the old place.'

'Which place?' murmured Sophie, going to the window. There now, she told herself. That wasn't so hard, was it?

'Old Mowat's place, of course. Arethusa.'

Sophie drew back the curtain and looked down into the street. The rain was coming down in sheets. She could see a stout old lady in a rain cape pulling a small bedraggled spaniel. A tall, very thin gentleman paying off a hansom cab. Daphne huddling beneath an umbrella as she ran to post the letter.

You did the right thing, she told herself. But she felt shaky and sick. And she couldn't get warm.

'I can't imagine whom they found to buy it,' said Sibella again, still at the looking-glass.

'Buy what?' said Sophie.

'*Arethusa*. Aren't you listening?'

'I expect someone took a fancy to it,' Sophie said with her eyes still on the street. 'A coffee planter or a rich American.'

Sibella snorted. 'Easier said than done in times like these.'

'Oh, I don't know,' said Sophie, turning back from the window. 'I've just sold Fever Hill.'

Sibella's expression would have made her laugh if she hadn't been on the verge of tears. Her friend's eyes opened theatrically wide and her jaw dropped, then shut with an audible click.

'Don't say a word,' said Sophie. 'I don't want to talk about it.'

'But—'

'Sib, *please*. Can we just go to Charbonnel's and have a quiet cup of chocolate, and pretend I didn't say it? I'll tell you all about it tomorrow. I promise. But not today. Tomorrow.'

Tomorrow – by which time Mr Fellowes would have received the letter, and no doubt muttered, 'Well, well, so at last she has made up her mind to go ahead.' And then he would send a man round to the purchaser's attorney with the papers she'd signed weeks ago, and then it would be done. And it really would be too late to change her mind.

To escape Sibella's pantomime astonishment, she turned back to the window.

The hansom was moving away, and the tall, very thin gentleman was unfurling his umbrella. He glanced at Sibella's brougham, gave himself a little shake, and walked off down the street.

Sophie dropped the curtain and turned back to Sibella.

CHAPTER NINETEEN

The Honourable Frederick Austen cast a wistful glance at the brougham waiting outside the elegant little town-house, then shook himself and walked round the corner into Mansfield Street.

What a confounded idiot he was. To have paid off his cab in the pouring rain three streets from his employer's house, simply for the chance of catching a glimpse of the fascinating young widow who seemed to be a daily visitor to New Cavendish Street.

He'd only seen her face once, but it had been enough. She was enchanting. Wide blue eyes; a small, soft mouth; and a truly magnificent figure. Surely one so beautiful must also be sweet-tempered?

But of course he would never find out, for he couldn't possibly seek an introduction. If she so much as looked at him – or, heaven forfend, *spoke* to him – he would die of fear.

And after all, why *should* she speak to him? He was the last man on earth to find favour with a lady. He looked like an ostrich. All the Austens did. It was a family trait. They had long thin necks and large beaky noses, and in his case pale eyelashes and red-rimmed insomniac's eyes.

So all things considered, it was better if they never met.

He turned left into Queen Anne Street, then right into Chandos Street, heading for the tall stone house in Cavendish Square of which his employer was already tiring.

A restless man, his employer. Moody. Discontented. Unpredictable. A rough diamond. Very rough indeed.

'We'll call you my secretary,' he'd said at that first extraordinary interview in the Hyde Park Hotel. 'I'll pay you three times over the odds, but you'll be earning it. It'll be your job to teach me whatever I want to know.'

A singular requirement, particularly when it was made by an ex-street-Arab (and probably worse) to a member of the aristocracy. But as Austen had four unmarried sisters, three penniless old aunts, and a ninety-room country seat in Tipperary which was largely lacking a roof, he took the position. And so began the most exhausting, alarming and entertaining year of his life.

Whatever I want to know turned out to be everything. What to read and how to talk; how to dress and what to eat; where to live and where to ride one's horses. In short, how to be a gentleman.

To begin with, it was like teaching a savage. History, religion and the arts were utterly unknown to him. He had no idea that one ought to go to Scotland in September for the shooting, and he'd never even heard of Ascot. But when a subject interested him, he would seize hold of it and make it his own.

To his surprise, Austen found himself enjoying the job. He enjoyed the discussions and the arguments. He enjoyed his employer's harsh, godless sense of morality. A few months ago they'd made a start on the Bible, and Austen had been astonished at his employer's flat condemnation of Jacob for tricking his brother out of his birthright – not to mention his scepticism about Original Sin. 'So according to this,' he'd said, jabbing the Book with his forefinger, 'because Eve took the apple, it's all their fault. Women, I mean.'

Austen was forced to agree that such regrettably was the case.

'But how does that square with what you call a "gentleman's duty to revere the weaker sex"?'

Austen was poleaxed. Until then, he'd kept Genesis entirely separate from the proper way to treat a lady.

'The weaker sex?' His employer snorted. 'They're the ones that have the bloody kids.'

'Children,' Austen gently corrected, for amending his employer's language was an important part of his duties.

His employer studied him for a moment. 'Austen, have you ever seen a woman giving birth?'

Austen blushed scarlet, and mumbled that he had not.

His employer's lip curled. 'No, I didn't think you had.'

But he didn't laugh, and Austen liked him for that. He liked him and was afraid of him in equal measure. He liked his cleverness and his flat-on view of the world. He liked his cavalier attitude to his enormous wealth – acquired, he vaguely explained, through a 'prospecting syndicate' with his business partner in Brazil. He liked the fact that although he worked to improve his accent, he didn't carry it to extremes. 'I can't be talking like I've just come out of Eton,' he said drily, 'because I haven't.' Most of all, Austen admired his employer's in-difference to the opinion of others, for that was so utterly unlike himself. Austen could suffer paroxysms of self-consciousness quite literally at the drop of a hat.

But there was another side to his employer which he found unsettling and incomprehensible. The black, silent moods which could last for days. And the distance which must never be crossed. Two months before, as they were preparing to leave Dublin, Austen had been astonished when his employer gave orders to sell every one of his prized thoroughbreds.

'But – I thought you were attached to them,' he had ventured.

His employer had looked at him with eyes grown suddenly cold. 'I'm not attached to anything,' he'd said softly. 'Not to my horses. Not to Isaac. Not to you. Remember that, my friend.'

Always that distance.

And it hadn't taken long to learn that *why* was not a question which one ought to ask. *Why do you never go out into Society? Why do you bother to improve your speech, when you don't care a pinch of snuff for what*

people think? Why have you hired a private detective?
And why, since we've been in London, do you go out
alone every afternoon?

True to form, his employer was out when Austen
reached the house. Only Mr Walker was at home, as
Austen discovered to his discomfort when he went
upstairs and opened the drawing-room doors.

He hung back, irresolute.

Mr Walker, in an easy chair, froze with a teacup in one
hand and the *Daily Mail* in the other.

Their unease was mutual. Mr Walker was far more conventional than his business partner, and far more cautious
– which was probably why they'd made such a good team
in Brazil. But that also meant that he was uncomfortable
with people like Austen, whom he knew to be his betters.

For his part, Austen simply didn't know how to behave.
Until a year ago he had never spoken to a black man in his
life – let alone lived with one under the same roof. He
liked the man well enough, and in a way he even respected
him. But he couldn't relax with him. It would be like
relaxing with one's butler.

Awkwardly, Mr Walker deposited the *Daily Mail* on the
tea table, rose to his feet, and rubbed the back of his head.
'The tea's gone cold. D'you want me to ring for some
more?'

Austen reddened. It would be dire for them both if he
sat down to tea. 'No, no,' he murmured, 'I wouldn't
dream of disturbing you.'

Downstairs the front door slammed, and moments later
Austen saw his employer coming up the stairs. He
breathed a sigh of relief.

His employer glanced from Austen to his business
partner, and he grinned. 'What's up, Austen? You been
squabbling with Isaac again?'

Austen's cheeks burned. 'Oh, I say, sir, I wouldn't
dream—'

His employer touched his shoulder. 'I didn't mean it.'
He went over and poured himself a cup of cold tea and
drank it off in one go, then threw himself down into a

chair with his usual grace. 'So what you been up to, mate?' he asked Mr Walker. Sometimes with his business partner he lapsed into his old mode of speech. Austen suspected that he did it to tease his secretary.

'Been down the docks,' said Mr Walker, with an embarrassed glance at Austen.

'Bloody hell, Isaac, what for?'

Mr Walker shrugged. 'I dunno. I went down the COS, too. Least, the COS as was.'

'But what for?'

'I dunno. Old times.'

His partner shook his head. 'God Almighty, Isaac, you got to start leaving it behind.'

Isaac grinned, and his partner reached over and gave him a good-natured cuff.

Austen felt obscurely left out. He liked his employer and he wanted his employer to like him. But this reminded him of school, when the other chaps used to send him to Coventry for enjoying Greek. From the doorway, he cleared his throat.

His employer turned his head. 'What is it, Austen?'

'Erm. Not "God Almighty",' said Austen gently. 'Might I suggest – "Dear Lord"?'

His employer studied him for a moment, then burst out laughing. 'Why don't you stop prossing about in that doorway and come and have some tea? And if you ever catch me saying "Dear Lord", you can shoot me. All right?'

Austen permitted himself a shy smile, and edged towards the sofa. 'Very well, Mr Kelly,' he said.

It's Sunday morning, and Ben's gone down the bakehouse with his big sister to fetch the dinner, and everything's topper.

The weather's a bit sharp, but the big tin of batter pudding's warming his hands nicely, and the smell of the meat pieces is twisting his belly into knots.

It's the best time of the week, as he's got Kate all to hisself. She says that when he's ten he can go to the bakehouse on his own, but not before, or some basher will give him a thrashing and click the lot. But Ben knows that's just an excuse. Truth is, she likes coming with him.

She's topper, is Kate. She's got bright blue eyes and hair like copper wire, and freckles all over, which she hates, but Ben thinks are bang-up. She can be a right Tartar, making him sluice his head every Sunday and walloping him if he don't. But she's the sharpest bit of muslin you ever met, and she's got the loudest laugh in East Street. And when she cracks a joke, she always looks at Ben before the others, like she knows he'll catch on first. Pa hates that, but it makes Ben so proud that it hurts.

Today she's all poshed up to meet her sweetheart. She's got her blue frock out of pledge, and she's even put on her stays. Which means that Jeb Butcher can't be far away.

And sure enough; he's waiting for them on the corner of Walworth Place. He's a costermonger, and until Kate got sweet on him Ben wanted to be a costermonger too, and wear a velveteen jacket, and kicksies that flare out below the knee like a candle-snuffer. But over the last month, Kate's been talking of going to live with Jeb. Of course she's only joking. But it gives Ben a pain in his chest just to think of it.

So now they've reached East Street, and when they're nearly at number 39, Jeb shoves off home. That's when Ben says to Kate, 'I got you a present.'

'A present?' She grins at him. 'That's nice.'

'Here you are,' he says proudly. It's a pipe, a proper white clay pipe with a long stem for a good sweet smoke, just how she likes it. He's been waiting for a chance to give it her for days.

She takes it, and her face goes still.

His heart sinks. Bugger. She don't like it.

'Where'd you get this, Ben?'

'Found it, didn't I?'

'You mean you clicked it.'

'I never.'

'You did. This is old Mrs Hanratty's pipe. I seen her smoke it.'

Ben don't say nothing. Him and Jack clumped the old biddy a few days ago, and clicked her savings that was sewn into her drawers. Laugh! Did they laugh! There she is lying in the gutter, yelling blue murder, and thrashing her skinny yellow pins like a beetle.

Turned out she only had a couple of bob and her lucky pipe, and a twig that Jack said was heather. So Jack took the rhino and give Ben the pipe, and chucked the rest down the drain. But afterwards Ben wished they'd left the old biddy her bit of heather.

Kate gives him back the pipe without a word, and they go indoors. She's well narked. But there's no time for him to say nothing, because they're home.

Kate shoves the pudding on the table and everybody grabs a spoon and digs in: Jack and Lil and Pa, and Ma with the baby asleep under her lotties. Robbie's off in his corner as per usual, watching the spider. He does that all day. Maybe he thinks the spider's going to do something, instead of just prossing about in its web.

Ben tries to catch Kate's eye, but she won't look at him. She's narked, and he knows why. Mrs Hanratty's a neighbour. You don't click from the neighbours.

He's all hot and prickly inside. And that makes him narked at Kate, cos she's the one making him feel like that. What's he sposed to do, say sorry? Well, bugger that.

Pa scrapes the last of the meat pieces out the tin, and shoots Kate a look. 'You was a long time coming. Where you been?'

'At the bakehouse,' snaps Kate, 'where d'you think?'

Jack and Lil and Ben keep their heads down. Ma looks from Pa to Kate, and twines a lock of orange hair round her skinny finger. Any moment now and she'll start snivelling.

Ben puts down his spoon – quietly, so as not to nark Pa. If only Pa could be in a good mood today, and tell stories and crack a laugh, like he does sometimes. If only he didn't fancy Kate.

'You been with that Jeb Butcher,' goes Pa, watching her.

'I never,' goes Kate.

'You was,' goes Pa.

Kate gets up and goes to stand at the window, with her arms round her waist. Pa looks at her. He looks at the way her skirts swell over her hips, and her lotties push up under her frock. Ben knows that look. It's the same as Jack give Lil last summer, when it was so hot that they slept in the altogether.

Oh well. After Jack got into Lil, they was friends again soon enough, so maybe it'll be like that with Pa and Kate? A bit of a blow-up, then everybody friends again. And then Kate won't go off and live with Jeb.

'You was out with that Jeb Butcher,' goes Pa again.

'She never,' goes Ben, covering for her. 'We come the long way home on account of – there was dray-horses in Walworth Place.'

Pa's green eyes turn on him like a searchlight. 'What you on about?'

Ben swallows. 'See, I don't like dray-horses. I get scared.' It's true, he does. Except there wasn't no drays in Walworth Place. Only Jeb.

Pa leans across the table towards him. He's so close that Ben can smell the coal on him, and see the black dust in the deep lines from nose to mouth. That mouth. Lips like a statue's, and the edges so sharp they could be knife-cut. He can give you a smile with that mouth that'll make you feel ten feet tall, or he can give you such an earful that you'll want to crawl down a sewer. And you can never tell which is coming next. You just know that you'd do anything to make him like you, if you only knew how.

'Scared?' goes Pa, in a sneery voice that makes Ben's belly clench like a rat trap. 'Scared of a couple of nags?'

'They got big feet,' mumbles Ben.

'Big feet!' goes Pa. 'They'll stomp all over you with them big feet if they catch on you're scared! But if you don't show them you're scared, you'll be all right. Don't you know that yet?'

Ben shakes his head. He hates for Pa to think he's yellow, but he's got to cover for Kate. 'It's not that I don't like horses,' he mutters. 'It's just that I don't like dray-horses.'

Pa snorts. But all of a sudden he's not sneery no more, he's laughing. 'Oh, so it's just dray-horses you got a down on?'

Ben chucks him a doubtful look, then nods.

'Well, well,' goes Pa, looking round at the others. 'We got ourselves a sodding attorney! A twisty-turny attorney, playing with words!'

Lil sniggers, and Jack and Ma join in, but it's more out of relief than cos it's funny. Kate comes back to the table and sits down again. And the spring in Ben's belly loosens up.

Everything would be all right if Kate would only look at him again. But she's still narked about old Mrs Hanratty's pipe.

So after supper he slinks out for a bit. And an hour or so later when he gets back, the curtain's down and Ma and Pa are in the back room, and the others are prossing about in the front. Jack's curled up asleep, and Lil's jiggling the baby on her lap, and Robbie's in his corner, watching the spider.

Kate's sitting by the window with her tray on her knees, making violets. She's folded back a bit of newspaper off the window to let in the light, and she looks pretty as a picture. That coppery hair and the paper violets on the tray, and the blue glass pot of paste. All the lovely colours.

Ben sidles up to her, steering clear of the violets so as not to dirty them. He goes, 'I took the pipe back to Mrs Hanratty.'

She finishes off another violet and puts it on the tray.

'I didn't say sorry,' he mutters. 'Just left it in her shake-down where she'll find it.'

'That's good,' she says without looking up.

Later, he's sitting with Robbie watching the spider, when she comes over and squats down and puts a mug in his hands. It's her own tin mug with the painted roses that Jeb give her. 'Kettle broth,' she says.

That's his favourite. And she made it just the way he likes it, with the water well mashed into the bread, and a dot of lard on top for a relish. She must of gone next door to get the water hot.

He scowls at it. 'This because of that sodding pipe?'

She puts her head on one side. 'Maybe. Careful with that, it's hot.'

'Piping hot,' he mutters.

She grins. 'Pipe up, you idiot, I can't hear you.'

'Pipe down,' he shoots back, 'or you'll wake the baby.'

She cuffs him round the head, and goes back to work.

Ben woke with a start as Norton drew back the curtains.

For a moment he didn't know where he was. His heart was pounding. He lay still, fighting the pull of the dream.

Outside it was still dark. Rain pattered against the window panes. The street-lamp shone in his eyes. Seven o'clock, and a fire was already blazing in the grate. Some time around five, a housemaid would have crept in and made it up. She hadn't woken him. Since coming to London, he'd slept like the dead.

And now he was dreaming of them, too.

Rubbing his face, he propped himself up on one elbow, and watched Norton setting the coffee tray on the table.

The dream clung to him. He couldn't shake it off. All the little details. That blue frock of hers. The roses on the mug. His terror that she might leave. Twenty years on, and he hadn't forgotten a thing. Christ.

The unflappable Norton poked the fire, turned the gas on low, then went through into the dressing-room to lay out his master's clothes. He did it all without a word. Ben hated talking in the morning.

Ben got out of bed and shrugged on his dressing-gown, and stood looking down at the fire. Even without it the room would have been warm, for he always took houses with hot-water pipes in every room. What was the good of being rich if you couldn't stay warm?

He turned to survey the bedroom. In the golden glow of the gaslight, the furnishings were opulent but not ostentatious. The deep patina of well-polished mahogany. The dark blue sheen of silk damask hangings. The rich gleam of morocco book-bindings. What would Jack have made of it? Or Lil, or Kate?

Christ, why dream of them now, suddenly, after all these years?

Norton appeared at the dressing-room door and discreetly cleared his throat. 'Shall you be going riding this morning, sir?'

'No,' snapped Ben.

'Very good, sir.'

Ben went to the window and looked out. The sky was lightening, the rain easing off. 'On second thoughts, yes.' He'd just bought a three-year-old at Tattersall's: a big flashy chestnut who needed taking in hand. It was a challenge, but he knew that when he sold her in a few months' time he'd be passing on a much better horse.

'Very good, sir,' said Norton, and silently withdrew.

Norton was the perfect servant. Soft-spoken, soft-footed, and utterly unperturbed by his master's moods. Of course, who knew what he really thought about Ben – a man he'd have crossed the road to avoid five years before? But who cared, so long as he did his job?

Sometimes, Ben still had to remind himself that he was rich. It felt like play-acting. Isaac felt the same. 'I dunno, Ben,' he'd said once. 'These days I'm "Mr Walker" or "sir", but inside I'm still plain old Isaac, the nigger-boy from Lambeth.' It was the same for Ben.

And a lot of things about being rich bored him. Changing your clothes all the time, and the ceremony of meals. Servants creeping about. Having to plan your day in advance. *Shall you be going riding this morning?* How the hell should I know, I've only just woken up.

He poured himself a cup of coffee and returned to the window. The coffee was good. It bloody well ought to be; he'd paid enough for it. Six shillings a pound in some fancy shop in Piccadilly. And then he'd got a telling off from the cook when he brought it home – although not to his face, of course; it had come through Austen. Apparently he wasn't supposed to go out and buy coffee on his own. For some reason a box of cigars or a crate of wine was fine, but nothing else.

Well, sod it, he'd buy what he liked. That was what

he liked doing: buying things. Then getting rid of them.

That was the good thing about money: it was entirely predictable. You buy a fine claret or a good cigar, and you know what you're getting. Money doesn't let you down, not like people.

But *six shillings* a pound! How d'you square that with Kate getting sixpence a gross for her paper violets?

Again the gnawing sense of loss. That bloody, bloody dream. Until he'd got to London he'd never had a single one. Panama. Sierra Leone. Brazil. He'd slept like a baby.

Maybe it was coming to London that had done it. After all, London held other memories apart from Kate and Jack and the others. Cavendish Square wasn't very far from the Portland Road. The other day he'd even thought of walking down it, just to see if the photographer's studio was still there. He'd stopped himself in the nick of time.

So maybe it was thinking of that – or trying not to think about her – that had got him all churned up.

Involuntarily he glanced at the picture above the chimneypiece. It was an oil painting of Montego Bay that he'd seen in Paris and taken a fancy to. It wasn't very good, but at least the artist knew what royal palms look like, and poinciana trees and bougainvillaea.

Funny, but he still missed Jamaica. It was probably why he'd ended up in Brazil: because he'd felt at home there, with the parrots and the darkies. And now that he was in London, he sometimes went all the way down to the gardens at Kew, just to stand in the Palm House and breathe in that hot, wet, green smell, and see if the vanilla was in flower.

'Norton,' he called over his shoulder.

The valet appeared. 'Sir?'

'I've changed my mind. No riding. I'm going to Kew.'

'Very good, sir,' said Norton.

CHAPTER TWENTY

'But Kew', said Sibella crossly, as the train rattled through the suburbs, 'is so frightfully middle class. I fail to see why we can't go to Richmond.'

'Because,' answered her brother with an amused glance at Sophie, 'it's a cold, dank morning, and we wish to be pleasantly warm in the Palm House, rather than shivering with a lot of undernourished deer.'

'They're hardly undernourished,' retorted Sibella. 'It's a Royal Park. As far as I'm aware, there's nothing royal about Kew.'

She turned to the window and studied her reflection. When she was satisfied with her new pouched walking-coat with the sable collar, she renewed the attack. 'All those ghastly terraced houses. And tramways, and – and day-trippers.'

Sophie wondered in amusement why Sibella believed that they themselves fell outside the term. 'I imagine,' she said, 'that we'll be safe from the crowds on a Wednesday morning in April.'

Sibella ignored her. 'I so much prefer Richmond. And I wanted to see that new theatre. Apparently it's the first kind of chic.'

'You can see the new bridge at Kew,' said Sophie.

'Don't try to humour me,' said Sibella, turning back to the window.

Again Sophie and Alexander exchanged glances, and

Alexander rolled his eyes. He'd joined them at the last minute, much to Sophie's relief. Sibella had been impossible ever since she'd heard about Fever Hill.

'But it's your family *seat*,' she had complained in a scandalized tone over her chocolate, having ignored Sophie's request that the subject be deferred.

'We don't have a family seat,' Sophie had replied, taking refuge in pedantry. 'We're not aristocracy. But even if we did, our "seat" would've been Strathnaw. And if you remember, Madeleine sold that years ago.'

She'd thought that a powerful argument in her favour, but Sibella had brushed it aside. 'I dread to think what Aunt Clemency will say.'

That put Sophie on the defensive. 'Clemency could hardly go on living at Fever Hill by herself. Anyway, I hear that she already spends a good deal of her time at Eden.'

'But still—'

'Sibella, it's done. I've signed the papers. I've—'

'But *why*?'

Then Sophie had gone into her prepared speech: about feeling morally obliged to repay Cameron for her education, and wishing to recompense Mrs Vaughan-Pargeter more adequately for her keep. Sibella had listened, and asked a sharp question about just how much Sophie felt compelled to repay Cameron, but had entirely missed the fact that Sophie was window-dressing.

Her real reason for selling Fever Hill was simple and stark. She needed to sever her ties with Jamaica. By getting rid of Fever Hill, she was cutting herself loose from all the pain and regret. She was finally setting herself free.

So why wasn't she feeling any better?

'When shall we tell Alexander?' Sibella had asked, stirring her chocolate.

'Not yet,' Sophie had said in alarm. 'First I've got to write and tell Madeleine and Cameron.'

Sibella had looked appalled. 'You mean you haven't told them? Oh, *Sophie*!'

Again she'd been on the defensive. 'Why should that matter? It was mine to do with as I pleased.'

'But—'

'Sib, *please*. Let's talk of something else. And not a word to Alexander until I say.' After that she'd extracted a solemn promise of silence, and then at last the subject was dropped.

You did the right thing, she told herself as she and Alexander wandered through the dripping green jungle of the Palm House. They were alone together, for Sibella had declined to 'play gooseberry', and had gone off to inspect an adjacent greenhouse. You needed to cut yourself off, and you did. And now you're free.

So what was she doing in the one place in the whole of London that reminded her of Jamaica?

She raised her head and studied the intricate green-gold fronds of a tree-fern which wouldn't have been out of place in the gardens at Eden. She took a deep breath, and the air was as hot and humid as the forest on Overlook Hill. Only the sounds were different. Instead of the rasp of crickets she could hear the soft hiss of humidifiers, and the discreet murmur of the well-to-do visitors admiring the palms.

Alexander reached up and held a frond out of the way of her hat. 'I'm told,' he said, 'that there's a rather fine display of orchids in Greenhouse Number Four. Shall you care to see it?'

'Not really,' she replied. 'To tell you the truth, I don't at all care for orchids.'

'To tell you the truth, neither do I. I dare say I'm the most dreadful philistine, but I've always thought that they look rather badly made.'

She smiled.

Charming, handsome, undemanding Alexander. How he had changed from the old days. If someone had told her two months ago that they would become friends, she wouldn't have believed it. Alexander Traherne? That indolent, conceited young man?

But as Sibella never tired of pointing out, Alexander had reformed. He'd given up gambling and cleared all his debts. He'd even become a frequent caller on his mother's wealthy Aunt Salomon. 'And as for that business of the groom,' Sibella had confided to Sophie, 'why, no-one could have been more mortified than Alexander when he found out that Papa had had the fellow thrashed. He moved heaven and earth to make amends, but of course by then he'd fled the country. Skipped off to Peru, or Panama, or some such place.'

The fellow. With her talent for rearranging the truth, Sibella had pretended to have forgotten Ben's very name – not to mention the fact that her friend had once been in love with him. But her quick sideways glance to see how Sophie was taking it gave her away.

They turned into one of the quieter paths running along the side of the Palm House, and Alexander tapped his cane on the flags and frowned. 'Sophie,' he began, without looking at her.

'Yes?'

He hesitated. 'That work you do. That – volunteer affair?'

'You mean at St Cuthbert's?'

He nodded. 'I suppose you're frightfully attached to it, and all that?'

She was surprised. He'd never mentioned it before, except to josh her about it. 'I don't know,' she said. 'I suppose I am. It makes me feel useful.'

He nodded. 'You see, I was wondering. Should you be fearfully unhappy if circumstances were to take you away from it?'

She saw where he was heading, and wondered how to put him off.

'I mean,' he went on, 'why the slums? You could be useful, as you put it, just about anywhere. Couldn't you? You're not inextricably linked to Lambeth, or – or even London?'

He was right, of course. But 'why the slums?' was a harder question than it appeared. She herself had never come up with a satisfactory answer, although sometimes in her darker moments she wondered if Lambeth wasn't some means of retaining a link with the past. A link with Ben.

But of course that was absurd. And the only reason she'd thought of it now was because she was still upset about Fever Hill. 'I could leave it tomorrow,' she said with a sharpness which made Alexander blink.

'Ah,' he said. 'I was rather hoping you'd say that.'

They walked on in silence. Then Alexander came to a halt and took off his hat, and ran his hand through his golden curls.

Why, he's nervous, she thought in surprise. But he was never nervous. She found that slightly touching.

He replaced his hat and gave her a rueful smile. 'I dare say you've some idea of what's coming next.'

'Alexander—'

'Please. Hear me out, old girl. I promise I shan't take long.' He paused. 'I know that in the past I haven't always run quite the right side of the post. I mean, I've dabbled a bit with cards, and – well, that sort of thing.'

She bit back a smile. *That sort of thing* probably encompassed champagne suppers in Spanish Town with ladies of doubtful reputation, and running up racing debts at the speed of a cane-fire.

'But I truly believe,' he went on earnestly, 'that at last I've got myself running straight. I know you don't exactly love me. I mean – not as such.'

'I'm very fond of you,' she replied. 'That's the truth. You do know that, don't you?'

He gave her a slight smile. 'You're a darling for saying so. But you see, old girl, I'm rather more than fond of you. And I do believe, though it sounds frightfully arrogant to say so, that I could make you happy.'

She believed it too. He was considerate, gentlemanly and handsome. And everyone she knew would thoroughly approve of the match. Of course he would make her happy. At least, as happy as she deserved to be. 'I think you're probably right,' she said.

Again that slight smile. 'Does that mean you'll consider it?'

She stood looking up at him. In the greenish light his eyes were a clear, arresting turquoise, and his face had the smooth planes of a classical statue. 'I'll consider it,' she said.

They moved along the narrow path towards the end of the Palm House. Ahead of them, a vanilla plant clambered up the fibrous trunk of a palm. A tangle of peacock ferns dripped moisture. Beneath its fronds, Sophie saw, with an unpleasant little jolt, a small clump of orchids.

They had tubular, leafless stems and insignificant pale green flowers. And they were not, she told herself in alarm, cockleshell orchids. Certainly not. They merely *resembled* cockleshells. But if one looked closely, they were really quite different.

Suddenly she wondered if people put orchids on graves. She wondered what sort of flowers Madeleine put on Fraser's grave: on the grave that she, Sophie, had never seen.

'You see,' she said without turning round, 'in the main, I'm happy as I am.'

'But are you?' he said quietly.

She bit her lip. 'I am – content.'

'And yet you miss Jamaica.'

'No.'

'Sophie – yes. I've seen how you fall silent when Sib talks about it; when we come here to look at the palms. You miss it, and you're afraid of it.'

She glanced at him in surprise. She hadn't thought he could be so shrewd.

'You're afraid of Eden,' he went on, 'because of what happened to your nephew. And yet you miss it terribly. But don't you see, here's your chance? You could go home, without going home. You could be happy at Parnassus, I'd make sure of it. And no-one would put the least pressure on you to go to Eden, not if you didn't want to.'

She turned her head and looked out through the glass walls of the Palm House. A pair of ladies in enormous hats and modish draped coats tottered across the lawns towards the tea rooms. An elderly gentleman paused on the gravel to lean on his cane. A slender dark-haired man in an astrakhan coat emerged from the adjacent green-house and walked swiftly away.

Something about the way he moved reminded her of Ben. He had the same grace. The same taut air of watchfulness.

What's wrong with you? she asked herself angrily. Why should every good-looking, dark-haired man suddenly remind you of Ben?

But of course she knew the answer. It was because of Fever Hill, and Isaac Walker, and those wretched cockleshell orchids. Because of the hundred little daily coincidences that were always reminding her of Jamaica.

Alexander was wrong. She couldn't go home. Not ever.

She turned her head and looked up into his face. 'Dear Alexander,' she said softly. 'I'm so sorry. But I can't marry you.'

He was too gently bred to take it other than well. His features contracted slightly, but he managed a strained smile. 'It's because you don't care for me,' he said quietly. 'That's it, isn't it?'

'That isn't it at all,' she said with perfect truth. On the contrary, the fact that she didn't love him was his main attraction. She didn't want love. She was done with that. She only wanted peace, and perhaps a little affection.

He squared his shoulders and gave her another slight smile. 'Well, I give you fair warning, old girl. I shall ask you again in a month or so. And who knows, if I'm very lucky, you might even say yes.'

She put all thoughts of Fever Hill and cockleshell orchids and Ben firmly from her mind, and returned his smile. 'Who knows,' she said, 'one day, I might.'

The headless angel sat very straight on the sarcophagus by the cemetery gate, its legs nonchalantly crossed beneath its flowing marble robe. It looked as if it had just alighted for a moment's reflection on one of the quality tombs.

The inscription read *George Solon Ladd, aged 47, of San Francisco. 1889.*

Long way from home, thought Ben.

He started slowly up the wide gravel avenue, between the tidy battalions of the better class of dead. Sharp granite obelisks and windowless mausolea. A whole convocation of angels, serenely ignoring each other.

Kensal Green necropolis. *Necropolis*. He'd had to look it up. It meant a city of the dead.

He tried to picture his family relocated here. Kate and Jack, and Lil and Robbie and Ma. He couldn't do it. They'd lived in a city all their lives, and it had killed them. How could he drag them into yet another city, and leave them here for eternity?

And even if he did, they'd be right at the bottom of the heap. Everywhere he looked there was a Sir William this and a Lord Justice that. A Member of Parliament, a Fellow of the Royal Society, a Commissioner of the Metropolitan Police. That last one brought a wry smile to his lips. He could just see Jack's face if he was put to rest beside a copper. Poor old Jack. He'd never catch a wink.

No, it had been a mistake to come here. Just as it had been a mistake to go to Kew. Bloody Kew.

Still, how was he to know that he'd see her there? How was he to *know*?

Sibella Traherne. *Miss Sibella*, he'd automatically called her in his mind, and then corrected himself. Besides, she wasn't a Traherne any more, she was a Palairet. And maybe a widow – unless she'd been in mourning for her father, or for that brother of hers.

Still, at least she hadn't recognized him. She'd only glanced at him as they'd passed each other in the green-house, with the casual appraisal which any young woman gives to any man under sixty.

She'd put on a bit of flesh since he'd last seen her, but she was still pretty enough in a bovine kind of way, although she'd acquired a line of discontent between the eyes, and was beginning very slightly to resemble the dear, departed old Queen. In her younger days, of course.

Well, well, he'd thought as he walked past her. Sibella Palairet in London. And when you think about it, why not? She probably comes over once a year for the shopping, and to keep in touch with her friends. She probably sees quite a bit of Sophie.

Christ. *Sophie.* That was when he knew that he had to get out of Kew.

Thinking of that now, he quickened his pace and walked rapidly up the main avenue of the necropolis, his footsteps crunching on the gravel. He passed a well-dressed couple taking a stroll, and gave them a sharp, angry stare.

Maybe it had been a mistake to come to London in the first place. After all, the idea that he might chance across her had kept him away for years. But then one morning he'd woken up and thought, bloody hell, you're letting her tell you what to do. If you want to go to London, then sodding well go. Don't let her dictate to you.

Fine words, he thought, as he walked across the gravel. But still a mistake. Grinding his teeth, he moved swiftly up the avenue between the silent yews and the whispering poplars, and finally emerged onto a well-tended lawn before the chapel.

He found himself looking up at an enormous twenty-foot plinth which occupied pride of place in the middle of the lawn. On the plinth stood an ornate sarcophagus supported by four winged lions. The inscription on the side read: *SOPHIA 1777–1848. Her Royal Highness the Princess Sophia, 5th daughter of His Majesty King George III.*

The Princess Sophia.

He forgot to breathe. It felt like a message. A message aimed directly at him. *You may think you've made something of yourself, Ben Kelly, but the truth is, you don't belong with the quality, and you never will. There are some things that'll always be as far out of your reach as a princess on a pedestal.*

The Princess Sophia.

Astonishing how it all came crashing back. The pain. The loss. The anger. Sophie's pale, determined face in the dappled shade of the forest. Telling him she was leaving, telling him it was over. Casually destroying his dreams, like a child smashing a sandcastle.

The Princess Sophia. For ever out of reach.

He turned up the collar of his astrakhan coat and walked swiftly through the Grecian colonnade of the chapel and down the steps on the other side. He walked fast, and almost fell over Austen, kneeling on the verge.

'You!' cried Ben. 'What the hell are you doing here? Are you following me?'

Austen flushed and nearly overbalanced in the grass. 'N-no, of course not,' he stammered.

'Then what the hell are you doing?'

Austen reached for a bunch of lilies he'd dropped in the grass, and his large Adam's apple bobbed up and down. 'Um. Visiting my grandmother?'

Ben blinked. 'Oh. Sorry. It's just that I didn't expect to see you.' He turned on his heel and started back the way he'd come. Bugger Kensal Green necropolis. Bugger the whole daft idea.

Behind him he heard hesitant footsteps, and turned to see Austen lagging a discreet distance behind, but definitely following. 'I thought you were visiting your grandmother,' Ben said roughly.

Austen gave the characteristic ducking nod that always reminded Ben of an ostrich. 'And also my mamma,' he said, wincing and holding up the lilies as evidence. 'In point of fact, she's just over there, past the chapel.'

Well of course she is, thought Ben. Where else would she be but in the main avenue with the rest of the top brass? Again he felt constrained to apologize. 'Sorry,' he muttered. 'I'll be off and leave you to it.'

'Oh please, not on my account,' said Austen.

Ben shrugged. 'Suit yourself,' he muttered, and slowed his pace a little.

Austen fell into step beside him. They passed the chapel again, and shortly afterwards Austen came to a halt before a hideous mausoleum of pink speckled granite, guarded by four sludge-green marble sentinels sporting turbans and heavy moustaches.

So not angels, then, thought Ben, moving away to give him some privacy.

Out of the corner of his eye he watched his secretary stoop to lay the lilies before the blank stone door.

In the pediment above the door, five lines of large Roman capitals trumpeted the achievements of *Major General the Honourable Sir Algernon Austen KCB, of the Bengal Army and Member of the Supreme Council of India, Knight of the Legion of Honour* . . . et cetera, et cetera, et cetera. Below it, an inscription in cramped Gothic lettering had been squeezed in: *Euphaemia, 1860–89, widow of the above, and beloved mother of five grieving children.*

Austen straightened up and came to stand beside Ben.

Ben nodded at the lilies. 'Are they for your old man too, or just your mother?'

'Just Mamma,' said Austen with startling promptness. He caught Ben's glance, and looked sheepish. 'To tell the truth, I never much cared for the governor.'

'Me neither,' said Ben.

Austen gazed thoughtfully at his father's epitaph. 'He couldn't abide children. We were always supposed to keep out of his way. And if we forgot, and he happened across us, he used to wave his hand and murmur, "Vanish, vanish," and we fled like hares.'

Ben thought that sounded like the upper class equivalent of a clip round the ear.

He had an odd feeling that he ought to match Austen's confidence with one of his own. So in a few words he explained his idea of having the family relocated to Kensal Green. 'Of course,' he added, 'I'll have to find them first. And that won't be easy. They weren't exactly buried in a mausoleum to begin with.'

Austen nodded vigorously. 'Hence, the, um, private detective?'

'That's right.'

'I did wonder.'

There was a silence. Then Austen said, 'I'm sorry. That was inappropriate.'

'What was? Wondering?'

'No. Saying that I did.'

Ben threw him an amused glance. That was what he valued about Austen. His discretion, and his precise way of expressing himself.

'So if the detective succeeds,' said Austen, emboldened by Ben's silence, 'do you think that you'll go ahead? I mean, with the – er – relocation to Kensal Green?'

'No,' said Ben. He looked about him. 'Too posh. Too built-up. And too bloody cold.'

Austen buried his large nose in the collar of his great-coat and nodded. 'So where else, do you think?'

Ben did not reply. He stopped, and looked back over his shoulder at the sarcophagus of the Princess Sophia. 'I don't know,' he said, unwilling to reveal more of his plans. 'I'll have to give it some thought.'

Chapter Twenty-One

Sibella took her brother's walking-stick and hammered on the roof of the brougham, and told the driver to keep circling the park. Then she turned back to Alexander and pursed her lips. 'It's high time that you faced it,' she said importantly. 'You've simply got to marry money.'

'But that's what I'm trying to do,' he protested. 'It's scarcely my fault if she said no.'

With cordial dislike he watched her settle back against the cushions. She was enjoying herself immensely. She adored it when he misbehaved, for then she could play the responsible daughter, and 'do her duty', as she called it, by relaying the governor's increasingly irate messages. 'I don't believe,' she said severely, 'that you fully appreciate the gravity of your position. Sophie Monroe is positively your last chance.'

'*My* last chance?' he said indignantly. 'What about her?'

'Whatever do you mean?'

'Well, hang it all, Sib. I'm fond of Sophie and all that, but you've got to admit she has some pretty serious drawbacks.'

'Such as?'

'Well, for one thing, she was born on the wrong side of the blanket. And she's a frightful blue. And definitely damaged goods, what with that illness, and that appalling business about the groom.'

'It's because of those "drawbacks",' she snapped, 'that

you even stand a chance. Any other girl with a fortune like hers wouldn't touch you with a polo stick.'

'Oh, I *say*—'

'Well it's true! Tell me, Alexander. Give me a rough estimate. How much do you actually owe on the horses?'

Alexander ran his forefinger along his bottom lip, and wondered what to tell her. 'At a rough estimate, I should say – about five thousand?'

His sister's eyes became enormous. '*Alexander!* I never *dreamed* it would be as much as that!'

Oh, yes you did, he told her silently. And wouldn't you be delighted if you knew that the real sum is actually four times as much.

Even he was well aware that twenty thousand was going it a bit strong. But it really wasn't his *fault*. It had been such an amusing little dinner, and the fellows had got to joshing each other, and before he knew it he'd bet Guy Fazackerly a ridiculous amount on his nag in the Silver Cup. And then the confounded beast had plunged, and he'd had no choice but to take it on the chin. Twenty thousand? Of course he could pay. Just let him put his name to a bill for a few months, to give him time to rustle it up.

And of course he would manage it, somehow. He could hardly welsh on a debt to one of the fellows in his own set. Besides, the bill only fell due on New Year's Day, and that was *eight months* away. Plenty of time for him to marry Sophie. And plenty of time for Sib to snag that rich admirer of hers, which would be an additional comfort. So why was she trying to worry him like this? Why were women such confounded fools?

He turned to her and gave her his most charming smile. 'Sib darling, isn't this a tad academic? After all, the governor won't live for ever, and then I shall be a landowner, just as the Almighty intended.'

'Haven't you been listening? *Papa is losing patience with you!*'

Alexander swallowed a yawn. 'I'm amazed he has any left to lose. He's been losing patience with me since I was eight.'

'Be serious. If you don't go back and square things with him at once, I can't answer for the consequences.'

'But – what does he wish me to do?'

'For a start, he wants you to send him a schedule of your debts.'

'How should I know what they are? I'm not a bank clerk.'

She heaved a theatrical sigh. 'Failing that, he wants your proposal, in detail, as to how you plan to settle them.'

'But I can't,' cried Alexander. 'I haven't any money. What does he want me to do, work in a shop?'

'Don't be ridiculous.'

'Then what? I've tried everything else.'

It was true. He had tried all the professions open to a gentleman. He'd taken a commission in the Guards, which had lasted a month. He'd sat at a desk in the City for a week. He'd even spent a fortnight in some appalling barrister's chambers. It simply wasn't for him.

'Why won't people understand?' he complained. 'I *can't* work. I wasn't born to it. It is an unkindness of Providence, but there we are. I was born to be a landowner.'

'That's all very well, but in the meantime you've got to get along somehow, haven't you?' She shook her head. 'Such a shame that you couldn't bring yourself to be attentive to Aunt Salomon.'

'But how could I? I wasn't made to associate with Jews.'

'If you'd handled her properly, she'd have made you her heir.'

He thought for a moment. 'I don't suppose there's any chance that the old girl—'

'None whatsoever. I called on her last week.'

And how you must have enjoyed that, he thought, eyeing her with dislike.

It was all so confoundedly disagreeable. Why was everyone so hard on him? His needs were so few. An agreeable house, a few decent horses and perhaps a string of polo ponies. To be tolerably dressed, and to give the odd dinner for one's friends. To keep a dear girl in a pretty little apartment, and perhaps frequent one of the better houses when the dear girl was indisposed.

He allowed his mind to wander to the dear girl he'd left behind in Jamaica. He ought to buy her a little something when he was next in the West End. Perhaps one of those Japanese paper sun-umbrellas? It wouldn't cost much, and she would be so grateful. Girls like that were easily pleased.

'What you have to appreciate,' said Sibella, 'is that Papa isn't going to stand much more of this.' She opened her new crocodile handbag and frowned at the contents, then shut it with a snap. 'He's talking seriously of cutting you out of his will, and making Lyndon his heir.'

Alexander's mouth went dry.

Lyndon, heir to Parnassus? Caddish little Lyndon, with his hooked nose and his greasy black hair? It was inconceivable. Surely the governor wouldn't sink so low?

'Of course we must put a stop to that,' said Sibella, thereby reminding him why he preferred her to Davina. 'And as a first step, you absolutely *must* clear your debts.'

Alexander thought for a moment. 'When you marry this financier fellow the governor's got in his sights, surely he—'

'Mr Parnell,' said Sibella severely, 'is quite horribly strait-laced. The merest hint of gambling debts and he'll be off for good. And if that were to happen, which God forbid, then I'd be without a husband, and Papa would be without a business partner, and you, brother mine, would be out in the cold for good.'

'Which brings us neatly back to Sophie Monroe.'

'Precisely.'

'Don't *worry*, Sib. She'll come round, given time.'

'Unfortunately, Alexander, time is not in abundant supply.' She paused for effect. 'She intends to give part of her fortune to her brother-in-law.'

Alexander stared at her. 'But – you told me she'd only *sold* the property. You never mentioned—'

'Well, I'm mentioning it now.'

He turned his head and looked out across the park. 'Of course, he'll never accept it.'

'Why not? Heaven knows, you would.'

'Yes, but I'm not Cameron Lawe.'

Sibella snorted, as if to say that the man wasn't born who would decline a gift of several thousand pounds. 'Be that as it may, I take it that you now appreciate the need for speed?'

Slowly, Alexander nodded.

'Good,' said Sibella briskly. 'And you agree that you must return to Jamaica as soon as possible, and square things with Papa, and put beastly little Lyndon in his place once and for all?'

'And the best way of achieving that,' supplied Alexander, 'is by bringing out Sophie Monroe as my affianced bride.'

'Precisely.'

Again he ran his forefinger along his lower lip. Then he glanced at her and smiled. 'Don't worry, old girl. It's as good as done.'

She threw him a sceptical glance.

'Don't *worry*,' he said again. 'I wasn't born to fail.'

'You can always tell the ones on the skids,' said Austen's employer, 'by the state of their windows.'

He glanced up at the narrow, soot-blackened houses that seemed to lean towards each other across the street. 'If you've got curtains *and* blinds, then you're in clover. If you've had to sell the curtains, then things are getting dodgy. And when you're down to newspaper, it's all over bar the shouting.'

He turned up his collar and narrowed his eyes against the rain. They'd come out without their umbrellas and were getting gently soaked, but he didn't seem to notice. 'It's a funny thing,' he went on, 'but between a scrap of newspaper, and curtains and blinds, there's nothing but a bit of bad luck. A fall off a ladder. A bout of the fever. And suddenly you're down the drain, and you can't get out again.'

He'd been in a strange mood for days. Restless and angry, and more unpredictable than ever. Twice when Austen had gone downstairs in the night for a book, he'd found his employer standing at the window in his long Turkish dressing-gown, gazing out at the glistening street.

And this afternoon he'd suddenly decided to take Austen on what he called a 'little tour'. 'Time you got to know your own city,' he'd said with an angry glint in his eye.

They left Denmark Street and pushed through the crowds into Shaftesbury Avenue, then turned into Monmouth Street. Suddenly Austen didn't know where he was. He'd never seen so many second-hand clothes: rack upon rack of limp, greasy skirts and frayed jackets turning sadly in the rain. 'Where do they all come from?' he wondered aloud.

His employer threw him an irritable look. 'Dead people. Where d'you think?'

Austen blinked. 'But – can that be healthy?'

'What makes you think it's any healthier if you go to a tailor?'

They stopped before a narrow shop-front and his employer jerked his head, as if to illustrate his point. Inside, Austen saw a young woman on a stool, sewing a Norfolk jacket. Despite the cold, she wore only a poplin skirt and a soiled blouse, but as she hadn't yet attached the sleeves of the jacket, she'd pushed her arms through them for warmth. Austen couldn't help noticing that she wasn't wearing any stays. When she coughed, her front swung freely beneath the blouse.

'That,' said his employer dispassionately, 'is why you should never skimp on your tailor. She's got a nasty cough and she can't afford any coal, so why wouldn't she put on the sleeves for a bit of warmth? And if the poor cow's coming down with something, it's ten to one that you will too, when you put on your nice new togs.'

Austen was silent. He was recalling how his sister Iphigeneia had narrowly survived a bout of typhus the previous Christmas, shortly after taking delivery of her new winter costume. He only remembered the connection at all because Iffy had complained about having to alter the wretched thing after she'd lost so much flesh.

'Come on,' said his employer. 'I want to take a look at my old beat.'

To Austen's relief, they hailed a cab. His employer told the driver to take them to East Street, south of the river. As they were passing the Strand, he said abruptly, 'D'you remember Holywell Street?'

Austen's ears burned. 'Um, I can't say that I—'

'Of course you do! Everyone knew Holywell Street. Best pornography shops in London. My sister Lil used to make a good living posing for photos. Shame they knocked it down to make way for the Strand.'

Austen felt his face growing hot. He was beginning to resent this 'little tour'. What did his employer hope to achieve, and why was he inflicting it on him? Did he wish to humiliate him? Did he hold him responsible, as a member of the peerage?

They crossed the river, and eventually the cab pulled up in a dingy part of Lambeth. Austen peered through the window with apprehension. But to his intense relief, his employer told the cabby to wait. 'Here we are,' he said with an ironic flourish. 'East Street. My God, but it's changed.'

For better or worse? wondered Austen, resisting the urge to take out his handkerchief and press it to his mouth.

Grimy tenement blocks towered overhead, criss-crossed with soot-streaked washing. In the middle of the street, an oily brown puddle spread outwards from a clogged drain, from which came a stink so powerful that it caught at the back of his throat and made black spots dart before his eyes. He fought the urge to retch.

Three urchins with fleabitten faces stared at them from a doorway. A frowzy woman scratched her arm with a vigour that could only mean lice. Above her ear was a bloody patch of naked scalp where a hank of hair had been torn out by the roots.

'This used to be just houses,' murmured his employer,

shaking his head. 'Five families to a house. None of these bloody tenements.'

'I thought you lived north of the river,' said Austen with an edge to his voice.

'Shelton Street? That was later, after Ma died.'

One of the urchins had sidled up for a closer look. He had scabby bare feet and a pinched, knowing face, and he seemed to be sizing them up for what he could steal.

Austen's employer had been gazing up at the windows, but somehow he sensed the urchin's scrutiny, and turned to look at him. 'I wouldn't,' he said softly.

The boy met his eyes, and backed away.

Austen said, 'You said your mother died. How did she – er?'

His employer shook his head, his face impassive. 'I don't know. One day she just didn't wake up. We thought maybe it was because Pa had knocked her about a bit worse than usual.' He paused. 'It was summertime. We couldn't afford to bury her for a week. Christ. That smell. I'll never forget it.'

Austen swallowed hard.

They turned and walked back towards the cab, but after a few paces Austen became aware that the urchin had followed them.

His employer laughed. 'He doesn't give up, does he? Here you are.' He tossed the boy a sovereign. 'That's for persistence.'

As they were nearing the cab, he glanced back for a last look. 'Look, d'you see over there?' he said to Austen, pointing up at one of the windows. 'Newspapers. I told you. It never fails. And that one over there,' he added with a touch of scorn, 'they've got pretensions. Bit of old wall-paper off a building site.'

Austen was nettled. 'What's wrong with that? At least they're trying.'

'To be what?' sneered his employer. 'Respectable?'

'Well, and what if they are?'

'*Respectable*. Respectable.' His green eyes glittered. 'It's hankering after respectability that keeps you in places like this. Isaac's ma was "respectable". He told me once that she used to put on her hat to scrub the sodding doorstep. And when she took a bundle of togs to the dolly – that's the pawnbroker's to you – she'd shove it under her coat so that nobody'd see.' He paused. 'Austen, if I'd been like that, I'd still be here, in East Street. I'd be in awe of people like you.'

Austen didn't know what to say.

They got back into the cab, and his employer gave directions for a Poor Law charity in Centaur Street. As they rattled over the cobbles, Austen cleared his throat. 'Forgive me, Mr Kelly, but I feel I must ask something. Why did you bring me along today?'

'What do you mean?'

Austen felt himself reddening. 'It's just that I can't help feeling that you're enjoying my discomfort, and I'm not at all sure that that's fair. I mean, clearly I know nothing about the Poor, but I don't believe that that in itself makes me worthy of blame, or – or humiliation. After all, until recently, you yourself didn't know a great deal about – well, about—'

'About gentlemen's clubs,' put in his employer, 'and Fortnum's, and riding in Rotton Row.' He tapped his fingernail against his teeth. 'Why did I bring you along? I've been wondering that myself. But you're wrong, it wasn't to humiliate you. I wasn't thinking of you at all.'

Austen blinked.

'I suppose – I wanted a witness.'

'A witness?' Austen was nonplussed.

His employer studied the crowds hurrying in the rain. 'So many changes,' he said quietly, as if to himself. 'Half the old slums cleared. The rookeries torn down. Even Holywell Street gone. It's as if none of it ever happened. It's as if none of them ever—' He broke off, shaking his head.

'I'm not sure that I understand,' said Austen.

'I'm not sure that I want you to,' his employer snapped.

Austen folded his hands about his walking-stick, and resolved to say no more.

Eventually the cab pulled up outside a dingy little house in a cobbled street just south of Waterloo, with a railway bridge at the end. Above the door hung a peeling sign: *St Cuthbert's Charity for the Deserving Poor.* Through the grimy windows Austen could just make out people moving around inside. He was about to remark that the place looked rather busy when he spotted the brougham parked across the street.

His heart skipped a beat. It was the same carriage that belonged to the fascinating young widow in New Cavendish Street. He was certain of it. He recognized the L-shaped scratch on the door panel. 'Shall we – go in and take a look?' he said in a strangled voice.

His employer shook his head. 'No, I just wanted to see it.'

Austen's disappointment was so sharp that he almost winced. 'It seems a shame,' he ventured. 'I mean, to have come all this way.'

Again the shake of the head. 'You go ahead, if you want to. I'll stay here.'

'No, no,' murmured Austen. If his employer didn't come too, he'd never have the courage to go in alone.

His employer leaned forward and tapped the roof of the cab to tell the driver to move on.

Another chance missed, thought Austen, shuddering with self-loathing. I mean, dash it all, that's probably the best opportunity you'll ever get. And now you've absolutely gone and let it slip.

As the cab rattled off down the street, Sophie fielded the Reverend Agate's exasperated plea for quiet, while straining to hear old Mrs Shaughnessy's whispered request for an infirmary certificate, and telling Mrs Carpenter to wait her turn, and trying to ignore Sibella, who was standing at the window with a handkerchief pressed ostentatiously to her mouth.

'Sophie, do hurry up,' said Sibella, raising her voice above the determined grizzling of Mrs Carpenter's baby. 'I can't let the carriage wait for much longer in a place like this.'

The Reverend Agate flung her an outraged glare, which she ignored.

'I'll be ready in a moment,' said Sophie, watching in relief as he beat a dignified retreat upstairs. She handed Mrs Shaughnessy her certificate, and took a bottle of quieting syrup from the shelf and gave it to Mrs Carpenter. 'A teaspoonful three times a day,' she said, trying not to look at the baby, which was particularly unappealing, and had a habit of trailing snot over everything.

'There,' she breathed, when the door tinkled shut. She sat down at her desk and put her elbows on the pile of Registers and her head in her hands. There was a rhythmic pounding in her temples. Her eyes felt scratchy with fatigue. She hadn't slept properly for days. She'd been worrying about Fever Hill, and whether Madeleine had got her letter yet.

Why was everything so mixed up? She longed for it to be next week, when Alexander and Sibella would be safely on the mail steamer bound for Jamaica. And she wished she'd had the strength of mind to throw out the rest of the Reverend Chamberlaine's Registers, instead of letting them pile up on her desk like this. She was beginning to find his relentless acidity strangely depressing.

Sibella stared in horrified fascination as Mrs Carpenter made off down the street, hoisting the wailing infant on her hip. 'Sophie, how can you *bear* this? I shouldn't have dreamed of coming if I'd known it would be half so appalling.'

'I never asked you to,' Sophie muttered ungraciously.

Sibella pursed her lips. 'Well, do forgive me for wanting to deliver a friend from the horrors of the Bakerloo line.'

Sophie did not reply. She was looking down at the topmost Register, lying open on the pile. 'Jan. 22nd, 1889,' she read. 'Mrs Bridget Kelly, 39 East Street.' Something about the address was vaguely familiar.

'Were you expecting visitors?' said Sibella.

'What?'

'That cab. It stopped outside, and then moved off.'

'Perhaps they were lost,' said Sophie.

East Street. The Kellys of East Street.

Oh, God. No.

We lived in two rooms on East Street, he'd told her that day at the clinic. She hadn't thought of it in years – hadn't wanted to think of it – but now the memory was so sharp that she could almost see him.

'If you've finished,' said Sibella impatiently, 'then we can go. Sophie? Are you listening?'

'What? In a moment.' She put out a tentative hand and touched the Register. Suddenly she was frightened. She didn't want to know what it said. Why should she? That was all over years ago.

Mrs Bridget Kelly, she read, *39 East Street. Immigrant Irish. Aged 32, but looks 50, she is so raddled & unkempt. Husband Padraig a coal-heaver & a low radical, currently 'indisposed' (i.e., he drinks), who got himself dismissed for attending a 'union' meeting, and is now learning that the world can do without him. The family owes 5 wks' rent at 10/- per week, landlady requires 15/- down, which Mrs Kelly says she has not got; she says they must remove to cheaper lodgings if it cannot be found. She makes 2/6d a week by piece-work, & the children contribute. The eldest boy, Jack, 14, works as a ganger at 4/- per week. The girls, Katherine, 15, & Lilian, 13, are silk-winders at 2/- each, but widely reported to be engaged in immoral activities, although Mrs Kelly of course denies it. Benedict, 8, is 'supposed at school'; Robert, 2, is a defective with rickets; and the babe in arms is yellow & ill-favoured.*

Benedict, she thought numbly. I always thought it would have been Benjamin. Or simply Ben.

She didn't attempt to convince herself that this was some other family. Of course it was his.

Was this the real reason she'd taken the position at St Cuthbert's in the first place? Was this why, without even admitting it to herself, she had trawled through volume after volume of the Reverend Chamberlaine's Registers?

Well, now she had her reward. This sick pounding in

her heart. This gnawing conviction that wherever she went and whatever she did, she would never be free of him.

'Sophie,' said Sibella. 'I really am about to lose my patience.'

'Coming,' she murmured.

Manifestly, wrote the Reverend Chamberlaine, *the Kellys are far from respectable, and quite undeserving of any kind of aid. I told Mrs Kelly so in no uncertain terms, and suggested that, as they are Catholics, she might apply to the authorities at St George's. She said that St George's had already turned her down, & that we were her last resort. Scarcely complimentary! Application refused.*

Sophie sat blinking at the crabbed, backward-slanting writing. She shut the Register, grabbed hold of the whole pile of volumes, and crammed them into the waste-paper basket. Then she stuffed an old newspaper on top, to cover them up.

She got to her feet, and wiped her palms on her thighs, as if to rub away the last trace of them. 'There,' she said. 'There.' Then she turned to Sibella. 'I'll fetch my hat, and we can go.'

CHAPTER TWENTY-TWO

Everything's different since Pa got the sack.

When they lived in East Street, Ben was always out on the click with Jack or Lil. But now they've moved north of the river, and Lil's down Holywell Street all the time, and Jack's got a job down the docks, and moved into a dosshouse on the West India Dock Road. Ben never thought he'd miss him but he does.

He never thought he'd miss Ma neither, nor the baby, but he does. Everything's different. Pa's down the Lion all the time, and when he's back he's yelling at Kate or watching her like a cat, which is worse. And Kate's different, too. She gets this wary look when Pa's around, and she don't laugh no more.

Robbie's the only one that's stayed the same. He never even noticed when they left East Street. Just found hisself a corner in their new room and settled down to wait for another spider.

Yesterday, Kate told Ben there's something wrong with Robbie. 'He's one button short of a row,' she said. 'You'll have to look out for him, Ben. You're the big brother now.'

The way she said it. It made him go cold inside. 'But you'll be here too,' he said. 'You'll be looking out for him too.'

She put down the violet she'd just finished and reached for another. 'Yes, but not for ever.'

'Why not?'

'Because I won't.'

'But you're coming hop-picking, yeh? End of summer, we always go down Kent for the hops.'

She opened her mouth, then shut it again. 'I will if I can.'

That was yesterday, and it's been eating away at him ever since. What did she mean, 'if I can'? What did she mean?

So this morning he went down the docks to ask Jack. But Jack wasn't up for talking. 'Shove off,' he snapped without breaking stride. 'If I blab on the job I get the boot. Don't you know that yet?' So Ben hung about all day, waiting for him to finish. But when the whistle went, Jack pushed past him and disappeared into the dosshouse.

Ben knew better than to follow. Jack's a docker now. He'll thrash the stuffing out of you soon as look at you.

Ben hates the docks – and not just because they've took his big brother. He hates all them tattooed Lascars and darkies and Americans. He hates the din of the steam cranes and the rattle of the trolleys. But most of all, he hates the sugar.

First day he come, he thought it was topper. Sacks and sacks of it. It's all over the quays, all brown and sticky, and the air's thick with the smell of it. So soon you're stuffing your pockets and cramming your gob – and then you're down on your knees, catting it up again.

It gets everywhere, the smell of that sugar. It gets into your togs and your skin and your dreams. It's on him now as he's padding the hoof back to Shelton Street.

He's all in, he is. Padders throbbing and sore, black dots darting in front of his eyes, and so hungry it hurts. But he's just turning into their street when he remembers he was to stop off at the chemist's and pick up a pennorth of blackstick for Lil. Bugger. She'll be well narked that he forgot.

'What's it for, anyhow?' he'd asked that morning when she give him the penny.

She rolled her eyes. 'Don't you know?'

'Come on, Lil. What's it for?'

She grinned. 'You pinch off a bit and roll it into pills and, hey presto, you're not in the family way no more.'

'Get along!'

'It's bible, honest. Works a treat. Only you got to take care cos it's lead, so if you eat too much you turn blue and snuff it. Horribly.' She pulls a face, and they both laugh.

Lil's all right. But she'll have to wait till tomorrow for her blackstick, cos he's too beat to go back for it now. Anyway, it's not his fault if she's got a dumpling on.

Soon as he gets into their house he knows there's trouble. All yelling and banging coming from upstairs – from their place.

He stops at the foot of the stairs, feeling suddenly blue. He don't want no trouble. He just wants to crawl into the corner with Robbie, and have a kip.

All of a sudden the door opens, and out comes Pa. He stumbles down the stairs, then sees Ben and lurches to a stop. He's well basted, and not too steady on his pins; but steady enough to grab Ben by the shoulder and shake him like a rat.

Ben knows better than to sing out. He don't breathe, don't move. Just waits for it to stop.

Pa puts his face down close and peers into his eyes. He looks angry, but also sort of ashamed. Then he chucks Ben against the wall, and lumbers out.

Rubbing his shoulder, Ben picks hisself up off the floor. No harm done, he thinks. Pa will be down the Lion for a couple of hours at least, so everything's topper.

Couple of minutes later, Kate comes out onto the landing. His heart goes still. She's all poshed up in her blue frock and the hat with the violets round the rim. One eye is swelling shut, and she's lost the buttons down the front of her jacket. Then he sees the carpet-bag in her hand, and it's like he's been kicked in the belly. No no no.

He shoves his cap back on his head and puts on a cheery look. Maybe if he's cheery, she won't go. 'Where you off to, then?' he goes.

She comes down the stairs, the carpet-bag bumping

against her thigh. Then she sits on the bottom step. 'Come here, Ben,' she goes, very low and quiet.

Close up, her good eye is very blue, but red round the rim. 'Ben,' she says, rubbing his arm as if to make it better. 'I got to go, Ben.'

He opens his mouth but nothing comes out. He just stands there gaping like a fish.

'I got to. I can't stop here no more.'

He tries to swallow but he can't. He's got this lump stuck in his windpipe. It's like a bit of bread or something.

'I'm going to Jeb,' she says, not looking at him. 'I'll send you word, soon as I know where we'll be. But you got to promise not to tell Pa.'

'Kate – no.' He reaches up to touch her face, and misses and knocks a violet off her hat. He picks it up and brushes it off, and tries to shove it back on again, but he can't. Everything's swimming. He can't hardly see.

'If I stop here, I'll end up killing him. Or he'll kill me.'

'I'll kill him for you,' he mumbles.

She touches his cheek. 'You would an' all, you daft little bugger. That's another reason why I got to go.'

He grabs her hand. 'I'll come with you.'

Her face crumples. 'You can't.'

'Why not? I'll be ever so—'

'Ben – no. Jeb can't take you too. How can he? He can't afford to take me, let alone you and Robbie.'

'I don't care about Robbie!'

'Well you got to. You got to stop here and look after him. You're the big brother now.'

'No – Kate, no. No!'

He's still yelling as she pushes past him and yanks open the door and runs out into the street.

Someone knocked on the door of the study, and Ben raised his head from his hands and looked about him without recognition. He drew a deep breath and rubbed his face. Then he cleared his throat. 'What is it?' he said.

The butler opened the door. 'Mr Warburton to see you, sir.'

Ben glanced at the clock on the desk. Ten o'clock in the

morning. Warburton was on time, as usual. Private detectives seemed to make a point of that.

He gazed at his hands on the green morocco desktop, and struggled to get back to reality. It was three hours since he'd woken from the dream, but he still couldn't shake it off. It had left him feeling drained, with a gnawing sense of loss.

Discreetly, the butler cleared his throat.

Ben looked about him and squared his shoulders. 'Send him in,' he said.

Sophie heard the front door opening and closing with stealthy, conspiratorial softness. She pulled on her dressing-gown and moved out onto the landing to listen.

Down in the entrance hall, Mrs Vaughan-Pargeter shooed away the housemaid and tiptoed forward to extend a tremulous greeting to Sibella Palairet. 'I'm *so* sorry, my dear,' she whispered, shaking her head so violently that her powdered jowls quivered and her jet beads glittered on her chiffon-clad bulk, 'but I'm terribly afraid that she won't see anyone at all.'

'Not even me?' murmured Sibella, aghast.

Mrs Vaughan-Pargeter shook her head. 'The thing is, she's still so frightfully *down*. Won't eat a morsel. Can't seem to get up an interest in anything. It's all the fault of that dreadful, dreadful man.'

'But surely . . .'

Their voices faded as they moved into the drawing-room.

Sophie went back into her room and shut the door, and stood leaning against it. The distance to the bed seemed endless. She slid down onto the floor and clasped her arms about her knees.

That dreadful, dreadful man.

But the Reverend Agate wasn't dreadful. He was simply right. He had been right to be angry and horrified, and relieved. He had been right to lose his temper. 'You could have *killed* that child!' he'd bellowed, brandishing the offending bottle. An opiate strong enough to put a grown man deeply to sleep – and Sophie had given it to Mrs Carpenter for soothing her baby.

You could have killed that child!

Of course the Reverend Agate had lost his temper. What did he care that Sophie had simply made a mistake? What did he care that the baby had eventually awoken with no ill effects, after giving his mother the first bit of peace she'd had in months? The point was, the Reverend Agate was responsible. There had been questions from the rector and the St Cuthbert's Guardians, and a stern note from the doctor at the infirmary. Mrs Carpenter had forced her way in and berated him like a fishwife in the hopes of eliciting a payoff.

You could have killed that child.

The words drummed in her ears. They reverberated round the walls.

She was haunted by the randomness of it, by the complete absence of warning. She had started that fateful day as she'd started countless others before: she had bathed and dressed and eaten her breakfast, and opened her letters. Then she'd made her way to St Cuthbert's with the usual sense of pleasant tedium and mild exasperation. She'd argued gently with the Reverend Agate. The afternoon had become busy. Sibella had arrived unannounced.

Then, without knowing it, she had stepped over the edge of a precipice. She'd handed the wrong bottle to Mrs Carpenter, and sent her away. Only the infant's iron constitution had prevented a charge of manslaughter. If the child had been a little weaker, or Mrs Carpenter a little more generous with the 'quieting syrup', Sophie Monroe would have killed a child.

Sophie Monroe, child-killer. Every time she thought of it she broke out in a cold sweat.

She could never go back to St Cuthbert's. She could never face anyone again. All thoughts of Ben, and the Reverend Chamberlaine's Register, had been pushed aside. Fever Hill no longer mattered. Nothing mattered but this.

The Reverend Agate was right. She had no business

trying to help people. No business going anywhere near the sick.

She felt as if she were standing at the edge of a volcano, looking down and watching the thin crust cracking open beneath her feet to reveal the churning orange lava below. All it took was a single mistake, and a child was dead. The wrong bottle taken from a shelf in an unguarded moment. The slightest symptom missed or mistaken. The seemingly innocuous stomach ache which turns out to be a deadly brain fever.

As if it were happening all over again, she remembered those first terrible days after Fraser's death. Everybody kept telling her that it wasn't her fault. But it was. She knew. *She knew.*

She glanced at her jewel box on the dressing-table. In the bottom tray lay a tiny envelope of ivory card containing a folded piece of blue tissue paper; and inside that, a lock of her nephew's hair.

Clemency had pressed it on her the day she'd left Eden; she hadn't known, this time, how to refuse it. All these years it had lain at the bottom of her jewellery case: unopened, unexamined, but never quite forgotten. Now she could almost see it opening of its own accord.

You could have killed that child.

How had she ever dared to help the sick? How had she ever dared to do anything?

The private detective perched on the edge of his chair and ran a finger inside his cheap celluloid collar. He was honest, painstaking, imaginative and anxious. Ben guessed that somewhere he had an anxious wife and a clutch of anxious children.

'To date,' said the detective, anxiously scrutinizing his notebook, as if it might contain some revelation that he'd hitherto overlooked, 'a degree of progress has been made on your – on – the mother, sir.' He paused. 'Unfortunately, the – er, remains, are proving somewhat inaccessible.'

Ben leaned back in his chair and tapped the desktop with his fountain pen. 'Meaning?'

Again the detective ran a finger inside his collar. 'I regret to inform— That is to say— There has been a degree of, er, construction work over what was once the churchyard.'

'What kind of construction work?'

'A – a brewery.'

Ben thought for a moment. Then he burst out laughing. Poor old Ma. She'd never had much luck when she was alive, and now they'd gone and built a bloody brewery on top of her.

The detective was disconcerted. He looked down at his notes, and then away. He pretended interest in the study's appointments.

Ben stopped laughing as abruptly as he'd started. Again he tapped the desktop. 'What about – the older daughter?' It annoyed him that he couldn't bring himself to say her name. But he couldn't. Not after that bloody dream.

'Ah, yes,' said the detective, relieved to be back on track. 'Katherine.' His face fell. 'I regret, sir. Nothing as yet.'

Ben put down the pen and kneaded his temple.

'But the younger brother,' said the detective, brightening, 'now that is beginning to look reasonably promising. Yes, I think I may go so far as to say that in a few weeks' time—'

Ben shot him a look. 'Are you sure it's him?'

'Why – yes, I believe so.'

'I don't want belief. I want certainty.'

The detective swallowed. He looked like a rabbit caught in a flashlight. 'Of course, sir. Sir has always been most clear about that. And I have noted down here all the – the means of identification. The name-plates, the crucifixes, and so on.' He held up the notebook as evidence. 'Depend upon it, sir. There will be no mistake.'

'There'd better not be,' said Ben softly, still holding the detective's gaze. 'I shall know it if you play me false. Remember that.'

A sheen of sweat broke out on the detective's forehead. 'Sir, I would never dream— Truly. I would never dream—'

Ben leaned back in his chair and passed a hand across his eyes. He was disgusted with himself for bullying this weak, honest man. Of course the poor bloke wouldn't dare to lie. That was why he'd got the job in the first place. 'Anything else?' he said curtly.

The detective studied his notebook with a hopeful look. Then his shoulders sagged. 'Not as such.' Suddenly the spirit seemed to go out of him. He seemed to think that he was going to get the sack.

Again Ben kneaded his temple. All this effort, and he still couldn't find Kate.

And she wanted him to. She did, didn't she? That was what this was all about. The dreams. And that time in Jamaica when she'd appeared to Evie.

But why Jamaica? he thought suddenly. Why only in Jamaica, and never Brazil or Sierra Leone or Panama?

Jamaica.

He sat up. Was that what she was trying to tell him?

His heart raced. He forgot about being tired. *Jamaica.*

He'd been planning on going back for some time now; just to show them what he'd made of himself, and maybe teach one or two of them a lesson. So why not take his dead along too?

Why had he never thought of it before? It was perfect. The clean, sweet air. The warmth. The colours. It was everything they'd never had when they were alive.

He glanced at the detective, who sat meekly with his head down, waiting to be sacked. 'In a few days,' said Ben, 'I shall be leaving London for good.'

The detective raised his head and gave him a small, defeated smile. 'Very good, sir.'

'I shall be going to Jamaica.'

The narrow shoulders sagged. 'Yes, sir. To be sure.'

'I shall want you to continue your work. Redouble your efforts. I'll pay you a monthly retainer. Say, ten pounds. Will that do?'

The detective's mouth fell open. Two spots of colour appeared on his sallow cheeks.

'Will that do?' Ben said again.

'Yes, sir. Of course, sir. And – if I may say so, sir, more than generous—'

'I shall want a report every week, without fail.'

Weekly reports, wrote the detective in his careful copperplate, and underlined it twice. Then he raised his head, eager for more. 'And where shall I, er—'

Ben waved a hand. 'My secretary will sort out the details. But be sure and address the reports to him, rather than to me. The Honourable Frederick Austen, Fever Hill, Trelawny.'

The detective nodded, and wrote it all down in his book.

The curtain had gone down on the first act of *Il Trovatore*, and Sibella had hurried away to talk to an acquaintance in another box, having despatched Alexander to order champagne.

Sophie didn't want any champagne, but Sibella insisted. 'You can't come to the opera and not have champagne.'

'Can't we have the champagne without the opera?' suggested Alexander.

'Ridiculous boy,' said Sibella. 'Now do what you're told and go and fetch.'

While they were gone, Sophie sat and fiddled with the tassel on her evening bag, and hoped they would come back soon. It was her first time out of the house in a fortnight, and she couldn't shake off the sense that everyone was looking at her. *There's that woman who almost killed a baby. Deplorable case. Deplorable.*

It was ridiculous, of course, for no-one knew about Mrs Carpenter's baby, and if they had known they wouldn't have cared. But she couldn't help herself.

To her relief, Alexander swiftly returned with a waiter in his wake bearing an ice bucket, glasses, and two bottles of Piper-Heidsieck.

As she watched him dealing with the waiter, she felt a surge of gratitude. How amazing to think that just two weeks before, she had longed to be free of the Trahernes. Then had come the horror at St Cuthbert's. And after that

Sibella had quietly extended their visit, to help her friend through what she called 'everything'. And now Sophie couldn't do without them. She didn't *want* to do without them, not ever again.

Sometimes, a part of her mind would warn that she was becoming dependent on them. But then reality swiftly returned. She wasn't *becoming* dependent. She already was. It had been self-delusion to imagine that she could be anything else.

Once, she had believed that she could be self-reliant, that she could achieve something by herself. Now she knew that to be a mistake. St Cuthbert's had taught her that.

'Sophie,' said Alexander, as he shooed the waiter out of the box and handed her a glass of champagne. 'Sophie – I wonder, could I talk to you for a moment?'

'That's what you're doing,' she said with a smile. She took a sip of champagne. It was just what she needed: icy and dry and delicious.

'Quite so,' he murmured. He paused, as if composing his words.

She knew what was coming next. She had thought about it a great deal. And she knew that what she was about to do was right.

'I don't know if you remember,' he began, 'but a few weeks ago, I said that I would wait a while, before I asked you whether you would—'

'Yes,' she said.

He gave her an enquiring glance.

'Yes,' she said again. 'The answer, Alexander, is yes.'

CHAPTER TWENTY-THREE

Fever Hill took Ben completely by surprise.

He had never expected to like it. He'd only bought it on a whim, because it amused him to imagine their faces when they found out. But when he got there, he fell in love with it.

He arrived in May, just after the rains, when the whole estate was bursting with life. The air buzzed and hummed and chirruped. The trees were in full flower: lemon-yellow cassias and dusty pink oleanders; vermilion poincianas and powder-blue jacaranda. One morning he stood on the great marble steps and looked out over the shimmering cane-pieces and thought in astonishment, Yes. I'm home.

For the first time in his life he was at peace. No more restlessness, no more black moods. No more dreams of the old days. He was finished with all that. He'd left it behind in London.

For two months he lived peacefully on the property. He left the running of the estate to the manager who'd handled it under Cameron Lawe, and bought half a dozen thoroughbreds, and set about schooling them. Isaac came to stay for weeks at a time, preferring to walk and survey the hills, rather than run his own place at Arethusa, on the other side of Falmouth. Even Austen was enjoying himself, having confessed somewhat sheepishly to a passion for bird-watching.

The weeks slipped by. Ben watched in amusement as

Isaac and Austen finally became used to one another, even venturing out on joint bird-watching and surveying expeditions. He himself spent his days on long solitary rides, and his nights sitting up late, drinking rum and working his way through the latest crate of books. He was at peace.

Then, in the middle of July, the telegram arrived from the private detective.

Your brother Robbie, sisters Lilian and Katherine found. Report follows. Request instructions.

Robbie and Lil and Kate. Found. After all this time.

He stood on the verandah blinking at the telegram; trying to suppress an odd, nagging sense of apprehension.

They *deserve* to be out here, he told himself angrily. They deserve to escape the stink and din of London for the peace of Fever Hill.

But he couldn't quite shrug off a suspicion that whatever had been plaguing him in London was now following him out.

Two days later, he and Austen caught the train to Kingston, and plunged headlong into arrangements for bringing out the bodies. They spent hours in shipping offices and the Telegraph Department. Ben forced himself to refer to his brother and sisters as 'the remains', slamming the lid down hard on thoughts of the rough, larky street kids he'd grown up with. Then, when he couldn't stand it any longer, he left the rest to Austen, and took Evie out to lunch.

He took her to the Constant Spring Hotel, six miles out of town, and sat back in the hired carriage, and enjoyed her enjoyment. She loved it all. She loved the drive through the foothills ablaze with poinciana and bougainvillaea. She loved the great hotel with its manicured gardens and magnificent dining-terraces, and the enormous French menu that was entirely free of any taint of Jamaica. She loved the fact that their fellow diners – mostly wealthy English and American tourists – were all white, except for one well-to-do coloured family whom she felt entitled to ignore, as they were darker than she.

She wore a narrow gown of pale green silk which suited her willowy figure, and a wide-brimmed hat of fine pale straw, elegantly trimmed with cream silk flowers. Both hat and gown looked expensive, and Ben wondered how she could afford them on a teacher's salary. But he dismissed that as none of his business, and told her that she looked enchanting.

She acknowledged the compliment with a stately little nod, then leaned towards him and whispered, 'Our fellow diners probably think I'm your mistress.'

'I wondered about that,' he replied. 'Do you mind?'

She put her head on one side and studied him. Then she smiled and shook her head. 'Just so long as you explain yourself to the school governors if word ever gets around.'

'I'm at your disposal,' he said with a mock bow.

She took a sip of champagne and threw him a mischievous glance. 'So what *about* that, Ben? Have you got yourself a mistress yet?'

'You know very well that I haven't,' he said mildly. He should have known that she would ask. It seemed to offend her sensibilities to see him still unmarried at the age of thirty.

'Cho!' she said, lapsing into *patois* to tease him. 'You fooling me up, boy? What are you waiting for? You must be the despair of every Society matron on the Northside!'

'Very sad, I agree,' he said drily. 'Now what about you? When am I going to be introduced to your mysterious sweetheart?'

Evie snorted. 'Never, if I have my way.'

'Why not?'

'Because you'd grill him like a snapper and chase the poor man away. Sometimes you act as if you're my big brother.'

He shifted his water glass a fraction to the right. 'Sometimes that's how I feel.'

'But Ben,' she said gently, 'I don't need a big brother. I'm twenty-eight years old.'

And of course she was right. She had done extraordinarily well for herself. She had an excellent teaching position in one of the best girls' academies on the island, and a pretty little house in a leafy, respectable street in Liguanea, on the slopes above Kingston. She even spoke differently: in an Anglicized Creole accent which only occasionally lapsed into *patois* for fun.

It was all a million miles away from the old slave village. And Ben knew better than to remind her of that. In seven years, she had never been back to Trelawny. She never mentioned her mother, or the visions she'd had as a girl.

Shortly after his arrival, he had asked her about that. She'd turned on him. 'That's over,' she'd snapped, her lovely face ablaze. 'I'll thank you never to mention it again.' Judging from the strength of her reaction, it wasn't over at all. But he'd refrained from pointing that out.

The waiter came and refilled their glasses, and Evie applied herself to her pineapple ice, stabbing at it delicately with her spoon. 'So why'd you buy it, Ben?' she said suddenly. 'Why'd you go and buy Fever Hill?'

He took a cigar from his case and turned it in his fingers. 'I felt like it,' he said sharply.

If she noticed his tone she gave no sign of it. 'But you could've had any estate in Jamaica. Why Fever Hill? Is it because of S—'

'I don't know,' he snapped. 'Can we talk about something else?'

She studied him for a moment, and her long almond-shaped eyes were impossible to read. Then she put down her spoon and took a sip of champagne. 'You bought it because it belonged to Sophie,' she said calmly.

'Evie—'

'– because you can't forget her. Because she broke your heart.'

'I bought it,' he said between his teeth, 'because it came on the market, and I liked the idea of annoying Cornelius Traherne. Now can we please talk of something else.'

She put down her glass and looked at him, and smiled. 'Annoying Cornelius Traherne. Now that's something with which I can truly sympathize.'

He pretended to be amused, but she wasn't fooled. She had spoilt the day, and she knew it – although she seemed unrepentant.

They finished their lunch with a strained attempt at good humour, then he drove her back to Liguanea and dropped her off at her pretty little house. She made him promise not to leave it too long before he came back to town, and when he told her that he was busy at Fever Hill she only smiled and wished him luck. He didn't ask her what she meant.

Back at the hotel, he found a note from Austen. *Complications re shipping have sent me back to Port Royal. Irritating, but capable of resolution. Should be back by six. A.* Ben cursed under his breath. He didn't want to be on his own just now. He didn't want a chance to brood on what Evie had said.

He went out onto the verandah and ordered tea and a newspaper, and stood with his hands in his pockets, gazing at the peaceful little groups of tourists strolling beneath the royal palms, and beyond them the fishing-boats bobbing in the harbour.

The Myrtle Bank Hotel was the best in town, and occupied a magnificent position on Harbour Street with far-reaching views of the sea. Like much of Kingston, it had been destroyed by the earthquake three years before, but had since been lavishly rebuilt. Everything about it was new and rich and recently established. Rather like me, thought Ben. The idea amused him, and made him feel a little better.

The tea arrived, and with it the *Daily Gleaner*. He sat down and forced himself to read every item on every page, determined to keep the black mood at bay. He ploughed through the foreign news which had come in over the wires, and the local happenings. He learned whose horse had won the King's Purse at the Spanish Town meeting, and that the Jamaica Coloured Choir was successfully touring England, and that the Governor's daughter was leaving on the *Atranta* for a holiday in the Mother Country.

Underneath that, there was a small paragraph which

he nearly missed, for a waiter came up and asked if he needed anything more. *Arrived by the mail steamer yesterday morning*, he read as he waved the man away, *Mr Augustus Parnell the noted City financier, travelling with Mr Alexander Traherne of Parnassus Estate, Mrs Sibella Palairet, and Miss Sophie Monroe, latterly of Fever Hill Estate. The party will be staying at the Myrtle Bank Hotel for a fortnight before travelling on to Trelawny. It is with great pleasure that this correspondent has learned that Mr Traherne and Miss Monroe have recently become engaged to be married.*

Dinner was over, and golden light streamed out onto the hotel lawns. Fireflies spangled the hibiscus bushes. Ratbats dived after moths besieging the electric globes on the terraces. The waters of the harbour shimmered in the cool blue moonlight.

It was a peaceful sight, and Ben, standing with Austen on the balcony of his suite, wished he could take pleasure in it. But his sense of enjoyment had drained away like water into sand. First Evie's cross-questioning; then half a dozen lines in a newspaper.

So much for peace, he thought, if that's all it takes to destroy it.

He lit a cigar and studied the little pools of yellow light on the terraces below, where dress-coated gentlemen and bejewelled ladies murmured over coffee and liqueurs. He couldn't see anyone he recognized. He despised himself for looking.

At his side, Austen asked if anything was wrong. Ben shook his head. 'Just run through what you were saying again?'

Austen hesitated. 'You mean, about the – er, arrangements?'

'Well of course,' snapped Ben. 'What d'you think I meant?'

Austen did not reply.

Ben ground out his cigar and reached for another. 'Just run through it again, will you?'

The waiter came and cleared away the dinner things, and set out coffee and brandy. Austen waited till the man had gone, then went through the arrangements again. Ben turned back to the terraces, and failed to hear a word.

They had dined in his suite because he disliked the idea of bumping into her in the public rooms. He hated himself for his cowardice – and even more for his stupidity. Why had it never occurred to him that she might return to Jamaica? Why had it never occurred to him that she might marry – and that when she did, she would be bound to pick that most appropriate of suitors, Alexander Traherne?

Half a dozen lines in a newspaper, and his peace was gone. Was that all it took?

But why should it matter where she was or what she did? Half a dozen lines about someone he hadn't seen for years? Why should it *matter*?

He smoked his cigar and paced the balcony, aware of Austen's scrutiny. He felt heavy with anger – and with something else: a kind of fear.

Fever Hill was only four miles from Parnassus. Would she live at the great house with her new husband, or would Cornelius give them the house at Waytes Valley? Would he be faced with breathless little bulletins in the *Falmouth Gazette* about the wedding celebrations, and – the christenings? Would the young Mrs Traherne force him out of Fever Hill as she'd forced him out of Jamaica?

No. *No.* He wouldn't let her do that.

Behind him Austen stopped his recital, and asked if he'd care for a brandy. Ben shook his head and continued to pace.

And yet when you think about it, he reflected as he watched a mongoose slipping silently across the lawns, you've had a lucky escape. If it hadn't been for that piece in the *Gleaner* you might have run into her anywhere. At least like this you can pick your own time, and get it over with in your own way.

Put like that, it didn't sound so bad. In fact, it might even be fun.

He ground out his cigar under his heel and turned to Austen. 'The arrangements sound fine,' he said. 'And on second thoughts, I think I will have that brandy.'

Sophie had been dreading her arrival in Jamaica.

The *Atranta* had been due to dock on the Friday at seven in the morning, and two hours before she was on deck with a scattering of sleepy American tourists awaiting their first glimpse of Kingston harbour. Neither Alexander, Sibella, nor Gus Parnell was awake yet, which was just as she'd planned. She needed to be by herself. When the sharp green mountains first rose above the horizon, she had to struggle to hold back the tears.

The sun climbed higher, burning off the haze. The colours grew so intense that it hurt to look. She saw searing emerald peaks against a sky of fierce tropical blue; a dazzle of white sand and shining red roofs, and tall, spiky royal palms; along Harbour Street, a flame-coloured blaze of poincianas. She felt a shock of painful longing, and a strange kind of dread: as if she'd woken from a grey, unthreatening dream which had lasted for years.

Later she stood on the quay with the others, engulfed in the familiar chaos of Kingston on a weekday morning. She smelt incense from the Chinese parlours, and spiced coconut from the hominy pots; dust and horse-dung and wangla nut brittle turning sticky in the sun. She was assailed by the din of the West India Regimental Band which had come to greet the packet, and the thunder of street cars and trams and drays. She picked her way past iridescent piles of snapper and parrotfish, and higglers' handcarts laden with the last of the June plums and the first of the oranges. In a haze of red dust she saw self-conscious tourists in new cork helmets and tropical whites, and businessmen in morning coats and black top-hats; Chinese men on bicycles and east Indian girls in brilliant saris; fishermen in blue dungarees and jippa-jappa hats. Pickneys darted about between people's legs. John crows hunched on telegraph poles, surveying the scene with the gravity of undertakers.

For the first time in seven years, the richness of *patois* filled her ears. *'Fippance a ride to hotel, me genkelman! Fippance, ongly fippance a ride!' 'Basket around, me lady! Fish-kind, all sorta fish-kind!' 'Paradise plum! Tambrin balls! Mango, ripe mango gwine past!'* She felt bruised and raw. She was only too glad to let Alexander take the lead.

He'd been taking the lead for the past two months, and after the initial strangeness she had discovered that it was a glorious relief. He'd seen to everything. He'd placed the engagement notice in *The Times*, and made arrangements with Mrs Vaughan-Pargeter about packing up her things; he'd even conspired with his sister over the trousseau. Finally, he'd booked their passage to Jamaica, and gently told Sophie that of *course* she must stay at Parnassus, she needn't think of going anywhere else.

They both knew that 'anywhere else' meant Eden, but that she couldn't face it yet. In her brief letters to Madeleine she'd avoided the question of a visit, and she noticed with a pang that her sister did the same, confining herself to expressions of slight surprise at the suddenness of the engagement, and cautious approval. Bizarrely, Madeleine said nothing about Fever Hill. And after her first letter announcing the sale, Sophie didn't have the courage to allude to it again.

But how extraordinary to be a tourist in Jamaica. To take rooms at a grand hotel on Harbour Street, instead of simply running up for the weekend and staying with Mrs Herapath's sister-in-law at Half Way Tree. To her surprise, Sophie found that she liked it very well. After all, a tourist is transient. A tourist can leave whenever she wants.

It was Monday afternoon, their fourth day in Kingston, and she and Sibella had just returned to the hotel after a day's shopping. They'd been to Dewey's in King Street for India gauze underthings, and Joseph's in Church Street for canvas shoes and galoshes, and half a dozen other shops which had merged into a blur. But now the streets had become unbearable, for the sea breeze which in Kingston they call 'the Doctor' had dropped, and the land breeze wouldn't start up for another couple of hours.

Both Alexander and Gus Parnell had taken themselves off 'on business', and Sibella had declared herself absolutely *finished*, and gone upstairs to lie down. Disinclined to do the same, Sophie wandered out into the grounds and found a little table in a shady corner, and ordered tea.

After the dust and din of the streets the gardens were deliciously cool, with only a sprinkling of well-bred tourists quietly admiring the views. She sat back in her chair and fanned herself with her glove, gazing up at the wild almond tree overhead: a shifting pattern of enormous dark green leaves and small pale green blossoms, and little chinks of hot blue sky.

A pair of yellowbacks chased each other furiously in and out of the branches, then flew away across the gardens. A doctorbird arrived to feed on the blossoms, its tiny wings a blur of dark green iridescence, its long, slender tail feathers floating on the faintest of breezes.

I can't believe it, thought Sophie as she followed the hummingbird's progress from flower to flower. I'm back in Jamaica. I can't believe it.

'I don't believe it,' said a man's quietly courteous voice directly behind her. 'Can this really be Sophie Monroe, back in Jamaica after all this time?'

The voice was startlingly familiar – and yet unfamiliar. She twisted round, shading her eyes with her hand, but he was standing with his back to the glare, and at first she couldn't see his face.

Then the sun went black. Dark spots darted before her eyes. No. Not him. It couldn't be him.

He was standing looking down at her with his head slightly to one side and an amused expression on his face. He wore a white linen suit and a panama hat, and he stood with both hands in his trouser pockets, completely at his ease. 'It is you, isn't it?' he said again. 'May I sit down for a moment, or are you expecting someone?'

She swallowed hard. Then, still unable to speak, she

shook her head, and clumsily indicated the cane chair on the other side of the little round tea table.

Nothing was real any more. She wasn't sitting under a wild almond tree in the gardens of the Myrtle Bank Hotel. Ben wasn't standing beside her. He couldn't be.

And yet he was. It really was him. The same narrow green eyes, the same sharply handsome face, the same lean, graceful figure. Even the same thin vertical scar cutting across the right eyebrow.

He was the same – but he wasn't. He was utterly changed. The last time she had seen him he'd been bruised and unkempt, his clothes crumpled after a hasty wash in the river, his face white with shock as she told him she was ending it between them. The slender gentleman before her now was completely self-possessed. He was dressed with a casual, unstudied elegance, and spoke with distant courtesy, and not a trace of a Cockney accent.

'*Ben?*' she said stupidly. It came out as a croak. She felt herself colouring.

He sat down and put his hat on the ground beside his chair, and crossed his legs, and leaned back and smiled at her. It was a charming smile with no feeling behind it – a social smile – and it was nothing at all like Ben. At least, not like the Ben she had known. In the old days there'd been either that wary feral snarl, or the genuine, breath-taking smile which would occasionally flash out and make her want to cry.

He told her that she was looking remarkably well, and asked what she'd been doing with herself since he'd last seen her. Had she ever got round to taking her degree?

No, she said. She mumbled something about St Cuthbert's.

A charity volunteer, he said, how interesting. And have you been in Jamaica long?

Four days, she said.

Indeed, he said. I was in London a couple of months ago, we must have been there at about the same time. Isn't it extraordinary how one's always missing people one knows, just by a whisker?

Then he noticed the sapphire and diamond cluster on her finger, and asked whom he ought to be congratulating, and she steeled herself and told him that it was Alexander Traherne. He looked mildly surprised, then faintly amused. I hope you'll be very happy, he said, with the counterfeit pleasure which one adopts when the marriage is that of an acquaintance for whom one doesn't really care.

'It was in *The Times*,' she muttered by way of justification.

'I imagine it was,' he said, 'but I'm afraid I don't always have the time to read the papers when I'm in London.'

The tea arrived, and she asked in a strangled voice if he'd care to join her. She thought she sounded like someone reading from a script, but if he noticed he gave no sign of it. He reached for his hat and got to his feet and said, thank you no, I ought to be going. But you go ahead, you must be parched.

She stared at the tea things. She couldn't touch them. If she did she would drop the teapot or break a cup.

There was an awkward silence. At least, she felt it to be awkward, but Ben merely stood with one hand in his pocket, slowly fanning himself with his hat.

'I don't understand,' she said suddenly.

He smiled down at her. 'What don't you understand?'

'I don't— I mean, you're – you're—'

'Rich?' he put in gently.

'Well – yes.'

'And you really haven't heard a whisper about it?'

She shook her head.

He gave a slight laugh. 'Well, then, it seems we're both hopelessly ill-informed! Although I have to say, I think I've more of an excuse than you. You see, I never bother with newspapers at Fever Hill.'

The ground tilted. 'Fever Hill?' she said.

He was laughing and shaking his head. 'Really, Sophie, don't you know about that either? I fancy you're going to have to administer a sharp rebuke to that sister of yours for not keeping you better informed!'

CHAPTER TWENTY-FOUR

'I thought it best to wait,' said Madeleine over tea at Parnassus, 'and tell you face to face.'

Sophie caught the glance which passed between her sister and Sibella, and realized with a jolt that Sibella had known about Ben all along. 'Well,' she said as lightly as she could, 'now that I'm here, you can tell me everything.'

Madeleine put her teacup to her lips, then set it down again. She was trying to appear at her ease, but she wasn't managing it any better than Sophie. It was the first time they'd seen each other in seven years. Sibella had offered to make herself scarce, but Sophie had begged her to stay. She was too nervous to be left alone with her sister.

'There's not a great deal to tell,' said Madeleine, stirring her tea and avoiding Sophie's eyes. 'According to Olivia Herapath, he knocked around Panama for a while, then took up with some coloured engineer – the one who's just bought Arethusa. They went to Sierra Leone to look for gold, but didn't find any, so they went to Brazil, where they did. At least,' she added, 'they found the *expectation* of gold. I don't quite understand it, but Cameron says they bought up the rights very cheaply, and then sold them on to mining companies at an enormous profit, and then sold the business itself at an even more enormous profit. It seems that Mr Walker – that's the engineer – had a minority share as he only provided the surveying expertise, while Mr Kelly,' her cheeks darkened, 'was the

283

brains behind it. He came up with the idea of selling the information rather than doing the mining themselves, and that's why he's so much the wealthier of the two.'

Mr Kelly. How bizarre to hear Madeleine calling him that. The last time she'd spoken of him, she'd been cold-eyed and savage with grief. *I'll never forgive him*, she had cried. *I hope he rots in hell.*

And what about me? Sophie wondered, watching her sister stirring her tea with elaborate care. Have you forgiven me? Or are you always going to keep me at a distance?

'It was something of a nine days wonder,' Madeleine went on evenly, 'but it's all blown over now. And of course, he never goes out into Society.'

'I should think not,' said Sibella, pink with indignation. Clearly, having Ben Kelly for a neighbour was wormwood to her.

Sophie pictured the consternation at Parnassus when they'd first got the news. An erstwhile groom – *their* groom – the new owner of Fever Hill! Cornelius would have been incandescent; poor Rebecca prostrated. 'But has it really blown over?' she said.

Madeleine bit her lip. 'There's been a certain amount of gossip,' she said carefully.

A certain amount of gossip. Sophie appreciated her sister's attempt to minimize it, but she could just imagine the nature of the gossip. Of course, no-one would say anything to her face, but everyone would be remembering her wildly inappropriate attachment to that good-looking young groom at Parnassus. How Olivia Herapath would relish it! 'My dear, isn't it killing? The boy from the wrong side of the tracks (so to speak) has absolutely gone and bought the railway! And just when she's about to be married, poor lamb. I'd give anything to be there when they meet.'

There was an awkward silence. Then Sibella stepped into the breach by loudly admiring the presents which Sophie had brought from London. There was a folding pocket camera for Madeleine, who had mentioned in one of her letters that she'd taken up photography again; a patented Thermos flask for Cameron; a picture frame for Clemency, and for Belle an Ever Ready electric battery torch which she was currently trying out in the croton bushes on the other side of the pergola.

Sophie did her best to join in, but she knew that she failed. She was painfully aware of how different this homecoming was from her last. Seven years before, she hadn't needed presents to buy approval. Her welcome had been genuine, Jamaican, and at Eden. Now they sat on Italian wrought-iron chairs under Rebecca Traherne's rose pergola, and skated like mayflies over the surface. Even when Sibella tactfully went inside – 'to fetch that copy of *Les Modes* for Madeleine' – they did not delve beneath. Madeleine asked about the trousseau, and Sophie told her what a godsend Sibella had been, and made a joke about Gus Parnell's horror of centipedes. They didn't mention Fever Hill. Or Ben.

They strolled the length of the pergola, and watched Belle emerging from the croton bushes, scowling as she beamed the torch directly into her eyes.

'She's going to be beautiful,' said Sophie for something to say.

Madeleine sighed. 'She's a dreadful tomboy. Rides all over the estate; always giving the grooms the slip.' She paused. 'Cameron wants to send her away to school. But I don't think she's ready.'

Of course not, thought Sophie with a pang. Madeleine had already lost one child. How could she lose another, even if it was only to a girls' academy in Kingston? 'I'm sure you're right,' she agreed.

'Am I? I don't know. Cameron has a point. She rarely sees children her own age, apart from the pickneys. And she's got a morbid streak which worries me.'

Sophie glanced at her in surprise. Was this her way of bringing the conversation round to Fraser?

'She never seems to *play* with her dolls,' Madeleine went on with her eyes on her daughter. 'Just holds funerals for them.'

'But lots of children do that. Don't they?'

'Yes, but Belle's are so elaborate. Proper Jamaican nine-nights, with parched peas in the pockets and cut limes on the eyes.'

'That's to stop them becoming duppies,' said Belle, who'd heard her name mentioned, and sidled up.

'Oh, I can understand that,' Sophie told her. 'At your age I was fascinated by duppies. I was very ill, you see, and I – well . . .' she broke off in confusion, 'I was simply fascinated.' She'd been going to say that she'd been scared of dying and becoming a duppy herself, but stopped just in time.

Belle was looking up at her with new respect. 'Mamma never told me you were ill,' she said with an accusing glance at Madeleine. Then she turned back to Sophie. 'How did you get better? Did you ask a duppy tree?'

'As a matter of fact, I did.'

Belle's mouth fell open. '*How?* Did you give it an offering? What did you—'

'Belle,' said her mother, 'that's enough.'

'But *Mamma*—'

'I said, that's enough. Now run along and ask Mrs Palairet if you can go to the stables and say hello to the horses.'

As Sophie watched Belle reluctantly trailing off, she felt a pang of recognition. She had been about Belle's age when she'd first come out to Jamaica. She'd adored Fever Hill, and lived in terror of the duppy tree across the lawn; she'd idolized her older sister, and – although she hadn't known it at the time – she'd had a hopeless crush on Ben.

He had been like some dark, bright-eyed spirit from another world: filthy, savage, and terrifyingly foul-mouthed, but always vividly aware of whatever she thought and felt. How could all that have changed so profoundly? How was it possible that he'd transformed into that polite, indifferent man in the white linen suit? How could anyone change so much?

At her side, Madeleine drew a cross on the flags with the point of her parasol, and asked when it was to be.

'When is what to be?' said Sophie.

'The wedding. I was talking of the wedding.'

'Oh. I don't really know. We haven't fixed a date.'

'Ah.'

They walked on a few paces. Then Madeleine said, 'Shall you care to be married from Eden?'

Sophie hesitated. 'Cornelius has suggested Parnassus.'

'What a good idea,' said Madeleine with an alacrity which gave Sophie a twinge of pain. 'That makes much more sense,' Madeleine went on without looking at her. 'The house and grounds are so much bigger, and it's far more convenient for people coming from town.' She paused. 'I wondered – there are still a few odds and ends of yours in the spare room. Shall I have them sent down, so that you can sort them out?'

'If you would.'

'I'll see to it directly.' She put on a brighter face. 'I was so looking forward to seeing Alexander, but I understand he's—'

'In Kingston, yes. You see, we'd been planning on staying there a fortnight, but then I changed my mind, and he still had business to complete, so he had to go back.' She knew she was talking too much, but this polite fencing was beginning to wear her down.

'Sophie,' said Madeleine, fiddling with her parasol, 'you do love him, don't you?'

Sophie was startled. She'd forgotten how direct her sister could be. 'What are you talking about?'

'It's just that it seemed – well, rather sudden. So I wondered.'

'I'm extremely fond of Alexander,' said Sophie, and confirmed that with a smile.

'Oh, Sophie.'

'Why "Oh, Sophie"? It's true. It really is.' Then an unwelcome thought occurred to her. 'I should perhaps mention – Alexander doesn't know anything about Ben. I mean, he knows that I was – attached to Ben. But he doesn't know anything about what happened – that night.'

Madeleine's face had gone still. 'I'm sure that's for the best,' she said, scarcely moving her lips.

'I thought so too,' said Sophie. 'I just thought you should know. That's all.'

Madeleine nodded, and they walked on in strained silence.

What happened that night. What an anodyne way of putting it. Sophie's spirits plunged. How could she put it like that, when she could still summon up the feel of his back beneath her hands. The clean, sharp smell of his skin. The heat of his mouth.

Suddenly she was alarmingly close to tears. She snapped off a rose and started pulling it to pieces. 'How could you not tell me?' she said harshly. 'How could you let me come back without warning me that he was here?'

Madeleine's face contracted. 'We thought you already knew.'

'What? What gave you that idea?'

'For heaven's sake, Sophie, you'd just sold him Fever Hill!'

'But I didn't know it was him. I had no idea.'

'And we had no idea that you were selling it.' She opened her parasol with a snap and walked a few paces, and then turned back. Her mouth was set, her eyes glittering with angry tears. 'I cannot *imagine* why you took it into your head to sell it. And I cannot imagine why you didn't tell us first.'

'Because you'd have tried to stop me.'

'Well of course we would!'

'Madeleine, I'm sorry. I'm sorry I didn't tell you. But you still should have warned me about Ben.'

'No,' said Madeleine, raising her hand as if to ward off an attack. 'No. We won't talk about him any more.'

'But Madeleine—'

'I *can't*,' said her sister, rounding on her. 'I just – can't. It's different for you, Sophie, you've been away, you've been out of it. But for me nothing's changed. Can't you understand? Nothing's changed.'

Sophie looked at her sister's beautiful, agonized face,

and wondered how she could ever have hoped that things might be different between them. 'Of course,' she said gently. 'I understand. Nothing's changed.'

So now I have my answer, she thought as she watched Madeleine walking swiftly away to find her daughter. She hasn't forgiven me. She may not even know it herself, but it's true. She hasn't forgiven me. And she probably never will.

Picking hops in Kent is Ben's best thing ever. At least it was till Kate went away.

Every September, him and Jack and Kate used to make the long walk down south, to save on the train fare. But this year it's only Ben. He's never been by hisself before, and it feels a bit rum. But he promised Kate he'd go, so he's got no choice. Besides, he's nearly ten, and it's not like he don't know the way.

Just thinking about Kate gives him a pain in the chest. He's hardly seen her since she left, as her and Jeb live miles away in Southwark, just off the Jamaica Road. Ben can only manage the odd half-hour of a Sunday, if he can slip away without letting on to Pa.

So Kent, now. It takes him two days of padding the hoof to get there, and of course he goes to the same farm they always do, Farmer Rumbelow's, couple of miles west of Leigh. He teams up with this old bloke name of Roger, and Roger does the pole-pulling while Ben does the picking. So there's Roger hooking down these long trailing branches, and here's Ben ripping off the hops till he can't hardly feel his arms. They're not so quick as the big men, and they can't keep going as long as the sodding families, but who cares? They do all right.

And when you get the hang of it, it's topper. All them clean yellow hops against the clean blue sky, and the flowery smell and the floaty gold dust. Then when the whistle goes, you stand by your bin and wait for the measurers to come round. The cold creeps up and your padders go numb, but soon it's time for grub, and at Farmer Rumbelow's it's bang-up, cos they fill your tin right to the top.

*Him and Roger manage about seven bushels a day,
which is a shilling between them, split sevenpence for Ben
and fivepence for Roger, cos Ben done most of the work.
So after tuppence each for food and a kip in the barn,
they're doing all right. In fact they're in clover.*

*And it's topper in Kent. One lunch-time, in the next-door
field, Ben saw a couple of horses playing. He never knew
horses could play, but these ones did: kicking up their
hooves and giving each other little play-bites on the neck,
and galloping about for no reason – or maybe just cos they
was happy. Watching them play was the best thing ever. Or
it would of been, if Kate was here to see it too.*

*So now the hops are picked and Roger's taken hisself
off down some town called Somerset to see what's what,
and Ben's off home again. Loads of rhino in his pocket,
but he still pads the hoof all the way back to London.
Well, it's half a crown for the train, and that's just chuck-
ing it away for no reason, isn't it?*

*It's cold, and there's a fog: one of them thick yellow
jobs that clogs your throat and stings your eyes like lime.
Ben's been beating the streets for a day and a half and he's
all in, so he goes into this coffee-house and asks for a
penny mix, but the skivvy just looks at him.*

*Don't she even know what a penny mix is? 'That's a
ha'porth of tea,' he snaps, 'and a ha'porth of sugar, and a
Woodbine. All right?'*

*So finally he gets his penny mix, and he's sat there
nursing his tea and getting the feeling back in his padders,
and looking about to see what's what. And sure enough,
this bloke gets up, leaving half a faggot on his plate.
Makes a nice little supper, that does.*

*'A penny a day is all you need,' he tells the pretend-Kate
in his head. 'You get yourself a penny mix and make it
last, and then you just watch and wait. You'll never credit
what people leave on their plates. Just a penny a day, and
you can eat like a king.'*

*Then all of a sudden it comes so strong upon him that
he nearly cries out. Here he is talking to a pretend-Kate,
cos the real one's not here.*

Slippers Place where she lives is miles out of his way, but he goes there just the same. Only she's out. The missis in the next-door room tells him she's got a job down a manufactory making umbrella covers, and won't be back for hours. So he tells her to tell Kate that Ben come by, and starts off home.

It's well dark by the time he gets to Shelton Street, and he's all in, and the pain in his chest is worse. He didn't know it down at Slippers Place, but he was counting on seeing Kate.

Pa's not home thank Christ, but Lil's there, getting ready to go out, and Robbie jumps up from his corner with a big gappy grin. 'Ben!'

'Well who'd you think it was?' laughs Ben, giving him a cuff round the ear.

'All right, Ben?' goes Lil, putting on her hat. She's thinner than when he left, and her cough's no better.

'All right, Lil,' he goes.

'How much d'you make, then?'

He does a low bow. 'Fifteen shillings and sixpence, my lady.'

'Well if I was you I'd stash it, or he'll have it off you in a trice.' They both know she means the old man.

'So how's he been, then?' goes Ben.

'I dunno. I make sure I'm out of here before he gets back.' She stops for a minute and shoots him a look. 'He's been on and on about Kate. He'd make me tell where she is if I hung around. And I mean it about that rhino, Ben. Stash it, or he'll knock you about and nick the lot.'

'He'll knock me about anyway,' goes Ben. And he's not worried about the rhino: he's already stashed ten bob in his special place behind the chimneypot, and just kept five and six in his pocket, so Pa will get something off him, and not boil over.

He gives Lil two bob as a present, then says to Robbie, 'Here, Rob, I got you something.' He reaches into his pocket and brings out a straw doll he clicked off a window sill in Kent. 'It's got spiky hair like yours, but this is gold and yours is red.'

'Gold,' breathes Robbie, taking the doll in delicate fingers.

Ben grins. 'Not real gold, you daft little bugger.'

But Robbie's not listening. He carries his treasure back to his corner and introduces it to the wall.

Well at least he's talking to something, thinks Ben. He turns back to Lil. 'So you seen Kate, then?'

She shrugs. 'Off and on.'

'She all right?'

She darts a glance at Robbie, then leans down close to Ben. 'She's in the family way.'

'Bugger.'

'Quite,' goes Lil. 'Just don't tell Pa.'

'Course not.'

'I mean it, Ben. Keep it dark. He's still funny about her. Look, I got to go. Just don't tell him where she is, all right?'

Ben's narked. 'What d'you take me for, a idiot?'

She bares her yellow teeth in a grin. 'Keep your shirt on, Ben.'

After she's gone, everything's dark and quiet. Ben curls up on the shakedown by the window, and after a bit Robbie comes over and snuggles against him like a skinny little kitten. Ben shuts his eyes and sets to thinking about the horses playing in the field.

Everything's starting to get well fuzzy, when all of a sudden he's yanked awake.

'Where is she?' yells Pa, shaking him like a rat.

The big face is so close that Ben can see the coal-dust ground down deep in the little pits. The breath stinks like a hot drain. The green eyes are swimming in red. He's well basted. Ben should of cut the lucky while he had the chance. 'Where's who?' he mumbles, pretending to be half asleep.

But Pa's not fooled. He gives Ben a shake that nearly yanks his arm from the socket. 'You know who, you fucking little sewer rat! Kate! Now you want me to bash your head in, or you want to tell me where she is!'

* * *

Ben opened his eyes and stared at the sunlight on the rafters. He lay watching the golden light on the golden wood while the dream slowly faded and his heartbeat returned to normal.

He heard the maidservant tiptoe in and set down the tray, then murmur, 'Mornin, Master Ben,' and tiptoe out again. He got up and pulled on his dressing-gown and went out onto the balcony.

When he'd bought Fever Hill, the first thing he did was to open out the galleries and let in the light. No more shadows, even if it did mean letting in the heat. He never minded heat. And now he had a clear view of the grounds, and the rust-red carriageway sweeping down between the tall royal palms; past the New Works at the foot of Clairmont Hill, and the old slave village on the other side, and the ruins of the Old Works beyond it; and on through the shimmering cane-pieces of Alice Grove, to the distant gatehouses that marked the northern edge of the estate. Beyond that he could just glimpse the rolling acres of Parnassus, and the grey-blue glitter of the sea.

Strange to think that this upper gallery on which he stood had once been the domain of Great-Aunt May. Here she'd sat in her straight-backed mahogany chair, watching all that went on: the nemesis of servants and field-hands alike. Sometimes, out of the corner of his eye, he thought he saw her. Can someone haunt you even before they're dead?

He pushed the idea aside. He didn't want to think about ghosts. He leaned over the balustrade and took a deep breath, and waited for the sea breeze to blow away the last dark shreds of the dream.

A month ago, it would have knocked him sideways. But now at last he was beginning to understand. Evie used to say that when a duppy has a message, it sometimes 'dreams to' a person. And to begin with, he'd thought that Kate was dreaming to him. Now he believed otherwise. He'd realized that he only ever dreamed of the old days when he'd been thinking of Sophie. In some way, the dreams were connected with her.

The first ones had come when he was concluding the purchase of Fever Hill. And then again, when he'd seen her in Kingston. They were connected in some way. But how? After all, he had loved Kate – he loved her still – and he didn't love Sophie. Not any more.

She was so utterly changed. In the old days she'd talked the hind leg off a donkey, particularly when she was nervous. But that day in the hotel garden she'd hardly said a word. It was as if all the spirit had leached out of her, leaving just this wan, submissive, frightened little thing.

That day in the hotel garden. Whenever he thought of it he winced. He'd laid it on far too thick. Especially the accent. *You're looking remarkably well . . . You must be parched . . . I fancy you're going to have to administer a sharp rebuke to that sister of yours . . .* God Almighty, he'd sounded like bloody Austen.

The old Sophie would have noticed that in a trice. She would have given him no quarter; she never did. The new Sophie had just sat there staring at him. Incredible to think that he'd loved her once.

But what did she have to do with Kate?

He ran his thumb along his bottom lip. Only one way to find out, he thought suddenly. Stop skulking at Fever Hill, and meet them all head-on. The Lawes. The Trahernes. Sophie Monroe. Meet them all head-on, and then have done with it.

He went back inside and poured himself a cup of tea, then lit a cigar.

Best china tea in a porcelain cup, he thought, and a fine Havana cigar. Not exactly a penny mix, but near enough.

That was almost enough to make him smile.

The early morning sun played prettily on Evie's blue and green chintz counterpane, and on the hat and gloves and parasol laid out in careful readiness.

Even though it was a Saturday, she'd been up for hours, for she always gave herself plenty of time to get ready when her sweetheart took her out. Saturday was their day. Sometimes he managed to slip away on weekdays too, but

Saturday was reserved for them. Which was why she'd had to do some fancy rearranging when Ben swooped down last week and carried her off to Constant Spring.

She smiled at the recollection. Lord God, if those two ever met, how the fur would fly!

That was the thing about Ben. He might look different from the way he had seven years before, he might dress and talk differently too; but underneath he was just the same. And you never knew what he might do.

Her sweetheart, on the other hand, was a perfect gentleman. In fact, he was perfect in every way.

Downstairs, the key turned in the lock. Her heart leaped. She'd made him a present of a latchkey two days before, but this was the first time he was using it. A latchkey for a lover. What a shocking, unteacher-like thing to do. But she couldn't help herself. She was in love with him.

She heard his well-known step on the stairs, and stared at her reflection as she listened to him reach the landing and come to a halt outside the door. In the mirror her eyes were bright, her lips moist and full and slightly parted.

On the other side of the door, the familiar voice called softly, 'Evie? Are you there?'

She waited a moment before answering, to savour the anticipation. 'I'm here,' she called as calmly as she could. 'You may come in if you wish.'

A muffled laugh. 'If I wish? Well, I rather think that I do!'

Then the door was flung open, and in a heartbeat she was in his arms, and he was holding her tight, and pressing his mouth to hers.

She sank her fingers into his golden curls and murmured, 'Alexander, Alexander. I've missed you so.'

CHAPTER TWENTY-FIVE

'I fail to understand,' said Miss May Monroe coldly, 'why you have done me the honour of calling, Mr Kelly. If that is indeed how I am to address you.' Her ice-blue gaze fixed on Ben, then slid sideways to Austen, who visibly shrank.

Ben repressed a smile. The old cat knew perfectly well why he'd come. She just liked her little game.

And why not? At ninety-one she was remarkable. She still held court in her shadowy drawing-room; still sat rigidly upright, scorning to touch the back of her chair; and still dressed impeccably, in a high-collared gown of pewter silk which made no concession to the stifling September heat. Perhaps she was just a little shrunken within her carapace of corseting; but clearly her mind was as hard as a diamond. And just as cold.

'It's good of you to see me, Miss Monroe,' he said evenly.

'So it is. Now answer the question. Why have you called?'

He met the unblinking blue gaze. 'I've a mind to go into Society. So naturally my first thought was to call on its *de facto* head.'

A wintry compression of the lips, which may have been a smile. 'You have acquired Latin, Mr Kelly. How very droll.'

Ben did not reply.

'But I regret that I cannot assist you. It is impossible for you to go into Society. You are a coachman.'

Beside him, Austen gasped. 'I've been a lot worse things than a coachman,' he said with a slight smile. 'But here's the thing, Miss Monroe. You could have declined to see me, but you didn't. So I think I can allow myself to hope.'

'That does not follow at all.'

'Then why did you let me come up?'

'Because it amuses me to see how you have turned out.'

There must be more to it than that. The old cat despised amusement.

'You are a very clever young man, Mr Kelly,' she said coldly, 'but I repeat, what is it that you want?'

Ben hesitated. 'No doubt you're aware,' he said, 'that this summer's ball at Parnassus was cancelled – out of respect for the death of the King.'

The old lady inclined her narrow grey head. 'So it was given out.'

He nodded. 'And it was the proper thing to do.' He paused. 'The fact that sugar prices are the lowest they've ever been is of course irrelevant to a man like Cornelius Traherne. Saving money had nothing to do with it.'

The gloved claws adjusted their grip on the ivory-headed cane. Now she was interested. Any chance to discountenance the Trahernes.

'So I was thinking,' continued Ben, 'that I might step into the breach, and give some kind of – entertainment. Perhaps at Christmas.'

The blue eyes glittered. 'But what is it that you want of me?'

Ben met her gaze. 'I was hoping you might agree to come. Then everyone else would too.'

'I never go out.'

'I thought you might make an exception. Or at least send your carriage and your man. I understand that you sometimes do that.'

With surprising force she rapped her cane on the parquet floor. 'I repeat. I never go out.'

Austen shifted uneasily on his chair, but Ben let the

297

silence grow. He'd expected this. No city falls at the first assault. And he was damned if he was going to beg.

When the silence had gone on long enough, he picked up his hat and rose to take his leave. But as he did so, the doors opened, and Kean announced Mrs Sibella Palairet.

Plump and pretty in modish black and white half-mourning, the young widow swept in, all smiles for Miss Monroe. She didn't notice Ben. Austen leaped to his feet and turned bright red as Miss Monroe introduced him. The young widow's smile became gracious when she learned that he was an Honourable. It congealed when she turned and recognized Ben.

'Mrs Palairet,' he said with a nod and a slight smile.

She drew herself up. 'I do not believe, sir, that we have been introduced.'

Ben laughed. 'One rarely is to one's groom.'

That earned him a wince from Austen and an unreadable look from Miss Monroe. Once again Ben asked himself what she was after.

The old lady flexed her claws on the head of her cane, and turned to him. 'Concerning your plans, Mr Kelly. It may be that I shall see fit to send my carriage and my man.' The ice-blue eyes held his for a moment, then slid to Mrs Palairet, and back to him. 'It may be,' she said again.

What the hell is she after? he wondered. He glanced at the little widow, then back to the old witch. Could it be, he thought suddenly, that she planned all this? That it wasn't mere chance that his visit coincided with that of Sibella Palairet?

Sibella Palairet – *née Traherne*.

Then understanding dawned. Jesus Christ. It was outrageous. It couldn't be. The old witch was proposing some kind of bargain. The social countenance of her carriage and her man at his Christmas entertainment, in return for a fling with the plump little widow.

No, that can't be it, he told himself. Not even Miss Monroe would . . .

And yet, when one thought about it, she might. And it would be savagely effective. A scandal like that would topple the Trahernes from social pre-eminence *and* frighten off the wealthy Mr Parnell, thereby scuppering Cornelius's hopes for shoring up his flagging finances. And seventy-three years after being insulted by a parvenu's offer of marriage, Miss May Monroe would finally have her revenge.

Provided, of course, that Ben decided to play along with it.

As he watched the young widow talking polite nothings to poor, smitten Austen, he remembered Mrs Dampiere. He remembered the feeling of being used. Suddenly he had to get out.

Abruptly he took his leave, giving Miss Monroe no sign that he'd understood her little game. And when they were once more down in the street, he muttered an excuse to a dazed and silent Austen, and walked on alone through the town to get some air.

He felt angry and disappointed. What an idiot he'd been. To have actually hoped that the old witch would admit him to her charmed circle simply on his own merits!

What naivety! He ought to have known that social acceptance was only ever going to be had at a price. And in his case, that price was a roll in the hay with Sibella Palairet. Once a groom, always a groom, it seemed.

Of course, if he decided to pay that price, there would be advantages. For one thing, he'd be outraging the Trahernes. But he didn't want to do it like this. This was – ignoble. An odd word for an erstwhile street-Arab to use, but there it was. He was still turning it over in his mind as he rounded the corner into King Street, and walked straight into Cameron Lawe.

Without thinking, Ben stepped back and touched his hat with a muttered apology. 'I was hoping to bump into you,' he said.

Cameron Lawe looked at him without expression. Then he touched his own hat, and stepped aside, and walked on without saying a word.

It was early afternoon, and King Street was empty, so there was no-one about to see him snubbed. Despite that, the heat rose to his face. It was one thing to be told that he didn't belong by some old witch up in Duke Street; quite another to be cut dead by a man he'd always respected. He despised himself for his weakness, but he wanted Cameron Lawe to like him. Or at least, to approve of him.

Feeling very much alone, he walked on up the street, and emerged into the square. It wasn't a market day, so there was only a sprinkling of higglers. He felt their eyes on him as he passed. They were probably only curious, but he couldn't shrug off the sense that they were judging him. *You don't belong*, they seemed to say. *You can try as hard as you like to fit in, but it'll never work. You'll always be the street-Arab who made good.*

But why should that bother you now? he wondered angrily. You've never belonged. You've never wanted to. Who are these people, that you should care what they think?

As he crossed the square, a memory floated to the surface. Fifteen years before, he had wandered across this same dusty space feeling just as angry and alone – and caught sight of a familiar face lighting with joy at seeing him there.

God, he thought savagely, why think of that now?

The bench on which she'd sat was still there outside the courthouse. But instead of a young Sophie Monroe, it was occupied by a pretty, dark-haired little girl of about twelve, who reminded him painfully of Madeleine.

She wore a white frilled pinafore over a red and green tartan frock, with a straw hat pushed far back on her head. She had her mother's vivid colouring, and something of her father's strong will in the modelling of the mouth. And she was watching Ben with intense curiosity, although trying not to show it.

He put his hands in his pockets and wandered over to her. 'Hello,' he said.

'Hello,' she said shyly.

'So. Have you still got that stripy horse of yours?'

She flushed with pleasure. 'I didn't think you remembered me.'

'I didn't think you remembered me either.'

'Of course I do. You told me that Spot had a broken cannon bone, and that I ought to shoot him.'

'And did you?'

She laughed. 'No! I've still got him. He lives on my bed. And I also have a real horse now. Actually, a pony.'

'What's its name?'

'Muffin. She's a chestnut, and she's *extremely* fiery.'

Ben tried not to smile at the thought of a fiery muffin. 'Chestnuts often are,' he said.

'I don't mean that she's bad-tempered,' she put in quickly, as if she'd been guilty of disloyalty. 'She's extremely obedient. At least, with me.'

'That's good to hear.'

It made a change to talk to someone who was pleased to see him, and he was tempted to stay a little longer. But he could hardly do that after what had just passed between him and her father. 'I think I'd better be going,' he said.

Her face fell. 'Oh, but I've bags of time, honestly. I'm waiting for Papa, and he always takes ages when he goes to the saddler's.'

'That's why I can't stay,' said Ben. 'You see, your papa and I don't quite see eye to eye. I wouldn't want to get you into trouble.'

'Oh.' She sucked in her lips. 'It's probably just the weather. Everyone's grumpy before the rains, even Papa. And then when it does start raining, everyone's *still* grumpy, *because* of the rain.'

Ben grinned. Suddenly he felt a lot better. 'That must be it, then,' he said.

'So I looked him up and down,' said Sibella with flashing eyes, 'and I told him very distinctly, "I do not believe, sir, that we have been introduced." Oh, you should have seen his face! He was absolutely lost for words. Quite put out of countenance.'

Sophie gritted her teeth and fought the urge to scream. Sibella must have told the story a hundred times. She had returned from Falmouth blazing with triumph, having royally snubbed 'that Kelly person'.

In the days which followed, she went on telling the story to anyone who would listen, until Sophie began to wonder if something more than mere outrage lay behind those flashing eyes and that heightened colour. Even Gus Parnell, the most phlegmatic of men, started giving his sweetheart thoughtful looks. Eventually Cornelius summoned his daughter to his study. When Sibella emerged she was pale and shaking, and she never again told the story of how she had cut Ben Kelly dead.

Sophie couldn't bring herself to sympathize. Every time Sibella had told that wretched story, everyone's attention had been focused on herself, to see how she was taking it. They all remembered that little episode seven years before – even if none of them knew quite how far it had gone.

September gave way to October, but still the rains didn't come. The heat increased. Tempers grew short. And Sophie began to realize that she'd made a huge mistake by agreeing to marry Alexander.

When they'd first arrived in Jamaica, she had simply been grateful for being cosseted and kept safe from the outside world. But as the months passed, she'd become increasingly restless. She wasn't used to doing nothing. And at Parnassus, ladies were not encouraged to be active. Alexander gently let it be known that he disapproved of her riding out alone; nor did he wish her to see her old friend Grace McFarlane. 'It doesn't do to fraternize with these people,' he said with his most winning smile. 'Particularly not the McFarlanes.'

'But why not?' she asked in surprise. 'I've been friends with Evie since we were children.'

'Yes,' he said patiently, 'but you aren't a child now.'

'But in a month or so she'll be back for the holidays. Surely you're not suggesting that I shouldn't see her?'

'I can't imagine why you should want to,' he said very gently, 'given where she'll be living.'

He didn't have to say any more. Evie's mother still lived

in the old slave village at Fever Hill. Of course Sophie wouldn't go anywhere near it.

He might be right about that, but it didn't alter her conviction that she was living a lie. She didn't belong at Parnassus. She didn't fit in. She'd been a fool to imagine that she could.

But how could she jilt Alexander – Alexander who was always so kind and considerate, and who hadn't done anything wrong. It would be the biggest and most humiliating about-turn of all.

She pictured the consternation at Parnassus. She had been their honoured guest for months. Rebecca had showered her with trinkets. Sibella had treated her like a sister. Cornelius had even bought her a horse. And everything was *arranged*. The lawyers had drawn up the settlements. The trousseau was bought. Everyone *expected* the marriage to go ahead.

Besides, even if she did get up the courage to break it off, where could she go? She still hadn't been back to Eden, not even for an afternoon; she couldn't face the thought of it. So seeking refuge there would be out of the question. That only left London, and Mrs Vaughan-Pargeter.

The days merged into weeks, and she did nothing. She had endless bitter arguments in her head. She called herself a liar and a hypocrite and a hopeless coward. She let things slide.

In the middle of October, the rains finally came, turning the roads to rivers and confining her to the house. She shut herself up in her room and went through the trunk of 'odds and ends' which Madeleine had sent down from Eden. She spent hours curled up with an old mildewed journal of some overseer from Fever Hill, which opened her eyes to the nature of true misfortune, and made her long for the real Jamaica, and the salty company of Grace McFarlane and Evie. She let things slide.

Finally, one afternoon during a particularly thunderous downpour, she couldn't take it any more, and determined to have it out with Alexander.

She found him in his study, reading a newspaper.

'Alexander,' she said as soon as she got in the door, 'we need to have a serious talk.'

'You're absolutely right,' he said, glancing up with a smile. 'I've been an utter brute. Going off to Kingston all the time, and leaving you on your own.'

'It's not about that—'

'But I *promise* it'll be different when we're married,' he cut in earnestly. 'For one thing we'll be living at Waytes Valley, so you'll have your own house. That'll give you something to do.'

She gritted her teeth and wondered how to begin.

Alexander must have seen something in her face, for he put down his newspaper and came over to her, and put his arms on her shoulders. 'You know, old girl, we really ought to fix a date. How about it, eh? When is it to be?'

As gently as she could, she twisted out of his hands. 'That's what I wanted to talk to you about.'

His face lit up. 'I can't tell you how delighted I am! So. When is it to be?'

She looked up into his face. He was so undemanding. So unfailingly good-natured. And so happy. 'Um – next spring?' she said. Coward, coward, coward. Now you've just made it ten times worse.

'Oh, I say,' he murmured with the slightest of frowns, 'isn't that an awfully long wait? I was thinking rather of November.'

Her stomach turned over. 'But – that's next month.'

He gave her his most charming smile. 'I know I'm a brute to press you, but it's just that I'm tired of waiting.'

'November's too soon,' she said, turning away so that he couldn't see her face.

'Very well. What do you say we split the difference, and make it December?'

'How about after Christmas?' she countered weakly.

For a moment he hesitated. Then he smiled. 'So be it. January. I'll run and tell the governor. He'll be over the moon.'

She gave him a tight smile.

When he'd gone, she went out onto the gallery and

stood watching the rain hammering the grounds and making the carriageway run red. She was the worst kind of coward. She had missed her chance, and now it was going to be even harder to break it off.

The weeks that followed were a whirlwind of activity. The invitations were sent out; the wedding breakfast was planned like a military operation; every day Sophie resolved to say something, and every day passed with nothing being said.

Then, on the twenty-fifth of November, something happened which made matters a great deal worse.

Scores of engraved, gilt-edged invitations of impeccable simplicity went out to everyone who was anyone in Trelawny. *Mr Benedict Kelly, At Home on Monday the twenty-sixth of December, at eight o'clock. Masquerade. Dancing. Rsvp.*

Northside Society had a wonderful time being completely appalled.

'*Outrageous*,' declared Sibella, opening her eyes very wide.

'The man's a cad,' said Gus Parnell with satisfaction.

'Of course he is, my dear fellow,' chuckled Cornelius, slapping him on the back. 'Only a blackguard would flout the rules by not bothering to make a single call, then expect everyone to kow-tow, simply because of his money. I call it caddish in the extreme.'

'But how can he *imagine* that we should wish to know him?' wondered his older daughter, Davina.

'And how is it conceivable that we could?' put in Olivia Herapath. 'A man of no blood? No breeding? Why, who were his people? What were his grandparents?'

'In my day,' said old Mrs Pitcaithley, greatly distressed, 'gentlemen were born, not made. I don't understand it at all.'

'I've always rather liked him,' said Clemency, startling everyone. She had adapted surprisingly well to the move from Fever Hill, and now often made the trip from Eden to Parnassus in her little pony-trap.

'Oh, Aunt *Clemmy*,' cried Sibella impatiently, 'you've never even met the man!'

'Yes I have, dear,' replied Clemency mildly. 'Years ago, when he was a boy. I gave him a ginger bonbon. In fact, I think he ate several. I wonder if he remembers.'

'What on earth does that signify?' snapped Sibella. 'The point is, no-one can possibly go. That's the point.'

'I agree,' said Alexander, glancing at Sophie. 'Don't you agree, my love?'

She put on her blandest smile and said that of course she agreed. And everyone nodded and tried not to show that they were desperate to discover how she really felt.

They would have been astonished if they'd known the savagery of her reaction. For a week she had been berating herself for her cowardice in not breaking it off with Alexander, but now all that was swept away in her fury at Ben. Boxing Day? *Boxing Day?* The very night when she'd gone to him at Romilly – when Fraser had died. How could he do it? How could he do it?

A week later, the fashionable world was set agog for a second time, when word got around that no less a personage than Miss May Monroe herself had *accepted* her invitation: at least to the extent of letting it be known that she would send her carriage and her man Kean.

'I suppose that that makes it all right?' asked Rebecca Traherne with her hand to her cheek.

'I should rather say that it does,' said Cornelius. 'One can hardly argue with a family as old as the Monroes.' And he gave Sophie a courteous little bow.

'That goes without saying,' said Olivia Herapath. 'Indeed, I consider it my duty to attend. Besides, it's too intriguing to miss. I hear he's desperately good-looking, *and* a Roman Catholic. I've always rather *liked* RCs. A whiff of incense is almost as exciting as sulphur, don't you agree?'

'I wouldn't miss it for worlds,' said Davina, eyeing Sibella with sisterly acidity.

Sibella made no reply. She was scanning the latest issue of *Les Modes* for ideas for new gowns.

'But do you think it's quite the thing?' bleated poor Mrs Pitcaithley.

'Depend upon it,' said Cornelius with a glance at Gus Parnell, who was sitting in moody silence. 'Everyone will go, simply because they can't bear to be left out. I hear that even old Ma Palairet hasn't the courage to stay away.'

Only Clemency declined, out of loyalty to Madeleine and Cameron, who had sent their regrets by return of post.

'We can't possibly go,' said Sophie later to Alexander, having sought him out in his study.

'Why not, my love?' he said, looking up with a smile from the letter he'd been writing. 'I rather think that we ought.'

She stared at him. 'But I couldn't. I couldn't possibly.'

He stood up and came round the side of the desk and took her hand. 'That,' he said gently, 'is precisely why we must. We must show everyone that the man means nothing to you now.'

'I could show that just as easily by staying away.'

'No you couldn't,' he said patiently. 'Darling, people have such long memories. It pains me to say this, but that little episode did rather demean you in their eyes.'

'Demean me?'

'Well, of course. It always lowers a girl to form an attachment outside her own degree.'

She opened her mouth to protest, but he talked her down. 'I don't say this to distress you, my love. It's in the past. But don't you see, that's precisely why we must go? To show everyone that it doesn't signify in the least.'

She felt her blood rise. 'So I am to attend Mr Kelly's Christmas Masquerade simply because he means nothing to me, while I'm barred from seeing Evie McFarlane, precisely because she's my friend. No, Alexander, I have to say that I don't see the logic at all.'

'I hardly think that you need to,' he crisply replied. 'All you need to do is to be guided by me.'

After Sophie had gone, slamming the door behind her with a force which reverberated through the house,

Alexander sat for a moment in silence, kneading his temples.

Confound it all. Everything was such a *muddle*. Sophie was dragging her feet, and the governor was looking thunderous, and there had been a quite startlingly uncivil letter from Guy Fazackerly, demanding to know when the debt would be settled. *TWENTY THOUSAND POUNDS*, he'd written in insulting capital letters, *absolutely due by New Year's Day*. What was the man worrying about? Didn't he realize that as the wedding was now fixed, Alexander could go to the Jews and borrow against the expectation? Didn't he realize that he would get his filthy money, every penny of it? People were so confoundedly disagreeable.

And now to cap it all, there was this other little unpleasantness.

On the blotter before him lay Evie's letter. He'd been rereading it when Sophie came in, and had only just had time to turn it over. Now he took it up again with weary distaste.

Dearest Alexander,
    Why have you not come to see me or written a line? It has been weeks since I told you my news, and I have heard nothing from you. Is that kind? You promised to visit me. You promised to help me. I am so alone. I can't tell anyone, and I can't think about anything else. I don't know what to do. My love, I need you now more than ever . . .

Confound it all. Why did women *get* themselves into such scrapes? After all, men handled far trickier matters every day, and never made such a fuss. Why, he himself had managed to square things with Evie over his engagement to Sophie almost as soon as he'd got off the steamer! It had been tricky, but he'd carried it off. So why couldn't Evie deal with this little difficulty of hers with similar finesse?

And really, when one thought about it, she had misled

him most dreadfully. He'd always assumed that a girl like her would know very well what she was about in these sorts of things. Surely she would either not allow herself to get *into* such a scrape – or, if she did, she would know how to get herself *out* of it? How could he possibly have known that she was so ignorant of the ways of the world? That she would be careless enough to get herself with foal?

No. When one looked at it in the round, he'd been most frightfully misled.

The clock on the bookshelf struck half past six. He heaved an enormous sigh. In another ten minutes he would have to go and dress for dinner. Dash it all, why was there never enough time for a fellow to draw breath?

With a sense of being greatly ill-used by the world at large and by women in particular, he took up his pen and began to write.

Dear Evie,

I particularly asked you never to write. By doing so, you have made things confoundedly difficult for me. I know that I said I would see you, and so I shall; given time. But you must understand that when you told me your news the other week, I was so taken aback that I scarcely knew what I was about. And forgive me, but I must ask you: are you absolutely sure that it is mine? If you tell me that it is, then of course I must take your word for it; nevertheless I feel it my duty to enquire.

Moreover I must confess that until this rude awakening, I had felt entitled to assume that you knew how to avoid this kind of unpleasantness. You must admit that you never led me to believe the contrary, and that I was therefore justified in my assumption. I might add that your timing in this matter could hardly be worse, given my impending marriage.

Here he paused. His marriage couldn't really be said to

be 'impending'. But let that pass. Besides, Evie probably didn't even know what the word meant.

> *However, no-one can say that I have ever neglected my obligations. I therefore enclose a five pound note, which I trust will enable you to take care of your little difficulty promptly, permanently, and to your satisfaction.*
>
> *I hope to look in upon you when I next run up to town. In the meantime, pray, pray, <u>pray</u>, do not write again. Yours, AT.*

CHAPTER TWENTY-SIX

Where are the spirits when you need them? thought Evie as she sat hunched on her grandmother's tomb.

Every night since she'd got back to Fever Hill she'd come out here to the bottom of her mother's yard, and asked the spirits for guidance: for some sign as to whether she should have the child, or get rid of it. But nothing came. Only the dark trees leaned over to listen to her thoughts.

Lord *God*, what a fool she'd been! How could she ever have imagined that she was good enough for Alexander Traherne?

A hot wave of shame washed over her as she recalled her secret fantasy: that he would realize that he couldn't marry Sophie, and marry her instead; that he would bring her proudly back to Parnassus and introduce her to his family. And she would turn to his father with a cold smile, and dare him to remember the frightened little girl he'd tried to rape in the cane-piece seven years before.

Lord God, what a fool.

The murmur of voices drifted over to her on the sweet night air. She glanced back to the house, where her mother sat smoking her pipe with Cousin Cecilia and old Nana Josephine. For the first time in years she wanted to join them. She wanted to kick off her shoes and feel the dust between her toes, and just sit and reason awhile. But she couldn't. What she carried inside her set her apart.

And time was running out. It had been the middle of October when she'd found out that she was carrying. She'd told Alexander three days later, and he'd promised to stand by her. And she had believed him.

At first when she didn't hear from him, she thought he'd fallen ill. Then after several desperate weeks, the letter arrived. *You have made things confoundedly difficult for me . . . Your timing could hardly be worse . . . Are you absolutely sure that it is mine? Pray, pray, pray, do not write again.*

Write again? How could he imagine that after such an insult she would ever contact him again? Every night she lay awake screaming at him inside her head. Every morning she got up heavy with tiredness, still silently screaming.

All the lies. The kisses, the caresses, the burning promises. Sophie didn't mean anything, he had said. It was just a marriage of convenience. It was Evie he loved.

What did it come to in the end? A sweaty embrace and a cheap dinner in an out-of-the-way dining-house. A paper sun-umbrella and a five pound note.

She had the money now, tucked into her bodice; just like that gold chain which his father had once given her, and which she'd lost in the struggle in Bamboo Walk. *His father.* Why hadn't she realized they were just the same?

A breeze stirred the pimento tree above her head. She pressed her knuckles to her eyes until she saw stars. Lord God, girl! Stop going over what's past, and *think!* Time's running out. It's already the fifteenth of December, and you're over three months gone. You've got to *do* something.

But what?

Get rid of it? But if she got caught she might be thrown in gaol. It would be the end of everything. And if she bore the child, it would still be the end of everything. She could never teach school again; never dream of a respectable marriage to a respectable man. Her life would be over.

She didn't know what to do. She longed to talk to someone. Ben maybe, or Sophie. Except that Sophie was the last person she could tell.

A noise behind her, and she opened her eyes to see her mother standing by Nana Semanthe's tomb, looking down at her with her hands on her hips. 'What's wrong with you, girl?' she said quietly.

'Nothing,' muttered Evie.

Her mother picked a shred of tobacco from between her teeth. 'You been back awhile, and hardly said two words. Got some big high thinking going on, and black feelings, too, besides. Not so?'

Evie shook her head.

'Sweetheart trouble? Sweetheart trouble out in foreign?'

Evie thought for a moment, then nodded.

'Some sugar-mouth buckra man.'

Evie's head jerked up. 'Why you say that, Mother?'

'Tcha! I not no fool. What the name he got, this man?'

But again Evie shook her head. One thing was certain: her mother must never find out. Grace McFarlane had done some dark things in her time. If she ever learned who'd done this to her daughter, he wouldn't live long. And then Grace would be hanged for murder. And the Trahernes would have won.

'Mother,' she said, swinging her legs off the tomb, 'don't worry about me. It's all over now.'

'Evie—'

'I said it's over. It's done. Now I'm tired, I'm going to bed.'

The next morning she awoke to a strange new clarity. It wasn't that she knew what to do; but she felt sure that today she would make her decision. As she lay watching Mr Anancy spinning his web in the rafters, she wondered how such certainty had come about. Had some spirit dreamed to her while she slept?

She put on her town clothes, and told her mother that she was going up to the busha house to see Mr Kelly.

'What you wanting with him?' said her mother narrowly. 'Is he the sweetheart?'

'Oh, Mother! Of course not!'

'True to the fact? Bible true?'

'He's like a brother to me. You know that.' And I hope to God, she added silently, that he'll be like a brother to me now.

But to her dismay, Ben wasn't at home. 'I'm afraid he's out riding,' said the ugly black man who came out onto the verandah. He was very dark, with a clever, bony face which reminded her uncomfortably of a younger version of her cousin, Danny Tulloch. She took an instant dislike to him.

'My name's Isaac Walker,' he said, smiling as he extended his hand.

She gave him the barest of nods and ignored the hand. 'Evie McFarlane,' she muttered. Black as a Congo nigger, she thought contemptuously. Too black, too ugly, and too damned polite. Who the hell does he think he is?

His smile widened as he took in the name. 'Grace McFarlane's daughter? I've been looking forward to—'

'Please tell Mr Kelly that I called,' she said coldly, and turned to go.

'Are you sure you won't wait? Or – d'you want me to give him a message?'

She looked him up and down with the disdain which only a beautiful woman can fling at an ugly man. 'No message. Good day to you, sir.'

She walked down the carriageway in a towering rage. Don't you start your sugar talk with me, she told Isaac Walker silently. You with your trickified smiles and your lying, sweet-mouth ways.

Now she knew what her mother had been muttering about the night before with Cousin Cecilia and old Nana Josephine. A well-to-do black man up at the busha house – and unmarried! What a fine thing if he made a match with their Evie!

And of course, she told herself, setting her teeth, their Evie isn't *good* enough for anyone better. Not good enough for a white man with blue eyes and golden curls.

Her anger lasted about a mile and a half. By the time she'd come out into the Fever Hill Road, all that remained was a cold, heavy dread. She realized now that her plan to see Ben had been nothing more than a delaying tactic. Ben couldn't tell her what to do. She had to decide that for herself.

It was dark by the time she got back to her mother's place, and the fufu was bubbling on the hearth. 'You know is past eight o'clock?' Grace said sharply. 'Where you been all day?'

'Out,' muttered Evie. She tossed her hat in the dust and threw herself onto the step. She was bone-weary, and she could still smell the stink of the bush-doctor's hut on her clothes. She wondered that her mother didn't smell it too.

'Where "out"?' demanded Grace.

'Just out. Cousin Moses gave me a lift to Montego Bay, and I did a little shopping.' Which, in a way, was true.

'Shopping? Cho! Don't seem to me that you bought anything.'

'I didn't.' That was a lie. The little brown bottle of physic in her pocket had eaten up over half of Alexander's five pounds. The rest had gone on a train ticket to Montpelier, and a seat on the mail coach home from Montego Bay.

She'd been travelling all day. All day she had felt people's eyes on her, and imagined their silent condemnation; even in Montpelier, where nobody knew who she was.

Her mother gave the embers a prod, and came to sit beside her. 'Evie,' she began, 'that sweetheart you got.'

Evie tensed.

'Now don't give me no back-answer, girl. Just listen.' She paused. 'You know it does no good to tangle-up with that kind a man.'

Evie gave a weary smile. 'Yes, Mother, I know.'

Grace studied her face. 'Evie – you got anything to tell?'

Evie met her eyes without blinking. 'No.' She was good at the blank eye, and it worked. Grace gave a curt nod, and went back to watching the fire.

Evie sat and watched it too. And it seemed that in the

embers she saw again the old bush-doctor's knowing leer as he'd handed her the physic.

His hut stood on the outskirts of Montpelier. To reach it one passed the gates of the Montpelier Hotel – *the most splendidly appointed hotel in Jamaica*, according to the guidebooks. A year ago in the first flush of their romance, Alexander had promised to take her there. Now all she'd glimpsed as she trudged past was a pair of enormous gates, and an avenue of stately yokewoods sweeping up towards some fairytale palace that she would never see.

The bush-doctor's hut had smelt of goats and press-oil and ganja. He had liquid yellow eyes and glistening tooth-less gums, which he bared in a constant grin. 'Likkle quinine,' he'd chuckled, tapping a long, sharp fingernail on the bottle, 'and oil a tansy; oil a parsley, and other things too besides. Mind you drink it down like a good girl-child!'

Oil of tansy and other things too besides. It sounded harmless, but she didn't doubt that if she decided to use it, it would work. Such mixtures were secret and hard to come by, but they'd been around for a very long time. She remembered a passage in the journal of Cyrus Wright. Congo Eve miscarried. He suspected her of taking 'foul potions' to bring it about.

Beside her, her mother took up a stick and drew a circle in the dust. 'You know, Evie, you father was a buckra gentleman, too.'

Evie bridled. 'I know that, Mother. But just because you took up with one doesn't mean that you can tell me what—'

'No, that's not what I intending.' She tapped the circle with the stick and frowned. 'I going to tell you a thing, Evie. I didn't take up with you father. He took up with me.'

Evie shot her a look. 'What do you mean?'

Grace shrugged. 'You know what I mean. Years back, I'm setting out for Salt Wash one afternoon. I'm cutting through Pimento Piece, heading over towards Bulletwood, and he's out riding and he sees me. And he's too strong for me.' She opened her hands to take in the rest.

Evie stared at her. Grace had spoken in the everyday tone she might use when talking of a spilt basket of yams. Evie tried to speak but no sound came. She cleared her throat. 'You mean – he forced you?'

Her mother snorted. 'Well I sure as hell didn't ask him,' she said drily.

Evie licked her lips. In all her musings about her father, it had never occurred to her that he might have forced himself on her mother. Grace McFarlane? The Mother of Darkness? It wasn't possible.

Her mother crossed out the circle and tossed away the stick. 'It happens,' she said flatly. 'Women need lot, lotta courage to live in this wicked world.'

Evie was shaking her head in bewilderment. 'But – did you ever tell anyone?'

Her mother snorted.

'But you could have gone to the magistrates—'

Her mother put back her head and hooted. 'Merciful peace, girl! You a teacheress, but you witless as a newborn pickney! What anybody coulda done if I did even tell? The man *too strong*! You hearing me? Too strong in every damn way.'

'But – what did you do?'

She shrugged. 'Thought about lot, lotta things. Thought about running away to foreign. Or letting the River Missis take care of it. Or going up into the far country and taking bush-medicine to kill it dead inside a me.' She frowned. 'To kill you, I meaning to say.'

Evie flinched. Until now she'd only thought of the thing inside her as the most desperate of problems. For the first time she realized it was a child. Would she have the courage – or the wickedness – to do what her own mother could not?

Grace pushed herself off the step and went to squat by the fire. She lifted the lid, and the familiar smell of thyme and callaloo and fragrant hot peppers filled the air. 'But I'm glad at the way it turned out,' she said as she stirred the pot. 'My own self daughter.'

Evie blinked. Her mother never said such things to her.

But why was she saying them now? Was this the sign she'd been waiting for? Were the spirits telling her to throw away the physic and have the child?

'Mother,' she said slowly. 'Why you telling me this now?'

Grace shrugged. 'You got to hear sometime. Too besides,' she added with a wry smile, 'you got sweetheart troubles. So maybe it only fair that I to tell you some of mine.'

'But why did you never tell me before?'

'Because it don't necessary! It all in the past.'

'Forgive and forget? That's not like you.'

She sighed. 'Sometimes you can get vengeance for you own self, Evie. Other times, not. That man – you father – he done a lot, lotta bad things. Vengeance will come to him in the end. But not from me.'

'Who was he?' Evie said abruptly.

Grace sighed. 'Now, Evie. What good—'

'Tell me.'

'No.'

'Yes. I'm a grown woman. I ought to know the name of my own father.'

A long silence. Her mother raised the spoon to her lips and blew off the steam to taste the fufu. Then she tossed in a little more thyme, gave a satisfied nod, and replaced the lid. 'Well all right, then,' she said. 'Maybe you right, maybe it time.' She got to her feet and took hold of Evie's wrist. 'Come.'

She led her through the trees to the tombs at the bottom of the yard. At great-grandmother Leah's she stopped, and put her daughter's hand flat on the cold stone. 'First you got to swear. Swear on great-grandmother Leah that you never will try for to confront him or face him down.'

'Why not?' said Evie harshly.

'You not hearing me, girl? He too *strong*! He do you harm!'

Evie thought for a moment. Then she swore.

Her mother gave a nod. 'Well, all right. So now I tell. You father. He's that Cornelius Traherne.'

Evie swayed. Then she leaned over the side of the tomb and began to retch.

The crossroads at the foot of Overlook Hill marks the edge of Eden land. If you stop there with the estate behind you, you have a choice of three ways.

To your right the track disappears into the deep woods on Overlook Hill, climbing all the way to the glade of the great duppy tree, then winding down the rocky western slope to the Martha Brae and the bridge at Stony Gap.

To your left runs the familiar, unthreatening dirt road which heads east past the works at Maputah, and then on towards Bethlehem, Simonstown and Arethusa.

But straight ahead – straight ahead and due south – that's the narrow, stony track which winds up towards the distant hamlet of Turnaround, and the start of the Cockpits.

The Cockpits belong to no-one. They're the province of mountain people and duppies. The Cockpits are a vast, hostile wilderness of deep ravines and tall, green, weirdly conical hills. Sudden precipices await the unwary, and haunted caves and hidden sink-holes. And if you get into trouble, you'll have to wait a while for help, and the mountain people don't welcome strangers. They're the descendants of runaway slaves, and as tough and silent as the land which made them. They only come down from the hills for an illness or a nine-night; for the rest, they keep to their remote, never-visited settlements. Look Behind. Disappointment. Turnaround.

'Turnaround,' Belle's mother always told her, 'means exactly that. So what do you do when you reach the crossroads?'

'*Turn around*,' Belle would reply.

Her mother hated the Cockpits. Belle didn't know exactly why, except that once, before Belle was even born, she'd had a bad experience there. That was why she'd made Belle promise never, ever to go beyond the cross-roads on her own.

And that was why Muffin now stopped out of force of

habit when they reached the crossroads after giving Quaco the slip.

It was half past ten in the morning, and Belle could feel the sun beating down on her hat and shoulders. The rasp of the crickets was deafening. So was the pounding of her heart.

Up ahead, the track climbed a narrow defile littered with thornscrub and tumbled boulders before disappearing round a spur on its way to Turnaround.

Turn around.

But surely, she reasoned, her promise to her mother could be set aside in an emergency?

In the pocket of her riding-skirt was the list of wishes she'd drawn up two weeks before. *Mamma and Papa to be happier and <u>never quarrel again</u>. Sugar prices to go up or treasure to be found, so that Papa will not have to work so hard. Aunt Sophie to come for a visit and make up with Mamma.*

She wasn't sure how she was going to achieve any of these, but she knew that she had to try. After all, there was nobody else to do it.

Two weeks before, she'd woken in the middle of the night to the sound of raised voices on the verandah. She'd lain in bed staring up at the mosquito net, hardly daring to breathe. Her parents never fought. Not properly *fought*.

Still holding her breath, she'd drawn aside the netting and shaken out her slippers, and hissed at Scout to *stay*. Then she'd tiptoed to the door of her room which gave onto the verandah, and peered out.

Her mother was pacing outside in her long rust-coloured dressing-gown. Her feet were bare, which Belle had never seen before, and her long dark hair was wild. 'Another child?' she cried. 'How could you even suggest it? How could you even think of mentioning that again?'

'Madeleine, hush,' said Papa. His voice was low, but Belle could tell that he was angry. He too was in his dressing-gown, and somehow that frightened Belle most of all. It was as if the fight had been too great to be contained within their own room, and had boiled over terrifyingly onto the verandah.

'D'you think we can just replace him?' her mother flung back at him.

There was a silence before her father replied. 'I think,' he said quietly, 'that when you reflect on what you've just said, you'll regret it.'

'Why? It's what you mean, isn't it?'

'My God, Madeleine, he was my son too!'

'Yes, and now you want to pretend that he never existed!'

'Madeleine – *stop*. Stop.' His voice was sharp. Belle had only ever heard him use that tone twice in her life. 'Don't do this,' he said. 'Don't push me away.'

Mamma turned and looked at him. She was breathing hard, with her arms rigidly at her sides, but Belle could see that she was trembling. It was as if she knew that she had gone too far.

For a moment they stood facing one another in silence. Then Papa went to her and put his hands on her shoulders, and drew her against him. After a moment she put her arms around him, and Belle saw how her hands clutched at his back. He rocked her gently in his arms, talking to her in a low voice. Belle saw her mother's shoulders begin to shake. Then she heard her deep, painful, uncontrollable sobs.

Belle was terrified. It was horrible enough to witness her parents fighting – fighting like two separate people. It was worse to hear her mother cry.

'I don't know what's happening,' her mother mumbled, her voice muffled against his chest. 'I thought we were through it, years ago. But now she's back, and suddenly it's all out in the open again, and I can't seem – I can't—'

Then Papa bent his head to hers and murmured something which Belle couldn't hear. And after a while Mamma nodded, and leaned against him as if she were exhausted, and they turned and walked slowly back to their room.

But now she's back.

That could only mean Aunt Sophie. And it astonished Belle, for she adored Aunt Sophie, and she knew that Papa and Mamma did too. But the fact remained that everything had been all right until Aunt Sophie had come back.

Hadn't it? Or had Belle only *thought* that everything had been all right?

Muffin tossed her shaggy head and snorted, impatient for some decision to be made about the crossroads. Belle stroked the pony's neck and told her to quieten down.

It was a week after the fight on the verandah that something else had happened to set her wondering. She'd accompanied her father on one of his rare calls to Parnassus, and he and Aunt Sophie had gone for a walk on the lawns, with Belle trailing behind.

Suddenly Papa had turned to Aunt Sophie and said quietly, 'Sophie, come to Eden. It's time. It really is.' Belle had the impression that this wasn't the first time he had asked.

But Aunt Sophie had crossed her arms about her waist and shaken her head. She looked sad, and so did Papa.

'Just for a few days,' he said. 'Or an afternoon.'

Aunt Sophie looked at the ground. 'She doesn't want me,' she said in a low voice.

'Yes she does. She may not even be aware of it herself, but she does. That's what's making her so unhappy.'

But Aunt Sophie was shaking her head. 'She still blames me.'

'For what? For Fraser?'

'She does, Cameron. I know she does.'

'Do you truly think so? Or is it that you still blame yourself?'

Aunt Sophie did not reply.

So in the end Papa had sighed, and bent to kiss her cheek, and then they'd left.

Belle couldn't understand it. Blame? What did they mean by blame? Nobody was to blame for what had happened to Fraser. She knew that because Papa had explained it to her when she was little. Fraser had become very ill and the doctors couldn't save him, so he'd

322

died. Just like the new mastiff puppy who'd got pneumonia last October.

Once again, Muffin tossed her head. Belle cast a doubtful glance up the track.

Her plan had seemed so easy in the safety of her own room. Of all the wishes on her list, *treasure to be found* was the most straightforward. In *Tales of the Rebel Maroons* there was a story about the Spanish Jars which the buccaneers had filled with gold doubloons and hidden in caves in the Cockpits. And according to the map in her father's study, there were several promising caves somewhere just off the track to Turnaround.

So why was she even hesitating? There was no other way. She knew that. She'd tried everything else. She'd prayed. She'd petitioned Aunt Clemmy's dead baby. She'd even tried to ask Grace McFarlane.

That had been the worst of all. She'd waited at the crossroads at midnight on the night when Braverly said Grace went to talk to the great duppy tree on Overlook Hill. But Grace had looked so different as she strode up in the blue moonlight: so like a real witch. She wore a ghostly white shift hitched up above her calves, and a white headkerchief, and a necklace of parrot beaks that made a horrible soft clicking as she walked. Belle hadn't dared to breathe. She'd hidden in the shadows until Grace had passed, and then run all the way home.

That had been two days ago. It was now the nineteenth of December – two whole weeks since the row on the verandah – and she was tired of calling herself a coward all the time.

Besides, she'd been enormously careful to protect herself and Muffin from the duppies: she'd pinned a sprig of rosemary and Madam Fate to her belt, and tied another big bunch to the pony's browband. They ought to be *fine*.

Thus telling herself, she gathered the reins and put Muffin forward up the track to Turnaround.

To begin with, the path seemed reassuringly like any other. She recognized honeyweed and a calabash tree; hogmeat and Jamaica buttercup and shame o' lady. But the ground climbed steeply, and soon she was on foot, leading Muffin between looming slopes of tumbled boulders and thornscrub.

There was no birdsong. Even the rasp of the crickets seemed hushed. She felt eyes on her, but when she stopped and looked back, she saw no-one – although she was alarmed to note that the crossroads had disappeared from view.

It grew hotter. The sun was high in the sky, the light so bright off the rocks that it hurt her eyes. Up ahead the path forked. From the map, she recalled that if one took the right-hand fork, one soon reached the speckled region marked *caves*. At least, she thought so.

It was noon when she found it. The path had forked often, but she'd made sure to mark each turn with a distinctive knot of grass, as her father had taught her. She was thinking of him as she rounded a corner and spotted it: a mouth of pure darkness about twenty yards up the slope. It was half hidden by a thorn tree, and curtained by strangler fig, but unmistakably a cave.

She touched the rosemary at her waist. It felt woefully inadequate. What use were herbs against duppies, and maybe Ole Higue herself? But she'd come too far to turn back now. She tied Muffin to a thorn bush, and crossed herself, and started to climb.

As she got closer, she saw that the mouth of the cave was fringed with spiky wild pine, and a small creeping plant with grey-green stems and tiny nubbly green flowers. Orchids, she thought, her heart pounding. *Ghost orchids*. She wished she hadn't remembered the name.

Inside the cave, something moaned.

Belle froze. Possibilities tumbled over in her mind. The Rollen-Calf? Ole Higue? *A duppy?*

Another moan. This time it sounded more like an animal. A wounded cat? A goat? But did wounded goats sound like that?

Clutching the herbs in her fist, she edged closer.

An uprush of cool, earth-smelling air swept her face. At first she couldn't see anything, but as her eyes grew accustomed to the dimness she made out rough walls streaked with ratbat dung, a dirt floor, and, in a corner, a crumpled blanket of homespun, spattered with a great dark stain.

Her heart lurched. Beside the blanket lay a woman: curled up, motionless, and as grey as a duppy. It was Evie McFarlane.

CHAPTER TWENTY-SEVEN

That girl sick bad, said the voices in the cave walls. *Baby dead, him dead inside of her. And sure as sin, that girl ready to dead too.*

Drip, drip, drip went the spring at the back of the cave. *Father, brother, lover. Sin, sin, sin.*

Pain burns her belly. She screams. But the only sound she makes is a nightmare wheeze.

A while back, a little girl came and gave her water. She felt the butterfly brush of soft hair on her neck, and the sweet child-breath on her cheek. But then the little girl pressed a sprig of rosemary into her palm and whispered that she was going for help, and then she faded back into the walls.

Now all Evie can hear is the *drip, drip* of sin, and the murmur of the cave people. *What you doing in this old stone-hole, girl? This no place for you . . . This a bad-luckid place full of spirits and dead-bury memories . . .*

Then comes a new voice, a woman's. *If this is living, then I want no more of it . . .*

Who said that? Was it Congo Eve, or Evie McFarlane?

A woman needs lot, lotta courage to live in this wicked world . . . You got courage, Evie? You got spine?

'Christ, Evie, Christ . . .' mutters the man kneeling beside her.

Ben? What's Ben doing up here in the hills? Is he dead

too? Is he stuck in this old stone-hole alongside Evie McFarlane and Congo Eve and all the jealous, whispering spirits?

She hears the skitter of pebbles as he scrambles down the drop at the back of the cave towards the spring. Then his returning footsteps, and the clink of the bucket as he sets it down. 'Christ, Evie, Christ...' His voice is shaking, and he's swearing continuously under his breath.

Coolness floods her mouth. She swallows, splutters, and tries to swallow again. Coolness curls down inside of her, deep down where the fire lives.

He starts washing her neck and arms, but she pushes him away – or at least, she tries to. 'Damn it, Ben,' she tells him, 'I'm a woman, not one of your damn horses.' But the words won't come out. All she hears is a low, cracked moan.

Where'd he get the bucket? Oh yes, she remembers now. She brought it with her, didn't she? She planned it all out. The bucket and the blanket, the stack of hard dough, and the little bottle of bitter brown physic. The thought of that makes her want to retch.

Ben raises her in the crook of his arm to help her drink. Pain flares in her belly.

She opens her eyes. But it isn't Ben looking down at her, it's Cyrus Wright. 'Go *way*,' she mumbles. 'You rascally whoreson crowbait – go *way*.'

But Cyrus Wright isn't listening. Still supporting her in the crook of his arm, he takes off his jacket and rolls it up to make a pillow. It feels soft as he lays her down on it. It smells of horses and cigars, and it's warm from his body.

She must have dropped asleep, for when she wakes again Cyrus Wright has gone back into the walls, and she's alone. It's so quiet that she can hear the dust whispering across the floor, and the *plick* of the spring, and the endless murmur of the cave people, spinning their spells to send her to sleep.

When she awoke again, the cave people were gone. All she could hear was the rustle of the wind in the thorn tree at the mouth of the cave, and the high, lonely cry of a red-tailed hawk.

The pain was still there, deep in her belly, but it was duller now, no longer burning her up. *Baby dead, him dead*. Tears stung her eyes. She blinked them back. More tears left hot, salty trails down her cheeks.

She turned her head, and the glare at the mouth of the cave sent splinters of glass into her brain. She moaned.

A dark rock by the thorn tree moved and resolved into Ben. He came and knelt beside her and held his cupped hand to her lips for her to drink. The water tasted of earth and iron. Again she felt its cold strength curling down inside her: the strength of earth and iron and the spirits who lived in the cave. The strength of the Cockpits.

'How long have you been here?' she said. She was astonished by the weakness of her voice.

'A few hours,' he replied.

'How did you find me?'

'How do you feel?'

She turned her head away.

At the mouth of the cave, a tiny green lizard was sunning itself on a rock. Evie watched the fleeting motion of its sides: in, out, in, out. She licked her lips. Without turning her head she said, 'What did you do with the blanket?'

'I burnt it,' he said.

She tried to swallow, but her throat was too tight. 'Was there anything – could you see anything?'

'No. Not much.'

She shut her eyes tight, but the tears squeezed out just the same.

There was silence, while he knelt beside her with his hand on her shoulder, and she cried. Again she heard the red-tailed hawk out in the hills: high and far away and lonely. The loneliest sound in the world.

When she'd stopped crying, Ben said, 'Evie. Tell me something.'

She turned back to him.

'When you were delirious, you called me Cyrus. I didn't catch the surname—'

'Wright. Cyrus Wright.'

'Is he the father?'

She shook her head. 'Cyrus Wright died a long time ago. At least, I hope so.'

There was a pause while he considered that. Then he said, 'So who is the father?'

She did not reply.

'Evie?'

'Ben – no. I'm not telling.'

'But—'

'I said no.'

Another silence. Then he said softly, 'Christ, Evie, what the hell were you thinking? Why didn't you come to me? I would have got you the best doctors.'

'The best doctors are white. They wouldn't treat a mulatto girl who's no better than she should be.'

'Then I'd have got you a black doctor.'

'There's only one black doctor on the Northside, and he's my cousin.'

'And you don't want anyone to know. That's it, isn't it? That's why you came up here?'

She nodded.

'Not even your mother?'

'God, no! Specially not her.' She paused to recover her strength. 'She thinks I'm up at Mandeville, seeing a friend. And it's got to stay that way, Ben. You've got to promise me that.'

He nodded. But something in his eyes made her uneasy.

'How did you find me?' she asked again.

He told her how he'd been riding in the hills, and met a frightened little girl on a pony. 'She was babbling about something she'd found in a cave, so we came back here, and – there you were.' He cleared his throat. 'I did what I could for you, then I took Belle home. Well, at least I saw her safely to the crossroads.'

She frowned. 'Her name was Belle?'

'Yes. Isabelle Lawe.'

She shut her eyes in dismay. She pictured Belle excitedly telling her parents all about her adventure in the hills;

which would mean that by now old Braverly knew, and Moses and Poppy, and most of Trelawny. Including her mother.

'Don't worry about Belle,' said Ben, guessing her thoughts. 'She won't breathe a word.'

She threw him a suspicious look. 'Why not?'

'Because once we reached the crossroads, all she could think about was how she was going to catch it from her parents for venturing into the Cockpits. So I suggested a pact. I wouldn't rat on her, if she didn't rat on you.'

'And you're sure she'll stick to that?'

His lip curled. 'Oh, yes.'

She studied his face. 'There's something you're not telling.'

He turned his head to look at the cave mouth, then back to her. 'I sent for help.'

Her heart sank. 'What sort of help?'

He ran his thumb across his lower lip. 'I met young Neptune Parker, and sent him for supplies and horses.'

Jesus God. Neptune Parker was her second cousin! She opened her mouth to protest, but again Ben read her thoughts. 'Don't worry, he doesn't know you're up here. As far as he's concerned I've just found something interesting in a cave.'

But still she sensed that there was more to come. 'Was it only for supplies that you sent Neptune?'

Again he glanced away. 'No. I also sent him to deliver a note.'

'A note?'

He did not reply.

'Who'd you send for, Ben? Who?'

He met her eyes. 'She won't tell anyone, Evie. You know you can trust her.'

In a horrifying flash she realized who he meant. But she should have known! With Ben it always came back to the same woman. Always. Even though he wouldn't acknowledge it to himself.

She tried to rise up on her elbow, but the pain forced her

back. 'Jesus God, Ben! Sophie's the last person you should have told!'

'Listen,' he said between his teeth, 'I don't want her here any more than you do. But I had to get someone. And at least she'll have some idea of what to do.'

Sophie had no idea what Ben imagined she could do, but his request was so extraordinary that she obeyed it at once.

E.M. needs you. Bring medicine. Tell no-one (including Neptune). B.K.

A pencilled scrawl on a scrap of notepaper. In the space of a few seconds, she went from astonishment that he should seek her help, to indignation at his arrogance, to sharp anxiety for Evie. *Bring medicine.* Medicine for what?

By great good luck she was alone when the note arrived. Alexander had gone to a polo match at Rio Bueno, Cornelius was with Gus Parnell in Montego Bay, Rebecca was having her after-luncheon rest, and to Sophie's intense relief Sibella was spending the day at Ironshore with Davina and the little Irvings. Lately she'd been impossible: moody, restless and excitable. But she'd barely noticed when Sophie pleaded a headache and stayed at home.

It had been surprisingly easy to get away without being seen – although that was probably due to the network of servants conspiring to help her. Neptune Parker was related to Danny Tulloch the head groom, and also to Hannibal, the second footman; and at Parnassus that counted for more than loyalty to the master and mistress.

But to her consternation, Neptune wouldn't tell her a thing about where they were going. He was polite and respectful, but immovable. In taut silence they rode south-east through the cane-pieces to the edge of the estate. By the time they'd reached the Fever Hill Road, Sophie had had enough. 'Neptune, what on earth is this about?' she demanded, reining in her horse.

The boy looked unhappily at the ground and shook his

head. Tall and solemn, with a narrow, clever face, he'd clearly been chosen for his silent disposition. 'I don't know, Miss Sophie,' he mumbled. 'Master Ben just said for to fetch you quick-time.'

'But where are we going? You've got to tell me something, or I shan't go any further.'

He looked so unhappy that she felt a twinge of guilt. 'Somewhere up near Turnaround,' he muttered.

'Turnaround? But that's miles away, in the Cockpits!'

'Yes, ma'am.'

'What's up there?'

'I don't know, ma'am.'

She gave up. It wasn't fair to cross-examine him. Besides, given Ben's warning about mentioning Evie, there wasn't much more she could ask.

They turned into the gates of Fever Hill and headed up the carriageway, stopping only briefly at the stables to collect fresh horses and what Neptune laconically called 'supplies', before putting the great house behind them, and following the narrow trickle of the Green River south towards the Martha Brae. Sophie didn't have time to look about her, or feel more than a faint regret at this fleeting visit to the estate where she'd begun her life in Jamaica.

But now as they rode south through the nursery cane-pieces of Glen Marnoch, she realized that they were heading straight for Eden. Once they reached the Martha Brae, they would have to turn either right towards Stony Gap, or left towards Romilly. And if they were making for Turnaround, the eastward route via Romilly would be the more direct.

Romilly was on Eden land. Merely thinking about it brought her out in a cold sweat. She was astonished at the strength of her reaction. More than ever, she knew that she couldn't go anywhere near Eden.

By the time they reached the Martha Brae, she was clutching the reins to stop her hands from shaking. Neptune stopped briefly to water the horses, but she remained in the saddle, ready to turn tail and run.

Eden was breathtakingly close. If she threw a stone at

the opposite bank, she would hit it. Through the overarching plumes of the giant bamboo she could see the young cane of Orange Grove, where she and Evie used to play hide and seek. Half a mile downstream lay Romilly. And on the soft red banks directly opposite, old Braverly had taught Fraser to fish, in the final summer of his brief life.

Too many reminders. Too many memories. She couldn't go back. Cameron hadn't known what he was asking.

'Miss Sophie?' said Neptune.

She started.

He was looking at her oddly, and she realized that he must have spoken her name several times. 'We go now? Yes?'

'That depends,' she said. 'Which way?'

He gave her a puzzled look, then turned his horse's head right, towards Stony Gap. Master Ben, he explained, had said to avoid Eden land.

She hardly heard him. She was shaking with relief.

They followed the river upstream to the bridge at Stony Gap, then Neptune took her on a track she didn't know, which skirted the bare western slope of Overlook Hill before looping south around its foot, and coming out just south of the crossroads.

Now that she could forget about Eden, she had time to wonder about Ben. She hadn't seen him since that day at the Myrtle Bank Hotel. She didn't *want* to see him again. Especially not after that invitation to his Boxing Day Masquerade. What was he playing at now? What was she getting herself into?

An hour later, Neptune reined in beside a stunted calabash tree, and dismounted, and indicated the half-hidden mouth of a cave some twenty yards above the track.

Ben was nowhere about. 'Is he up there?' Sophie asked, pointing to the cave.

Neptune shook his head. Ben's hat was no longer on the boulder by the thorn tree, which apparently meant that he'd gone elsewhere.

His absence astonished her. She'd just ridden ten miles cross-country in the baking sun, and he didn't even have the decency to be here when she arrived. Setting her teeth, she dismounted, tethered her horse, and stiffly asked Neptune to lead the way. He politely declined. He had strict instructions not to go near the cave.

She didn't know if that made her feel better or worse. But as she unbuckled the saddlebag containing the hasty collection of medicines she'd cobbled together with the help of the Parnassus housekeeper, she felt the first bite of real alarm. She glanced at the mouth of darkness gaping in the hill. It looked horribly quiet and still. What would she find inside? And what did Ben imagine she could do? She wasn't a doctor. She wasn't even a nurse.

She drew a deep breath and gave Neptune what she hoped was a reassuring smile. 'Well, then,' she said briskly. 'If Master Ben comes back from wherever on earth he's got to, perhaps you'd be kind enough to tell him where I've gone.' Then she shouldered the saddlebag and began to climb.

After an hour she emerged from the cave, drying her hands on her handkerchief. And there he was: sitting on the ground halfway down the track, with his back to her and his elbows on his knees.

When he heard her he jumped to his feet. 'How is she?' he demanded.

No greeting. No *Thank God you came*. What did he care that she'd dropped everything for a one-line summons, and ridden ten miles in the afternoon sun? What did he care that she felt shaky and sick from the stink of blood and hopelessness in that cave?

Biting back her anger, she put her finger to her lips and motioned to him to follow her down the slope.

Neptune must have gone off to water the horses, because all that remained beneath the calabash tree was a neat stack of supplies. Sophie found a low wooden box in the shade, and sat down and put her head in her hands.

'How is she?' Ben said again.

'I gave her a febrifuge and a sleeping powder,' she muttered.

'And?'

'And she's asleep,' she snapped. She took off her hat and tossed it on the ground, and kneaded the back of her neck. 'She's extremely weak, and very low in spirits – which is hardly surprising. And furious with you for summoning me.'

She intended 'summon' as a reproach, but he ignored it. 'But she'll be all right?' he insisted.

'As far as I can tell, yes.'

His face was taut. He didn't seem to believe her.

She said sharply, 'I was surprised not to find you here when I arrived. Where were you?'

He blinked. 'What? Oh. She wanted some Madam Fate. I went to look for it.'

She glanced at his empty hands. 'No wonder you didn't find any. It doesn't grow round here.'

He wasn't listening. He was looking up at the cave, his face sharp with concern.

Not for the first time, she wondered if he was the father of Evie's child. But if he were, surely he would have looked after her better than this?

He turned back to her. 'Did she tell you who the father is?'

She shook her head. 'Who is he? D'you know?'

'Of course not. That's why I'm asking you.' He saw something in her face, and tossed his head. 'You thought it was me.'

'It crossed my mind.'

'Do you honestly think that if I were the father, I would have let her come up here?'

'I only said that it crossed my mind. I didn't—'

'Sooner or later,' he cut in, 'she'll have to tell me his name. And when she does, I'll rip his spine out.'

She could see that he meant it. She almost envied Evie for inspiring such fierce concern.

He turned back to her and searched her face. 'Are you absolutely sure that she's going to be all right?'

'I told you, I'm as sure as I can be.'

He looked at her for a moment. Then he threw himself onto a boulder and put his elbows on his knees and his head in his hands. 'God,' he muttered. 'God.'

It was only then that she realized just how worried he'd been.

And as she watched him, something stirred at the back of her mind. That day at the clinic, when she'd asked him about his sister. *Did she get pregnant? Did she have to go to a – an angel-maker? Isn't that what they call them?* He had flinched as if she'd struck him. Clearly it had touched a very raw nerve. So perhaps what had happened to Evie had touched a raw nerve too. Perhaps it had brought bad memories to the surface.

That day at Bethlehem. She remembered every detail. Belle squatting beneath the breadfruit tree with Spot. Ben turning the toy in his hands, and suddenly smiling. That brief, astounding moment when he'd kissed her for the first time.

Suddenly she felt an enormous sadness. She thought, What children we were. And look at us now. Evie up in that cave, crying for her dead child; me stuck at Parnassus in an impossible engagement. And Ben – what about Ben?

As he straightened up, she looked at his face. Wealth seemed to have given him authority, but it didn't seem to have brought him either happiness or peace.

He was hatless and dishevelled, in riding-breeches, dusty topboots and shirtsleeves rolled to the elbow. He looked just the same as he had in the old days. It was almost as if the last seven years had never happened – as if she'd simply gone riding one afternoon, and come across him up in the hills. Only the scar bisecting his eyebrow bore witness to the passage of time.

She looked at the dark hair falling into his eyes. It seemed cruel that she could remember exactly how it felt if one brushed it aside. It was so unfair. What was the good of remembering? He clearly did not.

There was an awkward silence. Then he said, 'I suppose I ought to thank you for coming.'

'Oh please,' she said tartly, 'don't do anything just because you "ought".'

That seemed to surprise him. Then his lip curled. 'I take it that this won't cause problems for you?'

'What kind of problems?'

'I mean, with your – fiancé.'

She felt herself reddening. Until that moment she'd forgotten all about Alexander. It simply hadn't crossed her mind that by coming here she had flouted every one of his prohibitions: not to go for long rides, not to see Evie McFarlane, and not to have anything to do with Ben Kelly. 'There won't be any problem,' she said firmly. 'Neptune was very discreet.' She paused. 'Speaking of Neptune, you told him to avoid Eden. Why?'

He shrugged. 'I'm not on very good terms with your brother-in-law. As I'm sure you already know.'

'As it happens, I didn't. I don't often see them.' As soon as she'd said it she wished that she hadn't. But she was tired, and the spirit of contradiction was strong in her. It always was when she was with Ben.

As she feared, he picked up on it. 'What do you mean, you don't often see them?'

'Just that. I haven't been back there in a while.'

'How long is a while?'

She did not reply.

'You haven't been back since you left. Have you?'

Damn him for jumping to the right conclusion.

'Seven years,' he said, incredulous. 'Good God Almighty.'

How pitiful she must seem to him. So terrified of the past that she couldn't even bring herself to go back once for a visit. He, on the other hand, seemed to have put it all behind him with remarkable ease.

She watched him draw out his watch and frown at it, then snap it shut. 'It's getting late,' he said, standing up and brushing off his hands. 'Neptune will be back soon with the horses. He'll take you home.'

'Thank you,' she replied, 'but I think I'll wait and help you bring Evie back.'

'She isn't coming.'

She blinked. 'What do you mean?'

'She wants to stay up here till she's better.'

'*What?* But she can't.'

'Try telling her that.'

'In a *cave*? But—'

'Look, she doesn't want anyone to know, especially not her own family. And in case you've forgotten, you've only got to spit in this damn country and you hit half a dozen McFarlanes or Tullochs or Parkers.'

'I haven't forgotten,' she retorted. 'I haven't forgotten anything.'

He threw her a curious glance. Then he said, 'You don't need to worry. She'll be all right. I'll stay with her tonight. And tomorrow—'

'Tomorrow I'll come up and see how she is.'

'That won't be necessary.'

'Oh, I think that it will.'

He sighed. 'You couldn't manage it without your fiancé knowing.'

'You leave that to me,' she snapped. She wasn't sure exactly how she *would* manage it, but she was damned if she was going to be dismissed like some servant who'd outlived her usefulness.

He put his hands on his hips and took a few paces up the track, then turned back to her. She thought he meant to remonstrate with her, but instead he said simply, 'I think I need to apologize to you.'

She was astonished. 'For what?'

'That day in Kingston. I gave you a bad time of it. I overdid things.'

She thought about that. Then she raised her chin. 'Do you know,' she said in a cut-glass accent, 'I rather fancy that you did.'

He laughed. 'All right, I deserved that. In my defence, I think I was still a bit angry with you. But that's all over now.'

She felt a gentle sinking in the pit of her stomach.

In the distance, Neptune appeared with the horses. Ben

watched them for a moment, then turned back to her. 'Seven years ago,' he began, then cut himself off with a frown.

'Yes?' she said. 'Seven years ago, what?'

Again he glanced at Neptune, who was still out of earshot. 'Just this,' he said. 'I was a fool, and you were right. You were right to break it off. It would never have worked.'

Slowly she pushed herself to her feet. Then she picked up her hat and dusted it off. 'Probably not,' she said.

He nodded, his face grave. 'I just thought it needed saying, that's all.'

'I see.'

'Well. I'll tell Neptune to take you back.'

'Yes. Thank you.'

He thought for a moment, then held out his hand. 'Goodbye, Sophie.'

She looked at it without speaking. Then she shook hands with him, and looked up into his face and tried to smile. 'Goodbye, Ben,' she said.

CHAPTER TWENTY-EIGHT

Christmas on the Northside is a strange time of year.

People celebrate in the usual way by going to church and eating too much Christmas pudding, and having Johnny Canoe parades, but there's always a ghost at the feast: the shadow of the great slave rebellion of Christmas 1831.

The white people call it the Christmas Insurrection; the black people call it the Black Family War. Everyone knows somebody who lived through it. Everyone knows the stories. Fifty-two Northside plantations destroyed. Dozens of great houses reduced to cinders, thousands of acres of cane put to the fire. Fever Hill, Kensington, Parnassus, Montpelier; even old Duncan Lawe's place out at Seven Hills – which two years later, in his bitterness at the emancipation of the slaves, he renamed Burntwood.

Great-Aunt May was twelve years old when she sat in the wagon beside her baleful old father, Alasdair Monroe, and watched their great house go up in flames. She saw the cane-pieces destroyed, and the sugar works at the foot of Clairmont Hill; she saw the huge boiling-house chimney come crashing down like a cathedral.

And seven weeks later, when the insurrection had been savagely crushed, she had sat beside her father again, and watched the hangings in the square. In the course of the rebellion, fourteen white people had died, and about two hundred slaves. Some four hundred more were killed in the reprisals which old Alasdair helped to orchestrate.

In the eighty years since then, Great-Aunt May had never spoken of what she'd seen – except once, to Clemency. And years later, on an overcast Christmas Eve when Clemency was being more than usually badgered for a bedtime story, she had told a thirteen-year-old Sophie.

Ever since then, Christmas for Sophie had possessed a dark undercurrent. It never felt completely real. It was a time when light and dark, life and death, past and present, danced side by side at the great masquerade.

Fraser's death had added another layer of darkness. Christmas had become a time when terrible memories broke the surface without warning. She might be sitting at tea with Rebecca Traherne, or reading to Clemency from the fashion report in the Saturday supplement, and suddenly she would be back on the steps at Eden in her nightgown, straining for the sound of carriage wheels in the dark. She would hear the soft whisper of the bronze satin evening mantle settling in the dust. She would see the blood drain from her sister's cheeks. And then would come that terrible, desolate, animal cry.

Light and dark, past and present, life and death. Not real, not real.

Now here she sat in her ballgown beside Alexander – this man who overnight had become a stranger to her – as the phaeton made its way slowly up the carriageway towards the great house on Fever Hill.

It had been seven days since that strange meeting with Ben up in the Cockpits, and since then she had led a double life. Polite, sleep-walking days at Parnassus were punctuated by wild rides into the hills to see Evie. No-one seemed to notice her absence. Nothing seemed real any more.

She turned and regarded Alexander. He was in a difficult mood, for Cornelius had taken the hated Lyndon in his brougham, and relegated them to the second carriage; but not even ill humour could spoil his good looks. He had chosen the Sailor for his costume, and the tight white uniform with its rich gold braiding suited him to perfection. No wonder, she thought, that Evie fell in love with him.

She still couldn't quite believe it. Two days before, she had taken Evie some books, and found her swiftly regaining her strength – and with it, her anger. An unguarded word about Parnassus had slipped out. Sophie had guessed the rest.

Evie and Alexander. All those visits to Kingston 'on business'. Of course.

Evie had lifted her chin and given her a look of cool defiance from which she couldn't banish the anxiety. 'If it's any comfort,' she'd said, 'it started long before you met him in London.'

'I don't need comfort,' Sophie had replied. 'It's just – unexpected. That's all. I don't even mind. I really don't.'

But in the days that followed, she discovered that that wasn't entirely true. She *did* mind. She minded that she'd been so wrong about him. She minded that she'd been so easily taken in. She minded that he'd only ever been after her money.

And what breathtaking hypocrisy! Calmly to caution her against the impropriety of befriending a mulatto girl, when he himself had impregnated that same girl, and then thrown her aside.

My God, she thought, as the phaeton trundled up the carriageway, how did everything get so twisted? Here you are with this weak, mendacious, unfaithful man, whom you intend to jilt as soon as decently possible after Christmas – here you are, making your way to *Fever Hill*, for a masked ball to be given by Ben. None of it makes sense. It isn't real.

The press of carriages was great, so their progress was slow. She turned her head and tried to lose herself in the flickering lights strung between the royal palms. Ruby, saffron, sapphire, emerald. She caught a glimpse of the great house on the hill, ablaze with electric light. That couldn't be Fever Hill. Not Fever Hill. Not real, not real.

They passed the pond and the aqueduct, and the creeper-clad ruins of the Old Works. Without warning, torches flared amid the tumbled cut-stone. A dark figure cut across the flames, bare-chested and inhuman in a fearsome bull-horned mask. She caught her breath. Suddenly it was seven years ago, and she was back at the Jonkunoo Parade at Bethlehem, looking for Ben. Not real, not real.

'Apparently,' said Alexander beside her, 'our Mr Kelly is letting the estate workers have their own parade – at the Old Works, if you please. Given that the beggars burnt it to cinders in the rebellion, I call that confoundedly poor taste.'

Sophie did not reply. She remembered the smell of pimento smoke at Bethlehem; the gnawing dread that she would never find Ben.

But that was then, she told herself, and this is now. *That's all over.* That's what he said.

She hadn't seen him since that day in the hills, for he'd contrived to be away whenever she visited Evie. But she was glad of that. She didn't want to see him again. And she didn't want to see him tonight. What was the point? It was all over now.

'Your grandpapa,' said Alexander, cutting across her thoughts, 'would never have permitted a thing like that.'

'A thing like what?'

'A Johnny Canoe parade down at the Old Works. Haven't you been listening?'

She looked down at her lap and realized that she'd been clenching her fists. Alexander didn't yet know that she knew about Evie. But he seemed to have sensed the change in her; he seemed determined to needle her into conversation.

'Apparently,' he went on, watching her, 'our Mr Kelly has brought his family out for Christmas. Isn't that sweet? Although of course, the fact that they're dead does rather put a dampener on things.' He paused. 'I hear he's got the coffins up at the hot-house ruins. Just beyond your family Burying-place.'

'I know,' she said with an edge to her voice. 'Sibella heard it in town three days ago and told us all about it. Don't you remember?'

'Ah yes, so she did. Darling Sib. She seems to have developed quite a fascination for our handsome Mr Kelly.' Lightly, he slapped his gloves against his thigh. 'It must have been devilish tricky, getting the blacks to handle the coffins at all. Don't you think?'

Again she did not reply.

'And I hear there's even talk of a mausoleum. I call that vulgar in the extreme.'

'Other people have mausoleums,' she said.

He smiled. 'I knew that in the end you'd leap to his defence.'

'Why do you say that?'

'My darling, I wonder you can even ask, when you've been meeting him in secret up in the hills.'

Ah. So that was it. She turned and met his eyes.

He was still softly slapping his gloves against his thigh, and looking very slightly pained. 'I'm sorry I had to bring it up,' he said, 'but I thought it for the best.'

'How did you know about it?' she asked. 'Did you have me followed?'

'Does it matter?'

Slowly she shook her head. After what he'd done to Evie, none of it mattered. And yet, ridiculously, she felt guilty. She had lied to him, and she'd been caught out. 'If it's any consolation,' she said, 'it wasn't an assignation. There's nothing between me and Mr Kelly.'

'I never for a moment imagined that there was. The problem is,' he added delicately, 'other people won't see it that way.'

She looked down at the mask in her lap. It was a deep midnight blue, like her gown, and edged in tiny brilliants. She couldn't wear it now. She was sick of masks.

What is the point, she wondered, of waiting till after Christmas to have it out with him? Why not do it now and get it over with?

She raised her head. 'I went into the hills to help Evie,' she said calmly. 'Do you remember Evie? Evie McFarlane?'

He took that without a flicker.

'She needed help,' she went on. 'You see, someone – some man – has let her down rather badly.'

'So she ran off into the hills?' He raised an eyebrow. 'Good Lord, the things these people do.'

'Alexander,' she said wearily, 'let's do away with the pretence. I can't marry you. I know about Evie.'

Another silence. He ran his thumb across his bottom lip, then gave her a small, rueful smile. 'Well? And what of that?'

She blinked.

'I'm most awfully sorry if I've hurt you, old girl,' he said gently, 'but what you must understand is that it didn't mean a thing. Those sorts of affairs never do.'

'It meant something to Evie.'

'Well it oughtn't to have done. She knew perfectly well what she was about. And I never made her any promises.'

'Does that make it all right?'

'It makes it – well, it makes it the sort of thing which happens all the time. Everyone knows that.'

When she did not reply, he took her hand and squeezed it. 'You want to punish me. I understand that. And I admit, I've been most frightfully wicked. But now I've been punished, and I promise that I'll never do it again. No more wild oats. I shall be the most faithful spouse in Christendom. You have my word.'

She opened her mouth to reply, but he put his finger lightly to her lips.

'Be reasonable, my darling. Forgive us our trespasses, and all that?'

'No, you don't understand—'

'Sorry to be a bore, but I really think I do. And I think you ought to forgive me *my* little trespass, as I forgive you yours.'

'You – forgive me?' she said in disbelief.

He smiled. 'Well of course.'

'For what? I told you, there's nothing between me and—'

'But there was, though, wasn't there?'

Again she met his eyes.

'Seven years ago,' he went on, still in that gentle, apologetic tone, 'you – how can I put this without descending to indelicacy – you knew the man, in the Biblical sense.'

She swallowed. 'How long have you known?'

He gave a little laugh. 'How very like you not even to attempt to deny it.'

'Why should I? How long have you known?'

'Oh, for absolutely ever. Darling Sib put two and two together from something your sister let slip just after you'd left for England. And of course she simply had to tell me.' He paused. 'But all that's beside the point, my love. The point is, you *mustn't worry*. I shall never breathe a word to a living soul.'

Something about the way he said it was anything but reassuring. 'What do you mean?' she said uneasily.

'It's really quite astonishing, the double standards which the world applies to this sort of thing. Don't you agree?'

She licked her lips. She was beginning to see where he was heading.

'Say we were to perform a small experiment: say we were to tell the fellows at the Caledonian a little story about Miss Monroe and some dreadful low brute of a groom – and then *another* story about Master Alex Traherne and some pretty little mulatto girl. D'you know what they'd say? They'd slap me on the back for being a jolly good fellow and a confoundedly lucky dog; while you, my poor darling – why, you would be utterly beyond the pale.' He shook his head. 'You wouldn't be able to show your face anywhere. And I shudder to think what the scandal would do to your sister, and that darling little girl of hers. People can be so horribly ill-natured.'

She opened her mouth to reply, but just then they swept up to the house, and liveried footmen ran forward to open the doors, and there was no more time for talk.

It looked to Ben as if everyone was having a bloody good time. Except, that is, for the host.

He watched old Mrs Palairet shuffling along on the arm of her nephew, a tall young lad out from England for the holidays. The old lady gave Ben a gracious nod, and the lad from England threw him a slightly long-suffering smile.

Ben inclined his head as they passed. He had no illusions that they'd accepted him as one of their own. Northside Society – the upper two hundred – had only come to his party in order to tear him to bits in its kid-gloved claws. But then a strange thing had happened. To Society's surprise, it had found that, thanks to Austen, everything was being 'done rather well'. So it had decided to enjoy itself instead.

Even Isaac and Austen were having a good time. Isaac – one of about a dozen fancy-dress Sailors – was chatting to a cluster of wealthy banana farmers from Tryall, and even Austen was circulating with that inborn sociability which the shyest of the gentry seems to know how to affect. He'd chosen the Doctor for his costume, and the dark frock coat and severe black mask suited him, and somewhat disguised his nose. And as he was a good dancer, he hadn't lacked for partners. He'd even stood up with Sibella Palairet, although he'd been too abashed to say a word.

Ben could see the little widow now, circling the ballroom with Augustus Parnell. She'd been one of the first to arrive, with her mother-in-law, with whom she was spending Christmas. Ben had been putting off talking to her ever since.

For the festivities she'd interpreted half-mourning liberally, and wore a heavily corseted creation of mauve satin, with a prettily ineffectual gold lace mask and a headdress of mauve silk lilacs. The lilacs reminded Ben of Kate's imitation violets. *Sixpence a gross, but you've got to stump up for your own paper and paste.* He put that firmly from his mind, and drained his glass.

The little widow had spotted him watching her. Self-consciously she turned and spoke to Parnell, with a sidelong glance of studied insouciance which must have fooled no-one.

Oh, God, thought Ben wearily. He'd been putting it off for weeks, but tonight he'd have to decide. Either he must keep his promise to that old witch down in Duke Street and seduce Sibella, or he must come clean and tell her he was going back on the bargain.

It was a humiliating thought, and it made him feel more apart than ever. He looked about him at the enormous, glittering ballroom. What was he doing here? How had it come to this?

Fever Hill – his beloved old house of peace and silence and mellow sunlight – had been overrun. Everywhere he turned he saw a blaze of electric chandeliers; a brilliant blur of satin; an artificial forest of ferns and huge oriental bowls of orchids.

Those bloody orchids. He'd intended them as a little dig at Sophie. 'Just keep the tone Jamaican,' he'd told Austen when they were discussing the arrangements. 'The food, the decorations, all of it Jamaican. And plenty of orchids. Make sure of that.'

That had been before he'd met her up in the hills. But since then he'd forgotten to change his instructions, so orchids were everywhere. Great showy scarlet Broughtonia; white, waxen Dames de Noce; the delicate veined petals of cockleshells.

The heavy perfume reminded him painfully of Romilly. It also underlined the fact that Madeleine and Cameron Lawe had not relented, as he'd been hoping they would, but had stayed away. And to cap it all, the party from Parnassus hadn't even turned up yet – and when they did, she probably wouldn't even remember. She'd forgotten about Romilly. Why else would she be marrying Alexander Traherne in a fortnight's time?

Yes, the whole thing had spectacularly backfired. A Boxing Day Masquerade! Why had it occurred to him to do it? Had he lied to her that day in the hills? Could it be that he *was* still angry with her, and didn't even know it?

Suddenly he felt breathless. Ignoring his guests, he

walked swiftly from the ballroom, and through to the back of the house.

Supper was being laid out on the newly landscaped south lawns. Down by the cookhouse, a whole jerked hog was crackling over a barbecue of pimento wood; nearer the house, liveried footmen were setting out great silver dishes of Jamaican delicacies on long damask-covered tables. Mountain mullet and turtle soup; oysters in hot pepper sauce; ring-tailed pigeons and baked black land-crabs.

When he was a boy, he would have given an arm for a spread like this. He pictured his brothers and sisters descending on it like a pack of scruffy little harpies, then piling together in a heap to sleep it off.

He longed to go up to the hot-house ruins on the other side of the hill, and be with them in the darkness. Three heavy mahogany coffins sealed with lead and, inside, what was left of Robbie and Lil and Kate. Thinking of them up in the ruins made him feel like a ghost. He couldn't fit it all together in his mind. His brother and sisters up there, and him down here.

On another table, two maids were setting out Bombay mangoes and figs next to a dish of preserved ginger. In the centre stood a great crystal bowl of purple star-apple and nutmeg and cream: an old Jamaican favourite, named matrimony. That was another little dig at Sophie. Not that she'd notice.

He thought how pitiful he must seem to her. All this, just to show her what he'd made of himself.

Why had it taken him so long to realize that? Even the other day, when Evie had pointed it out once again, he'd hotly denied it. 'Ben,' she'd said, 'when you going to face up to it? All you do, you do because of her.' He'd been speechless with anger. If she hadn't been so weak, he would have shaken her.

And yet she was right. Buying Fever Hill. Coming back to Jamaica. Throwing this bloody party. It was all because of Sophie. But what did she care? She was going to marry Alexander Traherne.

349

He thought of her that day in the hills, snapping at him like a vixen. He'd been wrong about her in Kingston. She hadn't changed at all.

A footman glided past with a tray of champagne, and Ben exchanged his empty glass for a full one, and went back into the house. It was time to be the dutiful host again: to return to his post on the north verandah, and greet the stragglers. Eleven o'clock. Another seven hours to go. Heigh-ho.

And there she was, coming up the main steps on the arm of her fiancé.

Ben saw her before she saw him, and he was grateful for that. She wore a narrow-skirted, high-waisted gown of midnight blue, shot through with changing sea-green. It was cut in a deep V at front and back – so deep that it left the pale shoulders bare – and was only held up by two slender blue straps. No jewels and no mask. The wavy light-brown hair was tied back at the temples and hung loose down her back, restrained only by a narrow bandeau of blue silk in which was set a tiny enamelled fish.

He knew at once what the costume was meant to be. She was the River Mistress – the shadowy siren who haunts Jamaican rivers and entices men to their doom. Years ago, she had told him that as a child she used to go down to the Martha Brae and ask the River Mistress to watch over him. Had she forgotten that? Or was this some kind of sly dig, just as the orchids and the matrimony were with him?

He moved forward to greet them. 'I thought the River Mistress only ever appeared at noon,' he said as he briefly took her hand.

She gave him a practised smile. 'Very occasionally I make an exception.'

'I'm honoured that you made one for me.' He turned to Alexander Traherne and held out his hand.

'How do, Kelly?' said the fiancé, just touching the tips of his fingers.

'How do, Traherne?' Ben replied, mimicking his tone.

Traherne ignored that. 'I see that you're exercising the host's prerogative, and eschewing both mask and fancy dress. I must say, I envy you the tailcoat. This sailor's uniform is confoundedly heating. And I never could abide a mask.'

'Then don't wear it,' said Ben with a smile. He turned back to Sophie. 'You know, I was surprised when I saw that you'd accepted. I never thought that you would.'

'Alexander said that we ought,' she replied sweetly.

She seemed on edge, and Ben wondered if they'd had a fight. A lover's tiff, he thought sourly; with all the fun of making up still to come. 'So you obeyed your fiancé,' he remarked. 'How very right and proper.'

She didn't like that. The little dents at the corners of her mouth deepened ominously. 'Was that Great-Aunt May's carriage we saw by the steps?' she asked. 'So she really has been as good as her word?'

God, she was quick. If you stung her, she stung right back.

'We're all agog,' she went on. 'What did you have to do to persuade her to send him?'

He flinched. She couldn't possibly know anything about that sordid little bargain. No-one knew except himself and Miss Monroe. 'I made her a promise,' he said lightly.

'What kind of promise?'

'I can't say.'

Alexander swallowed a yawn. 'How desperately intriguing,' he murmured. 'Come along, darling, we oughtn't to monopolize our host.'

But Sophie had seen Ben flinch, and she was on to it. 'And shall you keep your promise,' she asked, 'whatever it is?'

At that moment Sibella Palairet appeared in the gallery, trotting out for air on the arm of the young lad from England, and resolutely not glancing at Ben. She looked flushed and pretty, and slightly pitiable.

'Shall you keep your promise?' said Sophie again.

'I don't know,' murmured Ben.

'You don't know? But when do you mean to decide?'

He turned and looked down into her honey-coloured eyes. He kept looking.

Years ago, when he'd first arrived in Jamaica, old Cecilia Tulloch had warned him about the River Mistress. *Don't you go meeting her eyes, bwoy*, she'd said, waggling her fat finger in his face, *or you done with everyting*.

Don't go meeting her eyes, bwoy. As he stood looking down into those honey-coloured eyes, he thought: Trust me to remember that sixteen years too late.

He glanced from Sophie Monroe to her fiancé, and back again. Ah, but what does it matter? he thought in disgust. She's getting married in a couple of weeks. What does any of it matter?

'I think,' he said slowly, 'that I probably shall keep my side of the bargain, after all.'

'When?' she asked.

'When what?'

'When shall you keep this mysterious "bargain"?'

He thought for a moment. 'Later tonight.'

CHAPTER TWENTY-NINE

Every time Sibella saw Ben Kelly, her stomach turned over.

She had never felt like this before, and she hated it. It was terrifying and humiliating. She didn't want it to end.

She could see him now, waltzing with Olivia Herapath. They made a curious couple: the little fat aristocrat, outrageously colourful in an obeah-woman's headkerchief and strident print gown, and the tall, slender adventurer in the immaculate black tailcoat and faultless white linen. One had to look closely to perceive the one detail in his dress which was deliberately off: the shirtstuds were not the plain pearls which were *de rigueur*, but very small black diamonds.

'Black diamonds,' Alexander had murmured to his friends. 'I call that devilish vulgar.'

'Or just plain devilish?' quipped Dickie Irving.

'What? Devilish?' said Walter Mordenner, who was always three steps behind. 'D'you imagine that's who he's supposed to be? By George, that's a pretty rum sort of joke!'

Sibella didn't think it a joke at all. Ben Kelly terrified her. He made her feel breathless and confused: desperate to see him again, but speechless with fear when she did. And since that never-to-be-forgotten episode on the Fever Hill Road three weeks before, she had dreamed of him every night. The most vivid, febrile, horrifying dreams, in which he did things to her which— No, no, she couldn't even think about it.

And yet in those dreams she let him do it. She whimpered and moaned for more. And when she awoke she was still whimpering, and desperate to get back into the dream. She didn't know herself any longer. There was another woman inside her: a savage female beast, fighting to get out.

It did no good telling herself that he was a gutter-born scoundrel with not a drop of decent blood in his body. She didn't care about that. She didn't want to *talk* to him. She just wanted him to kiss her again.

That was why she was here now, in this great crowded ballroom, counting the minutes until she could go to him. *The Burying-place, midnight*, his note had said. Every time she thought of it she felt faint.

He hadn't danced with her or said a word to her all evening, apart from the briefest of greetings when she'd arrived. If it hadn't been for that note slipped inside her invitation, she could have pretended that she'd imagined the whole thing. But there it was in that bold black scrawl. *The Burying-place, midnight; if nothing else, to return that token you let fall the other day.*

'If nothing else'? What did that mean? The Burying-place? *At midnight?* They would be alone together. Absolutely alone. She pictured the long pale grass glowing in the moonlight. She saw herself laid out like a sacrifice on a marble tomb: eyes closed, hands crossed beneath her breasts. Passive. Surrendering to him.

Suddenly she couldn't bear the ballroom a moment longer. She pushed through the crowds and ran out to the verandah, then down the steps onto the lawns.

She took deep breaths of the warm night air. The scent of star jasmine clogged her throat. The lights strung between the trees became a coloured blur.

'Are you unwell?' said a man's voice behind her.

She spun round. Her heart jerked with disappointment. Gus Parnell stood on the bottom step, watching her. 'N-no,' she stammered. 'That is, I am quite well. Thank you.'

His costume was that of the Doctor: the same as poor ugly Freddie Austen. But unlike Austen, it didn't suit Parnell. It made him look like an undertaker. 'Forgive me,' he said, 'but you appear a trifle flushed.'

'It was the crush in the ballroom. Such an unseasonably hot night. Don't you agree?'

'I'm afraid I'm not in a position to say what is seasonable and what is not, since this is my first Christmas in the tropics.'

'Oh, of course. I was forgetting.'

'However, if you find it too exciting, perhaps you would care for an ice?'

She forced a smile. 'How thoughtful. Would you be so kind as to fetch me one?'

'I should consider it a privilege.'

She watched him go. Then she picked up her skirts and ran round the corner of the house and onto the lawns on the west side, so that he wouldn't be able to find her when he returned.

Every time she thought about Gus Parnell, her spirits sank. If she wasn't very careful, she would begin to hate him.

They had known each other for seven months, they were on the point of becoming engaged; but he still talked to her as if they'd only just met. She tried to tell herself that things would improve once they were married, but she knew that they wouldn't. One might as well ask such a man to befriend his valet as to make genuine conversation with a woman.

And yet when he did propose, she intended to accept. If she didn't marry again, she would be nothing; she might as well be dead. And Papa expected it of her. He'd made it very clear in that awful interview in his study. He needed Parnell to shore up the estate.

Besides, why was she hesitating? Gus Parnell was a gentleman, and enormously rich. She would have everything she wanted. Houses in Belgrave Square and Berkshire; an *hôtel* in Neuilly and a hunting-lodge in Scotland; accounts at Worth and Poiret. She would be the envy of all her friends.

'But you don't love him,' Sophie had said the other day, in that infuriating way she had of speaking her mind.

Sibella had turned on her. 'What does that matter? I didn't "love" Eugene, but we got along perfectly well.'

Sophie had looked at her doubtfully. 'But – did Eugene make you happy?'

'Oh, Sophie, stop being such a child! What has that to do with anything?'

After that Sophie hadn't said a word. She'd merely touched Sibella's shoulder and looked at her with a sympathy which had made Sibella want to shake her.

What did Sophie know about anything? She knew nothing. She still believed that marriage was about wedding presents and 'making people happy'. Well, it was time that she found out the truth. Marriage means a great red-faced man thrusting into you as he grinds his palm down on your mouth to stifle your cries. Marriage means nine months of the most appalling indignities. It means being treated like an animal by disapproving old doctors with stale breath and liver-spotted hands. It means two days of squalor and agony, and then a dead infant; and being told not to dwell on it, because there'll be more babies soon enough. That's what marriage means. And it was high time that Sophie found out.

A burst of music from the ballroom. She turned and saw Ben Kelly on the verandah, moving silently among his brightly costumed guests like a wolf in a sheepfold.

All thoughts of marriage fell away. Gus Parnell ceased to exist. She could think of nothing but how she had felt when that man had kissed her on the Fever Hill Road.

It had begun so innocently. And no-one – *no-one* – could say that her behaviour had been in any way to blame. She'd thought about that a lot, and was quite certain. It was a great comfort.

She'd been in Falmouth, and was just coming out of Olivia Herapath's little studio when she'd bumped into him on the pavement. For a moment she'd been alarmed. She was quite alone, with no allies in sight and not even a passerby for protection. And the last time they'd met she had tried to cut him, and he'd laughed at her.

But to her relief, he didn't laugh now. He merely lifted his hat with grave courtesy and asked how she was, and then walked with her the few yards to her pony-trap. Then he handed her in, made a compliment about Princess, her little grey mare, and took his leave.

But after a few steps he turned back, and casually suggested that as it was market day and there was such traffic on the Coast Road, she might do better to take the Fever Hill Road home, thus reaching Parnassus by the back way, through the cane-pieces. It was a perfectly proper suggestion for a gentleman to make to a lady, and she thanked him, without indicating whether she intended to follow his advice.

But as her little equipage bowled along the Fever Hill Road, her heart began to pound. And by the time she'd left town and reached the section of road which giant bamboo turns into a shadowy green tunnel, she was light-headed with anticipation.

It's simply the lack of air, she told herself. But she slowed Princess to a walk, and strained for the sound of a horseman behind her. Of course there was nothing.

Then she began to fancy that the mare had developed a limp. Not a pronounced limp, but nevertheless Sibella judged it prudent to pull up in the shade of the giant bamboo and wait until someone should come by to assist her. Otherwise Princess might go lame.

And after a few minutes, he came.

'It's probably just a stone,' he said, dismounting and coming round to take a look at the mare. 'But we don't want her to get a stone-bruise, do we?'

She sat very straight in the pony-trap and hardly moved her head. 'Oughtn't you first to tie up your horse?' she suggested timidly, for he'd left his reins carelessly trailing on his saddle.

He glanced at her over his shoulder, and smiled. 'Don't worry, she knows not to stray.' And sure enough, the big, sleek chestnut stood patiently by her master, like a dog.

For some reason, that made Sibella blush. She watched him drawing off his gloves and tossing them in the grass with his hat, then gently lifting the grey's off foreleg and exploring the tender underside with his fingers.

She began to feel dizzy. No gentleman, she told herself, has brown hands like that, with black hairs on the wrists. Her heart began to pound.

'Here we are,' he said. He took a small pearl-handled knife from his pocket and deftly prised out a pebble, then set down the mare's hoof and gave the leg an absent caress.

Sibella looked at the line of his jaw, and the way the dark hair fell into his eyes, and her stomach turned over.

'You'll be able to walk her home now,' he said, flicking back his hair as he looked up into her face. 'But go gently. She mustn't be rushed.'

She nodded. She couldn't trust herself to speak.

'And when you get back to Parnassus,' he went on, still looking into her eyes and caressing the mare's neck with one hand, 'you might tell old Danny that she's taken a slight cut in the sole. Get him to wash it out with a little carbolized oil.'

'Carbolized oil,' she murmured, watching his mouth. He had a beautiful mouth: chiselled, like the mouth of a statue.

'That's right,' he said. 'Carbolized oil.'

She tried to swallow. 'The whole hoof?' she mumbled. Her lips felt hot and swollen.

He shook his head. 'Just the cut. Here, shall I show you?'

She didn't say yes. At least, she couldn't remember saying yes. But the next moment he was lifting her down from the pony-trap – respectfully, there was nothing wrong in it – and she was standing beside him in that whispering, shadowy tunnel beneath the giant bamboo.

He stooped to pick up the mare's hoof in order to show her, and she saw how the muscles of his shoulders strained his jacket. Then he set down the hoof again and straightened up, and repeated the instructions for Danny.

She watched his mouth and didn't hear a word. Then he took out his handkerchief and brushed off his hands. 'You know,' he said calmly as he pocketed the handkerchief, 'I've been thinking about you.' Then he put his hands lightly on her shoulders and bent and kissed her.

She'd been over it a hundred times, but she could never recall exactly how it happened. One moment she was standing beside him, thinking that he was taller than she remembered, and that the green of his eyes had little flecks of russet, and was that a sign of danger; and the next moment, without any force or compulsion, he'd placed his hands on her shoulders – *gently, gently, she mustn't be rushed* – and covered her mouth with his own.

Never in her life had she experienced anything so wonderful as that kiss. The heat, the dizziness, the spiralling down into a pleasure she'd never known or imagined could exist. He parted her lips with his own and invaded her mouth – *gently, gently, she mustn't be rushed* – and her knees buckled and she moaned like an animal and threw her arms around his neck. She opened her mouth fiercely wide to take him in. She clung to him until she could no longer breathe, until black spots darted before her eyes. Then he broke from her and his mouth moved down to the tender spot beneath her jaw and he sucked at her pulse, and the pleasure was so intense that she nearly passed out.

Suddenly, but as gracefully as he'd begun, he stopped. 'I'm sorry,' he murmured. 'I suppose I shouldn't have done that.'

She couldn't speak. She was still clinging to him, panting and shuddering like an animal.

Without another word he led her back to the pony-trap and took her by the waist and lifted her lightly into the seat. Then he put the reins into her nerveless hands, and told her to make the mare go gently on the way home. He seemed quite unruffled, and merely concerned that she and her equipage should get safely home.

She sat trembling in the pony-trap. She could still taste him; still feel the strength of his hands on her shoulders, and the heat of his mouth on her throat.

In a blur she watched him walk to his horse. But then he stopped and stooped for something in the dust. It was the little pink foulard scarf that she'd been wearing about her neck.

He walked back to her as if to return it, then seemed to think better of it. He folded the scarf and put it in his breast pocket. 'Perhaps some other time,' he said with a curl of his lip.

She did not reply. She couldn't. The words wouldn't come.

It was only after she'd reached the turn-off for the estate that she remembered that the scarf had been a gift from Gus Parnell, as was the little diamond brooch with which it had been fastened.

But what does that matter now? she'd thought as Princess plodded through the cane-pieces. Everything is different. Everything.

That had been three weeks ago. Since then she'd lived in a whirlwind of terror and remorse and sudden, shameful heat. She kept reliving that kiss. How could it have happened? How could she have *let* it happen? She cared nothing for him. He was so far beneath her that it was a degradation to be in the same room. And yet – she wanted him so.

But to kiss a woman like that! Was it some vile guttersnipe talent? Or did gentlemen also know how to give such pleasure? Eugene certainly hadn't. He'd regarded kissing as a distasteful waste of time. He'd only known how to hurt.

Every Sunday in church, she had prayed that she might forget all about Ben Kelly. But instead, to her horror, she found herself thinking of him all the time. And she found herself studying men's mouths. It didn't matter where she was or who they were; she couldn't help looking at them and comparing. Her brother Alexander's upper lip made a self-indulgent 'M' like a permanent sneer. Her father had a fleshy lower lip that went dark plum when he was vexed. Gus Parnell had no lips at all.

How could that be? How was it possible for a man of

birth and breeding to have no lips at all, while a scoundrel from the gutter had a mouth as beautiful as a statue's?

'Here you are,' said Gus Parnell behind her.

She spun round.

'Did I startle you?' he said as he handed her the ice. 'I do apologize.' He paused. 'Such a pleasant air on this side of the house. I quite understand why you should have preferred it.'

She muttered her thanks and bent over her ice. The first spoonful felt wonderfully cold against her swollen lips.

'I fancy you were in danger of becoming too heated,' said Parnell, watching her narrowly.

She forced a smile.

Midnight at the Burying-place, she thought. And it's still only half-past eleven.

She wondered how she might contrive to get rid of Parnell. She wondered how she was going to get through the next half-hour.

Alexander watched his sister despatching Gus Parnell on yet another pretext, and swore under his breath. What did the stupid little bitch think she was playing at? Couldn't she see that Parnell wouldn't stand for much more of this? Did she imagine that rich, admiring bankers grew on trees?

He snatched another brandy from a passing tray and downed it in one. Then he descended the steps to the lawns, to smoke a cigar.

Everything was going to blazes, and he didn't know what to do. Good God Almighty, he *needed* Sib to make this match. Once Parnell was safely hooked, he'd be a sure touch for a loan. But did she ever think of that? Did she ever consider anyone but herself?

He needed Parnell, and he needed Sophie. But now Sophie was cutting up rough because of that wretched little mulatto. *God*, women were such infernal hypocrites. He couldn't count the number of times Evie had said that she loved him. Love? Was it love to ruin his prospects over a tiff?

He turned and gazed up at the great house, ablaze with light. It didn't seem possible that God could be so unfair. That a low scoundrel like Ben Kelly should have the power to squander thousands!

The house was unrecognizable from the peeling ruin of a year ago. The galleries had been opened up, the woodwork restored, the grounds landscaped and new terraces cut. Even old Jocelyn's aviary had been rebuilt. It was so horribly unfair. What had that scoundrel done to deserve it?

The world had gone mad. It was only five days till the debt fell due, and none of the filthy Jew money-lenders would advance him a penny. They'd all heard rumours that things weren't running straight with Sophie, and that the governor was thinking about taking back his gift of Waytes Valley. Everything was going to blazes. And ghastly little Lyndon was loving every minute of it, sneering at him down his greasy Jew-boy nose. Even Davina had begun to make sharp little jokes about careers in sheep-farming in Australia. Dear *God*, what was he to do?

He could hardly force Sophie to marry him. Despite his attempt in the phaeton, they both knew that.

But was it possible that he might still bring her round? Or if not, might they remain friends – at least to the extent that she'd simply *lend* him the money? He'd thought about that a great deal in the course of the evening, and at times it had seemed like a goer. But there was always that damned brother-in-law of hers. Cameron Lawe was sure to ruin the whole thing.

So what was he to *do*? What if Sib made a fool of herself and Parnell slipped the hook? What if Sophie couldn't be brought round? What if New Year's Day came and went and the money remained unpaid?

He would be finished. Utterly smashed. Word would spread like wildfire that Alexander Traherne had welshed on a debt. He would be black-balled at every club he'd ever put his name to. The governor would cut him off without a penny. He'd be a nobody. He might as well slit his throat.

And all for a paltry gambling debt. It was so outrageously unfair.

He threw away his cigar and stood for a moment, irresolute. He must do something. But what?

At his feet, the cigar flared briefly in the darkness. Frowning, he ground it out under his heel, and turned back to the house.

It was all so outrageously unfair.

It was a quarter to midnight, and Sophie had had enough.

She had danced a slow gavotte with Cornelius, and another with Alexander, who'd scarcely spoken a word to her all evening. She had encountered Ben Kelly's business partner Mr Walker at supper, and been astonished to recognize him as the mysterious black gentleman from St Cuthbert's, eight months before. But he had spoilt things by asking after 'Miss McFarlane', and she'd felt obliged to deny all knowledge, so he'd given her a strained smile and gone away, snubbed. It was a small wrong note in an evening composed of nothing but wrong notes.

She hated being back at Fever Hill. For her it would always be a magical place of shadows and whispers, wearing its dilapidation with a faded elegance. She hated to see it brightly illuminated and swarming with brittle, inquisitive gossips. It was like watching the foibles of some ancient aunt exposed to an uncaring public. And what was worse, it reminded her of Maddy. Maddy, a thousand miles away at Eden. It was all wrong.

She hated being back, and she hated being in fancy dress. At supper her train had snagged beneath a chair, and as she'd sat in the ladies' cloakroom while the maid sewed up the rent, she'd caught sight of herself in the looking-glass. What had possessed her to come as the River Mistress? She looked thin and hollow-eyed: like something drowned.

After that, she had returned to the ballroom, and stood for hours with a fixed smile on her face, listening to the gentle complaints of old Mrs Pitcaithley, and watching Ben Kelly dancing. And gradually, as she listened to the gossip, public sentiment swung round in his favour. Well, of course, she thought sourly. He's rich, good-looking and single, and there are daughters to be married off.

To be sure, my dear, there is that question of birth to be considered – but as I've always said, although lack of breeding is a misfortune, *it's hardly a* fault. *After all, how is Society to renew itself without new blood? What were the Trahernes three generations ago? And even the Monroes – I mean today's Monroes, not dear old Jocelyn – why, they can scarcely pretend to have been born on the right side of the blanket . . .*

How fickle people are, she thought as she moved from the ballroom out onto the north verandah, nearly knocking into one of those wretched bowls of orchids. Seven years before, everyone had thrown up their hands in horror at the notion of Sophie Monroe befriending a groom. Now they were only too happy to drink his champagne and dance in his ballroom.

She caught sight of Alexander at the other end of the gallery, and moved back behind the orchids. Why, she wondered, had he thought it necessary to make that clumsy attempt at a threat? He must know that he couldn't force her to marry him.

But what about Eden? There was the rub. Alexander was vindictive enough to start some scandalous rumour about her and Ben. And when Cornelius, the most powerful financier on the Northside, learned that she wasn't going to marry his son, his goodwill towards the Lawes would evaporate like morning mist. And again she would have brought trouble to Eden.

She minded that more than anything. More than the outrage of the Trahernes. More than the humiliation of the cancelled invitations, and the polite little notes returning the wedding presents, and the gossip.

And after Parnassus, where would she go? Eden was out of the question. But she could hardly stay anywhere else on the Northside. Back to England? Her heart sank. Something told her that if she left Jamaica again, she would never return. It would be the ultimate defeat.

She pictured herself living with Mrs Vaughan-Pargeter, and paying for her keep out of the sale of Fever Hill. She would be living on Ben's money.

She could see him now, standing by the doors amid a throng of people, watching the waltz. He hadn't spoken to her since that edgy greeting out on the steps. Not once had he come up to her and said a quiet word about Evie, as she had thought he might. But he hadn't avoided her, either. Several times in the course of the evening their paths had crossed, and he'd simply given her a polite nod, and moved away. Clearly, as far as he was concerned they had made their goodbyes up in the hills, and there was nothing left to say.

She watched him stoop to speak to the woman at his side. The woman turned to listen, and with a shock Sophie recognized Sibella Palairet. She was looking up at Ben with total concentration, her lips slightly parted, her eyes fixed on his mouth.

Sophie glanced from Sibella to Ben, then back again. She remembered the ancient brougham stationed at the edge of the carriageway, with Great-Aunt May's man inside. She had a sensation of falling. Could it be that this was the mysterious 'bargain'?

It wasn't possible. And yet the pieces slotted into place as precisely as a Chinese puzzle. What a fine revenge for Great-Aunt May that would be: to put an end to the Parnell–Palairet match and bring down scandal on the Trahernes at a single stroke. And all it would take was one vain, stupid, self-deceiving little widow, prettily gift-wrapped in mauve satin and gold lace.

And Ben would do it, too. He couldn't have forgotten what the Trahernes had done to him.

That, she thought suddenly, is what this whole wretched ball has been about: to show the Trahernes how far he's come, and to bring them down.

And the worst of it, she thought, plucking an orchid from a bowl and shredding it in her fingers, the very worst of it is that he must have known all about it that day in the hills.

She felt shaky and sick. She'd never imagined that he could have changed so much – that he could be capable of an act so calculated, so sordid and so destructive.

This, she told herself in disbelief, really is the end. The Ben you knew is gone for ever.

She opened her hand and watched the shredded petals drifting down around her feet. Then she raised her head and searched for him through a blur of tears.

He was no longer there. Neither was Sibella.

CHAPTER THIRTY

'For the last time,' yells Pa, 'where's Kate!'

'I don't know,' mumbles Ben.

Pa grabs his arm and yanks him to his feet and wallops him. Bam, bam, bam. The room goes round. Lights burst in his eyes.

Robbie's hunched in the corner with his face to the wall, rocking from side to side. Good boy, Ben tells him silently. Stay there and let me take care of this.

'Where's she fucking gone?' goes Pa, shaking him by the arm till it's near out of its socket.

'I don't know,' mumbles Ben between his teeth.

Pa knocks him about some more, then slams him against the wall. More lights flare. Salty-sweet blood fills his mouth. He slides down in a heap. One good kick, he thinks fuzzily, and it's all up with you.

Pa stands over him, swaying. The brewery stink is hot and strong, but he's miles from passing out, worse luck for Ben. 'So you're not going to tell me, eh?' he says, very low and quiet.

Shakily, Ben wipes his face on his sleeve. He tries to move but he can't. His legs are bits of string.

Pa turns and stumbles over to the corner and grabs Robbie by the ankle, and hoists him upside down. Robbie don't say nothing, not even a yelp. He just dangles there like a sewer rat, clutching his straw doll to his chest.

'Leave him alone,' mutters Ben, wiping the blood

from his eyes. 'He don't know nothing, he's just a idiot.'

'So you're still not going to tell me, eh?' goes Pa over his shoulder. He swings Robbie round by the legs, like he's going to take a bash at the door frame with Robbie's head. 'You sure about that?'

'Pack it in,' whispers Ben.

'Robbie or Kate? What's it to be?'

Ben struggles to his feet and props hisself against the wall. Pain bursts in his head. 'Pack it in!'

'Why should I? Robbie don't mind, do you, Rob?' And all the time he's swinging round and round, taking that little carroty head closer to the door; and Robbie's clutching his doll and not making a sound, but his mouth's going big and square. 'Come on, Ben,' goes Pa. 'You got to choose.'

Ben twists round and grinds his forehead into the wall. Mouldy plaster flakes off, and crusty bits of bedbug. His eyes are stinging and hot, and there's a lump welling up in his throat. How can he choose? How can he fucking choose?

Kate's big and strong, he tells hisself. She can hold her own against Pa; and she's got Jeb to look after her, too. But Robbie can't hold his own against anyone. And he's only got Ben.

'Come on, Ben,' goes Pa. 'Which is it to be? Robbie or Kate?'

'Ben?' wails Robbie. 'Ben!'

'Slippers Place,' croaks Ben through big jerky sobs.

'What?' goes Pa. 'What's that you say?'

Ben grinds his head against the wall, mashing the plaster to a soggy pulp of blood and tears. 'She's at Slippers Place. Slippers Place off the Jamaica Road. Now let him go!'

Sunlight hit him in the eyes and he woke up. He was sweating. His heart was pounding. He didn't know where he was.

You shouldn't have told him, Ben. You made the wrong choice, didn't you? You shouldn't have told him about Kate.

Under his hand the crusted bedbugs resolved into the lacquered surface of the bedside table. He put his hand to his cheek and wiped away tears.

You lost Kate, he told himself, and then you lost Sophie. That's why the dreams keep coming. One loss conjuring up another.

The silent maidservant moved from the window to the bed, and held out a salver on which lay a small cream-coloured envelope.

'What's that?' he muttered, propping himself up on his elbow. On the bedside table his watch told him that it was nine o'clock in the morning. Christ. He'd only been asleep for just over an hour. The last guest had left sometime after seven.

'Message, Master Ben,' murmured the maid, her eyes politely averted. 'Carriage waiting for reply. They says it's urgent.'

Cursing under his breath, he snatched the envelope and tore it open. He scanned the contents. It was from the little widow. He crumpled the note and threw it across the room.

Well, who did you think it was from? he told himself in disgust. Sophie Monroe, writing to thank you for the party?

He remembered how she had looked as she'd ascended the steps with her fiancé. The sardonic gleam in her honey-coloured eyes; the twist of mockery in that mouth of hers. *And when shall you keep this mysterious bargain?*

He rubbed a hand over his face. He felt exhausted and still slightly drunk; heavy with fatigue and self-disgust. The dream dragged at his spirits. Wrongdoing and loss, he thought. Is that all there is?

Beside the bed, the maidservant cleared her throat. 'Carriage waiting, Master Ben, waiting for reply.'

He thought of the little widow in her over-upholstered dress and her artificial flowers. She'd worn a mauve satin ribbon around her neck, like a dog-collar. Just like a little dog. *You shouldn't have done it, Ben.*

There was a sour taste in his mouth. He reached for the

carafe and poured himself a glass of water and drained it in one go. 'Tell the boy there's no reply,' he muttered.

Half an hour later, he was dressed and coming downstairs when he saw Isaac in the hall. His partner was in his town clothes, and there was a large portmanteau at his feet.

Ben stopped on the bottom stair, and gripped the banister with a sudden, surprising clutch of panic. Isaac had been threatening to leave for days – they hadn't been getting along too well since he'd got some ridiculous idea into his head about Ben and Evie – but he'd always allowed himself to be talked round again into staying. At least, until now.

Don't go, Ben told him silently. Not now. Not today. Please. Out loud he said, 'So you're going, then.'

Isaac turned his head and waited while a trio of manservants passed through with potted orange trees in their arms. When they'd gone he said, 'I'll be at Arethusa for another week or so. Then I'm off.'

'Where?'

'I don't know. That depends.'

'Isaac—'

'I'm thinking of selling up. If I do, I'll get the lawyer to give you first refusal on Arethusa.'

'For Christ's sake, Isaac! I don't care about that.'

Isaac looked up at him, and his face was taut. 'What do you care about, Ben?'

Ben ignored that. 'For the last time, there's nothing between me and Evie McFarlane. Nothing but friendship.'

'Then tell me where she is.'

Ben hesitated. 'No.'

'Why?'

'She doesn't want to be found.'

'I don't believe you. I will find her, Ben. With or without your help. That girl's in some sort of trouble. I could tell when she came up here that day. She needs a friend.'

'She's got a friend.'

Isaac shook his head sadly. 'You still don't trust me, do you?'

'Of course I trust you.'

'No you don't. You don't trust anyone. You never have.' He put on his hat and picked up his portmanteau. 'Goodbye, Ben. And good luck. Something tells me you're going to need it.'

Ben stayed on the stairs, listening to the clatter of the carriage dying away. Wrongdoing and loss, he thought. He couldn't remember when he'd felt so bleak.

Ah, sod it. If Isaac wanted to leave, then let him. Besides, he wasn't a friend. He was just a bloody business partner.

He forced a shrug, and put his hands in his pockets, and wandered through the house and out onto the south lawns, where the clearing-up was in full swing. In the harsh December sunlight the lawns offered a dismal prospect of overturned chairs and smeared glasses, and great bowls of orchids turning brown at the edges. Everywhere he looked he saw footmen and maids clearing away, picking up, and setting to rights. None of them met his eyes.

He wondered if they were afraid of him. Or did they resent him because he had once been a servant too? Because he wasn't and never would be a gentleman?

He wandered round the side of the house, and found a patch of shade on the bench beneath the breadfruit tree, and sent for a bottle of champagne. Then he sat back and watched a couple of lovebirds having a spat in the aviary.

The strange thing was, he could easily have put Isaac's mind at rest about Evie, for she was coming down from the cave that very morning. So why hadn't he told Isaac? Was it because Isaac was in love? Because that was the last thing he, Ben, needed to see right now? Was that it?

The champagne arrived, and he drank off the first glass in one, and waited for the artificial lightening of the spirits. The lovebirds erupted into full-blown war.

There'd been an aviary out here for as long as anyone could remember, but until Ben had had it rebuilt it had always been a ruin. Old Master Jocelyn had built it back in the forties for his young bride, Catherine McFarlane –

and then had destroyed it a year later, when she'd died. It was said that he'd never got over her death; that he'd never looked at another woman for the rest of his life.

More fool him, thought Ben sourly as he poured himself another glass.

A shadow cut across his sun, and he glanced up to see Austen standing before him. 'Hello, Austen,' he said. 'Sit down and have a drink.'

Uncertainly, Austen perched on the far end of the bench, but waved away the champagne. 'No thank you, Mr Kelly.'

Ben shot him a look. These days, Austen only called him 'Mr Kelly' when he was on his dignity. And it wasn't hard to guess what was troubling him this morning. 'So,' he said, pouring himself another drink. 'What's on your mind?'

Austen cleared his throat and frowned at his feet. 'I understand that there was a carriage here. And a note from – from a lady.'

'That's right.'

'May I ask what it was about?'

'I don't think so,' said Ben.

More throat-clearing. 'Mr Kelly. I need to talk to you.'

'That's what you're doing, isn't it?'

'Not as employer and secretary. Man to man.'

Ben sighed. 'The thing is, Austen, I haven't had much sleep, and I'm feeling a bit rough. Can it wait?'

'I'm afraid not.'

Ben glanced at him in surprise. He hadn't given his secretary credit for such strength of purpose. Or perhaps for such depth of feeling. Oh God, he thought, not another one in love. I seem to be surrounded by bloody lovebirds. He blew out a long breath. 'Go on, then,' he said.

Austen's narrow cheeks became mottled with red, and his Adam's apple bobbed up and down. 'Last night I saw something. I mean, I saw you and Mrs Palairet – talking, and then – then you both disappeared. So I thought . . .' his face was burning, 'that is to say, I witnessed enough to give me cause for concern.'

Ben found such delicacy intensely irritating. 'Well, of course you did,' he snapped. 'You saw, but you didn't take part. That's the story of your life, isn't it?'

Austen pulled at his nose. 'Mr Kelly. I need to ask – are you – that is, do you intend to marry her?'

Ben blinked. 'Who?'

'Mrs Palairet.'

Ben looked at him, then burst out laughing. 'Sibella? Of course not!'

Again Austen pulled at his nose. Then he put both hands on his knees, and stood up very quickly. 'Then I regret to inform you that I cannot remain in your employ for another day.'

Ben looked up at him for a moment. Then he waved his hand. 'Don't be ridiculous, Austen. You don't even know what—'

'With respect, Mr Kelly, it's not ridiculous at all. It's the only honourable thing for a fellow to do.'

Ben was astonished. He'd read about men who put women on pedestals – he'd often teased Austen for being one – but he hadn't really believed it until now. 'Austen,' he said wearily, 'don't be an ass. There really is no need for us to quarrel.'

'On the contrary, Mr Kelly,' Austen said quietly, 'I'm as certain as I could be that there is.'

He was in earnest. Ben's spirits plunged. First Isaac, now Austen. Wrongdoing and loss. No, no, no.

He leaned forward with his elbows on his knees. 'I can explain about Mrs Palairet,' he said in a low voice. 'But please. I'm asking you – I'm *asking* you – to stay.'

Austen's face worked. Then he shook his head, and turned and walked away across the lawn.

Ben sat back on the bench and watched him go. A few minutes later, the trap came round to the front steps, and Austen descended with his bags, and rattled off down the carriageway.

Two down and none to go, thought Ben. Now you're all alone. He was surprised at the strength of his regret.

He poured himself another drink and listened to the

crickets gathering force, and watched the lovebirds waging war. Out of nowhere, an image came to him of Sophie at supper the night before. Someone had just trodden on her train and ripped it, and for a moment, before politeness had got the better of her, she'd been ready to snap. He knew that expression so well: the flashing eyes, the shadows at the corners of her mouth deepening ominously. He used to love that look.

He stood up quickly and walked a few paces across the lawn, then returned and threw himself down onto the bench again. In the carriageway, a workman dismantling lights cast him a curious glance.

He could do anything he wanted, but there wasn't anything he wanted to do. He could go for a ride on one of his beautiful thoroughbreds. He could stay here and drink champagne all day. He could go to his study and look at the plans for the mausoleum. Or he could go up to the hills and collect Evie, and bring her back to her mother's place.

But he didn't want to do any of it. He could do anything he liked, and there was nothing – absolutely nothing – that he wanted to do. He felt utterly wretched. He had no idea how he was even going to get through the day.

The night of Ben's Masquerade, Sophie sat on the upper gallery at Parnassus and waited for the sun to come up.

She'd hung on grimly at Fever Hill in the hope that Sibella would reappear, but that had never happened. Around two o'clock, when she couldn't take any more, she'd left Alexander still drinking brandy with a group of old racing cronies, and gone home in the brougham with Rebecca and Cornelius.

'There's nothing wrong, is there, dear?' Rebecca had whispered as they'd settled themselves inside.

Sophie had pressed her hand and tried to smile. What could possibly be wrong? she thought. I've just jilted your son, and Ben Kelly is having an affair with Sibella. Of course there's nothing wrong.

As soon as they'd reached Parnassus she'd gone straight

to her room. She hadn't even tried to sleep, but had sat up on the gallery, listening to the whisper of the wind in the cane, and the distant cries of Patoo.

It was the morning of the twenty-seventh of December. Seven years ago she'd been with Ben at Romilly. She remembered every detail. The smell of the orchids. The secret rustle of the night creatures on the riverbank. How young he had looked: how careful and grave as he peeled back her stocking and touched her knee.

She tried to think of him as he was now, but she couldn't. Every time she conjured up the image, another imposed itself. Ben as he'd been in the clearing on Overlook Hill seven years before. Pale, shaken, and unable to comprehend that she was ending it between them.

Until now she'd never allowed herself to wonder what would have happened if she'd had the courage to be with him. What was the point? She'd been right to put an end to it.

But – what if?

They might be man and wife, and living together at Fever Hill. They might have children. She tried to imagine what their children would be like. Would they be dark and beautiful like him? Or mousy and plain like her?

Around five o'clock, the song of the crickets changed from a low, pulsing night-ring to an early-morning rasp. A breeze began to blow off the sea. A flock of grassquits descended on the hibiscus bushes around the steps.

She drew up her knees beneath her nightgown and pulled her shawl closer around her. December the twenty-seventh. Seven years ago, she'd spent the night with Ben, and Fraser had died.

She wondered if Madeleine was sitting on the verandah at Eden among the tartan cushions, with her knees drawn up beneath her nightgown, thinking of Fraser. She pressed her knuckles to her eyes. Everything was wrong, wrong, *wrong*. Why was she down here in this great cold-hearted house, while Ben was up there with Sibella? Why was she down here, while Madeleine was at Eden without her?

How had she let this happen? And how could she make it right?

Around eleven o'clock she was woken by a maidservant tapping her on the arm.

Blearily she raised her head. Her eyes felt scratchy, her neck sore from sleeping curled up.

The maid told her that Miss Sibella was downstairs in the blue drawing-room, and that she needed to speak to her 'quick-time'.

Sophie was instantly awake.

'I had to see you,' cried Sibella as soon as Sophie reached the drawing-room.

Sophie glanced over her shoulder to check that the door was closed, then turned back to Sibella. She looked terrible, her gown haphazardly fastened, her face puffy and blotched from crying.

Sophie couldn't find it in herself to feel sorry for her. She could only remember how Sibella had gazed up at Ben as they'd stood together in the ballroom; how she had watched his mouth as he spoke. 'What d'you want?' she said harshly.

Sibella twisted the rings on her plump fingers. Then she threw herself onto the sofa and burst into tears.

Sophie stood in stony silence, wishing she were a million miles away.

'I feel so *ashamed*,' sobbed Sibella. 'So dirty and – and humiliated. I – I wrote to him. I begged – I even waited at the house for a reply.' She made a gobbling sound in her throat. 'Do you know what he did?' She pushed back her hair from her face, and her eyes were red-rimmed and out-raged. 'He sent word that there was no reply. Can you *imagine*? *No reply*.'

Sophie didn't want to imagine anything. She was trying hard not to picture Ben and Sibella together.

But Sibella clutched her hand and pulled her down beside her onto the sofa. 'You've got to go and talk to him.'

'*What*? But—'

'Sophie, you've got to! There's no-one else who can help.'

Sophie tried to withdraw her hand from the feverish grasp, but Sibella clung to it. 'You're not making any sense,' Sophie told her as gently as she could. 'You're tired and overwrought. You need to go to bed.'

Sibella stared at her with incomprehension. Then she broke down again.

The maid put her head round the door, but Sophie motioned her out, while Sibella clutched her hand and sobbed.

Gradually, reluctantly, Sophie pieced together the story. There was something about a missing scarf and a diamond brooch – both gifts from Gus Parnell – and a promise by Ben to return them: a promise which hadn't been kept; and a midnight tryst at the Burying-place. The idea of the tryst hurt more than anything. A lovers' tryst among the Monroe tombs. It felt like a calculated stab at herself.

And now, according to Sibella, Parnell was 'cutting up rough' and demanding that she produce the wretched things, and Papa was being horrible to her, and what was she to *do*?

'You've *got* to get them back,' she cried, clutching Sophie's hand so tightly that her rings bit into the flesh. 'He's a liar and a scoundrel, but he'll listen to you, I know he will. He'll give them back if you ask him to.'

'Sibella,' she said wearily, 'he won't listen to anyone. Least of all me.'

Sibella took a shaky breath and wiped her eyes with her fingers. 'But there's no-one else. You're my only, only friend.'

Her only friend?

Sibella pounced on her hesitation. 'Say you'll go. Oh, Sophie, *do* say you'll go!'

What can you possibly say to him? she wondered as she rode between the great cut-stone gatehouses of Fever Hill.

For the Masquerade the gatehouses had been cleared of creepers, and for the first time since she'd known them, the Monroe crest could plainly be seen. She wondered when Ben would get round to having it removed. For a man who had kept a lovers' tryst at the Monroe Burying-place, it was presumably only a matter of time.

Slowly she rode up the carriageway. Twice she reined in and resolved to turn back. Let Sibella sort out her own sordid little affairs. Thoughtless, insensitive Sibella, who – if she remembered it at all – had doubtless assumed that Sophie had got over her feelings for Ben years ago.

The men taking down the coloured lanterns strung between the palms watched her pass with undisguised curiosity. She ignored them. For the hundredth time she cursed Sibella. For being vain. For being weak. For being pretty.

At last she reached the house, and there was no more time for second thoughts. A boy ran out to take her horse. A maid came down the steps to conduct her inside. She was shown straight into his study.

It had been her grandfather's study, and she was surprised to see how little it had changed. It still had books from floor to ceiling, and oil paintings of Jamaica on the walls, and at the far end, in front of the doors leading onto the south verandah, a great walnut desk.

Ben was sitting behind it with a sheaf of what looked like blueprints spread out before him. When she was shown in, he stood up, and his face briefly lightened. Then he caught her stony expression, and his own became unreadable. He looked pale and tired, with dark shadows under his eyes.

As well he might, she thought grimly, remembering Sibella's blotchy, tear-stained face. *I feel so humiliated. So dirty and ashamed.*

Ben and Sibella at the Burying-place. It didn't seem possible. She pushed away the images that kept floating before her eyes. 'I didn't think you'd see me,' she said as she walked the length of the study.

'I didn't think you'd come,' he replied. He motioned her to a chair on the other side of the desk, and resumed his own.

She sat down and clasped her hands in her lap. They felt

shaky and cold. 'How could you do it?' she said quietly.

He raised his eyebrows. 'What have I done this time?'

'Don't try to get out of it. I've just come from Sibella. She's in a terrible state.'

'I take it that means she didn't enjoy the party.'

She looked down at her hands. It didn't seem possible that he could treat this as a joke. 'I know it's because she's a Traherne,' she said in a low voice. 'I know that's what this is all about. But I never thought – I never imagined you'd sink this low.'

'And you do now?' He gave her a slight smile. 'You're quick to believe the worst of me, aren't you?'

'You *used* her. You used her to curry favour with Great-Aunt May.'

A flush darkened his cheekbones. But he recovered swiftly. 'And of course in polite society,' he said drily, 'nobody ever uses anyone. I'm always forgetting that.'

'The least you can do,' she said between her teeth, 'is give me back those trinkets of hers.'

'Ah, so that's why you've come.' He leaned back in his chair. 'She's in trouble with her sweetheart – her sweetheart whom, I might add, she cordially detests – and now she's sent you to do her dirty work.'

Sophie coloured.

'You see,' he went on, frowning, 'you indicated just now that I was a blackguard for using her. But to the uninitiated, it might appear that *she* was using *you*. Although that's impossible, isn't it, because, as I said before, in polite society nobody ever uses anyone. I mean, she isn't *using* Gus Parnell to buy herself a comfortable future. And her father isn't *using* her, or Parnell, to buy himself back to financial security. And her brother certainly isn't *using* you to get out of his own little spot of trouble.'

'Alexander isn't in any trouble,' she snapped. Then she felt annoyed with herself for standing up for him.

'That shows how much you know,' he remarked. Thoughtfully he tapped his fingernail against his teeth. 'And what about you?' he said suddenly. 'What are you using Alexander for?'

'What do you mean?'

'Why are you marrying him? Is it to buy yourself a bolt-hole? Somewhere safe and secure and far away from Eden, so that you won't ever need to—'

'I didn't come here to fight,' she broke in. 'Just give me the scarf and the brooch and I'll go.'

'Why should I?'

'Because you don't need them! You've got what you wanted. You're just keeping them to make a point.'

'Am I? And what point is that?'

'To show us all how powerful you've become.'

He laughed. 'And you think I need a couple of trinkets to do that?'

'Apparently, yes.'

Abruptly his smile vanished. He got to his feet and came round to her side of the desk and leaned against it with his arms crossed on his chest, looking down at her. His eyes were glittering. With a flicker of alarm she wondered if he'd been drinking. 'You're so quick to think the worst of me,' he said in a low voice.

'You're not giving me much choice.'

For a moment longer he looked down into her face. Then he pushed himself off the desk, moved past her to the bookshelf, opened a large cedarwood box, and took out a small brown paper parcel. He tossed it onto the desk in front of her. 'There you are,' he said. 'One scarf. One brooch. Both slightly used. Just like their owner.'

She took the parcel and stood up to go. 'Thank you,' she muttered. She felt sick.

He moved back behind the desk, and opened the doors onto the south verandah, and stood with his back to her, looking out. 'If she's angry with me,' he said over his shoulder, 'it's not because I met her at the Burying-place. It's because I didn't.'

She stared at the package in her hands, then back at him. 'What? You mean—'

'She waited, but I didn't turn up. There. Now you know.'

She thought of Sibella's outraged face. *I feel so*

380

humiliated. I begged – I wrote to him. There was no reply.
'You – you never intended to meet her there. Did you?'

He laughed. 'Oh, I wouldn't go that far. The truth is, I didn't think too much about it. It was sort of a spur-of-the-moment decision.'

'She waited for hours. In the dark.'

'Did she really?'

'Then she risked scandal to come here and beg for her things.'

'So?' He turned to face her. 'It'll do her good. The silly little cow's probably never had to beg for anything in her entire life. Now she knows how it feels.'

Again she looked down at the parcel in her hands. Somehow it almost made it worse that he'd been playing with Sibella. 'If I hadn't come and asked for this,' she said slowly, 'would you have sent it back anyway?'

'Probably not.'

'Why not?'

'Why should I?'

'But – you would have ruined her.'

Again he laughed. 'Isn't that a bit melodramatic?'

She shook her head. 'What's happened to you, Ben?'

He shot her an impatient glance.

'Look at you. You've got everything. An enormous house. Fine clothes. Beautiful horses. But inside, something's gone.' She tapped her breastbone. 'In here. It's gone.'

In the glare from the doorway his face was dark. 'I think you'd better go,' he said quietly.

'What happened to you? Did getting rich burn it all away?'

He turned back to the verandah. 'It wasn't the money which did that.'

CHAPTER THIRTY-ONE

From the Journal of Cyrus Wright – Volume the Second

January 28th, 1832 Terrible, terrible calamity. I write this from Falmouth, whither I have removed with Mr Monroe & Family, as the country has been over-run with havoc. Slaves running amok with irresistible fury. Fever Hill burnt all to ashes, & Seven Hills, Parnassus, & countless others. Only Mad Durrant's place at Eden spared, for he always was unnatural soft to his Negroes, & never would flog the women but only the men.

The militia patrol night and day. I pray to God to deliver us from the evil designs of our slaves. Have put Congo Eve in the collar to prevent her going runaway, for Mr Traherne's Strap is among the rebels.

Plick! A swallow dipped to drink from the aqueduct. Evie glanced up from the page.

She'd only been back an hour or so, but already she was in her old place on the wall, leaning against the trunk of the ackee tree, with her bare shins stretched out in the sun. To her relief, her mother had been out when she'd arrived.

Strange. She'd been eager to get home, but now that she was, she longed to be back in the hills. Up in the cave, she'd felt safe. It was as if there were a presence watching over her: a shadow at the corner of her eye. Down here she felt exposed. And what was more, she had a strange, taut sense of suspense. She'd felt it as soon as she woke up that morning. She'd felt it all through the ride down from the hills with Ben. She felt it now. A prickling in the air. A sense of something ready to happen. She glanced down at the book in her lap. Was this it?

The second volume of the Journal of Cyrus Wright. Sophie had brought it to her as a present, a few days before Christmas. She'd told Evie that she'd found the first volume a few weeks ago among some things Madeleine had sent to her, and read it in one sitting. Then she'd got Miss Clemmy to ferret through the boxes of Master Jocelyn's books up at Eden, and this second volume had emerged.

Sophie had been quietly triumphant, and Evie had been touched. But she hadn't wanted to read it in the cave. She'd been afraid of what she might find. She didn't want to learn that Cyrus Wright had finally broken the spirit of Congo Eve, or that he'd beaten her once too often and left her dying in a ditch.

And yet – she *needed* to know. More than that: she sensed that Congo Eve was trying to tell her something. Maybe that was why the journal had found its way to her in the first place.

With a shiver of apprehension she opened it again, and began to read.

February 22nd, 1832 *Have just been delivered from exceeding peril. Was returning to Falmouth from Salt Wash when a Negro leaped out and dragged me from my horse. It was the Negro Strap, much altered & terrible of visage. He struck at me with all violence, shouting 'This for what you done to Congo Eve', but by the mercy of Providence his blows glanced off my stick. He drove me back into the Morass & I called out Murder, and some militia men rode up & laid hold of the villain & beat him till he knew no more. I sustained a bruised elbow, very sore, & was much befouled by the Morass. Altogether put beside myself with fright.*

March 7th *By the mercy of Providence I am now fully restored, & greatly rejoiced, for the Rebellion has been quelled. Mr Monroe exceeding active at the assizes. I myself have been at the square many times to view the punishments, and yesterday I watched Strap flogged and hanged. The brute made a tolerable good death. Dined with Mr Monroe: broiled conch, a ham, & good porter. Cum Congo Eve in the undercroft,* supra terram. *Told her of her paramour's end. I said, Now he is gone for ever. Let that be a lesson to all Negroes who would raise their hand against the white man. She replied not a word. I shall keep her in the collar overnight.*

March 14th *Since the last entry a sennight ago, I have been sick near unto death with the bloody flux. I believe it was some foul Negro poisoning by Congo Eve, for she went runaway the very night I was took sick. Have not been able to learn how she broke free of the collar, but suspect the other Negroes of assisting her. They fear her for knowing Obiah, Mial, &c.*

July 28th *Congo Eve still runaway. It has been over four months, & all attempts to recover her have failed. Find myself exceeding low in spirits, & much troubled by the Night Mare. Doubtless I am not yet fully recovered from the flux. Cum Jenny in Bullet Tree Piece,* sed non bene.

August 5th *One of Mad Durrant's field Negroes saw a woman 'very like to Congo Eve' some weeks past, heading south into the Cockpits! Have sent men after her & posted a reward.*

August 6th *Have myself questioned Mad Durrant's field Negro. He did indeed see the woman heading south, towards the region known as Turn Around. Have sent more men with hounds.*

'There you are,' said Grace McFarlane.

Evie jumped. She shut the book with a thud and clasped

it tight. Her heart was pounding. *The region known as Turn Around.* Of course. Of course.

'So,' said her mother. 'You been away.' She took in her daughter's bare feet and naked shins and her wary expression, but she made no remark.

Evie nodded. Yes, she thought, I've been away. I've been in *the region known as Turn Around* – perhaps in the very cave in which Congo Eve stayed hidden all those years ago.

She was shaken, but not deeply surprised. Some part of her – the four-eyed part that she used to hate – had perhaps guessed it all along.

Grace ran her tongue around her teeth, and spat. 'You're looking meagre, girl. Look like you been ill, up at Mandeville with that friend of yours.'

'I had a fever,' said Evie.

'Hn,' said Grace.

'But I'm better now. I'm much stronger.'

Grace gave her a long, searching look. Then she nodded. 'That I can see.' She indicated the book. 'You got much more of that?'

'I don't know.'

'Well, when you done, come along back a the house. I'm making red peas soup.'

Evie nodded.

Her mother turned to go. 'So Evie,' she said over her shoulder. 'You back now. Yes?'

'Yes, Mother,' she said. 'I'm back.'

When her mother had gone, Evie sat in silence by the aqueduct, watching the dragonflies skimming the opaque green water. I'm back, she thought. But for how long? And what am I going to do?

Again that sense of tautness and suspense. The air felt hot and heavy, crackling with energy. She opened the book.

Surprisingly, there were only about five more pages of script, and the rest was blank. She resisted the urge to read the last page first, and went back to where she'd left off.

It appeared that when Cyrus Wright had sent out the

hounds in August 1832, he'd sent them out in vain. The next entry was a pair of small, mildewed clippings from the *Daily Gleaner*, carefully pasted in. Both were from a column advertising for the return of strayed stock and runaway slaves. *January 1st, 1835. Escaped: Congo Eve, five feet five inches high & branded with the mark CW on left shoulder, belonging to Mr Cyrus Wright of Fever Hill Estate. Whoever shall lodge the said Negro with the subscriber shall receive a reward of ten shillings. Cyrus Wright (sub).*

The second clipping contained an identical advertisement dated the following year. The reward was doubled.

There followed two pages of spare one-line entries, often only one per year. There was no more mention of the weather, or of his sexual conquests, or what he'd had 'to his dinner'. Cyrus Wright had lost his taste for the minutiae of his life. But every so often he would tersely record that his health and spirits remained 'indifferent'. And each year there was a stark note that Congo Eve had not yet been found.

The penultimate entry was longer, but tremulous. By then, Cyrus Wright had been an old man of eighty.

November 13th, 1849 *Congo Eve not yet found, but rumoured alive and in the hills. This day, Master Jocelyn Monroe was wed to Miss Catherine McFarlane. Miss McFarlane brought with her several Negroes from her father's estate, including Leah, the sister of Congo Eve, and Leah's daughter Semanthe. The daughter is blind, but has a look of Congo Eve. Both mother & daughter are said to be in contact with Congo Eve, & to have learned from her the unclean secrets of Obiah & Mial. I questioned them strenuously, but the wretches refused to tell of her.*

The final entry was six weeks later, and in another hand, large and untutored. *January 2nd, 1850. This day Cyrus Wright Esq. died in his sleep. By Elizabeth Mordenner, his wife.*

Evie closed the book and put her hands on the cover. So Cyrus Wright had died in his sleep, with a wife at his side – a wife he'd never even bothered to mention in his journal.

The fact that he'd died peacefully after escaping punishment for all his cruelties would once have outraged Evie. Now she almost felt sorry for him. It was clear from his bitter little notations that he'd spent the rest of his life – all eighteen years of it – tormented by the knowledge that Congo Eve was living freely in the hills, in *the region known as Turn Around*. He might have survived an attempt to poison him; he might have escaped Strap's attack on his life; but in the end, Congo Eve had had her revenge.

Evie had thought a lot about revenge while she was regaining her strength up in the cave. She'd promised her mother that she would never confront her father, Cornelius Traherne, and she intended to keep that promise. *And yet* – she craved justice from the Trahernes. Justice for herself and for her mother, and for that child begotten in incest, whom she'd sacrificed in the cave.

But what should she do? Should she emulate her ancestress and try a poisoning? Or should she act the civilized twentieth-century teacheress, and turn the other cheek?

Who was she? That was the question. Until she decided that, she wouldn't know what to do.

All her life she had wanted to be white. All her life she had envied Sibella Traherne – rich, pretty, thoughtless Sibella, who had everything Evie had always wanted. Sibella Traherne. Her half-sister.

But strangely, Evie didn't envy her any more. How could she? Sibella was just a poor, weak woman who was terrified of her own father, and detested the man she was going to marry. And if Evie couldn't envy her, then why try so hard to be white?

She wasn't white. She was mulatto. She was the four-eyed daughter of Grace McFarlane, and a kinswoman of Congo Eve. Wasn't that something to be proud of? Wasn't that what Congo Eve had been trying to tell her all along?

A gust of wind stirred the ackee tree above her head. She looked about her at the creeper-clad ruins of the old slave village – the village which Alasdair Monroe, in his murderous rage, had burnt to the ground after the Rebellion. Then an idea came to her.

Pensively she traced a triangle on the cover of the journal. Maybe that's it, she thought. Her heart quickened with excitement. Maybe it's time to get up a little Christmas Rebellion of your own.

To reach the Burying-place at Fever Hill, one crossed the lawns at the back of the house, and took the path over the crown of the hill and halfway down the other side.

But if one then continued on past the Burying-place, the path snaked through a thicket of ironwoods, and finally ended at a creeper-choked ruin in a dark little dell. People shunned this place, for it was the ruin of the old hot-house or slave hospital. A place of duppies and evil memories: some long-ago, some not so long-ago.

Precisely because no-one went there, it also possessed a curious kind of peace. At least, it did for Ben. That was why he'd caused the three coffins to be placed here beneath a temporary bamboo shelter, until the mausoleum could be built. It was also why he'd come here to be alone, after fetching Evie.

He sat on a block of cut-stone with his elbows on his knees, watching a centipede working its way along the coffin which held his brother's remains. It was peaceful in the clearing, but not at all quiet. The rasp of the crickets rose and fell like the soughing of the sea. A flock of jabbering crows flew raucously overhead. A mongoose emerged from beneath a dumb-cane leaf, spotted Ben, and vanished into the undergrowth.

Life was going on all around him. Busy, indifferent, beautiful. So why couldn't he find peace? After all, he'd achieved what he wanted. He'd found Robbie and Lil and Kate, and brought them out to the warmth and the light. Why wasn't that enough?

'What do you want from me, Kate?' he said aloud.

A cling-cling flew down onto the roof of the shelter and regarded him with a beady yellow eye.

'I made the wrong choice and you paid for it,' he said. 'I'm sorry. I've tried to make amends. What more do you want?'

The cling-cling hopped along the roof and flew away.

Ben sat on in the clearing, while the rasp of the crickets intensified. He was dizzy with fatigue and still half drunk – and still disgusted with himself. That look on Sophie's face. *What happened to you, Ben? Inside, something's gone.*

He'd bought Fever Hill in order to get her back. He saw that now. He'd bought it because she'd lived here once; because she loved it. Perhaps that was why he'd fallen in love with it too. *What happened to you, Ben? Inside, something's gone.*

Was she right? Was that why Isaac had left, and Austen? Ah, but what was the good of wondering? What was the point?

Slowly he got to his feet, and started back up the path.

He'd crested the hill and was wading through the long grass towards the Burying-place when a flash of white caught his eye. He stopped. His mouth went dry. Below him, sitting on the bench beneath the poinciana tree, was a ghost.

She was dressed in vaporous white, in the fashion of twenty years before. A high-necked blouse with leg of mutton sleeves, a bell-shaped skirt cinched in at the waist, and a beribboned straw bonnet. What little he could see of her face was a waxen yellow.

Then she turned and smiled at him, and he glimpsed an escaping lock of dyed grey hair, and breathed again.

'Hello, dear,' she said calmly. 'I was wondering when we'd bump into each other.'

He took off his hat and went down towards her. 'Hello, Miss Clemmy.'

'I hope you don't mind my coming unannounced? But your letter did say that I might visit at any time.'

'I meant it,' he said. 'I'm glad to see you, Miss Clemmy.'
He meant that too. He didn't want to be alone any more.

He'd only met her once before, and that had been years ago when he was a boy, and she'd summoned him to Fever Hill on an errand. At the time he'd thought her mad and slightly pitiful. But she'd treated him with the instinctive courtesy with which she treated everyone, and he'd never forgotten.

She patted the bench beside her and asked if he'd care to sit down. She sounded as cheery as if she were at a tea party; not communing with the spirit of her infant son.

Ben hesitated. 'Wouldn't you rather be alone with Elliot?'

She smiled. 'You know, he's not actually down here. He's up in heaven. This is just the place I come to, because it's nice and quiet, and so much easier to get his attention.'

Ben couldn't think of anything to say to that. So he tossed his hat in the grass and sat down.

Miss Clemmy folded her pale hands in her lap, and watched a yellow butterfly sunning itself on a large barrel tomb at the far end of the Burying-place.

Ben said, 'You're looking very well, Miss Clemmy.'

'Thank you, dear,' she said, still watching the butterfly. 'I've been busy, and I fancy it agrees with me. *So* much to do, what with looking after Belle – strange child – and of course, dear Madeleine.'

'How is she? Madeleine, I mean?'

Her pretty young-old face contracted. 'She misses her sister dreadfully. But they're both too proud to make amends. Or perhaps too frightened of what would happen if it didn't work. I don't know. But I do know that nothing will be right until it's sorted out.'

Ben made no reply.

'Madeleine's down in Falmouth,' Miss Clemmy went on with a smile. 'She's spending the day with the Mordenners. I'm going down to join her after I finish here, and dear little Belle's going along for tea, on her pony! She absolutely pestered Maddy to let her.'

Ben broke off a grass stem and turned it in his fingers.

'Would you – would you send Madeleine my regards?'

Miss Clemmy's china-blue eyes became troubled. 'Oh, I'm sorry, dear, but I don't think that would be wise. You see, she associates you with such painful memories.'

He bit back his disappointment. 'Of course. I understand.'

She patted his knee, as if to make him feel better. 'Now then,' she said brightly. 'I hear that you've brought out your brother and sisters to be with you. I call that *very* nice.'

She made it sound like a jolly sort of picnic, and he had to smile.

'And where shall you put the mausoleum?' she asked.

'To tell the truth, Miss Clemmy, I don't think I'll build it.'

'But why? I'd heard that the plans are all drawn up.'

'They are. And on paper it seemed like a good idea. But it's not for them. It's too grand.' He looked about him at the simple barrel tombs dreaming away the decades in the long grass. 'Maybe the Monroes got it right after all,' he said, indicating the big barrel tomb where the butterfly was still sunning itself. 'Maybe I'll build something like that instead.'

'Oh, don't copy that one,' said Miss Clemmy with startling energy. 'That's old Alasdair's tomb. That wouldn't do at all.'

'Why not?'

'Oh, he was a dreadful old man. Perfectly dreadful. Died of apoplexy just after they freed the slaves. His servants hated him so much that they built that tomb especially for him. Walls two feet thick, and special cement made with ashes from his own great house, and a few other things which it doesn't do to mention.'

He glanced at her in surprise. 'How do you know all this?'

'Why, because it was Grace's mother, old Semanthe, who helped them build it. The aim was to keep him inside, you see. To stop him walking.'

Ben considered that. 'Did it work?'

'Oh, heavens, yes. Jamaicans know a thing or two about ghosts.'

Watching the butterfly lift off from the tomb, Ben thought how odd it was – how odd but how universal – that people attributed such importance to a corpse. Most people probably paid lip service to the idea that once the spirit had departed, what was left was merely 'clay'. But it wasn't. Semanthe McFarlane had gone to enormous lengths to keep old Alasdair's corpse from walking. And he, Ben, had gone to endless trouble to find what remained of his brother and sisters and bring them out. For what? To set them free? To have them with him? To atone for the crime of being alive, while they were dead?

He turned to Miss Clemmy, and asked if she believed in ghosts.

'Why of course, dear. Don't you?'

'I don't know. I never used to. When my brother Jack was killed down at the docks, I remember thinking, Well that's that, then. Like a lamp going out. It was the same when Lil got the con.' He coloured. 'Sorry, I mean consumption.'

Miss Clemmy smiled and nodded, and waited for him to go on.

'But then a few years ago, Evie saw something. Something I can't explain. Since then, I haven't known what to believe.'

Miss Clemmy was shaking her head. 'That poor child. She was always seeing things. Absolutely hated it. Used to come to me in tears.'

It was Ben's turn to smile. 'Did you give her ginger bonbons?'

She looked delighted. 'As a matter of fact, I did.' She studied his face. 'You were such a fierce little boy. And you cared so deeply about Madeleine and Sophie.'

Ben did not reply. He threw away the grass stem and reached for another, and began stripping off the bracts.

A cling-cling – perhaps the one from the hot-house ruins – alighted on the tomb of Alasdair Monroe, and extended a glossy blue-black wing and began to preen.

Miss Clemmy lightly touched Ben's shoulder. 'Who is Kate?'

Ben opened his mouth to reply, then shut it again. He shook his head.

'It's just that I saw you at the old hot-house,' she said. 'I always come that way, from the Eden Road – it's so much less intrusive than coming up by the house – and as I was passing, you were saying sorry to Kate.'

Ben reached for his hat and turned it in his hands. Then he tossed it back into the grass. 'Kate was my older sister,' he said.

'Ah. And why were you saying sorry?'

He had never told anyone about it. Not even Sophie. But there was something about Miss Clemmy's gentle directness which made one feel that one could say almost anything.

So he told her. About his father, and the day Kate left, and about Pa forcing him to choose between her or Robbie. 'So I told him where she was,' he said simply. 'I thought she'd be able to look after herself better than Robbie.'

'And – were you right about that?'

'No. I couldn't have been more wrong.'

She waited for him to go on.

'You see, I'd forgotten that she was in the family way. I'd forgotten about the blackstick. That's a kind of lead, Miss Clemmy. The girls buy it and roll it into pills, to get rid of – well, to get them out of trouble.'

'Oh,' said Miss Clemmy, and folded her hands neatly in her lap.

'It turned out that she'd taken too much, and it had made her sick. Really bad. Cramps and that. So when Pa – my father – when he caught up with her, she was too weak to protect herself.' He drew a deep breath. 'I thought Jeb would be around to look after her, but he wasn't, he was out somewhere. She was alone when Pa found her.'

'What happened then?'

He shook his head. 'I don't know. She was dead when I

got there. Lying in the gutter with one side of her face smashed in.' He cleared his throat. 'She'd gone through the window. I supposed he must have thrown her out. Or she fell. I don't know. When I got there he was in the gutter, holding her in his arms. He was crying his heart out.' He paused. 'Funny, that. I never remembered it till now.'

Miss Clemmy made a clucking sound which was both wholly inadequate and extremely comforting.

'I made the wrong choice,' he said, frowning down at his hands. 'I should've found a way to save them both. To save Robbie and Kate, both.'

'But how could you have done that? You were only a child.'

'I could've taken him on. Not just cowered against the wall and told him where she was. If I'd taken him on, Robbie could've got away. Then it wouldn't have mattered what he did.'

'But surely – surely then your father would have killed you instead.'

He nodded. 'That's what I mean. I made the wrong choice.'

The cling-cling spread its wings and lifted off from the tomb of Alasdair Monroe, and headed north.

It flew over Fever Hill great house, and over the cane-pieces of Alice Grove. It crossed the Fever Hill Road and flew west into Parnassus Estate. But as it was passing over the cane-pieces of Waytes Valley, something glittering caught its eye. It swept down – then abruptly swerved up again. What from the sky had looked like a seductive, glowing thing was in fact a lighted match in human hands. With an indignant squawk the cling-cling headed east, towards the stables at Parnassus.

Back in Waytes Valley, a breeze from the sea ruffled the uncut cane, and the flame crackled and spat as the hands put it to a cluster of dry leaves.

This year, the weather had been perfect, with good strong rains in October, then a couple of hot, dry months to bring up the sugar. But while some planters had started taking off the crop before Christmas, at Parnassus things had been slower, and much of the cane remained uncut. It was even rumoured that Master Cornelius might have trouble paying his field-hands.

The breeze fanned the flames higher. A hand fed more dry leaves to the fire. The leaves blackened and curled and smoked. Sparks flew upwards.

The wind carried the sparks inland. They flurried south, into the dry, rustling, uncut cane.

CHAPTER THIRTY-TWO

'When there's a duppy around,' Quaco had told Belle as he helped her up onto Muffin, 'you get a sudden hot wind in you face, and a sweet-sweet smell. That's when you got to run quick-time and throw lot, lotta salt. But you know all this, Missy Belle. Why you wanting to hear it over again?'

'Just to make sure,' she'd told him.

But he was right, she did know it already. She knew that duppies live in ruins and burying-places, but mostly in silk-cotton trees. She knew that on moon-full, all the duppy trees in Trelawny remove from their own place, and go up to the forest to reason with each other. All except the great duppy tree on Overlook Hill. The other trees come to him.

It wasn't going to be moon-full tonight, which was good. Besides, darkness was hours away, for it was still only tea-time. At least, it was tea-time in the outside world. But here in the forest on Overlook Hill, it was half dark. And there was a horrible listening stillness which made her catch her breath.

It shouldn't *be* so quiet in a forest. There should be birdsong, and the buzz and hum of insects. But the small creatures knew to keep away from the glade of the great duppy tree. All Belle could hear was her own breathing; and a leaf dropping from the canopy and softly striking the undergrowth.

She raised her head and gazed into the upside-down world of the duppy tree. The great outstretched limbs blotted out the sky: wide enough to accommodate a whole nest of duppies. Ropes of purple thunbergia hung down about her, and the tortured cords of strangler fig. Ghostly Spanish moss clogged the fingers of the branches, and vicious green spikes of wild pine, and scarlet orchids like vengeful darts of flame.

She swayed. The duppy tree leaned closer. On the enormous buttressed trunk she saw the black, sunken pits where nails had been hammered in. Quaco said that when somebody got sick bad, it was because the obeah-man had stolen their shadow and nailed it to the tree. She wondered if the shadows were still here, wriggling on the nails.

Her heart began to pound. She wondered if the duppies were here too, watching her. Was Fraser among them? Was he one of the rare *good* duppies, the kind Quaco called a 'good death'? Would he protect her because she was a relative? Or was he the other kind of duppy, who threw rockstones and put hand on people?

She felt in her pocket for the rosemary and the bag of salt. She wished she'd brought Muffin along instead of leaving her tied up at the crossroads so that she wouldn't get scared. She wished she could run away. But she had an offering to make.

Her hands were slippery with sweat as she slid the satchel off her shoulder and took out the bottle of proof rum she'd bought from a higgler near Bethlehem. That had only been a couple of hours ago, but it felt like days.

She had slipped away from Quaco just as she'd planned. They'd set off for town after lunch, and stopped halfway at the village of Prospect for a cool-drink. It had been easy to persuade Quaco to take a little nap. Then she was off.

The quickest route to Overlook Hill would have been straight up the Eden Road, across Romilly Bridge, then down to the crossroads and turn right. But she couldn't go that way for fear of bumping into Papa. So instead she'd turned *east* through Greendale Wood, crossed Greendale Bridge, and then looped south-west through Bethlehem, keeping to the cane-tracks so as to avoid passing too near the Maputah works or home. She'd been proud of herself for finding her way, and when she'd stopped at Tom Gully to give Muffin a drink, it had felt like an adventure. But all that seemed a world away now.

She cast a doubtful glance at the bottle of rum in her hand. What was she doing here? How dare she ask the duppy tree for help? And how did one make an offering, anyway? Should she pour the whole bottle onto the roots? Or just leave it uncorked, so that the duppy tree could have it when it liked?

She decided to compromise by pouring half onto the roots, then propping the bottle against the trunk. She did it all with the greatest of care. If you knock against a duppy tree, it might get vexed, and put hand on you. How does a tree 'put hand on you'? She didn't like to think.

When the half-full bottle was resting securely in a fold of the trunk, she took her list of requests from the satchel and unfolded it. Her heart was pounding so hard that she felt sick.

'This is my list,' she said. Her voice sounded horribly loud in the stillness, and she could feel the duppy tree leaning closer to listen. She didn't dare look up from the page. '*Mamma and Papa to be happier and never quarrel again,*' she mumbled. '*Sugar prices to go up or treasure to be found, so that Papa will not have to work so hard. Aunt Sophie to come for a visit and make up with Mamma.*' She cleared her throat. 'That's the end of my list.'

She wondered if she should say any more. It seemed presumptuous to say 'thank you' when she didn't know if the duppy tree intended to help. But it would be awful to appear ungrateful. 'Thank you, great duppy tree,' she said, and gave a respectful bow. Then she folded the list and tucked it behind the half-full bottle of rum.

The stillness was deeper than ever. All she could hear was her own breathing, and the fall of another leaf in the undergrowth. Then another one brushed her hand. Glancing down, she saw that it wasn't a leaf at all, but a large black flake of ash.

Puzzled, she looked up.

The duppy tree was dripping with black ash. Big black flakes, some as long as her forefinger, rocking silently down through the canopy, and coming to rest with a soft pattering on the ferns and creepers of the forest floor.

For one terrible moment she thought this must be some kind of sign that the duppy tree was angry with her. Then one of the flakes of ash brushed her face, and she smelt the bitter tang of burnt sugar. *Cane-ash*, she thought in a rush of relief. It's just someone setting a cane-fire, silly. Just a normal, everyday cane-fire to burn away the trash and make it easier to take off the crop.

And yet – there was still something a little odd about it. For one thing, it was too early in the day for setting a cane-fire. For another, who was doing it, and where? Papa hadn't said anything about setting a fire. And Fever Hill wasn't due to start taking off the crop for another couple of weeks; Papa had mentioned that at breakfast.

And she needed to know where the fire was, because it would affect her route back to Falmouth. She'd been planning to nip back to collect Muffin, and then avoid home altogether by sneaking west around the bottom of Overlook Hill, and then crossing the river at Stony Gap. From there she could follow the Martha Brae round on its opposite bank – which was actually trespassing on Fever Hill land, but no-one would mind – and then cut east through the Bellevue cane-pieces and out onto the Eden Road somewhere north of Romilly. She might even reach the Mordenners' without Mamma finding out where she'd been.

But the trouble with that plan was that if Papa was setting a fire in one of the Orange Grove cane-pieces on this side of the river, then he'd be bound to see her, and she'd be most horribly told off.

For a moment her fear of the duppy tree was sidelined by the prospect of being told off by Papa. She wondered what to do. Of course, she could just brazen it out, and ride openly north from the crossroads: past home, past Romilly, and right down the Eden Road to town. But it would be horribly risky.

Another idea would be to make a quick reconnaissance on foot from here to the western edge of the forest, and get a bird's-eye view of which cane-piece Papa was burning, so that she could avoid it.

She bit her lip. It would take her about a quarter of an hour to walk to the western edge of the forest, and poor Muffin had already been waiting long enough. But on the other hand, if it stopped her getting caught by Papa . . .

Around her the forest was hushed and breathless, waiting to see what she would decide. The only sound was the gentle pattering of ash.

Down on the Fever Hill Road, a clump of giant bamboo caught fire. Flames scurried up the canes like lizards. The dry leaves crackled and flared. Then the culms exploded in a deafening fusillade of rifle-shots. Ben's big bay gelding skittered and squealed.

'Shut up, Partisan,' he said between his teeth, 'it's not here yet.' But the bay had sensed his master's tension, and sidestepped in alarm. Ben reined him in and drew out his watch. Half past four. Christ. Only half an hour since they'd first got news of the fire. It felt like hours. A blur of orders and snap decisions and hurried evacuations. Scarcely time to take it in. *Cane-fire*. A vast, hungry animal sweeping towards them from Waytes Valley.

He yanked Partisan's head round and put him into a canter up the track to the New Works. Already he could smell smoke, and he had to keep the bay on a short rein to stop the canter degenerating into a gallop. A light scattering of black ash floated down into the red dust like hellish snow. Not long now, he thought. Jesus, it travels fast.

To his relief, the New Works were deserted, and so was the field-hands' settlement behind it. He doubled back to the carriageway, then cantered along the track by the aqueduct to check the old slave village. That too was empty, thank God. So Neptune had finally prevailed on Grace and Evie, and got them out.

Once again Ben cantered back to the carriageway, this time putting Partisan up the hill towards the great house. A glance over his shoulder told him that the royal palms down by the gates were already blazing like torches. It didn't seem possible.

The first they'd known of the fire had been a scent of burnt sugar in the air and a light sprinkling of ash. Minutes later, a panicky field-hand had clattered in from Waytes Valley on a mule. The fire was sweeping south towards them at terrifying speed. Two months of hot, dry weather had created the perfect conditions; and now a gentle breeze was wafting in from the sea, and fanning the flames steadily south and east.

Parnassus had been caught completely unawares, and so was Fever Hill. There was no time to set a controlled fire along the Fever Hill Road, and thereby burn a fire-break to contain the blaze. No time to do the same around the New Works and Fever Hill great house. It was a question of deciding how far to retreat, and where to stand and fight.

In the end he'd sent half his men out west to burn an east–west break to protect the cane-pieces of Glen Marnoch, and the other half to start burning a break along the Eden Road, from the edge of Greendale Wood all the way south to Romilly Bridge. He wasn't too hopeful about saving Glen Marnoch, but if the second break held, it would at least save the eastern cane-pieces of Greendale, as well as Cameron Lawe's land at Bullet Tree Walk.

He'd also sent a handful of riders on all available horses to warn Isaac at Arethusa and Cameron Lawe at Eden, and to evacuate the settlements in between. Finally he'd sent a rider to Parnassus – ostensibly for more inform-ation on the fire, but really to check that Sophie was safe.

As he'd hoped, he found the great house deserted. He'd evacuated it immediately, despatching the men to help with the firebreaks, and the women in a wagon across country. Now he checked the cookhouse, the laundry-house, the servants' quarters. All deserted. Someone had even remembered to fling open the aviary doors and let out the birds.

Back in the carriageway, he reined in for a last look at the house. After the months of renovation it appeared stately and serene: like an elderly lady who'd once been beautiful, and still possessed a faded elegance.

For the first time the enormity of the fire came home to him. This house which he loved was right in its path, and there wasn't a damn thing he could do to save her. This house which had been entrusted to him. This house in which a twelve-year-old Sophie had lain for months in bed, a prisoner of her illness. This house where a fourteen-year-old Ben Kelly had waited in trepidation for the mad Miss Clemmy. This house which, only a few months ago, had welcomed him back with gentle old-fashioned grace, and made him feel at home for the first time in his life. And now he was losing it.

Far off on the Fever Hill Road, more giant bamboo went up in flames. Partisan snorted and fought the reins.

Everything's going up in smoke, thought Ben.

But not quite everything, he reminded himself. At least Kate and Robbie and Lil are still all right.

With a last look at the house, he turned and dug in his heels and cantered off towards the stables. Then, having satisfied himself that they too were deserted, he crossed the trickle of the Green River and headed east through the cane-pieces of Bellevue.

He'd gone less than a quarter of a mile before he caught up with the ox-wagon bearing the coffins. To his horror, he saw that the wagon was tilting dangerously, with one back wheel stuck in an irrigation ditch. The four field-hands who'd been detailed to get it to safety were standing around shaking their heads.

'Hey, Amos!' he shouted as he skittered to a halt. 'What the hell are you doing?'

Amos looked guilty. 'Just fixing to pull her out of the hole, Master Ben.'

'So what's stopping you?'

'That fire's running quick as black ant, Master Ben. Why, we just seen Garrick and Caesar come through here. They say that firebreak over at Alice Grove never go hold, they say the whole of Glen Marnoch go burn for sure.'

'Then thank your lucky stars that you're not in Glen Marnoch,' snapped Ben. 'Now forget about that and get that wheel out of the ditch!'

Gingerly the men moved forwards and put their shoulders to the wagon. With a sinking feeling Ben realized that if he hadn't happened along, they'd probably have abandoned the wagon and run. They were good, conscientious, hardworking men, but they were also terrified – and not only of the fire. It was asking too much of any country Jamaican to escort three coffins containing powerful, untrammelled buckra duppies.

He bit his lip and glanced back over his shoulder. To the north he could see a vast pall of grey smoke at least a mile wide. Amos was right. The fire was scything through Alice Grove towards the house, and after that it would swallow Glen Marnoch to the west, and Bellevue here in the east.

He glanced at the coffins on the wagon. Out here in the open they looked much smaller and more vulnerable. And with only oxen to draw the wagon, progress would be achingly slow, much slower than the fire. If they had horses, they could make it. But all the horses had been needed by the messengers. Where was he going to get any more?

A couple of miles up ahead, he could just make out the guango tree and the giant bamboo that marked the Eden Road. 'Right,' he said to Amos, 'here's what we do. You get the wagon back on the track, no hanging about, and I'll go and see if I can't borrow a couple of horses from someone. Then I'll come back and ride along with you, and we can all get to safety, quick-time.' Without waiting for an answer he dug in his heels and put Partisan into a flat gallop along the cane-track towards the Eden Road.

Oh, thank God. There was a carriage in the distance, coming from town. Whoever it was, they'd lend him the horses without question. An uncontrolled cane-fire threatens everyone, so everyone helps.

But as he drew nearer, he saw to his horror that the 'carriage' was Miss Clemmy in her pony-trap.

It can't be, he told himself. She'd left for town three hours ago. He'd seen her go.

It couldn't be, but it was. And she was calmly trotting south down the Eden Road, heading straight for the path of the fire.

When she recognized Ben she reined in, and politely waited for him to approach.

'Miss Clemmy,' he panted when he reached her, 'what the hell are you doing?'

She blinked. 'Why, dear, I'm going to Eden—'

'There's a *fire*, Miss Clemmy. Can't you see? It'll cut off the Eden Road before you get there.'

'Oh, I know that,' she said, startling him. 'I met a boy on a mule and he told me all about it. He said that Cameron and that nice Mr Walker's men from Arethusa are burning a firebreak along the western edge of the road, from Romilly all the way down to—'

'I know,' he broke in impatiently. 'I've sent men to help. And that's just why you've got to turn round and go back. It'll be chaos up there.'

'But I won't be *taking* the Eden Road,' she insisted. 'In about a quarter of a mile I shall turn off and take the track east through Greendale Wood, and then loop round via Bethlehem—'

'Miss Clemmy—'

'But I must,' she said with surprising firmness. 'You see, Belle has gone off on one of her secret missions into the hills, so I—'

'What? Belle Lawe? Madeleine's little girl?'

'She can be so frightfully naughty! She was supposed to join Madeleine for tea at the Mordenners' – but I think I told you that? Anyway, somehow Quaco lost sight of her on the way, and then his horse went lame, so he couldn't go after her or even reach Madeleine to raise the alarm – he's quite beside himself, poor lamb – and that's when I bumped into him, on my way to the Mordenners'. Wasn't that lucky? Of course he was wild to go after her himself, but I didn't think he'd know where to look, so I thought I'd better go instead. So here I am.' She looked up at him with a triumphant smile.

Ben kneaded the point between his eyes. 'And you think you do know where to look?'

'Oh yes. She's either gone to that cave at Turnaround – yes, dear, she did mention it to me, but I haven't told any-one and neither has she – or to Fraser's Burying-place on the slope at the back of the house, or to any of half a dozen other places I can think of.' She leaned forward and added in a conspiratorial whisper, 'Madeleine's still with the Mordenners, and doesn't know a thing, thank heavens. But I really do feel that I ought to go and help Sophie look.'

'*Sophie?*' cried Ben.

Miss Clemmy looked worried. 'Didn't I mention that? I met her just after I'd bumped into Quaco. She was going into town, but of course as soon as I told her, she turned round and headed off to find Belle, so I—'

'Where? Where was she heading?'

'Why, to Eden, of course. I told her to go via Greendale, so—'

'On horseback or in a trap?'

'On that little grey mare of hers. I think she calls her Frolic?'

'When? When did you see her?'

'I really couldn't say. A while ago, I think.'

Far in the distance, another fusillade of rifle-shots split the air. More giant bamboo, but closer this time. Not the Green River already, thought Ben. From here he should be able to see Fever Hill great house in the distance, but all he could see was the vast pall of smoke. Again that twist of guilt. He'd left the old house to face the fire alone. There was nobody there to watch her burn.

Christ, Sophie, what are you thinking? Eden on your own in the middle of a cane-fire?

His thoughts raced. He glanced at the brave, silly

woman in the pony-trap, then back over his shoulder to the cane-pieces. Far in the distance, and out of sight in the man-high cane, the ox-wagon with his brother and sisters was lumbering to safety. If the men hadn't already abandoned it.

No time, no time.

Sophie was heading into the path of the fire. But surely as soon as she realized how bad it was, she'd turn round and head back to town to fetch help? Where was the sense in his going to look for her now? He'd never find her in all this chaos. And as for Belle Lawe, he could get a message to her father, and he'd be sure to find her; he wouldn't need or want Ben Kelly getting in the way.

He thought of Robbie and Lil and Kate, stuck out in the middle of Bellevue with the fire scything towards them. He couldn't lose them again. Not all over again.

And Sophie will be all right, he told himself. Besides, she'll never dare go all the way to Eden. She can't bring herself to go back there, she told you so herself.

He turned to Miss Clemmy, who was waiting obediently for him to decide. 'Miss Clemmy,' he said, 'you've got to turn round and go back to town. Right now.'

'But—'

'No buts. Listen to me. I've just come from Bellevue. I've—'

'I know, the boy on the mule told me. You're getting your brother and sisters to safety.'

He licked his lips. Then something behind her caught his eye, and he froze. Thank God. About a quarter of a mile down the road, a cartload of field-hands was coming from Prospect – no doubt to help with the firebreaks. He turned back to Miss Clemmy. 'The thing is, I've got to ride back to the ox-wagon, or the men will abandon it. So I need you to *promise* me that you'll turn round and go back to town.'

'But what about Belle?'

'There's a party of field-hands coming up behind you, d'you see it? I'll ride over now and get them to unhitch their horse, and send a man up the road to Mr Lawe, quick as he can, to tell him that Belle's gone missing.'

She opened her mouth to protest, but he talked her down. 'Miss Clemmy, a man on a horse will get there a whole lot faster than you ever could in your pony-trap. Now you've got to *promise* me that you'll turn round and go back. If you don't promise, I can't leave you on your own and go back to my brother and sisters.'

She gazed up at him with worried, china-blue eyes. 'Of course I promise. But are you sure that you're doing the right thing?'

'What?' he snapped, impatient to be off.

She gestured towards Bellevue. 'I mean, for *you*. I should hate for you to make the wrong choice all over again.'

He reined in and brought Partisan about. 'What d'you mean?'

'Well, you seem to think that Sophie might be in some kind of danger,' she said in her gentle, devastating way. 'So going back to the ox-wagon might be the wrong choice. Mightn't it?'

Partisan was angrily tossing his head, and when Ben glanced down he saw that he'd been unconsciously sawing at the reins. It took an effort of will to loosen his grip. 'Sophie,' he said quietly, 'is in no kind of danger. She'll be fine. Now please, Miss Clemmy, turn round and go back to town.'

Sophie will be fine, he told himself again, as he dug in his heels and headed up the road towards the field-hands. She'll turn back when she sees the fire. She isn't completely mad.

CHAPTER THIRTY-THREE

How bizarre, thought Sophie as she cantered through Greendale Wood, that you chose this of all days to go and see Maddy at Falmouth.

It was supposed to have been an opportunity to meet her sister on neutral ground, and re-establish some kind of contact. Instead here she was crashing through a wood with a cane-fire somewhere behind her, on her way to Eden.

Eden. She still didn't want to think about it. Perhaps something would happen to prevent her getting there. Perhaps she'd catch up with Belle on the way, or learn from someone on the road that she'd already been found, and taken back to town. She hated herself for such cowardice, but she couldn't stop praying for something like that to happen.

Nothing did. She clattered across Greendale Bridge, then turned Frolic south and started along the track towards Bethlehem. The cane-pieces were eerily deserted, the black ash softly falling. Ash this far east? But surely Clemency had said that the fire had started at Waytes Valley? That was miles away.

She didn't want to think about what it meant – or about what might be happening elsewhere. 'Fever Hill all ablaze, Missy Sophie,' the boy on the road had said. *Fever Hill ablaze*. So where was Ben?

And what about Cameron? And *Belle*?

She didn't meet anyone on the road until about a quarter of a mile from Bethlehem, when she rounded a bend and came upon a small party of men with bills over their shoulders, heading south at a tireless lope.

They told her they were from Simonstown, on their way to lend a hand. None of them had seen Belle, or even heard that she was missing. But they'd heard tell that the whole of Orange Grove had been given up to the fire, and that Master Cameron was burning a firebreak in a great north–south line, to protect the house and the eastern cane-pieces and the Maputah works.

If it could be finished in time, the firebreak would stretch from Greendale Wood in the north, all the way past the crossroads in the south. And if it held, then the fire would have nowhere to go except south into the hills. 'Master Camron fixing to *push* that fire south,' said the eldest man, 'south inna the bush. And when it reach there, it burn itself out in the bare rockstones, if it please Master God.'

'Where's Master Cameron now?' she said. 'D'you know?'

He shook his head. 'Maybe down at Romilly? Maybe further north? But it don't necessary for you to go on, Missy Sophie. You better turn back now, too much smokes up ahead. And not to frighten about Missy Belle. She soon going safe, for Master Camron go find her quick-time.'

She bit her lip. In the distance up ahead she could see the roof of Bethlehem chapel pushing above the trees. Three miles beyond that lay Eden great house. The man was probably right: she should turn round now, and go back to town. She certainly wanted to. And in all probability, Cameron would find Belle without any help from her. He'd probably found her already, and sent her off in disgrace to her mother.

But what if he hadn't? What if the news that she was missing hadn't even got through?

There didn't seem to be any way out. If she turned back now and something happened to Belle, she'd never forgive herself.

She wished the men luck, and told them to keep an eye out for Belle. Then she gathered the reins and put Frolic into a canter towards Bethlehem.

When she reached the village she found it deserted. She slowed to a trot, and crossed the silent clearing in front of the chapel. She passed the old clinic – long since abandoned by Dr Mallory – and the breadfruit tree under which, seven years before, a young groom had stooped to examine a five-year-old's beloved toy zebra.

'Belle?' she shouted. Her voice echoed eerily from house to house. But no-one came out. Not even a dog. All she could hear was the insidious whisper of falling ash.

She trotted to the edge of the village and reined in at Tom Gully, the shallow stream which marked the boundary between Bethlehem and Eden land. Frolic put down her head to drink.

Sophie was thirsty too, but she knew that she couldn't drink. Her throat was too tight to swallow. No more than a yard away, on the other side of this shallow ribbon of rusty brown water, lay Eden.

It's only land, she told herself as her heart began to thud. There's no *need* to feel like this.

It didn't work.

The mare finished drinking and shook her head, scattering droplets.

You're just a miserable coward, Sophie told herself. Belle needs you. How can you even hesitate?

She glanced over her shoulder at the deserted village. Then she looked ahead to the track that led to the works at Maputah, and on to Eden great house. Then she took a deep breath and put the mare forward across the stream.

Nothing is real any more, she thought, as she cantered up to the house. She felt as if she were trapped in a dream: as if she were the only one left alive.

From force of habit, she rode round the side of the house and into the garden, where she dismounted and tethered Frolic at the bottom of the steps. It all looked achingly familiar, and eerily untouched by the catastrophe which threatened to sweep it away.

'Belle?' she called.

No answer.

The garden was just the same as she remembered. The same scarlet hibiscus and greenish-gold tree-ferns; the same spiky royal palms and white bougainvillaea. And down by the sliding river, the same great banks of torch ginger and scarlet heliconia, and the nodding plumes of the giant bamboo, which would ferry the fire across the river in a heartbeat if Cameron's firebreak didn't hold.

Everything was weirdly peaceful, and alive with birds. She caught the emerald flash of a doctorbird; the smoky blur of a bluequit. She heard the rapid *zizizi* of sugarbirds in the hibiscus, and the high-pitched trill of a grassquit. At Eden life was going on in terrifying innocence of the fire about to sweep it away. It was almost as if there was no fire. Except for the black ash, softly falling.

She turned and ran up the steps.

'Belle?' Her voice echoed in the empty house.

Everywhere she looked she saw traces of lives interrupted. A maid's coconut-fibre broom discarded on the tiles. A copy of the *Daily Gleaner* tossed across the tartan cushions on the sofa.

Quickly she checked the bedrooms, in case Belle was hiding, and afraid to come out. The spare room and the nursery were empty. Feeling horribly intrusive, she ran into Cameron's and Madeleine's room. It too was empty – but it felt unsettlingly as if someone had only just left. The bird-feeder at the open door was gently rocking. One of Cameron's shirts lay crumpled on the floor.

She was turning to go when a group of photographs on the bedside table caught her eye. There were three of them, in a little tortoiseshell cluster beside a yellow-backed novel and a lacquered ring-stand that she remembered giving Madeleine for her birthday years before.

The first photograph was of an eight-year-old Belle, scowling into the camera, with Spot firmly gripped beneath her chin.

The second was of Fraser. He wore his beloved sailor suit, and he was hatless, his curly hair a pale halo around his eager little face. He was standing proudly behind Abigail the mastiff, with one small hand on her massive black head and the other on her back, as if he was about to climb aboard and ride her like a pony.

He used to do it, too, Sophie remembered. And when he fell off, Abigail would nose him to his feet and chase him round and round the house, wagging her tail and pretend-biting him, while he squealed with delight.

Grief welled up in her throat and lodged there like a piece of meat.

She dragged her eyes away from Fraser to the third photograph. With a jolt she recognized herself. She hadn't expected that. Since Fraser's death, Madeleine could hardly look her in the eye. And yet here was her photograph on Madeleine's bedside table.

Madeleine had taken it seven years ago, on the day of the Historical Society picnic. In the photograph Sophie stood beneath a tree-fern, looking painfully self-conscious in her unflattering pale green dress.

That picnic. She remembered the drive back to Eden with Ben. He hadn't spoken a word all the way to Romilly, and then she'd forced him to talk, and they'd had a row.

She pressed her hands to her mouth. First Fraser. Then Ben. Not *now*. There wasn't time.

She ran out onto the steps at the back of the house, and stood irresolute, not knowing which way to turn. Clemency had said that Belle had gone off on a 'secret mission into the hills'. But where?

Would she really have gone to the cave at Turnaround, as Clemency believed? That seemed unlikely, given that coming across Evie in the cave had given Belle the fright of her life.

So what about somewhere closer to home? Where would a child with a morbid streak go on a 'secret mission'?

She was debating this when a flicker of movement in the undergrowth caught her eye.

There it was again: something pale in the dense greenery of the slope. It had only been a flicker, but something about it made her catch her breath. For a moment – just a moment – she thought she'd glimpsed a child's fair head.

Not possible, she told herself, feeling suddenly cold. There are no fair-haired children at Eden. Not any more.

'Belle?' she called. In the stillness her voice sounded shaky and scared. She cleared her throat. 'Fraser?'

Crows exploded from the trees in a flurry of wings. When they'd gone there was a taut, listening stillness. It was as if the trees, and the very house itself, had tensed when she'd said the name.

She moistened her lips and forced herself to stay calm. Think of Belle, concentrate on Belle. Where would she go on a secret mission?

Fraser was buried quite close to the house, only a short way up the slope. From where she stood, she could see the path: a narrow but well-worn track disappearing into a shadowy green jungle of sweetwoods and breadfruit trees and huge-leaved philodendron.

Could Belle be up there?

She never seems to play *with her dolls*, Madeleine had said once. *She just holds funerals for them.*

A cold sweat broke out on her forehead. She couldn't go up there. No, no, no. Not to the grave.

Oh, it's beautiful, Sophie, Clemency had assured her. *Maddy's made it into a little secret garden. She's planted all sorts of flowers. She told me once that after he died, she just wanted to make things grow. That was all she could bear to do. Just make things grow.*

Again Sophie caught that pale flicker of movement. Her mouth went dry. *No*. It was just a bird. Or a yellowsnake, or – or something. Not the gentle, grey-eyed, fair-haired little boy who had died in her arms seven years before.

Again she called for Belle. Again that taut, listening stillness. A stillness broken only by the lazy fluttering of ash.

She drew a deep breath and ran up the track to the Burying-place.

413

It really was just as beautiful as Clemency had said. A small oval clearing enclosed by tree-ferns and wild almond and cinnamon trees, and planted with a dazzling profusion of flowers. She saw powder-blue plumbago and jasmine and hibiscus; the subtle mauves and greenish whites of orchids, and the brilliant cobalt and orange of strelitzia, Fraser's favourites.

In the midst of it stood a small, plain white barrel tomb with a stark inscription:

Fraser Jocelyn Lawe
1897–1903

Finally, after all these years, she was standing by his grave.

She watched a flake of black ash float down and settle on the marble. Tentatively, she put out her hand and brushed it off. The stone felt smooth and cool. Not terrifying at all, but strangely comforting.

'I'm so sorry, Fraser my darling,' she whispered. 'I'm so sorry I couldn't save you.'

She looked about her, and stooped and broke off a sprig of orchids, and laid them on the marble. And as she did so, something inside her lifted and broke free.

Now at last she understood what had compelled Ben to bring his dead out to Jamaica. He had decided to stop running from them. He had invited them back.

She squared her shoulders and wiped her eyes with her fingers. Then she began to make a search of the clearing. But she could find no sign that Belle had been here. No ritual herbs. No cut limes or other anti-duppy measures such as a child might be able to muster.

And she, Sophie, should know all about that. As a child, she too had had a morbid streak. She'd lived in terror of duppy trees, and had never been without her sprig of rosemary or Madam Fate.

She froze. *Duppy trees.*

A snatch of conversation came back to her. *Did you ask a duppy tree?* Belle had asked at Parnassus, as she gazed intently at Sophie with her big dark eyes. *Did you give it an offering?*

Suddenly, Sophie knew. Belle's 'secret mission' had nothing to do with Fraser's grave. She'd gone to make an offering to the great duppy tree on Overlook Hill. She was up there right now.

A cold wave of dread washed over her as she realized what that meant. As she stood here beside Fraser's grave, Cameron was somewhere to the north, hard at work with his men to burn a firebreak all the way from Greendale Wood to the crossroads and beyond. His aim was to block the fire's eastward march, so that it had nowhere to go but south.

South to Overlook Hill.

CHAPTER THIRTY-FOUR

Belle wasn't at the duppy tree.

But she'd been there recently. Sophie was sure of it. There was a half-full bottle of proof rum propped up against the trunk, and around its neck a scarlet hair ribbon tied in a neat, crisp bow.

'Belle?' she shouted. '*Belle!* It's Aunt Sophie! Where *are* you?'

Nothing. Ash pattered down into the undergrowth. To the north she could hear a distant roar. The roar of the fire.

Ahead of her the track wound on through the trees towards the western edge of the forest. Surely Belle wouldn't have gone that way? But where else *could* she have gone? If she'd been anywhere near the track leading up from the crossroads, Sophie would have found her.

No time to think about that now. She put Frolic forwards, heading west.

It was hard going, for the path was overgrown, and she was forced to dismount and lead, stopping often to untangle the stirrups from the undergrowth, and talking to the mare to calm her. But Frolic would not be calmed, for she'd scented smoke. Her ears were flattened against her skull, and she kept tossing her head and tugging the reins, making progress agonizingly slow.

Ben, reflected Sophie, would have had the mare trotting calmly at his heels like a retriever. She pushed the thought aside. She didn't want to think about him now. *Fever Hill all ablaze, Missy Sophie*. But he'll have got out all right, she told herself. There can't be any doubt about that.

A parrot flew over the canopy – *ah-eek, ah-eek*. A pulse beat in her throat. Was she imagining things, or was it getting hotter? Certainly the stink of burnt sugar was stronger, and the air was becoming hazy. And still she could find no sign that Belle had been this way. No snapped branches, no horse droppings. Nothing.

After ten minutes' hard going she caught a glimmer of dirty white sky between the trees. She quickened her pace, dragging the reluctant Frolic after her.

She reached the edge of the forest with startling suddenness, and the stench of burnt sugar hit her like a wall. Frolic squealed and jerked back, nearly pulling Sophie off her feet.

The fire was terrifyingly close: a roaring, crackling wall of fierce-burning orange, only half a mile distant. Behind it the cane-pieces of Orange Grove had disappeared in a dirty grey pall of smoke.

Tugging Frolic after her, she picked her way between the boulders and the thorn scrub, and round the flank of the hill. Somewhere on the south-west slope was a track that wound down to the bridge at Stony Gap.

On this side of the hill, the fire wasn't quite so close. But through the bitter blue haze she could only just make out the giant bamboo that marked the Martha Brae, little more than a mile from where she stood.

'Belle!' she shouted. 'Belle!' Her voice sounded weak and ineffectual in the roar of the fire.

'*Here!*' yelled a voice, so close that she nearly fell over.

Belle was about twenty feet below her on the track. She was filthy, her face and riding-costume covered in dust and soot. 'Aunt Sophie, I'm *really* sorry!' she cried. 'I was trying to get round to see how far it had gone and I slipped and bumped my knee and then I tried to find another way up and sort of got lost.'

She seemed exasperated rather than frightened, and after the first shattering upsurge of relief Sophie was tempted to run down and give her a good shaking. Then she noticed that Belle's shoulders were hunched up around her ears, her fists clenched at her sides. 'It doesn't matter,' she said, raising her voice above the roar of the fire. 'Are you all right?'

Belle gave a tight nod. 'What do we do now?'

Sophie licked her lips. 'Stay where you are. I need to think.'

From where she stood, the path wound steeply down the bare western slope of the hill towards Belle. It was loose stony ground, with a steep drop on the left of about fifty feet into a thorny defile. But if they could make it down to the bottom of the hill, they might reach Stony Gap before the fire closed off their escape, and then cross to the safety of the cattle pastures on the other side of the river.

The alternative was to head back up the track and into the forest again, retracing their steps past the duppy tree, and down to the crossroads.

Every nerve in her body cried out for the primeval shelter of the forest. And yet, she thought, what if we can't make it through in time? As she was setting out from Eden, she'd heard the shouts of Cameron's men, hard at work burning the firebreak. There'd been no time to ride down and question them, but they hadn't sounded that far off. What if, by the time she and Belle reached the crossroads, they found themselves cut off by the very firebreak intended to protect Eden?

Or what if they never got that far, but were overtaken by the cane-fire while they were still in the forest? With terrifying clarity she saw herself and Belle wading through the tangled undergrowth. She saw burning branches crashing down on them. The heat and smoke becoming unbearable. Overwhelming.

'Stay where you are,' she told Belle. 'I'm coming down to you.'

Belle looked horrified. 'But what about Muffin? We can't leave her!'

'What?' shouted Sophie, intent on picking her way

down without losing her footing. Behind her a reluctant Frolic snorted and tugged on the reins.

'I tied her up!' cried Belle, jumping up and down. 'She won't be able to get away! She'll be burnt!'

'No she won't,' said Sophie unconvincingly. She slipped on a loose stone and nearly lost her footing. A trickle of pebbles rattled and bounced down the slope and lost themselves among the boulders at the bottom. She licked her lips. The track was steeper than it looked. God, she thought, I hope this isn't another of Aunt Sophie's mistakes. 'I didn't see Muffin as I was coming up,' she called down to Belle, 'so she must have broken free and run away.'

'Are you sure?' said Belle doubtfully.

'Absolutely.' Again Frolic tugged on the reins.

'Aunt Sophie—'

'*What?*' she snapped. Yet another tug on the reins. Dust and pebbles rained down on her. 'Frolic, come *on*,' she shouted without turning round.

'Aunt Sophie!' screamed Belle. 'Look *out!*'

A rock struck her shoulder with bruising force. She glanced back just in time to see the mare going slowly down onto her knees – slowly, slowly, as if in a nightmare – then tumbling neck over crop, and sliding down the track towards her.

Ben reached the crossroads before Cameron Lawe's men, but with not much time to spare.

He could hear them through the thickening haze of smoke, a few hundred yards to the north. The air was acrid with the stench of burnt sugar. To the west he could hear the crackling roar as the fire engulfed Orange Grove and swept towards them.

The men didn't stop working when he rode up, nor did he expect them to. It wouldn't be much longer before the fire reached them, and if the break didn't hold the flames would burst through and engulf the great house, the works at Maputah, and the rest of the estate.

To his dismay, none of them had seen either Sophie or

Belle. But they told him that Master Cameron was further down towards Romilly, so maybe he should ride over and talk to him in person?

No time, thought Ben as he yanked Partisan's head round and galloped back towards the crossroads. No time to get into an argument with Cameron Lawe. Besides, Romilly was on the Eden Road, and Sophie hadn't come that way. She'd ridden cross-country through Greendale, as he had himself.

Don't make the wrong choice again, Miss Clemmy had told him. Why hadn't he listened to her at once, instead of wasting time riding back to the wagon? Maybe those few minutes' hesitation would mean the difference between finding Sophie and Belle, and – not. Maybe he'd already made the wrong choice all over again, and there was no going back. Always the wrong choice. Christ, did it never stop?

In his mind he saw Sophie as she'd looked that day in his study – no, that was this morning, wasn't it? Only this morning. She'd been angry with him, but there had been tears in her eyes. He told himself that that must mean something – that maybe she still cared about him.

But even if he was wrong – even if all her feelings for him had died years ago – it didn't matter. What mattered was that he still loved her, and she needed his help.

He reached the crossroads and skittered to a halt in a shower of dust and ash. Which way? Which *way*?

According to Miss Clemmy, Belle was heading for the cave near Turnaround. But what if Miss Clemmy was wrong? Or what if Belle had gone one way, and Sophie another?

He dismounted and started circling the crossroads, looking for tracks. Partisan threw down his head to cough, then plodded wearily after him.

He knew that Sophie had been at Eden great house, but after that the trail had gone cold. And the only reason he was so sure about Eden was because of a fluke.

At first when he'd got there, he'd had his doubts that she'd even reached it, despite what the men from Simonstown had said when he'd overtaken them. But then he'd remembered what Miss Clemmy had told him about the little boy's grave. And when he'd finally found it, he'd also found, lying on the smooth white marble, a sprig of cockleshell orchids. Sophie had been there, and no more than an hour before. The broken stem was still oozing sap.

In the dust near the crossroads he spotted a hoofmark: a mare's, by the size of it. A few yards further on he found the small, neat crescent moon of a pony's print. He kept looking, but the ground was too dry and stony to find any more. And from the little he'd found, it was impossible to tell whether Sophie and Belle had been together, or which way they'd gone.

Come on, Ben, which way? Turnaround? It had to be. Where else would Belle have gone?

He got back into the saddle and was heading east when a terrified squeal behind him pulled him up short. Partisan pricked his ears and gave an answering whinny.

Belle had hidden her pony with care, tethering her securely to a young guango tree in a clearing just off the track which led up the wooded eastern flank of Overlook Hill. The fat little chestnut had long since smelt smoke, and was white-eyed with terror and tugging frantically at the reins. A bundle of wilted herbs on her browband was tossing wildly.

Ben's heart sank. Wherever she was, Belle must be well out of earshot. She'd never leave her beloved pony squealing in terror.

'You must be Muffin,' he said as he jumped down, tethered Partisan, and advanced towards the pony – forcing himself to go slowly, so as not to panic her further. 'Where's your mistress gone, eh, Muffin? Where's she gone, then?'

The pony sidestepped and rolled her eyes, but her ears swivelled round to listen to him.

'Rosemary and Madam Fate,' he remarked to the pony, as he unbuckled the girth and slipped the saddle off the broad, sweaty back. 'What did she want with that lot, eh, Muffin?'

Talking continuously, he unbuckled the cheekband and slipped off the bridle, keeping the reins looped over the pony's neck so that he could still control her. Then he led her – or rather dragged her – back onto the open track. 'Go on, then,' he said, slipping the reins over her head and giving her a slap on the rump. 'And don't hang about!'

Muffin didn't need to be told. She flicked up her tail and clattered off down the road towards Maputah.

Rosemary and Madam Fate? thought Ben as he got back into the saddle and started once again for Turnaround. What did Belle want with that? Was she warding off duppies? But what duppies? And where?

Suddenly he remembered Sophie's childhood terror of duppy trees, and the pieces fell into place. *One of her secret missions into the hills.* Duppies. The duppy tree on Overlook Hill.

Oh, Christ. Christ. Straight into the path of the fire.

He turned Partisan round and galloped back to the crossroads, and put the gelding up the track to Overlook Hill.

He crouched low against the hot, sweaty neck as the gelding heaved through the undergrowth. Branches whipped at his face. Memories crowded in. Sophie's expression as she'd stood in the glade of the duppy tree, seven years before.

It's over, Ben, she had said.

No it bloody well isn't, he told himself grimly. There's still time. There's still time.

Another parrot flew screeching over the canopy. *Ah-eek! Ah-eek!* Belle and Sophie exchanged taut glances and ran on through the forest.

Surely, thought Sophie, the duppy tree can't be much further ahead? Did you do the right thing, going back into the forest? Or is this the last of your about-turns to go catastrophically wrong?

The breath rasped in her lungs. Her forearm throbbed where she'd fallen on the rocks and scraped it raw. She was tired. She was beginning to limp.

The roar of the fire was closer now – she could hear branches crackling somewhere to her left – but how close? At the foot of the hill? Halfway up the slope? Fifty feet away? She felt as if they were being stalked by some great cat that might leap out at any moment.

'Are you sure Muffin will be all right?' said Belle in a small voice. She was clutching Sophie's hand so hard that it hurt.

'I don't know,' muttered Sophie, too exhausted to lie.

'But you *said*.'

'Belle, I don't know. With any luck, the men will find her when they come to set the firebreak.'

Belle looked slightly mollified. Sophie wished that she herself was as easily reassured. The firebreak was now one of her greatest fears. What if the men reached the cross-roads before them, and they were cut off? Trapped between an uncontrolled fire at their backs, and a controlled but none the less deadly one up ahead?

She pushed aside the tattered leaves of a philodendron, and burst through into the clearing of the duppy tree. 'Thank God,' she panted, stumbling over to the tree and collapsing onto one of the great folded roots. From here it couldn't be more than twenty minutes to the bottom of the hill. Provided, of course, that they still had twenty minutes.

Belle looked frightened. 'You shouldn't sit there,' she said, hardly moving her lips.

'Just for a moment, to catch my breath.'

'You shouldn't sit on its roots. It isn't safe.'

Sophie gave a spurt of laughter. Safe? Nowhere was safe.

She was dizzy with fatigue, and her knee was beginning to stiffen. It seemed impossible that in a moment she would get to her feet and run all the way down the hill.

Belle tugged at her hand. 'Please can we go now? Please?'

Sophie drew a deep breath. Ash pattered down around her. Up ahead, a horse squealed.

A *horse*?

Suddenly a big foam-flecked bay gelding crashed through the ferns into the clearing. Sophie leaped to her feet as Ben – *Ben* – jumped down and ran over to her and gripped her shoulder so hard that it hurt. 'Christ, Sophie, Christ. What the hell d'you think you're doing, just sitting there on a fucking tree root?' He was out of breath and covered in soot and sweat, and there was a long bloody slash down his cheek.

'I wasn't – I mean – I found Belle.' She held up Belle's grimy little fist as proof.

'I'm *really* sorry,' muttered Belle with a sideways glance at the duppy tree.

'Christ,' said Ben to no-one in particular. He let go of Sophie and turned away, and put both hands on the bay's sweaty neck, and shook his head. Over his shoulder he said, 'What did you do to your arm?'

'I fell,' said Sophie. 'How did you find us? Did you—'

'Did you find Muffin?' said Belle. 'I tied her to a tree where nobody would see, and she'll be really sca—'

'I found her,' he said. He turned back to Sophie, and whipped out his handkerchief and wrapped it round her forearm so tightly that it hurt.

She yelped, but he ignored her. He'd already turned back to Belle. 'I untacked her and let her go,' he told her. 'She'll be halfway to Simonstown by now.'

'Oh, *thank* you!' Belle sighed with relief. Clearly she was no longer worried, now that her pony was safe, and she had two adults to look after her.

Sophie struggled to loosen the handkerchief on her forearm. 'Have the men reached the crossroads yet?' she asked Ben.

'Not yet, but soon.' He threw the reins over the bay's head in readiness to mount.

'How soon?' said Sophie.

'Ten minutes? I don't know.'

'We won't make it.'

'Yes we will, if we ride hard.' He turned and met her eyes. 'What the hell were you doing, riding around in a sodding cane-fire?'

She didn't get a chance to reply. A flurry of rifle-shots echoed through the forest, as somewhere a clump of bamboo went up in flames. Belle screamed, the bay reared, and the trees exploded with birds.

For a moment Ben had his hands full, calming his mount. Then he turned back to Sophie. 'Come on, it's time we were off. Where's your horse?'

Sophie opened her mouth, then shut it again.

'She fell,' said Belle.

He stared at them blankly. 'What d'you mean?'

'We were trying to get down the western slope,' said Sophie, 'towards Stony Gap. It was too steep and she fell. It was all I could do to get out of the way.'

He looked down at her as if he couldn't understand what he was hearing. For the first time she saw how exhausted he was. His face was drawn, and there were bluish shadows beneath his eyes.

'She twitched when she hit the rocks,' muttered Belle, 'and then she stopped. We think she broke her neck.'

Ben wasn't listening. He was looking from Sophie to Belle, and back to the gelding. Then he rubbed a hand over his face. 'Right,' he said. 'Right.'

He went over to Belle and grabbed her under the arms and swung her up into the saddle. Then he turned to Sophie, and before she knew what he was doing he'd given her a leg-up and propelled her into the saddle behind Belle. 'Keep your head down,' he said as he shortened the stirrups for her, 'and use your heels. His name's Partisan and he's had enough, but he'll get you past the crossroads. Whatever you do, *don't stop*. Just keep going – and yell, both of you, so that the men know you're coming. You'll make it through all right.'

Then it dawned on her that he wasn't coming with them. Until that moment she couldn't have imagined that things could get any worse. She leaned down and grabbed his shoulder. 'What about you?'

'I'll take my chances,' he muttered as he flicked up the saddle flap and started tightening the girth.

'I'm not leaving you here.'

'Yes you are.'

'No!'

'For Christ's sake, Sophie,' he burst out, 'use your head! One knackered horse isn't going to carry a man, a woman and a child!'

'I'm not leaving you,' she said again. Her eyes were beginning to burn.

'So what are you going to do?' he retorted. 'D'you fancy putting Partisan into a nice, slow trot, so that I don't get left behind, and we can all go up in smoke?'

Tears stung her eyes. In front of her, Belle clutched handfuls of mane and started to shake.

'Look,' said Ben more quietly, 'for once in my life I'm making the right choice. I'm not going to let you spoil it now. All right?'

'Choice? What choice? What are you talking about?'

But he only shook his head, and threw the reins over Partisan's neck, and closed her hands over them with his own.

Another explosion of bamboo. The gelding snorted and sidestepped in alarm.

'Go on,' said Ben, grabbing hold of the bridle and turning Partisan round. 'Get out of here.'

But Sophie reined in, and leaned down and grasped his hand. 'There's something you've got to know,' she said fiercely. 'Nothing's changed. I mean, about you and me. What I feel – it's just the same as it's always been. Always.'

He looked up at her and his eyes were glittering. 'I know, sweetheart. Same with me.' Then he pulled her down towards him and kissed her hard on the mouth. 'Better late than never, eh?'

'Promise me – *promise* you'll be right behind us.'

He didn't reply.

'Ben, I won't go unless—'

'Just keep going and don't look back. Now go on, go.'

'Ben, *please*—'

He slapped Partisan on the rump. 'Go *on*!'

Still crying, she dug in her heels and started off through the undergrowth.

She looked back once, and her last sight of him, through a stinging blur of tears, was as he stooped for the bottle of rum by the duppy tree, and took a long, slow pull.

Then the bitter blue smoke closed in around him.

CHAPTER THIRTY-FIVE

It was still raining when Sophie and Belle left Eden great house and started slowly along the riverbank towards Romilly.

The wind had changed a couple of hours before, bringing in rain from the north. Not a tropical downpour, but a steady, penetrating drizzle: 'old woman rain', as they called it in Jamaica, for it went on and on until you thought it would never stop.

'Shouldn't we have waited at the house?' said Belle in a small voice. She was huddled in front of Sophie in her mackintosh, and clutching handfuls of mane, for Partisan was stumbling with fatigue.

'Your papa needs to know that you're safe,' muttered Sophie. It was true, but it wasn't the whole truth. The fact was, she couldn't have stood the empty house another moment.

They had reached the crossroads at the same time as Cameron's men, and made it across to the sound of ragged cheers. Cameron himself wasn't to be found, and no-one seemed to know where he was. The men had suggested that she go and wait at the house. They said he'd be sure to turn up soon.

She'd found the house deserted, and just as she'd left it, hours before. After fetching bread and milk for Belle, she'd run out onto the verandah to wait for Ben.

He didn't come. She'd leaned out as far as she could,

straining to penetrate the cloud of smoke and steam and drizzle which shrouded Overlook Hill; telling herself that of course he'd got through.

But nobody came. And she kept remembering the look on his face as he'd told her to go without him. *For once in my life I'm making the right choice.* What did he mean? It sounded horribly like an epitaph.

A gust of wind shivered the giant bamboo, showering them with raindrops. Partisan shook his mane and plodded on, and Sophie gritted her teeth. Dimly she perceived that she was wet and cold and exhausted, but she didn't really feel it. She was in a long, dark tunnel with only one way forward: find Cameron, leave Belle with him, then go and look for Ben. Nothing else mattered, because it was outside the tunnel.

She turned her head and saw on the other side of the river the bright, untouched cane of Bullet Tree Piece, preternaturally green in the rainy light of the failing day. That's good, she told herself numbly, it means the fire-break has held. She knew it was good, but she didn't really feel it. It was outside the tunnel.

Voices up ahead. They must be nearing Romilly. They reached the creeper-clad enclosure of tumbled cut-stone in which, seven years before, Ben had built himself a fire. She looked for cockleshell orchids, but couldn't see any. It felt like the worst kind of omen. She lacked the strength to convince herself that it didn't mean anything.

Suddenly they were out of the bamboo and into the clearing, and Partisan was picking his way between little groups of astonished field-hands resting on the ground.

'Look, there's Papa!' cried Belle, squirming in front of her in the saddle.

Cameron was down by the bridge, and hadn't seen them yet. He was hatless and soaked, and had plainly just run down to meet the rider who'd ridden up from town. It took Sophie a moment to recognize her sister. Madeleine too was hatless and soaked, and incongruously dressed in a bronze-coloured afternoon gown which was smeared with soot, and had been hitched up to her knees so that she could ride astride. She must have just dismounted, for she was gripping Cameron's shoulders, and they were staring into one another's face, appalled and oblivious of their surroundings. As Sophie rode down towards them, their voices drifted over to her.

'But I thought she was with you,' said Cameron.

'She *was*,' cried Madeleine, 'at least, she was with Quaco till she gave him the slip. God knows where she is by now—' Her voice broke.

At that moment Belle scrambled down into the mud. 'I'm fine! Here I am! I'm saved!'

They turned and saw her at the same time. Madeleine pressed both her hands to her mouth. Cameron went forward and scooped up his daughter and held her up fiercely, high above him, as if he couldn't believe it was really her. Then he set her down with a splash, and Madeleine went down onto her knees in the mud and seized her by the shoulders. 'Where have you *been*?' she cried, shaking her.

Belle was disconcerted. 'The duppy tree,' she mumbled.

'The *duppy tree*?' cried her parents in horror.

'Jesus Christ,' said Cameron. 'What were you doing up there?'

'I was making an offering,' said Belle, who was beginning to realize the depth of trouble she was in. 'There was nobody at home so we thought we'd better come and tell you.' She glanced at Sophie for corroboration, but neither Madeleine nor Cameron took their eyes from their daughter's face. 'You're all sooty,' Belle said to her mother. 'Did you ride through the fire to save me?'

'Of course not,' snapped Madeleine, who was fast recovering her composure. 'It was over by the time I got there. What sort of offering?'

'I had a list,' said Belle defensively. 'Aunt Sophie was absolutely *brilliant*! She followed me all the way to Eden, *and* guessed about the duppy tree, *and* found me in the forest – well, not actually *in* the forest, because by then I'd . . .' While she went on breathlessly, Madeleine raised her head and spotted Sophie.

Sophie dismounted and handed the reins to Moses, and went over to her. She felt numb and cold and distant, as if she were seeing her sister from a long way away.

Still on her knees in the mud, Madeleine reached up and grasped her hand. Her face worked. 'Your hand's like ice,' she said. 'And you forgot your mackintosh.'

Sophie didn't reply. She knew that if she tried to speak she would burst into tears.

'Thank you,' whispered Madeleine.

Sophie shook her head. She tried to pull away, but Madeleine kept hold of her hand. '*Thank* you,' she whispered again.

'. . . and Mr Kelly was *so* brave,' Belle was telling her father. 'He lent us his horse, his name's Partisan, because Aunt Sophie's had fallen down a ravine, *and* he saved Muffin – have you found her yet?'

Cameron shook his head, clearly struggling to take it all in.

'And he wouldn't come with us because he said he'd slow us down and then we'd all go up in smoke. He said a knackered horse can't carry a man, a woman, and a child. So we had to leave him behind.'

Cameron turned to Sophie. 'Is this true?'

She nodded. 'That's his horse,' she said, jerking her head at Partisan. 'He was supposed to follow us on foot,' she went on, her teeth beginning to chatter, 'but I don't think he got through. He can't have done, can he? We waited at the house for hours.'

Madeleine came and stood behind her and put her hands on her shoulders.

'There wouldn't have been time for him to get out, would there?' Sophie said shrilly. 'I mean, we only just made it ourselves, and we were on horseback. Did the fire – did it go all the way to the hill?'

Cameron nodded.

'Perhaps he found another way down,' said Madeleine. 'If anyone knows his way around, it's Ben.'

Sophie's teeth were chattering so hard she could

scarcely speak. 'I'm going to look for him,' she said, turning back to Partisan.

Cameron stepped in front of her. 'No, Sophie,' he said.

'But I've got to. I've got to find him—'

'Sophie,' he said gently, 'in ten minutes it'll be dark. You're exhausted. And this horse isn't going anywhere.'

'But—'

'I'll send a man out to look for him.'

'Come on, Sophie,' said Madeleine behind her. 'There's nothing more you can do tonight. Come back to the house.'

Sophie looked from Cameron to her sister, then back to Cameron. 'Does he have a chance?'

'I don't know,' he said bluntly. 'We'll know by morning.'

She was in her old room at Eden, trying to sleep. She was also at Romilly, curled up on Ben's blanket, waiting for him to return.

After a while she felt him behind her, settling down against her back. She was so tired that she couldn't move. She wanted to put out her hand and touch him, but her arm was too heavy. She couldn't even summon the energy to open her eyes. 'I'm glad you're back,' she mumbled.

'Sophie,' whispered Madeleine.

She woke up with a start. 'What? What?'

It was dark in the room. By the light of the single candle on the bedside table Madeleine's nightgown was a pale blur. 'He's all right, Sophie,' she said, sitting down beside her. 'Ben's all right. We've just got word.'

Blearily, Sophie rubbed her face. She felt heavy and sick with fatigue. 'Where? Where is he? Is he hurt?'

Madeleine shook her head. 'I think he's spending the night somewhere in the cattle pastures. He sent a boy to check that you and Belle were all right.'

Sophie leaned forward and put her face on her knees.

'After you left him on the hill, he found his way down to Stony Gap,' said Madeleine, putting her hand between Sophie's shoulder blades and gently rubbing up and down.

'He got there just before the fire. Apparently he jumped off the bridge into the river. That's what the boy said. Anyway. He sent a note.'

Sophie drew a deep breath. 'What does it say?'

'D'you want me to read it?'

She nodded. She heard the rustle of Madeleine's nightgown as she leaned closer to the candle. *In the end, the River Mistress saw me through. Ben.* Madeleine paused. 'That's all there is. Does it mean anything to you?'

Sophie nodded. After a while she said, 'What time is it?'

'Three in the morning.' Madeleine folded the note again and handed it to her. 'It'll be light in a few hours. Then you can go and see him.'

Sophie took the note and nodded.

'You'll be all right now,' said Madeleine, stroking her hair. 'Now you can get a proper sleep.' She rose to go, but Sophie grasped her hand.

'What about you? Are you all right? And Cameron? And Belle?'

She saw the gleam of Madeleine's smile. 'We're all fine, thanks to you.'

'No, I didn't mean that—'

'Yes, but I do. I do.'

There was a silence. Then Sophie said, 'What about the estate?'

Madeleine laughed. 'The estate! Oh, don't worry about that. Cameron says if he works round the clock he can get in quite a bit of Orange Grove before it spoils. And we've still got Bullet Tree Piece. So it seems that we're not absolutely ruined just yet.' She paused. 'You know, there's a rumour that it was started deliberately.'

Sophie yawned hugely. 'Really?' Sleep was stealing up on her again. She could hardly keep her eyes open.

Madeleine patted her shoulder. 'I expect it's just a rumour. You go back to sleep.'

CHAPTER THIRTY-SIX

On the morning after the fire, Alexander Traherne awoke from his first decent sleep in weeks, feeling peaceful and relaxed. Still in his nightshirt, and before even tasting his cup of chocolate, he dashed off three short notes.

The first was to Sophie, telling her that she was absolutely right, and releasing her from her promise.

The second was to his insurers, informing them of the destruction of his house and property at Waytes Valley, and instructing them to pay the compensation monies forthwith to his account.

The third was to Guy Fazackerly, announcing that the whole of the debt would be repaid on New Year's Day.

Then, business concluded, he went down to breakfast.

To his surprise there was no-one about; not even his mother, who always poured his tea. At length the butler brought a message from his father, to say that he was wanted in the study.

To his relief, the governor hailed him cheerily and seemed in an excellent humour, although Bostock, his man of business, wore the haggard look of a man who'd been up all night.

Cornelius lit a cigar for himself and indicated the humidor to his son, and for a while they smoked in silence. Bostock sat a little apart, staring at the floor.

Alexander felt mildly curious as to what this was about. He and the governor weren't in the habit of sharing companionable silences. When it had gone on long enough, he flicked a speck of lint off his knee and remarked that it was a bad business about that fire.

To his surprise, the governor waved that away. 'These things happen. It simply means that I shall be taking off the crop a little quicker than I'd intended, and spending a lot more on labour to do it.' He leaned back in his chair and chuckled. 'Just as well Waytes Valley ain't yet yours, eh, my boy? Or you'd be getting a snap introduction to the art of taking off the crop at speed!'

Alexander paused with his cigar halfway to his lips. 'I rather thought that it was mine,' he said with careful nonchalance.

'Oh, no, old fellow. Not until you're actually married.'

'Ah,' murmured Alexander. A setback. Definitely a setback. Particularly since he'd just sent that note to Sophie.

But still. She could be brought round easily enough. Although it was a confounded shame about the insurance monies. Out loud he said, 'So crop-time will cost you a bit, will it? Shall you be put to much expense?'

'Quite considerable, I'm afraid. I shall need to bring in hordes of coolies from St Ann to get it done, and those brutes never come cheap.'

'But won't all that be covered by the insurance?' said Alexander.

'I doubt it,' said the governor, examining his cigar. 'They tend not to pay up when it's a question of arson.'

Alexander nearly choked on his cigar. 'Arson?'

'Odd, isn't it?' said his father without looking at him. 'Bostock tells me that a man was seen with a box of matches, "acting suspicious", as they say.'

Alexander shot a startled glance at Bostock, but the man of business went on staring at the floor.

'Of course,' he continued, turning his cigar in his fingers, 'if they find the fellow who did it, he'll hang. And I shall take the greatest pleasure in going along to watch.'

Alexander ran his tongue over his lips and forgot to breathe.

'Still,' said the governor briskly, 'that's not what I wanted to talk to you about.'

'It isn't?' Alexander said faintly. 'You mean there's more?'

'Oh, decidedly,' and this time when Cornelius looked at his son his small blue eyes were markedly less genial than before. 'I don't suppose you saw Parnell this morning?'

Alexander shook his head. How could he think about Parnell at a time like this? *Hanged?* For a few miserable sticks of cane?

'That's because he left,' said his father. 'Rather early this morning. In an absolute funk.'

Alexander dragged his mind back to the present. 'What?' he murmured. 'Where did he go?'

'Back to England. At least, that's what his note said. Some balderdash about urgent business. Didn't even have the courage to tell me to my face.' He drew on his cigar, narrowing his eyes against the smoke. 'It goes without saying that the match with your sister is off. In fact, everything's off. Including my own spot of business with him. Which, I might add, puts me in a decidedly tricky position just at present.'

'I'm sorry,' said Alexander mechanically.

'So am I. Particularly as it seems that I have you to thank for it all.'

Alexander went cold. 'I?'

He wondered how Parnell could possibly have found out about the fire – and indeed, why it should have put him into a funk. What did it matter to Parnell if a few acres of cane went up in smoke? It didn't make sense.

'D'you know what put him in a funk?' said the governor. 'No? Shall I tell you? It seems that he got to hear about you and some little mulatto girl.'

Alexander's stomach lurched.

'Frankly,' said Cornelius, fixing him with his hot blue gaze, 'I'd have thought it would take more to frighten him off than a trifle like that. But perhaps it was the way in which the little strumpet broke it to him.' He paused. 'It's a shame he didn't tell me who she was. I should rather like to get my hands on her.' He shot Alexander an enquiring look.

But Alexander made no reply. He wasn't that stupid. If Evie had been vile enough to shop him to Parnell, there was no telling what she might do if he shopped her to the governor.

'So you see, Alexander,' said his father, stubbing out his cigar, 'thanks to you, your sister has just missed out on a most advantageous match, and I shall be compelled to draw in my horns rather considerably. I may even have to sell some of the property.'

Alexander's thoughts darted in panic. In four days the world would know that he'd welshed on a debt of twenty thousand pounds. Added to which was the threat of unpleasantness – he couldn't bring himself to be more specific – over that wretched fire. And clearly he could expect no sympathy at home. Despite the governor's false calm, he was incandescent. It was all so horribly unfair.

Cornelius got to his feet and drew out his watch. 'I'm glad we've had this little chat,' he said, 'but I mustn't keep you any longer. Your boat leaves in just over an hour.'

'My boat?' said Alexander weakly.

'Coastal steamer to Kingston. It should get you there in time to catch the packet to Perth.'

'*Perth?*' cried Alexander. 'But – isn't that in Australia?'

'Well *done*, Alexander.' The governor went over to the humidor on the side table and selected another cigar. 'You can check the details with Bostock on your way to town,' he said, without turning round. 'Oh, and he has some papers for you to sign. Relinquishing your rights. That sort of thing.'

A spark of rebellion kindled in Alexander's breast. 'I shall relinquish nothing, sir,' he said proudly.

His father laughed. 'Oh, I rather think that you will! Insurers can be horribly persistent in investigating a fire.'

Alexander opened his mouth to protest, then shut it again.

'Chin up, old man,' said the governor crisply. 'You'll get an allowance of twenty pounds a month—'

'Twenty pounds a month?' cried Alexander. 'But I can't possibly live on that!'

'– twenty pounds a month,' went on the governor imperturbably, 'on condition that we never – never – see you again. Now off you go.' He shut the lid of the humidor with a thud. 'And say goodbye to your mother on your way out.'

It's mid-morning at Salt Wash, and Evie's helping to dole out a late breakfast for the field-hands before they make a start on taking off the crop.

There's sort of a holiday feeling in the village. Everybody's staying with everybody else, and they're all pulling together to help out. It's like Free Come Day and Christmas and crop-over, rolled into one. Even her mother's not taking the loss of her place so bad as she'd expected. 'I can get new things,' she said with a shrug. 'Too besides, it's time for a change.'

Yes, thinks Evie as she spoons a great dollop of green banana porridge into each outstretched bowl. It's time for a change. And she bites back a smile.

Inside, she can't stop smiling. For the first time in months, she's fizzing over with good humour. Revenge tastes *good*. A little while ago she went out for a walk along the Coast Road, and two carriages passed her by, and now the memory of them is like a kernel of heat in her belly. Yes, revenge tastes good.

The first carriage carried Alexander on his way to the quay. Lord God, but that man was white! Staring, staring in front of him, like he'd just seen his own self duppy. The carriage had almost passed her by when he glanced down and saw her – and that was best of all: seeing the knowledge in his face that she was the one who'd brought him down.

Neptune said that when Master Cornelius got word that Mr Parnell had fled, he'd smashed every last thing on his mantelpiece. Every last thing. It's almost enough to make you feel sorry for Alexander. Well. Almost.

The second carriage came along a little later, when she'd

already turned back for Salt Wash. It was heading in the opposite direction, towards Montego Bay, and in it sat that Mr Austen who used to be secretary to Ben, and his new employer, Mr Augustus Parnell.

Mr Parnell glanced at Evie as he passed, but he didn't really see her. Why should he? To him she was just some coloured girl on the road. How was he to know that she was the writer of the little note which had finished it all?

Strange, strange, how simple it had been, and how effective! Over the past few months, Mr Augustus Parnell had been perfectly happy to overlook all kinds of irregularities in his prospective in-laws: the determined womanizing of father and son; his own sweetheart's infatuation with Ben. But what had plunged him into blank white terror – what had made him turn tail and scurry back to England – was the prospect of having a coloured girl for a sister-in-law. All it had taken was the simple revelation that Cornelius Traherne had a coloured daughter – a darkie half-sister for Miss Sibella – and he had fled. Apparently, the notion of being connected to a mulatto was just too horrible to bear.

Strange, strange. Over the past few days she'd toyed with all kinds of moonshine schemes for revenge on the Trahernes. Poison. Shadow-taking. Each notion crazier than the one before. Then it had come to her in all its simplicity. What Congo Eve and Great-grandmother Leah had handed down to her – indeed, what her own mother had passed on – wasn't just about being four-eyed and putting hand on people. It was about being her own self. Evie Quashiba McFarlane. And once she'd got that sorted out, everything else just fell into place.

Humming under her breath, she went to the cookhouse and fetched more porridge, then returned to the head of the queue. She was just getting back into the rhythm of doling it out again when the next man in line snarled things up by not moving along. 'Go on now,' she said without looking up.

The bowl stayed where it was.

'What's the matter with you?' she said. 'You want breakfast or not?'

'Yes, ma'am,' said Isaac Walker, 'I certainly do.'

She blinked.

He looked tired, and his fancy clothes were crumpled and black with soot. And he was just standing there at the head of the queue: not smiling, but looking as if he was ready to smile.

Evie's good humour evaporated. There was something about this man which made her afraid. Something about the way he looked at her with his small, clever eyes: not as a man usually looks at a pretty woman – or not only that – but as one human being looks at another when they want to make friends.

But she didn't want to make friends with him. She didn't want to make friends with anyone. 'If you want your breakfast,' she said tartly, 'you'd better go and eat it, Master Walker. Now move along, I've got work to do.'

'I just wanted to make sure,' he said in his quiet, gentle way, 'that you and your mother are all right.'

'We're fine,' she snapped. 'Mother's over at Cousin Cecilia's. That's the second house on the right, by the breadnut tree. Why don't you go and look in on her?'

'No thank you,' he said politely. 'I came to see you.'

Her hackles rose. 'I'm busy,' she snapped.

'I can see that,' he replied.

His expression was hard to read, but he was clearly undeterred. Suddenly she wondered how many people in the past had mistaken his gentleness for weakness.

She frowned, and glanced down at the porridge in the pot, and began scraping it into a neat mound. 'I'll be a very, very long time,' she said forbiddingly.

'Take as long as you like,' he said. 'I can wait.'

It was an eerie experience to ride north along the Eden Road. On the right lay the fresh, rainwashed cane of Bullet Tree Piece – untouched except for a sprinkling of ash – while on the left lay the desolation of Bellevue.

Life and death side by side, thought Sophie, with only a narrow strip of red road in between.

It was a horrible thought. It kept coming back to her that if things had been just a little different yesterday – if Ben had been a little slower in deciding what to do or where to go – she wouldn't be heading up the road to see him. She'd be going to his funeral.

It was too narrow an escape for her to feel joy or even relief. She felt as if she were standing at the edge of a great black hole, leaning over and watching the bottom rushing up towards her.

She reached the gaunt, burnt-out hulk of the guango tree which marked the turnoff onto Fever Hill land, and started across the cane-pieces. She rode through acre upon acre of silent desolation. Endless ranks of burnt cane, standing like an army of blackened skeletons. Nothing moved. Her horse trod gingerly over the crisp black ground, stirring up a bitter tang of ash. A solitary john crow lifted off from the ground and wheeled away.

She found Ben a couple of miles in, by the blackened ruins of the wagon which Clemency had told her about. He was hatless, sitting on the ground with his knees drawn up, contemplating the remains. The heat of the fire must have been intense, for all that was left of the coffins was a pile of smoking cinders.

At her approach he turned and watched her, but to her surprise he didn't get up and come towards her.

Feeling suddenly awkward, she dismounted. 'I got your note,' she said.

He nodded. He wore the same riding-clothes as the day before, but with a clean calico shirt, obviously borrowed. He'd washed but he hadn't shaved, and his face looked shadowed and drawn. The cut on his cheek had dried to a crusted scab.

She stopped a few feet away from him. 'According to Madeleine, you jumped in the river to escape the fire.'

He nodded. 'It seemed the best thing to do.' His voice sounded rough. She wondered if that was from the smoke or from crying. His eyes were red-rimmed, the eyelashes spiky.

She tried to imagine what it must be like to have brought the remains of one's brother and sisters all the way from London, only to have them swept away by a cane-fire. She badly wanted to go down on her knees and put her arms round him, but something told her to keep her distance. He didn't seem to want her here. He wouldn't even meet her eyes.

As lightly as she could, she said, 'Belle wants to know if you met an alligator.'

He tried to smile, but it wasn't very successful. 'How is she?'

'Contrite. And she keeps telling everyone that Partisan's a hero. This morning she made him and Muffin one of her special hot-molasses mashes, and when I left she was braiding their manes.' She knew she was talking too much, but she couldn't help it. He was beginning to worry her.

'So you're back at Eden now,' he said.

'Yes. Well. It's a start.'

He nodded. 'That's good. It's good that you're back.'

'Madeleine wants you to come and stay, until you can rebuild. So does Cameron.'

'Do they?' He shook his head. 'I don't think they do. Not really.'

'You're wrong. And Madeleine knew you wouldn't believe me, so she wrote you a note.' She handed it to him, and watched him get to his feet and walk a few paces away to read it. He stood there reading it for a long time. Then he folded it carefully and put it in his breast pocket. He cleared his throat. 'Tell her thank you,' he said over his shoulder, 'but it's better that I don't.'

'Ben, what's wrong?'

He flicked her a glance. Then he stooped for a handful of ash, and opened his hand and watched it drift away on the breeze. 'Look around you, Sophie. It's all gone.'

'But – surely you can get in at least some of the cane? And—'

'It's not that,' he broke in. 'Of course I can get in some of the cane. Of course I've still got money in the bank. It isn't that.' He paused. 'It was the Monroe great house. Your grandfather's house. Then it was mine, and now it's gone.' He glanced at the blackened remains of the coffins. 'It's all gone. I couldn't save any of it.'

'What do you *mean*? You got every single person out alive. You got me and Belle out alive.'

He did not reply. She watched him walk to the other side of the wagon and break off a fragment of charcoal and crumble it in his fingers. And at last she began to understand. This wasn't about the destruction of the great house, or even the loss of his brother and sisters' remains. Or rather, it wasn't *only* about those things. He'd simply reached the end of his resources. She had always thought of him as someone with an unlimited capacity for fighting back. No matter what happened to him, he would always get up and start again, because that was who he was. Now she realized that nobody can do that; not all the time.

She followed him round to his side of the wagon. 'Yesterday on Overlook Hill,' she began, 'you told me that this time you were making the right choice. I didn't know what you meant until this morning.' She paused. 'Clemency came to me just after breakfast. She told me about Kate. About the choice you had to make when you were a boy.'

Again he forced a smile. It was painful to see. 'Everything I do turns to ashes.'

'If you weren't so exhausted, you'd know that's absolutely not true.'

He nodded, but she could see that he didn't believe her.

She tried a different tack. 'You said once that you're like your father. That you destroy the things you love. Do you still think that's true?'

He didn't answer at once. 'Poor bastard,' he said at last. 'You know, when he died, he was only a couple of years older than I am now. He didn't live long after Kate.'

'Does that mean you've forgiven him?'

'I don't know. Maybe.'

'Don't you think it's time you forgave yourself?'

He hesitated. 'Sophie, I brought them out to be with

443

me. I know it sounds odd, but it meant something. Now look at them. Just ashes, blown away.'

'What's so bad about that?' she said with deliberate bluntness. 'They're out here in the sun and the fresh air. It's a good place to be.'

He did not reply.

'Ben . . .' She put her hands on his shoulders and turned him round to face her. 'Look at you. Coming out here all on your own, when you're exhausted. When did you last get any sleep?'

He frowned.

'Added to which, you probably haven't eaten anything since God knows when, and you've just lost your home. Of course you're feeling low.' She put her palm against the roughness of his cheek. Then she stood on tiptoe and kissed his mouth.

He didn't return her kiss.

'Come back to the house,' she said quickly, to cover her confusion. 'I mean, come back to Eden. Have something to eat, and a proper sleep, and I promise you'll feel better.'

He was looking down at her, still frowning. Suddenly he took a deep breath and put his arms about her, and pulled her hard against him. He held her so tightly that she could hardly breathe.

She could feel his heart racing, and the heat of his breath on her temple. She could smell his clean sharp smell of windblown grass and red dust and Ben. She put her arms round him and buried her face in his neck.

When at last they drew apart, they were both blinking back tears.

'Whatever happens,' he muttered between his teeth, 'you're not going to marry Alexander Traherne.'

It was so unexpected that she laughed. 'What?'

'I mean it, Sophie. He—'

'I know! I broke it off on Boxing Day.'

He looked bemused. 'What?'

'At your Masquerade.'

'But – you never told me.'

444

'You never gave me the chance. You were too busy seducing Sibella.'

'I didn't actually seduce her—'

'I know, I know.' She was starting to feel happy again. Bickering was always a good sign.

'Tell me honestly,' he said, looking into her eyes. 'Do you truly not mind about the house?'

She gave his shoulders another shake. 'No! We'll build another house. And next Christmas we'll give an enormous party, and invite everyone in Trelawny. Including Great-Aunt May.'

He was watching her intently, as if he still wasn't quite ready to believe that she was in earnest.

'And we'll sort the replies into three piles,' she went on. 'One pile for acceptances, and one for regrets, and one for "never in a million years".'

Ben laughed.

THE END

ACKNOWLEDGEMENTS AND AUTHOR'S NOTE

As with *The Shadow Catcher*, I must thank my cousins Alec and Jacqui Henderson of Orange Valley Estate, Trelawny, Jamaica, for their help when I was researching this book, as well as my aunt, Martha Henderson.

I should also deal with a few points concerning the story itself.

The principal Jamaican families and properties featured in the book are entirely fictional, and I have taken some liberties with the local geography around Falmouth in order to accommodate the estates of Eden, Fever Hill, Burntwood and Parnassus.

As regards the *patois* of the Jamaican people, I haven't attempted to reproduce this precisely, but have instead tried to make it more accessible to the general reader, while retaining, I hope, at least some of its colour and richness.

Michelle Paver

THE STORY OF FEVER HILL
CONTINUES IN
MICHELLE PAVER'S
BREATHTAKING NEW NOVEL

THE SERPENT'S TOOTH

NOW AVAILABLE FROM BANTAM PRESS

HERE'S THE FIRST CHAPTER AS A TASTER . . .

CHAPTER ONE

Eden Estate, Jamaica, 1912

Belle had never wanted anything so much as the black onyx inkstand. Lyndon Traherne said she'd never win it because she was only a girl. He was wrong. She would take the first prize from right under his nose, and present the inkstand to Papa, and together they would place it on his desk, where it belonged.

Papa absolutely deserved the best. He was always working on the estate – at the boiling-house or in the cane-pieces – but however late he got home he always came in to kiss her goodnight. She would pretend to be asleep, and wait for the scratch of his whiskers, and his smell of horses and burnt sugar. And whenever she had the nightmare she would pad across to his study, and he would give her a thimbleful of rum and water and a puff at his cigar. Then she'd curl up on the Turkey rug beneath the oil painting of the big house in Scotland, and ask him impossible questions about robins and snow.

So the first prize in the Historical Society Juvenile Fancy Dress Ball had to be hers. Her costume had to be the best in Trelawny. Best on the Northside. Best in Jamaica.

To create a sense of drama, she announced that she'd be going as a fairy, when in fact she intended to make a surprise entrance as the Devil. She'd worked it all out. Saved her pocket money, and secretly bought a remnant of crimson sari silk at Falmouth market. She had every detail clear in her mind: the horns, the tail, the flickering flames of Hell. It would be *perfection*.

The day before the party found her furious and tearful amid a storm of botched fragments and crumpled fencing-wire horns.

Her mother came in, and gave her a long, steady look. 'Why didn't you ask me for help?' she said quietly.

'Because I wanted to do it myself!'

Her mother bit her lip and studied the remains. She looked tired, her dark hair coming down from her chignon in wisps. This was the first time she had hosted the Juvenile Ball, and she wanted it to be a success. But their house at Eden wasn't really big enough, so they'd had to move the furniture off the verandah, and erect an awning in the garden. She'd been working for days. And the twins were colicky, which didn't help.

Belle felt a pang of guilt at giving her this added trouble. 'It doesn't matter,' she muttered, aiming a kick at a nearby horn. 'It's my fault for choosing the Devil. I'll just go as a wretched fairy.'

Her mother stooped and picked up a scrap of sari silk. 'You always punish yourself.'

Belle thrust out her lower lip. 'Well, because I deserve it.'

'No you don't. We can use my old dressing gown. The one Papa bought in Kingston that was a mistake? And these can be flames.' She picked up the sari silk. 'A nice, fiery ruff to hide that new bosom you're so embarrassed about.'

Belle's face burned. She'd been worrying about that.

'But you'll have to help,' said her mother. 'You do the horns, the tail, and the hooves.'

'*Hooves*?' said Belle.

'Well, of course. All devils have hooves.'

Somehow, it was finished in time – and it was magnificent. Layer on layer of spangled scarlet flames. Plump red felt horns fixed to an Alice band. Cunning little hooves of crimson satin which fitted over her button boots like demonic spats. And best of all, a three-pronged tail that would be perfect for spiking air-balls, and Lyndon Traherne's pride.

Then, on the morning of the party, disaster struck. Belle got her monthly cramps – what her mother called her *petit ami*. An odd name for bleeding and stomach ache and appalling embarrassment.

She told her parents that she had a headache, and sneaked a Dover's powder from the bath-house cupboard. She didn't want *anyone* to know. She hated the idea of growing up.

'But you're nearly fourteen,' her mother would say when she was trying to persuade Belle into grown-up combinations, or gently mooting the notion of school in England.

'Thirteen and five months,' Belle would snap back. 'That's nowhere near fourteen.' But even thirteen sounded too old.

She lay curled on her bed, watching the tree-ferns dip and sway against the louvres, and listening to the slap of the servants' slippers and the *chup-chup-zi* of the sugar-quits under the eaves.

She felt sore and churned up inside. And that wasn't the worst of it. Ever since she'd started getting the cramps, she'd developed a terrible compulsion: an irresistible urge to picture every man she saw without any clothes. It didn't matter who it was. Old Braverly the cook. Her dashing uncle Ben. Even *Papa*.

And she knew very well what to imagine, because last year she'd seen a group of field-hands cooling off at the swimming-hole by the Arethusa Road. At the time, they'd looked so happy that she'd simply envied them their freedom. But a few months later, when the cramps started to come, the memory had returned to haunt her. It was awful. Shameful. There must be something wrong with her.

She slept away the morning, and felt a little better, and got dressed and went to the party.

She didn't win.

Everyone agreed that hers was by far the best costume.

Better than Dodo Cornwallis's genial, large-footed fairy; better than Sissy Irving's slyly pretty little Pierrot; better even than Lyndon Traherne's steeplechase jockey, in genuine racing silks made specially for him, with real spurs and soft boots of Italian kid.

But it was Lyndon who won.

'Because,' said old Mrs Pitcaithley, the senior judge, 'boys can be jockeys, but girls can't be devils.'

Her mother shot Belle an anxious look, but she was too proud to let her feelings show. She put on a smile and gave Mrs Pitcaithley a regal nod, while in her head she was taking aim with Papa's rifle, and blowing a great hole in Lyndon's narrow, silk-clad chest.

He didn't *need* the inkstand. His papa was the richest man in Trelawny. Lyndon could buy ten inkstands out of his pocket money. He'd probably just lose this one on the steamer when he went back to school.

For her mother's sake, Belle sat through tea under the awning with the other children. She even managed a square of sweet-potato pie with coconut syrup. Then, when the Reverend Prewitt was setting up the magic lantern display, she fled.

She took the path by the river, into the airless green tunnel of the giant bamboo, until she reached her special place under the duppy tree.

Her heart was thudding with rage. She peeled back her stocking and scratched a tick-bite on her knee until it bled. Snatched a handful of ginger lilies and crushed them, breathing in the sharp spicy scent to make her eyes sting. *Why* had she chosen the Devil? If she'd picked any other costume she would have won, and Papa would have got his inkstand. It was all her fault.

Mosquitoes whined in her ears, but she let them bite. The rasp of the crickets was deafening. She welcomed it. Distantly, she could hear the murmur of the party. She ground her teeth. She didn't belong back there. She didn't know the rules.

Girls can't be devils. Why hadn't she known that?

'Because you're *stupid*,' she said aloud. Raising her

head, she glared at the spreading branches of the duppy tree.

It was only a young one – not nearly as tall or frightening as the ancient silk-cotton on Overlook Hill – but it was hers, and she felt safe in the folds of its buttressed trunk, with the purple-flowered thunbergia and the white star jasmine festooning its branches, and the big green cotton-cutter beetles patrolling its trunk. A little of the rage lifted from her and floated away.

She ran her hand over the rough bark – and something snagged her skin, making her wince.

It was the head of a nail that had been hammered into the trunk. Someone must have been casting spells again. Perhaps one of the McFarlanes, mother or daughter, paid by a smallholder to catch a person's shadow, or set a love-charm.

The nail had drawn blood. Belle scowled at it. Then she ground her palm onto the rusty iron, to hurt herself some more. That'll teach you, she told herself. You chose the wrong costume, and because of that Papa lost his inkstand—

'Oh, I say,' said a voice behind her. 'Don't hurt yourself. Please.'

She spun round. Blinked in astonishment.

It was Lyndon's father, Mr Traherne. He didn't often attend Historical Society gatherings, but he'd come to Eden as a favour to her mother, whom he'd always admired.

'How d'you do, Mr Traherne,' Belle said politely. She wondered how much he'd heard, and felt herself redden.

He inclined his head in a courtly nod, and went on smoking his cigar. He was sitting on the bench which Papa had built for her last birthday. Belle hadn't spotted him before, because they'd been on opposite sides of the trunk.

'Is this your sanctum?' he asked. 'If so, I apologize for trespassing.'

Awkwardly, she shook her head.

'Bad luck about the prize,' he added, and, to her

surprise, he sounded as if he meant it. 'You looked . . . cast down when they awarded it to Lyndon.'

She was embarrassed, but flattered that he'd noticed. And she liked it that he talked to her as if she were a grown-up.

With her heel she dug at the ground, and her red cloven hoof sank into the softness of rotten leaves. 'It's just . . .' she began, 'I didn't know that girls can't be devils.'

Mr Traherne chuckled. 'Oh yes they can!'

She wasn't sure what he meant.

He asked if his cigar smoke troubled her, and she told him no, and that sometimes Papa let her try one of his.

'Well, I shan't let you try one of mine,' he said with a smile. 'It's far too strong. It would make you unwell.'

She wondered if he meant that Papa's cigars were weak by comparison – then told herself not to be such a muff. He was only making conversation. 'When I was little,' she volunteered, 'I wanted to be a boy, you know.'

He raised an eyebrow. 'Did you really?'

She nodded. 'I made everyone call me Bill, and refused to wear frocks or play with dolls. It was after my brother died, and I thought . . . well, that I ought to be a boy. To make up for it to Papa.'

He took that with an understanding nod.

Pressing her lips together, she perched on the end of the bench, arranging her tail carefully beside her.

He offered her his handkerchief to bind up her hand, and she said thank you. In silence they sat side by side, but without any awkwardness, and Belle watched him blowing smoke rings across the river. It was April, and the rains were weeks away, so the Martha Brae was a slow, sludgy olive green that smelt a little off. But Belle was used to it, and Mr Traherne didn't seem to mind.

She cast him a shy glance. He was very old, at least sixty, and acknowledged by everyone to be the most powerful man on the Northside. But she'd never really noticed him before. It was a relief that he was so old. She'd found that with old men she didn't imagine what they were like naked. She simply couldn't.

She reflected that she liked his face. He had strong, almost Roman features, with silver hair and a white moustache, and slightly bulging light blue eyes.

Yes, she thought, a Roman senator. She pictured him walking nobly in the Forum, making laws.

'You know,' he remarked with a curl of his red lips, 'when my son went up to accept the prize, you didn't merely look cast down. For a moment, you looked as if you wanted to kill him.'

She opened her mouth to protest, then shut it again. 'I'd never have carried it out,' she mumbled.

He laughed. 'No attempt to deny it! I like that. You seem rather to enjoy breaking rules.'

Did she? She'd never thought about that before.

'Oh, don't worry,' he said gently. 'All girls like breaking rules. It's in their nature.'

Belle frowned. 'What about boys?'

Again he laughed. 'Oh, they *make* the rules.'

That didn't seem at all fair, but she thought it might be rude to say so.

Suddenly Mr Traherne got to his feet. 'Oh, do look, there's a yellowsnake!'

'Ooh, where? Where?'

He gestured with his cigar, then put his hand on her shoulder to shift her a little to the right. 'Other side of the river, under the heliconia – d'you see?'

'. . . Oh, yes! I just caught the tail!' She was elated. It's good luck to see a yellowsnake, and she hadn't seen one since the year before last, when her uncle had taken her shooting in the Cockpits.

That had been such a wonderful day. It was just after the twins were born, and she'd been feeling a bit left out, when suddenly her uncle had swept in from Fever Hill, and taken her off riding for the day. They'd taken a packed lunch, and ridden all over the hills, and she'd felt proud to see him sit his horse so well, for Ben Kelly was the best rider in Trelawny, better even than Papa. They'd yelled insults at the john crows till they were weak with laughter, and he'd taught her to jump.

She was thinking of that when she felt Mr Traherne's hand move slowly down from her shoulder, under the neck of her frock, and onto her breast.

He didn't say anything. Neither did she. She froze. Couldn't look at him. Couldn't breathe.

Keep perfectly still, she told herself. Stare straight ahead. Pretend you haven't noticed. This is a mistake. His hand has slipped by mistake, and he doesn't know it yet. If you stay perfectly still, he'll realize, and take it away. And then we can pretend that it never happened.

She stared straight ahead of her at the great, curved scarlet flowers of the heliconia on the other side of the river.

But they're not flowers at all, she thought in horror. They're claws. Blood-red claws for tearing flesh.

A choking smell of rottenness rose from the green water. She felt sick. She swayed. The heavy hand held her back, pressing painfully into her breast.

This is a mistake, she told herself over and over.

She tried to take refuge in the thought; to make it push away what was happening. Mistake, mistake, mistake.

It was stifling inside the bamboo tunnel. The crickets were deafening. The bitter smell of his cigar caught at her throat.

A burst of laughter from the party made her jump.

Slowly he withdrew his hand. 'I wonder,' he said calmly, 'if we were to wait here very quietly, should we see it again? The yellowsnake. What do you think?'

She clasped her hands in front of her to stop them shaking. She tried to say something, but her tongue wouldn't come unstuck from the roof of her mouth.

From the corner of her eye she saw him toss his cigar in the river. Then he withdrew a silver case from his jacket pocket and opened it, and chose another. 'You know,' he went on in the same easy, conversational tone, 'poor old Lyndon must seem the most awful muff to you, but in fact he's rather an admirer of yours.'

She tried to swallow. What was he talking about? What did he mean?

He sighed. 'I suppose I oughtn't to have told you that. Poor little Lyndon. He'd be mortified if he ever found out.'

She watched him light his cigar. The way he narrowed his eyes against the smoke, and tossed his match into the river. She watched its sure, steady arc.

'You shall have to be very kind,' he went on, 'and promise me that you'll keep it a secret. Will you do that for me?'

There was a silence.

At last she raised her eyes to his face.

He was looking down at her, smiling as he waited for her to reply. His face looked just as it had before: the light blue eyes crinkled and genial. Until you noticed the pupils, which were blank and black as a goat's.

But it *must* have been a mistake, she told herself. He simply didn't realize—

'So what do you say, hm? Are you going to be a good girl, and keep our secret?'

She looked up into his eyes, and slowly nodded.

'That's my clever girl. Now. Let's go and see if they've left us any tea.'

Read the complete book – now available from Bantam Press

THE SERPENT'S TOOTH
Michelle Paver

Since she was twelve years old, Belle has lived with a secret –
a secret which cuts her off from her family, and isolates her
wherever she goes. Against the unfolding horror of the Great
War, her search for peace takes her from the brittle gaiety of
English country house society to the remote Scottish mansions
where her grandmother's tragedy was played out, and to the
battlefields of Flanders. As the scarred and shattered men
return from the trenches, and an influenza epidemic scythes
across the country, Belle must finally discover a way to break
free of her secret – or lose her last chance of happiness.

A MAGNIFICENT NEW NOVEL ABOUT LOVE,
FRIENDSHIP AND A WORLD CHANGED FOR EVER,
FROM THE ACCLAIMED AUTHOR OF *THE SHADOW
CATCHER* AND *FEVER HILL*

0 593 05394 X

NOW AVAILABLE FROM BANTAM PRESS

BANTAM PRESS

THE SHADOW CATCHER
Michelle Paver

EDEN. In the depths of the lush Jamaican forest stands a
ruined house of haunting beauty – the last remains of a
great estate founded on slavery. Abandoned for decades, it
still casts its spell down the generations. A place of dreams,
magic and madness.

Worlds away, ten-year-old Madeleine's untroubled Scottish
childhood is cut short by a fateful encounter with the
handsome, disenchanted Cameron Lawe. Left alone to raise
her new-born sister Sophie, growing up an outcast in Victorian
London, she seizes her chance to escape and returns to the
decaying Jamaican plantation where she was conceived. There
she finds a people haunted by a savage legacy; a family torn
apart by obsession and betrayal; but there too she finds Eden –
where she must finally confront the shadows of her past.

'A RICHLY ATMOSPHERIC BOOK, FULL OF MENACING
SECRETS AND BETRAYAL'
Sunday Mirror

'EPIC . . . FULLY IMMERSES THE READER'
Good Housekeeping

0 552 15152 1

CORGI BOOKS

WITHOUT CHARITY
Michelle Paver

Now was the time for him to leave. If he did not leave now, if he allowed her to catch sight of him, there would be no going back. She stood before the great stone horse, absorbed and unaware. She looked small and upright and brave. And easily hurt. He took in the slow sweep of her lashes as she traced the line of the horse's neck. The clarity of her profile. The warmth and tenderness of her mouth. All his careful reasoning collapsed about him.

When Sarah first saw Harlaston Hall, its grandeur unnerved her. How could this great mansion have anything to do with her family, and in particular with her grandmother Charity? Reluctantly, Sarah had taken on the job of writing up the history of the hall, mainly so that she could get away from London and the misery of her broken love affair. But as she became immersed in the poignant story of the house, and in particular of Robert, the last Lord Harlaston, it became vital that she uncovered the truth.

From present-day London to the windswept Lincolnshire fens, from the battles of the Boer War to the rigid hierarchies of a small village in Edwardian times, this sweeping novel tells a breathtaking story of a family and its long-buried mysteries.

0 552 14752 4

CORGI BOOKS

A PLACE IN THE HILLS
Michelle Paver

A LOVE BEYOND TIME

A PASSION BEYOND REASON

A TREASURE BEYOND PRICE

One long look and I was brought down.
She entered my blood . . .

Be careful how you dig up the past.

In the splendour and savagery of ancient Rome, Cassius, the greatest poet of his age, lost the only woman he ever loved. Two thousand years later, in the foothills of the Pyrenees, Antonia is driven to solve the riddle Cassius left behind. Her chance comes when she and her father, both archaeologists, excavate the sun-baked valley where Cassius lived and died.

This is the heartbreaking, heartwarming story of what Antonia found, and of all that followed. For Antonia there is a chance – one final chance – to undo the mistakes of the past, and to solve the age-old, all-pervading mystery that binds past and present together.

0 552 14753 2

CORGI BOOKS

PLANTS
AND
ANIMALS

A Field Guide in Colour to

PLANTS
AND
ANIMALS

Text by Jan Toman and Jiří Felix

Illustrations by Květoslav Hísek,
Libuše Knotková, Jaromír Knotek
and Jiří Polák

BLITZ EDITIONS

PV Přírodou

Text by Jan Toman and Jiří Felix
Translated by Olga Kuthanová
Illustrations by Květoslav Hísek,
Libuše Knotková, Jaromír Knotek
and Jiří Polák
Graphic design by Josef Dvořák

Designed and produced by Aventinum
Publishing House, Prague,
Czech Republic
This English edition published 1998
by Blitz Editions,
an imprint of Bookmart Ltd.
Registered Number 2372865
Trading as Bookmart Limited
Desford Road, Enderby,
Leicester LE9 5AD

ISBN 1-85605-437-3
Printed in the Czech Republic
by Polygrafia, a.s., Prague
3/07/01/51-02

CONTENTS

Plants

Animals

Foreword

The present make-up of Europe's flora and fauna is the result of a lengthy and complex evolution in the distant past. This present-day composition of plants and animals was primarily influenced by changes that occurred from the end of the Tertiary period to the beginning of the Quaternary, in other words, approximately during the last two million years. One determining factor was extreme changes in climate that occurred: from the subtropical or nearly tropical, when palms grew in central Europe and even monkeys could be found there, to cold, sometimes near arctic, conditions. Glacial periods, with conditions similar to the present-day Siberian tundra, were interspersed at lengthy intervals with warm interglacial periods, comparable in climate to the Balkans of today. Of necessity, such climatic changes resulted in the extinction of numerous species, or even whole genera, of plants and animals, as the prevailing climate proved intolerable for their existence. There was also a great migration of species, allowing the spread of hitherto exotic animal and plant groups to biotopes that they now found congenial. The present European flora and fauna is the result of all these changes and is formed by representatives of dry, warm, cold or wet periods that prevailed thousands of years ago.

Also affecting the composition of the flora and fauna are the many differences in the make-up of the soil throughout Europe and also the topography of the land, which ranges from spreading lowlands to rolling hills, highlands and mountains including high mountain peaks. In Europe one can find the remains of sand dunes, large bodies of water, artificial ponds and dams, tumbling mountain streams and lowland winding brooks and rivers as well as the calm, unruffled waters of oxbow lakes. One may admire the gloomy, hushed environment of

Fig. 1. The Common Tern (*Sterna hirundo*) not only nests on the seacoast and on islands but also by inland lakes and ponds.

Fig. 2. The Marmot (*Marmota marmota*) feeds on seeds from the cones of the Mountain Pine (*Pinus mugo*).

deep forests, stroll across sun-dappled glades and escape the huge city conglomerates to seek green fields and meadows. Nature in Europe wears many garbs—from alder groves, pastureland and forest-steppes to mountain beech woods; from rock steppes covered with oak and pine to mountain spruce forests and alpine grasslands; from mountain tarns and glaciers to vineyards on sunny hillsides—all part of the varied landscape that is to be found on this continent rimmed by seacoast to north, south and west.

Naturally, such widely varied biotopes are home to a huge diversity of plant and animal communities. Many plants and animals have no special requirements in terms of habitat and thus may be found in several biotopes. Some, on the other hand, have very specific requirements and are closely bound to a particular environment. The scope of this book makes it impossible to examine all of Europe's many and diverse biotopes, so we shall say a few words only about the most typical biotopes and their plant and animal communities.

Broad-leaved Forest

The character of Europe's broad-leaved forest differs from lowland to mountain elevations. Near flowing waters, in regularly, or at least occasionally, water-inundated lowlands it bears the character of a flood-plain forest, with alder, willow and poplar predominating. The greater the distance from regular water courses, the greater is the number of oak, elm, ash trees, lime trees and maple trees. At median elevations oak and hornbeam predominate, lingering remnants of once-extensive oak and hornbeam forests that have, today, to a great extent, been cut down and replaced by planted conifers. At submontane elevations, beeches are found in increasing numbers among the oaks and hornbeams until, eventually, they predominate and form typical mountain beech forests with an admixture of firs and spruces.

The broad-leaved forest is arranged in distinct layers, generally divided into three: the tree layer, the shrub layer and the herbaceous layer. This arrangement allows for the growth of a greater number of plants on a small area and for the best utilization of the space above, as well as below, ground, without the plants being mutually competitive. This layering provides similar advantages for animals.

The shrub layer of flood-plain forests is often impenetrably dense. It is composed of small, young trees (such as elm and poplar, growing from the root suckers of old trees, or willow, readily spreading by vegetative means from broken-off fragments) and true shrubs. The latter include Common Elder (*Sambucus nigra*), Dogwood (*Cornus sanguinea*), Guelder Rose (*Viburnum opulus*), Alder Buckthorn (*Rhamnus frangula*), European Spindle Tree (*Euonymus europaeus*), and others. Also characteristic of the flood-plain forest are climbing plants, mainly Hop (*Humulus lupulus*), English Ivy (*Hedera helix*), and Traveller's Joy (*Clematis vitalba*).

The herbaceous layer of the flood-plain forest is also rich in flora, despite the fact that little light penetrates through the dense cover of

Fig. 3. The Slow-worm (*Anguis fragilis*) is ovoviviparous, which means that the female generally produces live offspring.

Fig. 4. *Ramaria aurea*, found mainly in broad-leaved forests in summer and autumn, is a tasty edible mushroom.

tion disappears to be replaced by shade-loving plants. Such seasonal variability is a specific characteristic of broad-leaved forests.

Early in the year spring is heralded in the oak-woods by the white flowers of the snowdrop, soon followed by the blue flowers of Noble Liverleaf (*Hepatica nobilis*), purple lungwort (*Pulmonaria*), the white, star-like flowers of the Wood Anemone (*Anemone nemorosa*), variously coloured fumeworts (*Corydalis*), asarabacca (*Asarum*), the changeably coloured Spring Vetchling (*Lathyrus vernus*) and many more. In summer these are replaced by diverse hawkweeds (*Hieracium*) and grasses, such as fescues (*Festuca*) and Chalk False Brome-grass (*Brachypodium pinnatum*).

Herbaceous plants characteristic of hornbeam and oak woods include Greater Stitchwort (*Stellaria holostea*), Wood Chrysanthemum (*Chrysanthemum corymbosum*), Hairy St John's Wort (*Hypericum hirsutum*), Mountain St John's Wort (*Hypericum montanum*), brooms (*Genista*), black brooms (*Lembotropis*) and Nottingham Catchfly (*Silene nutans*).

Found in both hornbeam-oak and beech woods is Herb Paris (*Paris quadrifolia*), Coral Root (*Dentaria bulbifera*), Sweet Woodruff (*Galium odoratum*), baneberry (*Actaea*), Cuckoo-

trees and shrubs. This layer is brightened by the flowers of the Yellow Wood Anemone (*Anemone ranunculoides*), Spring Snowflake (*Leucojum vernum*), Water Forget-me-not (*Myosotis palustris*), Cowslip (*Primula veris*), Common Lungwort (*Pulmonaria officinalis*), Ramsons (*Allium ursinum*), Marsh Marigold (*Caltha*), Bog Arum (*Calla palustris*), and other, often rare and protected, plants.

Despite occasional flooding, the fauna of the flood-plain forest includes a wealth of species. The same species of game are found here as in the forests of higher elevations, including red deer and roe deer. Wild boar, in particular, find the conditions of the flood-plain forest extremely congenial. Typical birds are the Blackcap (*Sylvia atricapilla*), Nightingale (*Luscinia megarhynchos*), Penduline Tit (*Remiz pendulinus*) and Golden Oriole (*Oriolus oriolus*).

Like the flood-plain forest, broad-leaved forests provide favourable conditions for the development of the shrub layer as well as the herbaceous layer. In spring the trees are without leaves and sunlight can penetrate all the way to the ground to warm the earth. Here the plants soon begin new growth. When the trees are in full leaf and their crowns shade the ground beneath them, the bright carpet of spring vegeta-

Fig. 5. The simple, almost stark beauty of the Lily-of-the-Valley (*Convallaria majalis*).

11

pint (*Arum maculatum*), Solomon's Seal (*Polygonatum*) and *Lysimachia nemorum*. These and other herbaceous plants are described in greater detail in the pictorial section.

Besides the popular woodland fruits — raspberries, blackberries and whortleberries — mushrooms are also abundant, although one will not find as many in broad-leaved forests as in coniferous or mixed stands. One of the handsomest mushrooms of all is found growing at the foot of large oaks—the brown-capped *Boletus aestivalis*. Beneath aspens one will find the Orange Cap Boletus. The most poisonous European mushroom—the Death Cap (*Amanita phalloides*)—also grows at the foot of oaks and may be found in all types of broad-leaved as well as mixed forests.

The shrub layer in oak-hornbeam forests is well developed. Well represented are the Hazel (*Corylus avellana*), Spindle Tree (*Euonymus*), Red Dogwood (*Cornus sanguinea*), Viburnum,

and Common Privet (*Ligustrum vulgare*). The shrubs are thickest at the forest's edge where thorny shrubs also often grow, such as Blackthorn (*Prunus spinosa*), Midland Hawthorn (*Crataegus oxyacantha*), Common Buckthorn (*Rhamnus catharticus*) and Dog Rose.

Beechwoods have a much thinner shrub layer, with Red Elder (*Sambucus racemosa*), Black Honeysuckle (*Lonicera nigra*) and the early-spring-flowering Mezereon (*Daphne mezereum*) predominating.

Oak and hornbeam woods are inhabited by a great many insects. Most people are familiar with the cherry-like galls found on oak leaves in which the larvae of the gall wasp *Cynips quercusfolii* develop. The predaceous ground beetles *Calosoma sycophanta* and *Calosoma inquisitor* hunt the caterpillars of gipsy moths (*Lymantria*) and other Lepidoptera. Broad-leaved forests are also inhabited by many long-horned beetles (Cerambycidae), most of which are named on lists of protected species. Carrion beetles (*Necrophorus*) bury small dead animals in the ground to serve as a later food store for their larvae. The larvae of the metallic-green dung beetles (*Geotrupes*) also feed on carrion as well as on excrement and decaying fungi.

From spring until autumn the broad-leaved forests are brightened by the appearance of countless butterflies and moths. Much damage is caused by the handsome Green Oak Tortrix Moth (*Tortrix viridana*), whose larvae are capable of stripping oak trees of their young leaves, leaving them completely bare.

The abundance of insects is welcomed by woodland birds. In old oak woods there are numerous tree cavities in which the birds can build their nests. Besides tits (*Parus*), nuthatches (*Sitta*), treecreepers (*Certhia*) and cuckoos, their number includes several species of woodpeckers (*Picidae*), with toes that are well adapted for climbing and a wedge-shaped beak for extract-

Fig. 6. The Fire Salamander (*Salamandra salamandra*) hunts earthworms, slugs, insects and spiders by clear streams. It emerges from its hiding place in the evening, and also in the daytime in rainy weather.

ing insects and insect larvae from beneath the bark of trees. Oak woods are also home to the Stock Dove (*Columba oenas*), the Jay (*Garrulus glandarius*) and the Raven (*Corvus corax*). Protected species include the Hazel Hen (*Tetrastes bonasia*), Black Grouse (*Lyrurus tetrix*), and Woodcock (*Scolopax rusticola*).

Many mammals are found in oak-hornbeam forests. Here and in beechwoods, one will find the squirrel, badger, fox, Pine Marten (*Martes martes*), European Polecat (*Putorius putorius*) and the Wild Cat (*Felis silvestris*). One common small mammal is the Common Dormouse (*Muscardinus avellanarius*).

King among the animals here is the red deer, although the roe deer is even more closely bound to the broad-leaved forest. The forest margins are often visited by hares. Small mammals inhabiting beechwoods include the Bank Vole (*Clethrionomys glareolus*), the Yellow-necked Field Mouse (*Apodemus flavicollis*), and

the Forest Dormouse (*Dryomis nitedula*) which is not often seen because of its nocturnal habits.

The bird population of beech forests is somewhat more distinctive. The Red-breasted Flycatcher (*Ficedula parva*) makes its home here, while owls, in particular the Tawny Owl (*Strix aluco*), also nest here. Submontane forests are inhabited by eagles — the Lesser Spotted Eagle (*Aquila pomarina*) and the Imperial Eagle (*Aquila heliaca*) — while mountain and submontane beechwood is where the Black Stork (*Ciconia nigra*) builds its nest.

Of all Europe's ancient forests, the original broad-leaved forests that once covered vast expanses of land were the ones most destroyed by people, particularly at lower elevations where humans settled close to the edges of open, broad-leaved woods in areas with congenial climates and good sources of food for themselves and their domestic animals.

Fig. 7. *Boletus aestivalis* is a favourite food of the Red Slug (*Arion rufus*).

Coniferous Forest

Fig. 8. A fully grown leaf and spirally furled young leaves of the Male Fern (*Dryopteris filix-mas*).

The importance of mountain coniferous forests in their effect on the water balance and their influence on the climate and in the prevention of soil erosion is inestimable. Mountain forests catch most rain and favourably affect the composition of the earth's atmosphere in vast areas; they are the sources of numerous rivers, and they prevent the washing away of humus. They are also irreplaceable as sources of quality wood. Coniferous forests are to be found at lower elevations, but, apart from the occasional exception, these are all spruce or pine monocultures artificially planted for the purpose of timber extraction. Original, natural coniferous forests are nowadays found only in the mountains.

Spruce stands often include scattered firs, larches and beeches; in pine stands one will also find oaks, birches, lime trees and poplars. The shrub layer of coniferous forests is quite sparse and that is why spruce and pine forests seem much more uniform and less diversified than broad-leaved forests. Only the Rowan (*Sorbus aucuparia*), whose young shrubs do not mind being shaded by the thick crowns of the spruce trees, is more plentiful in spruce forests, while the Juniper (*Juniperus communis*) is often found among pines. Occurring in large numbers at higher elevations is the Red-berried Elder (*Sambucus racemosa*). The bottom layer in coniferous forests is mostly composed of perennial grasses, mosses and ferns, occasionally with heather and small whortleberry and cranberry bushes.

Growing in damp, open locations are dense, spreading carpets of small-reed (*Calamagrostis villosa*); in more shaded places that are not too damp, Wavy Hair-grass (*Avenella flexuosa*) is found. As well as these two dominant plants, which are found in other types of forests as well, there are rarer species that are dependent on the specific conditions of the coniferous stands. Bound to spruce forests in this way are Hard Fern (*Blechnum spicant*), Male Fern (*Dryopteris filix-mas*) and Stag's-horn Clubmoss (*Lycopodium clavatum*). Of the herbaceous plants there is Common Wood Sorrel (*Oxalis acetosella*), One-flowered Wintergreen (*Moneses uniflora*), *Streptopis amplexifolius*, Purple Coltsfoot (*Homogyne alpina*) and Willow Gentian (*Gentiana asclepiadea*). The moss layer is likewise well developed, particularly in spruce forests where *Polytrichum commune, Polytrichum formosum* and *Sphagnum* grow.

Numerous medicinal herbs grow in coniferous forests, such as St John's Wort (*Hypericum*), Lungwort (*Pulmonaria obscura*) and Common or Lesser Centaury (*Centaurium minus*). Rare and protected plants include Common Helleborine (*Epipactis helleborine*) and the Lesser Butterfly Orchid (*Platanthera bifolia*). In pine stands Box-leaved Milkwort (*Chamaebuxus alpestris*) and Flesh-coloured Heath (*Erica carnea*) are found.

Fungi abound in coniferous forests. Their number includes the handsome Edible Boletus (*Boletus edulis*) and *Boletus pinicola*, plus various species of *Suillus, Russula* and other edible mushrooms. The Honey Fungus (*Armillaria mellea*) is a parasite of forest trees and poses a grave danger; it grows on tree stumps and roots as well as on live trunks and is capable of destroying them completely. Even more dangerous is the bracket fungus (*Fomes annosus*), which often causes the decay of spruce wood.

Pests of the coniferous forest include numerous insects. Most dreaded of all is the Spruce Bark Beetle (*Ips typographus*), which multiplies with extraordinary rapidity. Its larvae make tunnels beneath the bark of spruce trees, in which they pupate. The newborn beetles then feed on the tree's phloem, making further tunnels, on the sides of which they again lay eggs three weeks later. Spruces that are severely infested by this bark beetle will dry up and die. Luckily, the Spruce Bark Beetle has many natural enemies, among birds chiefly the Coal Tit (*Parus ater*), Crested Tit (*Parus cristatus*) and woodpeckers (*Picidae*); among insects the checkered beetle *Thanasimus formicarius*, rover beetles (*Staphylinidae*) and certain hymenopterous insects (Hymenoptera).

The caterpillars of the Pine Sawfly (*Diprion pini*) feed on pine needles and on the bark of young pine shoots. In the case of overpopulation, they may cause complete defoliation of the tree. Pine Sawfly populations are kept in check by numerous insect parasites as well as other natural enemies among the vertebrates.

Striking scaly swellings at the tips of small branches are galls caused by *Dreyfusia nordmannianae*. It is fondest of young trees and is

Fig. 9. The Yellow-necked Field Mouse (*Apodemus flavicollis*) inhabits rather damp forests with a thick shrub undergrowth.

spread from one place to another by birds or animals. The females of the horntail *Urocerus gigas* resemble large wasps. With their long ovipositors they pierce the wood of spruce trees to a depth of as much as 15 mm and lay their eggs there. The newly hatched larvae then bore tunnels in the wood. Many Lepidoptera, but mainly moths, are dreaded pests of coni-fers, particularly in monocultures. The Black Arches Moth (*Lymantria monacha*), whose lar-vae feed on the tree needles, may be a veritable scourge. Its natural enemies include tits, cuck-oos, bats, and predacious beetles.

On the other hand the widespread Wood Ant (*Formica rufa*) is extremely beneficial. The Wood Ants' nest, a mound of pine needles and

Fig. 10. The Red Wood Ant (*Formica rufa*) is usually found in sunny spots in coniferous for-ests. In such places one may also come across the inconspicuous Common Helleborine (*Epi-pactis helleborine*).

18

small twigs over 1 m high, is visible from afar. Ninety per cent of their diet consists of woodland pests, such as larvae, caterpillars and adult insects. It has been discovered that the ants capture all pests within 20 m of their nest, thereby effectively protecting the nearby trees from being defoliated by caterpillars. They also greatly limit the occurrence of harmful insects for a radius of a further 15 m beyond this limit.

It is mainly in coniferous forests that one will find many of the striking, long-horned beetles (*Cerambycidae*), now on the list of rare species. The larvae of *Leptura rubra* usually develop in the decaying stumps and trunks of pine and spruce trees. On newly felled trunks one will find *Rhagium inquisitor*, whose larvae live beneath the bark of dry conifers that have been attacked by bark beetles. Also frequently found on newly felled pines is *Acanthocinus aedilis*, whose males sport antennae several times longer than their bodies. The stumps of spruce, pine and fir are where the development of the larvae of *Toxotus cursor* takes place. These forests are also inhabited by other species of long-horned beetles.

Coniferous forests are the home of numerous birds. They are the nesting grounds of tits (*Parus*), woodpeckers (*Picidae*), the Bullfinch (*Pyrrhula pyrrhula*), Mistle Thrush (*Turdus viscivorus*) and Common Crossbill (*Loxia curvirostra*), which feed on the seeds of the conifers. The Common Treecreeper (*Certhia familiaris*) climbs upward and around the tree trunks in a spiral and extracts insects and insect larvae from cracks in the bark with its awl-shaped beak. Often heard in the treetops is the twittering note of the smallest European bird—the Goldcrest (*Regulus regulus*), weighing a mere 5—6 g. Open, dry coniferous forests are frequented by the European Nightjar (*Caprimulgus europaeus*), and the predacious Sparrowhawk (*Accipiter nisus*) builds its large nest in the branches of spruce trees. Coniferous forests in mountain districts are frequented by the Nutcracker (*Nucifraga caryocatactes*), a native of the northern taiga. One of the most popular game birds with hunters is the Capercaillie (*Tetrao urogallus*), the largest European grouse; the male may weigh as much as 6 kg.

Fig. 11. A Silver-washed Fritillary (*Argynnis paphia*) resting on flowering Box-leaved Milkwort (*Chamaebuxus alpestris*).

One will not find many mammals that are specifically bound to coniferous forests. Like broad-leaved forests, they are inhabited by red deer and roe deer, the Pine Marten (*Martes martes*), European Badger (*Meles meles*), fox, wild cat, and the ubiquitous squirrel. Typical inhabitants of mountain coniferous forests include the European Lynx (*Lynx lynx*), which hunts mammals as well as birds, and the now relatively rare wolf. The Northern Birch Mouse (*Sicista betulina*), which is rather like an ordinary mouse, inhabits thinner stands of spruce above the upper forest limit.

Meadows and Pasturelands

Fig. 12. The Small Tortoiseshell (*Aglais urticae*) is one of the commonest butterflies.

Not all meadows are alike. Much depends on how and to what degree they have been affected by people, and, accordingly, they may be divided into three groups. The first comprises natural meadows that formed as treeless grassy tracts located mostly in river valleys. These valleys were regularly flooded for lengthy periods and thus afforded no opportunity for the successful development of forests in the belt of land bordering the rivers. Such meadows are practically non-existent now and the few that do remain are valued as relicts of natural meadows, often containing rare plant species. They are of great importance in our understanding of the evolution of the landscape.

Most of today's meadows belong to the second group, that of semi-cultivated and cultivated meadows. These came into being alongside smaller water courses through the agency of people, by felling trees, clearing land and regularly mowing the resulting vegetation. The more people affected the composition of these meadows by sowing other, economically more important grasses, and by enriching the soil with fertilizers, the more these semi-cultivated meadows became transformed into true meadow cultures.

The third group — mountain meadows — are fully dependent on the intervention of people. These meadows are relatively recent for they were formed only when humans settled in mountain districts. In order to earn a livelihood in the mountains and to be able to graze cattle, farmers had to fell trees and clear the land in places suitable for the purpose. In the mountains, however, a meadow generally cannot be tended with the aid of machines; here it can be maintained only by laborious mowing by hand or by grazing. If left ungrazed for just a few years, however, the forest will begin to encroach upon it once again. Abandoned mountain meadows are soon covered with the seedlings of woody plants and, before long, those beautiful, brightly coloured grassy tracts containing countless rare herbaceous plants are no more and the forest again reigns supreme.

In drier locations grazing gave rise to pasturelands in those places where the poor soil was not conducive to the development of rich meadow vegetation. Less-demanding grasses tolerate cropping, trampling down and natural fertilization by the manure of grazing cattle. Regular, yearly and long-term grazing thus not only has a beneficial effect on the condition of the cattle but also serves to maintain the composition of the vegetation in pasturelands and mountain meadows.

The vegetation of these areas is characterized by the absolute predominance of grasses over other herbaceous plants. Even in meadows with a brightly coloured carpet of flowers, grasses predominate. Woody plants are non-existent here. The occasional solitary trees to be seen in pasturelands were planted by farmers as points of orientation or else for ornament to break the uniformity of the meadow. Only the boundaries between meadows, fields and pastures were left to woody plants, mostly small shrubs.

Common grasses in semi-cultivated and cultivated meadows are mostly members of the Poaceae family, such as Timothy Grass (*Phleum pratense*), fox-tail grass (*Alopecurus*), Crested

Dog's-tail (*Cynosurus .cristatus*), quaking grass (*Briza*), Cocksfoot (*Dactylis glomerata*), Tufted Hair-grass (*Deschampsia cespitosa*) and others. Herbaceous plants of flowering meadows include Ragged Robin (*Lychnis flos-cuculi*), buttercups (*Ranunculus*), Meadow Cranesbill (*Geranium pratense*), Lady's Mantle (*Alchemilla*) and many more.

Fig. 13. A sunny, grassy slope dotted with White Campion (*Melandrium album*) is host to the Sand Lizard (*Lacerta agilis*) which suns itself on a stone.

In pasturelands one will often find Narrow-leaved Meadow-grass (*Poa angustifolia*), Perennial Rye-grass (*Lolium perenne*), bent grass (*Agrostis*), Field Woodrush (*Luzula campestris*), Sweet Vernal-grass (*Anthoxanthum odoratum*), and other, mostly more dry-loving (xerophilous), grasses. Herbaceous plants growing here include Yarrow (*Achillea millefolium*), Dandelion

Fig. 14. On sunny summer days burnets (*Zygaena*) fly in their rather cumbersome way in meadows and on grassy slopes.

(*Taraxacum*), Ribwort (*Plantago*), Knotgrass (*Polygonum aviculare*) and the like. In hilly country and mountain districts pastureland vegetation also includes Mat-grass (*Nardus stricta*) and *Phleum alpinum*.

The fauna of meadows is extremely varied, especially in spring and summer when the meadows are carpeted with brightly coloured

flowers that attract large numbers of insects. Most conspicuous are the butterflies. Various species of blues (*Polyommatus*) and gold-coloured coppers (*Lycaena*) flutter from one flower to another. In dry meadows small burnets (*Zygaena*) are seen resting on the flowers of thistles, while flying about in the air are countless yellows (*Colias*) and browns (Satyridae) as well as brightly coloured admirals (*Vanessa*) and fritillaries (*Argynnis*). During the daytime a number of moths remain concealed beneath the broad leaves of herbaceous plants, for example tiger moths (Arctiidae). They emerge when darkness falls and fly about close above the ground in search of suitable plants on which to lay their eggs.

On warm sunny days large numbers of flies buzz about above the meadow and in the grass. In late summer, particularly, one will often find huge numbers of small grasshoppers, which make welcome food for insectivorous birds. Practically all the meadows are visited by spittle-bugs (*Cercopis*) that leap up out of the grass like huge fleas only to land and hide again a short way off. On tall herbaceous plants one may see the striking frothy secretions that contain the larvae of the spittle-bugs.

Innumerable insects hover around grazing cattle. Hundreds of small beetles lay their eggs in the pats of cow dung where the larvae will develop and feed. Flies are the troublesome and constant companions of grazing cattle, but horse-flies (Tabanidae), which mercilessly stab and suck the blood of their victims, are veritable pests, often for people as well.

Sun-warmed, grassy places are also inhabited by reptiles. The Sand Lizard (*Lacerta agilis*), adroitly capturing insects that alight in its vicinity, likes to sun itself here. When danger threatens, it disappears at lightning speed into a hole in the ground or between stones, but soon comes out again into the sunlight. In damp meadows one will also find amphibians such as frogs (*Rana*).

Of the many rodents that inhabit meadows, a typical steppe-dweller is the slender European Ground Squirrel (*Citellus citellus*), which lives on grass, fruit and insects and usually forms colonies. Once very common and widespread, it is now declining in numbers.

Forest creatures avoid meadows during the daytime but as soon as dusk falls and they are no longer conspicuous in the open, many venture forth to feed there.

Meadows are visited by many birds, particularly insectivorous species. The Yellow Wagtail (*Motacilla flava*), Whinchat (*Saxicola rubetra*)

24

and others build their nests there, concealed by the clumps of grass. Even certain predators find the open, grassy tracts to their liking; the Hen Harrier (*Circus cyaneus*), for example, builds its nest here on the ground. Of the owls, the one most often encountered in damp meadows is the Short-eared Owl (*Asio flammeus*). The meadows are also regularly visited by the Hoopoe (*Upupa epops*), which feeds on the larvae of insects, mainly beetles. Another common sight in meadows is storks, strolling about in search of larger insects and small rodents.

Fig. 15. The Blue-headed Wagtail (*Motacilla flava*) inhabits lowland meadows, often near water.

Fields

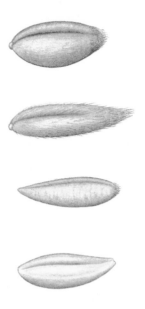

Fig. 16. Comparison of grains (from top to bottom): wheat, oat, rye, barley.

The vast areas of forest that covered both the lowland and the hilly landscapes of Europe in the distant past were transformed by farmers into what is termed cultivated steppe. The farmers cleared the land either by felling or burning, drained the swamps, ploughed the earth and sowed seeds. A cultivated steppe or field may be defined as an area of land fully exposed to sun and wind, regularly ploughed, enriched with fertilizer, treated with chemicals and harvested every year.

Besides cultivated plants, however, fields also contain a wide variety of weeds, which form an inseparable part of even the best-cared-for land. A typical feature of field weeds is that they are capable of adapting to the growth cycle of cultivated plants as well as to many agrotechnical procedures. Some weeds readily multiply vegetatively by means of their roots or rhizomes, for example Common Couch (*Agropyron*

repens); others do so by means of underground tubers — Earth-nut Pea (*Lathyrus tuberosus*) — or bulbs — Star-of-Bethlehem (*Gagea arvensis*). The roots of some weeds extend so far down into the earth that they remain untouched even by deep ploughing. Examples are Common Horsetail (*Equisetum arvense*), Field Bindweed (*Convolvulus arvensis*) and Creeping Thistle (*Cirsium arvense*).

There are also differences between the weeds of winter and spring crops. Winter crops usually have far more weeds than spring crops, because most weeds are destroyed by the ploughing of the soil in spring. Generally to be found in spring crops are plants with a short growth cycle, such as Wild Mustard (*Sinapis arvensis*), Scarlet Pimpernel (*Anagalis arvensis*) and Field Madder (*Sherardia arvensis*). Weeds of winter crops are usually annuals that germinate in the autumn and grow and flower in the spring of the following year. These species include certain speedwells (*Veronica triphyllos, Veronica arvensis*) and Annual Knawel (*Scleranthus annuus*).

Most weeds can be classified into one of four groups. The first includes species that mature in spring, long before field crops are harvested, such as Common Whitlow Grass (*Erophila verna*), Wall Speedwell (*Veronica arvensis*) and Star-of-Bethlehem (*Gagea arvensis*). The second group includes weeds that mature at the same time as grain, their ripe seeds falling to the ground when the crop is harvested, such as Corn Cockle (*Agrostemma githago*), nowadays rapidly disappearing from the scene, and the more common Corn Crowfoot (*Ranunculus arvensis*). The plants of the third group are perennial weeds that, even though they may be damaged during harvest, immediately grow again from their undamaged roots and flower a second time that same year, for example Field Bindweed (*Convolvulus arvensis*). The fourth and last group contains species that do not mature until after the harvest. Included in this group may be those weeds that can repeat their growth cycle several times during the growing season, such as Wild Pansy (*Viola tricolor*) which often produces several generations in a single year.

In root crops the number of weed species is relatively small, often with only one predominant species, such as All-seed (*Chenopodium polyspermum*) or Redleg (*Polygonum persicaria*).

Some weeds will only occur in certain crops that suit their needs. This goes hand in hand with differences in the manner of cultivating different crops and the particular conditions under which they grow. Hop fields, vineyards, tobacco fields, fields of flax and medicinal herbs, as well as fields of nectar-secreting plants all have typical, specific associations of weeds. Examples of such specialized weeds are Branched Broomrape (*Orobanche ramosa*), a parasite mostly of tobacco only, but very occasionally of sunflowers or other plants, and *Cuscuta epilinum*, a parasite solely of flax.

Over the past decades farmers have perfected methods of protecting and influencing crops by spraying them with herbicides and pesticides, treating seeds against infection and removing the seeds of weedy plants before sowing. Perhaps one day Corn-cockle, Field Fennel (*Nigella arvensis*) and Forking Larkspur (*Consolida regalis*) will no longer be seen in fields.

The transformation of forested areas into cultivated steppe brought with it a change in the composition of the animal communities. The original animals migrated or were exterminated and were replaced by new creatures, mainly native steppe species. Many adapted rapidly to the changed conditions and the fields soon became the source of a rich supply of food. These animals sometimes multiply to such a degree that they reach plague numbers, especially in dry years which they find exceedingly favourable.

Fields provide ideal conditions for various rodents that feed on cereal grains and other field crops. The Common Hamster (*Cricetus cricetus*) consumes a large amount of grain during the summer and, in addition, stores several kilograms of seeds in its underground burrow as a reserve food supply for the winter.

Fig. 17. The caterpillar of the Convolvulus Hawk (*Herse convolvuli*) feeds on Field Bindweed (*Convolvulus arvensis*).

Fig. 18. The Common Vole (*Microtus arvalis*) readily overmultiplies; the female produces up to twelve litters of more than ten young a year. It is as well that it has many natural enemies.

Even more troublesome is the Common Vole (*Microtus arvalis*), whose overpopulation is reason for much concern among farmers. Luckily, the fields are visited by raptorial birds, such as the Common Buzzard (*Buteo buteo*) and Eurasian Kestrel (*Falco tinnunculus*), which can decrease the number of voles considerably. Small weasels (Mustelidae), as well as foxes, also regularly prey on harmful rodents. The most important game animal of fields is the European Hare (*Lepus europaeus*).

Insect pests are very common in extensive tracts of cultivated monocultures, both above and below ground. The larvae of the Wheat Wire-worm (*Agriotes lineatus*) nibble the roots as well as the top parts of cereal grasses and the larvae of *Zabrus gibbus* gnaw at young spring shoots, while the adult beetles feed on the ripe seeds in the spikes. Also found on cereal crops are various species of heteropterous insects (Heteroptera). The Colorado Beetle, brought to Europe from Mexico many years ago, is a troublesome pest of potatoes. Hop fields are inhabited by many species of harmful aphids (Aphidoidea), which multiply at a rapid rate and damage plants by sucking their juices and with their spittle and excrement. Their greatest natural enemy is the ladybird and its predacious larvae which feed on aphids. In spring and summer the fields of clover and alfalfa present the brightest scene, with countless fritillaries (Nymphalidae), yellows (*Colias*), blues (*Polyommatus*) and other butterflies converging there to suck the sweet nectar of the flowers.

For insectivorous birds, fields are a veritable paradise. The liquid song of the Skylark (*Alauda arvensis*) fills the air as it hovers high in the sky, and the Crested Lark (*Galerida cristata*), originally a native steppe bird of the east, frequents the edges of the fields. Among typical field birds, the Partridge (*Perdix perdix*) is one of the most popular game birds. Due to the use of chemicals in farming, however, the partridge population has decreased alarmingly in many European countries. Even worse has been the fate of the Quail (*Coturnix coturnix*), at one time

Fig. 19. The Rose Chafer (*Cetonia aurata*) visits flowering plants on sunny days.

one of the commonest birds in Europe. In the countries of southern Europe and northern Africa, where its meat is considered a great delicacy, more than twenty million quail used to be captured in nets every year during the migrating season. Nowadays this bird is on the list of protected species in most European countries and, as a result, its numbers have increased slightly in recent years.

Mountains

Environmental conditions in the mountains differ markedly from those of lowland and foothill districts. The climate here is completely different. There is lower atmospheric pressure, strong prevailing winds, a low mean annual temperature of air as well as soil, high intensity of solar radiation and high rainfall. Winter in the mountains is relatively long and harsh, thick snow often covers the ground for as long as seven months or more; on mountain glaciers it stays there permanently.

For a long time mountain plant and animal communities remained untouched by people. Farmers penetrated the mountains relatively late, long after they had transformed vast expanses in the lowlands and foothills into fields and meadows. Mountains are used primarily for grazing cattle, to a lesser degree for logging and mining relatively rare ores, and also as a place for recreation, the clean air and relatively unspoiled wilderness making them ideal for this purpose.

Above the upper forest limit one will encounter only the occasional tree, a larch or stone pine perhaps. Most woody plants here are of shrubby habit, the principal species being the Mountain Pine (*Pinus mugo*), an important plant of the alpine belt. As for herbaceous plants, low, often cushion-like, types prevail, such as Moss Campion (*Silene acaulis*), mountain saxifrages (*Saxifraga*), Least Primrose (*Primula minima*) and several others. The small, often prostrate, shrubs of Reticulate Willow (*Salix reticulata*), Least Willow (*Salix herbacea*) and *Salix serpyllifolia* trail over rocks and boulders in screes. Many mountain plants have adapted to the harsh conditions by remaining permanently green even beneath the blanket of snow. Some even flower under the snow or push their stems up through the snow cover and start to flower very early in spring, for example tassel-flowers (*Soldanella*).

Annuals are only rarely seen in the mountains for the summer there is too short for the plants to complete their life cycle within a single growing season; that is, germination of the seeds, growth of the top parts, development of the flowers and ripening of the seeds. On the other hand, plants that flower before their leaves are fully developed are common in the mountains, for example butterbur (*Petasites*).

The composition of mountain flora is readily observed as one climbs from mountain forests up to alpine grasslands and meets the fountainheads of streams beneath the steep peaks. Predominant here are robust herbaceous plants and grasses, with, here and there, the occasion-

al 'flag-form' tree, its branches pointing leeward as it braves the force of the strong winds. Mountain slopes and rocky screes are inhabited by plant communities composed primarily of low, prostrate or cushion-like species. On the highest rocky peaks one will find only lichens with corky thalli pressed to the rock substrate. Only very occasionally will one find undemanding and hardy flowering plants in rock crevices, such as *Veronica aphylla*, Small Gentian (*Gentiana nivalis*), *Androsace lactea* and *Androsace helvetica*.

Mountains also have their typical animal inhabitants, creatures that have adapted to life on rocky, often very steep, inaccessible slopes and cliffs. Some animals, such as the Chamois (*Rupicapra rupicapra*), inhabit the highest rocky regions. Here they are well protected from predators that do not possess the nimbleness of foot with which a herd of Chamois moves about over the slopes and rock ledges. In summer Chamois remain near the snow line; in winter they descend to lower elevations. They are extremely adept at climbing the steep slopes and will leap as much as 8 m across deep ravines and gorges. Even the smallest rock ledge makes a springboard for their breakneck jumps. Herds of Chamois are generally headed by an experienced female, the males living separately for the greater part of the year. The young, wobbling at first on weak legs, soon scamper fearlessly in their mothers' wake, often within a few hours of birth.

The Austrian, Italian, Swiss and French Alps are home to the Ibex (*Capra ibex*), which remains above the upper forest limit, generally at elevations of 2,300—3,200 m. It often stays there even during the cold winter months. The Ibex lives in small herds comprising females, young males and young. Older, adult males live separately in small bands, and old males live singly, except during the mating season when they visit the females. The Ibex is protected by law throughout its entire range; there are some 3,000 specimens in the national parks of the alpine region.

A typical inhabitant of mountain districts in the Alps and Carpathians is the Marmot (*Marmota marmota*), one of Europe's largest rodents. It was also introduced to the Pyrenees, the Black Forest and other places. It lives on rocky slopes at elevations of 800—3,000 m, in colonies of up to eighteen individuals, all usually related.

Mountains also have a characteristic bird population. The rocky mountain localities of the Alps, Pyrenees and Carpathians is where the beautifully coloured Wall-creeper (*Tichodroma muraria*) makes its home. Only in winter does it descend to the lowlands for more readily obtainable food. It can be identified at a glance by its red wings spotted with white.

Wheeling and gliding above mountain cliffs, one may see the Golden Eagle (*Aquila chrysaetos*), a magnificent bird with a wingspan of about 2 m. The courtship flights of eagles may be observed in spring high up above the peaks. Rocky mountain slopes and cliffs are also the nesting site of the Griffon Vulture (*Gyps fulvus*), found in Spain, northern Italy, Austria, Switzerland, south-eastern France and south-eastern Europe; it may also be seen in other European countries, where it occurs as a guest.

The Chough (*Pyrrhocorax pyrrhocorax*) lives in rocky sites in the Alps and in Spain, as well as in Britain. The Ring Ouzel (*Turdus torquatus*) is partial to mountain slopes thinly covered with dwarf pine and low spruce, where it may be spotted in the vicinity of tumbling mountain streams. It occurs in the Alps, Pyrenees and Carpathians, as well as in England and Scandinavia.

Grassy mountain slopes abound with many species of insects. In particular, butterflies add beauty and colour to the scene, for example the Apollo (*Parnassius apollo*), a large butterfly with a wingspan of up to 70 mm.

Fig. 20. The Wallcreeper (*Tichodroma muraria*) is a rare, protected bird of rocky mountain districts.

Built-up Areas

Fig. 21. Blues (*Maculinea*) flit about close above the ground on summer days, visiting one flower after another.

People live surrounded by countless cultivated plants and domestic animals. Our houses are covered with climbing plants; our neighbourhoods are made attractive by neat gardens with decorative flowers, trees and shrubs. Fruit trees hold promise of a rich harvest, in the kitchen garden we try our hand at growing the latest kinds of vegetables, and in our homes the rooms are brightened by lovely house plants.

Beside plants, our companions include animals. Dogs and cats keep us company day in and day out, our homes are brighted by aquariums filled with tropical fish, cages of exotic birds or even terrariums containing small reptiles. Our children are made happy by having a guinea pig or hamster for a pet. The range of purely utility animals we use to provide our

food, be they mammals or birds, is continually extended by breeders through the introduction of new types.

However, in spite of this great number of cultivated plants and animals our immediate neighbourhood also abounds in wild flora and fauna. Some, such as birds, are quite obvious. Others, however, are inconspicuous. Some of these plants and animals are unwelcome guests that are difficult to get rid of.

All gardeners are well acquainted with the weedy plants that invade their beautifully kept gardens, such as Canadian Fleabane (*Conyza canadensis*), Common Groundsel (*Senecio vulgaris*) and galinsogas (*Galinsoga*). The queen of weedy plants is Goatweed or Ground Elder (*Aegopodium podagraria*); it is unbelievable how tenaciously it resists all attempts to eradicate it from the garden. Some weeds are small herbaceous plants with lovely flowers, for example Common Speedwell (*Veronica persica*), *Veronica sublobata*, Common Chickweed (*Stellaria media*), Shepherd's Purse (*Capsella bursa-pastoris*) and Henbit Dead-nettle (*Lamium amplexicaule*).

The most troublesome weeds are perennials with long underground rhizomes by means of which they spread through the soil. When digging the ground we often cut up the rhizomes of Couch (*Agropyron repens*) and Goatweed, thereby actually aiding and abetting their spread.

Weedy plants growing in the garden or by waysides are generally distinguished by immense vitality, in particular those that were brought to Europe from other continents, for example Small-flowered Balsam (*Impatiens parviflora*) and Canadian Fleabane. These plants are so very invasive because Europe's native plants are unable to compete with their great reproductive powers. The ripe capsules of Impatiens, first brought here from Central Asia, burst at the slightest touch, ejecting the seeds far from the parent plant. In the case of galinsogas, brought to Europe from Central and South America, during a single growing season one plant produces thousands of light, minute achenes furnished with an ingenious apparatus called a pappus, that serves as a parachute, carrying the achenes great distances from their parent plant. A few such invasive plants are all that is needed in order for them to dominate a large area within just a few years.

Not all weedy plants are to be disdained. Many have useful characteristics. Some may be made into tasty dishes, others may contain medicinal substances of importance in the

Fig. 22. Dense thickets of Stinging Nettle (*Urtica dioica*) are where the European Hedgehog (*Erinaceus europaeus*) hides until dusk, when it emerges in search of prey.

pharmaceutical industry or are used in home remedies. The young spring leaves of Stinging Nettle (*Urtica dioica*) and Small Nettle (*Urtica urens*) are widely used in salads and stuffings and valued for their high vitamin C content. A tasty salad may also be made from Lamb's Lettuce (*Valerianella locusta*) or from the leaves of Dandelion (*Taraxacum officinale*). Delicacies with a therapeutic effect include dandelion wine or a wine or compote made from elderberries, the fruits of the Common Elder (*Sambucus nigra*). Scented Mayweed (*Chamomilla recutita*) and Coltsfoot (*Tussilago farfara*) are among the most widely used, commonly known medicinal herbs, and we could cite many more examples.

Special mention should be made of the flora of dumps, rubbish heaps and waste places. Typical are spreads of orache (*Atriplex*), chenopods (*Chenopodium*) and numerous other plants.

Fig. 23. The flea (*Pulex irritans*) is a parasite of humans. Other species of fleas parasitize domestic animals.

Most plants found growing in the neighbourhood of human dwellings, by waysides and in waste places are extremely hardy. They are able to withstand all kinds of unfavourable conditions: toxic substances in the atmosphere, high concentrations of nitrogen in the soil and even daily trampling. They are covered in detail in the pictorial section, along with plants that have spread widely as escapees from gardens. Nor should we forget the trees and shrubs planted in parks and avenues to improve the dust- and fume-polluted atmosphere of cities and built-up areas.

The development of civilization was accompanied by the disappearance of many animals from the vicinity of human dwellings and by the arrival of others to take their place. Here they found suitable hiding places and better conditions for obtaining food or for propagation. In the favourable conditions that we unwittingly prepared for them, many species have multiplied in such numbers as to reach plague proportions, and have often caused irreparable damage.

Among the small mammals it is mainly the rodents that find built-up areas to their liking, above all the House Mouse (*Mus musculus*), Black Rat (*Rattus rattus*) and Brown Rat (*Rattus norvegicus*), feeding industriously on food stores and household scraps. They are capable of causing untold damage. Attracted by the rodents, came small beasts of prey, such as the

Weasel (*Mustela nivalis*), European Marten (*Martes foina*) and European Polecat (*Putorius putorius*), which hunted and fed on the rodents. They themselves, however, also became pests after a time as polecats and martens eventually began to specialize in easier prey such as chickens, hens and ducks and their eggs.

Built-up areas also attracted numerous species of insects, chiefly flies but also butterflies, moths and beetles. Vegetable gardens are visited by countless parasites, such as whites (*Pieris brassicae*), whose females deposit hundreds of eggs on the leaves of cabbages and other cruciferous plants and whose larvae then devour the leaves right down to the leaf stalks. Decorative flowering plants in gardens and on patios and windowsills are visited by many insects, including many butterflies, that suck sweet nectar from the blossoms.

Human dwellings are visited in the autumn by numerous species of insects attempting to survive the winter in congenial conditions. These include various fritillaries (*Vanessa*), the Green Lacewing (*Chrysopa vulgaris*), ladybirds (Coccinellidae) and the ubiquitous flies. Places that are not often aired are the favourite haunts of the House Spider (*Tegenaria derhami*) which spins dense webs. Even today one will often encounter such unpleasant parasites as fleas (*Pulex irritans*) and bedbugs (*Cimex*) in warm places, as well as cockroaches. Of late, households in the large cities of Central Europe have also been invaded by the Pharaoh Ant (*Monomoria pharaonis*), introduced only recently from the south. It spreads rapidly and is very difficult to exterminate. Wardrobes and stores of flour, vegetables and other foodstuffs are visited by many storehouse pests, of which moths (Tineidae) are the most familiar, their larvae feeding on whatever they find.

In the garden slugs and snails are troublesome pests that feed on tender young vegetable plants when darkness falls. However, they may be kept in check by the frogs and toads that often visit gardens in search of a tasty morsel. Attics, steeples and other high structures are often inhabited by insectivorous bats. Nowadays some species may also be seen in large cities where they may be found in such places as the ventilation shafts of modern buildings. In many countries bats are on the list of protected species.

Last of all we come to the birds, welcome companions, whose songs brighten the built-up areas where we live. The House Sparrow (*Passer domesticus*) probably first accompanied people when they began to cultivate grain, and was probably the first bird to settle permanently in the neighbourhood of humans. Nowadays it may be seen in the very heart of cities, on busy streets and town squares. The Blackbird (*Turdus merula*) is also our constant companion today, but this bird arrived in town at a much later date than the sparrow. As late as 1855 it was still described by ornithologists as a very shy woodland bird. Now it may be seen in town gardens and parks as well as in small courtyards where it builds its nest on windowsills and balconies.

Fig. 24. The Common Toad (*Bufo bufo*) is often found not only in gardens but also in cellars and sheds where it hides during the daytime. It also overwinters in damp country cellars.

The Swallow (*Hirundo rustica*) has almost to-
tally abandoned its native cliffside habitat and
moved to the neighbourhood of people, often
settling directly inside our houses—in a hallway
or even in a bathroom. Built-up areas are also
inhabited by the Swift (*Apus apus*) and House
Martin (*Delichon urbica*) which builds its nest
on the outside walls of houses, under balconies,
cornices and eaves. Worthy of particular notice
is the Starling (*Sturnus vulgaris*) which will
make its home wherever one hangs a nestbox,
be it in a garden, park or courtyard.

Other species of birds are also moving into
the neighbourhood of people in increasing numbers. They include the Black Redstart (*Phoenicurus ochruros*), Redstart (*Phoenicurus phoenicurus*), Great Tit (*Parus major*) and Blue Tit (*Parus caeruleus*). The Jackdaw (*Corvus monedula*)
sites its nest in church steeples in cities. In

Fig. 25. The European Blackbird (*Turdus merula*)
has become a constant companion of people. It
often builds its nest directly on a windowsill, on
a beam or even in a wicker basket. In the garden it nests in the forked branch of a shrub or
small tree.

parks the Rook (*Corvus frugilegus*) nests. Another recent arrival in cities is the Kestrel (*Falco tinnunculus*) which is now a permanent resident. It nests in church steeples and on the cornices of tall buildings. On the other hand the Barn Owl (*Tyto alba*) builds its nest in attics, barn lofts and dovecotes. In recent years, city parks and gardens have become the nesting place of the Song Thrush (*Turdus philomelos*), while the Collared Dove (*Streptopelia decaocto*) is a permanent year-round resident of built-up areas.

In winter bird-feeders in cities are often visited by woodland birds, but even in summer one may often see typical woodland birds in a park or garden, such as the Golden Oriole (*Oriolus oriolus*) and the Green Woodpecker (*Picus viridis*). Other woodland creatures visit cities too; the squirrel, for instance, is a common sight.

Fig. 26. The Golden Oriole (*Oriolus oriolus*) suspends its hammock-shaped nest, made of long thin stalks and grasses, between the forks of branches so that the young will not fall out even in strong winds.

43

Flowing Waters

The vast network of blue lines drawn on a map may show all the water courses in a given region, but they can give no idea of their great diversity. Cool, clear water has its source primarily in mountain forest districts, where mountain streams force their way down through rocky troughs, rushing and tumbling over rocks and boulders that block their path. These streams converge to form larger streams and brooks and then large rivers. The rivers take on a new and different aspect in their lower reaches where their banks are often artificially strengthened. At the mouths of rivers one can see the influence of the sea — the flow of the river slows and the fresh water mingles with salt seawater.

Throughout the journey from its source to the sea, the flow of water carries with it sand, mud and soil, which it then deposits lower down in the backwaters and mouths of rivers in the form of alluvium. The amount of oxygen in the water decreases over its course from mountain region to lowland country and at the same time there is a considerable increase in the degree of the water's pollution. All of these factors — flow, the changing swiftness of the current, the removal and deposition of alluvium, amount of food, variability in the concentration of oxygen and degree of pollution — make adaptation on the part of the river's living organisms a necessity.

In clear, flowing waters at higher elevations *Fontinalis antipyretica* grows, an aquatic moss with branching stems thickly covered with keeled leaves. River Crowfoot (*Batrachium fluitans*), which has submerged stems with much-divided leaves floating on the surface, is also a common plant of slow-flowing water.

The banks of streams and rapid-flowing rivers do not have such greatly developed waterside vegetation as backwaters, ponds and boggy pools. However, even alongside flowing waters one will find interesting vegetation. Masses of *Rumex aquaticus* are often seen growing by water courses in valleys. Slow-flowing rivers are bordered by Amphibious Bistort (*Polygonum amphibium*), while on their surface the leaves of Shining Pondweed (*Potamogeton fluitans*) float. Meadowsweet (*Filipendula ulmaria*) grows in large masses by the waterside, as do other plants such as *Myricaria germanica*, found on stony, alluvial river deposits together with Sea Buckthorn (*Hippophaë rhamnoides*). Lowland rivers are bordered by typical flood-plain forests and waterside thickets composed of willows, poplars and alders. Here and there the blue-violet flowers of Bittersweet (*Solanum dulcamara*) are visible, replaced in the autumn by poisonous dark red berries. One may also find the large whitish flowers of Larger Bind-

Fig. 27. The River Crowfoot (*Batrachium fluitans*) grows in slow-flowing waters. The Blue Damselfly (*Calopteryx virgo*) lays its eggs on the plant's submerged parts.

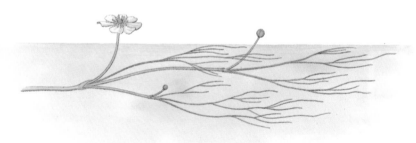

weed (*Calystegia sepium*). Often to be seen twisting and twining through waterside thickets is wild hop (*Humulus lupulus*).

Animals that live in flowing waters, particularly in swift streams, are specifically adapted to life in this environment. They often have flattened bodies and other well-developed features that help them to hold on fast to vegetation. Fish are without doubt the most familiar denizens of this aquatic environment. The cold, clear waters of the upper reaches of rivers are visited by some marine fish that may travel many hundreds of kilometres upstream from the sea to spawn. Some fish spend their youth here, only swimming downstream in maturity.

Once vast numbers of salmon swam up Europe's rivers to spawn, but people blocked the return of these beautiful fish to their spawning ground by putting dams and high weirs in their path — obstacles that the salmon found insurmountable. In many rivers salmon 'leaps' or 'ladders' have been built to allow the fish to climb up over the weirs. Much the same happened in the case of young eels (elvers), which used to leave the sea and swim upriver where their further development took place. Nowadays fishermen transport the eels inland from river mouths by various means, even by aeroplane, to release them in the places the young eels previously reached under their own steam. Only in some rivers in western and northern Europe do eels still migrate freely without outside help.

Flowing waters are also inhabited by many species of crustaceans (Crustacea) and molluscs (Mollusca) as well as large numbers of insect larvae, such as caddis flies (Trichoptera), giant dragonflies (Anisoptera), mayflies (Ephemeroptera), water beetles and the like. Streamsides and riversides also have their typical denizens. Damselflies (Zygoptera) and giant dragonflies (Anisoptera) flit about above the vegetation. Also found here are such unpleasant insects as greenflies (*Chrysops*) and gadflies (*Tabanus*), whose females suck the blood of people. They are most obnoxious pests, particularly on warm summer days before a storm. By watersides one may also find many handsome butterflies and beetles, their larvae developing on willows, poplars, aspens, willowherbs (*Epilobium*) and spurges (*Euphorbia*).

The shores of flowing waters are brightened by numerous species of birds. Wagtails (*Motacilla*) are the most common species to be seen at, or close by, the water's edge. Dippers (*Cinclus*) are good divers, plunging underwater to gather insect larvae and crustaceans on the bottom as well as to collect material for their nests,

Fig. 28. The European Eel (*Anguilla anguilla*) grows to maturity in brooks and streams.

which they build close to the water. Riverbanks are inhabited by the Little Ringed Plover (*Charadrius dubius*) which runs rapidly over the pebbles in search of insects and worms. It nests on the stony banks, making a small scrape in washed-up gravel or amid pebbles where its brownish, speckled eggs are practically indistinguishable from their surroundings.

Flowing waters also have typical mammal populations, some of which may be found on calm bodies of water as well. The European Beaver (*Castor fiber*) is partial to slow-flowing streams where it builds its characteristic dams of twigs and small stones. The Common Otter (*Lutra lutra*) excavates simple burrows in the banks of streams and rivers, while the Muskrat (*Ondatra zibethicus*) may be seen by slow-flowing streams and larger brooks.

Still Waters

Fig. 29. The Little Bittern (*Ixobrychus minutus*) builds its nest on flattened reeds.

The range of aquatic and bog plants and animals that inhabit calm bodies of water is extremely diverse and differs in many ways from the communities of streams, brooks and rivers. There is less oxygen in pools, ponds, lakes and large dams than in flowing water; with increasing depth there is less light in the water and there are increasing deposits of nutrients from decomposed dead organisms that have not been carried away by the current.

The aquatic microcosm is extraordinarily rich. A single drop of water examined under a microscope reveals a vast number of protozoans (Protozoa), otherwise invisible to the naked eye, whirling about with the aid of typical appendages such as flagella or cilia. The plant plankton is composed of microscopic green algae, blue-green algae and bacteria; the animal plankton is chiefly composed of millions of minute crustaceans (Crustacea), and is found everywhere, in ponds and pools, as well as in small water reservoirs. These creatures are well adapted to life in water. Some move with the aid of paddling feet, others, such as water-fleas (Cladocera), leap rhythmically with the aid of enlarged forked antennae that function as oars. Small crustaceans form the main food of commercially important fish.

Still stretches of water are a congenial environment for many plants with floating leaves, such as duckweed (*Lemna*), and submerged plants, such as Canadian Waterweed (*Elodea canadensis*), Water-milfoil (*Myriophyllum*) and certain pondweeds (*Potamogeton*). On the surface of calm water float the leaves of yellow water lilies (*Nuphar*) and white water lilies (*Nymphaea*) as well as those of Water Crowfoot (*Batrachium aquatile*). Most plants root in the bottom and form typical masses by the edges of still bodies of water.

The occurrence of damp-loving plants depends on the water level. Some, such as sweetflag (*Acorus*), reedmace (*Typha*), bur-reed (*Sparganium*), common reed (*Phragmites*) and Yellow Flag (*Iris pseudacorus*), form large masses at the water's edge only in places that remain permanently underwater even in periods of extreme drought. Damp-loving sedges (*Carex*) and club-rushes (*Scirpus*) grow on watersides that remain wet throughout spring or autumn and their occasionally flooded masses give way to meadow communities, which is why one will find numerous plants both by the waterside and in wet meadows or marshes.

The draining of bogs and marshes gives rise to new meadows or fields. This has led in the past to the irrevocable disappearance of many rare aquatic and bog plants, although nowadays these are generally protected by law, for example flowering rush (*Butomus*), *Iris sibirica,* Snake's Head (*Fritillaria meleagris*), Orchis, Dactylorhiza, Marsh Helleborine (*Epipactis palustris*), bogbean (*Menyanthes*), bladderwort (*Utricularia*), sundew (*Drosera*), butterwort (*Pinguicula*) and other damp-loving gems of the plant world.

Darting about above the surface of still stretches of water are predacious pond skaters (Gerridae). Below the surface live countless water beetles, superbly adapted to their aquatic environment, with hind legs serving as powerful oars, for example the back-swimmers (*Notonecta glauca*). Also found here are bloodthirsty leeches (Hirudinea), lying in wait for their prey.

Fig. 30. The leaf of Yellow Flag (*Iris pseudacorus*) serves as a launching, as well as landing, pad for the dragonfly *Libellula depressa*.

Calm bodies of water are inhabited by large numbers of amphibians. The larval development of newts (*Triturus*) takes place here, as does that of tadpoles. Some species of toads, for example Red- and Yellow-bellied Toads (*Bombina*) stay in the shallows even as adults, seeking a hiding place on dry land only during the winter. The Edible Frog (*Rana esculenta*) also stays by the water all the time, leaping into it in a flash when danger threatens.

Birds requiring an aquatic environment also possess certain adaptations. Their legs are short but strong and the toes are equipped with broad webbing. Some diving birds have legs located at the very rear of their body to serve as oars that propel them swiftly along in pursuit of underwater prey. The greatest number of bird species is to be found on large lakes and ponds which are bordered by thick vegetation to provide the birds with ample places of concealment. In damp meadows near water shorebirds (Charadriiformes) build their nests, as do various species of duck and other birds. Thickets on islands or near water are sought out by waders (Ciconiiformes) which build their nests in the branches of trees and shrubs, often forming large colonies. Cormorants (*Phalacrocorax*) are also to be seen in such places. The dense vegetation in shallows and at the water's edge is where rails (Rallidae) and warblers (*Acrocephalus*) congregate. The Great Crested Grebe (*Podiceps cristatus*) and Little Grebe (*Podiceps rufi-*

Fig. 31. The Edible Frog (*Rana esculenta*) perches on aquatic plants.

collis) conceal their floating nests amid reed-mace or reeds. Also found here is the Black-headed Gull (*Larus ridibundus*). Reedbeds provide shelter for large flocks of songbirds to roost in at night before their migratory flight south in the autumn.

Certain mammals are able to swim, having long ago moved from dry land to water and adapted to the new environment. They, too, have webbed feet to help them to swim. One such specialist is the beaver, whose flattened tail serves as a rudder.

Fig. 32. When it occurs in large numbers, the Musk Rat (*Ondatra zibethica*) can do considerable damage to the dams of ponds with its several-metre-long corridors.

Seashores

Seashores are marked by great diversity. Rocky shores are common, with cliffs rising straight up from the water. Low plateaux, regularly washed over by water and constantly pounded by the surf, bear evidence of marine life. Amid the shells and cases of animals cast up on the shore by the sea, one may find the thalli of algae and seaweeds, torn by the surf from the submerged rocks on which they grow, for example *Xanthoria*, *Lecanora* and the minute shrub-like *Ramalina*.

Salty shores, where the seawater continually soaks into the sandy soil, have a richer flora. Among the first to become established in these sandflats were the glassworts (*Salicornia herbacea* and *Salicornia prostrata*). Related to these herbaceous plants are Herbaceous Seablite (*Suaeda maritima*), *Suaeda prostrata*, Saltwort (*Salsola kali*) and *Basia hirsuta*. Sea Rocket (*Cakile maritima*) grows in salty soil from the surf line to the sand dunes. Very common in such habitats is the salt-tolerant (halophilous) and sand-tolerant (psammophilous) Common Saltmarsh Grass (*Puccinellia maritima*), which forms characteristic stands together with other halophilous species — Mud Rush (*Juncus gerardii*), Sea Rush (*Juncus maritimus*) and Sea Club-rush (*Bolboschoenus maritimus*). Sea Milkwort (*Glaux maritima*) stands up well to flooding by salt water, as well as to burial in sand. Halophilous plants are well adapted to the extreme conditions of their environment: they contain a greater concentration of salt in their cell plasma than other plants so that the greater osmotic pressure inside the cells enables them to absorb salt water more readily. For inland plants this salty, damp environment would seem extremely dry; they would be unable to absorb the water that is so saturated with salt and would suffer from both thirst and hunger. Furthermore, halophilous plants have fleshy stems and leaves and the special construction of their epidermis prevents the excessive evaporation of water.

Another type of coast landscape is spreading sandflats. A typical feature of these sandy coasts is the pronounced and continuous movement of the sandy substrate, caused by the wind. Sand is poor in nutrients, water readily seeps to great depths and the sand is a poor conductor of heat. Plants growing in these sandflats live in an unnourishing and extremely cold environment which hampers their absorption of water via their roots. Winds generally blow in from the sea, carrying the sand away from the shore to form sand dunes. On the leeward side of an obstacle, such as a stone, a clump of plants or a small heap of shells, the sand blown by the wind piles up and the dune gradually becomes bigger. Plants then grow up through the small dune or else new plants become established there, creating a new obstacle, and the dune thus increases in height as well as breadth. It is then shifted farther from the shore by the wind, most of the salt in the sand is washed out by rainwater and a secondary dune is formed. Decomposed plant remnants and the calcareous rubble from the shells of marine animals enrich this secondary dune with calcium and other elements; the sand becomes richer in nutrients and the resulting humus finally enables the growth of more demanding plants. Those that thrive here include Sand Couchgrass (*Elytrigia juncea*), Sea Aster (*Aster tripolium*), Sea Plantain (*Plantago coronopus*), Sea Pink (*Armeria maritima*), Sea Holly (*Eryngium maritimum*) and Scentless Mayweed (*Matricaria maritima*), along with grasses such as Lyme Grass (*Elymus arenaria*) and the related *Ammophilla arenaria*.

On dunes and salt-free sand farther away from the shore one may find plants with much more demanding requirements, such as Sand Sedge (*Carex arenaria*). On such firmed sands even shrubs such as Sea Buckthorn (*Hippophaë rhamnoides*) and Creeping Willow (*Salix repens*) may grow. Sands held firm by the roots of herbaceous plants and shrubs no longer shift, thus making it possible even for trees to grow there, for example the Scots Pine (*Pinus sylvestris*), a familiar inland tree that thrives in sandy soils where it forms typical pine woods.

The sea provides food for countless animals. Every day in these limitless expanses millions of tonnes of minute plankton, algae, crustaceans, molluscs and other animals serve as food for fish. In their turn the fish become food for pinnipeds and fish-eating seabirds.

High up on the seaside cliffs the gannets (*Sula bassana*) build their nests. Gannet colonies may be found on the coasts of England, Scotland, Ireland, Iceland and Brittany. Rocky islands off the northern and western coasts of Europe are the breeding grounds of the Razorbill (*Alca torda*) and the plentiful Guillemot (*Uria lomvia*). One of the most interesting seabirds is the Puffin (*Fratercula arctica*), whose European population numbers several million birds.

Gulls and terns are also common inhabitants of rocky coasts and islands. Thanks to protective measures, the Kittiwake (*Rissa tridactyla*), which forms large closed colonies, has recently even moved into ports where it builds its nest on the windowsills of tall buildings. Many species of graceful terns (Sterninae) nest on large sandy or stony beaches; here the Sandwich Tern (*Sterna sandvicensis*) forms dense colonies numbering many thousands of birds.

Numerous marine invertebrates are found on the seashore, such as crustaceans (Crustacea), molluscs (Mollusca), echinoderms (Echinodermata) and small fish left stranded in little pools or depressions in rocks when the tide ebbs. Some, for instance crabs (Brachyura), are very active on the damp sand at low tide, where they forage for food. At ebb tide flocks of birds converge on such places to feast. These include primarily gulls and terns, herons (Ardeidae) and also shorebirds (Charadriiformes), chiefly plovers (Tringinae) and sandpipers (Calidrinae). The robust Oystercatcher (*Haematopus ostralegus*), a handsome black and white bird with a red beak, cannot escape notice. It runs about in small groups on sandy beaches and shallows seeking food. When it comes upon a mollusc it pries the shell open with its beak and devours the succulent meat inside.

A typical mammal found off the coasts of Europe is the Common Seal (*Phoca vitulina*), which inhabits the coastal waters of the north Atlantic and is occasionally seen in the western Baltic. Sometimes it even strays up rivers and has been spotted 700 km inland up the Elbe.

Fig. 33. Seashores abound in countless species of crabs that feed on animal and plant remnants. This picture shows *Cancer pagurgus* and a typical plant of the North Sea coast—Thrift or Sea Pink (*Armeria maritima*).

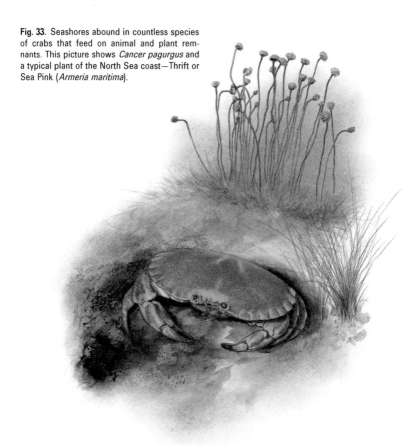

Fungi

The fungi with which we are most familiar are mushrooms with typically shaped caps, such as the Edible Boletus, Orange Cap Boletus, Chanterelle, Parasol Mushroom and toadstools. However, fungi also include yeasts, rusts, smuts and mildew. What all these organisms have in common is that they completely lack the green colouring matter called chlorophyll, by means of which green plants are able to make food through the action of sunlight. Fungi must obtain their food supply by other means. Saprophytic fungi take nourishment from organic compounds that result from the decay of dead organisms. Parasitic fungi obtain nourishment from green plants or else they may be parasitic on animals including humans. Some species of fungi live in a mutually beneficial, or symbiotic, association with other plants; such a symbiotic

Fig. 1. The striking Edible Boletus is one of the most sought-after mushrooms.

association of the mycelium of a fungus with the roots of a seed plant is termed a mycorrhiza.

Saprophytic fungi are usually ground plants, but some, such as the saprophytic bracket fungus *Fomes fomentarius,* also grow on the wood of fallen trees. The thin-walled mycelium of these fungi absorbs water and, with it, the dissolved nutrients from decomposed humus, as well as the decaying bodies of dead plants and animals.

The mycelium of parasitic fungi invades the tissues of the living plants from which it obtains nourishment. This, of course, weakens or even completely destroys the host plant. Parasitic pests of trees are mainly the Honey Fungus (*Armillaria mellea*), some *Pleurotus* and many bracket fungi (Polyporaceae).

Mycorrhitic fungi are the ones we know best and the ones most eagerly sought by mushroom pickers. *Suilus luteus* grows beneath pine trees, *Suilus grevillei* lives symbiotically with larches. *Boletus edulis, Boletus pinophilus* and *Boletus aestivalis* were all named after the tree with the roots of which their mycelium lives in a symbiotic association that is beneficial to both the fungus and the tree. The fibres of the mycelium envelop the tips of minute rootlets, penetrate their cells, from which they absorb certain substances, and in return transfer other substances into these cells.

Many fungi are important agents in the food industry. All types of fermentation, be it in the making of beer, wine or vinegar, or in the leavening of dough, are made possible by the action of microscopic fungi known as yeasts. Some yeasts cause undesirable fermentation, for example the clouding of beer, others may even cause skin diseases in people and animals.

Other fungi (moulds) may cause food and other products to become mouldy, for example spoiling camera film in the tropics. Others, as pathogenic organisms, may cause disease in animals and people. Some moulds give cheeses their specific smell and taste during the ripening process. These moulds are mainly members of the genus *Penicillium,* such as *P. camembertii, P. gorgonzola, P. roquefortii.* Ranking high on the list of useful moulds are those that produce antibiotics such as penicillin (*P. notatum* and *P. chrysogenum*), patulin (*P. patulum*) and griseofulvin (*P. griseum*) which has a fungicidal effect.

There are fungi that are edible and tasty, some that are inedible, unappetizing or bland, others that are revoltingly bitter, and some that are extremely poisonous. Boletus mushrooms, most of which are edible and very tasty, also include several inedible species, for example

Fig. 2. *Tylopilus felleus* is often mistaken for an edible mushroom. It can be readily identified, however, by the prominent network on the stipe and also by its sharp burning taste — tasting just a tiny piece suffices!

Boletus albidus and *B. calopus,* as well as species that vary from slightly to extremely poisonous — *B. luridus, B. satanas.* On the other hand, among toadstools, which are generally inedible and which also include the deadly *Amanita virosa* and the Deathcap (*A. phalloides*), one will find species that are extremely tasty, for example the Blusher (*A. rubescens*). The tastiest of the lot is *A. caesarea,* highly prized as far back as the days of the ancient Romans but nowadays, alas, very rare.

Fig. 3. *Macrolepiota rhacodes* can be readily distinguished from *Macrolepiota procera* by the pronounced colour reaction of the flesh, which turns orange-red to brownish-red when pressed or cut. Both parasol mushrooms are edible.

Some lower fungi are dangerous pests of important crops. Particularly harmful to vineyards, especially in damp, warm summer weather, is *Plasmopara viticola*. This pest was introduced into Europe from America in the mid-nineteenth century. In the first years, before the application of an effective pesticide, it caused great worry to vintners by making the grapes shrivel, turn

a leathery brown and fall prematurely. Also introduced into Europe from America, at the beginning of the nineteenth century, was the potato blight caused by *Phytophtora infestans*. Affected leaves first develop dark spots and later a white coating on the underside; the potato tubers become dry, leathery and mummified.

Some fungi may be harmful in one respect and beneficial in another. Ergot (*Claviceps purpurea*) is harmful in grain crops because it is poisonous, but is beneficial in that its alkaloids may be used in the pharmaceutical industry in the preparation of valuable medicines. *Apiocrea chrysosperma* is harmful to various boletus mushrooms, in particular *Xerocomus chrysenteron*. The related *Byssonectria luteovirens* attacks russulas and other gill fungi. *Morchella* and *Helvella* sp. number among their relatives not only *Rhytisma acerinum* but also the dangerous *Monilinia furstigena* which causes a dis-

60

ease of fruit that spreads from rotting apples and pears to ripening fruits. The diseased fruits then fall or else remain, dried and mummified, on the tree throughout the winter. If the infected fruits are not burned, the disease spreads and attacks the branches which, in the case of cherry trees, will then die back.

Common to all fungi are two types of spore production. In the fruiting body of Ascomycetes there are sac-like structures called asci, in which the propagating bodies, or spores, are formed. Basidiomycetes produce spores at the end of special cells called basidia. In gill fungi these form on the edge of the lamellae (gills); in tube fungi they form inside the tubes.

The thallus of fungi is generally fibrous. Fungal filaments, called hyphae, form a mycelium from which small propagating organs or large fruiting bodies grow.

The classification of fungi into families is based on the identification of features on the fruiting bodies and on the structure and production of spores.

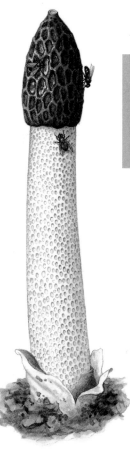

Fig. 4. Development of the fruiting body of the Stinkhorn (*Phallus impudicus*). The spores are dispersed by flies that lick the malodorous, slimy layer on the cap.

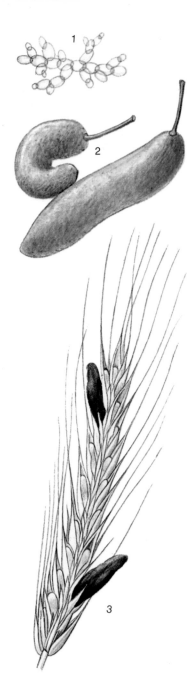

Division: **Fungi**—Mycophyta

Class: Ascomycetes

Subclass: Protoascomycetidae

Family: Saccharomycetaceae

1 *Saccharomyces cerevisiae*. Unicellular fungus, known as yeast, visible only under microscope. Of considerable economic value as it is used to leaven dough. Other species are used to ferment wine, cider and beer. In the wild it lives on fruits and other parts of many plants. Propagates by budding; the dividing cells mostly remaining together and forming branched strings.

Family: Taphrinaceae

2 *Taphrina pruni* (syn. *Exoascus pruni*) ('bladder plum'). Attacks fruits of plum-trees causing them to grow large, lop-sided and bladder-like. *T. deformans* ('peach-leaf curl') causes the leaves of peaches and almonds to curl and swell, finally turning bright red. Dense bunches of twigs — witches brooms — are formed on trees attacked by *T. insititiae*. Related species of this fungus cause similar deformations on birches and hornbeams. The mycelium grows through branches or fruits of host plant and terminal cells develop into asci with spores on surface. Asci grow so close to each other that they appear as fine hoar frost on branches or fruits of afflicted plants.

Subclass: Euascomycetidae

Family: Clavicipitaceae

3 Ergot *Claviceps purpurea*. Parasitic on seeds of grasses, particularly rye. Infection is caused by spores producing hyphae which consume ovary and form a black, horny, seed-like sclerotium. This falls to ground and winters in soil. Red-stalked fruiting bodies (*ascophores*) with club-like tips grow from them the following year and produce more spores which are dispersed by wind or insects when the grasses or grain crops are flowering. Ergot is deadly poisonous; its alkaloids are used in the preparation of valuable medicines.

Family: Phacidiaceae

4 *Rhytisma acerinum* ('tar spot'). Parasitic on maple leaves. Forms irregular to rounded, conspicuously large, black, yellow-bordered spots on upper surface of leaves. In spring these

black fruiting bodies produce asci full of slender spores. Parasitic also on sow-thistle leaves. Related *Rhytisma punctatum* grows parasitically on sycamore and another member of the genus causes spots on willow leaves.

Family: Morchellaceae (syn. Helvellaceae)

5 Morel *Morchella esculenta*. Fruiting body consists of cap and stalk. Cap mostly ovoid or globose, up to 8 cm high, yellowish to brownish, with irregular, deep and broad cavities that do not form continuous rows, rather recalling a crumpled honeycomb. Well-known spring mushroom, grows in April and May in open deciduous or mixed forests but also in old gardens, parks and yards. Edible only when young.

Old fruit bodies, in which decomposition of albumins takes place, may cause serious poisoning.

Family: Helvellaceae

6 *Gyromitra esculenta*. Brown to dark brown hollow cap, irregularly lobed and wrinkled, up to 10 cm. wide. Stalk whitish to yellowish, hollow, sometimes wrinkled on surface and shorter than cap. Grows in spring in sandy pine-woods, also in other coniferous forests. Sensitivity of man to it varies; it is poisonous to some, even deadly. Therefore, this fungus should never be eaten. Related species *Gyromitra gigas* with lighter cap may be eaten without danger after scalding.

6

4

5

Class: Basidiomycetes

Subclass: Heterobasidiomycetidae

Family: Pucciniaceae

1 *Puccinia graminis.* Parasitic on cereals as well as on barberry. Rusty patches of powdery spores on under surface of barberry leaves. Spores spread by wind on to cereals or other grasses where they germinate. On leaves of these plants so-called summer spores are formed during the growing season. In summer rust spreads by these spores and causes infection of neighbouring plants. At the end of growing season black patches of winter spores form; they overwinter and the following spring each one germinates to produce a basidium with four stalked spores. These are spread by wind and again infect barberry leaves. The sequence of various spore types and alternation of host plants is characteristic of many species of rusts.

Subclass: Homobasidiomycetidae

Order: Hymenomycetales

Family: Corticiaceae

2 *Stereum hirsutum.* Grows on trunks and stumps of deciduous trees. The stemless, shell-like fruiting bodies are yellowish-grey and somewhat leathery, often with a paler zoned striping; the surface varies from soft velvety to shaggy felt in texture. Under surface grey-yellow when dry, reddish in wet weather. A similar species, *Stereum sanguinolentum*, has fruiting bodies with greyish surface. Turns blood-red when injured.

Family: Polyporaceae

3 *Trametes versicolor.* Somewhat fleshy to leathery fruiting bodies form fan-shaped, often overlapping clusters, ornamented with concentric dark and light stripes of brown, grey, orange or yellowish velvety hairs; whitish beneath. Abundant on stumps and decayed trunks of deciduous trees and shrubs, also on dry branches. Related species *Trametes zonatus* has no conspicuous striping. Both species are inedible.

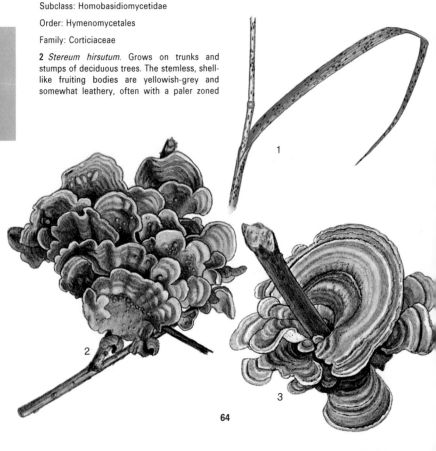

4 *Polyporus squamosus.* Young fruiting bodies convex, older ones widely expanded with a depressed centre; stalk (stipe) short and thick. Whitish to brownish-yellow, roughly circular cap thinly covered with darkish, mostly brown, relatively large scales. Flesh white, whitish to yellowish or slightly brown. Grows on branches, trunks, roots and stumps of deciduous trees, especially nut-trees, individually or in groups, from spring to winter. Young, crisp and still not leathery fruiting bodies edible. Strikingly cucumber-like, floury taste.

5 *Grifola sulphurea* (syn. *Laetiporus sulphureus*). Fruiting bodies fleshy, juicy when young, later tough and brittly crumbling. Cap flat against the tree, usually in tufts densely set one above another. Young fruit bodies bright sulphur yellow, mature even orange, old ones brownish. Grows abundantly on stumps, branches and trunks of deciduous trees in woods but also in parks and gardens. Edible when young, but has a slightly acid, woody taste and seldom eaten.

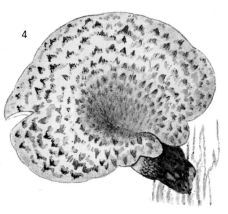

6 *Phellinus igniarius.* Hoof-shaped fruit bodies on trunks of poplars, willows and other trees where they often grow to large size. Cap flat against the tree without stipe, consists of layers; upper surface greyish to blackish. Fruit bodies of this fungus and of its relative *Fomes fomentarius* served once as fuel. In poor mountainous regions fruiting bodies of the latter used to be processed into fine, leathery sheets from which caps and waistcoats were made.

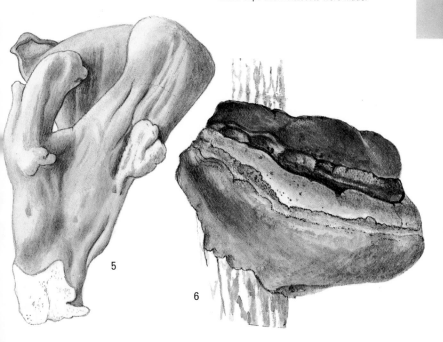

Family: Hydnaceae

1 *Sarcodon imbricatus* (syn. *Hydnum imbricatum*). Shallow, funnel-shaped cap with rim inrolled when young, 6—18 cm wide, brownish to grey-brown, thickly covered with large, black-grey scales, thickest in centre. Underside of cap thickly covered with greyish to brownish bristles. Grows in coniferous woods, especially pine-woods, in late summer and autumn. In places used for preparing soups and sauces. Only young specimens are suitable, old ones tough.

Family: Clavariaceae

2 *Ramaria flava* (syn. *Clavaria aurea*). Edible species with dense coral-like tufts of fruiting bodies. Distinguishable from other inedible *Ramaria* species by yellow colour of branches which do not turn red on bruised spots. The stalk and flesh are white. In places, especially in warm regions, it occurs abundantly in forests at beginning of autumn and end of summer. Related *Sparassis crispa* is edible. Its fruiting body formed by flattened undulate branchlets weighs up to several kilograms.

Family: Boletaceae

3 *Boletus felleus* (syn. *Tylopilus felleus*). May easily be mistaken for edible boletus. Differs from it by more striking olive-brown network on stipe. Under surface pinkish, when bruised turning rusty brown. Hot bitter taste, quite inedible, even if not poisonous. Abundant forest mushroom, especially in coniferous woods in higher altitudes; in lowlands and deciduous woods occurs only occasionally.

4 Edible Boletus *Boletus edulis*. Most sought after and most frequent of three similar boleti. Pine boletus and oak boletus are differentiated, apart from colouring, by symbiosis with roots of different trees. Stipe of edible boletus has white network in upper part and the smooth cap

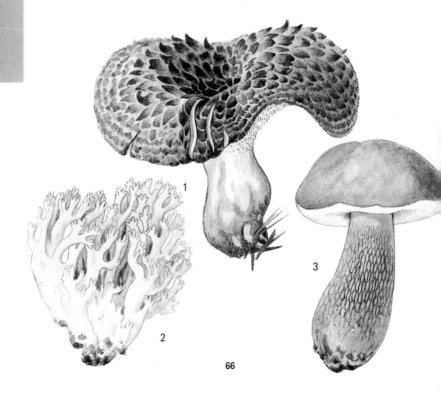

is pale brown; more frequent summer oak boletus has network with large mesh on whole of stipe; pine boletus has fine, thick network. Edible boletus is found especially in pine-woods from July to October, from lowlands to mountains; oak boletus from spring to September in deciduous forests, occasionally under other trees; pine boletus grows during summer as well as in autumn in sandy pine-woods, rarely in other woods in lower altitudes.

5 *Boletus luteus* (syn. *Ixocomus luteus*). Chocolate brown to brownish-yellow cap with easily peelable, membranous skin. In wet weather stickily slimy; shiny and smooth when dry. Young fruit bodies have cap connected with stalk by a membranous skin (volva). After the cap has burst through, the remains of volva appear as a ruff-like ring on the stipe. Stipe above ring whitish-yellow, with a darker speckling. Found in grassy places at outskirts of pine forests, usually during whole summer and autumn, from lowlands to mountains. Excellent edible species.

6 *Boletus chrysenteron.* Cap of young fruiting bodies dark brown, smooth, of older ones yellow-brown with an irregular pattern of reddish cracks. Stalk relatively thin, dirty yellow to yellow-brown with touch of red. Under surface yellow, later olive, taking on a blue tint when bruised. Frequent summer and autumnal mushroom. Grows in all woods, more abundant in pine-woods, from lowlands to foothills. Frequently sought after but not very valuable due to considerable fragility.

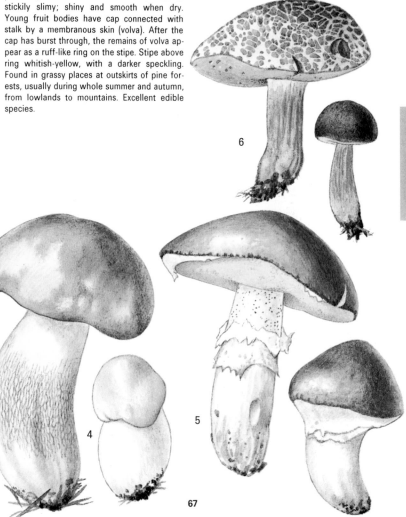

6

5

4

Family: Boletaceae

1 *Boletus scaber.* Fleshy cap greyish to dark brown, often cracked in dry conditions, pulp watery whitish, early becomes soft; under surface greyish to buff, also soon becoming soft. Stalk long, tough, whitish to brownish-grey, fibrous, covered with tiny blackish scales, flesh when cut turns faintly rosy. In summer and autumn found frequently under birches or aspens.

2 *Boletus aurantiacus.* Fruit body with dark orange to maroon cap. Stipe long, tough, white to greyish, at first covered with whitish, later with reddish to brownish flaky scales. White flesh turns greyish to black. Occurs abundantly in woodland of various types but usually under aspen and birch. Grows from summer to autumn from lowlands to mountains. A similar species, *Boletus testaceoscaber*, has lighter, rather orange cap; young fruiting bodies have blackish scales on stipe.

Family: Cantharellaceae

3 Chanterelle *Cantharellus cibarius.* Young fruit bodies with a convex cap: as it matures, the margins grow up to form a shallow funnel shape. Whole fruit bodies almost yolk yellow, flesh whitish to yellowish. Found from summer to autumn very abundantly in coniferous woods, most frequently in pine-woods. Sought after for preparing fried dishes and pickling in vinegar.

Family: Agaricaceae

4 *Agaricus campestris.* Young fruit bodies have elongated globose cap, later fibrous, brownish and scaly. Whitish flesh; the gills beneath pinkish, maturing to chocolate brown. Whitish stalk with conspicuous ring encircling it in upper third. Never has sheath at base of stalk as is characteristic of deadly poisonous species such as Fool's Mushroom (*Amanita verna*) and

4

5

6

Avenging Angel (*Amanita virosa*). Both differ from *Agaricus campestris* by always having white gills and the fact that they grow largely under deciduous trees. *Agaricus campestris* is found in grassy places, mostly out of woods. In forests, especially spruce-woods, it is replaced by Horse Mushroom (*Agaricus arvensis*).

Family: Lepiotaceae

5 Parasol Mushroom *Lepiota procera.* Stalk up to 35 cm high; cap at first convex, sometimes with small central swelling or umbo, later widely expanded, brownish with torn scales on surface. Flesh and gills white or whitish. Bulbous based stalk has a loose ring. Grows from summer to autumn in spruce-woods but also in other conif-

erous or mixed forests and in grassy places from lowlands to mountains. Commonly prepared in various ways for its attractive meaty flavour.

Family: Tricholomataceae

6 St. Georges Mushroom *Tricholoma gambosum.* Popular spring delicacy; grows from April in grass or sparse woods under deciduous trees and shrubs. Cap whitish, yellowish to brownish, gills white or grey-yellow. Short cylindrical whitish stipe. Flesh has a mealy taste and smell. Young fruiting bodies easily mistaken for poisonous *Rhodophyllus sinuatus* (syn. *Entoloma lividum*) which, however, does not grow until summer and has salmon-pink gills when mature.

69

Family: Russulaceae

1 *Russula cyanoxantha.* Cap violet, green, violet-green or greenish with violet tint. Flesh whitish, gills white to yellowish, flexible and not brittle, unlike other members of this genus. Grows abundantly in summer and autumn in mixed or deciduous woods, from lowlands to foothills. Suitable mainly for preparing soups and sauces and for pickling in vinegar in a mixture containing boleti.

2 Sickener *Russula emetica.* Strikingly red cap hardly confusable with edible mushrooms. Young fruiting body has convex cap, old ones flattened, often shallowly concave in centre. Gills and stipe white to light yellowish, flesh whitish. May cause vomiting if eaten raw. Edible when cooked, but best avoided. Found from summer to autumn in all woods with acid soils, especially in mixed and coniferous forests.

3 Saffron Milk Cap *Lactarius deliciosus.* Young fruiting bodies have convex cap, in maturity expanded, concave in centre, red-orange, as a rule with several dark, mostly green, concentric circles. When cut, flesh releases orange milk, gills become greenish on bruising. Grows mainly in autumn in grassy places in coniferous woods, especially in young spruce-woods. Commonly pickled in vinegar for its characteristic spicy taste. It can hardly be confused with inedible *Lactarius torminosus* which exudes white milk and mostly grows under birches.

Family: Amanitaceae

4 Death Cap *Amanita phalloides.* Most poisonous European mushroom. Yellow-green, pure green or brown-green cap is convex at first, later flattened. Stipe, flesh and gills whitish to greenish. Stipe with white skirt-like ring has a cup-shaped base and a conspicuous whitish to greyish sheath, torn at tips. Grows quite abundantly in summer and autumn in deciduous or mixed woods in warmer regions, in coniferous forests especially under pines. Inconspicuous, rather sweetish, treacherous taste. Contains at least two deadly poisonous substances.

5 Blusher *Amanita rubescens.* Fleshy cap is rose to maroon with brownish warty scales. When cut, the flesh is reddish, gills whitish with pink tint. Strong, slender stalk with swollen base. Beneath the cap there is flared whitish to grey-rose ring, usually thickly grooved on upper side. Distinguishable from similar inedible toadstools by reddening of pulp and by ring grooving. *Amanita rubescens* grows in summer and autumn from lowlands to mountains in all types of forests, especially under spruces.

6 Fly Agaric *Amanita muscaria.* Much less poisonous than Death Cap or Avenging Angel, being of rather intoxicating character. Cap ornamented with whitish or yellowish warty patches on coral-red surface. Flesh and gills whitish to yellowish, stalk white, with concentric rings of volva remains at base. Ungrooved wide ring under cap. Summer to late autumn in coniferous and birch woods.

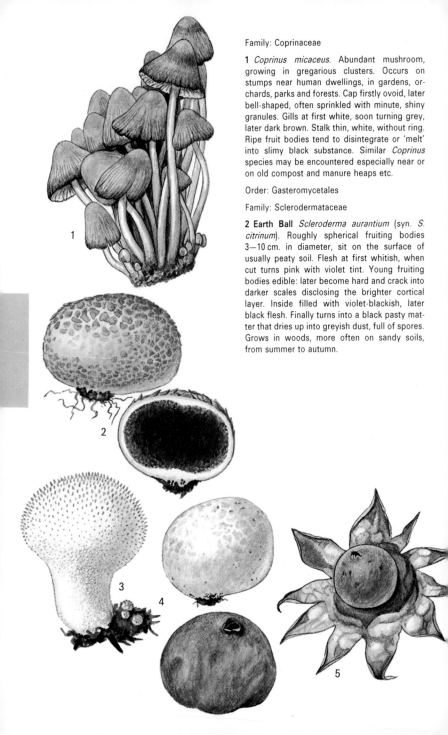

Family: Coprinaceae

1 *Coprinus micaceus.* Abundant mushroom, growing in gregarious clusters. Occurs on stumps near human dwellings, in gardens, orchards, parks and forests. Cap firstly ovoid, later bell-shaped, often sprinkled with minute, shiny granules. Gills at first white, soon turning grey, later dark brown. Stalk thin, white, without ring. Ripe fruit bodies tend to disintegrate or 'melt' into slimy black substance. Similar *Coprinus* species may be encountered especially near or on old compost and manure heaps etc.

Order: Gasteromycetales

Family: Sclerodermataceae

2 Earth Ball *Scleroderma aurantium* (syn. *S. citrinum*). Roughly spherical fruiting bodies 3—10 cm. in diameter, sit on the surface of usually peaty soil. Flesh at first whitish, when cut turns pink with violet tint. Young fruiting bodies edible: later become hard and crack into darker scales disclosing the brighter cortical layer. Inside filled with violet-blackish, later black flesh. Finally turns into a black pasty matter that dries up into greyish dust, full of spores. Grows in woods, more often on sandy soils, from summer to autumn.

Family: Lycoperdaceae

3 Warted Puffball *Lycoperdon perlatum* (syn. *L. gemmatum*). Narrowed bases of pear-shaped fruiting bodies grow from soil. Surface of young body whitish or creamy, yellowish with pointed warts. Ripe fruiting body smooth with irregularly round aperture on top; when pressed or stepped on, a cloud of brownish spores is puffed out of this opening. Summer and autumnal, growing from lowlands high up to mountains, in meadows, pastures and spruce-woods, often in great numbers. Young fruit bodies with white flesh edible.

4 *Bovista plumbea.* Young fruiting bodies almost globose, slightly compressed on top; outer surface whitish, inside pure white. Ripe ones dark grey, filled with brown dust-like spore mass; when pressed, spores fly out through oval opening on top. In summer and autumn found abundantly in grassy places, at the edges of meadows and pastures and on the outskirts of forests, from lowlands to mountains. Edible when young; has excellent delicate taste.

Family: Geastraceae

5 *Geastrum fimbriatum.* Young fruiting bodies more or less globose; in maturity outer layer cracks into four ray-like segments which turn inside out thrusting up the ovoid fruiting 'capsule' on a short stem-like neck. Grows in summer and autumn from lowlands to mountains with other species of earth-stars, often in groups, especially in spruce-woods. Unsuitable for eating.

Family: Phallaceae

6 Stinkhorn *Phallus impudicus.* Conspicuous for its appearance and in maturity also for the disgusting smell of decaying flesh. Slightly reminiscent of morel with long, cylindrical stalk and conical, pitted cap. Globular fruiting bodies rather resemble small puffballs when young as they are covered with white-skinned jelly-like layer. In mature specimens only conspicuous sheath at stalk base remains of this layer. Stalk up to 25 cm high, thickly and shallowly porous. Cap covered with olive greenish slime which attracts insects that normally feed on carrion. Grows from summer to autumn in deciduous woods and in gardens on humus-rich soil. Mature fruiting bodies inedible because of bad odour.

6

Lichens

Lichens are also called lichenized fungi. In lichens a fungus tissue lives in a symbiotic association with an alga. This dual association is different from the saprophytic, parasitic or symbiotic properties of fungi.

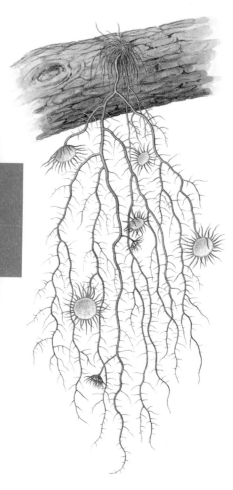

Even though both fungi and lichens can live independently, albeit with difficulty, it is only when the hyphae of fungi are joined with the cells of algae that the typical thallus of a lichen is formed. The symbiotic association of fungus and alga is also of physiological importance. Although the fungus takes the products of photosynthesis from the alga, it also provides the latter with water and essential salts. Symbiosis is distinguished by certain products of the metabolism, for example lichen acids, which neither the fungus nor the alga is able to produce by itself — these are formed in the thallus or plant body of the lichen.

In most lichens the fungal component, called the mycobiont, is generally composed of ascomycetes; in tropical regions it also contains basidiomycetes. The algal component, phycobiont, may consist of green algae, especially Chlorococcales, or blue-green algae, for example colonies of *Nostoc* or *Chrococcus* sp. Despite their great diversity of shapes, lichens may be roughly divided into three groups: having a crusty thallus, laminar thallus or forked thallus. The internal structure of lichens is also very diverse but usually the fungal component prevails. The tangled hyphae of the fungus form a dense outer layer. Beneath this is a looser layer of fungal fibres and algae, then a loose layer of fungal fibres and often, on the bottom, another layer of thickly intertwined fungal fibres from which individual fibres or clumps of fibres grow into the substrate on which the lichen lives.

The propagating bodies of the fungus are important in the classification of lichens, because the alga remains in a vegetative state. This explains why lichens are called lichenized fungi. The fungal component may be classified according to the fruiting body in the system of fungi, but the lichen thallus can be formed only if the fungus spores develop into fibres that meet up with the respective alga.

Lichens may be found in widely diverse situations and on varied substrates. They commonly grow on the bark of trees, on rotting wood, on rocks, boulders and walls. Individual species sometimes have special requirements, some growing only on limestone rocks, others only on siliceous substrates. Some lichens may be found high up in the mountains, others in lowland country; some species prefer sunny locations, others need habitats that are shaded and damp. Different species grow on broad-leaved

Fig. 1. The striking *Usnea florida* cannot escape notice. It is an extremely sensitive indicator of atmospheric pollution in the mountains.

74

Fig. 2. The thalli of the various species of *Cladonia* differ in shape as well as colour. *Left: Cladonia sylvatica; right: Cladonia coccifera.*

trees and on the bark of conifers. Most European lichens are extremely sensitive to atmospheric pollution.

Lichens growing on the bark of fruit trees are considered harmful for they may have a detrimental effect on the respiration of the tree as well as promoting dampness and the presence of harmful insects. In Scandinavia ground lichen, especially Reindeer Moss (*Cladonia rangiferina*), are eaten by reindeer, in deserts they may serve as food for people. In the Bible we are told of the 'manna' that was miraculously supplied to the Israelites on their journey through the desert — possibly the thalli of *Lecanora esculenta* that had been uprooted and blown there by the wind.

Roccella tinctoria, which grows on the Mediterranean coast, *Ochrolechia tartarea* and *O. parella*, lichens of the tundra, yield compounds that are used to make the colouring matter litmus and orcein. Lichens also yield polysaccharides and alcohol. They are used in the perfume industry in some countries, and some species even produce substances with antibiotic properties. Lichens also contain several specific compounds that are not found in other organisms.

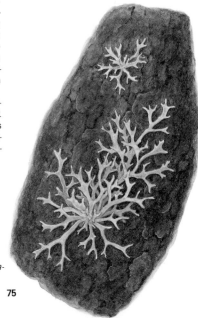

Fig. 3. A young fruiting body of *Evernia prunastri* growing on the bark of a tree.

75

Division: **Lichens**—Lichenes

Class: Ascolichenes

Family: Buelliaceae

1 *Rhizocarpon geographicum.* Appears as yellow-green, black striated patches on non-limestone rocks. Irregularly lobed thalluses form striking designs resembling maps. Thin, corticular thallus contains in addition to algal cells also hyphae of an Ascomycetes. (Basidiomycetes are a component of tropical lichens.) Tiny fruit bodies of fungal component are black with multicellular spores. Grows mainly in mountains, most often on granite boulders.

2 *Cladonia arbuscula* (syn. *C. sylvatica*). Very abundant species, resembling Reindeer Moss from which it differs especially in colouring; it is yellow-green or straw-yellow, its podetia are narrower and slightly brownish at the shoot

ends. Fungal component sometimes forms tiny maroon thalluses on twig tips. Grows in similar places as reindeer moss, together often forming extensive carpets.

3 Reindeer Moss *Cladonia rangiferina*. Forms conspicuous whitish or greyish bushes, abundantly branched. Twigs bent to one side, with brownish tips. Often grows in great quantity in dry pine-woods and on heathland, from lowlands to mountains. Can survive long periods of drought; in rain takes in moisture very quickly again.

4 *Cladonia fimbriata.* 1—3 cm high cups, olive or grey-green on upper side, whitish on under side, grow from a basal scaly podetium. Fungal component forms short-stalked, brownish fruit bodies on margins of cups. Cup surface covered with powdery segments, containing alga cells wound around with fungal hyphae. Grows on dry sites, in open woods, heathlands, on decayed stumps and mossy rocks from lowlands to mountains. Related species have fungal fruit bodies scarlet-red and cup rims strikingly notched.

Family: Peltigeraceae

5 *Peltigera canina.* Thallus broadly lobed, sometimes with lobes up to 5 cm wide, upper side grey-white or brownish, finely felt-like, underside whitish, covered with numerous bunches of fungal rhizoids. Fruiting bodies of fungal component brown, tubular, erect at end of lobes. Common lichen from lowlands high up to mountains. Grows in sunny spots, on mossy rocks, on putrefying trunks as well as in meadows.

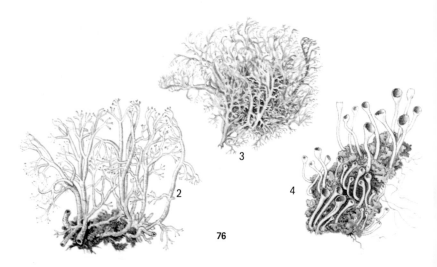

Family: Parmeliaceae

6 *Hypogymnia physodes* (syn. *Parmelia physodes*). Probably the most frequently found lichen. Its rosette-like thallus is greyish to grey-green on upper surface, dark brown to black on underside, bordered with white. Fruiting bodies of fungal component appear only rarely. Grows abundantly from lowlands to foothills. In suitable places forms extensive coatings on tree trunks and branches. Also grows on stumps, dead trunks, less often on rocks and earth.

7 Iceland Moss *Cetraria islandica*. Thallus chestnut to dark brown, sinuately branched, spiny margined, ascending, up to 10 cm high, or more. Grows on moorland and heathland and in forests and peat-bogs; indicator of poor soils.

Family: Usneaceae

8 *Evernia prunastri*. Grows from lowlands to mountains on bark of deciduous trees, old shrubs, also on trunks of felled trees, in orchards, parks, gardens and open woods; abundant everywhere, rare only on rocks. Soft thallus is many-branched, often more or less pendent, grey-green to yellow-green, lighter on underside, white-spotted edges and upper side. Similar species, *Evernia furfuracea,* with black-violet underside of thallus, grows in similar places and on rocks and walls at higher altitudes.

Family: Teloschistaceae

9 *Xanthoria parietina*. Brightly coloured thalluses are light to orange-yellow, arranged in rosettes, forming neat patches on trees rocks and walls. Dish-like fruiting bodies of fungal component are very frequently seen. Grows from lowlands to mountains, but particularly near the sea.

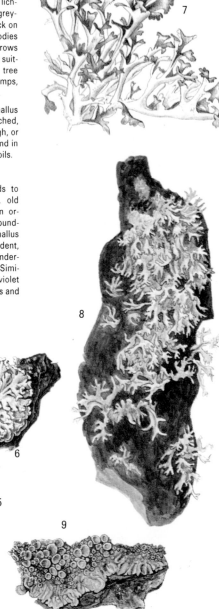

Bryophytes—Mosses and Liverworts

Mosses and liverworts (Bryopsida, Marchantiopsida) are green, mostly ground-dwelling plants that have much in common with other higher green plants, having spore-bearing pteridophytes and gymnosperms as well as angiosperms. They contain chlorophyll and so are capable of photosynthesis, the product of this process being the starch found in liverwort oil. However, their external resemblance to higher plants is deceptive. A moss plant does not have true roots, only underground root-like structures called rhizoids. Even its stem is not a true stem

Fig. 1. *Polytrichum commune* is the most robust European moss, reaching a height of 40 cm. The capsule is closed by a lid covered by a calyptra that falls at maturity.

Fig. 2. Section of the capsule of *Polytrichum commune*. Beneath the lid are locules separated by partitions and filled with spores.

Fig. 3. The stem as well as the branches of *Sphagnum palustre* are covered with minute leaves.

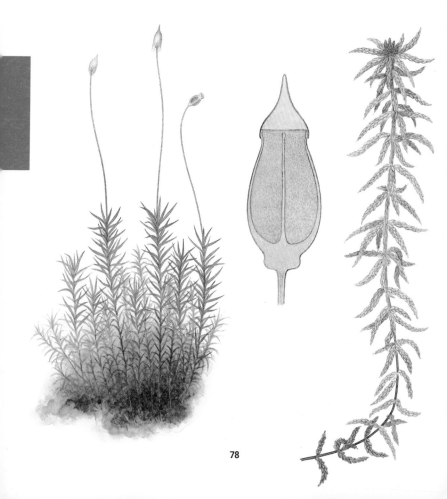

for it has few differentiated tissues, lacks true vascular bundles and the leaves are generally composed of only a single layer of cells. Sometimes the thallus is not differentiated into a stem and leaves at all, as in Anthocerotopsida and some liverworts. The propagating and reproductive organs, on the other hand, resemble those of pteridophytes.

Monoecious species have both male and female sex organs in the same individual; dioecious species have male reproductive organs in one individual and female organs in another. Following fertilization, an asexual sporophyte develops, connected to the plant by a stalk through which it draws nutritive substances. This filamentous stalk is terminated by a capsule containing spores. On germination, each spore produces a protonema from which the plant proper grows — this is called the sexual stage.

Bryophytes have no medicinal or edible uses by people. However, clumps of moss do have an extremely beneficial effect on the amount of water in the soil. Mosses have no roots and thus absorb very little moisture from the soil; furthermore, they prevent excessive evaporation of water from the soil. Sphagnums (Sphagnidae) are also important for many other reasons. They grow on poor soils in districts with great amounts of rainfall, or with plenty of underground water. Sphagnums will grow only above the water level; below it they die and partially decompose, forming a small layer of peat every year. In a single year they grow up to 1 cm above ground, and in that same period the layer of peat is increased by an equal amount below the water level because of the inability of decomposition to take place without the access of air. This process has been going on for centuries, which should give one some idea of the great depth of the layers of peat that have formed on high moors. Other, undemanding plants that grow in these localities also contribute to the formation of peat, for example sedges (*Carex*), cotton-grass (*Eriophorum*) and rushes (*Juncus*).

Extracted peat is a very important product. In gardening it is used to lighten the soil. In health hydros it is used in peat baths and body packs. Natural moors are reservoirs of water for the creation of rivers, and these also have a determining effect on the climate.

Bryophytes may be found in widely diverse situations. Liverworts generally grow in damp and shady places, but are also found on rocks, in dry soil and on the bark of trees. Some even grow in ponds, for example *Riccia fluitans*. Stubble

Fig. 4. The reproductive organs of *Marchantia polymorpha* are on stalks; the female ones are star-shaped, the male organs umbrella-shaped. Vegetative propagation is by tiny bodies embedded in shallow cups.

and damp fields are the preferred habitat of *Anthoceros punctatus*, the thalli of which are marked with black dots — mucilaginous cells inside which the blue-green alga *Nostoc* lives in symbiosis.

Mosses also occur in diverse localities, on tree trunks and stumps, on rocks, on walls and roofs and in woodland as well as meadow soils. They include species that form floating clumps in woodland streams, such as *Fontinalis antipyretica*, as well as ones that grow in bogs, at the edge of water and in many other places.

It is estimated that there are some 25,000 species of bryophytes. Their differentiation into families is based on the morphology of the capsules and on the anatomical structure of the leaves.

Division: **Mosses and Liverworts**—Bryophyta

Class: **Liverworts**—Hepaticopsida

Family: Marchantiaceae

1 *Marchantia polymorpha.* Lamellar thallus broadly ribbon-shaped, forked, ground hugging. The upper side has conspicuous air chambers just beneath the surface, each having a breathing pore. Dioecious plant with sexual organs on stalked discs; male discs irregularly lobular, female ones star-shaped. Vegetative propagation by special tiny bodies (*gemmae*) embedded in shallow cups. Forms dark green coatings everywhere in moist places; particularly in gardens and greenhouses. Grows from lowlands to mountains in sunny or semi-shaded places.

Class: **Mosses**—Bryopsida (syn. Musci)

Subclass: Sphagnidae

Family: Sphagnaceae

2 *Sphagnum palustre.* Requires plenty of light as do majority of bog-mosses. Forms soft pale green carpets. Stems 10—40 cm high with clustered side branches rosetted towards the tips; more frequently than in other bog-mosses stem bears round brown capsules at apex which explode on ripening. All members of this genus are important for creation of moss peat.

Subclass: **True Mosses**—Bryidae

Family: Polytrichaceae

3 *Polytrichum commune.* Stout moss whose simple, erect stems can reach a length of 25 cm. Sharply notched leaflets thickly overlap and cover stem during dry spells, standing out and apart in wet weather. Red stalk about 10 cm long. Large capsule covered with hairy, yellow to reddish brown calyptra. Grows in mountains, hill country, heathland, along forest streams and in clearings. Tiny relative *Polytrichum formosum* is more frequent in lowlands. Its leaves stand apart even during dry conditions.

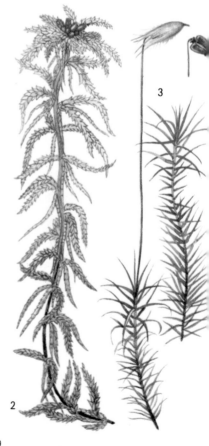

Family: Dicranaceae

4 *Dicranum scoparium.* Erect stems up to 10 cm high, thickly set with sickle-bent, blunt leaflets, finely notched at tip. Stems 2—4 cm high, reddish, with brown, cylindrical, slightly bent capsule having a long-beaked reddish lid. Cap overlaps from lid to capsule. A moss of coniferous woods, growing abundantly on ground, tree stumps, trunks, boulders and rocks, from lowlands to mountains.

Family: Ditrichaceae

5 *Ceratodon purpureus.* Erect stems, sparsely covered with narrow, finely pointed leaves, having inrolled margins; they twist up together in dry weather. Stalk shiny dark red, erect at first, but leaning over horizontally as the capsule ripens. Cap overlaps lid and covers over half of capsule. Grows abundantly from lowlands to mountains, on burnt ground, in clearings, on heathland, rocks and walls.

Family: Leucobryaceae

6 *Leucobryum glaucum.* Forms dense rounded hummocks of distinctive grey-green foliage. Stems bear entire leaves with upturned rim that lack a central rib. Dioecious moss, only very rarely fruitful; female plants have dark purple stems 1—2 cm high. Grows in moist woods and on moorland.

5

6

4

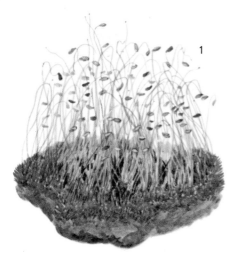

Family: Funariaceae

1 *Funaria hygrometrica*. Grows on bare ground, heathland, walls and roofs, and is one of the first colonizers on burnt ground. Simple stems are not more than 3 cm high, upper leaves rolled and bud-like when dry, short-pointed and entire. Sporophyte stalk is yellow to red, twisted, nodding at the tip with a grooved brown capsule.

Family: Bryaceae

2 *Bryum argenteum*. Tiny moss forming pale to silvery-green cushions. Stems only 1—2 cm high with ovate and pointed leaves. Pendent capsule is red-brown, elongated cylindrical to ovoid, with small pointed lid; the short (about 1 cm) stalk is also red. Grows from lowlands to foothills but is more frequent in lower altitudes on walls, rocks, along roads, among paving-stones and in similar places. It is one of the very few mosses found in big cities.

Family: Mniaceae

3 *Mnium punctatum*. This and other species of *Mnium* are frequent from lowlands to high up in mountains. Reddish stems are up to 5 cm high with relatively large, almost rounded leaves which are covered with pellucid dots. Stalk 2—4 cm high, usually reddish, at top yellow, with drooping or horizontal capsule. Capsule with elongated and sharply beaked lid and a shiny brown cap. Grows abundantly in moist woods, on bank of forest streams and in mountains. Often fertile.

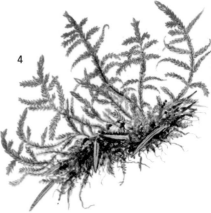

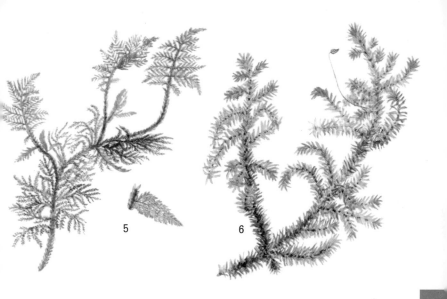

5   6

Family: Hypnaceae

4 *Pleurozium schreberi* (syn. *Hypnum schreberi*). Stems red, up to 15 cm long, ascending, pinnately branched, in two regular rows; branches at top recurving. Leaves overlapping, convex, broadly ovate, with double veins; those on branches are smaller than on main stems. Dioecious, fertile only in places. Then a thin, corrugated red stalk with elongated, curved capsule develops on female plant. Grows not only in coniferous and mixed forests but also in meadows, on grassy slopes and rocks where acid conditions are found.

Family: Hylocomiaceae

5 *Hylocomium splendens*. Stems red, up to 20 cm long, rigid, bi- to tripinnately branched, conspicuously flattened. Main stem leaves sessile, overlapping, ovate, elongated, abruptly tapering to long points; margins of upper third finely serrate; leaves of branches oval, smaller, abruptly tapering to a fine point, serrate. Dioecious species; female plant up to 4 cm high, with pendent, ovoid capsules. Grows in forests, on grassy slopes, among rocks overgrown with vegetation and in meadows. Often fertile.

Family: Rhytidiaceae

6 *Rhytidiadelphus triquetrus*. Reddish stems are densely leaved, up to 15 cm long, erect or semi-prostrate, irregularly branched. Leaves lanceolate, pointed, spreading, in upper part finely serrate and grooved. Dioecious plant, stalk about 2—5 cm high, sinuously corrugated, red. Capsule shortly ovate, pendent, red, with warty navel-shaped lid. Common in shady places in mixed forests, especially on limestone in spruce-beech growths; also on grassy slopes, sand dunes and sometimes on moorland.

Pteridophytes—Clubmosses, Horsetails and Ferns

The Ginkgo (*Ginkgo biloba*) could be considered a 'living fossil' for it has been part of the world's flora for 200 million years. Even further back, in the Palaeozoic era, the typical palaeophytic formations were 'carboniferous forests', composed of tree-like clubmosses, horsetails and ferns. Over the long period of 350 million years, these sporophytes evolved, died out or adapted to the change from life in water and bogs to life on dry land.

The pteridophytes changed over time. Their tree-like forms were replaced by low herbaceous plants that were sometimes even prostrate but nevertheless retained many of their distinguishing features. First and foremost of these is their manner of propagation in a damp environment.

The plant bodies of clubmosses, horsetails and ferns are the asexual phase, which is entirely independent of the sexual phase. These plant bodies are already clearly differentiated into a root, stem and leaves and hence also have a relatively complicated morphological and anatomical structure. Running throughout the entire body, a conductive system of vascular tissues distributes water and food around the body. Be-

Fig. 1. *Isoëtes lacustris* is a rare relict of extinct Palaeozoic pteridophytes that grows on the floor of mountain lakes.

sides leaves which manufacture food, the plants also have leaves called sporophylls that develop sporangia. Sometimes the spore-bearing leaves are arranged in a cone-like cluster.

Pteridophytes, then, are ancient sporophytes that evolved in the Palaeozoic period and apparently attained the peak of their development in the Carboniferous period. We shall deal with the more common present-day examples of European clubmosses, horsetails and ferns later in this book, but here let us take at least a passing look at some of the rarer and less conspicuous groups. Growing among the Palaeozoic, extinct clubmosses were tree-like sigillarias and lepidodendrons. Many had leaves with a short tongue (lingula) on the upperside and this same feature may still be found on present-day selaginellas, moss-like plants that grow in mountains. Another group survived only in damp places or directly in water. These are the rare *Isoëtes*, with awl-shaped leaves less than 20 cm long, that are found growing on the floors of mountain lakes.

You would not find such curious groups among the horsetails, but if you came across a mass of *Equisetum telmateia*, in which most of the plants will be nearly 2 m high, you would probably get a better, albeit remote, idea of what the tree-like ancestors of present-day species looked like.

Present-day ferns are not as large as their ancestors. In the tropics, however, they still find conditions favourable for the growth and development of immensely large fronds. Such ferns — up to 20 m high, with leaves up to 3 m long — are to be found in Australia (*Alsophila*) and South America (*Cyathea*). However, ferns also include among their number dwarf species only 5 cm high, more like a liverwort or moss in appearance, that grow on rocks. They are aptly named *Hymenophyllum*, meaning membranous-leaved, for their leaves are composed of only a single layer of cells.

Last but not least, ferns also include plants that long ago gave up life on dry land and went back to living in water. Many people are acquainted with the water-fern *Salvinia* as a plant grown in aquariums. Only in an aquarium, hardly ever in the wild, will you see the popular *Marsilea*. In special aquarist shops one may also purchase *Azolla caroliniana*, which spreads rapidly by vegetative means, soon covering the surface of the aquarium with its leaves.

84

Fig. 2. The young leaves of Common Brake (*Pteridium aquilinum*) are characteristically spirally coiled, opening into coarse flat fronds when they mature. Clearly evident in a cross-section of the stem is the typical pattern of the cavity with its vascular bundles.

85

Division: **Vascular Plants**—Tracheophyta

Sub-division: Pteridophytina

Class: **Clubmosses**—Lycopodiopsida

Family: Lycopodiaceae

1 Stag's-horn Clubmoss *Lycopodium clavatum.* Creeping stems of up to 1 m long, forked into shorter erect stalks. Leaves linear lanceolate, entire to irregularly notched, hairy. Spore-bearing spikes arranged usually in pairs on thin stalks with tiny, sessile leaflets. Sporophylls widely ovate, with colourless, soft spicule. Grows in open forests, on heathland and among rocks in mountains, from lowlands to mountains. Sporangia ripen from June to August.

Family: Huperziaceae

2 Fir Clubmoss *Lycopodium selago* (syn. *Huperzia selago*). Erect, tufted, branched stems up to 25 cm high. Leaves erect, spreading, soft, linear-lanceolate, entire. Sporangia do not form terminal spikes; they are placed mostly in upper part of stem on sporophylls, similar to other leaflets. Often produces bulbils in leaf axils at the end of branches. Grows in humid, shady woods, among rocks and on ledges, particularly in mountains. Sporangia mature from July to October.

Class: **Horsetails**—Sphenopsida (syn. Equisetopsida)

Family: Equisetaceae

3 Common Horsetail *Equisetum arvense.* Species with two types of stems: spring stem terminates in spore-bearing spike, summer stem sterile. Spring stems are 10—20 cm high, yellowish to brownish, with cylindrical, slightly inflated, light green, notched sheaths. Spore-bearing spike up to 3 cm long, brownish; after spores are released in March and April, spring stems die. Summer stems about 50 cm high, with distinct ribs. Both stems and branches have ribbed brownish sheaths. Common weed in fields and gardens, by the roadside and in open woods from lowlands to mountains.

4 Wood Horsetail *Equisetum sylvaticum.* Stems of two types: spring stem up to 50 cm high, at first wax-pink, during ripening of sporangia turns green, later resembles summer stems. These grow almost simultaneously with spring stems; are regularly branched, branches are slender and pendent and further branched. Sheaths slightly inflated, funnel-shaped, teeth tinted with red. Grows gregariously in moist places in forests from lowlands to mountains on poor soils. Sporangia ripen from April to June.

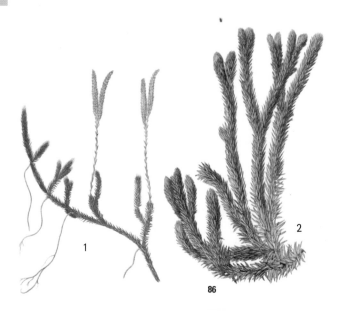

1   2

5 Water Horsetail *Equisetum fluviatile*. Robust stems over 1 m high with fine ribs, often unbranched and shiny, submerged parts maroon. Sessile sheaths glossy, lower ones reddish, upper green with black, awl-shaped teeth bordered with white. Spore-bearing spike short and ovoid. Sporangia mature from May to July. Grows from lowlands to mountains, in wet places, bogs, and on muddy banks of rivers and lakes.

Class: **Ferns**—Filicopsida (syn. Polypodiopsida)

Subclass: Ophioglossidae

Family: Ophioglossaceae

6 Adder's Tongue Fern *Ophioglossum vulgatum*. Small fern, about 8—20 cm high, with underground rhizome and one single leaf. Sterile part of leaf leathery, ovoid, entire, yellow-green and mat-shiny; spore-bearing part with sporangia, arranged in two parallel rows close together. Sporangia ripen from June to August. Grows in marshy and mountain meadows, and moist clearings in woods, more frequently on limestone. A very small form (*O. lusitanicum*) is found on grassy cliff tops in the Channel Isles and Scilly Isles and in Mediterranean regions.

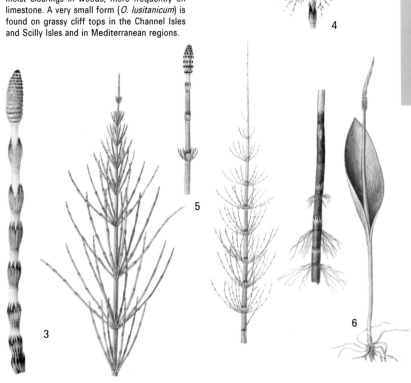

4

3

5

6

Family: Ophioglossaceae

1 Common Moonwort *Botrychium lunaria.* Small fern up to 5—15 cm or more high. Sterile part of single leaf simply pinnate, spore-bearing part bi- to tripinnate. Sterile part composed of 4—7 or more pairs of fan-shaped, entire or scalopped, leathery segments. Spore-bearing part long-stalked, terminating with sporangia arranged in two rows on linear segments. Sporangia yellow-brown, later of cinnamon shade, ripen from May to June. Grows from lowlands to high up in the mountains, in meadows, pastures and among rocks; generally of localized distribution.

Subclass: Polypodiidae

Order: Polypodiales

Family: Matteuciaceae

2 Ostrich Fern *Matteuccia struthiopteris* (syn. *Struthiopteris germanica*). Fan up to 150 cm high, sterile leaves, grows from robust rhizome. Blades simply pinnate, segments fine, linear-lanceolate. Spore leaves only 50—60 cm high, grow in centre of sterile fronds and have segments at first rolled, later unrolled. Sori ripen from June to August. Grows in moist places, along streams and rivers, in forests, from lowlands to mountains. Also cultivated for ornament.

Family: Blechnaceae

3 Hard Fern *Blechnum spicant.* A fern with leaves of two types; the sterile ones over-wintering, leathery, pinnately divided to mid-rib. Segments dark green, linear-lanceolate, entire. Non-leafy sporophylls, growing from centre of tuft, are longer, erect, up to 40 cm high, with interrupted pinnate to linear segments, bearing sori which ripen from July to September. Grows, often gregariously, in woods, on moors, heaths, mountain grassland and among rocks.

Family: Aspidiaceae (syn. Dryopteridaceae)

4 Male Fern *Dryopteris filix-mas.* Robust fern over 1 m high, with rusty-scaly rhizome. Leaf stalks bearing pale brown scales. Leaf blade deeply pinnately divided, pinnules dark green, lighter on underside, with toothed margins. Large sori adhere to mid-rib of pinnules; indusia kidney-shaped. Sporangia ripen from June to September. Grows in shady woods, among boulders and in hedgerows, from lowlands to mountains.

5 Beech Fern *Thelypteris phegopteris* (syn. *Phegopteris polypodioides*). Long-stalked leaves, up to 10—30 cm or more high, grow from long rhizome. Blades simply pinnate, lanceolate leaflets deeply pinnately lobed, more or less hairy. Conspicuous backward slant of lowest pair of leaves and fusion of lowest pinnules with mid-rib aid in identifying this fern. Sori rounded, light brown, on border of pinnules; no indusia. Sporangia ripen in June and July. Grows in moist, shady woods, among rocks and on banks of forest streams, from lowlands to mountains.

Family: Athyriaceae

6 Brittle Bladder Fern *Cystopteris fragilis.* Long-stalked fronds, 8—25 cm or more high, grow from short rhizome. Fragile, dark brown petioles usually shorter than bipinnate blades, with deeply lobed and notched leaflets; sori in two rows either side of pinnule mid-rib. Sporangia ovoid pointed, ripening from June to September. Grows on walls, rocks and screes, also in shady woods, from lowlands to mountains. Only found in the north and west of Great Britain.

4

5

6

Family: Athyriaceae

1 Lady Fern *Athyrium filix-femina.* Leaves 20—100 cm or more high, with stalk and mid-rib often purplish and bearing a few chaffy scales. Grows from short, dark brown, scaly rhizome. Freshly green, bi- to tripinnate leaves with alternate, lanceolate, long-pointed leaflets; pinnules ovate to lanceolate, toothed. Margins of pinnules with crescent or kidney-shaped sori; sporangia ripen from July to September. Grows abundantly and often gregariously from lowlands to mountains, in moist forests, and shady places on acid soils.

Family: Aspleniaceae

2 Forked Spleenwort *Asplenium septentrionale.* Small evergreen fern, 4—15 cm high, short, black-brown scaly rhizome and narrow blades, black-brown at base. Blades have slender, forked pinnules. Sori cover almost whole under surface of pinnules. Sporangia ripen from June to October. Grows in sunny places, in cracks of acid rocks, rarely on walls, from lowlands to mountains. Rare in Britain.

3 Wall Rue *Asplenium ruta-muraria.* Long-stalked evergreen leaves, bipinnate, dark green, up to 3—12 cm high, grow from creeping rootstock. Pinnules obovate to lanceolate with crenate or dentate margins. Linear, coalescent sori ripen from June to October. Grows in cracks of rocks, walls, and screes, almost always on limestone, from lowlands to mountains. Related Maidenhair Spleenwort, *A. trichomanes*, has leaves simply pinnate and oval or oblong pinnules.

4

5

Family: Pteridaceae

4 Bracken *Pteridium aquilinum.* A deciduous fern up to 2 m high with stout cylindrical petioles up to 1 m long, which grow from thick, black, creeping rhizomes. Blades triangular bi- to tripinnate, light green, lanceolate to oblong pinnules, lobed at the base, with marginal sori. Sporangia ripen from July to September. Grows gregariously in open woods, especially pine-woods, and on heath and moorland, usually on acid soils, from lowlands to mountains. This fern and its subspecies are distributed all over the world; important cosmopolitan species.

Family: Polypodiaceae

5 Common Polypody *Polypodium vulgare.* Long-petioled evergreen leaves, pinnately divided into alternate, lanceolate and entire, somewhat leathery blunt-tipped pinnules, grow from creeping rhizomes. Two rows of relatively

large, rounded sori without indusia on under surface of pinnules. Sporangia ripen from May to September. Grows in woods, on shady, mossy rocks, and on trunks and branches of deciduous trees.

Order: Salviniales

Family: Salviniaceae

6 Water-fern *Salvinia natans.* Tiny floating 'fern'. Stem 5—15 cm long, bears leaves in whorls of three of which two are always floating, short-stalked with undivided blade, tufted with hair-like papillae on upper surface; third leaf transformed into numerous, root-like submerged segments. Sporangia of two types: small male and large female ones, closed in sporocarps. Ripen in August and September. Grows locally, in lakes and slow flowing rivers, mainly in central and southern Europe. Often grown as aquarium plant.

Grasses and Grass-like Plants

Grasses are a typical example of plants found growing in large communities — in savannahs in tropical regions, in pampas, steppes or prairies in the temperate zone. In Europe, grasses are a familiar sight in the semi-cultivated and cultivated meadows of lowland districts, in mountain meadows and in rolling pastureland. Grasses are distributed throughout the world, from the tropics to the arctic regions of both north and south, from seacoasts to mountain

Fig. 2. Detail of a spikelet of Sweet Vernal-grass: awnless lemma, spiny palea, two feathery stigmas and two pendulous stamens with versatile anthers (most grasses have three stamens).

peaks, in deserts as well as in forests. They are one of the largest families of flowering plants, comprising an estimated 10,000 species.

Grasses are members of the Poaceae family — monocotyledonous herbaceous plants with fibrous roots. The stems, or culms, are unbranched, usually hollow, jointed, cylindrical and firm. Only occasionally do they become woody, for example in bamboo stems used as walking sticks or fishing rods. The leaves of grasses are alternate, without a stalk and sheathed; sometimes there is a small leaf-like outgrowth called the ligule at the point where the leaf blade emerges from the sheath. The inflorescences, often very dense, are composed of spikelets. The fruits are grains, one-seeded achenes with a pericarp closely adhering to the seed coat (testa).

Grasses are important as fodder for domestic animals, in the fresh as well as dried state. For people also they are an important source of food. Rye, wheat, oats, barley, maize, rice and millet are the best-known grasses that are grown as cereals for their starchy grains, which are ground in mills into flour or eaten whole, for example rice. Besides starch, gluten and proteins, spirits, starch sugar, dextrin, vegetable oil and other products are also obtained from grains. Today barley grains are less often used to make flour because barley bread is less tasty than wheat bread and rapidly becomes hard. Barley groats, grits and meal, however, are still popular, and barley is used in the preparation of

Fig. 1. A flowering tuft of Sweet Vernal-grass (*Anthoxanthum odoratum*).

Fig. 3. Detail of a spikelet showing awnless lemma and palea, two feathery stigmas and three stamens.

malted coffee substitutes. However, most barley is now made into malt for use in brewing beer (the grains are allowed to germinate and are then lightly roasted). Oats are used to make ground or rolled oats for oatmeal and muesli. Millet was formerly cultivated much more widely. Nowadays it is used only rarely, mostly as bird-seed.

Many alcoholic beverages are dependent on cereals. What would beer be without malted barley or whisky without rye? Japanese sake and Malaysian arak are well-known alcoholic beverages that are made from rice. Maize, too, is fermented for use in making alcoholic beverages.

Grasses are also sugar-yielding herbaceous plants, the most familiar being sugarcane (*Saccharum officinarum*). Sugar is prepared from the juice obtained from the crushed cane. Excellent Jamaican and Cuban rums are obtained through the distillation of molasses and cane syrups following their fermentation.

The leaves of some grasses have cells that contain fragrant essential oils. *Cymbopogon nardus*, for example, is cultivated in Java, Malaysia and elsewhere for its high concentration of citronella oil, other species of *Cymbopogon* yield other essential oils, and some are used in perfumery.

There are certain common European grass-like plants which, though not true grasses, can readily be mistaken for them because of their resemblance in appearance and habit of growth as well as their occurrence in large masses— namely sedges (*Carex*) and rushes (*Juncus*). These, however, do not have jointed stems. Plants of the sedge family (Cyperaceae) have three-sided stems and those of the rush family (Juncaceae) often have leaves with an undifferentiated upper and under surface. The members of these two families also differ from true grasses in their flowers and fruits. Rushes bear capsules; sedges achenes. Of course, reedbeds composed primarily of the Common Reed (*Phragmites australis*), one of the most robust of European grasses, often contain damp-loving sedges and rushes, and other species of sedges, and perhaps also the Field Woodrush (*Luzula campestris*), often intermingle with the numerous true grasses in drier meadows and pastures.

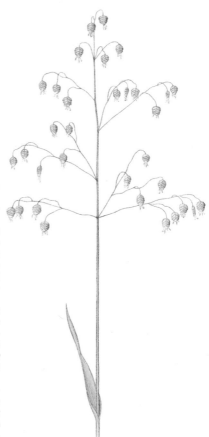

Fig. 4. A flowering branching panicle of Common Quaking Grass (*Briza media*).

Subclass: **Monocotyledones**—Butomidae

Family: **Rush**—Juncaceae

1 Field Woodrush *Luzula campestris.* Perennial, tufted herb, up to 15 cm high, with erect stems and shortly creeping rhizomes. Linear leaves have sparse but long white hairs. Tiny flowers in few-flowered panicle, usually nodding. Tepals six, brown, equally long, lanceolate, pointed, with a membranous border. Flowers from March to June. Grows in meadows, open woods and on grassy banks and lawns from lowlands to mountains. The similar hairy woodrush (*L. pilosa*) is larger, with distinctly stalked flowers in a lax cyme and rather more hairy leaves. It is usually found in woods and hedgerows only.

2 Soft Rush *Juncus effusus.* Perennial herb almost 1 metre high, densely tufted. Erect stems filled with spongy pith. Leaves grow direct from rhizome, cylindrical, resembling stems. Inflorescences apparently lateral, emerging below the top of the stem. The apparent stem tip is, in fact, a cylindrical bract. Small, six-lobed flowers are brownish. Flowers from June to August. Grows in damp meadows and near water from lowlands to mountains. *Juncus conglomeratus* is similar, but inflorescence is a dense, rounded head. Jointed Rush (*J. articulatus*) has distinct stem leaves and a terminal, open inflorescence. Toad Rush (*J. bufonius*) has very slender branched stems, and filamentous leaves.

Family: **Sedge**—Cyperaceae

3 Common Cottongrass *Eriophorum angustifolium.* Perennial grassy herb, sparsely tufted, up to 50 cm high, with erect stems. Leaves grooved, narrowly linear, slender pointed. Stalked ovate spikelets in pendent clusters of 3 to 5; tiny lanceolate bracts with white membranous border. Perianth of numerous fine bristles which elongate and become white and cottony after flowering. Flowers in April and May. Grows in bog pools on heaths and moorland and in acid fens, from lowlands to mountains.

4 Bulrush *Schoenoplectus lacustris.* Perennial herb 1—3 metres high, with thick, creeping rhizomes and rounded stems. Sheathed leaves with linear triangular blades. Spikelets in large terminal clusters; glumes broadly ovate, often fringed. Fruit a trianglular ovoid nut. Flowers from May to July. Grows in wet soil and near or in water at lower altitudes, often gregariously.

94

5 Wood Club-rush *Scirpus sylvaticus*. Perennial herb up to 1 metre high, sparsely tufted, with short rhizomes and usually erect stems. Leaves widely linear, flat, rough on margins. Dense, large, well-branched inflorescence of sessile spikelets in clusters. Glumes ovate, entire, greenish-brown. Nuts broadly ovoid. Flowers from June to August. Grows in damp meadows, ditches, and on river or lake banks from lowlands to mountains.

6 Common Sedge *Carex nigra*. Perennial herb up to 70 cm high, with creeping rhizomes and triangular stems, rough textured in upper part. Flat, linear, grey-green leaves often rolled when dry. Spikelets in terminal raceme, the topmost ones male, lower ones female. Black-brown glumes obovate, with a pale mid-rib. Female flowers with two stigmata each. Flowers in May to July. Grows in wet meadows and near water, from lowlands to mountains.

7 Spring Sedge *Carex caryophyllea*. Perennial herb 20—40 cm high, with branched rhizome and slender, bluntly triangular stems. Leaves flat, keeled, stiff, rough textured. Spikelets close together, sessile; sometimes lowest one distant and short-stalked; male spikelet terminal; others female. Glumes rusty brown, glossy with green mid-rib. Nut ovoid, triangular, brownish. Flowers in April and May. Grows in dry grassland and margins of woods, particularly on limestone, from lowlands to foothills. At least 100 species of sedges grow in central Europe.

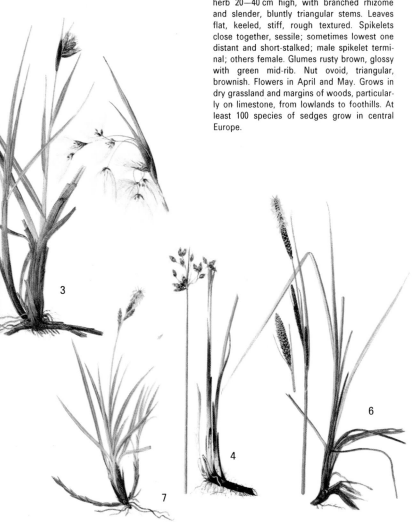

Family: **Grass**—Gramineae (syn. Poaceae)

1 Feather-grass *Stipa capillata*. Perennial herb, densely tufted, up to 80 cm high, with erect stems. Bristly leaves grey-green, rough on margin. Panicles greenish, spikelets with shortly awned glumes, lemma with wavy awns, up to 15 cm long. Flowers in July and August. Grows on sunny, grassy and stony slopes in lower altitudes of milder regions. Common Feather-grass (*S. pennata*) has straight awns and silvery white hairs. It is sometimes grown in gardens but not recorded as a genuine escapee in Britain.

2 Meadow Fescue *Festuca pratensis*. Perennial tufted herb, up to 80 cm high, with erect stems. Leaves narrowly linear, upper side rough, underside smooth. Panicles sparse and open; spikelets up to 10-flowered. Flowers have three stamens with pendulous anthers on long slender filaments; two stigmata; lanceolate glumes, lemma usually awnless. Flowers in June and July. Grows in meadows and other grassy places from lowlands to mountains.

3 Annual Meadow-grass *Poa annua*. Annual or short-lived perennial herb, up to 30 cm high, branched. Ascending or erect stalks, rooting at lower nodes. Blades slightly rough on margins. Open, often one-sided panicle with few-flowered spikelets. Bottom glume single-veined, upper one three-veined, both smooth, lemma has dry-membraneous margin similar to palea. Flowers almost all year round. Grows in lawns, pastures, on wasteland, and as a weed of farms and gardens, almost everywhere.

4 Common Meadow-grass *Poa pratensis*. Perennial, tufted herb, up to 80 cm high, with shortly ascending or erect, smooth, rounded stalks and creeping stolons. Blades flat or rolled, stem leaves usually erect and stiff. Open erect panicles of 3- to 5-flowered spikelets. Glumes equal, lemmas five-veined, hairy at base. Flowers in May to July. Grows in meadows and other grassy places, and on dunes, from lowlands to mountains.

5 Quaking-grass *Briza media*. Perennial, tufted herb, up to 50 cm high, with short, branched rhizome. Slender, smooth, erect stalks. Flat blades, stem ones short, rough on margin. Open sparse panicles of drooping, quaking spikelets often of purplish hue, broadly ovoid. Glumes asymmetrically obovate, keeled, lemma inflated, with a paler border. Flowers in May and June. Grows in all kinds of grassy places, from lowlands to mountains.

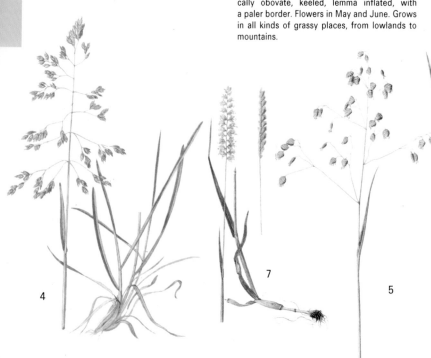

4

7

5

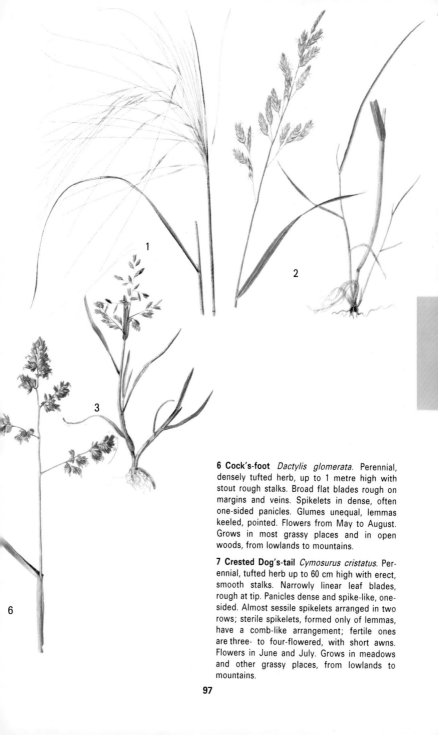

6 Cock's-foot *Dactylis glomerata*. Perennial, densely tufted herb, up to 1 metre high with stout rough stalks. Broad flat blades rough on margins and veins. Spikelets in dense, often one-sided panicles. Glumes unequal, lemmas keeled, pointed. Flowers from May to August. Grows in most grassy places and in open woods, from lowlands to mountains.

7 Crested Dog's-tail *Cymosurus cristatus*. Perennial, tufted herb up to 60 cm high with erect, smooth stalks. Narrowly linear leaf blades, rough at tip. Panicles dense and spike-like, one-sided. Almost sessile spikelets arranged in two rows; sterile spikelets, formed only of lemmas, have a comb-like arrangement; fertile ones are three- to four-flowered, with short awns. Flowers in June and July. Grows in meadows and other grassy places, from lowlands to mountains.

Family: **Grass**—Gramineae

1 Blue Mountain-grass *Sesleria albicans* (syn. *S. caerulea* and *S. calcarea*). Perennial, tufted herb up to 40 cm high with stalks leafy only in lower part. Blades with distinctly cartilaginous border, rough, flat. Two scaly bracts beneath short spike-like inflorescence. Spikelets glistening blue-grey, rarely yellowish, usually with two flowers. Shortly awned glumes, toothed tipped lemmas, paleas with two terminal teeth. Flowers from March to June. Grows in hill pastures and on stony slopes, usually on limestone, in foothills and mountains.

2 Perennial Rye-grass *Liloum perenne*. Perennial, densely tufted herb, with erect stalks, up to 50 cm high. Smooth, flat linear leaves. Spikelets arranged in an open two-ranked spike. Each spikelet flattened, with 8—11 florets. Single glume longer than half of spikelet, lemmas shortly pointed. Flowers from May to September. Grows in most grassy places, from lowlands to foothills. Much sown as a fodder crop and for rough lawns.

3 Common Couch *Agropyron repens*. Perennial herb with far-creeping, stiff rhizomes and erect stalks, up to 150 cm high. Leaf blades sparsely veined. Slender spike two-ranked, rhachis rough. Spikelets compressed, three- to five-flowered, with equal, veined glumes and shortly awned lemmas. Flowers from June to September. Pernicious weed of farms and gardens; grows in fields, on wasteland and in hedgerows, from lowlands to mountains.

4 Barren Brome *Bromus sterilis* (syn. *Anisantha sterilis*). Annual herb, somewhat tufted, up to 90 cm high, with stiff stalks. Flat leaf blades rough on margins. Large, open, spreading panicles, with pendulous, narrowly wedge-shaped spikelets. Each spikelet up to six-flowered, often flushed dull purple; awn-like pointed glumes and lemma with awn up to 3 cm long. Flowers in May and June. Grows on wasteland, by roadsides and as a farm and garden weed, at lower altitudes.

5 Tufted Hair-grass *Deschampsia cespitosa*. Perennial, densely tufted herb, up to 2 m high, with rough stalks. Leaf blades flat, rough on upper surface, smooth beneath, with sharp ribs. Large, open panicles with arching or lax branches. Spikelets two- or three-flowered, short-stalked, usually violet-tinted; blunt, membranously bordered glumes and shortly awned, toothed lemmas. Flowers from June to August. Grows in damp meadows and open woods from lowlands to mountains. Wavy Hair-grass (*D. flexuosa*) has bristly leaves and very distinct lemmas.

6 Yorkshire Fog *Holcus lanatus*. Perennial herb of tufted habit, up to 1 metre high, softly short-hairy, with erect or asceding stems. Leaves flat, sheaths inflated. Panicles spreading only during flowering; two- to three-flowered stalked spikelets with coarse bristly glumes and tiny lemmas with awns not projecting beyond the upper glume. Flowers from June to September. Growns in meadows, open woods and waste places, from lowlands to mountains.

Family: **Grass**— Gramineae

1 Sweet Vernal-grass *Anthoxanthum odoratum.* Perennial herb, densely tufted and sweetly aromatic, with erect, smooth stalks, up to 50 cm high. Leaves with flat, usually hairy blades. Panicles spike-like compressed. Spikelets yellow-green, very shortly stalked, bearing 2 sterile and one hermaphrodite florets; lanceolate glumes, lemmas awned, hairy; two stamens only. Flowers in May and June. Grows in dry meadows, pastures, open woods, heaths and moors, from lowlands to mountains. Contains coumarin, which provides the new-mown hay smell.

2 Wood Small-reed *Calamagrostis epigeios.* Perennial herb, tufted and robust, up to 2 m high, with erect, reedy, grey-green stalks. Leaf sheaths and blades rough. Dense, well-branched panicles. Spikelets stalked, greenish or brownish with violet tint. Awl-pointed glumes, lemmas three-veined, membranous, awned and with a basal tuft of hairs. Flowers in July and August. Grows in damp open woods, ditches and fens, mainly in lowlands.

3 Meadow Foxtail *Alopecurus pratensis.* Perennial herb up to 1 metre high, loosely or compactly tufted, with short rhizomes and erect, smooth stalks. Leaf blades flat, rough, the sheaths somewhat inflated. Dense, cylindrical, spike-like inflorescence. Spikelets very shortly stalked; pointed glumes fused together at their bases, the keeled back silky-hairy, lemma almost the same length as glumes, with protruding awn. Flowers in May and June. Grows in damp meadows and other grassy places, from lowlands to mountains. Related *Alopecurus aequalis* is much smaller, with whitish anthers, turning orange.

5   1   6

4 Timothy *Phleum pratense*. Perennial herb up to 1 metre high, densely tufted, with erect stalks. Leaf blades very rough. Dense grey-green, spike-like inflorescence, with almost sessile spikelets. Glumes whitish dry-membranous, on greenish keel bristly hairy and shortly awned; white-membranous lemma, violet anthers. Flowers from June to August. Grows in meadows and other grassy places from lowlands to foothills, more frequent in lower altitudes. Extensively sown for hay and forage.

5 Mat-grass *Nardus stritla*. Perennial, densely tufted herb, up to 30 cm high, with short rhizomes and erect slender stems. Grey-green leaves, filiform, prickly pointed, with conspicuous basal sheaths. Flowering spike sparse, one-sided, spikelets single-flowered. Glumes miss-

ing, lemma with short rough awn; three stamens, one stigma. Flowers in May and June. Grows on heaths and moors, sometimes locally abundant, from lowlands high up into mountains, usually on acid soils.

6 Common Reed *Phragmites communis*. Perennial robust herb up to 3 metres high, with tough, long-creeping rhizome and erect, grey-green stems. Conspicuously double-ranked leaves of sterile shoots; blades flat, rough beneath, gradually tapering to point. Large, dense panicles; spikelets grey, sometimes purple-tinted with long silky hairs. Unequal glumes, lemmas long-pointed, awnless. Flowers from July to September. Grows in marshes, swamps and shallow water, often gregariously, forming extensive colonies.

Herbaceous Plants

Fig. 1. In the Common Dandelion (*Taraxacum officinale*) one may often see inflorescences at all stages of development on a single plant.

When you hear that the banana is a robust herb and, on the other hand, that whortleberry and cranberry are shrubs, you may be surprised. Herbs cannot have trunks, can they? And as for whortleberry and cranberry, what kind of shrubs are they? What actually is the difference between herbaceous and woody plants?

Herbs are annual, biennial and plural-yearly to perennial plants with a non-woody stem that does not thicken and dies at the end of the growing season. In the case of plural-yearly and perennial herbs in temperate regions, their underground parts — roots, rhizomes, tubers or bulbs — live over from season to season and make new growth the following year. Woody plants, on the other hand, have woody stems — trunks in the case of trees, stems and twigs in the case of shrubs and sub-shrubs. Semi-shrubs have stems that become woody, but their tips or young sections die and fall. All woody plants grow thicker with age. Because bananas, which are perennial and thus grow for a long time, have stems that are not woody and do not thicken and their seeming 'trunks' are merely the remains of leaf sheaths pressed closely together, they are neither trees nor shrubs but robust herbs, the largest in the plant realm.

The life forms of herbs may be divided into four groups. Annual herbs germinate, grow, flower and bear fruits within a single growing season. They include numerous weeds that must complete their life cycle within a single year, for example Common Poppy (*Papaver rhoeas*) and Cornflower (*Centaurea cyanus*).

Biennial herbs germinate and produce only a basal leaf rosette or the first vegetative structures the first year, passing the winter in this phase. Then, in the second year, they continue growth, produce flowers and bear fruit. Examples are Mullein (*Verbascum*) and Foxglove (*Digitalis purpurea*), as well as certain winter crops, such as cereals sown in the autumn, mainly wheat.

Plural-yearly herbs also first germinate and form vegetative organs and then overwinter in this phase. However, a plural-yearly herb may remain in this state for several more growing seasons or else may form further vegetative structures. Not until the last year of its life does it flower, produce seeds and then die. Most people are acquainted with the agaves that are cultivated for ornament, especially the American species *Agave americana*, which forms large rosettes of succulent leaves edged with prickly spines along their entire length and with a larger terminal spine at the tip. Agaves live in this state for many years, sometimes even do-

Fig. 2. Flowering Field Poppy (*Papaver rhoeas*) with a bud enclosed by the calyx and a ripening capsule with a dried remnant of the stigma.

zens, and only then do they produce an inflorescence on the huge axis, after which they die; in other words they flower only once in their lifetime, at the end of their life cycle. European plants that have a similar life cycle are the broomrapes (*Orobanche*). For several years they live as parasites on their host plant, forming only underground vegetative structures. Then, all of a sudden, they flower and die within a single year.

The last group are perennial herbs that live for several years, producing flowers and seeds each year. They die down to ground level for the winter and grow again the following year from their underground parts — roots, rhizomes, bulbs or tubers — which have survived the cold season unharmed below ground. Examples are certain campions of the genus *Silene*, such as Nottingham Catchfly (*Silene nutans*), *Silene otites*, Moss Campion (*Silene acaulis*), Maiden Pink (*Dianthus deltoides*), German Pink (*D. cartusianorum*) and Ragged Robin (*Lychnis flos-cuculi*).

Among the most remarkable of the aquatic perennial herbs are plants related to Europe's water-lilies (*Nymphaea* and *Nuphar*), such as *Victoria amazonica* (syn. *V. regia*) from the Amazon River region and *V. cruziana* from the Paraná River region. Both are grown in hothouses in Europe and their 2-m leaves are

Fig. 3. Longitudinal section of the head of a dandelion. The involucral bracts are green, the yellow strap-shaped florets are longer towards the edge of the inflorescence.

Fig. 4. On the flower head of the Ox-eye Daisy (*Leucanthemum vulgare*) one can clearly see the two types of florets of certain composite flowers. Unlike the dandelion, for example, the outer florets are ligulate, the inner florets tubular.

Fig. 5. A leaf of Common Sundew (*Drosera rotundifolia*) with long-stalked, sticky glands and short digestive glands.

and Sikkim at elevations of 5,600 m. *D. glomerata* and *D. lasiophylla* grow at elevations of 6,000 m; *Ermania koezlii* was collected in Kashmir at an altitude of 6,300 m above sea level. These undemanding and hardy plants also hold a further record — that of conquering the Arctic. *Draba groenlandica* was found by the Koch fjord in northern Greenland as far north as 82°48′ latitude North; *Braya purpurascens* occurs in Grinell Land at the eastern tip of Ellesmere Island in northern Canada, at 83°24′ latitude North.

However, how many people will ever have the opportunity to look for drabas in the mountains of Kashmir or near the North Pole? On the other hand, we can all admire the largest fruits in the plant realm in our own gardens! *Cucurbita maxima* is not native to Europe; it hails from Central America. Sometimes grown is its large-fruited

Fig. 6. Cowslips (*Primula veris*) are a common sight in spring in open woods.

among the largest in the plant realm. The fragrant flowers measure 35 cm. They open in the late afternoon and close again towards morning. They are a delicate pink at first. Once pollinated, they close immediately; when they open again the following afternoon they are coloured a reddish-pink. These beautiful nocturnal flowers are far above average in size but still cannot begin to compare with *Rafflesia arnoldii* of Sumatra. This is a parasitic plant whose fleshy flowers measure up to 1 m in diameter, have a circumference of 3 m and may weigh over 5 kg — truly the largest flowers known to botany.

At the other end of the scale, the smallest flowering dicotyledonous plant is a member of the Loranthaceae family. This is *Arceuthobium minutissimum* which lives as a parasite on the Himalayan pine *Pinus griffithii*. This miniature parasite lives beneath the bark of the tree, displaying only its 2—3-mm-long flowering stems.

P. griffithii grows at elevations of about 3,000 m, but other small herbs have climbed twice as high. Heading the list of plants that have conquered the Himalayas are members of the mustard family (Brassicaceae). *Braya oxycarpa* and *Draba altaica* grow in western Tibet

In central Europe, too, there are rarities among the herbaceous plants. Leaves that are turned edgewise, in the north-south direction, with leaf surfaces facing east and west, are an unusual characteristic of Prickly Lettuce (*Lactuca serriola*) which grows in sunny waste places.

Even in Europe one may come across plants that are carnivorous, although these are quite rare nowadays. Most familiar is the Common Sundew (*Drosera rotundifolia*). Less familiar is the Common Butterwort (*Pinguicula vulgaris*) which has a basal rosette of oblong-ovate leaves with edges curled upward and an upper surface covered with numerous stalked glands that secrete a sticky fluid on which small insects become caught. Even some aquatic, rootless herbs have leaves adapted for capturing and digesting insects. These are the bladderworts (*Utricularia*) which have minute translucent follicles

Fig. 7. The fleshy outgrowths on the seeds of Sweet Violet (*Viola odorata*) are a favourite food of ants which contribute to the spread of the violets by dispersing the seeds.

variety *gigantea*, with fruits measuring up to 80 cm in diameter and weighing 100 kg. In the European garden it is impossible to provide this plant with tropical, damp, warm conditions throughout the year, as in its native land, where fruits have measured up to 150 cm in diameter and weighed up to 125 kg! These berries are the largest of all known fruits.

Having mentioned one member of the gourd family (Cucurbitaceae), let us take a look at a few more. There is no need to describe the Cucumber (*Cucumis sativus*) or the Sugar Melon (*Melo saccharinus*). However, *Ecbalium elaterium* might catch your attention in the Mediterranean region and might even give you a bit of a fright during an evening stroll. This trailing or climbing herbaceous plant has fleshy leaves and oblong to ovoid fruits that, when ripe, break off with a loud pop when touched, ejecting their seeds and mucilaginous pulp far from the plant.

Fig. 8. The terminal leaf of Meadow Vetchling (*Lathyrus pratensis*) is modified into three twining tendrils by means of which the plant attaches itself to the stems of grasses or other plants.

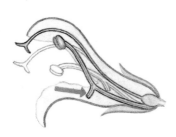

Fig. 9. The pollination mechanism of Sage (*Salvia officinalis*). Normally the style with bifid stigma, as well as the stamen, is pressed to the flower's domed upper lip. An insect, trying to get to the nectar at the bottom of the corolla tube, presses its body against the outgrowth on the stamen, thereby tilting the stamen and the stigma. The pollen from the stamen spills onto the body of the insect while pollen that has been brought by the insect from another flower is pressed onto the stigma.

amid their thread-like leaf segments. The bladder has a small opening encircled by irritable ciliae and furnished with a lid that only opens inward, thereby blocking the escape of any small aquatic insects or crustaceans trapped inside. The inside walls of the bladder are covered with four-branched glandular hairs and nearer the mouth there are stalked glands that secrete digestive substances and also absorb the decomposed organisms. Observing the minor dramas of captured insects on the leaf of a sundew or bladderwort may cause one to reflect on the ingenious equipment with which nature has provided plants in order that they may obtain essential nutrients that are lacking in nitrogen-poor soils and nutrient-poor water.

The realm of herbaceous plants is extraordinarily rich and diverse. To discuss their useful and medicinal properties in detail would require more than one book.

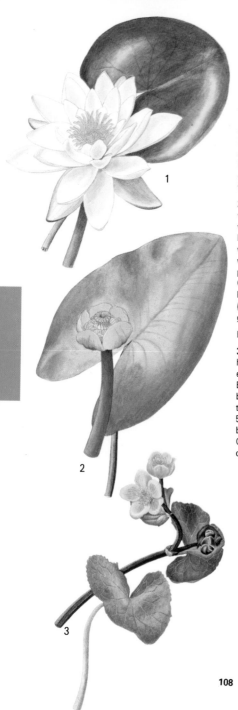

Herbaceous Plants

Class: **Angiospermous Plants**—Magnoliopsida

Subclass: **Dicotyledones**—Magnoliidae

Family: **Waterlily**—Nymphaceae

1 White Waterlily *Nymphaea alba*. Perennial aquatic herb with stout, creeping rhizome. Long-petiolate leaves, narrowly cordate, have circular blades, floating on water surface. Flowers large, cup-shaped, petals white, of the same length as four green sepals. Stamens have linear filaments. Flowers from June to August. Grows in lakes and ponds, at low altitudes; often cultivated.

2 Yellow Waterlily *Nuphar lutea*. Aquatic plant with stout perennial rhizome, similar to white waterlily. Long-petiolate leaves with ovate-oblong blades are leathery, smooth, floating on water surface. Flowers yellow, strongly fragrant, with disc-like stigma. Fruits are bottle-shaped, pulpy capsules. Flowers from June to August. Grows in lakes, ponds and slow flowing rivers at lower altitudes. Related Least Yellow Waterlily (*N. pumila*) has smaller flowers, slightly fragrant, with a somewhat lobed stigma.

Family: **Buttercup**—Ranunculaceae

3 Marsh Marigold *Caltha palustris*. Perennial, hairless herb 30—40 cm high with fibrous roots, erect stems, sometimes ascending and rooting. Bottom leaves petiolate, top ones sessile, blades cordate, rounded to bluntly triangular, toothed and glossy. Flowers yellow, glossy, with 5—8 golden yellow petals. Fruit a cluster of beaked follicles. Flowers from March to July. Grows by the waterside, in damp meadows and ditches, from lowlands to mountains.

4 Globe Flower *Trollius europaeus.* Robust perennial herbs with erect stems, 30—60 cm high, and terminal, solitary flowers. Leaves deeply palmately lobed with 3—5 segments, each deeply cut and toothed; lower leaves long-petiolate, upper ones sessile. Large flowers up to 3 cm in diameter, globose, light to golden yellow, composed of 5—15 petaloid sepals. Fruit a cluster of beaked follicles. Flowers in May to July. Grows in wet meadows in foothills and mountains; in places extinct through over-picking, therefore it deserves strict protection. Hybrids of this and Asiatic species with orange flowers are cultivated in gardens.

5 Common Baneberry *Actaea spicata.* A somewhat foetid perennial, poisonous herb with erect, unbranched stems, 30—60 cm. high. Basal leaves bi- to tripinnate, leaflets ovate, pointed and toothed. Small flowers, yellowish-white, in long-stalked terminal racemes. Fruit a glossy black berry. Flowers in May and June. Grows im shady, deciduous forests from hills to mountains; in lowlands only rarely.

6 Columbine *Aquilegia vulgaris.* Perennial herb, up to 50 cm high. Leaves composed of 3—9 somewhat glaucous leaflets, ovate, deeply to shallowly lobed; upper stem leaves smaller and less divided. Flowers long-stalked, pendent, blue-violet, rarely white or pink; sepals flared, coloured, petals elongated into curved spurs. Garden varieties of various colouring. Flowers from May to July. Grows in deciduous woods from lowlands to highlands. Much and long-cultivated in flower gardens, along with some equally pretty Siberian and North-American species.

Family: **Buttercup**—Ranunculaceae

1 *Aconitum vulparia* (syn. *A. lycoctonum*). Poisonous, variable perennial herb with fibrous root system and widely branched stem, up to 1 metre high. Leaves palmately parted, segments 3—5 wedge-shaped, downy or smooth. Inflorescences of branched racemes, with well-spaced yellow, hairy flowers with long, cylindrical helmet-shaped spur. Flowers from June to August. Grows in deciduous woods and thickets from highlands to mountains. Sometimes cultivated.

2 Common Monkshood *Aconitum napellus.* A poisonous, perennial herb, with tuberous roots and erect, branched inflorescences. Leaves palmately divided, 3—5 lanceolate to widely linear segments. Dark violet flowers in dense racemes, the 'helmet' almost of the same height and width. Flowers from June to August.

Grows in moist woods and on banks of streams; also cultivated in gardens; occasionally becoming naturalized. Related Lesser Monkshood (*A. variegatum*) with 'helmet' much taller than its width grows in similar places in mountains. Both strictly protected.

3 *Delphinium elatum.* Perennial herb up to 150 cm high, with simple stem, branched only at the inflorescence. Basal, long-petiolate leaves, smooth on the upper side, downy beneath, deeply palmately parted into widely wedge-shaped, deeply cut segments. Flowers dark blue to blue-violet, long-spurred, in dense raceme. Flowers in June and July, in original mountain habitats till September. Grows along mountain streams. Hybrids with this and two other species have given rise to the giant border delphiniums of gardens.

4 Larkspur *Consolida regalis* (syn. *Delphinium consolida*). Annual plant with erect stem, up to 50 cm high and branched only in upper half. Leaves much divided into linear segments; bracts linear, shorter than flower-stalks. Flowers in branched racemes, usually blue, spur reddish. Hairless follicles. Flowers from July to September. A field weed in southern Europe at lower altitudes; grown in gardens. This and the related species *C. ambigua* have given rise to the popular garden larkspurs.

5 Wood Anemone *Anemone nemorosa*. Up to 25 cm high herb with thin rhizome and solitary basal leaves. Stem simple, unbranched, with 3 petiolate leaves. Each leaf trifoliate, the segments bi- to trilobed. Flowers solitary, long-stalked, with usually six white tepals with pink flush outside. Hairy achenes with curved beak. Flowers from March to May. Grows in deciduous woods, thickets and damp meadows; almost common. Related Yellow Wood Anemone (*A. ranunculoides*) has yellow flowers and almost sessile leaves.

6 Snowdrop Wind-flower *Anemone sylvestris*. Herb up to 35 cm high with creeping rhizome and rosette of leaves. Leaves palmately 3—5 parted, segments toothed. Stem leaves divided into 5 oblong, lanceolate, deeply toothed segments. Flowers usually solitary, long-stalked, white, with five widely ovate tepals, hairy outside. Hairy achenes. Flowers from April to June. Grows on sunny, bushy slopes, in open woods, mostly on limestone soils, from lowlands to foothills, in milder regions. A protected plant.

by wind. Flowers from May to August. Grows on rocky mountain slopes, in meadows and amongst knee-pine. Strictly protected, similar to other pulsatillas.

3 Pasque Flower *Pulsatilla vulgaris.* A variable species with large flowers in shades of purple and violet. Illustrated species has stem up to 50 cm high. Basal leaves develop as the first flowers fade. They are long-petiolate, at first densely hairy, later thinly hairy, simply or twice pinnate, each leaflet deeply dissected; floral bracts divided into narrowly linear segments. Flowers with 6 tepals outside silky hairy, at first tulip-shaped, later opening wide, light to misty violet. Flowers from March to May. Grows on grassy slopes, on limestone soils. Also cultivated as rock-garden plant and occasionally escaping.

4 Fair Maids of France *Ranunculus aconitifolius.* Perennial, robust herb up to 1 metre high or more, with short rhizomes and a well-branched stem. Basal, long-petioled leaves are palmately five-parted, the segments lobed and deeply serrate; stem leaves similar to basal ones, mostly sessile. Flowers white, with 5 pe-

Family: **Buttercup**—Ranunculaceae

1 *Anemone narcissiflora.* A variable tufted perennial. Stem up to 40 cm high, hairy; basal leaves palmately 3–5 parted, each segment deeply toothed. Floral bracts usually in 3- to 5-lobed whorl. Flowers arranged in a several-stemmed umbel, erect; tepals white, sometimes flushed purple. Achenes hairless. Flowers from May to July. Grows in mountain meadows of the Alps and other central-European mountains. Poisonous plant, strictly protected.

2 Alpine Anemone *Pulsatilla alpina.* Up to 30 cm. high herb with branched rhizome, rosette of basal leaves and several simple, hairy, single-flowered stems with whorl of bracts. Basal leaves long-petiolate, stem ones shortly petiolate, with deeply dissected segments. Flowers long-stalked, with 6 white tepals often flushed outside with pink or violet; sometimes yellow. Achenes have long, hairy awn to aid dispersal

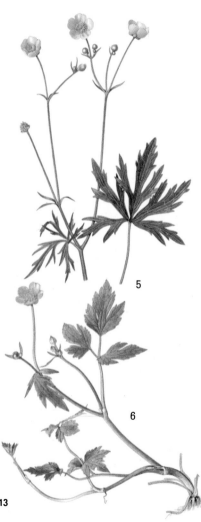

tals. Achenes shortly beaked. Flowers from May to August. Grows in mountain forests, along streams and in knee-pine. Poisonous.

5 Meadow Buttercup *Ranunculus acris.* Poisonous perennial herb, up to 1 metre high. Basal leaves long-petiolate, palmately five-parted, segments lanceolate, dissected and toothed. Stem sometimes with spreading hairs. Stem leaves similar to basal ones, upper leaves cleft into linear segments. Flowers with 5 glossy golden yellow petals. Achenes shortly beaked. Flowers from May to September. Grows abundantly in meadows and moist grassy places.

6 Creeping Buttercup *Ranunculus repens.* Perennial plant with erect flowering stems up to 50 cm long, and creeping stems rooting at the nodes. Basal leaves trifoliate, each leaflet petiolate, lobed and toothed; stem leaves similar to basal ones, upper leaves sessile, cleft into lanceolate or linear segments. Flowers glossy golden yellow with 5 petals. Achenes smooth, with curved beak. Flowers from May to August. Grows abundantly in wet meadows, fields, along banks of streams and ponds; also a garden weed.

Familly: **Buttercup**—Ranunculaceae

1 Water Crowfoot *Batrachium aquatile* (syn. *Ranunculus aquatilis*). Perennial aquatic plant with floating, smooth, branched stem to 1 m. Submerged petiolate leaves much divided into linear, forked segments which collapse after being taken out of water. Leaves floating on water surface are long-petiolate, rounded to reniform, cordate, palmately three-to five-lobed. Long-stalked flowers above water surface, with 5 white petals. Achenes wrinkled, bristle tipped. Flowers from June to September. Grows in lakes and ponds at lower altitudes. Related River Crowfoot (*B. fluitans*) has much longer segments to submerged leaves; segments of Rigid-leaved Crowfoot (*B. circinatum*) do not lose shape when taken out of water.

2 Noble Liverleaf *Hepatica nobilis* (syn. *H. triloba, Anemone hepatica*). Perennial herb with shortly creeping rhizome and single-flowered stems. Leaves trilobed, leathery, softly hairy on underside. A whorl of 3 calyx-like bracts immediately beneath the flower. Flower stalks hairy; flowers with 6—10 tepals, blue to light or dark violet, less frequently rosy or whitish. Achenes without appendages. Flowers in February to April. Grows in deciduous groves and bushy places from lowlands to foothills; locally abundant only. A protected plant.

3 Lesser Celandine *Ficaria verna* (syn. *Ranunculus ficaria*). Perennial herb with tubers among fibrous roots. Smooth stem up to 20 cm high. Basal and stem leaves petiolate, cordate, rounded to reniform, scalloped to notched,

smooth, glossy. Some forms have tiny tubers in axils of basal leaves. Flowers solitary, with 8—12 tepals of glossy yellow. Achenes small, ovoid. Flowers from March to May. Grows commonly in open woods, meadows, ditches and along banks.

4 Spring Pheasant's Eye *Adonis vernalis*. Poisonous perennial plant, up to 40 cm high, with thick rhizome. Erect stem scaly at base. Leaves sessile, up to four cleft into linear segments. Flowers solitary, large, of 10—20 narrowly elongated bright glossy yellow petals. Flowers in April and May. Grows on sunny slopes, bushy ravines and in pine-woods, as a rule on limestone soils. Occasionally cultivated for ornament. Strictly protected plant.

5 Summer Pheasant's Eye *Adonis aestivalis*. Annual herb up to 50 cm high with erect, little branched stem. Basal leaves petiolate, upper ones sessile, as a rule cut into many linear seg-

ments. Flowers individual, smallish, petals red, rarely pale yellow, at base usually with a black spot. Achenes smooth, oblong-ovoid, beaked. Flowers from May to July. Grows as field weed at lower altitudes in milder regions.

6 Upright Clematis *Clematis recta*. Perennial herb up to 1.5 m high, with erect, non-climbing stems. Basal stem leaves simple, upper ones odd-pinnate, leaflets ovate to lanceolate, entire, petiolate. Flowers arranged in terminal panicles; white, composed of 4 petal-like sepals. Achenes have long, hairy style. Flowers in June and July. Grows on bushy slopes, in open woods and meadows, at lower altitudes, mainly on limestone soils. The climbing, white to green-white flowered Traveller's Joy (*C. vitalba*) of Europe (including Britain) and northern Africa is more abundant and flowers from July to September. Many exotic species and cultivated varieties and hybrids are grown in gardens.

1

2

3

Family: **Buttercup**—Ranunculaceae

1 French Meadow-rue *Thalictrum aquilegiifolium.* Robust herb up to 1 metre or more high with erect stem, branched in the upper part, grooved and hairless. Leaves bi- to tripinnate, leaflets obovate, lobed, smooth and grey-green, resembling those of columbine. Flowers in dense corymbose panicles; no petals and the small whitish sepals soon falling; stamen filaments violet, thickened. Ovaries and achenes long-stalked, pendent. Flowers from May to July. Grows in moist forests and thickets and by the waterside from foothills to mountains. Similar but much smaller Lesser Meadow-rue (*T. minus*) has yellow stamens and greenish sepals.

Family: Aristolochiaceae

2 Asarabacca *Asarum europaeum.* Perennial evergreen herb with branched, scaly rhizome. Stems prostrate, each lateral shoot usually with two long-petiolate, reniform, entire, glossy deep green leaves. Fleshy bell-shaped flowers with 3 lobes brownish outside, dark violet within, are hidden by leaves. Flowers from March to May. Grows in humid groves and among bushes from lowlands to mountains.

3 Birthwort *Aristolochia clematitis.* Foetid perennial herb with erect, unbranched stems, up to 50 cm or more high. Leaves alternate, long-petiolate, rounded cordate. Flowers in small groups in axils of leaves; at first erect, later drooping. Corolla tubular, slightly curved, swollen at base, dull yellow. Capsule pear-shaped. Flowers in May and June. Grows in thickets, in hedges and vineyards at lower altitudes, in temperate regions. Formerly cultivated as a medicinal plant and later escaping to become naturalized.

Family: **Poppy**—Papaveraceae

4 *Papaver alpinum.* Perennial tufted herb, with unbranched flowering stems up to 20 cm high. Leaves petiolate, simply pinnate, segments linear to linear-lanceolate, deeply lobed, grey-green. Flowers white or yellow, calyx, with black bristles, falls off as flower expands; petals widely obovate. Seed-heads small, obovate with a flat top. Flowers in July and August. Grows on screes and among rocks at high elevations of the Alps and Carpathians.

5 Field Poppy *Papaver rhoeas.* Annual herb with erect, simple or little branched stems, bristly, leafy, up to 1 metre high. Leaves pinnate, segments deeply lobed and toothed, lower ones petiolate, upper sessile and bristly. Solitary flowers on long stalks with bristles; drooping in bud, erect in bloom. Calyx green, bristly, falling as flower opens. Corolla of 4 bright red petals; stigma usually ten-lobed. Seed-heads obovate, flat topped. Flowers from May to September. Grows as weed in fields and gardens, on spoil heaps and wasteland, from lowlands to foothills in temperate regions; locally abundant, elsewhere missing.

6 Greater Celandine *Chelidonium majus.* Perennial herb releasing orange latex when cut. Stem up to 60 cm high, erect and branched. Leaves somewhat hairy, lower ones petiolate, odd-pinnate, upper leaves sessile, deeply cut; segments lobed and toothed, underside grey-green. Flowers in umbels, yellow, petals soon falling. Capsule linear. Flowers from May to October. Grows in open woods, thickets and hedgerows, from lowlands to foothills.

1

2

6

Family: **Fumitory**—Fumariaceae

1 Common Fumitory *Fumaria officinalis.* Annual, grey-green herb, up to 30 cm high, with erect or ascending stem, branched and leafy. Leaves petiolate, bipinnate; petiolate leaflets palmately parted into linear segments. Flowers in upright racemes, small and narrow, rosy red, dark purple at tip; tiny sepals persistent. Fruits globular, single-seeded. Flowers from May to October. Grows commonly as weed in fields, gardens and on wasteland from lowlands to foothills.

2 *Corydalis cava.* Perennial herb up to 30 cm high, with hollow-topped underground tuber and erect stem, as a rule with two leaves. Leaves cut into several lobed leaflets. Flowers in erect raceme, bracts under flowers entire; corollas rosy-purple, yellow-white, spurred. Capsules long and narrow, beaked. Flowers from March to May. Grows in woods and thickets, from lowlands to foothills. Related *Corydalis fabacea* has pendent, few-flowered raceme while *Corydalis solida* has palmately lobed bracts beneath the flowers.

Family: Cruciferae (syn. Brassicaceae)

3 Charlock or **Wild Mustard** *Sinapis arvensis.* Annual plant up to 50 cm high with erect, little branched stem, irregularly hairy. Leaves mostly unparted, irregularly toothed, lower ones lyre-shaped, pinnatisect. Flowers have expanded, yellow-green sepals, corollas yolk-yellow, of four petals. Seed pod, either somewhat hairy or not at all, with short beak. Flowers from June to October. Grows fairly abundantly as field weed in lower altitudes. Related *Sinapis alba*, cultivated for seeds, has stem leaves lyre-like, pinnatisect to pinnately divided.

4 Wild Radish *Raphanus raphanistrum.* Annual herb with erect, slender, bristly stem. Leaves petiolate, lower ones lyre-shaped to pinnately lobed, unequally dentate; top leaves often undivided and irregularly toothed. Petals sulphur-yellow, violet-veined, sepals erect. Fruit is a pod

118

or loment, dehiscent, with beaked last segment. Flowers from June to October. Grows fairly abundantly as weed in fields and on wasteland. Related Radish (*R. sativus*) with flowers white or violet-tinted and non-dehiscent loment is cultivated as vegetable.

5 Hoary Cress *Cardaria draba*. Perennial, grey-downy herb, up to 50 cm high. Basal leaves ovate, stem ones usually shallowly toothed, clasping, arrow-shaped. Flowers in branched, crowded racemes, corollas white. Siliqua (pod) heart-shaped with long, persistent style. Flowers from May to July. Grows as weed in fields, on wasteland and trenches. Native of eastern Mediterranean, today abundantly naturalized, especially in milder regions.

6 Field Pennycress *Thlaspi arvense*. Annual hairless herb, up to 30 cm high, after bruising gives out a foetid smell. Stems slender, leaves distantly toothed, dentate, arrow-shaped, stem clasping. Flowers in erect racemes; calyx yellow-green, corolla white. Siliquas large, flat, ovately rounded, with wide rim, deeply dissected. Flowers from May to October. Commonly grows as weed in fields, fallows and on wasteland.

Family: Cruciferae

1 Shepherd's Purse *Capsella bursa-pastoris.*
Annual to biennial herb, up to 50 cm high, stem
often branched. Basal leaves pinnatisect to almost entire, arranged in rosette, stem leaves
clasping. Many-flowered inflorescences;
flowers small, white, occasionally petal-less. Siliquas roughly triangular with many small seeds.
Flowers from February to November, sometimes whole year round. Grows as common
weed in fields, gardens, on wasteland and along
paths from lowlands to mountains.

2 Perennial Honesty *Lunaria rediviva.* Perennial
plant up to 140 cm high, with creeping rhizome
and erect, unbranched stem. Leaves petiolate,
cordate, upper ones triangular, toothed. Flowers
light violet, rarely whitish. Siliquas large, elliptical, tapering to both ends, with membranous
partition and stiff valves. Flowers from May to
July. Scattered on screes, in open mountain forests and in ravines from foothills to mountains.
Protected plant. Cultivated Honesty (*L. annua*),
native of eastern Mediterranean, has sessile upper leaves and large, broad siliquas.

3 Golden Alison *Alyssum saxatile.* Evergreen
sub-shrub with oblanceolate, grey-felted leaves.
Stems up to 30 cm high, upright, few-leaved. Inflorescence branched; flowers in dense corymbs; petals shallowly lobed, golden yellow,
siliquas hairless. Flowers in April and May.
Grows on sunny rocks. Also cultivated as rock-
garden plant.

4 Mountain Alison *Alyssum montanum.* Perennial sub-shrub, 10—20 cm high. Stems and grey-
green leaves have grey hairs which are
branched and distinctly star-shaped under lens.
Lower leaves obovate or spatulate, upper ones
oblanceolate. Flowers in simple racemes; sepals as well as petals soon fall, corollas golden
yellow. Raceme during fruition much elongated,
siliquas almost round. Flowers from April to
June. Grows on rocks, dry and sunny slopes,
sandy places and margins of pine-woods at
lower altitudes, in warm regions.

5 Common Whitlow-grass *Erophila verna*. Tiny, annual, only 2—10 cm high with basal rosette of leaves and simple, leafless, filamentous stem. Leaves elliptic or lanceolate, entire or toothed. Few-flowered inflorescences; upper side of sepals hairy, margins white or light violet, membraneous. Petals distinctly cleft; white; siliquas elliptic to almost rounded, without style. Flowers from March to May. Grows gregariously in places from lowlands to mountains, on slopes, in fields, meadows, fallows, and on walls.

6 Lady's Smock *Cardamine pratensis*. Perennial herb, 20—40 cm high, with short rhizome and erect, hollow stem. Basal leaves in rosette, odd-pinnate, with up to 8 pairs of ovate leaflets, angularly toothed. Stem leaves pinnately divided, with linear, usually entire segments. Flowers often in dense racemes, lilac or violet-tinted, distinctly violet-veined. Anthers yellow; siliquas linear without beak. Flowers from April to June. Grows abundantly in damp meadows, from lowlands to mountains. Related Bitter Cress (*C. amara*) has rather weak, semi-decumbent stems and white flowers with violet anthers.

Family: Cruciferae

1 Common Winter-cress *Barbarea vulgaris.* Biennial, almost hairless herb up to 50 cm high. Lower leaves lyre-shaped, pinnately lobed, terminal leaflet broadly ovate, somewhat lobed or toothed; base of leaf stem clasping. Racemes dense, branched; flowers golden-yellow, petals almost double length of sepals. Siliquas erect on short stalks. Flowers from May to July. Grows in meadows, ditches, along streams, and also in fields and on wasteland.

2 *Hesperis matronalis.* Perennial, robust herb, up to over 1 metre high, hairy. Lower leaves oblong-ovate to lanceolate, upper ones smaller, almost sessile, all distantly toothed. Raceme long, sometimes branched; flowers large, fragrant, usually violet, rarely reddish or white, petals somewhat shallowly toothed. Siliquas cylindrical, up to 10 cm long. Flowers from May to July. Grows wild in the Mediterranean; often cultivated and becoming naturalized on waste ground, along hedges, in thickets and open woods.

3 Garlic Mustard or **Jack-by-the-Hedge** *Alliaria petiolata* (syn. *A. officinalis*). Biennial herb, smelling of garlic when bruised. Stems erect, often branched at the top. Lower leaves long-petiolate, cordate, irregularly sinuate toothed; stem leaves shortly petiolate, ovate to triangular, irregularly toothed. Flowers small, white; siliquas long, stalked, erect. Flowers from April to June. Grows in open woods, thickets, in hedgerows and on wasteland, abundant from lowlands to foothills.

1   2   3

Family: **Mignonette**—Resedaceae

4 Wild Mignonette *Reseda lutea.* Perennial herb with erect stems, little or not branched, up to 50 cm high. Leaves once pinnately cut into linear segments, with wavy margins. Flowers in dense racemes, during fruition becoming elongated. Each floret yellow-green, with 6 narrow petals, the 4 upper ones lobed. Upright oblong capsules. Flowers from May to September. Grows on grassy slopes and waste ground and as weed of cultivated land at lower altitudes in milder regions. Garden Mignonette (*R. odorata*), a North-African species, is cultivated in gardens; it has almost undivided leaves, reddish anthers and pendent fruits.

Family: **Rockrose**—Cistaceae

5 *Helianthemum chamaecistus* (syn. *H. nummularium*). Procumbent, evergreen, hairy shrublet 10—20 cm high. Leaves oval or oblong-ovate, densely white, hairy beneath. Inflorescence a few-flowered raceme, flowers large, 2—2.5 cm in diameter. Two minute outside sepals linear, three inner ones larger, ovate. Corolla of five yellow, rarely yellowish white petals. Flowers from June to October. Grows on sunny grassy slopes and in open scrub, from lowlands to mountains.

Family: Silenaceae (syn. Caryophyllaceae)

6 Corn Cockle *Agrostemma githago* (syn. *Lychnis githago*). Annual plant with erect stem up to 1 metre high, grey hairy. Leaves opposite, linear-lanceolate, hairy. Long-stalked flowers solitary; calyx bell-shaped, with five slender lobes; corolla red-purple, petals obovate. Capsules ovoid with black, reniform, poisonous seeds. Grows as weed in cereal crops in lower altitudes; formerly more abundant. Native probably of eastern Mediterranean.

Family: Silenaceae

1 Ragged Robin *Lychnis flos-cuculi.* Perennial plant up to 80 cm high. Stems of two sorts; decumbent and leafy and erect flowering. Opposite leaves narrowly to oblong lanceolate, entire. Open dichasial inflorescence; calyx bell-shaped, with 5 triangular teeth. Petals rose-red, cleft into four linear segments. Capsule broadly ovoid. Flowers from May to July. Grows in damp meadows, marshes, fens and open wet woods, from lowlands to mountains.

2 *Lychnis alba* (syn. *Silene alba, Melandrium album*). Annual to perennial herb, up to 1 metre high, softly downy, stems erect, branched. Lower leaves petiolate, oblanceolate, upper ones lanceolate to elliptic, sessile, all opposite. Flowers arranged in open dichasia. Flowers dioecious, stalked, opening in afternoon, slightly fragrant, calyx bell-shaped, inflated, with 5 pointed teeth; petals white, lobed. Capsule widely ovoid, enveloped in persistent calyx. Flowers from June to September. Grows in hedgerows, meadows, on waste and cultivated land, from lowlands to foothills. Related *Silene dioica* (syn. *Melandrium rubrum*) has red flowers and hairy stems.

3 Red German Catchfly *Lychnis viscaria* (syn. *Viscaria vulgaris*). Perennial plant up to 50 cm high, with smooth stem, having sticky zones beneath each pair of the upper leaves. Bottom leaves oblong-lanceolate, upper ones linear-lanceolate, all opposite, often with red tint. Inflorescence an interrupted spike-like panicle of axillary cymes. Calyx tubular, reddish, corolla bright red; ovoid capsules. Flowers from May to July. Grows in pastures, on stony slopes and dry rocks, from lowlands to foothills; very rare in Britain.

4 Moss Campion *Silene acaulis.* Perennial plant, cushion-like, densely leafy with numerous stems, only 2—4 cm high. Leaves spreading, linear, pointed, sessile. Flowers solitary, short-stalked. Calyx narrowly bell-shaped, petals bright to dark rose; capsules stalked, ovoid. Flowers from June to September. Grows on stony slopes and ledges, screes and among rocks above forest zone in mountains of western and central Europe.

5 Bladder Campion *Silene vulgaris* (syn. *S. cucubalus*). Herb up to 50 cm high, perennial, grey-green and smooth. Leaves elliptic lanceolate, entire, lower ones almost, upper leaves distinctly sessile. Flowers arranged in corymbose cymes, lower ones with long stalks, upper flowers short-stalked. Calyx inflated, ovoid, strikingly net-veined, yellowish green or with tint of purple. Petals usually white, deeply bilobed. Capsules broadly ovoid. Flowers from June to September. Grows on grassy slopes, by the roadside, on margins of woods, and on cultivated land, from lowlands to mountains.

6 Nottingham Catchfly *Silene nutans.* Up to 50 cm high, perennial, with erect and unbranched stems. Lower leaves spathulate, upper ones with short petioles, lanceolate to linear-lanceolate, with short hairs. Inflorescence a lax panicle of dichasial cymes, glandularly hairy; flowers long-stalked, more or less drooping. Calyx cylindrical, petals whitish, deeply bilobed. Capsules ovoid. Flowers from May to August. Grows on sunny slopes, among rocks, at outskirts of woods and on screes, from lowlands to foothills.

4

5

6

Family: Silenaceae

1 German Pink *Dianthus carthusianorum*. Perennial, tufted herb, over 25 cm high, with slender flowering stems and short, leafy, non-flowering ones, little branched. Leaves linear, fused at the base into a short sheath, pointed, stiff, rough on margins. Inflorescence a dense corymbose head, flowers almost sessile, bracts under calyx leathery, brown to red-brown, bluntly obovate, with awn-like point. Calyx cylindrical, smooth with maroon tint; petals purple-red, with toothed tip; capsules narrow oblong. Flowers from June to September. Grows on grassy, stony dry slopes and field boundaries.

2 Maiden Pink *Dianthus deltoides*. Perennial, sparsely tufted herb, with prostrate leafy stems and erect flowering ones. Leaves linear-pointed, opposite, roughly hairy on margins. Flowers long-stalked, solitary, bracts under calyx membranous. Calyx cylindrical, sometimes reddish; petals carmine-red, toothed at tip; conspicuously bristled and white-dotted at base. Flowers from June to September. Grows in dry pastures, banks and field boundaries, from lowland to foothill country. Some related species, e.g. Carnation (*D. caryophyllus*) and China Pink (*D. chinensis*), are cultivated in gardens.

3 Soapwort *Saponaria officinalis.* Perennial robust plant, up to 75 cm high, erect, usually with finely downy stem, branched only in upper part. Leaves ovate to elliptic, pointed, sessile, three to five-veined. Flowers pink, sometimes white, in terminal corymbs. Calyx usually light green, hairy; petals blunt or square tipped. Capsules oblong ovoid. Flowers from June to September. Grows in hedgerows, by streams and in open moist woods, from lowlands to foothills. A double-flowered form is sometimes cultivated and becomes naturalized on banks and wasteland.

4 Greater Stitchwort *Stellaria holostea.* Perennial, sparsely tufted plant with creeping rhizome and erect, square stems, up to 30 cm high. Leaves spreading, narrowly lanceolate, pointed, opposite, underside and margins rough. Flowers in an open, terminal, few-flowered dichasia. Petals white, double the length of calyx, almost deeply bilobed. Flowers from May to September. Grows in hedgerows, on bushy slopes and in open woodland from lowlands to foothills. Related Common Chickweed (*S. media*) has much smaller flowers and petals of the same length as calyx.

5 Field Mouse-ear *Cerastium arvense.* Perennial herb, sparsely tufted, up to 30 cm high, with numerous stems creeping or ascending, with sterile leafy shoots. Leaves narrowly oblong to linear-lanceolate, pointed, hairy. Flowers in lax dichasia. Sepals hairy, with whitish membranous margins; petals double the calyx length, white, bilobed. Flowers from April to July. Grows in dry grassland and on banks, from lowlands to mountains.

6 *Cerastium holosteoides* (syn. *C. vulgatum*). Perennial tufted herb up to 30 cm high, with ascending, flowering stems and semi-prostrate, leafy, sterile shoots. Leaves oblanceolate to elliptic, bluntly pointed, with short hairs. Flowers in open dichasia. Petals slightly longer than calyx, small, white, bilobed. Flowers from May to October. Grows by the roadside, on dunes, in dry meadows and on grassy slopes, from lowlands to mountains.

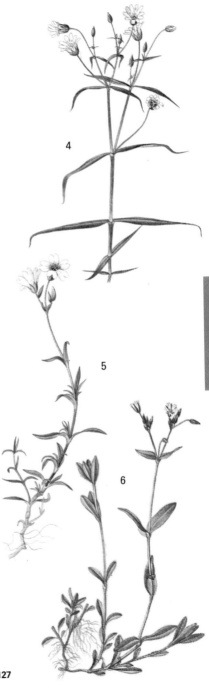

node, silvery membranous. Flowers in a small terminal cyme; flower stalks nodding, after fertilization again erect, and elongated when capsule is mature. Petals pink, usually shorter than sepals. Flowers from May to September. Grows in sandy or gravelly soils, from lowlands to foothills.

Family: **Violet**—Violaceae

2 Sweet Violet *Viola odorata*. Perennial herb with short, thick rhizomes and long prostrate stolons. Basal leaves ovate-orbicular, cordate, sparingly hairy. Stems up to 10 cm high, with widely ovate stipules, entire or glandular fringed. Fragrant flowers blue-violet or white, rarely pink; petals whitish at base, the lowest one spurred; calyx has appendages which are much shorter than the spur. Flowers in March and April. Grows in woods, thickets and hedgebanks at lower altitudes; often cultivated in gardens. Related Heath Violet (*V. canina*) is distinctly hairy and has narrower leaves, and unscented flowers with a whitish spur.

3 Common Violet *Viola riviniana*. Perennial plant with short rhizome and basal rosette of leaves. Stems erect, usually 10—15 cm high. Leaves long-petiolate, ovate-orbicular, deeply cordate, crenate; stipules lanceolate, deeply fringed. Flowers large, various shades of blue-violet, spur paler. Calyx with angularly rounded

Family: Stellariaceae (syn. Alsinaceae)

1 Sand Spurrey *Spergularia rubra*. Annual or biennial plant, somewhat tufted, decumbent or ascending. Stems 5—25 cm long; leaves narrowly linear, sharply pointed, shorter than stem internodes. Stipules ovate, fused around the

5

6

appendages. Flowers in April and May. Grows in open woods, hedgebanks, heaths, pastures and among rocks, from lowlands to mountains. A very variable species; the smaller forms distinguished as *V. riviniana* ssp. *minor.*

4 Heartsease or **Wild Pansy** *Viola tricolor.* Annual or perennial herb, usually tufted, up to 20 cm high, with branched, erect or ascending stem. Leaves petiolate, ovate to lanceolate; stipules deeply lobed. Flowers on long stalks; lanceolate sepals have blunt to rounded appendages. Petals often double calyx length, two upper ones mostly violet, others light yellow, or entirely blue-violet or yellow; spur longer than calyx appendages. Flowers from May to September. Grows in fields and meadows, on wasteland, from lowlands to foothills. Related Field Violet *V. arvensis* has much smaller light yellow flowers, the calyx and corolla of equal length. *Viola* × *wittrockiana* is the cultivated hybrid garden pansy with large flowers of varied colours.

Family: **Goosefoot** —Chenopodiaceae

5 Good King Henry *Chenopodium bonus-henri- cus.* The only perennial goosefoot; stem up to

50 cm or more high, unbranched. Petiolate leaves triangular, with pointed basal lobes and a wavy margin. Globose clusters of flowers arranged in dense, terminal, leafy, pyramidal panicle. Flowers have minute five-lobed perianth which enfolds the base of the tiny ovoid capsule. Flowers from May to August. Grows abundantly near human dwellings and by roadsides from lowlands to foothills. Related Sowbane (*C. hybridum*) and especially Stinking Goosefoot (*C. vulvaria*) are slightly poisonous and distinctly malodorous.

6 Shining Orache *Atriplex nitens.* Annual herb up to 150 cm high, with branched stems. Leaves triangular, lobed, on upper surface glossy, dark green, on underside silvery grey with a mealy coating. Inflorescence drooping, especially during fruiting. Pair of enlarged bracts in which fruit is enclosed, is rhomboid, entire, longer than fruit stalks. Minute flowers are greenish. Flowers from July to September. Grows on wasteland and by roadsides at lower altitudes. Related Common Orache (*A. patula*) has rhomboid-lanceolate to linear-oblong leaves and floral bracts with one or two small teeth on each side.

Family: **Knotgrass**—Polygonaceae

1 Sheep's Sorrel *Rumex acetosella*. Perennial plant, often with red tint; stem up to 25 cm high, decumbent or erect. Lower leaves long-petiolate, hastate, upper ones linear-lanceolate. Inflorescence a small branched raceme; flowers have small greenish perianth; during fruition this enlarges and more or less encloses the fruit. Flowers from May to August. Grows on heaths and pastures, and as a weed in fields and gardens from lowlands to foothills.

2 Common Sorrel *Rumex acetosa.* Over 50 cm high, perennial. Lower stem leaves narrowly ovate, arrow-shaped, with pointed basal lobes. Stipules fused as a fringed sheath. Inflorescence a branched raceme; flowers have green perianth. Inner segments rounded cordate with tiny, round swelling, enlarging during fruit development; outer segments reflex back. Flowers from May to July. Grows in light woodland clearings, in damp meadows, and by roadsides, from lowlands to mountains. Eaten in salads and sauces. Related Curled Dock (*R. crispus*) has a triangularly ovate fruiting perianth and the lower leaves with waved and curled margins.

3 Bistort or **Easter-ledges** *Polygonum bistorta.* Perennial herb with thick rhizome and simple stems up to 1 metre high. Basal leaves long petiolate, ovate, pointed, entire, stem leaves triangular-ovate, sessile. Inflorescence a dense terminal spike, individual flowers rosy, rarely whitish. Flowers from May to July. Grows in damp meadows, pastures and by roadsides, often in dense colonies or clumps, from lowlands to mountains. *Polygonum persicaria* has leaves with large, horseshoe-shaped maroon blotch.

4 Knotgrass *Polygonum aviculare.* An annual, decumbent plant with branched stem, up to 50 cm long, often forming dense mats. Leaves elliptic, spathulate, lanceolate or linear with membranous stipules, fused into sheaths, usually lacerated. Flowers in clusters of one to six in leaf axils; perianth whitish, often pink tinted; enlarging during fruition and becoming red. Flowers from May to October. Grows in waste places, by roadsides, along paths and as farm and garden weed, from lowlands to hills.

5 *Polygonum convolvulus.* Annual, prostrate or twining, with angular stems up to 1 metre long. Leaves ovate-acuminate to triangular, arrow-shaped. Flowers in an interrupted, terminal raceme; perianth of 5 segments, the outer two somewhat keeled. Flowers from July to October. Grows as field and garden weed, and on wasteland at lower altitudes.

Family: **Nettle**—Urticaceae

6 Hop *Humulus lupulus.* Twining, perennial, dioecious plant with coarsely hairy stems, 2—6 metres long. Stipules triangular-ovate; leaves opposite, long-petiolate, lower ones palmately three- to five-lobed, cordate, upper leaves more shallowly lobed to ovate, all boldly toothed. Male flowers in axillary panicles, female ones in ovoid, cone-like spikes. Fruiting heads pendent, pale greenish-yellow, their scales covered with golden-yellow glands. Flowers from July to August. Grows in hedgerows, amongst scrub, and at edges of woodland at lower altitudes. Has been cultivated since 8th century in fields for flavouring beer.

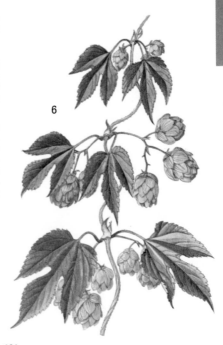

6

Family: **Nettle**—Urticaceae

1 Small Nettle *Urtica urens.* Annual herb, 10—30 cm high, with erect, little branched stems. Leaves ovate to elliptic, serrate. Erect inflorescences of the same length as petioles or shorter; tiny flowers have light green perianth. Fruit a tiny ovoid nutlet. Whole plant covered with stinging hairs; sharply 'burns' on touch. Flowers from June to September. Grows abundantly as weed in fields and gardens, on wasteland and by rubbish tips at lower altitudes.

2 Stinging Nettle *Urtica dioica.* Robust, perennial, dioecious herb with a far-creeping rhizome. Stems erect, rarely branched, up to 150 cm tall. Leaves petiolate, ovate, cordate, pointed, serrate. Male inflorescences spreading or pendent panicles, longer than leaf petioles; female always drooping and longer. Perianth greenish, nutlet ovoid. Whole plant covered with stinging hairs, but sometimes without. Flowers from June to October. Grows as a farm and garden weed on waste ground, in thickets, damp woods, ditches and in hedgerows, from lowlands to mountains.

Family: **Sundew**—Droseraceae

3 Common Sundew *Drosera rotundifolia.* Perennial herb, forming solitary or tufted rosettes. One to several erect stems, 10—20 cm high, usually red tinted, bearing a few-flowered spike of tiny, white flowers. Leaves rounded and fleshy, long-petiolate, reddish, with long, glandular hairs; fruit is a capsule. Flowers in July and August. Grows in bogs and wet peaty places, on moors and heaths, from lowlands to mountains. Grows in sites with soil poor in nitrogenous substances; acquires missing compounds from bodies of insects. Sensitive, glandular hairs exude sticky liquid which traps insects; special glands secrete substances for digesting soft parts of insects body.

Family: **Crassula**—Crassulaceae

4 Orpine or **Livelong** *Sedum telephium*. Perennial herb with thick rootstock and erect stems up to 50 cm high. Leaves ovate to oblong-lanceolate or obovate, toothed, tapered to sessile base, alternate, opposite or in whorls of three, fleshy grey-green. Inflorescence flattened and compact, composed of numerous cymes; sepals 5, green, corollas reddish purple. Flowers from July to September. Grows among rocks, on hedgebanks, walls, and in light dry woods from lowlands to mountains.

5 Wall Pepper *Sedum acre*. Perennial, mat-forming plant, 5—10 cm high, with prostrate, much branched stems. Leaves widely ovate to ovoid triangular, blunt, sessile, thickly set and usually overlapping, having a sharply burning taste. Inflorescence a few-flowered cyme; flowers short-stalked, corollas bright yellow, star-shaped. Flowers in June and July. Grows on sunny slopes, among rocks, in sandy places, on wasteland, walls and dunes, from lowlands to foothills.

6 *Sempervivum soboliferum*. Perennial herb with leaves arranged in a dense basal rosette. Leaves ovate, reddish brown at tip, margins shortly bristled. Flowering stems glandular-hairy, up to 20 cm high, thickly leaved. Calyx also glandular, sepals red-tipped. Petals six, pointed, greenish yellow. Flowers in July and August. Grows on rocks, stony slopes and walls, from lowlands to mountains. Protected plant. Common Houseleek (*S. tectorum*), bearing rosy flowers, and other species are cultivated in gardens.

133

Family: **Saxifrage**—Saxifragaceae

1 Meadow Saxifrage *Saxifraga granulata*. Perennial, somewhat tufted plant, up to 40 cm high, with basal rosettes and stems usually branched. Overwinters as a cluster of small bulbils from the axils of the basal leaves. These leaves are reniform, cordate, glandular-hairy, usually with large crenations. Stem leaves almost sessile, much smaller. Inflorescence a loose terminal cyme. Flowers shortly glandular, petals white, at least three times longer than calyx. Capsules ovoid or sub-globose. Flowers in May and June. Grows in well-drained grassland and on margins of woods at lower altitudes.

2 Livelong Saxifrage *Saxifraga paniculata* (syn. *S. aizoon*). Perennial herb with stiff, grey-green leaves in numerous basal rosettes. Basal leaves obovate to ligulate, serrate; the margins with small glands which secrete calcium carbonate.

Stem up to 30 cm tall, leaves small, ligulate, finely serrate. Inflorescence open, paniculate, corollas white, often red-dotted. Capsules globose. Flowers in June and July. Grows scattered on rocks, screes and stony barrens in mountains. Many related species grow in Alps, some of them cultivated in gardens.

3 Grass of Parnassus *Parnassia palustris*. Perennial herb with few-leaved basal rosette and stems 10—20 cm high. Basal leaves long-petiolate, ovately cordate, smooth. Single-flowered stems with one sessile clasping leaf. Flowers of five white petals; five gland-fringed staminodes alternate with five stamens. Capsule ovoid. Flowers from June to September, in lowlands much later than in mountains. Grows in damp meadows and on heaths and moors from lowlands to foothills, in mountains, in peaty meadows and among wet rocks.

4

5

Family: **Rose**—Rosaceae

4 Wood Goatsbeard *Aruncus dioicus* (syn. *A. sylvester*). Perennial, clump-forming herb up to 2 metres high, with erect, smooth stems. Leaves long-petiolate, two or three times pinnate, the leaflets ovate to lanceolate, shortly petiolate to almost sessile, pointed and unequally toothed. Inflorescence a large, dense, terminal panicle, composed of numerous minute, unisexual or dioecious cream-white flowers. Fruits are tiny brown follicles. Flowers in July. Grows in damp mountain forests and thickets and often naturalized by roadsides, from hilly country to mountains.

5 Meadowsweet *Filipendula ulmaria*. Perennial, clump-forming plant up to 150 cm high, with short rhizomes and erect, stiff, seldom branched stems. Leaves odd-pinnate, with double-toothed ovate leaflets, terminal one larger, palmately three- to five-lobed. Flowers in large, dense, terminal cymes, creamy-white, fragrant. Flowers from June to September. Grows in swamps, marshes, fens, damp or wet woods, and in lowlands and foothills. Dropwort (*F. vulgaris*) thrives in dry habitats, is smaller and has a tuberous rootstock.

6 Marsh Cinquefoil *Potentilla palustris* (syn. *Comarum palustre*). Perennial, woody-based herb up to 1 metre high. Leaves odd-pinnate with 5—7 oblong, toothed leaflets, dark green above, hairy on veins and grey-green beneath. Flowers in sparse terminal cymes, the five-lobed calyx outside green, inside red-purple. Petals smaller than calyx lobes, deep purple, stamens dark red; achenes ovoid. Flowers in June and July. Grows in fens, bogs, marshes, and by water, from lowlands to foothills.

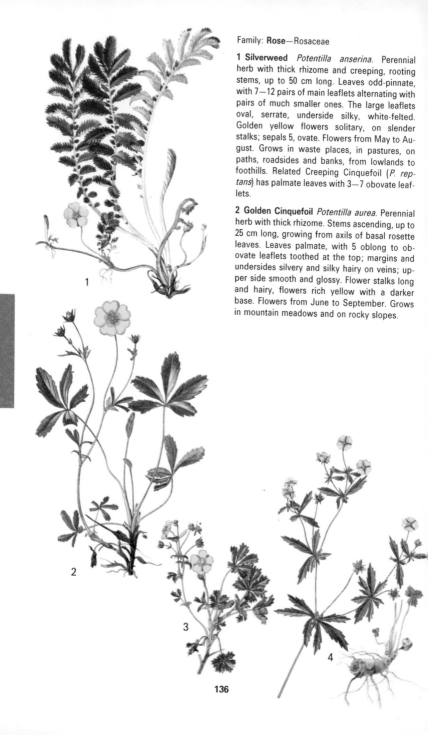

Family: **Rose**—Rosaceae

1 Silverweed *Potentilla anserina*. Perennial herb with thick rhizome and creeping, rooting stems, up to 50 cm long. Leaves odd-pinnate, with 7—12 pairs of main leaflets alternating with pairs of much smaller ones. The large leaflets oval, serrate, underside silky, white-felted. Golden yellow flowers solitary, on slender stalks; sepals 5, ovate. Flowers from May to August. Grows in waste places, in pastures, on paths, roadsides and banks, from lowlands to foothills. Related Creeping Cinquefoil (*P. reptans*) has palmate leaves with 3—7 obovate leaflets.

2 Golden Cinquefoil *Potentilla aurea*. Perennial herb with thick rhizome. Stems ascending, up to 25 cm long, growing from axils of basal rosette leaves. Leaves palmate, with 5 oblong to obovate leaflets toothed at the top; margins and undersides silvery and silky hairy on veins; upper side smooth and glossy. Flower stalks long and hairy, flowers rich yellow with a darker base. Flowers from June to September. Grows in mountain meadows and on rocky slopes.

3 *Potentilla tabernaemontani* (syn. *P. verna*). Perennial mat-forming plant with much branched rhizome and numerous prostrate shoots, often rooting at the nodes. Leaves long-petiolate, palmate, with 5 somewhat hairy, toothed, wedge-shaped to obovate leaflets. Stalked flowers with shallowly notched yellow petals. Flowers from March to June. Grows on sunny, grassy slopes, in sandy places and among rocks from lowlands to foothills. Related Hoary Cinquefoil (*P. argentea*) has leaflet margins recurved and undersides white-felted similarly to stems.

4 Tormentil *Potentilla erecta*. Perennial herb with short, thick, branched rootstock and erect or ascending leafy stem, up to 30 cm long. Basal leaves petiolate, stem ones almost sessile, usually trifoliate; leaflets wedge-shaped, obovate, toothed, lobed stipules large and conspicuous. Flowers slender, stalked, small, with 4 rounded, faintly notched yellow petals. Flowers from June to August. Grows on heaths, heather moors and in rocky and grassy places, from lowlands to mountains.

5 White Cinquefoil *Potentilla alba*. Perennial herb with much-branched rhizome and numerous flower stems, about 10 cm high, from axils of basal leaves. Leaves palmate, with 5 lanceolate leaflets, finely toothed at tip; upperside dark green, underside silvery, silky-hairy. Flowers white; sepals of the same length as epicalyx. Achenes hairy. Flowers from May to July. Grows in dry woods, meadows and on grassy slopes at lower altitudes, in milder regions.

6 Wild Strawberry *Fragaria vesca*. Perennial tufted herb with branched rhizome and creeping, rooting stolons. Stems up to 20 cm high emerge from axils of leaves. Leaves trifoliate, leaflets obovate to ovate, toothed, lateral ones sessile. Flower stalks have appressed hairs, flowers are white; ripe strawberries sub-globose to bluntly conical, red. Flowers in May and June. Grows in woodland clearings, open woods, on bushy slopes, banks and hedgerows, from lowlands to mountains. Related *Fragaria moschata* is larger, has flower stalks with spreading and lateral leaflets shortly petiolate. Fruits whitish, on sunny side red flushed.

5

6

Family: **Rose**—Rosaceae

1 Mountain Avens *Dryas octopetala*. Plant with woody stems forming cushion-like tufts, several centimetres high. Leaves petiolate, ovate-oblong, with rounded teeth, leathery, on underside white, upper surface dark green, glossy. Flowers solitary on erect, up to 10 cm long stalks; petals 7—10, white, obovate. Achenes have long, hairy appendages and resemble those of Pasque Flower. Flowers from June to August. Grows on rocks, screes, and grassy slopes in mountains and by the sea, predominantly on limestone soils.

2 Common Avens *Geum urbanum*. Perennial tufted herb, up to 50 cm high, with thick rhizome and basal rosette of leaves. These are petiolate, odd-pinnate, with lanceolate lateral and broadly ovate to orbicular terminal leaflets, irregularly double-toothed. Stem leaves trifoliate or trilobed. Flowers erect, calyx after flowering reflexing; petals yellow. Achenes bristly hairy with a sharp hook on the modified style. Flowers from May to August. Grows in open woods, thickets, along hedgerows and on wasteland, from lowlands to foothills.

3 Water Avens *Geum rivale*. Perennial plant up to 1 metre high, with thick rhizome. Stems erect, hairy, often red flushed. Basal leaves in a rosette, long-petiolate, lyre-like, pinnate, terminal leaflet large, rounded, trilobed; lateral leaflets ovate, all hairy and toothed. Stem leaves are trifoliate. Flowers drooping; calyx purple, petals orange-pink; after fertilization flowering stem erect. Achenes hairy, with a stalked hook. Flowers in May and June. Grows in wet meadows, marshes, streamsides and damp woods, from hilly country to mountains.

4 Common Agrimony *Agrimonia eupatoria*. Perennial plant up to 1 metre high, hairy, with thick rhizome. Stem little branched. Basal leaves odd-pinnate, leaflets elliptic, toothed; stem leaves smaller, with few leaflets. Flowers short-stalked, arranged in simple, erect raceme; corollas small, yellow; calyx hairy, with numerous deep grooves and bearing hooked spines. Flowers from June to August. Grows on hedge banks, along field boundaries, by roadsides and on bushy and grassy hills, from lowlands to foothills.

5 Great Burnet *Sanguisorba officinalis* (syn. *Poterium officinale*). Perennial herb up to 1 metre high, with thick rhizome and erect, branched stems. Basal leaves odd-pinnate in basal tufts; leaflets shortly petiolate, oblong-ovate, toothed, upper side glossy dark green, under side blue-green, hairless. Floral heads oblong-ovoid, dull crimson; flowers very small, without petals. Flowers from July to September. Grows fairly abundantly in damp meadows, from lowlands to foothills. *Sanguisorba minor* grows in well-drained hill grassland, has globose, reddish green heads, and leaflets widely ovate with green undersides.

6 Common Lady's Mantle *Alchemilla vulgaris.* Perennial herb, with a thick, somewhat woody rhizome and tufts of basal leaves. Stems ascending or erect, 10—30 cm high, hairy to smooth. Petiolate basal leaves rounded or reniform, palmately lobed and toothed. Flowers without petals, yellow-green, in open panicles; sepals either smooth or hairy. Flowers from May to September. Grows in meadows, pastures, along brooks and at outskirts of woods, from lowlands to mountains.

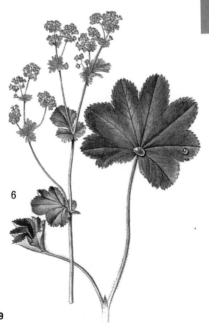

5

4

6

139

Family: Fabaceae (syn. Papilionaceae)

1 Common Lupin *Lupinus polyphyllus.* Perennial plant up to 150 cm high. Stems leafy, erect, unbranched. Leaves petiolate, palmate, with cuneate, elliptic, hairy leaflets. Pea-shaped flowers in dense, upright racemes; corollas blue or blue and white. Pods large, hairy and many-seeded. Flowers from June to August. Native of North America; at one time cultivated as forage for farm animals and for green manuring in gardens. Also grown for ornamental purposes and often going wild. South-European species are sometimes cultivated as forage, having white or yellow flowers.

2 Common Melilot *Melilotus officinalis.* Biennial herb with erect, branched stems up to 1 metre high, angular, usually smooth. Leaves petiolate, trifoliate, with oblong-elliptic, toothed leaflets, the central one distinctly petiolate; stipules lanceolate, entire. Dense axillary stalked racemes bearing tiny yellow drooping flowers. Pods ovoid, smooth and black. Flowers from June to September. Grows in fields, wasteland and by roadsides, from lowlands to hilly country. Related White Melilot (*M. albus*) has white flowers.

3 Lucerne *Medicago sativa.* Perennial herb, up to 80 cm high, with erect, smooth stems and trifoliate leaves; leaflets narrowly obovate, central one distinctly petiolate. Flowers purple, rarely whitish, in dense, short racemes. Pods spirally twisted, two to three turns. Flowers from June to September. Native of eastern Mediterranean and western Asia; long cultivated for forage and often well naturalized. Related Sickle Medick (*M. falcata*) is native of central Europe, has yellow flowers and sickle-shaped pods. Hybrid populations are often encountered.

4 White Clover *Trifolium repens.* Perennial herb with creeping, rooting stems, ascending at the tips, up to 30 cm long. Leaves long-petiolate, trifoliate, leaflets sessile, obovate to obcordate, finely toothed at tip, with lighter angled band towards the base. Flower heads globose; florets white or pink; after flowering light brown. Flowers from May to September. Grows in meadows, lawns and ditches. Cultivated as a fodder crop.

5 Red Clover *Trifolium pratense.* Perennial herb almost 50 cm high, with erect, little-branched stems. Leaves in basal tuft are trifoliate and long-petiolate; leaflets sessile, obovate to elliptic, entire, usually with a whitish or red-brown crescent-shaped spot on upper surface. Stem leaves smaller, sessile. Flower heads globose to ovoid, flowers purple-pink or pale red, rarely whitish. Flowers from June to September. Grows in meadows, by the roadside and in forest clearings, from lowlands to mountains. Often cultivated for forage. Cultivated *Trifolium incarnatum* has striking cylindrical heads. Tiny Haresfoot Trefoil (*T. arvense*) has small hairy heads and palest pink flowers.

6 Kidney Vetch *Anthyllis vulneraria*. Perennial herb with hairy stem, up to 30 cm high, ascending to erect. Odd-pinnate basal leaves; 11—15 leaflets, elliptic to linear-oblong, terminal one much larger than lateral ones. Globose flower heads singly or in clusters. Flowers light yellow to reddish. Flowers from May to August. Grows on sunny grassy banks and slopes.

4

6

2

3

5

Family: Fabaceae

1 Common Birdsfoot Trefoil *Lotus corniculatus.*
Perennial herb, well-branched rhizome, decumbent or ascending stems, up to 30 cm long, distinctly angular. Leaves odd-pinnate, the 5 leaflets smooth, entire, broadly ovate to lanceolate, underside grey-green. Flowers short-stalked, in 3—10 flowered umbels, corollas intense yellow, outside usually reddish. Flowers from May to September. Grows in pastures and on grassy and bushy slopes from lowlands to mountains. Related Marsh Birdsfoot Trefoil (*L. uliginosus*) has hollow, round stems, larger inflorescence and grows in moist habitat.

2 Common Crown Vetch *Coronilla varia.* Perennial, robust herb with numerous stems, decumbent or ascending, often climbing, branched, up to 1 metre long. Leaves odd-pinnate, the 9—17 leaflets shortly petiolate, oblong elliptic with a short point. Long-stalked inflorescence erect; white, pink or purple flowers in 10—20 flowered umbels. Pods slender, breaking up into one-seeded sections. Flowers from June to August. Grows on field boundaries, bushy slopes and by the roadside, from lowlands to foothills. Slightly poisonous.

3 Sainfoin *Onobrychis viciifolia.* Perennial, robust herb, scattered with hairs, up to 50 cm. high, with stiff, erect stem. Leaves odd-pinnate, the 11—25 leaflets obovate to linear-oblong. Racemes ovoid to cylindrical, flowers bright red or pink, the standard petal purple-striped. Pods short, flat, one-seeded. Flowers from May to July. Commonly cultivated forage since 16th century; often becomes locally naturalized. Found along field boundaries, by the roadside and on dry slopes at lower altitudes.

1

2

3

4 Bush Vetch *Vicia sepium*. Perennial herb with branched rhizome and erect or climbing stem up to 50 cm high. Leaves pinnate, terminated in branched tendril; the 10—18 leaflets ovate to elliptic, mucronate, and pointed. Flowers in threes to sixes in axils of leaves; corollas pale purple, calyx teeth unequal, shorter than calyx tube. Flowers from May to August. Grows in hedgerows, thickets, open woods and meadows, from lowlands to mountains. Related Common Vetch (*V. sativa*) has larger flowers in groups of one to three in the leaf axils. Large forms cultivated as forage and well naturalized by roadsides and on waste ground.

5 Tufted Vetch *Vicia cracca*. Perennial herb with strong, creeping rhizome and angular, softly hairy stems, up to 1 metre or more high. Pinnate leaves terminate in branched tendril; the 12—30 leaflets oblong to linear-lanceolate, underside usually hairy. Inflorescence a 10- to 40-flowered, one-sided raceme, stalked, almost as long as leaves; corollas blue-violet, rarely whitish. Pods short-stalked. Flowers from June to August. Grows in hedgerows, thickets, along field boundaries and in grassy places, from lowlands to mountains.

6 Hairy Milk Vetch *Oxytropis pilosa*. Perennial herb 15—30 cm high, densely hairy. Erect, ascending stems bear odd-pinnate leaves with narrowly lanceolate leaflets. Dense inflorescence an elongated raceme; flowers light yellow. Pods linear with white hairs. Flowers in June and July. Grows on sunny grassy slopes at lower altitudes, in milder areas.

4

5

6

143

Family: Fabaceae

1 Earth-nut Pea *Lathyrus tuberosus*. Perennial, hairless, grey-green herb with creeping rhizome and tuberous, thickened roots. Stems climbing, up to 1 metre long, square. Leaves with one pair of obovate leaflets and branched tendril. Long-stalked inflorescences bear a few-flowered raceme; flowers fragrant, light purple, standard crimson. Flowers from June to August. Naturalized in Britain in fields and hedgerows especially on calcareous soils, at lower altitudes. Related Annual Sweet Pea (*L. odoratus*) with large flowers of various colours is native of southern Europe and cultivated in gardens.

2 Narrow-leaved Everlasting Pea *Lathyrus sylvestris*. Perennial, robust plant with long, creeping rhizome. Numerous stems are ascending or climbing, up to 3 metres long, keeled or winged. Leaves with branched tendril, the 2 leaflets linear-lanceolate, petioles widely winged. Axillary, long-stalked inflorescences, with 3—8 rose-pink flowers. Pods to 8 cm long, winged. Flowers in July and August. Grows in open woods, on bushy slopes and in hedgerows from lowlands to foothills. Related Meadow Vetchling (*L. pratensis*) is much smaller with attractive yellow flowers.

3 *Lathyrus vernus* (syn. *Orobus vermus*). Perennial herb with erect, self-supporting stems up to 40 cm high. Pinnate leaves bright green, without tendrils, the 2 or 3 pairs of leaflets ovate and long-pointed. Inflorescence a few-flowered raceme. Flowers red-violet, later blue-green, wings with blue tint. Flowers in April and May. Grows in open woods, from lowlands to foothills.

4 Milk Vetch *Astragalus glycyphyllos*. Perennial herb with decumbent or ascending, hairless stems, sometimes creeping, up to 1 metre long. Leaves odd-pinnate, the 11—21 leaflets oblong-elliptic. Axillary, stalked inflorescences in racemes, shorter than leaves; flowers creamy-white, tinged greenish. Pods linear, sickle-shaped. Flowers in June and July. Grows in open woods, thickets and rough grassy places, from lowlands to foothills. Related Alpine Milk Vetch (*A. alpinum*) has light blue flowers and violet-red keel.

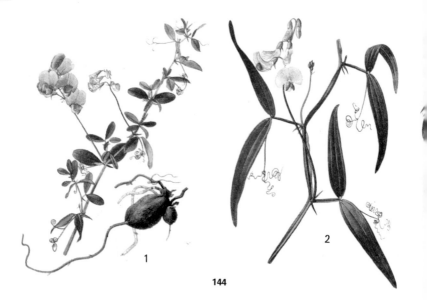

Family: **Geranium**—Geraniaceae

5 Bloody Cranesbill *Geranium sanguineum*. Perennial herb with thick, creeping rhizome. Stems ascending, up to 50 cm long, hairy. Basal leaves die early; stem ones are opposite, petiolate, deeply palmately lobed into five to seven narrow segments, which are further cut or lobed. Solitary, axillary, long-stalked flowers have 5 purple-crimson petals. Flowers from June to August. Grows in open bushy places, on stony slopes and in grassland, at lower altitudes.

6 Herb Robert *Geranium robertianum*. Annual or biennial herb, red-tinted, hairy, somewhat foetid. Erect or decumbent stems up to 40 cm long. Leaves palmately lobed, petiolate leaflets once or twice pinnately dissected, segments toothed. Rose-pink flowers in pairs; corollas less than 15 mm in diameter. Flowers from May to October. Grows in open woods, on screes and walls, from lowlands to mountains. Wood Cranesbill (*G. sylvaticum*) has purple flowers; Meadow Cranesbill (*G. pratense*) has violet-blue and *Geranium phaeum* brown or black-purple flowers. All have strikingly beaked fruits.

3

4

5

6

145

Family: **Geranium**—Geraniaceae

1 Common Storksbill *Erodium cicutarium.* Annual or biennial herb with erect or inclined stems, hairy, up to 25 cm long. Basal, long-petiolate leaves in rosette, upper ones are shortly petiolate; all leaves odd-pinnate, segments pinnatisect, hairy. Inflorescence a several-flowered, stalked umbel with rose-violet corollas; downy, long-beaked fruits follow. Flowers from April to October. Grows in fields, waste places, dry grassland and downs, from lowlands to mountains.

Family: **Oxalis**—Oxalidaceae

2 Common Wood Sorrel *Oxalis acetosella.* Perennial tufted herb up to 10 cm high. Leaves and long-stalked flowers grow directly from stiff, creeping rhizome. Leaves trifoliate, leaflets sessile, obcordate and entire, underside usually reddish. Flowers white, veined lilac or purple. Fruit an explosive capsule. Flowers in April or May. Grows in damp forests or thickets and among rocks from lowlands to mountains. Introduced, yellow-flowered species: Upright Yellow Wood Sorrel (*O. europaea*) with leaves in whorls and Procumbent Yellow Wood Sorrel (*O. corniculata*) with prostrate stems and alternate leaves often purple-flushed.

Family: Linaceae

3 Flax *Linum usitatissimum.* Annual herb, up to 50 cm high with erect, leafy stems. Leaves linear-lanceolate to linear, pointed, three-veined, entire. Flowers in cymose inflorescences; corolla of 5 light blue petals. Fruit a globular capsule. Flowers in June and July. Long cultivated for linen fibre; native of Asia Minor; mainly cultivated in foothills. Purging Flax (*L. catharticum*) is a small slender plant with tiny white flowers and forked stems with opposite, obovate leaves.

Family: **Rue**—Rutaceae

4 Burning Bush *Dictamnus albus*. Perennial, aromatic plant with whitish, branched rhizome. Erect stems up to 1 metre high, inflorescence reddish glandular. Odd-pinnate leaves, the 9—15 leaflets ovate or lanceolate, finely toothed, with translucent dots; dark green. Flowers in terminal racemes; calyx dark-veined, rarely whitish, petals purple or white, outside glandular hairy, similarly to capsules. Flowers from May to June. Grows only rarely on sunny slopes and forested steppes in temperate regions. Also often cultivated in gardens. Strictly protected plant.

Family: **Milkwort**—Polygalaceae

5 Common Milkwort *Polygala vulgaris*. Perennial, tufted herb. Ascending, erect or decumbent stems up to 25 cm long, usually simple and hairless. Leaves linear-lanceolate, pointed; bracts shorter than flower buds. Flowers are blue, rarely rose or white, with two enlarged sepals. Flat, obcordate capsule. Flowers from May to August. Grows in dry meadows, on grassy slopes and on outskirts of forests. *Polygala amara* has basal leaves in rosette.

Family: **Spurge**—Euphorbiaceae

6 Dog's Mercury *Mercurialis perennis*. Perennial plant with far-creeping rhizome and usually erect, round, unbranched stems. Petiolate leaves dull green, lanceolate to elliptic-ovate, toothed, as a rule with spreading hairs. Unisexual, minute, greenish flowers; pistillate ones long-stalked, solitary or in twos, male flowers in small clusters forming sparse racemes. Capsules globular, bristly. Flowers in April and May. Grows in shady deciduous woods and among rocks from lowlands to mountains. Related Annual Mercury (*M. annua*) has pale green glossy leaves, square, branched stem and almost sessile pistillate flowers.

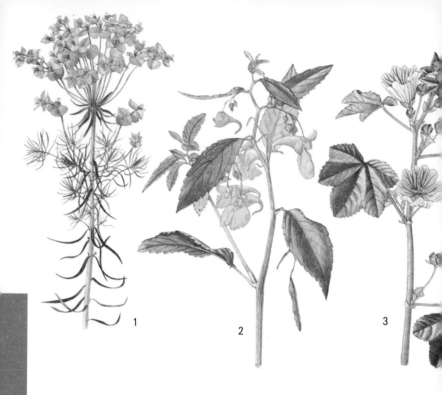

Family: **Spurge**—Euphorbiaceae

1 Cypress Spurge *Euphorbia cyparissias.* Perennial plant up to 30 cm high, with woody, branched rhizome. Stems tufted, erect, soon leafless at bottom, with red tint; densely leaved above, especially the lateral, non-flowering twigs. Narrowly linear leaves; yellowish bracts, after flowering reddish. Inflorescence a branched umbel with petalless flowers bearing wax-yellow glands. Capsules finely warty. Flowers in April and May. Grows in dry grassland and scrub and by roadsides from lowlands to foothills. All species of spurge have a white milky sap (latex).

Family: Impatientaceae

2 Touch-me-not *Impatiens noli-tangere.* Annual up to 1 metre high with erect stem, thickened at the nodes. Leaves petiolate, alternate, ovate-oblong, pointed, toothed, with glands at the base. Flowers in axillary few-flowered racemes, bright yellow, the mouth red-dotted, drooping, with curved spur. Cylindrical to ovoid explosive capsule. Flowers in July and August. Grows in damp woods and on the banks of rivers and streams, from lowlands to mountains. Related *Impatiens parviflora* has small, erect flowers with straight spur; Siberian plant, introduced to central Europe and now naturalized.

Family: **Mallow**—Malvaceae

3 Common Malow *Malva sylvestris.* Perennial herb with ascending or erect, tough stems, up to 1 metre long. Leaves palmate, petiolate, shallowly 5—7 lobed and toothed. Stalked flowers in small axillary clusters. Calyx flattened, with triangular lobes; corollas rose-purple, striped darker, petals spathulate, notched at tip. Stamen filaments fused into tube. Fruit a disc-shaped schizocarp, when ripe splitting into single-seeded, disc-shaped nutlets. Flowers from June to September. Grows by roadsides, in hedgerows, on wasteland, at lower altitudes of temperate regions.

4 Dwarf Mallow *Malva neglecta*. Annual to perennial with decumbent or ascending, branched stems, almost 50 cm long. Long-petiolate leaves, shallowly palmately lobed and toothed, with hairy underside. Axillary, stalked flowers reflexed during fruiting; sepals flat, corollas twice the calyx length, pale lilac to whitish, darker-veined, notched at tip. Fruits smooth. Flowers from June to October. Grows on waste ground, by roadsides and in fields, from lowlands to mountains. Similar Small Mallow (*M. pusilla*) is smaller, lighter green and little branched, with the corollas same length as calyx; fruits wrinkled.

Family: Hypericaceae (syn. Guttiferae)

5 Common St. John's Wort *Hypericum perforatum*. Perennial herb with erect stems, 50 cm or more high, with two longitudinal, narrow ridges and numerous lateral, non-flowering, leafy twigs. Leaves ovate-elliptic, hairless, with conspicuous translucent dots. Flowers arranged in terminal inflorescences; stalks usually dotted with black. Corollas golden yellow, sepals and petals black-dotted; stamens in three bundles. Capsule conical, glandular, dotted. Flowers in July and August. Grows abundantly in woodland clearings, on bushy slopes, by the roadside and in fields, from lowlands to mountains. Related Mountain St. John's Wort (*H. montanum*) has rounded, sparsely leaved stem and fringed glandular sepals.

Family: Lythraceae

6 Purple Loosestrife *Lythrum salicaria*. Robust woody-based perennial up to 1 metre or more high. Erect, hairy stems, sharply square in section. Leaves ovate to lanceolate, base rounded or cordate, sessile, almost hairless. Terminal, dense, spire-like inflorescence. Flowers small, purple, with 6 obovate, waved petals. Fruit a small ovoid capsule. Flowers from July to September. Grows by water, in fens, marshes, swamps and in damp meadows, from lowlands to foothills.

149

Family: Onagraceae

1 Rosebay Willowherb *Chamaenerion angustifolium* (syn. *Epilobium angustifolium*). Perennial herb up to 1 metre or more high. Erect stems usually smooth and unbranched. Leaves oblong-lanceolate to linear-lanceolate, entire, or with a few distant teeth. Flowers in long dense racemes; calyx dark purple, petals 4, obovate, rose-purple, rarely whitish. Long, slender, cylindrical, downy capsules. Minute seeds, with long white hairs. Flowers in July to September. Grows in woodland clearings, on margins of woods and on wasteland, often gregariously.

2 Broad-leaved Willowherb *Epilobium montanum*. Perennial herb up to 80 cm high; erect or shortly ascending stems, simple or sparingly branched in inflorescence, with appressed hairs in two rows, before flowering usually drooping. Opposite, shortly petiolate leaves, elliptical-ovate, pointed, toothed, usually downy. Flowers in leafy terminal raceme; corollas up to 1 cm, petals notched at tip, pink, dark-veined. Stigma four-lobed, capsules downy and glandular. Flowers from June to September. Grows in woods, in bushy slopes, in hedgerows, on walls and as a weed in gardens, from lowlands high up into mountains. Many related species, e.g. Great Hairy Willowherb (*E. hirsutum*) with flowers up to 2 cm across and softly hairy stem.

3 Common Evening Primrose *Oenothera biennis*. Biennial plant up to 1 metre high. Erect stems, as a rule unbranched. Leaves in basal rosette, lanceolate; stem leaves smaller, alternate, finely toothed. Flowers up to 2 cm in diameter are arranged in terminal, leafy racemes. Lanceolate sepals reflexed, petals obcordate, light yellow. Capsules cylindrical, finely hairy. Flowers from June to August. Native of North America, introduced to Europe and much cultivated in gardens. Now well naturalized in waste places, by the roadside and on banks, from lowlands to foothills.

Family: Trapaceae

4 Water Chestnut *Trapa natans*. Annual herb with long, submerged stem. Leaves of two types: submerged ones pinnately divided, with linear segments; rosette leaves floating on water surface with rhomboid blades, sharply toothed at apex; petioles slightly inflated. Axillary, solitary flowers with 4 small white petals. Fruit is conspicuous small edible nut with oily seed surrounded by the enlarged, woody, spiky, four calyx lobes. Flowers in July and August. Grows in still waters of lower altitudes; formerly more frequent.

Family: Umbelliferae (syn. *Apiaceae*)

5 Field Eryngo *Eryngium campestre*. Perennial herb, robust, spreading, up to 50 cm high, grey-green, with well-branched stem. Leaves with bipinnate, spire-tipped segments. Flowers in ovoid capitula, bracts and sepals spiny; corollas small, white or purplish. Flowers in July and August. Grows in dry grassy places in milder regions of lower altitudes.

150

6 Wood Sanicle *Sanicula europaea.* Perennial herb with short, creeping rhizome. Erect, angular stems, up to 40 cm high. Basal leaves petiolate, palmately 3—5 lobed, cordate, the segments again divided and sharply toothed; one or two sessile on flowering stem. Flowers small, arranged in several umbels grouped together. Corolla tiny, white or pinkish with protruding stamens. Flowers in May and June. Grows in deciduous woods, particularly on chalk and limestone, from lowlands to mountains; only locally frequent.

Family: Umbelliferae

1 Masterwort *Astrantia major*. Perennial herb with a somewhat woody rhizome. Erect stems up to over 50 cm high, each with one or two leaves. Basal leaves petiolate, palmate, deeply five- to seven-lobed, segments ovate, toothed; stem leaves more deeply dissected, segments wedge-shaped with trilobed tip. Bracts lanceolate, white or flushed pink. Flowers in simple umbels, corollas white, stamens protruding from flowers. Flowers from June to August. Naturalized in Britain, growing on margins of forests and in meadows in a few places from lowlands to mountains.

2 *Falcaria vulgaris*. A perennial, grey-green herb with erect, much-branched stems. Leaves stiff, doubly trifoliate (each lobe or leaflet again 3-lobed), segments linear-lanceolate, pointed, sharply serrate. Several small secondary umbels form sparse compound umbels; tiny, white flowers. Flowers from July to September. Grows on dry grassy slopes and on field and meadow margins. Only just naturalized in eastern England and Guernsey.

3 Burnet Saxifrage *Pimpinella saxifraga*. Perennial plant up to 50 cm high, with finely grooved, branched stems. Bottom leaves odd-pinnate, long-petiolate; leaflets more or less deeply lobed, sessile; blades of stem leaves smaller, lobed less or not at all. Inflorescence of compound umbels without bracts. Very small flowers, corollas white, rose or yellowish. Fruit a double, ribbed schizocarp. Flowers from July to September. Grows on grassy slopes, field boundaries, in pastures, and by the roadside, from lowlands to mountains.

152

3   5   6

4 Goutweed *Aegopodium podagraria*. Robust perennial plant, almost 1 metre high, with hollow, angular stems and far-creeping rhizomes. Leaves have stem-sheathing petioles; bottom ones twice, upper leaves simply trifoliate; leaflets ovate, petiolate, lateral ones usually lobed, toothed. Inflorescence of compound umbels without bracts; small white or rose-tinted corollas. Schizocarp brown with paler ribs. Flowers in June and July. Grows on waste ground, in damp woods and ditches; also a common garden and farm weed.

5 Wild Angelica *Angelica sylvestris*. Perennial, robust plant, up to 150 cm high, with thick rhizome. Petiolate leaves have shallowly grooved petioles and inflated sheaths; bottom leaves two to three times pinnate, upper ones smaller and simply lobed; leaflets ovate, almost sessile, toothed. Dense compound umbels without bracts; small white or rosy corollas; three-ribbed schizocarp, somewhat winged on margin. Flowers from July to September. Grows in damp woods, thickets and hedgerows, from lowlands to mountains.

6 Fine-leaved Water Dropwort *Oenanthe aquatica*. Perennial, well branched, robust herb with erect stems, up to 1 metre or more high, hollow, at base up to 5 cm in diameter. Leaves sheathed, petiolate, three times pinnate; segments lobed and toothed, lanceolate; submerged leaves filamentous. Numerous compound umbels, umbellets with bracts; small corollas white. Schizocarp narrowly ovoid, ridged. Flowers from June to August. Grows near or in water at lower altitudes and in moist places in hilly country. Related Fool's Parsley (*Aethusa cynapium*) has glossy coarser leaves and long slender floral bracts. It is a weed of cultivation on well-drained soils.

153

Family: Umbelliferae

1 Wild Parsnip *Pastinaca sativa*. Robust biennial herb up to 1 metre high; stem with angular grooves, more or less hairy. Odd-pinnate leaves; the leaflets ovate, serrate, lobed to pinnately divided. Secondary umbels on angular stalks, without bracts; small yellow flowers. Schizocarps elliptical, over 0.5 cm large, flattened and winged. Flowers from July to September. Grows on grassy slopes, in meadows and ditches, along roads, from lowlands to foothills, particularly on chalk and limestone. Caraway (*Carum carvi*), grown as a culinary herb, has upper leaves divided into filamentous segments and white flowers. The cultivated parsnip, with a thick fleshy root, is derived from this species.

2 Wild Carrot *Daucus carota*. Biennial herb almost 1 metre high, with erect, branched, hairy stem. Leaves twice or three times pinnate; pinnatisect segments of upper leaves linear. Dense, compound umbels have numerous pinnate bracts with linear segments. Flowers white, sometimes rosy, central umbels usually red or violet. Schizocarp ovoid, with hooked bristles. Flowers from June to September. Grows in dry meadows, field boundaries and on slopes from lowlands to mountains. *D. carota* ssp. *sativus* is the cultivated carrot.

3 Hogweed *Heracleum sphondylium*. Robust perennial herb up to 150 cm, somewhat foetid. Erect, grooved stems bristled and hollow. Large leaves, lower ones having a grooved petiole, upper leaves sessile with inflated sheaths, pinnate; segments asymmetrically lobed to pinnatisect, toothed. Large compound umbels usually without bracts; corollas white or pinkish. Flowers from June to September. Grows in damp meadows, on waste ground, by roadsides, from lowlands to mountains.

Family: **Primrose**—Primulaceae

6 Mountain Tassel-flower *Soldanella montana*.
Small perennial herb with creeping rhizome and
basal rosette of long-petiolate, reniform, faintly
toothed and somewhat leathery leaves. Stems
10—30 cm high, bearing umbels of up to six
pendent flowers on finely glandular stalks. Violet-blue flowers, calyx five-parted, corolla bell-
shaped. Ovoid capsule, opening through ten
blunt teeth. Flowers in May and June. Grows in
mountain and foothill forests and mountain
meadows.

4 *Anthriscus sylvestris*. Perennial, robust plant
up to 150 cm high. Grooved, hollow stems usually bare or bristly at bottom. Pinnate leaves with
toothed segments; bottom leaves are petiolate,
upper ones sheathing and sessile. Long-stalked
compound umbels, secondary umbels having
bracts. Small flowers with white corollas. Schizocarps glossy, black, oblong-ovoid, pointed.
Flowers from April to June. Grows in meadows,
hedgerows and by roadsides. Poisonous Rough
Chervil (*Chaerophyllum temulentum*) differs
from it by fruits which are distinctly ribbed.

Family: Plumbaginaceae

5 Thrift or **Sea Pink** *Armeria maritima*. Perennial plant, 10—50 cm high, with cushions of linear, single-veined leaves, usually with bristled
margins. Stems solitary, erect, smooth, with
a globular head of rose-pink, occasionally white
flowers. Funnel-shaped, persistent, chaffy calyx
acts as a wing when the fruit is ripe. Bracts beneath capitulum sometimes red tinted. Flowers
from May to October. Grows in sandy places,
dunes, on rocks and screes, in meadows and
pine-woods, from lowlands to mountains.

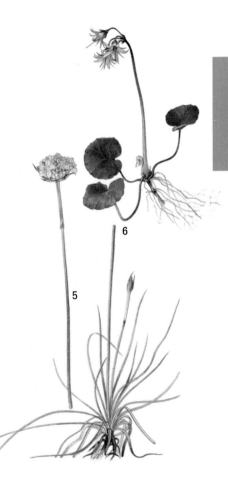

Family: **Primrose**—Primulaceae

1 Cowslip *Primula veris*. Perennial plant, up to 30 cm high. Leaves in basal rosette, wrinkled, hairy beneath, ovate-oblong, with winged petioles. Stem with umbel of several shortly stalked, fragrant flowers. Bell-shaped calyx, corolla yolk-yellow, with an orange spot at the base of each lobe. Corolla tube slightly longer than five-toothed calyx. Flowers from April to June. Grows on banks, in meadows and pastures, from lowlands to foothills.

2 Oxlip *Primula elatior*. Similar to preceding species. Leaves of basal rosette less wrinkled, grey-green on the underside, irregularly toothed. Flowers not scented, with longer stalks. Calyx tubular, corolla pale yellow, larger and flatter than in cowslip. Corolla tube double the length of five-toothed calyx. Cylindrical capsules longer than calyx. Flowers from March to May. Grows in deciduous woods, thickets and damp meadows, from uplands to mountains.

3 Bear's-ear *Primula auricula*. Perennial herb more than 20 cm high, finely and shortly glandularly downy and often somewhat mealy. Basal rosette of almost fleshy leaves with cartilaginous margin, rounded to ovate-obovate, tapering to wide petiole, usually entire, grey-green. Stem bears umbel of yellow, fragrant flowers, having a whitish throat; widely funnel-shaped corollas with the lobes notched at the tip. Capsules ovoid. Flowers from April to June. Grows on limestone rocks in Alps, Carpathians and their foothills; also cultivated. Protected plant.

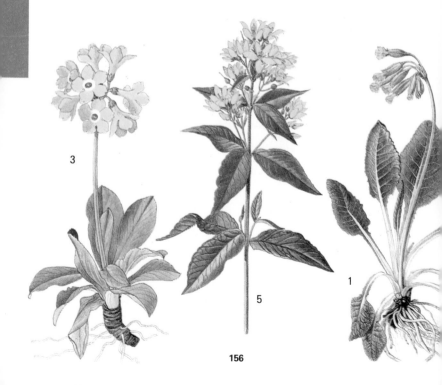

4 Purple Sowbread *Cyclamen purpurascens* (syn. *C. europaeum*). Perennial plant with underground, flatly globose tuber. Leaves in basal rosette are long-petiolate, cordate, rounded, somewhat leathery, shallowly toothed; on upper surface dark green with silvery white patterning, underside carmine. Pendent, pink to carmine, fragrant flowers, the corolla reflexed sharply back. Globose capsule. Flowers from July to September. Grows in deciduous woods and among bushes, usually on limestone soils, only in eastern Bavaria, scattered in neighbouring Austria and southern parts of the Czech Republic. Protected plant.

5 Yellow Loosestrife *Lysimachia vulgaris*. Perennial herb up to 150 cm high, with creeping rhizome and erect, leafy stems. Leaves opposite, or more frequently in whorls of three, downy, shortly petiolate, ovate-lanceolate, pointed, entire. Golden yellow flowers, calyx and petals sometimes bordered with red. Flowers from June to August. Grows in fens, beside water, and in damp forests from lowlands to foothills.

6 Creeping Jenny *Lysimachia nummularia*. Perennial, creeping herb with stem up to 50 cm long, rooting. Leaves broadly ovate to sub-orbicular, entire. Flowers solitary or in twos in leaf axils; corollas rich yellow, inside dotted with dark red. Capsule globose but seldom forms. Flowers from May to July. Grows in damp meadows, open woods and ditches. Related Wood Pimpernel (*L. nemorum*) has ovate, pointed leaves, flower stalks longer than leaves, with smaller, more starry flowers.

Family: **Wintergreen**—Pyrolaceae

1 Larger Wintergreen *Pyrola rotundifolia.* Evergreen perennial up to 30 cm high. Ascending, triangular stems. Leaves in sparse basal rosette, widely ovate to rounded, petiolate, indistinctly toothed, leathery; stem leaves scale-like, clasping. White flowers in dense, short raceme. Bracts usually of the same length as flower stalks. Open, broadly bell-shaped corolla, petals double the length of lanceolate sepals. Flowers in June and July. Grows in woods and on moors, from lowlands to mountains. Protected plant.

2 One-flowered Wintergreen *Moneses uniflora.* Evergreen perennial, up to 10 cm high. Round, petiolate, finely toothed, leathery leaves in basal rosette. Solitary, drooping flowers are fragrant, on long stalks; yellowish calyx, white corolla. Five-lobed stigma, ovoid capsule. Flowers from May to July. Grows in mossy forests from hilly country to mountains. Protected plant.

Family: **Gentian**—Gentianaceae

3 Spring Gentian *Gentiana verna.* Small evergreen perennial plant, up to 10 cm high. Rhizome bears numerous basal leaf rosettes. Leaves elliptic to oblong-ovate, pointed. Erect, short stems, with one to three pairs of smaller leaves, bear solitary erect flowers; corolla tubular with five brilliant deep blue lobes. Flowers from March to May, in high mountains till August. Grows in meadows and on rocks from hilly country to mountains. Protected. Very rare in Britain. Marsh Gentian (*G. pneumonanthe*) has corollas green-spotted at the throat and slender erect, often branched stems.

4 Spotted Gentian *Gentiana punctata.* Perennial, up to 60 cm high plant with thick, branched rhizome and erect, hollow stem. Ovate to broadly elliptic leaves, pointed and sessile. Flowers in axils of upper leaves, sessile, erect, bell-shaped. Corollas yellow, dotted with dark purple. Flowers in July and August. Grows on barrens, in meadows and mountain pastures of Alps and Carpathians. Great Yellow Gentian (*G. lutea*) is gathered for its bitter roots, although it is protected; it has unspotted golden yellow petals not joined into a tube.

5 *Gentiana acaulis.* Evergreen perennial tufted to mat-forming, up to 10 cm high, with basal rosette of almost leathery, ovate-lanceolate leaves. Short-stalked, large flowers, up to 6 cm long, erect; corolla funnel-shaped, rich blue, of lighter shade at mouth, often dark green spotted within. Grows in Alps and on their foothills in alpine meadows, also on screes and rocks. *G. acaulis* is nowadays considered as obsolete and used for a group of species. Three main species are now recognized: *G. clusii*, *G. kochiana* and *G. angustifolia.* Trumpet Gentian (*G. clusii*) has stemless flowers; Broad-leaved Trumpet Gentian (*G. kochiana*) has flowers on a short leafy stem and with a bell-shaped calyx; Narrow-leaved Gentian (*G. angustifolia*) is quite similar, but has markedly narrower leaves and deep sky-blue flowers. These species are strictly protected.

6 Willow Gentian *Gentiana asclepiadea*. Perennial herb, up to 80 cm high, often in dense tufts, with erect stems arching at the top. Ovate-lanceolate leaves, long-pointed and sessile. Axillary short-stalked flowers are borne in the upper leaf axils. Corollas funnel-shaped, azure blue, spotted purple within; rarely white. Flowers from July to September. Grows in Alps and Carpathians in woods, and along banks of streams.

Family: **Gentian**—Gentianaceae

1 *Centaurium erythraea* (syn. *C. umbellatum, C. minus*). Annual herb up to 50 cm high. Erect, square stems, forked above. Obovate to elliptic leaves in basal rosette; stem ones smaller and narrower, pointed, sessile, entire. Short-stalked to sessile flowers are pink, rarely whitish, with a five-lobed tubular corolla. Capsules cylindrical. Flowers from July to September. Grows on margins of forests and thickets, in dry meadows and on grassy slopes.

2 Marsh Felwort *Swertia perennis*. Perennial herb up to 50 cm high. Erect stems, often with violet tint. Basal leaves elliptic, petiolate, stem leaves lanceolate, sessile to semi-clasping. Flowers on winged, square stalks, in panicles. Corollas have five lobes, violet to light blue, dotted black-purple, greenish within. Fruit a capsule. Flowers from June to August. Grows in mountains, in peaty meadows and by streams.

Family: Menyanthaceae

3 Bogbean *Menyanthes trifoliata*. Perennial herb up to 30 cm high, with thick, creeping rhizome and erect, leafless flowering stems. Basal leaves, direct from rhizome, have long petioles, trifoliate leaflets almost sessile, obovate. Conspicuous flowers in dense raceme. Corollas broadly funnel-shaped, divided into five fringed lobes, white or pinkish; violet anthers. Capsule broadly ovoid. Flowers in May and June. Grows in marshes, bogs, fens and in ditches, lakes and ponds, from lowlands to mountains.

Family: Apocynaceae

4 Lesser Periwinkle *Vinca minor.* Evergreen perennial with long, creeping, rooting stems. Non-flowering stems are creeping and rooting; flowering ones are short, not more than 20 cm high, erect or ascending. Leathery leaves are opposite, lanceolate to elliptic, entire. Long-stalked flowers are axillary, tubular, with five angular lobes, light blue to blue-violet, rarely white or pink. Fruit formed of two slender, cylindrical follicles, fused at the base. Flowers in April and May. Grows in deciduous woods and thickets, from lowlands to foothills; also cultivated in gardens and becoming naturalized in hedgerows.

Family: **Milkweed**—Asclepiadaceae

5 Swallow-wort *Cynanchum vincetoxicum* (syn. *Vincetoxicum officinale, V. hirundinaria*). Perennial herb up to 1 metre high, poisonous, with rhizome and numerous thick roots. Erect, simple stems with opposite, ovate-lanceolate, entire leaves, hairy on veins beneath. Inflorescences in upper leaf axils, flowers bell-shaped, corollas white, greenish or yellowish, small. Fruit a slender pod-like follicle; seeds have white, silky plumes. Flowers from May to August. Grows on sunny slopes and among rocks, on margins of woods and thickets, more frequently on calcareous soils, from lowlands to foothills in milder regions.

Family: **Convolvulus**—Convolvulaceae

6 Field Bindweed *Convolvulus arvensis.* Perennial, prostrate or twining plant, up to 1 metre long. Rhizomes extensive, penetrating to depths of 5 cm. Stems climb by twisting counterclockwise. Leaves arrow-shaped, entire. Axillary flowers usually solitary, on short stalks, with widely funnel-shaped corollas, white or pink. Flowers from June to September. Grows in fields, on waste ground, roadsides, dunes, and in gardens as a pernicious weed.

4

6

5

1

2 Corn Cromwell *Lithospermum arvense.* Annual herb up to 50 cm high, with erect stems simple or branched towards the top. Leaves lanceolate to obovate, sessile. Inflorescence a leafy cyme; corollas white to bluish, their tubes sometimes with violet tint. Brown, wrinkled nutlets not glossy. Flowers from April to July. Grows as field weed, by roadsides and on wasteland, at lower altitudes. Related *Lithospermum purpureocoeruleum* is perennial, with purple flowers, later turning blue.

3 Common Forget-me-not *Myosotis arvensis.* Annual herb, rarely biennial, up to 40 cm high, with greyish hairs and erect or ascending stems. Oblanceolate, densely hairy leaves. Inflorescence a bractless, dense cyme; flower stalks spreading. Calyx deeply lobed into lanceolate sepals, hairy. Nutlets ovoid, keeled, dark glossy brown. Flowers from August to October. Grows along paths and in meadows, on wasteland, in sandy places, and as weed in fields. Related Yellow and Blue Forget-me-not (*M. discolor,* syn. *M. versicolor*) has fruit-stalks shorter than calyx and corollas coloured according to age of flower, from yellow through to blue.

4 Wood Forget-me-not *Myosotis sylvatica.* Perennial herb up to 50 cm high, fresh green, softly, usually densely haired. Erect stems with obovate to lanceolate leaves. Inflorescence a dense cyme, calyx with thick, hooked hairs; shorter than stalks; during fruition closed. Small corollas are over 5 mm in diameter, azure blue, with a yellow eye. Glossy, black-brown nutlets. Flowers in May and June. Grows in woods and meadows from lowlands to mountains; often cultivated in gardens and several forms known. Related Water Forget-me-not *Myosotis scorpioides* (syn. *M. palustris*) has calyx with appressed hairs, divided only to one third, and an angular stem.

5 Lesser Honeywort *Cerinthe minor.* Biennial, rarely perennial herb, up to 50 cm high, with erect stems. Leaves grey-green, ovate, clasping, lower ones usually white-spotted and warted. Calyx bristly-hairy; sulphur yellow corollas deeply cut into pointed lobes and drooping. Nutlets two-seeded. Flowers from May to July. Grows scattered in pastures, on field boundaries, slopes and along paths in lower altitudes of temperate regions and Alpine foothills.

Family: **Borage**—Boraginaceae

1 Hound's Tongue *Cynoglossum officinale.* Biennial herb up to 80 cm high, with erect, leafy, branched stems. Lanceolate, pointed leaves, basal ones petiolate, stem leaves sessile to clasping, all entire, softly densely grey hairy, especially on under surface. Inflorescence of dense cymes. Corollas small, red-purple, rarely whitish. Nutlets ovate, flattened, margins thickened and bearing short barbed spines. Flowers from May to July. Grows on grassy slopes, field boundaries and by roadsides at lower altitudes of milder regions.

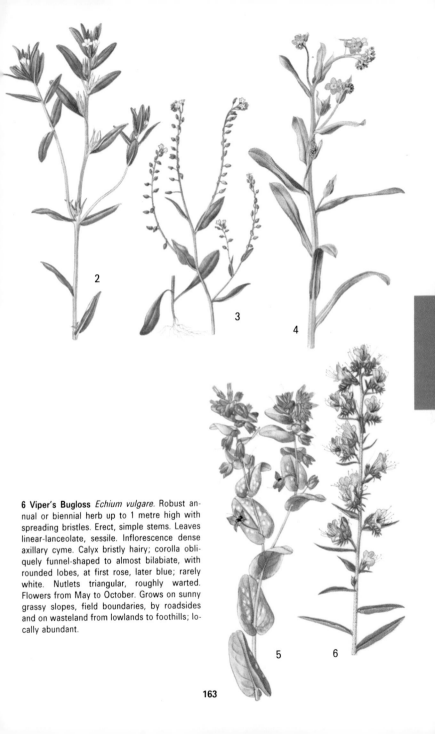

6 Viper's Bugloss *Echium vulgare*. Robust annual or biennial herb up to 1 metre high with spreading bristles. Erect, simple stems. Leaves linear-lanceolate, sessile. Inflorescence dense axillary cyme. Calyx bristly hairy; corolla obliquely funnel-shaped to almost bilabiate, with rounded lobes, at first rose, later blue; rarely white. Nutlets triangular, roughly warted. Flowers from May to October. Grows on sunny grassy slopes, field boundaries, by roadsides and on wasteland from lowlands to foothills; locally abundant.

Family: **Borage**—Boraginaceae

1 True Alkanet *Anchusa officinalis.* Biennial or perennial plant up to 80 cm high, with spreading hairs, rough. Erect much-branched stems with oblong-lanceolate leaves, entire, sessile with rounded base. Dense, short, axillary cymes bear five-lobed flowers, at first reddish, later dark blue-violet, rarely white, dotted. Nutlets brown, flowers from May to September. Grows in pastures, fields, by roadsides, on field boundaries and wasteland, from lowlands to foothills in milder regions. Related Italian Alkanet (*A. italica,* syn. *A. azurea*) has large, light blue corollas.

2 Wrinklenut *Nonea pulla.* Perennial, grey-haired herb up to 50 cm high, with erect, stiff stems. Leaves oblong to lanceolate, top ones semi-clasping, entire, bristled to glandular hairy. Inflorescence of several dense, axillary cymes bearing short-stalked flowers. Calyx bell-shaped, enlarging after fertilization. Corolla tubular, funnel-shaped, brown-violet, rarely yellowish or whitish, tube white. Nutlets ovoid. Flowers from May to August. Grows on field boundaries, by roadsides and on wasteland, often on calcareous soils at lower altitudes of milder regions.

3 Common Lungwort *Pulmonaria officinalis.* Perennial herb, up to 30 cm high. Bottom leaves ovate-cordate, abruptly narrowed into petiole, pointed, usually spotted silvery-white; stem ones almost sessile, ovate to lanceolate. Bracted cymes short and dense. Flowers short-stalked, calyx enlarging after fertilization. Corolla purple-rose to pink, later turning violet-blue. Dark brown nutlets. Flowers from March to May. Grows in light woodland and bushy places from lowlands to foothills.

164

Family: Labiatae (syn. Lamiaceae)

6 Common Bugle *Ajuga reptans.* Perennial herb up to 30 cm high, with creeping shoots and long-petioled, obovate basal leaves. Erect, simple, square leafy stems, bearing short-stalked flowers in the axils of leafy, purple-tinted bracts. Calyx bell-shaped with triangular-ovate teeth; corolla violet-blue, rarely pink or white; lower lip deeply three-lobed. Fruit of four smooth brown nutlets. Flowers from May to August. Grows in meadows, thickets and woods from lowlands to mountains. Related Upright Bugle (*A. genevensis*) has no creeping stems, but underground stolons; upper floral bracts are shorter and usually three-lobed, corollas bright blue.

3

2

4 Common Comfrey *Symphytum officinale.* Perennial herb with robust, bristly, hairy stems up to 1 metre high. Stems usually well-branched, and keeled or winged. Long tapering, broadly lanceolate leaves with winged petioles. Inflorescence of dense, bracted cymes. Short-stalked flowers purple, rarely rose or whitish. Corolla tubular; calyx with long-pointed lobes. Nutlets brown-grey, glossy. Flowers from May to July. Grows abundantly in damp meadows, on banks and in ditches from lowlands to foothills.

5 *Symphytum tuberosum.* Perennial herb up to 50 cm high, with short bristly hairs. Thickened, tuberous rhizome. Erect, almost unbranched, indistinctly angular stems. Shortly tapering leaves, widely lanceolate with winged petioles. Inflorescence of few-flowered cymes. Flowers yellowish white with short hairs. Corolla tubular, with recurved lobes; calyx deeply cleft. Nutlets cuneoid, brown, wrinkled. Flowers in April and May. Grows from lowlands to foothills in damp woods and thickets, rarely in meadows.

6

Family: Labiatae

1 Ground Ivy *Glechoma hederacea* (syn. *Nepeta hederacea*). Perennial herb up to 30 cm high, with long-creeping prostrate stems, rooting at the nodes. Leaves petiolate, reniform to broadly ovate-cordate, having rounded teeth. Axillary flowers usually in twos; calyx tubular, hairy, indistinctly bilabiate; corollas blue-violet with a bilobed upper and trilobed lower lip bearing dark purple pattern. Flowers from April to July. Grows in woods, bushy places, grassy slopes, on wasteland, and sometimes as weed in gardens, from lowlands to mountains.

2 Common Self-heal *Prunella vulgaris*. Perennial herb, somewhat hairy or glabrous, up to 30 cm high, with short leafy rhizomes and ascending, often brown-violet stems. Petiolate, ovate to elliptic leaves, entire or irregularly toothed. Inflorescence of axillary, bracted flowers arranged in short, dense, oblong head. Corollas blue-violet, rarely pink or white; upper lip hooded and bristly-hairy. Glossy nutlets. Flowers from May to September. Grows in pastures, dry meadows, open woods and by the roadside. Related Large-flowered Self-heal (*P. grandiflora*) is more robust and has larger flowers. It is sometimes grown in garden.

3 *Melittis melissophyllum*. Perennial herb up to 50 cm high, with erect stems and soft hairs. Erect, unbranched stems bear cordate-ovate, toothed and pointed leaves. Scented flowers are borne in axils of upper leaves. Corollas long-tubular, white or pink, lower lip rosy, central lobe usually yellow and with deep pink spots. Triangular, smooth nutlets. Flowers in May and June. Grows in open woods and hedgerows especially on limestone soils, at lower altitudes in milder regions. Sometimes cultivated for its distinctive flowers.

4 Large Hemp-nettle *Galeopsis speciosa*. Robust annual herb, up to 1 metre high with branched stems swollen at nodes. Leaves petiolate, ovate, serrate, long-pointed. Flowers in whorls in the upper leaf and bract axils. Corolla longer than calyx, light yellow, central lobe of lower lip violet. Flowers from June to September. Grows in open woods, clearings, bushy places and on wasteland. Common Hemp-nettle (*G. tetrahit*) has smaller light purple or whitish flowers with the lower lip purple-spotted.

5 Black Horehound *Ballota nigra.* Perennial herb up to 1 metre high, stems and leaves grey-hairy. Ovate to orbicular leaves wrinkled, pointed and toothed. Calyx bell-shaped; corolla purple, central lobe of lower lip mottled whitish. Flowers from June to September. Grows on wasteland, edges of fields, among bushes and along hedgerows, from lowlands to foothills.

6 Yellow Archangel *Galeobdolon luteum* (syn. *Lamium galeobdolon*). Perennial plant up to 50 cm high, with far-creeping leafy stolons and erect, simple flowering stems. Leaves petiolate, ovate, pointed, toothed. Flowers in whorls in the upper leaf axils. Calyx bell-shaped with pointed triangular lobes. Corolla yellow with large, hooded upper lip. Nutlets smooth, trigonous. Flowers from April to July. Grows in damp woods and thickets from lowlands to mountains. Related White Dead-nettle (*Lamium album*) lacks stolons and bears white flowers.

Family: Labiatae

1 Spotted Dead-nettle *Lamium maculatum*. Perennial herb up to 50 cm high. Petiolate leaves ovate-cordate to toothed, pointed, usually with a central silvery-white zone. Flowers in whorls in the upper leaf axils. Corollas purple, lower lip dark violet-spotted; tube curved. Triangular-obovoid, black-green nutlets. Flowers from April to September. Grows in open woods, on wasteland and by roadsides. Only naturalized in Britain as an escapee from gardens. Similar Red Dead-nettle (*L. purpureum*) with red-purple flowers, almost straight corolla tubes and plain green leaves is a common annual weed.

2 Hedge Woundwort *Stachys sylvatica*. Perennial herb up to 1 metre high, with creeping rhizomes and erect stems. Leaves long-petiolate, ovate-cordate, toothed and pointed. Flowers in bracted whorls, red-purple or crimson. Flowers from June to September. Grows in damp woods, among bushes and in hedgerows from lowlands to mountains. Related Marsh Woundwort (*S. palustris*) has almost sessile, lanceolate leaves with rounded teeth and pale purple flowers.

3 Wood Betony *Betonica officinalis* (syn. *Stachys betonica*). Perennial herb up to 1 metre high, with erect stems, having long internodes. Leaves petiolate, ovate-oblong, cordate, with rounded teeth; upper ones almost sessile and smaller. Dense oblong inflorescence with linear bracts. Corolla purple-red, tube whitish. Flowers in July and August. Grows in open woods, on hedgebanks and on grassy slopes from lowlands to foothills.

4 Whorled Clary *Salvia verticillata*. Perennial herb up to 50 cm high, hairy and foetid. Basal leaves ovate with rounded teeth, usually fading or dead at flowering time. Stem leaves petiolate, smaller, sometimes pinnately lobed. Inflorescences spike-like, composed of several bracted whorls. Corolla violet, rarely whitish or pink. Flowers from June to September. Grows by the roadside, on grassy slopes and rocky places in the mountains of central Europe, west to Spain; often naturalized elsewhere.

5 Meadow Clary *Salvia pratensis*. Perennial herb up to 50 cm high, with erect stems. Leaves long-petiolate, ovate to oblong-cordate, shallowly lobed with irregular rounded teeth, wrinkled. Inflorescence spike-like, formed of several whorls of blue, rarely pink or white flowers; upper lip of corolla hooded, lower one small and rounded. Flowers from May to August. Grows on dry slopes, in meadows, bushy places, hedge banks and on field boundaries, mainly in milder regions.

6 Pot Marjoram *Origanum vulgare*. Perennial aromatic herb up to 50 cm high with a woody rhizome. Stems erect, leafy. Short-petiolate leaves ovate, almost entire, glandular. Inflorescence a dense corymbose cyme. Flowers rose-purple, rarely white. Nutlets ovoid, smooth, brown. Flowers from July to September. Grows fairly abundantly on sunny grassy slopes, in bushy places, and on margins of forests, mainly in milder regions.

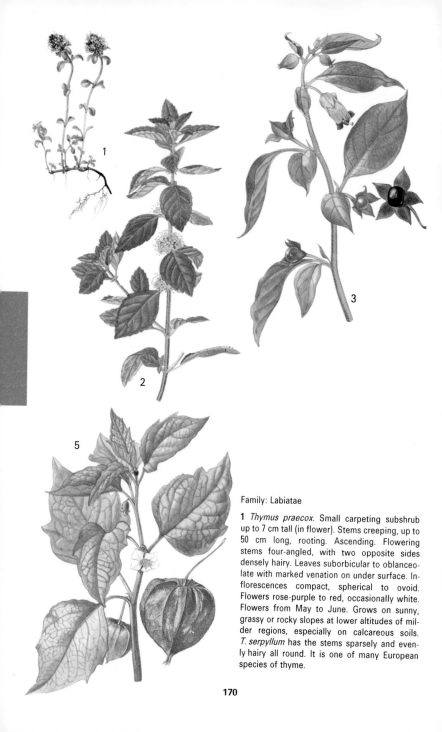

Family: Labiatae

1 *Thymus praecox.* Small carpeting subshrub up to 7 cm tall (in flower). Stems creeping, up to 50 cm long, rooting. Ascending. Flowering stems four-angled, with two opposite sides densely hairy. Leaves suborbicular to oblanceolate with marked venation on under surface. Inflorescences compact, spherical to ovoid. Flowers rose-purple to red, occasionally white. Flowers from May to June. Grows on sunny, grassy or rocky slopes at lower altitudes of milder regions, especially on calcareous soils. *T. serpyllum* has the stems sparsely and evenly hairy all round. It is one of many European species of thyme.

170

Family: Solanaceae

3 Deadly Nightshade *Atropa bella-donna.* Perennial herb, glandular-hairy, up to 150 cm high with thick, erect, branched stems. Leaves alternate, or on the flowering stems in unequal pairs; ovate to elliptic, entire, with a winged petiole. Flowers drooping, solitary, seemingly axillary, having bell-shaped corollas, outside brown-purple, inside yellowish. Berries globose, black, subtended by the star-like enlarged calyx. All parts of the plant are poisonous. Flowers from June to August. Grows scattered in woodland clearings, on margins of forests and wasteland from lowlands to foothills.

4 Henbane *Hyoscyamus niger.* Annual to biennial herb, up to 80 cm high, sticky glandular-hairy and foetid. Erect, densely leafy stems bear alternate oblong-ovate, somewhat irregularly lobed leaves, the lower ones petiolate, top ones semi-clasping. Flowers in axils of upper leaves. Calyx bell-shaped, glandular-hairy, prominently net-veined; corolla funnel-shaped, dull yellow, violet-netted. Anthers violet. Capsules with lids contain black-brown seeds. Whole plant poisonous. Flowers from June to October. Grows on wasteland, by roadsides, and on sandy ground, often near the sea, in lowland areas, more frequently in milder regions.

5 Winter-cherry *Physalis alkekengi.* Perennial herb up to 60 cm high, with creeping rhizome. Erect stems somewhat angular, upper part downy. Petiolate broad leaves ovate, usually entire, pointed. Flowers solitary, axillary, stalked; globular lantern-shaped inflated calyx; dull white or yellowish-green corolla. Berries orange, enclosed in the enlarged inflated calyx, both red when ripe. Flowers from May to August. Grows in deciduous woods, bushy places and on waste ground, in central and southern Europe. Cultivated and escaping here and there.

6 Black Nightshade *Solanum nigrum.* Annual herb up to 60 cm high. Erect or decumbent branched stems. Leaves widely ovate or rhomboid, shallowly lobed or with a sinuate margin. Flowers in small leafless cymes. Corollas white, with 5 spreading pointed lobes. Berries usually black, rarely greenish or yellowish. Flowers from June to October. Grows as weed in fields, gardens and on wasteland from lowlands to foothills. Related Bittersweet or Woody Nightshade (*S. dulcamara*) is a semi-climbing shrub with violet flowers and yellow anthers fused into a cone, protruding from reflexed corolla; berry translucent red. Both species poisonous.

2 Corn Mint *Mentha arvensis.* Perennial herb up to 50 cm high, often purple-tinted, aromatic, with underground rhizomes. Decumbent or ascending stems are densely leafy. Leaves narrowly to broadly ovate, toothed. Inflorescence of several axillary whorls. Calyx with triangular teeth. Corolla lilac to blue-purple. Flowers from June to October. Grows in damp fields, ditches, and in open wet woods from lowlands to foothills. Peppermint (*Mentha× piperita*), a hybrid of Water Mint and Spearmint (*M. aquatica× M. spicata*) is often cultivated for flavouring.

Family: **Snapdragon**—*Scrophulariaceae*

1 Common Mullein *Verbascum thapsus*. Biennial herb up to 2 m high, covered with dense whitish-felted hair. Leaves in basal rosettes obovate to oblong; stem ones lanceolate, with winged stalks that run down the stem. Light yellow flowers in a spire-like panicle; corollas up to 2 cm in diameter. Filaments of two longer stamens smooth, those of three shorter ones hairy. Flowers from July to September. Grows on hedgebanks, sunny slopes and wasteland, from lowlands to foothills. Related Large-flowered Mullein (*V. thapsiforme*) has flowers up to 4 cm in diameter, and filaments of bare stamens are double the anther length.

2 White Mullein *Verbascum lychnitis*. Biennial herb up to 1.5 metre high, with short hairs. Oblong to lanceolate basal leaves have small rounded teeth or are entire; stem leaves almost sessile, ovate, pointed. Inflorescence a narrow erect panicle; flowers white or yellow; stamen filaments of almost equal length, white-woolly. Flowers from June to August. Grows in waste places, on sunny slopes, forest margins and by roadsides, from lowlands to foothills. Related Dark Mullein (*V. nigrum*) has bottom leaves usually cordate and filaments of stamens violet-woolly.

3 Purple Mullein *Verbascum phoeniceum*. Biennial herb up to 1 m high, with stem usually densely glandular. Leaves of basal rosette ovate, stem ones sparse, cordate and sessile. Flowers in terminal raceme; dark violet corollas up to 3 cm in diameter. Flowers from May to July. Grows scattered at outskirts of forests, on bushy, sunny slopes and in sandy places at lower altitudes in milder regions. Cultivated in Britain and occasionally escaping.

4 Toadflax *Linaria vulgaris.* Perennial herb up to 40 cm high, usually unbranched. Alternate, sessile leaves linear-lanceolate, entire, grey-green. Flowers in dense terminal raceme; corollas snapdragon-like, sulphur yellow, with palate of lower lip orange; corolla tube with long spur. Ovoid capsule. Flowers from June to October. Grows abundantly in fields, on wasteland, by roadsides and among rocks from lowlands to foothills. Sometimes a weed of gardens. Tiny Alpine Toadflax (*L. alpina*) is grey, decumbent, with leaves in whorls; violet flowers have lower lip with orange palate.

5 Field Cow-wheat *Melampyrum arvense.* Annual herb up to 40 cm high, downy. Opposite, lanceolate leaves; bottom ones entire, upper leaves have several long, large teeth at the base. Flowers in dense spike, bracts purple. Corollas tubular bilabiate, pink, with yellow throat and deep pink lips. Flowers from May to September. Grows in fields, on slopes and margins of woods, mainly in the lowlands. Rare in Britain. Related Crested Cow-wheat (*M. cristatum*) has reddish crested bracts, smaller yellow and purple flowers and grows mainly in open woods.

6 Common Cow-wheat *Melampyrum pratense.* Annual herb up to 50 cm high with spreading branches. Linear-lanceolate to narrowly ovate, entire leaves. Flowers arranged in a sparse, one-sided spike, the lower ones well spaced. Calyx lobes unequal, pointed; corollas whitish to lemon yellow, with a narrow mouth. Flowers from May to September. Grows in forests and in clearings, from lowlands to mountains. Wood Cow-wheat (*M. sylvaticum*) has triangular-lanceolate sepals and yellow to orange-yellow flowers with wide open mouths.

5

4

6

Family: **Snapdragon**—Scrophulariaceae

1 Germander Speedwell *Veronica chamaedrys*. Perennial herb up to 25 cm high, little branched. Prostrate or ascending stems have hairs in two rows. Leaves are opposite, ovate to elliptic, toothed. Sparse floral racemes in axils of upper leaves; corollas sky-blue with a white eye. Capsules obcordate, shorter than calyx. Flowers in May and June. Grows on field boundaries and grassy banks, in meadows, open woods and among bushes. Thyme-leaved Speedwell (*V. serpyllifolia*) has white or pale blue flowers and rounded to oblong leaves.

2 Common Speedwell *Veronica officinalis*. Perennial herb with rooting prostrate stems up to 30 cm long. Finely serrate leaves elliptic to ovate or obovate, shortly petiolate, toothed. Racemes form in upper leaf axils. Flowers light violet to lilac. Capsules obcordate, glandular. Flowers from June to August. Grows in dry woods, clearings and on heaths and moors. Buxbaum's Speedwell (*V. persica*) has stalks longer than ovate, toothed leaves and sky-blue and white flowers formed singly in leaf axils.

3 Spiked Speedwell *Veronica spicata*. Perennial herb, up to 50 cm high, downy, on top glandular. Leaves opposite, oval or ovate, blunt, toothed along the sides. Flowers in dense, terminal racemes; corollas violet-blue. Obcordate, glandular capsules. Flowers from June to August. Grows in rocky places, on sunny grassy slopes, in pastures and on field boundaries from lowlands to foothills, mainly in milder regions. Rare in Britain.

4 Yellow-rattle *Rhinanthus minor*. Annual herb with a simple or branched stem up to 60 cm. Leaves linear-lanceolate with rounded teeth. Inflorescence a terminal bracted raceme. Calyx inflated; corolla yellow, hooded, just protruding from calyx. Flattened capsules hidden in calyx. Flowers from May to July. Grows scattered as field weed, in meadows and heaths, from lowlands to mountains.

5 Lousewort *Pedicularis sylvatica*. Perennial herb with decumbent stems, only at tip ascending, up to 20 cm high. Alternate, pinnately lobed leaves, the segments toothed. Inflorescence a few-flowered terminal raceme. Inflated, unequally five-toothed calyx; corollas pink. Flowers from May to July. Grows scattered in damp meadows and on moors and heaths from lowlands to mountains.

6 Yellow Foxglove *Digitalis grandiflora* (syn. *D. ambigua*). Perennial herb up to 1 metre high. Erect stems glandular-hairy. Alternate leaves, bottom ones oblanceolate, upper leaves ovately lanceolate, sessile. Flowers in one-sided, dense raceme. Corollas tubular, bell-shaped, somewhat flattened and lobed, light yellow outside, brown-netted inside. Flowers in June and July. Grows in clearings, on overgrown rocky slopes, and in open woods from hilly country to mountains. Grown in gardens and very rarely escaping.

Family: **Plantain**—Plantaginaceae

3 Ribwort *Plantago lanceolata.* Perennial herb up to 45 cm high, with deep green leaves in basal rosette and simple, erect flowering stem. Leaves lanceolate, sometimes obscurely toothed. Grooved stem and dense, ovoid to cylindrical spike. Corollas brownish with white anthers. Capsule with ovoid lid. Flowers from May to September. Grows as a weed in meadows, fields, pastures, by roadsides, on wasteland, from lowlands to mountains. Related Hoary Plantain (*P. media*) has elliptic to ovate hoary leaves, round stems and filaments of stamens light violet.

Family: Orobanchaceae

1 Toothwort *Lathraea squamaria.* Perennial whitish or pinkish parasitic herb, up to 25 cm high. Stout branched rhizome with fleshy, white scale leaves. Erect stem is fleshy, unbranched, with a few scale leaves. Flowers in one-sided, dense raceme, at first drooping at tip. Corollas tubular, bilabiate, dull purple, lower lip reddish. Capsules explosive, with large seeds. Flowers from March to May. Grows in deciduous woods at lower altitudes; parasitic on roots of deciduous trees, especially hazel and elm.

2 Red Broomrape *Orobanche alba.* Perennial yellowish parasitic herb up to 30 cm tall. Slender stems unbranched, thickened underground, glandular hairy. Stem bracts ovate-lanceolate; flowers in sparse raceme with reddish bracts. Calyx bilabiate. Corolla tubular, curved, labiate, upper lip dark glandular-hairy purple-tinged, rest of corolla whitish. In Britain flowers reddish throughout. Flowers in June and July. Grows on sunny grassy slopes, mainly in milder regions; parasitic on thyme and other members of the Labiatae.

4 Great Plantain *Plantago major.* Perennial herb up to 30 cm high. Broadly ovate to elliptic leaves in basal rosette narrow abruptly to a cordate base and winged petiole. Erect stems bear a long, dense, narrow spike of small yellowish white flowers; anthers lilac, turning to dull yellow, filaments whitish. Capsules broadly ovoid with lids. Flowers from June to October. Grows as a weed in pastures, fields, on wasteland and by roadsides, from lowlands to mountains.

Family: **Madder**—Rubiaceae

5 Field Madder *Sherardia arvensis.* Annual herb with slender, generally prostrate stems, up to 30 cm long, branched and square. Leaves in whorls of 4—6, with tiny prickled hairs, lanceolate to elliptic, pointed, single-veined. Inflorescence a few-flowered umbel terminating the branches. Corollas with 4 narrow cross-like lobes. Fruit of 2 obovoid mericarps. Flowers from June to October. Grows as a weed in fields, on wasteland and by roadsides, from lowlands to foothills, more frequently on calcareous soils.

6 Woodruff *Galium odoratum* (syn. *Asperula odorata*). Perennial herb up to 40 cm high, with far-creeping rhizomes and erect, square, smooth flowering stems. Leaves lanceolate to elliptic, with marginal prickles, tip usually with small hard point, in whorls of up to 6. Flowers in terminal, long-stalked cymes. Corollas small, white, funnel-shaped, with 4 blunt lobes. Double mericarp has hooked bristles. Flowers in May and June. Grows in deciduous woods and among bushes, from lowlands to mountains.

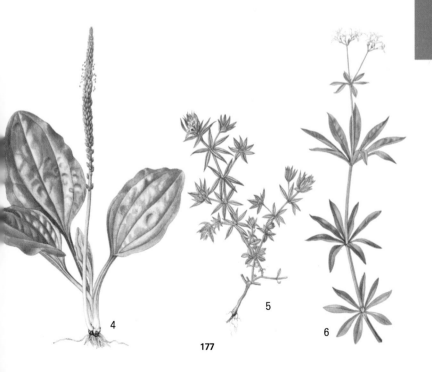

4

5

6

Family: **Madder**—Rubiaceae

1 Goosegrass or **Cleavers** *Galium aparine*. Annual herb with stems bearing hooked bristles, prostrate or climbing, square, up to 120 cm long. Leaves in whorls of 6—8, linear, oblanceolate, margins with small, curved bristles. Flowers in stalked, axillary cymes; four-parted corollas very small, whitish, with spreading lobes. Double mericarps with small white hooks. Flowers from June to October. Grows in hedgerows, thickets, on wasteground and in fields, and at outskirts of forests, from lowlands to mountains.

2 Lady's Bedstraw *Galium verum*. Perennial herb with creeping rhizome and prostrate to erect, angled stems, up to 60 cm long or more, branched at the top. Leaves narrowly linear, single-veined, in 8—12 whorls. Bright yellow cross-shaped flowers in dense terminal panicles. Flowers from May to September. Grows abundantly in meadows, on sunny grassy banks, field boundaries, in hedgerows and on dunes. Low-growing *Galium cruciata* has unbranched stems with spreading white hairs and three-veined ovate-elliptic, hairy leaves; flowers pale yellow.

3 Hedge Bedstraw *Galium mollugo*. Perennial herb up to 1 metre long with decumbent, ascending or erect stems, often climbing, square, smooth. Leaves linear to obovate, edge finely prickly, tip pointed. White cross-shaped flowers in long, terminal panicles. Corolla lobes prolonged into slender point. Double mericarps wrinkled. Flowers from May to September. Grows in meadows, on field boundaries, in hedgerows, at outskirts of forests and on dunes, from lowlands to mountains.

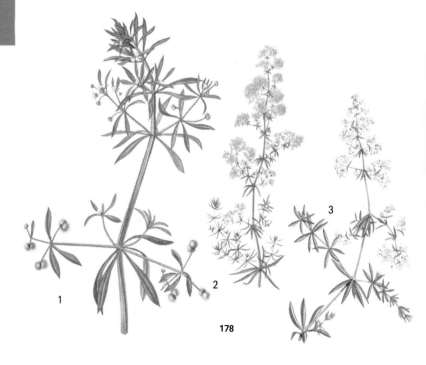

178

Family: Loniceraceae

4 Danewort *Sambucus ebulus*. Perennial herb, malodorous, poisonous, up to 150 cm high with erect, grooved stems. Leaves petiolate, odd-pinnate, leaflets 7—13, sharply serrate, oblong-lanceolate. Dense flat-topped, panicle-like cymes bear small 5-petalled, white or pale pink flowers; anthers violet. Fruits are glossy black globose drupes. Flowers in June and July. Grows in woodland clearings, margins of forests, among bushes and in hedgerows, from lowlands to foothills. Related species are woody plants.

Family: **Valerian**—Valerianaceae

5 Smooth-fruited Cornsalad *Valerianella dentata*. Annual herb up to 30 cm high, with erect, repeatedly forking stems, usually with single flower in forks of branches; further flowers in terminal heads. Tiny bluish white flowers; calyx margin with one tooth longer than others.

Leaves spathulate, blunt, opposite, sometimes toothed at the base. Flowers from June to September. Grows in fields, wasteland, on rocky slopes and old walls, from lowlands to foothills. Related Common Cornsalad (*V. locusta*) has forked branches without flowers and entire leaves.

6 Common Valerian *Valeriana officinalis*. Perennial herb up to 1 metre high, with stout erect stems and shortly creeping rhizomes. Pinnately divided leaves, bottom ones petiolate, upper leaves sessile. Flowers in dense cymose head with usually two main branches. Corollas white or pink, tubular, with 5 lobes. Achenes conical with crown of pappus. Flowers from June to September. Grows in damp meadows, and in bushy places from lowlands to mountains. Smaller Marsh Valerian (*V. dioica*) has almost entire, ovate to spathulate basal leaves, stem ones pinnately lobed, and unisexual flowers.

179

Family: **Scabious**—Dipsacaceae

1 Teasel *Dipsacus fullonum* (syn. *D. sylvester*). Biennial herb up to 200 cm high with robust, angled stems, prickly on the angles. Basal leaves in rosette, oblong to elliptic, stem ones lanceolate, opposite, fused at base, prickly on margins and central rib. Stalks of inflorescences densely prickly, flowers in a dense ovoid head, rose-purple, rarely whitish. Involucral bracts linear, pointed, prickly, longer than head. Flowers in July and August. Grows in open woods and thickets, on stream banks and wasteland, in ditches and by the roadside, usually at lower altitudes. *D. fullonum* ssp. *sativus* is cultivated for napping cloth. It has larger heads and stiff, spiny floral bracts.

2 Field Scabious *Knautia arvensis*. Perennial herb almost 1 metre high with spreading hairs and erect stems. Basal rosettes of somewhat grey-green leaves, oblanceolate to obovate, stem ones pinnately lobed, segments lanceolate. Long-stalked flowering heads; corollas bluish-lilac, rarely pink, whitish or yellowish; outer florets with 2 enlarged petals. Achenes ovoid, hairy, with a crown of persistent calyx lobes. Flowers in July and August. Grows in meadows, on field boundaries, grassy slopes and margins of forests from lowlands to mountains.

3 Yellow Scabious *Scabiosa ochroleuca*. Perennial herb up to 50 cm high, with erect stems. Leaves of basal rosettes obovate, lyre-shaped, pinnately lobed, terminal lobe toothed; stem leaves with linear, toothed segments. Long-stalked flower heads; outer florets with 2 enlarged petals. Light yellow corollas; calyx bristly hairy, at first reddish. Flowers from July to October. Grows on sunny slopes, field boundaries, rocky slopes and margins of forests, in lower altitudes of milder regions. Sometimes grown in gardens.

2   3   1

Family: **Campanula**—Campanulaceae

4 Peach-leaved Bellflower *Campanula persicifolia*. Perennial plant up to 1 metre high, with shortly creeping rhizome and erect stems. Glossy, smooth leaves are shallowly toothed; basal ones lanceolate to oblanceolate, top ones narrowly lanceolate. Flowers up to 4 cm long, in an open raceme. Corolla broadly bell-shaped, blue-violet to white, with 5 broad lobes. Erect capsules with three basal openings. Flowers from June to September. Grows in woods, thickets and on bushy slopes, from lowlands to mountains. Often cultivated in Britain and escaping; well naturalized in a few places.

5 Clustered Bellflower *Campanula glomerata*. Perennial herb up to 40 cm high, usually with downy hairs and erect stems. Basal leaves petiolate, ovate-cordate, stem ones sessile, lanceolate, toothed. Sessile flowers in terminal and/or axillary heads; corollas erect, bell-shaped, dark blue to blue-violet, less frequently white. Flowers from June to September. Grows on bushy or grassy slopes, in open woods and clearings from lowlands to mountains. Several forms are grown in gardens.

6 Alpine Bellflower *Campanula alpina*. A perennial herb up to 15 cm high, with basal rosette of hairy, oval leaves, toothed at the tips. Stem leaves lanceolate, usually toothed, rarely entire. Drooping flowers on hairy stalks; corollas broadly bell-shaped, light blue, with recurved lobes, woolly hairy on margins. Flowers in July and August. Grows on screes and among rocks in mountains. In the Alps accompanied by Bearded Bellflower (*C. barbata*) with larger, pale violet-blue flowers having prominently woolly hairy corolla lobes.

4   5   6

Family: **Campanula**—Campanulaceae

1 Spiked Rampion *Phyteuma spicatum*. Perennial herb up to 80 cm high, with erect stems. Long-petioled bottom leaves are cordate-ovate, with rounded teeth; stem leaves lanceolate. Flowers in dense, cylindrical head; corollas whitish-yellow, tubular; petals linear. Capsule ovoid, with two openings. Flowers from May to July. Grows in deciduous woods and thickets, from lowlands to mountains. Rare in Britain. Related Round-headed Rampion (*P. orbiculare*) has dark blue flowers in globose heads.

2 Common Sheepsbit *Jasione montana*. Biennial herb with erect hairy stems up to 50 cm high. Basal leaves, linear to oblong, hairy, mostly withered at flowering time; stem ones smaller with wavy margins. Flowers in globose heads, bracts triangular-ovate, pointed. Corollas bright blue, rarely rosy or whitish; petals linear. Capsule ovoid. Flowers from June to August. Grows in grassy places, dunes, on rocky slopes and on cliffs, especially on non-calcareous soils, from lowlands to foothills.

Family: Compositae (syn. Asteraceae)

3 Chicory *Cichorium intybus*. Perennial herb, up to 150 cm high, with a milky sap. Stiff, erect, branched stems. Basal leaves petiolate, in rosette, oblanceolate, irregularly lobed, bristle beneath; stem leaves sessile, upper ones lanceolate. Inflorescence a capitulum, involucral bracts in two rows. All florets strap-shaped, five-toothed at the tips, blue, rarely rose or whitish. Achenes without hairs, crowned with short scales. Flowers from July to October. Grows by roadsides on waste ground and in pastures, from lowlands to foothills. Much cultivated for roots (chicory) and as salad vegetable (chicons).

4 Mouse-ear Hawkweed *Hieracium pilosella*. Perennial herb with long, leafy stolons and leafless, single-headed flowering stems, up to 30 cm high. Leaves in basal rosette linear to obovate-oblong, white hairy floccose beneath, sparingly so above. Linear involucral bracts grey-green, hairy on margins. All florets ligulate, five-toothed, yellow, outer ones reddish, striped. Achenes purple-black, with pappus. Flowers from May to October. Grows in meadows, on grassy slopes and banks, and by roadsides, from lowlands to mountains.

5 *Hieracium aurantiacum*. Perennial herb up to 50 cm high, with creeping stolons and erect stems. Leaves of basal rosette oblong to lanceolate, hairy, glandular, woolly hairy beneath. Flower heads in a terminal cluster covered with black-based glandular hairs. Capitula have dark orange florets. Flowers from June to August. Grows in mountain meadows of central Europe. Sometimes grown in gardens and escaping; can become an aggressive weed.

6 Common Dandelion *Taraxacum officinale*. Perennial herb with a milky latex-like sap, 20—40 cm high. Leaves of basal rosette are angularly, pinnately lobed, either deeply or shallowly. Leafless stems with single capitula; outer involucral bracts linear, spreading or reflexed; inner ones erect and longer; strap-shaped florets golden yellow. Achenes with pointed tubercles, beaked, crowned by parachute-like pappus. Flowers from April to September. Common in meadows, pastures, lawns, by roadsides and as field weed, from lowlands to mountains.

4

5

6

183

Family: Compositae

1 Prickly Lettuce *Lactuca serriola*. Biennial herb up to 150 cm high, with a milky sap and prickly hairs. Bottom stem leaves pinnately lobed and toothed; upper leaves lanceolate, clasping. Leaf blades vertical, usually in a north-south plane (Compass Plant). Capitula in large panicles; all florets strap-shaped, yellow. Achenes with small points and stalked pappus. Flowers from July to September. Grows on wasteland, banks, dunes and walls at lower altitudes in milder regions. Related *Lactuca sativa* is cultivated as a salad vegetable.

2 Giant Cat's-ear *Hypochoeris uniflora*. Perennial herb up to 40 cm high, with erect stems bearing a solitary capitulum, usually leafless. Leaves of basal rosette lanceolate, toothed, coarsely hairy. Large capitula up to 5 cm in diameter, the involucre bearing soft blackish hairs; florets yellow. Achenes beaked, crowned with pappus. Flowers from July to September. Grows in mountain meadows, in rocky places and in clearings of knee-pine.

3 Greater Goatsbeard *Tragopogon dubius*. Biennial herb up to 50 cm high, with erect, branched and leafy stem. Leaves linear-lanceolate, sharply pointed, usually grey-green. Stems thickened and hollow beneath capitula. Solitary capitula with yellow florets. Involucral bracts longer than outer florets. Achenes up to 4 cm long, with spiny projections and stalked pappus. Flowers from May to July. Grows on sunny, grassy slopes, field boundaries and by roadsides at lower altitudes of milder regions.

4 Common Vipersgrass *Scorzonera humilis*. Perennial up to 40 cm high, with brownish-black rhizome and erect, simple, almost leafless stems, usually with single capitulum. Basal leaves petiolate, linear-lanceolate, woolly hairy when young, later smooth. Capitula with a bell-shaped involucre and yellow florets. Achenes ribbed and crowned with pappus. Flowers in May to July. Grows in damp meadows, on moors and in open forests, from hilly country to mountains. Rare in Britain. Related Purple Vipersgrass (*S. purpurea*) has lilac flowers and linear leaves.

5 Hemp Agrimony *Eupatorium cannabinum*. Perennial, robust herb up to 150 cm high with erect, leafy stems. Leaves short-petiolate, hairy, opposite, three- to five-lobed and toothed. Dense inflorescences, small, few-flowered capitula, narrowly cylindrical involucre. Florets pink or whitish tubular, with five corolla lobes. Achenes black, crowned with pappus. Flowers from July to September. Grows in damp open woods, on banks, in ditches and marshes, from lowlands to mountains.

6 Golden-rod *Solidago virgaurea*. Perennial herb up to 75 cm high. Stems erect, simple, leafy. Basal leaves obovate to oblanceolate, petiolate, toothed; upper ones lanceolate, sessile. Small yellow capitula arranged in dense, erect raceme or panicle. Outer ligulate florets longer than involucre, disc florets tubular. Achenes downy, crowned with pappus. Flowers from July to October. Grows in open woods, among rocks, in hedgerows, on cliffs and dunes, from lowlands to mountains. A very variable plant with several distinct forms varying from 5 to 75 cm in height.

6

4

5

Family: Compositae

1 Daisy *Bellis perennis.* Perennial herb up to 10 cm high. Leaves in basal rosette, obovate to spathulate, widely toothed. Erect stems with single capitula. Conical receptacle hollow, involucral bracts lanceolate, blunt. Disc florets tubular, yellow; ray ones ligulate, white, often red-tinted at the tip. Flowers from March to November. Grows in grassy places from lowlands to mountains. Large-flowered forms are cultivated, some with 'double' flower heads (all florets ligulate).

2 Alpine Aster *Aster alpinus.* Perennial herb up to 20 cm high. Erect, unbranched stems with single capitula, few-leaved. Three-veined, hairy, entire leaves; basal ones spathulate, stem leaves lanceolate, sessile. Capitula up to 4 cm in diameter, involucral bracts lanceolate, hairy. Disc florets yellow, tubular, ray ones strap-shaped, violet-blue, rarely rose. Flowers from June to August. Grows in rocky, stony places or on grassy slopes in mountains. Also grown in gardens.

3 *Erigeron canadense.* Annual or biennial plant, up to 1 metre high, with erect, densely leafy, simple stems and a large paniculate inflorescence. Leaves lanceolate; bottom ones petiolate, upper leaves sessile. Tiny capitula with membranous bordered involucral bracts. Disc florets yellowish white, tubular; ray ones dirty white, slightly longer than involucral bracts. Fruit is an achene. Flowers from July to October. Native of North America but extensively naturalised on wasteland, by roadsides, on dunes and walls. Also a weed of farmland and gardens.

4 Blue Fleabane *Erigeron acer*. Biennial to perennial herb, up to 30 cm high, with erect, reddish, leafy stems, all coarsely hairy. Leaves usually entire, bottom ones obovate-lanceolate, petiolate; upper leaves lanceolate, sessile. Capitula at the end of upper lateral branches, 1 cm in diameter; cylindrical involucre has linear bracts with grey hairs. Central florets whitish to yellow-green, tubular; outer ones short-ligulate, filamentous, slightly longer than central flowers, purple. Flowers from June to September. Grows particularly in limestone areas, on dry, grassy slopes, dunes, banks and walls, from lowlands to foothills.

5 Cat's-foot *Antennaria dioica*. Perennial evergreen plant with stolons up to 20 cm high, with stems and leaves white-woolly beneath. Basal leaves spathulate, stem ones lanceolate to linear. Separate-sexed capitula in close terminal cluster, stalked; involucral bracts overlapping, chaffy in texture, whitish or pink; florets usually whitish. Flowers in May and June. Grows in hill pastures, rocky places, in open pine-woods and on heaths and moors, from foothills to mountains.

6 Edelweiss *Leontopodium alpinum*. Perennial herb up to 20 cm high, thickly white woolly hairy. Erect simple stems sparsely leaved. Basal leaves in rosette, oblanceolate, petiolate, entire; stem ones alternate, smaller. Small hemispherical capitula grouped at end of stem into a dense cluster, surrounded by star-like unequal bracts which are lanceolate and white-felted; florets tiny, yellowish white. Flowers from June to September. Grows in mountain pastures, on limestone rocks and screes in central and southeastern Europe. Protected plant in some countries.

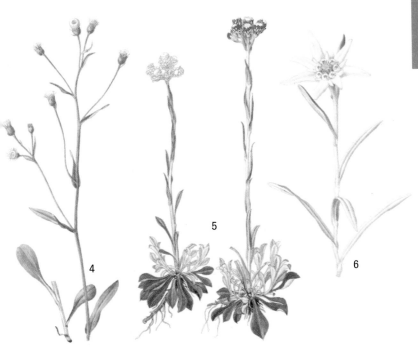

Family: Compositae

1 Wood Cudweed *Gnaphalium sylvaticum*. Perennial herb up to 50 cm high, erect, simple leafy stems. Single-veined, entire leaves on upper surface downy or bare, underside grey-felted; bottom ones lanceolate, upper leaves linear. Small capitula clustered in axils of upper leaves; involucral bracts bordered light brown. Tiny florets narrowly tubular, pale brown. Flowers from July to September. Grows in open woods, clearings and on heaths and moors, from lowlands to mountains.

2 *Inula britannica*. Perennial herb up to 60 cm high, with appressed hairs and erect, leafy stems. Hairy basal leaves oblong-ovate to lanceolate, toothed or entire; upper ones sessile, cordate and clasping. Capitula solitary or in groups of up to four at end of branches. Widely ovoid involucre, bracts linear-lanceolate, glandular-hairy. Florets yellow, central ones tubular, outer ones long ligulate. Flowers from July to September. Grows scattered in damp meadows, ditches, streamsides and damp woods, from lowlands to hilly country. Probably now extinct in Britain.

3 Common Cocklebur *Xanthium strumarium*. Annual, grey-green herb, up to 75 cm high, with a stout, sparsely leaved stem. Leaves cordate triangular, lobed and toothed. Axillary capitula unisexual; male ones with several flowers, greenish female capitula have two flowers enclosed in spiny involucral bracts. Achenes enclosed in spiny, woody involucre. Flowers from July to October. Native of South America, introduced and established on wasteland, by roadsides and on tips, usually at lower altitudes in temperate regions.

4 Tripartite Bur-marigold *Bidens tripartita*. Annual herb up to 60 cm high, with maroon-tinted, much branched stems. Opposite, petiolate stem leaves three- to five-lobed, segments lanceolate, toothed. Capitula solitary at ends of branches; outer involucral bracts enlarged and leafy, inner ones ovate, brownish. Disc florets yellow, ray ones absent. Achenes obovoid, flattened, edges barbed, with two to three straight barbed awns. Flowers from July to October. Grows in ditches, by ponds and rivers and in damp meadows, from lowlands to foothills. Related Nodding Bur-marigold (*B. cernuus*) has larger nodding capitula.

5 Corn Chamomile *Anthemis arvensis*. Annual herb, up to 50 cm high. Erect, much-branched stems. Twice or three times pinnately divided leaves, segments linear. Solitary, long-stalked capitula; receptacle conical, bearing lanceolate, pointed, chaffy awns. Disc florets yellow, tubular, ray ones white, ligulate. Achenes truncate ovoid, without pappus. Flowers from May to October. Grows in fields, on waste ground and by roadsides from lowlands to foothills.

6 Stinking Mayweed *Anthemis cotula*. Foetid annual herb, up to 50 cm high, with much-branched stems. Leaves twice to three times pinnately divided, with narrowly linear, toothed segments. Solitary stalked capitula, bracts of involucre with wide membranous rim. Tubular disc florets yellow, ray ones ligulate, white. Achenes lop-sided, ovoid, ribbed, without pappus. Flowers from June to October. Grows in fields, on wasteland and by roadsides, from lowlands to foothills.

2

5

6

189

Family: Compositae

1 Gallant Soldier *Galinsoga parviflora.* Annual herb up to 70 cm high, with erect, branched, leafy stems. Leaves opposite, ovate, pointed, sharply toothed. Small capitula in terminal, leafy clusters. Tubular disc florets yellow, ray ones shortly ligulate, white. Achenes with scaly pappus. Flowers from May to October. Native of South America, introduced to Europe and now a familiar weed in fields, gardens and on wasteland, from lowlands to foothills. Related Hairy Galinsoga or Shaggy Soldier (*G. ciliata*) is similar, but more or less densely covered with long hairs.

2 Sneezewort *Achillea ptarmica.* Perennial up to 60 cm high, with woody creeping rhizome and erect, leafy stems. Leaves linear-lanceolate, sessile, sharply toothed. Capitula in a loose terminal cluster, involucral bracts bordered with dark brown. Central florets whitish, surrounded by up to 12 ligulate flowers of the same length as involucre. Flowers from July to September. Grows on heaths, in ditches and damp meadows from lowlands to foothills. Double forms are often cultivated in gardens.

3 Yarrow *Achillea millefolium.* Perennial up to 50 cm high, with far-creeping stolons and erect flowering stems. Leaves twice to three times pinnate, segments linear-lanceolate, spreading. Small capitula in dense flattened corymbs. Disc florets creamy, surrounded by up to five ligulate ray florets coloured white, sometimes pink or cerise. Flowers from June to October. Grows in meadows, pastures, woodland clearings, among rocks and by the roadside from lowlands to mountains. Pink- and cerise-flowered forms are grown in gardens.

5

6

4

4 *Matricaria recutita* (syn. *M. chamomilla*). Annual herb, up to 50 cm high, pleasingly aromatic with branched stems. Leaves alternate, sparse, up to three times pinnately divided into narrow, linear segments. Individual long-stalked capitula at end of upper branches, disc florets yellow and tubular, ray ones white and ligulate, soon reflexing backwards. Receptacles of capitula hollow, conical. Achenes ovoid, ribbed, without pappus. Flowers from March to August. Grows as a weed in fields, gardens and by roadsides, from lowlands to foothills, mainly in milder regions. Once much cultivated as a medicinal herb and still used as a substitute for true Chamomile.

5 Pineapple Weed *Matricaria matricarioides.* Annual herb, up to 30 cm high, sweetly aromatic, with branched, densely leafy stems. Sessile leaves up to three times pinnately divided into linear-lanceolate segments. Flower stalks short, thickened at top; involucral bracts with translu-

cent membranous rim. All florets yellow-green, tubular. Receptacles hollow, conical. Achenes ovoid, truncate, ribbed, pappus absent. Flowers from June to August. Native of north-eastern Asia, introduced and now a common weed of cultivated land, roadsides, wasteland and along paths, from lowlands to foothills.

6 Scentless Mayweed *Tripleurospermum maritimum* ssp. *inodorum.* Annual or biennial herb, up to 50 cm high, with erect stems usually branched only on top. Leaves up to three times pinnately divided into narrowly linear segments. Long-stalked capitula. Disc florets yellow, tubular; ray ones white, ligulate. Achenes ovoid, truncate, ribbed, without pappus. Flowers from June to October. Grows in fields, fallows, on wasteland and by roadsides, from lowlands to foothills. *T. maritimum* ssp. *maritimum* is perennial and more or less prostrate, growing only near the sea.

Family: Compositae

1 Tansy *Tanacetum vulgare* (syn. *Chrysanthemum vulgare*). Perennial, with creeping rhizomes and erect stems up to 1 metre high. Leaves twice pinnately divided, segments lanceolate, toothed; pleasingly aromatic when bruised. Numerous capitula in dense corymbs. All florets yellow, tubular, five-lobed. Achenes ovoid, crowned with a short membranous cup. Flowers from July to September. Grows by the roadside, on wasteland, and in hedgerows, from lowlands to mountains. Formerly much grown as a medicinal and pot-herb.

2 Ox-eye Daisy *Chrysanthemum leucanthemum*. Perennial herb up to 70 cm high, with erect, simple stems, occasionally sparsely branched. Bottom leaves simple, spathulate, petiolate, shallowly lobed and toothed; upper ones oblong-lanceolate, sessile, clasping. Long-stalked capitula; disc florets yellow, tubular, ray ones white, ligulate. Achenes obovoid, grooved. Flowers from June to October. Grows in meadows, on grassy slopes, banks, and by the roadside.

3 Wood Chrysanthemum *Chrysanthemum corymbosum*. Perennial up to 1 m high, with erect, densely leafy stems. Bottom leaves petiolate, stem ones sessile, all pinnately lobed, the segments double-toothed. Capitula in corymbs. Disc florets yellow, tubular, ray ones white, narrowly ligulate. Flowers from June to August. Grows in open woods and among bushes, on sunny slopes, from lowlands to mountains, mainly on limestone, in milder regions.

4 Mugwort *Artemisia vulgaris*. Perennial herb up to 120 cm high, with erect, stiff, branched stems. Leaves pinnately lobed, underside thinly white-felted, segments lanceolate to oblong,

lobed, toothed, upper leaves simply pinnate with entire segments. Small capitula arranged in long, dense, pyramidal panicles. Minute, tubular florets reddish-brown. Flowers from July to September. Grows on waste ground, by roadsides and in hedgerows, from lowlands to mountains.

5 Coltsfoot *Tussilago farfara*. Perennial herb, up to 25 cm high, with creeping rhizome and erect, simple stem, bearing single capitulum. Basal tufts of leaves develop after flowering period. Leaves long-petiolate, rounded, polygonal, shallowly 5—12 lobed, cordate, shallowly black-toothed, underside grey-felted. Scale leaves on flowering stems ovate, numerous, yellowish.

Capitula solitary; bracts linear, sometimes with red tint. Yellow florets, disc ones tubular, ray ones linear-ligulate. Achenes cylindrical, ribbed, with crown of pappus. Flowers in March and April. Grows in fields, on wasteland, on banks and in ditches, from lowlands to mountains.

6 Purple Coltsfoot *Homogyne alpina*. Perennial evergreen herb up to 15 cm high with thin creeping rhizome. Stems with thick, grey hairs are erect, bearing a single capitulum, usually with two ovate, sessile, clasping leaves. Long-petiolate leaves in basal tufts are almost leathery, cordate-orbicular or reniform, shallowly sinuate toothed. Capitula with linear bracts; florets pale violet, slightly longer than involucral bracts. Achenes cylindrical, ribbed, crowned with pappus. Flowers from May to July. Grows in mountain forests, meadows and on barrens. Very rare in Great Britain, being found in Scotland only and even there not native.

Family: Compositae

1 Common Butterbur *Petasites hybridus* (syn. *P. officinalis*). Perennial herb up to 1 metre high, partly dioecious. Thick, branched rhizomes strikingly aromatic if bruised or cut. Erect, simple flowering stems often violet-tinted. Basal leaves long-petiolate, cordate, angularly rounded to reniform, bluntly toothed. Lanceolate stem bracts clasping, bottom ones sheathed. Capitula in dense racemes, during fruition elongated; involucres flushed purple. Florets pink, seemingly bisexual, tubular, five-lobed, pistillate ones shortly tubular. Achenes cylindrical, with pappus. Flowers in April and May. Grows gregariously on river and canal banks, in ditches and damp meadows from lowlands to mountains.

2 White Butterbur *Petasites albus.* Perennial herb up to 80 cm high, with far-creeping rhizome. Very similar to preceding species. Stem and scales light green. Leaves in basal rosette rounded, reniform, cordate, angularly lobed, sharply toothed, grey-felted to smooth on underside. Florets yellowish-white, seemingly bisexual; five-lobed, pistillate ones shortly tubular. Flowers in April and May. Grows in open woods, along streams and on wasteland, from foothills to mountains; in higher altitudes more frequent and often gregarious.

3 Mountain Arnica *Arnica montana.* Perennial herb up to 50 cm high, with far-creeping rhizome. Erect stems glandular hairy, usually with only one capitulum. Basal rosette leaves ovate, entire; stem ones opposite, oblong-lanceolate. Involucral bracts lanceolate; florets orange-yellow, disc ones tubular, ray ones ligulate. Achenes with a crown of pappus. Flowers in June and July. Grows in meadows, forest glades and on margins of peat-bogs from foothills to mountains, mainly at higher altitudes. Protected plant in some countries.

4 Austrian Leopards-bane *Doronicum austriacum*. Perennial herb up to 150 cm high, with short rhizome and angular, erect, hairy stems bearing several capitula. Basal leaves petiolate, ovate-cordate, toothed; stem ones elongated, cordate to auriculate, clasping. Long-stalked capitula with linear-lanceolate involucral bracts. Florets yellow, disc ones tubular, ray ones long-ligulate. Achenes of central flowers with pappus, outer ones without. Flowers in July and August. Grows in open woods and river banks, from foothills to mountains.

5 Common Ragwort *Senecio jacobaea*. Perennial up to 1 metre high, with erect, densely leafy stems branched in upper part. Basal leaves pinnately lobed, stem ones usually sessile, smaller. Capitula in flattened compound corymbs; florets yellow, disc ones tubular, ray ones ligulate. Flowers from July to September. Grows on grassy slopes, in meadows, on margins of forests and by roadsides, from lowlands to foothills.

6 *Senecio nemorensis*. Perennial herb up to 150 cm high, usually hairy. Stem leaves oblong-ovate to lanceolate, stalkless, semi-clasping, toothed, underside downy. Capitula in flattish compound corymbs. Florets pale yellow, disc ones tubular, surrounded by five ligulate ray ones. Achenes with long pappus. Flowers from May to July. Grows in forests and clearings from foothills to mountains.

6   4   5

Family: Compositae

1 Lesser Burdock *Arctium minus*. Biennial herb up to 1.5 m high, with erect, stout, much-branched stems, woolly-hairy. Leaves petiolate, ovate-oblong, cordate, entire or shallowly toothed, on underside thinly grey-felted. Capitula in racemes, involucral bracts with sharply hooked tips. Tubular, red-violet florets. Achenes ovoid, without pappus. Flowers from July to September. Grows in light woodland, on wasteland and by roadsides from lowlands to foothills.

2 Musk Thistle *Carduus nutans*. Biennial herb up to 1 metre high, with winged, spiny stems. Leaves elliptic, cottony-hairy, pinnate-lobed, with a spiny toothed margin. Capitula solitary, nodding, long-stalked; involucral bracts spine-tipped, webbed with cottony hairs. Florets tubular, red-purple. Achenes grey, smooth, with a light spherical pappus. Flowers from July to September. Grows on sunny grassy slopes, in pastures and by the roadside, from lowlands to foothills.

3 Welted Thistle *Carduus acanthoides*. Biennial plant up to 1 metre high, with winged, spiny stems. Leaves lanceolate, pinnate-lobed, the margins wavy and set with spines. Capitula on short, erect, winged spiny stalks; involucral bracts spiny. Florets red-purple. Flowers from June to September. Grows in pastures, on wasteland and by roadsides, from lowlands to foothills, especially in milder regions.

196

4 Creeping Thistle *Cirsium arvense.* Biennial plant up to 1 metre high or even taller with erect, leafy stems and far-creeping rhizomes. Leaves oblong-lanceolate, pinnately lobed, spiny toothed, upper ones smaller and sessile. Capitula in terminal clusters, sometimes violet-tinted; bracts pointed or shortly spined. Imperfectly dioecious pale purple florets. Achenes ovoid with long white pappus. Flowers from July to September. Grows on wasteland, as field and garden weed, in forest clearings and by roadsides, from lowlands to mountains. Spear Thistle (*C. vulgare*) is a biennial herb, with spiny-winged stems, and the leaves thinly grey-felted beneath.

5 Marsh Thistle *Cirsium palustre.* Biennial herb up to 1.5 m high, with little branched spiny winged stems. Basal leaves sometimes red-tinted, oblanceolate; stem leaves pinnate-lobed with winged bases, spiny-toothed. Capitula in crowded leafy clusters, somewhat cottony hairy and purple tinted; florets red-purple. Flowers from July to September. Grows in marshes, damp meadows, woodland clearings and in hedgerows from lowlands to mountains.

6 Cabbage Thistle *Cirsium oleraceum.* Perennial herb up to 120 cm high with erect, distantly leaved, rarely branched stems. Softly spiny leaves, bottom ones deeply pinnately lobed with toothed segments, upper leaves smaller, cordate, sessile. Capitula in clusters subtended by enlarged yellowish bracts. Yellow-white florets. Flowers from June to September. Grows in damp meadows, marshes, open moist woods and by streams, from lowlands to foothills. Naturalized in a very few places in Britain.

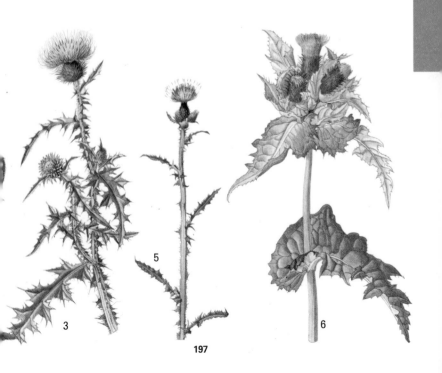

Family: Compositae

1 Brown-headed Knapweed *Centaurea jacea.* Perennial herb up to 50 cm high, with erect, branched stems, sparsely leaved. Upper leaves oblanceolate, sessile, with one or two large teeth. Capitula solitary at end of branches, bracts with distinct dry-membranous, fan-shaped appendages. Florets red-purple. Achenes ovoid, grey, glossy, without pappus. Flowers from June to October. Grows in grassland and waste places from lowlands to mountains. Only naturalized in a few places in southern Britain. Greater Knapweed (*C. scabiosa*) has pinnate-lobed leaves and larger heads. It is found in grassy places and by roadsides throughout lowland Britain.

2 Cornflower *Centaurea cyanus.* Annual or overwintering herb up to 60 cm high, with erect, branched stems. Leaves lanceolate, the basal ones often with narrow pinnate lobes. Capitula solitary at ends of branches, cottony hairy, central one with narrow-toothed appendages. Central florets violet, marginal ones much larger, spreading, bright blue, rarely whitish or rosy. Achenes with a brush-like crown of stiff hairs. Flowers from June to October. Grows in cornfields and waste places. Formerly a common weed of cornfields throughout Europe, but now on the decline where good farming practices prevail.

3 Mountain Cornflower *Centaurea montana.* Perennial herb up to 60 cm high, with erect, little-branched stems. Leaves lanceolate, entire, underside cobwebby hairy, upper surface smooth, stem leaves sessile with winged bases. Stalked capitula often solitary, bracts with black, short-toothed border. Central flowers violet, outer ones larger, blue, sometimes rose or white. Flowers from May to October. Grows in mountain meadows and forest clearings, from foothills to mountains. Grown in gardens in Britain and sometimes escaping.

6

2

1

198

4 Stemless Carline-thistle *Carlina acaulis*. Perennial plant with usually very short flowering stems, only a few centimetres tall. Leaves in basal rosette pinnate-lobed and spiny toothed. Capitula solitary, over 15 cm in diameter; outer involucral bracts leaf-like, inner ones linear, upper surface silvery glossy, underside yellowish, in sunshine widely expanded, in wet weather rolled tightly closed. Tubular, whitish or pinkish florets. Achenes with hairs. Flowers from July to September. Grows scattered in dry pastures and on stony slopes from lowlands to foothills.

5 Common Carline-thistle *Carlina vulgaris*. Biennial herb up to 50 cm high, with erect, purplish, cottony hairy stems. Under surface of leaves cobwebby woolly, later bare, oblong-lanceolate, with undulate margins densely spiny toothed. Basal leaves in rosette, dying before flowering starts. Stem leaves cordate, sessile, the topmost ones transformed into bracts. Capitula terminate lateral branches; inner involucral bracts straw-yellow, spreading and resembling ray florets. Florets purple. Achenes with short hairs and crowned with pappus. Flowers from July to September. Grows on sunny grassy slopes and banks, particularly on limestone, from lowlands to mountains.

6 Great Globe-thistle *Echinops sphaerocephalus*. Perennial herb up to 2 m high, with robust, woody, white-woolly stems. Bottom leaves petiolate, stem ones sessile, lanceolate, pinnate-lobed and spiny toothed. Single-flowered, narrow capitula aggregated into dense globose heads. Florets bluish or white, tubular. Achenes oblong-ovoid, with a cup-like crown of partly fused hairs. Flowers from June to August. Grows on forest margins, in vineyards, quarries, on river banks and wasteland, and by roadsides, in lower altitudes of milder regions. Grown in gardens in Britain and sometimes escaping.

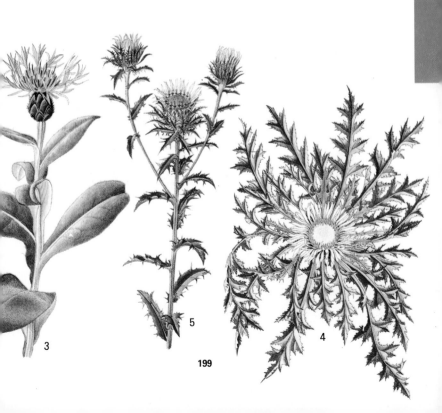

Orchids, Lilies and Related Plants

Without doubt, the most striking plants are those that belong to the order Orchidales. Everyone has marvelled at the exotic tropical orchids in florists' windows or in the glasshouses of botanical gardens. It is amazing to find flowers with so many bizarre shapes and widely diverse colour combinations in a single family. One must realize, of course, that the plants belonging to the orchid family (Orchidaceae) are estimated to number as many as 25,000, making it the largest family in the whole plant kingdom.

Orchids have an extremely wide range of distribution. Although they grow mainly in damp tropical forests, their range reaches far into the Arctic and extends from coastal rain forests high up into the mountains.

Just as their habitats are marked by great diversity, so is the structure of their bodies, their manner of obtaining nourishment and their life forms. European orchids are mostly green autotrophic ground orchids, with only occasional supplementation of their diet by saprophytic means. Practically all species are mycorrhizal. Only a few central European species lack chlorophyll and are entirely saprophytic, for example *Neottia, Corallorhiza, Epipogium* and several others. Tropical orchids are mostly epiphytic, which means that they grow on other plants, usually on tall trees, although a few genera are ground plants.

Many European orchids have underground tubers. Those belonging to the genus *Orchis* (which gave the whole family its name), have a typical pair of tubers, while the tubers of *Dactylorhiza* orchids and some others are digitately lobed. The food reserves in the tubers enable the plants to survive cold winter months or periods of drought. These reserves are more readily and more quickly transformed into nourishing substances than starch. Epiphytic orchids also have tubers, but these developed from stems, not from roots, and can thus reproduce by vegetative means. A common feature of epiphytic orchids is their aerial roots, through which respiration takes place and through which atmospheric moisture, which is nearly 100 per cent in tropical rain forests, is absorbed. Some epiphytic orchids have no leaves whatsoever, their function having been taken over by the aerial roots which are rich in chlorophyll.

Fig. 1. One of the loveliest European orchids, Lady's Slipper (*Cypripedium calceolus*). The conspicuously inflated, originally upper, lip assumes its position at the bottom as the flower develops.

200

The flowers of orchids exhibit perhaps the greatest diversity of shape of all plants. Usually there are several to dozens of blossoms on a single plant; sometimes they grow in clusters that hang in drooping racemes from the crowns of the trees on which tropical epiphytic orchids grow. These may form garlands up to 4 m long, as in the species *Renanthera lowii* of New Guinea. The European orchids with the largest flowers are Lady's Slipper (*Cypripedium calceolus*), with a flower up to 9 cm long, and *Himantoglossum hircinum*, with a flower up to 5 cm long, strap-shaped and twisted, with a violet-spotted lip. All the other European orchids have much smaller flowers; those of some species of *Epipactis, Listera, Spiranthes* and *Herminium* are extremely small and inconspicuous. The interesting and diverse shapes of the flowers of certain *Ophrys* species fully justify the names given to the respective plants: *O. insectifera, O. sphecodes, O. fuciflora* and *O. apifera*.

The flowers of orchids are extremely interesting. Before they open, the flower-peduncle is twisted round a full 180 degrees, so that the spurred, lip-shaped, upper perianth segment becomes the bottom segment. Only rarely are the pollen grains free, mostly they are in a coherent cluster, called a pollinium, with a sticky pad at the end of a stalk. The pollinia adhere to the bodies of insects that visit the flower, so that when they visit another, the pollinia are transferred to its stigma, thereby pollinating the flower.

Orchid seeds are the smallest and lightest in the plant realm and their number is the greatest. Of the European species the smallest number is produced by *Coeloglossum virida* — only about 1,330! The ovary of the South American orchid *Cychnoches ventricosum*, on the other hand, contains more than four million seeds! Despite this astounding quantity the chances of the development of a new plant are extremely small, for the seed must find conditions that are suitable for its germination and most orchids, including tropical species, require a mycorrhizal association to obtain their nourishment.

In no other family have so many hybrids been developed by selective breeding than in the case of orchids. In the continual quest for ever-new combinations of colour and form, not only have breeders crossed numerous species of the same genus but also some belonging to different genera. The genus *Cattleya* alone, which numbers 60—70 species, has more than 5,000 hybrids. As for the Indomalaysian genus *Vanda*, its species and varieties have been successfully crossed with members of eleven other genera.

Fig. 2. The flowers of Flowering Rush (*Butomus umbellatus*) adorn waterside meadows and wet places.

Numerous varieties have been developed among the popular orchids of the genera *Dendrobium, Catasetum, Cymbidium, Oncidium, Odontoglossum, Laelia, Phalaenopsis, Miltonia, Stanhopea* and dozens of others.

Despite the fact that all species of orchids are on the list of protected species in Europe, they are declining in number every year due to the disappearance of their natural habitats through land reclamation and runoffs from fields treated with chemicals. Even tropical orchids are not safe from human activity, for a portion of the tropical forest in the Amazon region, central Africa and south-east Asia is irretrievably lost every hour as a result of the unscrupulous felling of trees whose crowns contain orchids that have climbed there in search of light and air.

In addition to the lily family (Liliaceae), the order Liliales also comprises garlic, onion, Lily-of-the-Valley, crocus, snowdrop and snowflake. As with orchids, we are more likely to be acquainted with the cultivated plants than with those that grow in the wild. The lily family includes lilies (*Lilium*), fritillaries (*Fritillaria*), tulips (*Tulipa*), *Erythronium*, *Gagea*, *Lloydia* and several other genera. These appear to be common and familiar plants but we do not know all of them as well as we know the cultivated ones, for example *Lilium candidum*, native to the Lebanon, southern Syria and neighbouring regions, and the east-Asian species *Lilium regale* and Tiger Lily (*L. tigrinum*). Probably loveliest of all is the Turk's-cap Lily (*L. martagon*) with its pendulous, light purple, dark-spotted Turk's-cap flowers with recurved petals. I know of a dappled glade where dozens of these flowers, their protruding stamens tipped with dark orange anthers, glow brightly in the shafts of sunlight.

The same is true of fritillaries. We are more apt to be familiar with the Crown Imperial (*Fritillaria imperialis*), native to Iran and Afghanistan, which is widely grown for its large yellow or brick-red flowers, but who can boast having seen the unusual flowers of Snake's Head (*F. meleagris*) in the wild? The unbelievable regularity of its brown and violet checkerboard pattern is one of the small miracles of the flora of damp meadows.

Dog's-tooth Violet (*Erythronium dens-canis*) is also familiar to us as a garden plant, but in southern Europe one may come across it in the wild, its pink, brown-spotted flower rising from between two marbled leaves. In central Europe Dog's-tooth Violet is a rare relict of Tertiary period flora and, as such, is on the list of rigidly protected species in several localities in Austria, the Czech Republic and Switzerland, where its distribution occasionally extends from the southern regions of its range.

Most familiar of all the plants of this group are the tulips, grown in a wide range of varieties and hybrids. Garden tulips are classed under the heading *Tulipa gesneriana* and their popularity, cultivation and spread throughout Europe is fairly recent, dating from the sixteenth century, although they were cultivated in the Middle East as far back as the tenth century. Also popular are the low-growing, early-flowering, botanical tulips such as *T. greigi, T. fosteriana* and *T. kaufmanniana*, native to central Asia.

All plants of the lily family may be seen only rarely in the wild and for that reason they are on the list of protected species. We must all be content with the beauty of their cultivated

Fig. 3. Autumn Crocus (*Colchicum autumnale*) flowers in the autumn and again in the spring of the following year.

forms as it is an offence to gather bulbs or tubers in the wild. Wild plants should be left where they belong, to enhance the beauty of their natural surroundings.

Plants of the order Butomales are aquatic or bog plants. The order Pandanales comprises solely bog plants with a typical globose or cylindrical inflorescence (spadix), for example Lesser Reedmace (*Typha angustifolia*), a robust plant that grows on the banks of still stretches of water.

The order Arales is extremely diverse. It includes Sweet Flag, Bog Arum and duckweeds (Lemnaceae). It is native to India but has long since been naturalized throughout Europe, where it is a common plant.

The simplest and smallest of all flowering plants belongs to the duckweed family. This is Rootless Duckweed (*Wolffia arrhiza*), a tiny, rootless aquatic plant with a body consisting of minute (1.5 mm) thalli without vascular bundles and without stomata. The male flower is concealed in a minute hollow on the upperside. This consists solely of a single stamen. In the same tiny hollow the female flower grows, consisting of a single pistil. Rootless Duckweed grows in southern and western Europe, was introduced into central Europe and is sometimes grown in aquariums. In south-east Asia it is cultivated for its high concentration of proteins and its thalli are being experimentally processed as food for manned space flights of long duration.

Fig. 4. The perianth segments of the pendulous flowers of Turk's-cap Lily (*Lilium martagon*) are conspicuously curved upward.

203

Family: **Orchid**—Orchidaceae

1 Large White Helleborine *Cephalanthera damasonium*. Perennial herb up to 45 cm high with slender leafy stem, scaly at bottom. Leaves ovate to lanceolate. Flowers 3—12 in a loose spike. Cream-white tepals, bracts usually longer than ovary. Flowers in May and June. Grows scattered in deciduous woods, from lowlands to foothills. Related Red Helleborine (*C. rubra*) has rose to purple flowers and stem glandularly downy above.

2 Common Helleborine *Epipactis helleborine* (syn. *E. latifolia*). Perennial herb up to 60 cm high, with erect stems, downy above. Broadly ovate green leaves mostly spreading, sessile, clasping, on under surface downy. Raceme one-sided, elongated, many-flowered. Each flower at first drooping, straightening up while flowering. Inner tepals greenish and dull purple-brown. Flowers from July to September. Grows in forests from lowlands to mountains. Related Dark-red Helleborine (*E. atrorubens*) has ovaries densely glandular downy, flowers dark purple, fragrant, and whole plant is purple-tinted; protected in some countries.

3 Lesser Butterfly Orchid *Platanthera bifolia*. Perennial herb almost 30 cm high, with tuberous rootstock and erect, hollow stems. Basal leaves, two opposite widely elliptic; stem bears up to three small, leafy bracts. Open spike of white, spurred, fragrant flowers. Flowers in June and July. Grows in open woods, among bushes and sometimes on heaths, from lowlands to mountains.

4 Fragrant Orchid *Gymnadenia conopsea* (syn. *Habanaria conopsea*). Perennial herb up to 40 cm high, with lobed tubers and erect stems. Leaves grey-green, narrowly oblong-lanceolate, bottom ones close to each other. Floral spike has lanceolate bracts, often with purple margins. Purple, rarely whitish tepals; spurs of double length. Conspicuously twisted ovary. Flowers from May to July. Grows scattered in open woods, meadows and on grassy slopes from lowlands to mountains, usually on limestone.

5 Green-winged Orchid *Orchid morio*. Perennial herb up to 25 cm high with undivided, globose tubers and green stem. Leaves grey-green, lower ones lanceolate, upper ones smaller and

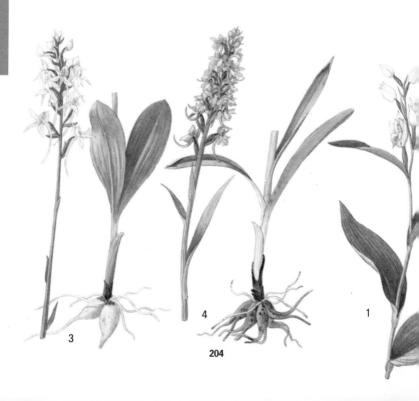

4

1

3

narrow. Flowers in short terminal raceme, purple, rarely whitish, green-veined. Helmet-like perianth, lip red-purple, dark-spotted; spur thick, cylindrical. Flowers from April to June. Grows in dry meadows and on grassy slopes, from lowlands to foothills. Related species of *Ophrys* have lip without spur but with striking design, simulating bee, bumblebee or other insect body.

6 Broad-leaved Marsh Orchid *Dactylorchis majalis* (syn. *Dactylorhyza majalis*). Very variable perennial herb up to 40 cm high, with finger-like divided tubers and erect, hollow stems. Leaves oblong-lanceolate, shortly sheathed, dark green, sometimes black-brown spotted. Dense

floral spike; flowers reddish to purple, with spotted outer petals, lip purple-red, three-lobed, spur shorter than ovary. Flowers from May to July. Grows in damp meadows, fens, marshes, dune hollows, from lowlands to foothills. Several forms are now given specific rank, *D. praetermissa* and *D. purpurella* being the most noteworthy.

7 Lady's Slipper *Cypripedium calceolus*. Perennial downy herb up to 50 cm high, with shortly creeping rhizome and erect stems, scaly at base. Only three or four leaves, alternate, ovate, prominently ribbed. Flowers solitary, or less frequently two, in axil of upper leaf. Lip light yellow, red-dotted, tepals maroon; three-lobed stigma. Flowers in May and June. Grows scattered in deciduous woods on calcareous grounds from lowlands to mountains. Almost extinct in Britain. Protected plant in some countries.

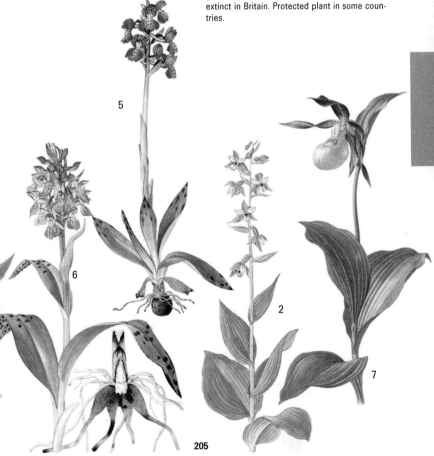

Family: Lily—Liliaceae

1 White False Helleborine *Veratrum album.*
Perennial herb, with stout erect leafy stems, up
to 150 cm high. Underside of leaves downy,
pleated, widely elliptical, upper ones lanceolate,
some in whorls of three. Flowers in dense, long
panicles, greenish-white or yellowish, bottom
ones bisexual, upper flowers mostly male. Cap-
sular fruits many-seeded. Flowers from June to
August. Grows in mountain meadows, pastures
and in rocky places, from foothills to mountains.

2 Meadow Saffron *Colchicum autumnale.* Perennial, poisonous herb with a large corm often
deeply buried. Basal, oblong-lanceolate leaves
develop in spring together with maturing capsule. Flowers pale purple, long-tubular, with 6
oblong, spreading tepals. The three-celled
ovary below ground; capsule ripens above
ground in spring. Flowers from August to November. Grows in damp meadows and open
woods, from lowlands to foothills.

3 Martagon or **Turk's Cap Lily** *Lilium martagon.*
Perennial herb with robust erect stems up to
1 metre high, and a scaly bulb. Leaves obovate-lanceolate pointed, mostly in whorls of
5—10. Flowers in open racemes, stalked and
nodding; tepals with reflexed tips, dull purple,
brown-spotted, sometimes white. Fruit an ovoid
ridged capsule. Flowers from June to August.
Grows in deciduous woods, thickets and pastures, more frequently on limestone soils, in
mountains. Protected plant in some countries. In
Britain often grown in gardens, escaping, and
now well naturalized in a number of wooded
areas.

4 Ramsons *Allium ursinum.* Perennial herb up
to 50 cm high with a bulbous rootstock and leafless stems. Basal leaves, two to three only, elliptic to lanceolate, long-petiolate. Umbellate inflorescence ensheathed while immature in two
or three bracts. Flowers up to 1 cm across, star-
shaped, with 6 pointed lobes, perianth white.
Fruit a flattened, 3-lobed capsule. Flowers from
April to June. Grows scattered in deciduous
woods, from lowlands to mountains, often gregariously. Related Crow Garlic (*A. vineale*) has
narrowly linear leaves and dense heads of bulbils and purple-red flowers; sometimes bulbils
only.

5 *Allium flavum.* Perennial herb up to 50 cm
high, with ovoid bulbs. Hollow channelled
leaves narrowly linear, grey-green. Spathe composed of two unequally long bracts. Stamens
project from bell-shaped, yellow perianth. Cap-

sules triangularly ovoid. Flowers from June to
August. Grows on sunny slopes, among rocks,
and in sandy places at lower altitudes of south-
eastern Europe. Related *Allium suaveolens* with
rosy flowers grows in the Alps.

6 May Lily *Maianthemum bifolium.* Perennial
herb up to 15 cm high with thin, creeping rhizome and erect stems, usually with two shortly
petiolate, cordate-ovate, pointed leaves.
Stalked racemose inflorescence bears small,
white starry flowers with 4 perianth lobes. Fruit
a small, red, globose berry. Flowers from May
to July. Grows in woods and among bushes
from lowlands to mountains. Very rare in Britain.

7 Common Solomon's Seal *Polygonatum multiflorum.* Perennial plant up to 80 cm high, with thick, creeping rhizome and smooth, rounded stems arching at the top. Leaves alternate, ovate to elliptic, bare. Axillary flowers usually in clusters of 2 to 5, pendulous. Perianth of six fused tepals, narrowly tubular, greenish white. Fruits are globular, blue-black berries. Flowers in May and June. Grows in shady woods and among bushes, from lowlands to foothills. Related Angular Solomon's Seal (*P. odoratum*) has angular stems and flowers solitary or in twos. *Polygonatum verticillatum* has narrowly lanceolate leaves in whorls. All species poisonous.

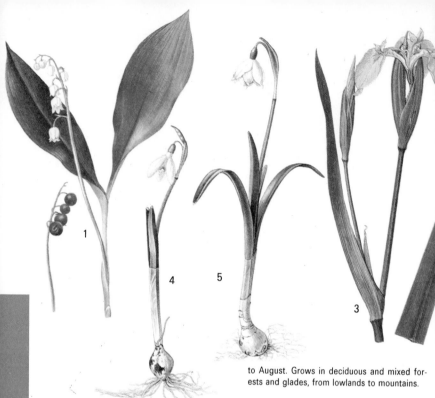

to August. Grows in deciduous and mixed forests and glades, from lowlands to mountains.

Family: **Iris**—Iridaceae

3 Yellow Flag *Iris pseudacorus*. Perennial herb up to 1.5 m high with thick, shortly creeping, branched rhizome and erect flowering stems branched at the top only. Leaves sword-shaped. Long-stalked flowers; perianth segments in two whorls of 3; outer tepals ovate, recurved, yellow, with violet-brown veining; inner tepals erect, obovate, yellow, shorter than crown-shaped stigma arms. Capsule bluntly triangular ovoid. Flowers in May and June. Grows in or close to water, rivers, ponds, lakes and ditches, mainly at lower altitudes. Related Siberian Iris (*I. sibirica*) has blue-violet flowers and linear leaves. Not native to Britain, but much cultivated in gardens and occasionally escaping.

Family: Amaryllidaceae

4 Snowdrop *Galanthus nivalis*. Perennial herb up to 20 cm high with brown-scaly bulb. Two basal leaves linear, grey-green, blunt, scale-sheathed at base. Erect stem with solitary pendent flower in axil of membranous bract. Outer perianth whorl consists of three obovate-ob-

Family: **Lily**—Liliaceae

1 Lily-of-the-Valley *Convallaria majalis*. Perennial, poisonous herb, up to 20 cm high, with creeping rhizome. Usually two petiolate leaves with sheathing scales at base, elliptic-lanceolate, entire. Erect stem, flowers in one-sided raceme, short-stalked, drooping, very fragrant, white or occasionally pinkish. Perianth broadly bell-shaped, consists of six short tepals. Fruits are sub-globose red berries. Flowers in May and June. Grows in open deciduous woods and among bushes, from lowlands to mountains.

2 Herb Paris *Paris quadrifolia*. Perennial herb up to 30 cm high, with creeping rhizomes and erect stems. Obovate-lanceolate leaves in one whorl of four. Flowers stalked, solitary, the perianth in whorls of four. Outer tepals lanceolate, green; inner ones narrowly linear, yellow-green. Eight stamens with anther connective awl-like. Fruits black globose berries. Flowers from May

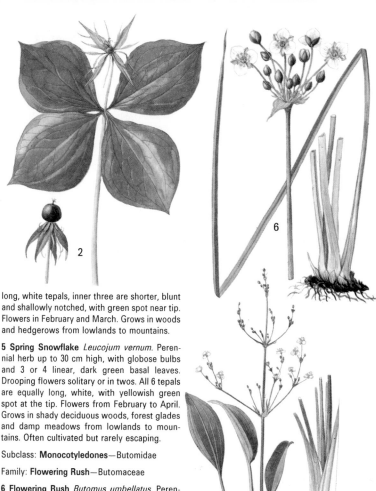

long, white tepals, inner three are shorter, blunt and shallowly notched, with green spot near tip. Flowers in February and March. Grows in woods and hedgerows from lowlands to mountains.

5 Spring Snowflake *Leucojum vernum*. Perennial herb up to 30 cm high, with globose bulbs and 3 or 4 linear, dark green basal leaves. Drooping flowers solitary or in twos. All 6 tepals are equally long, white, with yellowish green spot at the tip. Flowers from February to April. Grows in shady deciduous woods, forest glades and damp meadows from lowlands to mountains. Often cultivated but rarely escaping.

Subclass: **Monocotyledones**—Butomidae

Family: **Flowering Rush**—Butomaceae

6 Flowering Rush *Butomus umbellatus*. Perennial herb up to 150 cm high, with creeping rhizomes and erect flowering stems. Basal tufts of leaves are sheathed, triangular at base, expanding to a linear blade. Pink flowers in many-flowered terminal umbels. Six obovate tepals, 3 smaller than the rest, and 6—9 stamens. Fruits a cluster of small ovoid follicles. Flowers from June to August. Grows in ditches and on margins of water bodies, from lowlands to foothills.

Family: **Water-plantain**—Alismataceae

7 Common Water-plantain *Alisma plantago-aquatica*. Perennial herb up to 1 metre high, with short, thickened rhizome and erect stems. Submerged leaves (when present) linear, those above the water are long-petiolate, prominently ribbed, broadly ovate, pointed. Flowers in well-branched, whorled panicle; both sepals and petals in threes; petals obovate, pale white, lilac or rarely pink. Fruit a doughnut-shaped schizo-carp. Flowers from June to September. Grows in shallow water and on banks of ponds, lakes, canals, slow flowing rivers, and in ditches, from lowlands to foothills. Related Arrowhead (*Sagittaria sagittifolia*) has arrowhead-shaped leaves, larger, fewer, white flowers and petals with black-violet spot at base.

Family: **Pondweed**—Potamogetonaceae

1 Broad-leaved Pondweed *Potamogeton natans*. Perennial submerged aquatic herb with stem up to 1 m long or more in deep water. Floating leaves long-petiolate, elliptic, pointed, cordate. Submerged leaves linear. Tiny, greenish flowers, without petals, in erect, cylindrical spikes, emerging above water surface. Flowers from June to August. Grows in lakes, ponds, rivers and ditches, from lowlands to foothills.

Family: **Arum**—Araceae

2 Sweet Flag *Acorus calamus*. Perennial iris-like herb up to 1 metre high, with thick, fragrant rhizomes. Sword-shaped leaves arranged in two ranks. Triangular stems with a bract similar to leaf continuing in stem direction. Minute flowers in apparently lateral spadix, with 6-lobed, green-yellow perianth. Fruits do not mature in northern Europe. Flowers from June to August. Grows near and in water, from lowlands to foothills. Native of southern Asia and northwestern U.S.A., introduced about 400 years ago and naturalized in Europe.

3 Bog Arum *Calla palustris*. Perennial aquatic herb, up to 30 cm, with hollow, green rhizome. Leaves broadly ovate-cordate. Axillary stems bear short, cylindrical, short-stalked spadix. Minute yellow-green flowers without a perianth. Fruits are red berries. Flowers from May to August. Grows in pools, bends of rivers and peat-bogs from lowlands to foothills, rarely at higher altitudes, in central and northern Europe. Naturalized only in Britain.

4 Lords-and-Ladies or **Cuckoo-pint** *Arum maculatum*. Perennial plant, almost 50 cm high, with short tuberous rhizome and erect stem. Leaves long-petiolate, triangular ovate to arrow-shaped. Spathe cyathiform, whitish or greenish, rarely red-tinted inside, with violet blotches. On spadix, lowest are female flowers, above them male ones; above these ring of sterile, bulb-like thickened 'flowers' modified into thick bristles; spadix tip violet-brown or yellowish. Fruits are red, poisonous berries. Flowers in April and May. Grows in open deciduous woods, in hedgerows and on hedgebanks, from lowlands to foothills.

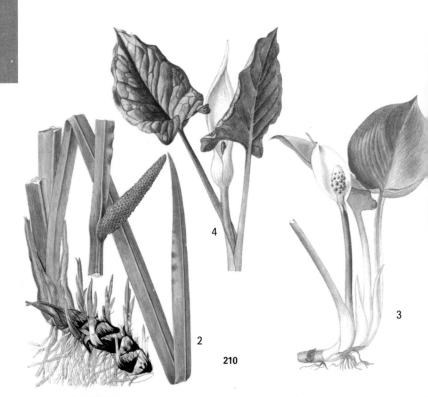

4

3

2

Family: **Bur-reed**—Sparganiaceae

5 Branched Bur-reed *Sparganium erectum* (syn. *S. ramosum*). Perennial aquatic herb up to 50 cm high with thick, spreading rhizomes. Stiff, erect leaves, triangular in section. Erect robust stems, with terminal stiff panicle. Flowers in globose heads, unisexual, bottom ones female, upper ones male; perianth much reduced, 3-lobed. Fruit ellipsoidal, shouldered yellow-brown nut. Flowers from June to August. Grows in shallow water and on mud or wet soil from lowlands to foothills.

Family: **Reedmace**—Typhaceae

6 Lesser Reedmace *Typha angustifolia*. Perennial herb up to 3 metres high, with extensively creeping rhizome and rigid erect, round stems. Erect, linear leaves not more than 1 cm wide. Inflorescence composed of two separate cylindrical spadices, one above the other; bottom one has female flowers, upper one male florets. Bottom spadix is narrow, red-brown. Unisexual flowers without any perianth. Fruits stalked with long pappus-like hairs. Flowers in June-July. Grows in water and wet soil, from lowlands to foothills. Related Great Reedmace (*T. latifolia*) has leaves up to 2 cm wide and spadices united one above other, bottom one dark brown and thick. This is much more common in Britain than *T. angustifolia*.

Family: Lemnaceae

7 Ivy Duckweed *Lemna trisulca* (a). Tiny perennial, aquatic herb, floating just beneath water surface. Leaf-like thalli ovate lanceolate, petiolate, branching from the middle. Flowering plants rare, smaller and floating. Grows in stagnant waters at lower altitudes. **Common Duckweed** *(L. minor)* (b) has floating thalli round to broadly ovate, usually growing gregariously. **Great Duckweed** (*L. polyrhiza*) (c) has roundly ovate thalli with reddish underside, each with bundle of rootlets.

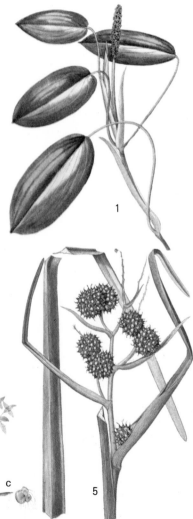

1

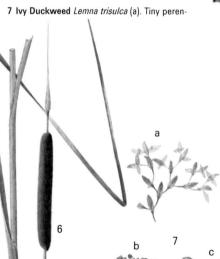

a

b

6

7

c

5

211

Trees and Shrubs

Woody plants are plants with stems that are, or become, woody and thicken secondarily. They may be deciduous or evergreen and include trees and shrubs as well as sub-shrubs ranging from huge forest giants to such tiny shrubs as the whortleberry and cranberry.

Trees are long-lived plants. Often we can only estimate the age of large oaks or lime trees. On the cross-section of the trunk of a felled tree one can count the annual rings, each produced by a single year's growth. This is quite laborious and, of course, it cannot be done in the case of

Fig. 1. A twig of Scots Pine (*Pinus sylvestris*) with male (*left*) and female (*right*) cones. *Below*. a ripe cone with fallen seeds.

Fig. 2. Male flowers of the Beech (*Fagus sylvatica*).

living trees. The true age of a living tree is scientifically determined in a quite different way. A bore is drilled in the trunk of the tree and a sample of the wood removed; once healed, the minute scars on the bark are practically unnoticeable.

In central Europe the only truly old trees are yews (*Taxus*), some believed to be over two thousand years old. Yews have a very slow rate of growth, their trunks increasing by only 0.5—1 mm in diameter each year. Larches rarely reach the age of 600 years, and as for oaks, 500 years is a record. Even the fantastically twisted, hollow trunks of the olive trees (*Olea*) that are cultivated in the Mediterranean region, are no more than a hundred years old.

On the other hand, North America has trees that were alive at the time of the growth of the civilizations of the ancient Egyptians and Sumerians. Still growing today in the White Mountains of California are specimens of the ancient Bristlecone Pine (*Pinus aristata*), less than 10 m high, their trunks' remnants deformed by gales and winds, yet with living green branches. With the aid of radiocarbon dating, probes have revealed that the famed Giant Sequoias (*Sequoiadendron giganteum*), hitherto believed to be the oldest living organisms (about 3,200 years old), are much younger than the Bristlecone Pine. The wood of the dead trunks of these pines remains undecayed, making it possible to date these remnants, and it has been determined that they are between 6,200 and 7,100 years old!

Fig. 3. An inflorescence of Small-leaved Lime (*Tilia cordata*).

213

Although the giant sequoias rank second in terms of age, they rank first in another respect, in that they are the largest and most massive of all existing plants. One Giant Sequoia, called 'Father of the Forest', was the tallest tree ever measured. It reached a height of 135 m and the trunk measured 12 m in diameter at ground level. The present-day record is held by 'General Sherman' in the Sequoia National Park. This tree is 83 m tall, measures 11 m in diameter at ground level and is more than 8 m in diameter 3 m above ground level; in other words this tree represents 1,400 cu m of wood. Currently, the tallest plant in the world is one American Coastal Redwood (*Sequoia sempervirens*), which reaches a height of 112 m. It grows in California's Redwoods State Park.

Competitors in height with these giant trees were the eucalypts (*Eucalyptus*). Earlier records gave their greatest height as being more than 150 m, but experts on Australian flora consider this improbable. According to present-day measurements eucalypts reach a maximum height of less than 100 m. However, they do have an extraordinarily rapid rate of growth, making as much as 3 m in height per year. Their wood is very dense, firm and highly prized.

The most primitive existing angiosperms are ever-green woody plants growing on the islands of Fiji in the Pacific. There, in 1934, the American A. C. Smith discovered a 14-m-high tree with unusual fruits. Its leaves are also unusual in the Pacific region. Not until 1941 did Otto Degener bring to the USA sufficient material, including flowers, according to which Smith and Bailey described a new family and new genus, consisting of a single species which they named *Degeneria vitiensis*. The discovery of this woody plant greatly contributed to a realistic idea of the general character of the very first angiosperms.

The most primitive flowering plants also include the members of the Winteraceae family, comprising six genera and approximately 60 species, found in the South Pacific region, and other families of the order Magnoliales. Certain species of the magnolia family (Magnoliaceae) are also grown in Europe's parks and gardens. Magnolias (*Magnolia*) have large, striking, fragrant flowers that often open before the leaves. Also grown in parks is the North American Tulip Tree (*Liriodendron tulipifera*) with its large, orange-spotted flowers. These woody plants also possess certain primitive features and are also related to the very first flowering plants.

Fig. 4. A fruit-bearing twig of Common Ash (*Fraxinus excelsion*).

The cranberry and whortleberry have already been mentioned as examples of the smallest woody plants. Also related to them are the heathers (*Calluna*) and heaths (*Erica*). The Tree Heath (*Erica arborea*), however, is a true shrub, 3—5 m high, which, in the Mediterranean region, is a woody component of the evergreen maquis. Below ground it has globose or tuberous roots of extremely hard reddish-brown wood which, because of its resistance to heat and fire, is used in the manufacture of tobacco pipes and briars.

The commonest trees and shrubs are discussed in greater detail on the following pages. They hold no records of size or age, but that does not make them any the less interesting.

Fig. 5. Branches of Broom (*Sarothamnus scoparius*) showing the typical flowers of papilionaceous plants.

Fig. 6. The hip, the aggregate fruit of the Dog Rose (*Rosa canina*), has long-haired fruits (achenes) enclosed in a fleshy receptacle.

Family: Pinaceae

2 Silver Fir *Abies alba.* Tall, stout tree up to 45 m or more, with pyramidal to cylindrical crown. Young shoots with fine, grey-brown tomentum, gradually changing into whitish, grey-green, smooth or scaly bark. Blunt, flat needles, with two white stripes beneath arranged in two rows, adhere to twig by disc-like bases. After they fall the twig remains almost smooth. Fir is monoecious, flowers from May to June. Male flowers have orange yellow anthers. Female flowers are borne on upper side of preceding year's stronger twigs and develop into erect cones, disintegrating at maturity. Grows in mountain or foothill woods and forms important component of beech-fir forests. Often planted. In parks cultivated in various forms, together with related species from North America, Asia and southern Spain.

Sub-division: **Gymnosperms**—Gymnospermae

Class: **Coniferous plants**—Coniferopsida

Family: Taxaceae

1 Yew *Taxus baccata.* Broad-headed tree up to 20 m, either in the open or as an understorey tree, mainly on chalk or limestone. Abundantly planted in many cultivated forms, often in parks. Grows slowly; therefore annual rings are very dense and even old trees are rarely very big. Only coniferous tree with resin canals. Wood and needles contain poisonous alkaloid toxin. Dioecious tree, flowers in March and April. Male cones grow in axils of needles and have shield-shaped stamens. Female cones have one ovule ripening into seed, enveloped in fleshy red cupule; only this is not poisonous.

3 Norway Spruce *Picea abies* (syn. *P. excelsa*). Tall tree up to 60 m or more, with shallow roots and slender pyramidal crown; young bark light brown, older greyish or maroon, scaly, changing into cracked bark. Branches in regular whorls, with pointed needles; when these fall they leave peg-like protuberances on twigs. Spruce is dioecious; flowers in April and May. Male flowers grow on preceding year's twigs; at first they are red, later yellowish and ovoid. Pendent female flowers at end of branches in upper part of crown are reddish before pollination. Mature cones also are pendulous and do not disintegrate. Originally native of mountain and foothill forests but generally planted also at lower altitudes; in many cultivated forms commonly planted in parks together with some North-American species. This is the popular Christmas tree of central Europe and Britain.

4 European Larch *Larix decidua*. A deep-rooting tree up to 45 m tall with spreading branches that droop at the tips in mature specimens. Grey-brown bark later becomes thick and irregularly scaly. The soft light green needles in clusters on shortened lateral shoots are of annual duration. Flowers from April to June; male flowers globose, sulphur-yellow, female ones red, ripening in autumn to small ovoid-globose cones. Larch is a mountain conifer, and needs high light intensity. For its valuable timber it is abundantly cultivated even at lower altitudes, especially on margins of coniferous woods and in parks. The evergreen Douglas Fir (*Pseudotsuga menziesii*) is also planted in woods. The pendent cones have trifid scales which project like three-pointed tongues; needles with two white stripes give out pleasant smell when crushed. Also cultivated in parks; native of western North America.

Family: Pinaceae

1 Scots Pine *Pinus sylvestris*. A tree up to 40 m, with a globose to flattened crown. Bark of young twigs green, later turning rusty; old trunks have a fissured, reddish-brown or grey-brown bark. Needles arranged in pairs on short shoots. Flowers from May to June; male flowers sulphur-yellow, female ones arranged individually or in twos or threes at ends of branches, reddish, ripen in two years. Originally grown in lowlands and hills, on sandy soils, rocks and heather moors. Commonly planted in poor, sandy soils. The Weymouth Pine (*P. strobus*) with grey-green, long needles in clusters of five, is often cultivated in parks; it is native to North America.

2 Austrian Pine *Pinus nigra*. A variable species ranging in height from 25—45 m, sometimes more. Bark rough, greyish to dark brown. Needles longer than in Scots Pine, 8—15 cm long, dark green, stiff and sharply pointed. Flowers in June and July. Male flowers cylindrical, yellowish, stamens with pink connective. Female flowers red to light violet during flowering, pruinous, ripen as late as third year into large, glossy, yellow-brown cones with seed-scales of dark brown beneath. Grows from limestone foothills of eastern Alps up to Mediterranean region. Often planted in dry forests of central Europe. Also cultivated for ornamental purposes in parks.

3 Mountain Pine *Pinus mugo.* A broad, bushy
shrub with irregularly branched trunk, or small
tree with erect trunk and pyramidal crown.
Mountain pine grows either as knee-pine in central-European mountains above tree line or as
bog-pine on peat soils and in hilly country.
Needles arranged in pairs, slightly twisted, rich
green, under lens distinctly toothed. Male
flowers yellow, with conspicuously large stamen connective. Female flowers on ends of
shoots, red to light violet. Knee-pine flowers
from June, bog-pine as early as May. Cones rip-
en third year, are conically ovoid to globose. Of
compact conical habit is the Arolla Pine (*P.
cembra*), reaching 20—25 m in height. Needles
usually in fives and cones containing large edible seeds; a native of Alps and Carpathians.

Family: Cupressaceae

4 Juniper *Juniperus communis.* A very variable
species, ranging in size from a prostrate shrub
to a small tree with conical crown up to 10 m or
more tall. Needles stiff, prickly pointed, grey-
green, in trimerous whorls; white stripe on upper side. Dioecious flowers; male flowers axillary, ovate, yellowish; female ones individual,
greenish. Flowers in April and May. Fruit matures into short-stalked, berry-like cone formed
by three fleshy, fused seed scales; at first
green, second year blue-black with a whitish
'bloom'. Forms undergrowth of coniferous forests, especially pine-woods, also occurs on
slopes and in pastures. Protected in many countries. Savin (*J. sabina*) with scaly, sessile
needles, and several American and Asian species, is also often cultivated.

Flowering Trees and Shrubs

Class: **Angiospermous Plants**—Magnoliopsida

Subclass: **Dicotyledones**—Magnoliidae

Family: **Barberry**—Berberidaceae

1 Common Barberry *Berberis vulgaris*. Shrub up to 2.5 m, with smooth bark and alternate leaves. Clusters of obovate sharply serrated leaves with short petioles arise in axils of branched spines (modified leaves). Yellow fragrant flowers in pendent racemes. Stamens sensitive to touch. Flowers during May and June. Fruit a red berry. Grows on sunny slopes and open groves from lowlands to foothills; most commonly seen in hedgerows in Britain. Also cultivated in various garden forms.

Family: Loranthaceae

2 Mistletoe *Viscum laxum*. Semi-parasitic evergreen shrub, of spreading habit up to 1 m in diameter in crowns of coniferous trees, especially pines. Branches by repeated forking; twigs brittle. Leaves opposite, yellow-green, longish obovate, entire, leathery texture. Tiny unisexual flowers are borne in small clusters in forks of branches. Fruits yellowish-white, globose berries. Flowers from March to April; berries mature as late as December. Stouter White Mistletoe (Common Mistletoe in G.B.) (*V. album*) with larger white berries, grows on a wide range of deciduous trees.

Family: **Elm**—Ulmaceae

3 European White Elm *Ulmus laevis* (syn. *U. effusa*). Robust tree with wide crown up to 35 m. Leaves with short petioles, sharply serrate, smooth above, usually hairy beneath. Flowers arranged in clusters on long stalks; anthers reddish. Achenes have wide cilious border, notched at tip. Flowers in March and April. Grows in meadows and moist forests; often also planted. Related Wych Elm (*U. glabra*) grows in woods, from hilly country to foothills, while *Ulmus carpinifolia* (syn. *U. campestris*) grows in river valleys; both species have flowers in sessile clusters.

Family: **Rose**—Rosaceae

4 Wild Raspberry *Rubus idaeus.* Branches somewhat thorny in lower parts, otherwise hairy to smooth. Leaves odd-pinnate, sharply toothed, underside white; terminal leaflet largest, sometimes rounded. Flowers white, arranged in pendent cymes. Fruits a cluster of red druplets — raspberries; easily separate from the plug-like receptacle when ripe. Flowers in June and July, sometimes later. Grows abundantly on heaths and hills, scrub and open woods. Often cultivated in gardens for its fruit.

5 Bramble *Rubus fruticosus.* A very variable species according to some authorities, split up into hundreds of microspecies. Native to woods, scrub, heaths, open hillsides and hedgerows. Most important common features: thorny branched stems and compound, mostly palmate leaves with 3—5 leaflets. Flowers white or pink. Globose druplets ripen to purple-black, pruinose blackberries. The related, smaller, thin-stemmed *Rubus caesius*, growing along roads, field margins, paths, has mainly trifoliate leaves and fruits with a waxy white 'bloom'.

6 Dog Rose *Rosa canina.* A variable spreading shrub up to 3 m tall; best known and most abundant of all wild central-European roses, characterized by arching, spiny branches. Leaves pinnate, with 5 to 7 ovate to elliptical, sharply serrate, smooth leaflets. Flowers solitary or in small clusters at end of branchlet. Sepals glandular on margins, outer ones usually cleft. Corollas white, flushed pink. Fruit an ovoid hip. Flowers from May to July. Grows in thickets on slopes, in hedgerows and forest margins from lowlands to foothills. The similar *Rosa dumetorum* has hairy leaflets and petioles.

1

2

Family: **Rose**—Rosaceae

1 Alpine Rose *Rosa pendulina* (syn. *Rosa alpina*). Widely expanded shrub up to 2 m tall, with pendent branches, sparsely covered with fine spines; upper branches are usually spineless. Leaves pinnate, with 7 to 11 elliptic, sharply serrate leaflets, dark green above, somewhat hairy underside. Flowers solitary, rarely in small clusters, on long stalks. Flowers purple-red; hips bottle-shaped, pendent, red. Flowers from May to July. Grows in hill and mountain forests and on bushy slopes.

2 Blackthorn or **Sloe** *Prunus spinosa*. Densely branched thorny shrub or small tree up to 4 m. Leaves elliptic, smooth, obovate with glandular margins. White flowers in small clusters often in profusion, before the leaves. Fruits are globose drupes, dark purple when ripe, usually with a waxy white 'bloom'. Flowers in March and April. Grows abundantly on sunny slopes, in hedgerows, at the edge of forests and in clearings from lowlands to foothills.

3 Gean or **Wild Cherry** *Prunus avium*. Tree up to 20 m or more tall, with widely expanded crown and smooth, grey branches. Entire, ovate leaves have two small, reddish, globose glands at base; blades serrate, smooth above, hairy beneath. Flowers white, opening from April to May. Fruit a globose drupe, yellow or red, sweet, with agreeable but slightly bitter taste. Found in woods, thickets and hedgerows, often on limestone or chalk soils. The cultivated sweet cherry is derived from this species.

4 Bird Cherry *Prunus padus*. Large shrub or tree up to 15 m with glossy brown branches. The leaves are obovate, abruptly pointed, finely serrate with two spherical glands on petiole. Flowers white, in pendent racemes; drupes small, black, astringent. Flowers and leaves give out pleasant bitter-almond smell. Flowers open in April and May. Grows in woods, scrub, and in hedgerows at lower altitudes. Sometimes forms of this tree are planted in parks and gardens.

5 *Cotoneaster integerrimus*. A low, spreading shrub with reddish branchlets. Leaves small, with short petioles, entire, rounded, smooth above, hairy beneath. Flowers in small clusters, somewhat pendent. Calyx maroon, persistent; corollas white or pink flushed, stamens red; fruits subglobose, red. Flowers in April and May. Grows on sunny, bushy, stony or rocky slopes, in open woods and steppes, from lowlands to foothills. Many Asiatic species are cultivated as ornamental shrubs, e.g. *Cotoneaster horizontalis*, *C. microphyllus*, and the tree-sized *C. frigidus*.

222

6 Midland Hawthorn *Crataegus laevigata* (syn. *C. oxyacanthoides*). Shrub or small tree up to 10 m, with red-brown, spiny branches. Leaves shallowly lobed and serrate. Flowers arranged in flattened clusters, stalks white or sometimes rosy. Globose to ovoid, red fruits (haws) have two stones each. Flowers in May and June. Grows wild in woods, on bushy slopes and in hedgerows. Several red, pink and double-flowered forms are cultivated in parks and gardens.

223

Family: **Rose**—*Rosaceae*

1 Wild Pear *Pyrus communis.* Broadly pyramidal tree, sometimes with spiny branches up to 15 m tall. Leaves with long petioles are ovate, pointed, finely serrate, glossy. Flowers, arranged in rounded corymbs, have long stalks. Corollas white or rarely pink-flushed. Fruits pear-shaped or globose, mature seeds black. Flowers in April and May. Grows wild in deciduous forests, on thickets and hedgerows at low altitudes. An allied species, *P. cordata*, is more bushy and spiny with smaller fruits. All the cultivated varieties of pears are derived from *P. communis*, which some authorities claim to be of multiple hybrid origin.

2 Crab Apple *Malus sylvestris.* Small tree up to 10 m tall. Young branches woolly, hairy, later more or less smooth. Leaves ovate, serrate, finely toothed. Petioles half of blade length. Flowers in small corymbs, pink in bud opening white; anthers yellow, lower half of styles fused together. Fruits almost globose, mature seeds brown. Flowers in May. Grows wild in hedgerows and woods. Cultivated apple-trees (*M.* × *domestica*) have no spiny branches; leaves are densely hairy on under surface, upper surface scattered with hairs; considered to be of ancient hybrid origin.

3 Mountain Ash or **Rowan** *Sorbus aucuparia.* A spreading tree up to 15 m or more tall, with felted winter buds. Leaves odd-pinnate, leaflets sessile, elongated, lanceolate, sharply serrate, hairy on underside. Flowers creamy white, arranged in wide, flattened, branched corymbs. Fruits red, berry-like, globose, slightly larger than pea. Rowan grows wild in open woods and on grassy and rocky slopes from lowlands to mountains; often planted in avenues.

4 Common Whitebeam *Sorbus aria.* A large shrub or small tree up to 15 m or more tall, with glossy, red-brown branches. Leaves irregularly serrate to shallowly lobed, under surface white, petals woolly at base. Fruits orange to reddish with yellow pulp. Flowers in May and June. Grows on sunny slopes and in open woodland from lowlands to mountains. Related Wild Service Tree (*S. torminalis*) has sharply pinnately cut leaves almost hairless beneath and fruits, yellow-brown, spotted with darker lenticels.

Family: Fabaceae (syn. Papilionaceae)

5 Broom *Sarothamnus scoparius* (syn. *Cytisus scoparius*). Shrub with angular green branches up to 2 m or more tall. Alternate leaves with short petioles composed of 3 lanceolate to obovate leaflets, silky hairy beneath. Flowers solitary or in small clusters, bright yellow. Style spirally twisted, protruding from keel, pods black, explosive when ripe. Flowers in May. Grows, often gregariously, at forest margins, sandy and stony slopes at lower altitudes, excluding limestone soils.

6 German Greenweed *Genista germanica.* Small shrub up to 40 cm or more, with ascending or erect, hairy, thorny branches. Leaves are ovate-lanceolate, pointed, and hairy. Flowers yellow, in leafy racemes at tips of shoots. Pods black-brown, hairy, exploding when ripe. Flowers from May to July. Grows in dry woods, especially pine-woods and in open sites on sandy soils from lowlands to foothills. Related Dyer's Greenweed (*G. tinctoria*) has thornless stems and hairless pods.

Family: Fabaceae

1 *Cytisus nigricans*. Deciduous shrub up to 2 m tall, with erect, green, hairy branches. Petiolate leaves of three pointed, obovate, dark green leaflets, paler beneath. Yellow flowers in bract-less racemes turn black when dried. Pods brown-black, smooth. Flowers from May to August. Grows on sunny slopes, among rocks and in dry woods from lowlands to foothills. Related Common Laburnum (*Laburnum anagyroides*), a tree up to 7 m tall with pendent racemes of large, yellow flowers, is often cultivated.

2 Spiny Rest-harrow *Ononis spinosa*. Sub-shrub up to 40 cm or more, with ascending or erect branches, mostly spiny, with one or two rows of hairs. Leaves of three leaflets, each narrowly obovate and serrate. Flowers pink, calyx bilabiate, hairy. One-seeded pods of the same length as or longer than calyx, softly hairy. Flowers from June to September. Grows in rough grassy places, field boundaries and on sunny slopes in lower altitudes of temperate regions. Related Common Rest-harrow (*O. repens*) is thornless, creeping or decumbent sub-shrub with underground rhizomes.

3 False Acacia *Robinia pseudoacacia*. Tree up to 27 m tall with deeply fissured bark. Leaves petiolate, odd-pinnate, stipules transformed into strong, curved thorns. Leaflets petiolate, oval to elliptic, entire. Flowers white, occasionally flushed pink, fragrant, in pendent racemes. Pods strongly flattened, hairless. Flowers in May and June. Native of North America, since 18th century planted in avenues together with other North-American species with pink or violet-rose flowers.

Family: Platanaceae

4 *Platanus hispanica* (syn. *P. × acerifolia*). Abundantly cultivated hybrid of eastern and western plane-trees, planted only rarely in parks. Robust tree up to 40 m with striking scaly fawn and grey bark peeling in flakes. Illustrated species differs from its parent species by hair-less underside of leaves; central lobes usually longer than their base width; globose inflorescences arranged mostly in strings of one to four. Oriental Plane (*P. orientalis*), native of eastern Mediterranean, has narrower lobes and inflorescences arranged in strings of up to six. Buttonwood or 'Sycamore' (*P. occidentalis*), native of North America, has leaves hairy on underside, central lobes wider and inflorescences in ones and twos. Plane-trees flower in May.

Family: **Hazel**—Corylaceae

5 Hornbeam *Carpinus betulus*. Tree up to 30 m
tall, with grey, smooth bark and glossy, brown
branches. Leaves narrowly oblong, doubly
sharply serrate. Male and female catkins cylindrical, female ones erect, with flowers in axils of
trilobed bracts; male pendulous. Ovary, with
two red stigmata, develops into a nut, attached
to the trilobed bract which enlarges and acts as
a wing for wind dispersal. Flowers from April to
May. Grows in woods and hedgerows at lower
altitudes, also planted for coppicing, hedging
and as a specimen tree.

6 Hazel *Corylus avellana*. Tall, well-branched
shrub up to 6 m. Leaves petiolate, glandular, obovate to rounded, doubly serrate, with short
hairs. Male inflorescences are catkins up to
5 cm long, female ones bud-like with two filamentous, red stigmata. Fruit is small nut enveloped in enlarged bracts, with white seed and
cinnamon-brown seed coat. Flowers from January to April. Grows fairly abundantly in open
woods and on sunny slopes from lowlands to
mountains. Once much planted for coppicing.
The cob nut of commerce is a form of this species.

4

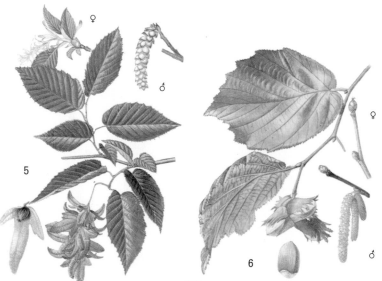

5

6

Family: **Walnut**—Juglandaceae

1 Common Walnut *Juglans regia*. Robust tree up to 30 m tall, with grey bark; branchlets at first green-brown, later ash-grey. Leaves odd-pinnate, with usually 5 to 7 pairs of obovate or elliptic, entire, smooth leaflets. Male catkins pendulous on previous year's twigs, female flowers at tips of new twigs with two lobed stigmata. Fruit globose to ovoid drupe with tough, somewhat fleshy exocarp and stony endocarp; seed coat membranous, lobed seed white.

Flowers in April and May. Native of south-eastern Europe and Asia Minor. Often cultivated for its edible nuts.

Family: **Birch**—Betulaceae

2 Silver Birch *Betula pendula* (syn. *B. verrucosa*). Slender elegant tree up to 25 m tall with straight trunk and white bark, transversely peeling in paper-thin bands; bark deeply fissured at base. Leaves usually rhomboid to triangular, ovate, with pointed tip, smooth, doubly serrate except base. Male as well as female catkins pendent, anthers yellow, stigmata purple. Seeds (nutlets) winged, wings wider than nutlet. Flowers in April and May. Grows abundantly in forests, on slopes and heathland, often planted. Related birch, *Betula pubescens*, has less pendent branches and leaves and twigs hairy when young.

3 Alder *Alnus glutinosa*. Tree up to 20 m or more tall, with slender, dark grey trunk with fissured bark; young branchlets glandular. Leaves broadly obovate, with notched point, doubly toothed, smooth, rich green; young ones sticky. Male catkins with red scales, female ones long-stalked, ovate, maturing to brown, cone-like fruits. Wingless achenes. Flowers in March and April. Grows in moist meadows and near water. Related Grey Alder (*A. incana*) has pointed leaves, grey-green on underside, downy; bark light grey and smooth.

Family: **Beech**—Fagaceae

4 Beech *Fagus sylvatica.* Robust tree up to 30 m or more, with slender trunk and smooth, pale grey bark. Buds long, slender, pointed, with red-brown ciliate scales. Leaves petiolate, almost entire, broadly ovate, pointed, with ciliate margins. Male flowers in long-stalked, pendent clusters; perianth red-brown. Female flowers in pairs are at ends of new twigs, enclosed in green cup. These mature red-brown and open by four valves. Fruits are triangular nuts or beech-mast. Flowers in April and May. Grows fairly abundantly from lowlands to highlands. Several forms are known, including red, purple and copper-leaved and the fern-leaved beech with deeply cut leaves.

5 Sweet Chestnut *Castanea sativa.* Tree up to 30 m or more, dark grey-brown bark often with spiral fissures. Leaves short-petiolate, oblong, lanceolate, stiff, sharply serrate. Flowers in erect spike-like clusters; female ones at the bottom, individual or in threes, enclosed in globose, prickly barbed cupule; male florets whitish, forming bulk of spike. Fruit — chestnuts — dark brown, glossy, leathery skin, with single seed. Flowers in July. Native of southern Europe; often planted for edible seeds and in parks for ornament. Naturalized in some territories, e.g. Carpathians and southern Britain where it was once extensively coppiced for fencing.

Family: **Poplar and Willow**—Salicaceae

6 White Poplar *Populus alba.* Rapidly growing suckering tree up to 25 m, with pale grey bark. Leaves ovate, orbicular, notched to deeply 5-lobed, undersides felted with white hairs. Male catkins long and thick, female ones shorter; flowers with two red styles and yellow stigmata. Long-haired seeds. Flowers in March and April. Grows in forests and near rivers; also much planted. Related Black Poplar (*P. nigra*) is often planted in avenues, mainly the Italian form with columnar crown.

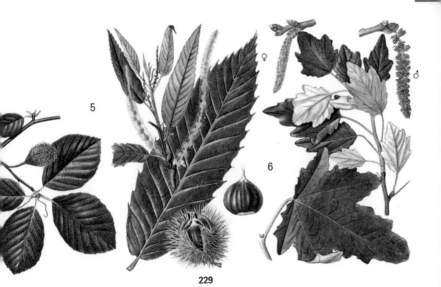

Family: **Poplar and Willow**—Salicaceae

1 Aspen *Populus tremula.* A suckering tree up to 20 m tall, with bark at first smooth, yellow-grey, later black-grey and fissured. Young twigs smooth or shortly hairy, buds sticky. Leaves almost round to rhomboid, shallowly notched. Long catkins with bracts palmately cut, anthers before releasing pollen red; purple stigmata in twos. Downy seeds. Flowers in March and April. Grows in open, moist places in woods, clearings, hedgerows, from lowlands to mountains.

2 Goat Willow *Salix caprea.* Large shrub or small tree up to 10 m tall. Leaves petiolate, ovate-oblong to obovate, pointed, narrowed or rounded at petiole, entire or irregularly toothed, upper side more or less hairy, under side felted with persistent grey hairs. Dioecious catkins appear before the leaves; male ones erect, thick, long silvery-haired, flowers with yellow anthers; female catkins similar, but are less hairy and remain grey-green, elongate when ripe and shed tiny seeds in cotton wool-like hair. Flowers from March to May. Grows abundantly at edges of forests, in clearings, on slopes, along brooks and in hedgerows from lowlands to mountains.

3 *Salix purpurea.* Shrub or small tree up to 3 m tall with thin, flexible and tough branches. Leaves shortly petiolate, obovate-oblong to linear oblanceolate, pointed, finely serrate, entire at petiole; somewhat blue-green above, glaucous beneath. Male catkins have stamens fused to filaments; red anthers, after pollination turning black; female catkins shortly conical. Flowers in March and April. Distinctive by having leaves and buds in sub-opposite pairs. Grows along streams and rivers and in wet meadows from lowlands to foothills. Also cultivated together with Osier (*S. viminalis*).

Family: **Beech and Oak**—Fagaceae

4 Common Oak *Quercus robur* (syn. *Q. pedunculata*). Robust tree up to 30 m or more tall with widely expanded, irregular crown; old branches strong, tortuous, old trunk has brownish-grey, deeply fissured bark. Buds ovoid, brown. Leaves shortly petiolate, pinnately lobed, blades cordate at petiole, hairy when young, soon becoming smooth, leathery, usually with five pairs of lobes. Male flowers in pendent catkins, female ones sessile, globular, in cupule; stigmata red. Acorns in twos to fives on long stalks. Flowers in April and May. Forms main component of oak-woods from lowlands to foothills. At one time commonly planted.

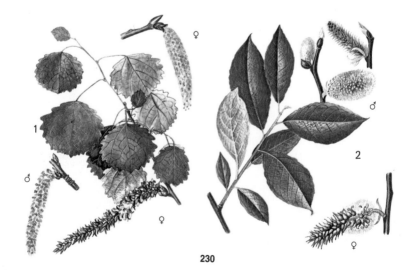

5 Durmast Oak *Quercus petraea* (syn. *Q. sessiliflora*). Differs from preceding species by ovoid crown, long-petiolate leaves, wedge-shaped blades at petiole and sessile acorns. Both species often hybridize and many trees are difficult to identify. In places the hybrid is more abundant than parent species. North-American *Quercus borealis* with red autumn leaves and *Quercus coccinea* with scarlet leaves are cultivated in parks; both have leaves larger than the native species and with bold, sharply pointed lobes.

6 Hairy Oak *Quercus pubescens*. Usually shrub with often distorted trunk and cracked bark. Young twigs and buds white-haired. Leaves obovate, pinnately lobed, blades wedge-shaped or cordate at petiole, lobes rounded or pointed, felted with grey hairs on both sides when young. In maturity upper surface almost smooth. Acorns long ovoid, pointed, in felted cupule. Flowers in April and May. Grows mainly on limestone soils, on sunny slopes in lower altitudes of warm regions.

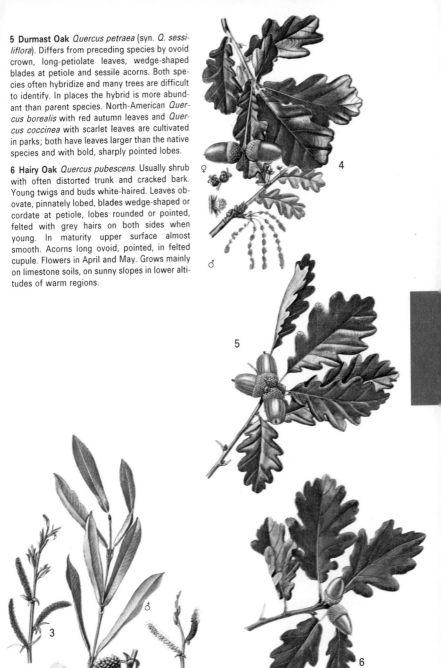

Family: Simaroubaceae

1 Tree of Heaven *Ailanthus peregrina* (syn. *A. altissima*). Robust tree up to 35 m or more; young branches reddish, hairy. Leaves up to 1 m long, odd-pinnate, reddish when young. Leaflets lanceolate with one to three glandular teeth at base. Tiny flowers yellow-green, arranged in large panicles; fruit winged, sometimes bright red. Flowers in June and July. Native of eastern Asia; cultivated as ornamental tree and often planted. Sometimes becomes naturalized.

Family: **Milkwort**—Polygalaceae

2 Box-leaved Milkwort *Polygala chamaebuxus* (syn. *Chamaebuxus alpestris*). Small sub-shrub, rarely above 20 cm. Stems decumbent, ascending, often rooting. Leaves almost sessile, persistent, evergreen, leathery, smooth, entire, oval, with a small point. Flowers arranged singly or in small groups in leaf axils; winged sepals white, sometimes buff-yellow or carmine. Petals yellow, reddening at tips after fertilization. Fruit a capsule. Flowers from March to September. Grows among rocks and in open forests, mainly pine-woods, on mountain slopes.

Family: Celastraceae

3 Spindle Tree *Euonymus europaea*. A shrub up to 3 m or more; young branches green, somewhat four-winged, smooth. Leaves petiolate, lanceolate to ovate, pointed, smooth. Flowers in axillary clusters; petals greenish. Square pink capsule with orange seeds. Flowers in May and June. Grows at outskirts of forests, on slopes and in hedgerows from lowlands to foothills. Several forms are cultivated in gardens.

Family: Hippocastanaceae

4 Common Horse-chestnut *Aesculus hippocastanum*. Robust tree up to 25 m or more; young branches brown, buds large and sticky. Leaves palmate, compound with 5—7 leaflets, each obovate, up to 20 cm long and irregularly toothed. Flowers in dense, pyramidal panicle, petals white, spotted with red and yellow. Fruit a somewhat spiny capsule with one or two glossy, dark brown seeds. Flowers in May and June. Native of Albania and Greece, but commonly cultivated in avenues, parks and gardens. Related species have red or rosy flowers.

2

3

1

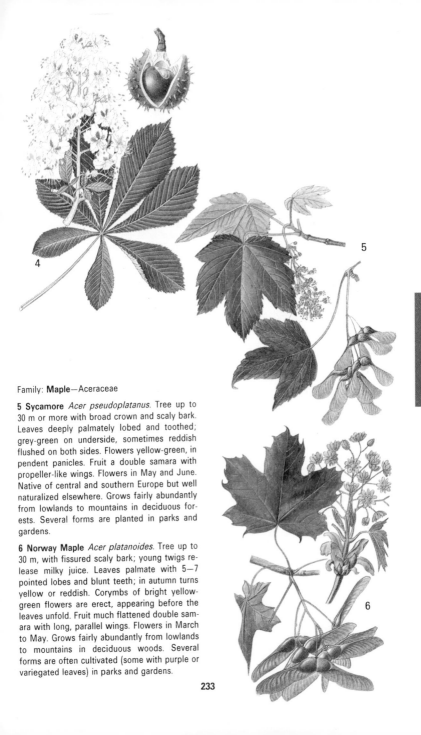

Family: **Maple**—Aceraceae

5 Sycamore *Acer pseudoplatanus*. Tree up to 30 m or more with broad crown and scaly bark. Leaves deeply palmately lobed and toothed; grey-green on underside, sometimes reddish flushed on both sides. Flowers yellow-green, in pendent panicles. Fruit a double samara with propeller-like wings. Flowers in May and June. Native of central and southern Europe but well naturalized elsewhere. Grows fairly abundantly from lowlands to mountains in deciduous forests. Several forms are planted in parks and gardens.

6 Norway Maple *Acer platanoides*. Tree up to 30 m, with fissured scaly bark; young twigs release milky juice. Leaves palmate with 5—7 pointed lobes and blunt teeth; in autumn turns yellow or reddish. Corymbs of bright yellow-green flowers are erect, appearing before the leaves unfold. Fruit much flattened double samara with long, parallel wings. Flowers in March to May. Grows fairly abundantly from lowlands to mountains in deciduous woods. Several forms are often cultivated (some with purple or variegated leaves) in parks and gardens.

233

Family: **Maple**—Aceraceae

1 Common Maple *Acer campestre.* Shrub or small tree up to 15 m or more; twigs sometimes with corky ridges. Leaves palmate, with 3 to 5 lobes, entire or bluntly toothed. Flowers yellow-green, downy, in small, erect, corymbose panicles. Fruit a hairy double samara with small blunt wings. Flowers from May to June. Grows in hedgerows on bushy slopes and in open forests mainly at lower altitudes.

Family: Rhamnaceae

2 Alder Buckthorn *Frangula alnus.* Smooth-barked shrub up to 5 m with slender branches. Leaves alternate, shortly petiolate, elliptic, entire, under side hairy when young. Small greenish flowers in axillary clusters; fruit a berry-like, black-violet, three-seeded drupe. Flowers in May and June. Grows in moist forests and near water, from lowlands to mountains. Related *Rhamnus catharticus*, usually with spiny branches, finely serrate opposite leaves and a more bushy habit grows on bushy slopes and in hedgerows on well-drained soils.

Family: **Lime**—Tiliaceae

3 Small-leaved Lime *Tilia cordata.* Tree up to 25 m tall with long-petiolate leaves, asymmetrically cordate, smooth above, on under side greyish, with tufts of rusty hairs in vein-axils. Flowers yellow-white, flower stalk bearing a large ligulate bract. Fruit a globose capsule, the bract persisting as a wing for wind dispersal. Flowers in early July. Grows in deciduous woods from lowlands to foothills; also often planted in parks and avenues.

4 Large-leaved Lime *Tilia platyphyllos.* A robust tree up to 30 m with black-brown bark. Leaves petiolate, cordate, usually asymmetric, dark green above, pale green beneath, somewhat hairy. Flowers white-yellow; capsule with three to five ribs, sub-globose. Flowers in late June. Grows in deciduous woods and on stable screes. Planted in parks and gardens, sometimes with other species; Silver Lime (*T. tomentosa*), having leaves white felted beneath; and the similar but pendulous branched *T. petiolaris.*

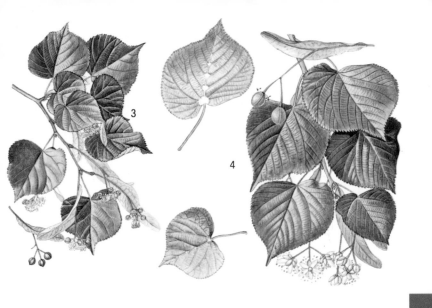

Family: Elaeagnaceae

5 Sea Buckthorn *Hippophaë rhamnoides*.
Spiny shrub up to 3 m tall with dense branches,
silvery-scaly when young. Leaves alternate,
linear-lanceolate, entire, under surface silvery-
scaly. Flowers greenish, in axillary clusters;
male and female on separate plants. Fruits
orange-red, rarely yellow, brown-dotted berries.
Flowers from March to May. In Europe native
only on sandy, gravelly river banks and stony
slopes. In Britain on dunes and cliffs by the sea.
Often planted for showy fruit, and as a hedge or
windbreak near the sea.

6 Oleaster *Elaeagnus angustifolia*. Shrub, less
frequently small tree, usually with spiny
branches. Leaves alternate, shortly petiolate,
narrow-lanceolate, upper side grey-green, under side silvery white. Tubular flowers silvery
yellowish, fragrant. Fruits are pale amber-yellow
berries. Flowers in May and June. Native of
Mediterranean; often cultivated in parks and
gardens. Not to be confused with the allied
E. argentea (syn. *E. commutata*) with wider
leaves, pendent flowers and silvery berries.

Family: Thymelaeaceae

1 Mezereon *Daphne mezereum*. Deciduous shrub up to 1 m, mostly with erect, little branched stems. Leaves alternate, lanceolate to oblanceolate, blunt-pointed, smooth, pale green. Strongly fragrant rosy-purple flowers appear before the leaves in lateral clusters. Fruits are globose, orange-red, poisonous drupes. Flowers from February to April. Grows in deciduous woods from lowlands to mountains. *Daphne cneorum* with terminal flowers and evergreen leaves grows at foot of Alps. Both species often cultivated. More common in Britain is the evergreen Spurge Laurel (*D. laureola*), with glossy dark green, oblanceolate leaves and yellow-green flowers from the leaf axils of the shoot tips.

Family: Araliaceae

2 Ivy *Hedera helix*. Evergreen climber up to 30 m with stems that cling by pads of short adhesive roots. Leaves leathery, opposite, long-petiolate, smooth, glossy, of two basic forms: non-flowering branches have leaves palmately three- to five-lobed, flowering ones have entire leaves, ovate to lanceolate. Flowers with five petals, greenish, arranged in rounded umbels. Fruit a globose, black berry. Flowers in September and October. Grows from lowlands to mountains in forests and thickets, climbs rocks and tree trunks. Flowers and fruits only at the top of its support. Many forms of varying leaf shape and colour are often cultivated for ornament.

Family: **Dogwood**—Cornaceae

3 Cornelian Cherry *Cornus mas*. Shrub or small tree up to 8 m. Leaves opposite, shortly petiolate, ovate to elliptic, pointed, with flattened hairs. Profuse yellow flowers in corymbs before leaves unfold. Fruits are oblong-ovoid red drupes. Flowers from February to April. Grows on bushy slopes and in open forests at lower altitudes. For long cultivated in parks and gardens for its distinctive early flowers.

4 Dogwood *Cornus sanguinea* (syn. *Svida sanguinea*). Shrub of bushy habit up to 3 m tall, with dark red branches especially during the winter. Leaves opposite, petiolate, ovate or oval, pointed, smooth. Flowers white in flat cymes, followed by black drupes. Flowers in May and June. Grows abundantly in deciduous woods, on bushy slopes and in hedgerows from lowlands to foothills. Related *Cornus alba*, with underside of leaves grey-green and hairy and bright red winter stems, a native of North America, is often cultivated.

Family: **Heath**—Ericaceae

5 Rusty-leaved Rhododendron *Rhododendron ferrugineum*. Small shrub up to 1 m tall. Tough, evergreen leaves are oblong-lanceolate, glossy, underside covered with rusty brown scales; margins inrolled. Flowers dark rose. Flowers from May to July. Grows on rocky slopes of Alps and in open woods on lower slopes. Related Alpenrose (*R. hirsutum*) with somewhat paler flowers and bristly margins of leaves, green on both sides, grows mainly in calcareous Alps. Many North-American and Asian species and especially their hybrids are cultivated in parks and gardens.

6 Marsh Tea or **Wild Rosemary** *Ledum palustre*. Low evergreen shrub to 1 m tall, with curious spicy fragrance. Young branches rusty hairy. Leaves alternate, sessile, linear to oblong, entire, the margins inrolled, under side rusty felted. Flowers fragrant, white, in dense terminal umbels; fruit an oblong capsule. Flowers from May to July. Grows in peatbogs, mossy rocks and at outskirts of wet forests from lowlands to foothills. Avoids limestone soils. Native of northern Europe and Asia. Poisonous, formerly used for protection against moths. In some areas now exterminated; a protected plant in certain countries.

Family: **Heath**—Ericaceae

1 Heather or **Ling** *Calluna vulgaris*. Low shrub up to ¹/₂ m, rarely to 1 m tall, sometimes decumbent, rooting and densely leafy. Leaves very small, linear, overlapping, with margins inrolled; glabrous or densely grey hairy in some forms. Flowers in one-sided racemes, drooping, pale purple, sometimes darker or white. Fruit a cap-

sule. Flowers from July to October. Grows abundantly on acid soils, in places dominant over vast areas — heaths and moors — also in open woods, on rocks, and in sandy places, from lowlands to mountain slopes.

2 *Erica carnea*. Decumbent, well branched, small evergreen shrub to 30 cm tall, with ascending, densely-leaved branches. Leaves linear, in whorls, smooth and glossy. Flowers in dense one-sided racemes. Stalked flowers drooping, rose-red, with narrow, bell-shaped carollas; capsule cylindrical. Flowers from December to May. Grows on screes, among rocks and in pine-woods, in the Alps and on their lower slopes. Many forms also cultivated. Related *Erica tetralix* has pink flowers in umbels and hairy leaves; *Erica cinerea* has flowers in dense racemes in summer.

Family: Vacciniaceae

3 Cowberry *Vaccinium vitis-idaea*. Low, densely branched evergreen shrub to 30 cm with creeping shoots and erect twigs. Leaves alternate, obovate, the apex rounded or with a short

point, slightly inrolled, margin dark green, glossy above, gland dotted beneath. Flowers in short terminal drooping racemes, corollas white or light rosy, bell-shaped. Fruit a berry, globose, red and glossy. Flowers from June to August. Grows in dry forests, especially pinewoods, on heaths, moors and peat-bogs, from hilly country to mountains.

4 Common Bilberry *Vaccinium myrtillus*. Low, densely branched deciduous bush with creeping stems and erect branches up to 60 cm tall. Leaves alternate, ovate, pointed, finely serrate, smooth, bright green, borne on green, angled twigs. Flowers solitary in leaf-axils, stalked, drooping; corolla globose, palest green with rosy flush. Mature berries globose, black, with a waxy 'bloom'; edible and tasty. Flowers from April to July. Grows abundantly in forests, from lowlands high up to mountains; in Britain mainly on heaths and moors, locally abundant, but only on acid soils. Related Cranberry (*Oxycoccus quadripetalus*), with evergreen leaves and prostrate stems and the corollas deeply four-parted, grows on peat-bogs.

Family: **Olive**—Oleaceae

5 *Forsythia suspensa*. Shrub up to 3 m tall, with long, pendent branchlets, hollow, angled and warty. Leaves simple or trifoliate, ovate, irregularly serrate, mostly unfold later than flowers. Flowers in lateral clusters before the leaves; bright yellow, bell-shaped with four lobes. Fruit a capsule. Flowers in March and April. Native of eastern China, but frequently cultivated in parks and gardens.

6 Common Privet *Ligustrum vulgare*. A semi-evergreen to deciduous shrub up to 3 m or more. Leaves opposite, shortly petiolate, lanceolate, entire, mostly pointed, bright green. Flowers in terminal, erect panicles; corollas cream-white and funnel-shaped. Fruit a glossy, black berry. Flowers in June and July. Grows on bushy slopes, in hedgerows and open woods, mainly at lower altitudes. Sometimes grown in hedges. The Japanese *L. ovalifolium*, a taller, more robust species with elliptic leaves, is now a popular hedging shrub.

5

6

239

Family: **Olive**—Oleaceae

1 Common Ash *Fraxinus excelsior.* Broad-headed tree up to 25 m tall. Branches grey-green, buds black-brown, broadly ovate. Leaves opposite, odd-pinnate; leaflets sessile, ovate to lanceolate, long-pointed, finely and sharply toothed, smooth. Flowers tiny, purplish, without petals, in axillary panicles before the leaves. Fruits are narrow, elongated, glossy samaras on slender, pendent stalks. Flowers from April to May. Grows fairly abundantly in woods, meadows, on screes, and in hedgerows, from lowlands to mountains. Also often planted, particularly the weeping form.

Family: **Nightshade**—Solanaceae

2 Bittersweet or **Woody Nightshade** *Solanum dulcamara.* Climbing deciduous subshrub up to 2 m, sometimes taller, with petiolate, entire, ovate, often pinnatifid leaves. Flowers in drooping panicles at end of branches. Corollas blue-violet with reflexed petals. Anthers yellow, a central yellow cone. Fruit a drooping, red, elliptical berry. Flowers from June to September. Grows fairly abundantly in thickets, hedgerows, woods and waste places, from lowlands to foothills.

240

Family: Loniceraceae

3 Common Elder *Sambucus nigra*. A shrub or small tree up to 10 m, with branchlets filled with white pith. Leaves odd-pinnate; leaflets ovate to elliptic, pointed, toothed, except at base. Inflorescence a large, flat-topped cyme with creamy flowers having a rank fragrance. Fruits are black, glossy druplets. Flowers in June and July. Grows abundantly in thickets, forests, on debris and along hedges from lowlands to foothills. Inflorescence and fruits edible and tasty, leaves poisonous.

4 Scarlet-berried Elder *Sambucus racemosa*. Shrub up to 4 m, with branchlets having yellow-brown pith. Leaves odd-pinnate, leaflets ovate to elliptic, finely toothed, on under side finely and thinly scalloped. Inflorescence a dense ovoid panicle with flowers greenish yellow. Red druplets. Flowers from April to May. Grows in clearings and at outskirts of woods, from foothills to mountains. Several forms, with deeply cut or golden leaves, are grown in parks and gardens.

5 Guelder Rose *Viburnum opulus*. A deciduous shrub or small tree up to 4 m tall. Leaves palmate with three to five lobes, sharply pointed and irregularly toothed. Inflorescences flat, cymose; inner flowers small, bell-shaped, hermaphrodite, whitish; outer flowers large, round, white and sterile. Mature drupes subglobose, red. Flowers in May and June. Grows fairly abundantly at woodland margins, in thickets and hedgerows, from lowlands to mountains. Several forms are cultivated in gardens and parks; one (the snowball tree), has all sterile flowers in globose heads. Related Wayfaring Tree (*V. lantana*) with oval leaves, felt-like on under side, and without showy sterile florets, grows in more open places, especially on chalk and limestone.

6 Snowberry *Symphoricarpos rivularis*. A deciduous suckering shrub about 2 m tall. Leaves oval, entire, rarely lobed. Flowers in small racemes; corollas bell-shaped, small, white with rosy tint. Fruit a white berry with spongy flesh. Flowers from June to August. Native of North America; commonly cultivated in woods for game birds, often becomes wild. Also often grown in gardens.

Gastropods and Bivalves

Gastropods (Gastropoda) are the best known of the molluscs. They may be found in woods, meadows, fields, gardens and often also in houses, in cellars and other damp places. They do not find dry conditions congenial, which is why they generally leave their damp hiding places only after dusk falls and dew has formed on the vegetation, or during the daytime after a rainfall.

The body of gastropods is divided into three parts — a head, foot and asymmetrical visceral sac. Many species have a shell, usually coiled in a spiral, inside which they can retreat. Some species, however, are without a shell. Gastropods are differentiated, according to their means of respiration, into three groups or subclasses: Pulmonata, Prosobranchia and Opistobranchia.

Best known are the Pulmonata, which have attained their greatest development on dry land. Only a few species inhabit fresh water, and a small number occur in the sea. The main distinguishing feature of pulmonate gastropods is the lung chamber, consisting of a dense network of branching blood vessels immediately beneath the fine skin of the mantle cavity, whose inner wall absorbs oxygen and releases carbon dioxide. The breathing hole (spiracle), through which air enters the cavity, is quite visible, for example in slugs, and can be opened and closed by the animal.

The shell of pulmonate gastropods is variously shaped and variously developed. As a rule, it is spirally coiled, but is sometimes only dish-shaped. In slugs, the remnants of the vestigial shell are found underneath the shield.

Commonest and most conspicuous are the gastropods of the order Stylommatophora, which have literally 'stalked' eyes. These are located on two long, retractable tentacles and look like black dots at the ends of the tentacles when they are extended. Below these tentacles are two further, shorter tentacles that can also be retracted. Stylommatophorous gastropods live on dry land but seek out moist locations. Some species have shells, others are without a shell. Some shells are conical-ovoid, such as the shell of Succinea, others are longish and spindle-shaped, for example Clausilia. The mouth of the shell is generally narrowed. Helicidae have spherical to flattened shells, often beautifully coloured as in the genus *Cepaea*. Helicidae, which are hermaphroditic, possess a special calcareous structure, sometimes

Fig. 1. *Cepaea nemoralis* has a beautifully coloured shell. The basic colouring may be different shades of yellow to reddish, striped with rich, dark brown bands.

called an 'arrow of love', which they use during copulation to pierce the body of their partner. Being hermaphrodites, one of them plays the role of the male and the other the role of the female, with only the latter being fertilized. The one that was the 'male' partner in this case, however, may be the 'female' partner in further acts of copulation.

Of all the members of the Helicidae family, the best known is the Edible Snail (*Helix pomatia*) whose shell may measure over 5 cm in diameter, thus making it one of the largest species. It is unjustly believed to be harmful by gardeners. In truth, not only are gardens undamaged by this snail, in fact they benefit from its presence because it feeds on and destroys many weeds. The worst that can be said of it is that it used to be partially harmful in the vineyards of southern Europe. The Edible Snail stays within a very limited area; often it will not even cross a path between two garden beds and may readily be lifted from a vegetable patch and placed elsewhere. During long dry periods, snails conceal themselves in a shady spot. There they retreat inside their shells and close the opening with a special membrane of hardened mucus. This enables them to survive the period of drought. During the winter they hide in loose soil, slowly digging their way into the earth using the edge of the shell. Once in the ground they form a hard and thick calcareous lid (operculum) which is porous, thus enabling the animal to breathe. In spring the snail presses the lid out and climbs out of the ground up into the air again. In many countries the flesh of the snail is considered a delicacy and this has been responsible for its disappearance in many places. For that reason it has been placed on the list of protected species. Nowadays snails are cultivated for food on special snail farms. Their flesh is tastiest in spring when it does not contain the calcareous salts required to form the operculum.

Also numerous are the 'naked' gastropods (slugs) without a shell, mainly members of the families Arionidae and Limacidae. These slugs have a dorsal shield at the front end of the body. In the Arionidae the spiracle is located on the lower right-hand edge of the front half of the shield; in the Limacidae it is located behind the midway point.

Fig. 2. The Roman or Edible Snail (*Helix pomatia*) is the largest European terrestrial mollusc.

Of the gastropods belonging to the order Basommatophora, which mostly comprises freshwater species, best known are the Lymnaeidae and Planorbidae. Lymnaeidae have a shell up to 6 cm high, a broad foot and a short head. They travel over the surface of the water by sliding along on the underside of a thin layer of mucus. They feed on algae and on decaying as well as fresh aquatic vegetation. Their eggs are deposited in cases on aquatic plants. In dry periods they form an operculum to prevent their bodies from drying out.

Planorbidae have a disc-like shell and a small head and foot. Their thread-like tentacles are extremely long. Unlike all other freshwater molluscs, these gastropods have red-coloured blood.

Prosobranchia gastropods have an operculum at the back of the foot with which they close the mouth of the shell when they retreat inside. The best known (*Viviparus*) have long tentacles. In males the right tentacle is thicker and is used as an organ of copulation. These gastropods are viviparous, which means that they produce living young.

Opistobranchia occur only in the sea and the main feature they have in common is that the gills are located behind the heart. The shells are often reduced or entirely absent.

Bivalves (Bivalvia) have a bilaterally symmetrical body consisting of only a trunk and a foot; the head is greatly reduced. They are devoid of a radula and tentacles and are generally also without eyes, whose function has been taken over by certain spots on the body that are sensitive to light. The soft body is enclosed by a mantle which secretes a substance that forms a paired shell consisting of two parts — a right and a left half. These are connected on the dorsal side via a strong elastic ligament. The two halves of the shell are usually equal in size and shape, which is dish-like. In some species, however, the valves are different, one being larger and more concave than the other and often with a patterned surface. Some bivalves are firmly attached to the substrate, to which the bottom half of the shell is cemented fast. In many species a thick layer of mother-of-pearl is formed on the inner side of the shell. On the dorsal side, at the apex, the two halves of the shell are joined by a ligament and often fasten by means of toothed edges which form a sort of interlocking system. The animal closes the shell halves by means of strong muscles.

Fig. 3. The Forest Slug (*Arion subfuscus*) is easily recognized by the traces of yellowish to orange slime it leaves behind it. It likes to feed on mushrooms.

Fig. 4. The Pearl Mussel (*Margaritana margaritifera*) inhabits small cold rivers and clear streams. It has disappeared from polluted waters in many places and is becoming increasingly rare.

In most bivalves the sexes are separate. In some species, however, their sex may change, sometimes several times, during their life cycle so that at certain periods they function as males, at others as females. The fertilized eggs develop into larvae.

Bivalves live only in water, most in the sea and only a small number in fresh water. There are some 25,000 species of bivalves worldwide. In the fresh waters of central Europe there are slightly more than 30 species. Bivalves are very important commercially. Many species are a common food in maritime regions and they are also shipped to inland countries where they are considered a great delicacy. The shells of many bivalves, even some freshwater species, yield mother-of-pearl, and certain species are highly prized as the source of precious pearls.

One of the best known marine bivalves is the Common or Edible Oyster (*Ostrea edulis*). The two parts of its shell are asymmetrical, the larger being deeper and thicker and firmly attached to the substrate, the smaller forming a lid to the cup. Because the oyster lives permanently in one spot, its foot has atrophied. The oyster grows to 8—10 cm and is able to reproduce when one year old. It forms large colonies.

Fig. 6. The marine gastropod *Natica millepunctata*.

Fig. 5. Great Ram's Horn (*Planorbarius corneus*) is found in pools, ponds, lakes and slow-flowing waters.

Class: **Gastropods**—Gastropoda

Family: **Amber Snails**—Succineidae

1 *Succinea putris.* Distributed in Europe, western and northern Asia. Common mainly in lowlands. Frequents lake- and pond-sides, ditches and marshes. Height 16—22 mm (in Danube basin up to 27 mm high and 13 mm wide). Life span up to 3 years. Lives on fresh and decaying vegetation. In pairing, one partner plays male and other female role. Each individual lays 50—100 eggs on damp ground. Spends winter and dry part of summer in crevices or among rotting leaves.

2 *Succinea pfeifferi.* Distributed in Europe and cool parts of Asia and northwest Africa. Occurs in low-lying country, lives on reeds and in waterside mud. Often found in large numbers on floating plants. Height 12—15 mm, width about 7 mm. Transparent shell. Similar biology to preceding species.

Family: Pupillidae

3 *Abida frumentum* Inhabits southern Europe and warm parts of central Europe. Frequents dry, grassy slopes. Height 6—10 mm, width 3 mm. Likes damp rocks, trees and other plants.

Family: Enidae

4 *Zebrina detrita.* Distributed over central, western and southern Europe, and south-western Asia. Common in limestone regions. Frequents warm spots. Plain-coloured or brown-striped shell. Height 18—25 mm, width 9—10 mm. Life span from 4 to 5 years. Shell often covered with dried slime and hardened soil.

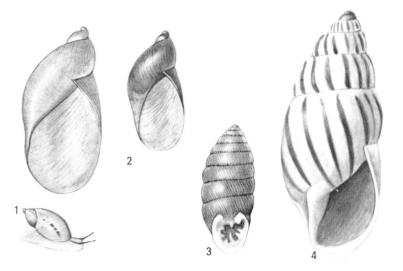

Family: Clausiliidae

5 *Laciniaria biplicata*. Distributed in central Europe, southern England, north-eastern France, Belgium; northern limit Sweden. Several subspecies. Very variable. Height 17—19 mm, width 4 mm. Inhabits forests, gardens, parks and hillsides, lives on tree-trunks, rocks, walls, etc. Usually produces live young, which take 5—10 months to develop. Life span about 3 1/2 years.

6 *Laciniaria turgida*. Inhabits eastern part of central Europe (chiefly the Carpathians), but exact distribution not known. Very variable. Height 12—17 mm Fusiform, transparent, glossy shell. Smaller shells at higher altitudes. Lives mainly in damp mountain forests; is especially abundant in thickly overgrown valleys, but also encountered in drier places. Several very similar species distributed all over Europe.

7 *Clausilia dubia*. Distributed in central, western and northern Europe as far as Sweden. Mainly inhabits mountains and rocky hills. Frequents rocks, ruins, walls, etc. Height 11 to 16 mm, width about 3 mm. Variably grooved. In winter hides under moss or fallen leaves.

Family: **Slugs**—Arionidae

8 Red Slug *Arion rufus*. Inhabits central and western Europe. Found in damp woods and meadows. Length 12—15 cm. Very large respiratory aperture. Variable colouring, from all shades of orange and brown to black. Black forms in colder areas, abundant local incidence of red forms in places. Border of foot usually red. Omnivorous. Often found on dead animals or excreta. Lays 300—500 eggs in piles, under stones, in moss, etc. Self-fertilization also observed.

9 Forest Slug *Arion subfuscus*. Distributed over whole of Europe. Chiefly inhabits lowland and mountain forests. Length 4—7 cm. Variable colouring. Basic colour yellow to reddish-yellow; back brown, sides often striped. Foot yellowish-white. Produces yellow or orange slime. Most frequently found on mushrooms, behind bark of tree-stumps, etc. Also eats fruit and parts of plants.

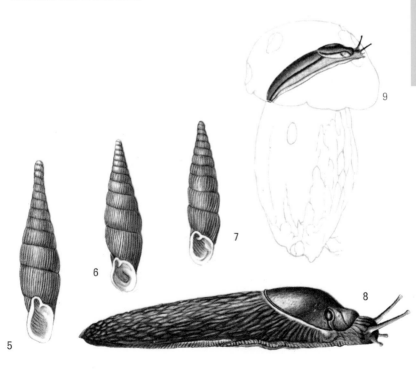

Family: **Keeled Slugs**—Limacidae

1 Great Greyslug *Limax maximus.* Distributed in southern and central Europe; extends to England and south of Scandinavia. Found in gardens, parks, cellars, etc. Variable colouring, often in association with differences in temperature. Length up to 15 cm. Frequently raids vegetable stocks in cellars, etc., but also eats other gastropods. When pairing, both partners hang twisted round a rope of slime attached to a twig. Active mainly at night and in damp weather.

2 Ash-blackslug *Limax cinereoniger.* Inhabits almost whole of Europe. Found mainly in deciduous woods in hilly and mountainous regions. Lives near trees, behind bark, under stones, etc. Colouring very variable (some specimens white), but mantle and foot always dark. Life span 3 years. Partners intertwine during pairing. Self-fertilization also known.

Family: Helicidae

3 *Helicodonta obvoluta.* Distributed in southern and central Europe and south-eastern England. Inhabits forests on warm limestone slopes. Lives under stones, leaves, etc. Forms white, parchment-like operculum in dry weather. Height 6 mm, width 13 mm. Thin-walled, discoid shell, hairy in young specimens.

4 *Helicigona lapicida.* Inhabits central and western Europe. Lives on damp rocks and tree-trunks in beechwoods. Often found on walls of ruins. Height 8.5 mm, width 17 mm. Shell partly transparent.

5 *Helicigona rossmässleri.* Inhabits the Carpathians. Lives on rocks and tree-trunks in damp forests. Commonest at altitudes of 800—1,400 metres above sea level. Attains 10—13 mm. Several tens of similar species occur in the Alps and mountains of central Europe.

6 White-lipped Snail *Cepaea hortensis.* Distributed over central and western Europe. Frequents damp spots in open woods, in gardens and at foot of rocks, etc. Shells of variable colouring; some specimens plain yellow or reddish, others striped. Width 15—25 mm, height 16 mm.

7 *Cepaea nemoralis.* Distributed in central and western Europe and Baltic coast. Lives in open woods and gardens and near human communities. Height 17—18 mm, width 20—24 mm. Basic colouring: different shades of yellow or red; usually striped with rich dark brown bands.

8 *Cepaea vindobonensis.* Inhabits eastern and south-eastern Europe; extends to the Alps and Danube and Vltava basins. Found primarily on limestone slopes, on outskirts of forests, etc., secondarily in vineyards and on banks. Width 19—25 mm, height 17—18 mm. Basic colour whitish to yellow; always striped.

9 Roman or **Edible Snail** *Helix pomatia.* Distribution area from south-eastern England across central Europe to Balkans. Is found today in places where it did not live originally. Inhabits open deciduous woods and thickets, chiefly in warm, low-lying country or hills. Frequents chalky regions. Often found on walls of ruins, etc. Height and width 40 mm; it is the largest European snail. Mean life span up to 6 years. Vegetarian. Pairing time May to August. After 6—8 weeks, each individual lays 20—60 eggs 5—6 mm in diameter in pits in the soil. In dry weather the shell is closed with a slimy secretion which looks like parchment when dry and ensures several months' survival. In winter a chalky operculum is added. Hibernates from October to April.

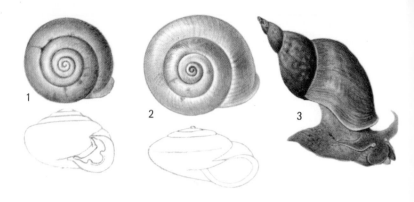

Family: Helicidae

1 *Isognomostoma personatum*. Distributed over central Europe, mainly the Alps, Pyrenees, Carpathians and German uplands. Does not occur in lowlands. Usually frequents rubble, hides under fallen trees and often under stones. Height about 6 mm, width 9—10 mm. Easily identified by three teeth on narrow aperture of rough, hairy shell.

2 *Zenobiella umbrosa*. Inhabits eastern Alps, German uplands, western Bohemia and Slovakia. Inhabits damp forest valleys, bogs and dense vegetation at foot of rocks, etc. Likes to climb tall plants where it can be found on leaves. Width of shell 9—13 mm, height 6—7 mm. Thicker shells in limestone areas.

Family: **Pond Snails**—Lymnaeidae

3 Great Pond Snail *Lymnaea stagnalis*. Its range of distribution includes whole of Europe, Morocco, northern Asia, North America. Lives in stagnant water at low altitudes. Has elongate, ovoid, pointed shell 45—60 mm high and 22—34 mm wide. Feeds on algae and parts of rotting vegetation. Eggs laid in capsules attached to aquatic plants. Life span 3 years.

4 Marsh Snail *Galba palustris*. Distributed over whole of Europe, Algeria, northern Asia and North America. Found in low-lying country in stagnant water, creeks and ditches. Has elongate, ovoid shell with dull lustre and finely grooved surface. Size very variable. Height 20—30 mm, width 10—18 mm. Colouring dark, inner surface usually deep violet.

Family: Planorbidae

5 Ram's Horn *Planorbis planorbis*. Distributed over almost whole of Europe. Found at low altitudes in stagnant and brackish water. Discoid shell about 3.5 mm high and 15—17 mm wide. Red blood. Frequents aquatic plants. Often seen surfacing for air. Feeds on algae, etc. Life span 2—3 years.

6 Great Ram's Horn *Planorbarius corneus*. Distributed over most of Europe except northern regions. Inhabits stagnant or slow-flowing, thickly overgrown water at low altitudes. Width of shell 25—37 mm, height 10—17 mm. Specimens in swamps and ponds small. Shells of young snails covered with bristles.

Family: Pomatiasidae

7 Round-mouthed Snail *Pomatias elegans*. Inhabits warm regions of Europe, particularly southerly areas. Lives under stones, fallen trees, on rocks and walls. Height 10—17 mm, width 8—13 mm.

Family: **River Snails**—Viviparidae

8 Common River Snail *Viviparus viviparus*. Distributed over large part of central Europe. Occurs in pools, ponds, creeks, etc. Lives at bottom in mud. Height 30—45 mm, width 25—35 mm. Specimens with shell of up to 50 mm are known. Has operculum with accretion grooves. Gives birth to live young with small shell. Feeds mainly on algae and organic debris.

9 *Viviparus fasciatus*. Distributed over whole of Europe except most northerly parts. Inhabits large rivers or river-fed reservoirs. Found between stones. Height 28—32 mm, width 22 to 24 mm. Likewise produces live young. Feeds on algae, organic debris in mud and occasionally plankton.

Class: **Bivalves**—Bivalvia

Family: **Freshwater Mussels**—Unionidae

1 *Unio tumidus.* Distributed over practically whole of Europe. Found in slow-flowing lowland rivers, lakes and ponds. Length of shell 70—90 mm. Annually lays up to over 200,000 eggs, incubated 4—6 weeks in female's gills. The hatched larvae (glochidia) hook themselves to fish gills, but after a few weeks drop to the bottom and live in the mud like adult animals. The adult mussel lives on microorganisms and debris.

2 *Anodonta cygnea.* Distributed over almost whole of Europe. Commonest in stagnant lowland waters. Length 170—260 mm. Hermaphroditic, lays up to 400,000 eggs a year. The eggs, produced in the winter, remain several months in the mussel's gills. The hatched larvae attach themselves to fish skin. When fully developed they leave their host and settle in the mud at the bottom. The adult animal lives on microorganisms.

Family: **Freshwater Pearl Oysters**—Margaritanidae

3 Pearl Mussel *Margaritana margaritifera.* Inhabits western, northern and occasionally central Europe. Scattered incidence. Inhabits small, cold rivers and clear streams. Length up to 150 mm, width 70 mm. Thick-walled valves. The small glochidia live as parasites in fish gills. Pearls may be formed in the mantle. Grows very slowly (only a few mm a year), but has life span of up to 80 years. Feeds on microorganisms and debris on bed of streams and rivers.

Family: **Orb Cockles**—Sphaeriidae

4 *Musculium lacustre.* Distributed over practically whole of Europe. Lives in rivers, streams, ponds and swamps. Common in lowlands. Length 8—14 mm, width 6—8 mm; 3—4 mm thick. Has thin-walled, transparent valves. Hermaphroditic and viviparous. Tolerates long droughts.

Family: **True Oysters**—Ostreidae

5 Edible Oyster *Ostrea edulis.* Distributed over European coasts from North Africa to Arctic Circle. Hermaphroditic, alternation of sexes in same individual. Free-swimming larvae hatch from the eggs. Up to 3 million eggs laid yearly by one oyster. Diet consists of plankton and debris. Collected as delicacy.

Family: **Cockles**—Cardiidae

6 Edible Cockle *Cardium edule.* Its area of distribution includes Atlantic, North, Baltic, Mediterranean and Black Seas. Diameter 3—4 cm. Lives in sand or mud in tidal zone, to depths of 10 metres. Can 'leap' distances of over 50 cm with long, bent foot. Lives on plankton.

Family: **Piddocks**—Pholadidae

7 Common Piddock *Pholas dactylus.* Distributed from Mediterranean to Norway. Tunnels in soft rocks and wood. Length up to 9 cm, width 3.5 cm. Secretes phosphorescent slime. Damages ships, but not seriously.

Family: **Scallops**—Pectinidae

8 *Pecten varius.* Its range of distribution includes Atlantic Ocean from Spain to western Norway and North Sea. Shell 3—7 cm in diameter. Colouring very variable. Adult sessile, young swim by snapping valves together.

Family: **Mussels**—Mytilidae

9 Blue Edible Mussel *Mytilus edulis.* Distributed in Arctic Ocean to North Africa, North and Baltic Seas. Forms large colonies, anchored to base by byssus. Settles in places with strong tides. Length 6—10 cm. One individual can lay up to 12 million eggs a year. Feeds on algae, debris and protozoans. Collected and sold as delicacy. Flesh rich in vitamins A, B, C and D. In many places piles are driven into the sea bed to provide the mussels with a ready-made base.

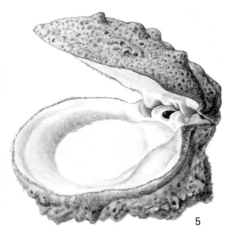

5

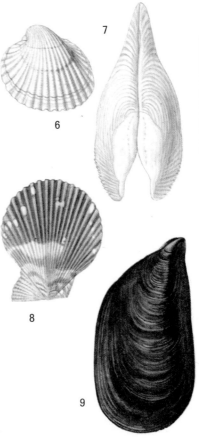

7

6

8

9

Spiders, Scorpions, Centipedes and Millipedes

The arachnids (Arachnidae) form a very large class of arthropods. Some 36,000 species have been described to date. These are divided into nine orders, of which the best known in central Europe are the spiders (Araneida), false scorpions (Pseudoscorpionidea), harvestmen (Opilionidea), and mites and ticks (Acari). Arachnids have four pairs of legs, one pair of chelicerae and one pair of pedipalps. The body is segmented but the segments are often fused together to form larger units. Arachnids live on dry land and in fresh water as well as in the sea. Many species are parasites of animals and humans as well as of plants.

Most familiar to us are the spiders (Araneida). The body of a spider consists of a cephalothorax and abdomen. The head is separated from the thorax by a suture. There are usually eight eyes, less often six or less. At the front of the mouth are claw-like fangs (chelicerae) which are connected to a venom gland. On either side of the mouth are the pedipalps, which resemble legs. The four pairs of legs are located on the thorax. The respiratory organs are either lung chambers or tracheae, sometimes both. The abdomen terminates in a spinneret that produces fine threads out of secretions from silk glands. The sexes are separate; the young that emerge from the fertilized eggs resemble the adults.

Some spider species are aquatic and spin their webs beneath the surface of salty coastal water. Best known of the freshwater species is the Water Spider (*Argyroneta aquatica*).

The best known spiders are the Araneidae. A typical representative of this large family (in central Europe there are more than 50 species)

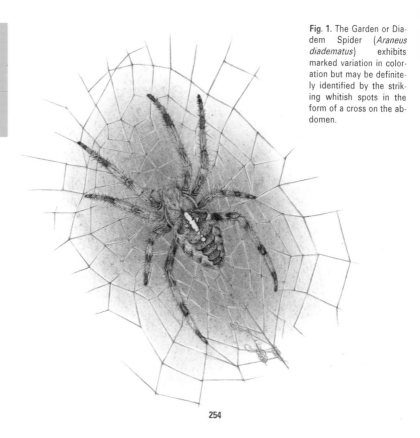

Fig. 1. The Garden or Diadem Spider (*Araneus diadematus*) exhibits marked variation in coloration but may be definitely identified by the striking whitish spots in the form of a cross on the abdomen.

is the Garden or Diadem Spider (*Araneus diadematus*). The concentric, outer threads of its web are dotted with tiny drops of a sticky substance. These threads trap and hold insects, while the spider usually sits in the centre of the web in a spot that is not sticky or else lies in wait near the web. As soon as the prey is caught fast, the spider hastens to it and either stuns or kills it with venom from its chelicerae. Then it winds threads round the victim's body and 'stores' it until it decides to feed. When that time comes, the spider injects digestive juices into the insect's body. These dissolve the tissues into a thick liquid which the spider then sucks out. The female usually remains in the same spot throughout her whole life. The male, much smaller in size, approaches the web and woos the female by shaking it. He places reproductive cells inside the female's body with his pedipalps and then departs quickly. It occasionally happens that a careless suitor is seized and devoured by the female. The female lays up to 700 eggs in a cocoon. Young spiders spin silken threads and wait for a breeze to carry them off to a different spot.

The young of other species of spiders (e.g. crab spiders — Thomisidae) spin silken parachutes or balloons on which they are borne far away by the wind.

Centipedes and millipedes belong to the group of tracheates (Tracheata) in which respiration is achieved by means of a system of air tubes called tracheae. These terminate in paired openings on the sides of the body segments and convey oxygen to all the body organs. Tracheates usually have a pair of antennae on their heads. The largest class of tracheates are the insects.

Centipedes (Chilopoda) have an extremely elongated, flat-backed and distinctly segmented body. The body consists of a head with a pair of long antennae and a large number of segments, each of which has a pair of legs. The mouthparts of centipedes consist of one pair of mandibles and two pairs of weak maxillae. The

Fig. 2. The Crab Spider (*Thomisus albus*) lies in wait for insects on a blossom. The splayed forelimbs serve to capture prey.

appendages of the first body segment have evolved into large pincer-like organs containing a venom gland. In central Europe there are more than 50 species of centipedes.

Millipedes (Diplopoda) are arthropods with the body segments fused into pairs so that there are two pairs of legs on each segment. The body is usually cylindrical and has a chitinous covering. The head usually has short antennae and a few simple eyes. The mouthparts consist of a pair of mandibles and a curious formation called a gnathochilarium, formed by the fusion of the maxillae. Millipedes have weak legs. In central Europe there are some 100 species.

Fig. 3. Centipedes (*Dermacentor pictus*) courting.

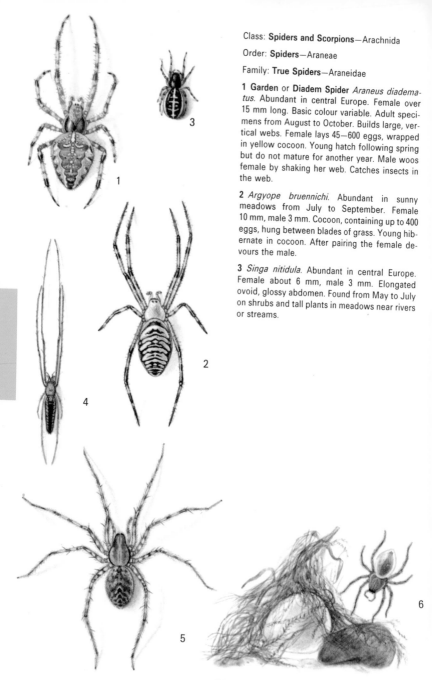

Class: **Spiders and Scorpions**—Arachnida

Order: **Spiders**—Araneae

Family: **True Spiders**—Araneidae

1 Garden or **Diadem Spider** *Araneus diadematus*. Abundant in central Europe. Female over 15 mm long. Basic colour variable. Adult specimens from August to October. Builds large, vertical webs. Female lays 45—600 eggs, wrapped in yellow cocoon. Young hatch following spring but do not mature for another year. Male woos female by shaking her web. Catches insects in the web.

2 *Argyope bruennichi*. Abundant in sunny meadows from July to September. Female 10 mm, male 3 mm. Cocoon, containing up to 400 eggs, hung between blades of grass. Young hibernate in cocoon. After pairing the female devours the male.

3 *Singa nitidula*. Abundant in central Europe. Female about 6 mm, male 3 mm. Elongated ovoid, glossy abdomen. Found from May to July on shrubs and tall plants in meadows near rivers or streams.

Family: Tetragnathidae

4 *Tetragnatha extensa.* Found all over central Europe. Up to 11 mm long. Strikingly elongated body. Builds web in damp spots between grasses and rushes. Attaches egg cocoon to rushes, etc.

Family: Agelenidae

5 House Spider *Tegenaria derhami.* Widespread all over Europe. Length 6—11 mm. Looks much larger because of its long legs. Frequents houses, cattle-sheds, etc. Builds dense, horizontal webs in corners. Can be found whole year round. Lives several years. Catches insects. Female suspends spherical egg cocoon from several webs disguising it with fragments of mortar, etc.

6 Water Spider *Argyroneta aquatica.* Inhabits whole of central and northern Europe. Body length 8—15 mm (male larger than female). The only subaquatic spider. Lives in clean pools. Weaves 'diving-bell' between aquatic plants and fills it with air. Bell also used as receptacle for eggs. Found whole year round. Life span two years.

Family: **Wolf Spiders**—Lycosidae

7 *Xerolycosa nemoralis.* Distributed over whole of central Europe. Length 5—7 mm. Common in woods, especially coniferous. Does not build web. Runs about among stones, pine needles, etc., catching small insects. Found from May to August. Egg cocoon carried attached to tip of female's abdomen. Female also carries young on its body for short time.

Family: Pisauridae

8 *Pisaura mirabilis.* Abundant in low-lying country. Length up to 13 mm. Elongated abdomen, long legs. Found on ground or leaves. Hunts prey. Male woos female with gift of fly; takes advantage of situation while female eats the fly. Does not build web. Female carries egg cocoon in jaws.

Family: **Crab Spiders**—Thomisidae

9 *Diaea dorsata.* Common everywhere in central Europe. Length 5—7 mm. Found on bushes in both coniferous and deciduous forests. Lies in wait for insects, with two pairs of long legs in typical splayed position. Walks sideways. Seen mainly in May and June.

10 *Misumena vatia.* Common in central Europe. Female 10 mm, male only 4 mm. Frequents tall plants and bushes, chiefly in May. Lies in wait for insects in flowers.

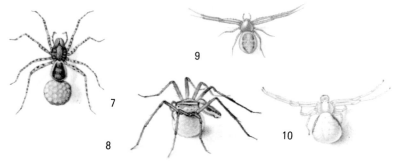

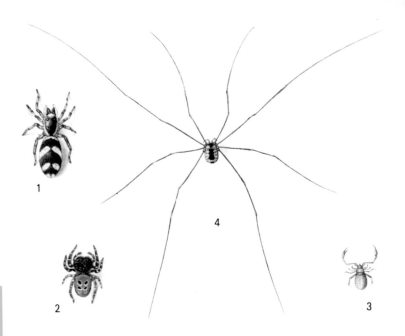

1

4

2

3

Family: **Jumping Spiders**—Salticidae

1 Zebra Spider *Salticus zebraneus*. Inhabits warm parts of Europe. Length up to 6 mm. Short legs. Appears in sunny spots early in spring. Male performs nuptial 'dance' in front of female. Female weaves nest and then lays eggs in it and guards them.

Family: Eresidae

2 *Eresus niger*. Inhabits warmer parts of Europe. Length 8—16 mm. Female velvety black. Male has red abdomen with 4 black spots. Found in sandy areas, lives in colonies. Scrapes holes 10 cm deep, lined with cobwebs. Erects porch over entrance and builds web traps in vicinity. Hunts tiger beetles. Female lives 3 years, male only one.

Order: **Pseudoscorpions**—Pseudoscorpionidea

3 Book Scorpion *Chelifer cancroides*. Very common. Length 3—4 mm. Lives among leaves, behind bark, in old books, etc. Catches small insects and mites. Spread by flies. Nuptial 'dances'. Female lays 5—18 eggs in pouch on underside of body. Able to spin cocoons.

Order: **Harvestmen**—*Opilionidea*

4 Common Harvester *Opilio parietinus*. Abounds in damp, shady spots. Hunts flies and ants. Males fight at pairing time. Female lays small piles of eggs in damp soil or cracked ground. Young hatch early in spring.

Order: **Mites and Ticks**—Acari

5 Sheep or **Castor-bean Tick** *Ixodes ricinus*. Inhabits almost whole of Europe. Male 1 to 2 mm, female up to 4 mm (several times larger when engorged). After fertilization and engorgement with vertebrate blood female lays up to 3,000 reddish eggs on ground or between stones. After sucking blood, the 6-legged larvae turn into nymphs, find fresh hosts and moult again to become adult males and females. Total time of development 178 to 274 days.

6 *Trombidium holosericum*. Very common. Length about 2.5 mm. Found on bushes, grass, ground, etc., from spring until autumn. Larvae 6-legged and bright red. Lives mainly on insects' eggs.

7 Common Beetle Mite *Parasitus coleoptratorum*. Occurs over most of Europe. Often found on dung beetles, used by adult female as means of transport to new dwelling-place, manure, compost, etc. Initial diet mouldy or rotting matter, later flies' eggs. Eggs usually unfertilized, but sometimes produce males.

Class: **Centipedes**—Chilopoda

Order: *Lithobiomorpha*

8 *Lithobius forficatus*. Common all over central Europe. Length 20—30 mm. Lives under stones, behind bark, etc., in woods and gardens. Solitary species. Can crawl both forwards and backwards. Bite harmless. Moults as it grows. Lives on insects, spiders, etc. Life span several years.

Class: **Millipedes**—Diplopoda

Order: Oniscomorpha

9 *Glomeris pustulata*. Widespread in central Europe. Length 4.5—14 mm. Resembles woodlouse, also able to curl up. Lives under stones, tree trunks, etc. in open country. Diet rotting leaves. Crawls very slowly. Eggs laid singly, in special nest made by female from damp clay. Life span 7 years.

Order: Opisthospermophora

10 *Julus terrestris*. Very common in central Europe. Length 20—50 mm. Coils itself up when disturbed. Lives under stones and leaves, behind bark, etc. Staple diet decomposing matter. Nocturnal animal. Female lays eggs in piles encased in capsule made of soil and secretion and fitted with ventilating shaft.

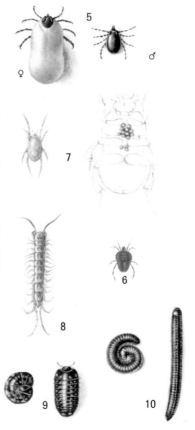

Crustaceans

Crustaceans (Crustaceae) belong to the sub-phylum Branchiata, in which respiration is achieved by means of gills. Crustaceans are mostly aquatic arthropods with two pairs of antennae, the first of which are simple, while the second, shorter pair are forked. The body segments exhibit marked diversity. The sexes are usually separate; only sessile forms, such as barnacles (Cirripedia), and some parasitic species are hermaphroditic. A few are parthenogenetic, that is the young develop from an unfertilized egg, as in water fleas (Cladocera). Some species of crustaceans care for their offspring.

Most crustaceans live in the sea, a smaller number in fresh water and only a few are terrestrial. Reproduction is by means of eggs. In many cases the larvae that hatch from the eggs resemble the adult—such larvae are called nauplii.

Fig. 1. The Common Hermit Crab (*Eupagurus bernhardus*) has a soft, vulnerable abdomen, which it protects by wearing the empty shells of various marine gastropods. When danger threatens, it closes the aperture of the shell with its large claw.

Fig. 2. Colonies of *Balanus tintinnabulum* are found on rocks, mollusc shells and even crabs' claws.

Some groups of crustaceans are important as the mainstay of the diet of numerous fish as well as some cetaceans; others, such as shrimps, lobsters and crabs, are a favourite food of people.

An interesting group of small crustaceans are the branchiopods (Anostraca), which are generally found in still bodies of fresh water. Only *Artemis salina* inhabits salt lakes, but not seas. In many places it forms the basic food of flamingoes. Branchiopods usually occur in small seasonal tracts of water that dry up. They pass the dry period in the egg stage, the larvae hatching as soon as their abode fills with water after a rainfall or after the spring thaw. They grow rapidly, reaching maturity within a short time and laying eggs that will again wait out the period of drought.

Water fleas (Cladocera) are a well-known group of crustaceans that usually live in fresh water. The head is free and the body encased in a translucent bivalvular shell. The second pair of antennae are branched, unusually large and are used for swimming. Water fleas occur in large numbers mainly in still or slow-flowing waters. Live, as well as dried, water fleas are commonly used as food for aquarium fish.

Another interesting group are the barnacles (Cirripedia), which mostly live in the sea. Some species are parasites on other animals. Usually they are hermaphroditic. Free-swimming larvae, known as nauplii, hatch from the eggs. Adult forms are anchored to a base, often a floating object or the body of another animal. The body of the barnacle is protected by a covering, usually consisting of calcareous platelets, in which the animal can enclose itself and thus prevent itself from drying out, for example when stranded by the tide.

The higher crustaceans (Malacostraca) have a constant number of body segments, usually twenty. The head is generally united with the thoracic segments to form a cephalothorax. All body segments, except the last, called the telson, have forked or simple appendages. These crustaceans live in the sea as well as in bodies of fresh water; some groups also live on dry land. Of commercial importance are, first and foremost, the decapods (Decapoda)—crayfish, lobsters and crabs. One feature they have in common is a very thick shell, usually united with the thoracic segments on the dorsal side. The first three pairs of thoracic appendages are converted to mouthparts. The body has five pairs of strong legs, the first three pairs being furnished with claws. The claws of the first pair are usually extremely powerful. In some species one of these claws is much bigger than the other. Crabs (Brachyura) have a short, square abdomen concealed beneath the cephalothorax, and large, occasionally asymmetrical, claws. Many species of decapods are a greatly prized catch in marine fishing.

Fig. 3. The Goose Barnacle (*Lepas anatifera*) does not look in the least like a crustacean. It is completely concealed inside a special shell and firmly anchored by a long, flexible stalk on its dorsal side to a solid object — a rock or stone or even the body of another animal such as a shark or whale.

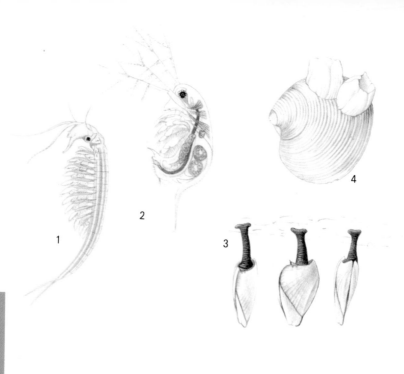

1

2

4

3

Class: **Crustaceans**—Crustacea

Order: **Branchiopods**—Anostraca

1 *Branchipus stagnalis.* Common all over central Europe. Length up to 23 mm. Found in wet ditches and pools. Occurs from April to September. Swims upside down. Lives on microorganisms. Female lays eggs in a special pouch on her abdominal segments, carries them a short time and then drops them into the mud. The eggs can survive five years of drought.

Order: **Water Fleas**—Cladocera

2 Common Water Flea *Daphnia pulex.* Abounds in stagnant water. Length about 2 mm. Fertilized hibernated eggs produce only females which reproduce further by unfertilized eggs. Eggs laid by the last generation also give rise to males and the females again lay fertilized eggs.

Order: Thoracica

3 Goose Barnacle *Lepas anatifera.* Lives off coasts from North to Mediterranean Sea. Length 3—4 cm. Locally abundant. Usually occurs in deep water but often found on floating objects. Anchored to base by thick, flexible stalk. Lives on plankton gathered by the gyrating movements of its six pairs of lash-like limbs. Hermaphroditic. Larvae hatch from eggs.

4 Acorn Barnacle *Balanus crenatus.* Inhabits tidal zone of North Sea and western Baltic. Very abundant. Lives in colonies. Attached to base over wide area of body surface. Often found on crabs' claws. Individuals in colonies stranded by tide enclose themselves in their shell, compound of 6 parts, by means of a leathery 'lid'. Size 10—20 mm.

Order: **Sea Lice and Allies**—Isopoda

Family: **Water Lice**—*Asellidae*

5 Hog-slater *Asellus aquaticus*. Plentiful in central and northern Europe. Length up to 13 mm. Lives at bottom of stagnant or slow-flowing water. Female carries the eggs or embryos in a brood pouch on the underside of her thorax. Lives on rotting vegetable debris. If water dries up, burrows in mud.

Family: **Sea Woodlice**—Ligiidae

6 Sea Woodlouse *Ligia oceanica*. Common on coasts from central Norway to Spain. Length up to 28 mm. Found under stones or among seaweed on rocky shores. Runs very quickly and dashes for water if in danger. Leads amphibian existence.

Family: **Land Woodlice**—Porcellionidae

7 Common Woodlouse *Porcellio scaber*. Abundant all over central Europe but has been carried to all parts of world. Length up to 16 mm. Colouring rather variable, but usually marbled. Lives in damp buildings, cellars, cracked walls, behind bark, etc. Large communities common. Breathes by means of gill plates on underside of abdomen. Lives on decomposing matter.

Order: **Flea Shrimps**—Amphipoda

Family: **Freshwater Shrimps**—Gammaridae

8 Common Freshwater Shrimp *Gammarus pulex*. Very common in central Europe. Length up to 24 mm. Inhabits shallow lakes, ponds and streams. Found under stones or among plants. Good swimmer. Mainly vegetarian. Usually winters on sandy bottoms, but often under stones. Sexes separate. Female lays eggs in brood pouch on legs where they are then fertilized. Young remain a short time with female.

Family: Caprellidae

9 *Caprella linearis*. Found off coasts of North and Baltic Seas as far as Kiel. Length up to 20 mm. Flat-sided, thread-like body. Legs terminate in prehensile claws. Frequents algae, seaweed, etc. Crawls swiftly over sea bed in search of prey. Predacious, catches small crustaceans, worms, polyps, etc. Deep red with light red eyes.

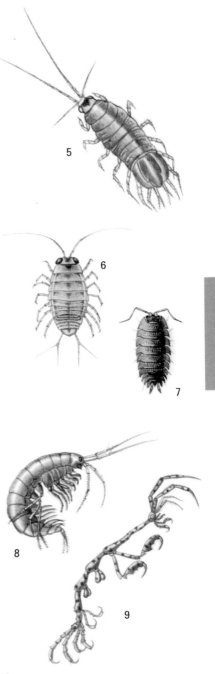

Order: **Decapods**—Decapoda

Sub-order: **Long-tailed Decapods**—Macrura

Family: **Crayfishes**—Astacidae

1 Common Crayfish *Astacus astacus*. Distributed in central Europe and southern Scandinavia. Length up to 22 cm. Occurs at low altitudes. Likes clean flowing water, but also found in ponds and lakes. Digs holes in banks to hide in during day. Hunts at night. Catches insects, gastropods, tadpoles and small fish. Also likes carrion. Occasionally eats green stuff. Eggs laid from October to December, attached in clumps to female's abdominal limbs. One female lays 6–150 eggs. Young hatched between May and July. They resemble the adult animals and remain attached to female's body for about 14 days. The young moult five times a year, adult specimens twice and old females only once.

Family: **Lobsters**—Homaridae

2 Lobster *Homarus gammarus*. Distributed from North Sea to Mediterranean and Black Sea. Length 35 cm, occasionally up to 50 cm. Takes 7–10 years to reach 20 cm. Inhabits rocks on sea bed. Nocturnal animal. Every two years, in July and August, lays up to 3,000 eggs which are carried on the underside of female's abdomen. Larvae hatch after 11 months. After four moults they resemble the adults. Life span 30 years. Caught in lobster-pots as delicacy.

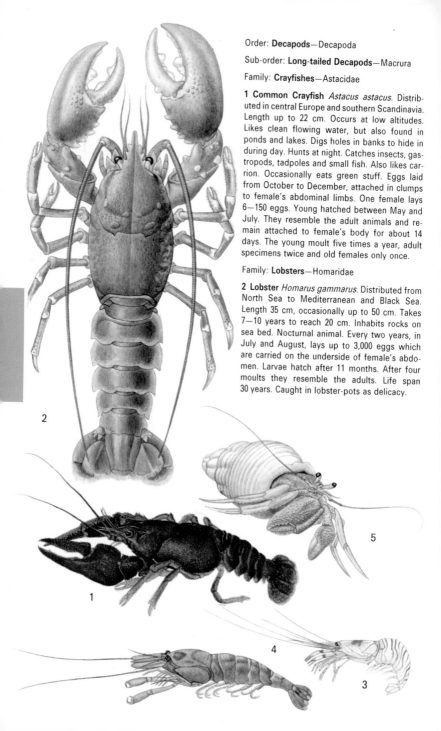

Family: **Prawns**—Palaemonidae

3 Common Prawn *Palaemon squilla.* Lives in North and Baltic Seas. Length 5—6 cm. Frequents seaweed near shore in summer, deeper water in winter. Lives on algae, debris, small crustaceans, etc. Eggs laid in summer. Almost transparent when alive, turns pinky-red when boiled. Delicacy.

Family: **Shrimps**—Crangonidae

4 Common Shrimp *Crangon crangon.* Distributed from North Sea to Mediterranean. Length 4—5 cm. Frequents coastal zone, enters brackish water in summer. Lives on small molluscs, fish roes, etc. Eggs laid April-June and October-November. Delicacy. Does not change colour when boiled.

Family: **Hermit Crabs**—Paguridae

5 Common Hermit Crab *Eupagurus bernhardus.* Distributed from Mediterranean to North Sea where it is very abundant. Length about 3.5 cm. Frequents shore but also found at depths of 450 m on sandy or rocky bottom. Wears marine gastropod shells to protect its soft abdomen. Closes aperture of shell with claw. Lives on small animals and debris. Large numbers of young may be found in shallow water.

Sub-order: **True Crabs**—Brachyura

6 Common Shore Crab *Carcinus maenas.* Its distribution area ranges from Mediterranean to Iceland. Abundant in North Sea, rare in Baltic. Length 5—6 cm, width up to 8 cm. Large well-developed nippers. Can swim short distances. Runs rapidly sideways on sea bed and on land. If stranded by tide, hides under large pebbles or burrows in sand. Lives on remains of different animals and plants.

7 Spider Crab *Macropodia rostrata.* Plentiful in North Sea and Baltic bays as far as Kiel. Also occurs in Mediterranean. Frequents coastal zone to depth of 100 m. Hides in rocks or sand. Length up to 18 mm. Rostrum formed of two long, joined spines. Eats small molluscs, crustaceans, algae, etc.

8 Mitten Crab *Eriocheir sinensis.* Native of rivers of northern China and shores of Yellow Sea. Brought to Europe, now lives in Elbe, Weser and other rivers. Locally abundant. Length up to 7.5 cm. Very wide chelae thickly covered with fine hairs. Travels long distances upstream. Attains adulthood after 4 years and then returns to sea where female lays eggs. Larvae can hatch only in salt water.

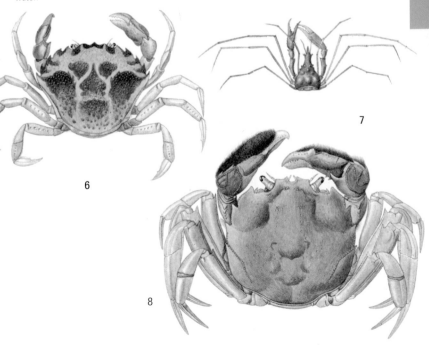

6

7

8

Springtails and Insects

Springtails (Collembola) were formerly classed among insects, but today they are in a separate class by themselves. They are primitive wingless creatures that never possessed even vestigial wings. They occur in large numbers in the ground as well as on the soil's surface in woods and gardens, on trees, leaves and on flowers, and they form large colonies. They usually measure 1—3 mm. Most species jump well, aided by a special forked appendage at the caudal end on the underside of the body. This generally lies folded under the body, facing forward. When suddenly extended, it hurls the springtail up and out. Springtails feed on rotting debris, fungi and the like; some species are also carnivorous.

The females lay eggs several times a year beneath stones and in holes in the ground. The young moult a number of times. Adult forms also moult, often reproducing missing organs, such as antennae or appendages, that have been lost one way or another. Springtails are important soil organisms which contribute to the decomposition of plant substances and thereby to the formation of humus. Some species may cause damage by nibbling parts of green plants. There are some 3,500 known species distributed throughout the world, from the tropics to the regions of permanent snow and ice. In central Europe there are about 400 species.

Insects are arthropods with a body that is divided into three distinct parts: the head, thorax and abdomen. The head generally bears large, compound eyes made up of many small prismatic eyes; however, some species have simple eyes. Attached to the front sides of the head are mobile antennae composed of several segments. The antennae are sensory organs, serving primarily as organs of smell and touch, and they may vary greatly in form. In some species they are thread-like (filiform), in others club-shaped (clavate), comb-like (pectinate), etc.

The mouthparts may be adapted for chewing or else for sucking or licking. Above the mouth opening is the upper lip or labrum, below it is the lower lip or labium, bearing small appendages known as the labial palps. The mouthparts proper consist of a pair of mandibles and a pair of maxillae to which are attached a pair of appendages known as the maxillary palps. Protruding from the mouth opening is a tongue-like appendage known as the hypopharynx.

Fig. 1. Developmental stages of the Swallowtail (*Papilio machaon*). The caterpillars like to feed on dill.

Fig. 2. Common Stag Beetles (*Lucanus cervus*) engaged in combat.

The thorax is composed of three segments: the prothorax, mesothorax and metathorax. The second and third segments both bear a pair of wings. Sometimes, however, one pair of wings is reduced, for example in flies, to form minute balancing organs (halteres). Some groups of wingless insects once had winged ancestors and their present wingless condition is an acquired one, for example in fleas. Wingless insects such as fish moths (Thysanura), however, never possessed wings in the first place. In many species of insects the wings are membranous, in others the front wings are thickened and serve to protect the hind wings; wings of this type are termed wing-covers or elytra, for example in beetles.

On the underside of each thoracic segment is a pair of legs, so that insects have six legs altogether. Legs are adapted for jumping, scraping, swimming, holding prey and so on. The abdomen may be of diverse shape, ranging from thread-like to broad and flattened. It is composed of a varying number of segments that look like rings.

The sexes are usually separate. In some species the male and female differ markedly in coloration or size or by having various appendages.

The development of insects is generally achieved by one of two methods: incomplete metamorphosis or complete metamorphosis. In the case of complete metamorphosis, the larvae that emerge from the eggs (caterpillars in Lepidoptera) do not resemble the adult at all. They shed their skin (moult) several times and then turn into a pupa, from which the adult, known as the imago, emerges after a time. In the case of incomplete metamorphosis, the larvae that emerge from the eggs slightly resemble the adult insect but are without wings. These larvae,

Fig. 3. Female Colorado Potato Beetles (*Leptinotarsa decemlineata*) lay orange eggs in piles. The red, black-spotted larvae gnaw the leaves of potato plants, often leaving only the skeleton.

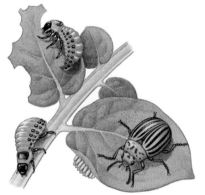

Fig. 4. The caterpillar of the Puss Moth (*Cerura vinula*) has prongs at the tip of the abdomen, from which it extrudes pink filaments to scare foes.

known as nymphs (in some species also as naiads), shed their skin a number of times, looking more like the adult with every moult, until they finally change directly into an adult. This is the basic scheme, but the development of some species or groups of insects is rather more complex.

Winged insects (Pterygota) have wings in the adult stage. In some species the adults have reduced wings, but this is an acquired condition. Fleas, for example, are wingless because they have adapted to a parasitic way of life.

Wings and their shape differ markedly in the various insect groups. In many species the front wings are not adapted for flight but form a hard, protective cover for the hind pair of membranous wings.

The pictorial section of this book does not include members of certain insect orders that occur rarely or are less well known—the enormous number of insect species makes this impossible. Furthermore, the individual orders are not presented according to the zoological system of classification; this has been done to show species that are similar (not related) alongside one another in the colour plates, for the purpose of easier orientation on the part of the reader. For example, springtails and fleas are not related at all, but members of the two groups might readily be mistaken for one another by the layman;

Fig. 5. The larvae of *Perla abdominalis* live in water, on or under stones. They like clear water and are therefore most often found in swift-flowing streams. The adult insects are on the wing from April until June in foothill districts, but fly only short distances.

Fig. 6. The development of a dragonfly (*Aeschna*).

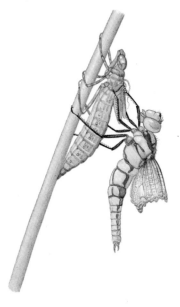

Insects make up the largest group of animals. The number of described species totals nearly a million, but the actual number is much larger.

Insects are divided into two sub-classes: wingless insects and winged insects. Wingless insects (Apterygota) never had winged ancestors and they undergo an incomplete metamorphosis. Fish moths (Thysanura), for example, belong to this group. These are small insects with a body that is narrowed toward the end and terminates in two cerci and a single long median caudal filament. The body is covered with fine scales. The antennae are usually quite long. The legs are slender and break off easily, but will grow again. Fish moths are nocturnal insects. Their development is slow and includes several larval stages. There are some 500 species worldwide; in central Europe there are over 20 species.

269

the same holds true for snoutflies (Mecoptera) and alderflies (Megaloptera), as well as for leaf beetles (Chrysomelidae) and ladybirds (Coccinellidae). The following are the insect orders found in central Europe, representatives of which appear in the pictorial section.

Mayflies (Ephemeroptera) are small insects with a 3—4-mm-long body. Their forewings are larger than the hind wings, which, however, may be absent in some species. When at rest, the wings are held upright above the abdomen, thus making it easy to distinguish mayflies from

Fig. 7. The larvae of damselflies (*Calopteryx*) live and develop in water.

Mayflies are widely known for their mass occurrence. In summer, when naiads complete their development, millions of mayflies may appear around rivers. Often they fly to streetlamps by the riverside or to lighted windows. Such hordes of mayflies are a sight that is becoming increasingly rare nowadays because they cannot live in polluted waters. There are some 2,000 known species of mayflies in the world; more than 80 are found in central Europe.

Stoneflies (Plecoptera) are smaller to moderately large insects with a wingspan of about 5 cm. There are some 90 species in central Europe. Their metamorphosis is incomplete. Their bodies are elongated and slightly chitinous. The forewings are narrower than the hind wings. Both wings are folded flat against the abdomen when resting. The flight of stoneflies is cumbersome. The mouthparts are usually vestigial in the adults. Development takes place in water where the females lay their eggs cemented to-

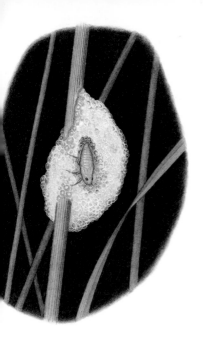

Fig. 9. Developmental stages of the Common Fire-bug (*Pyrrhocoris apterus*).

Fig. 8. The larvae of spittle-bugs (Cercopidae) develop in a large mound of froth attached to a plant.

other insects. The abdomen of mayflies is terminated by a pair of long cerci with a third, long caudal filament in the middle. The mouthparts are vestigial in the adults and that is why they do not feed. The metamorphosis of mayflies is incomplete; the developmental stages are called naiads. The larvae of mayflies show little resemblance to the adults and live in water. However, there exists a transitional stage between the naiad and the adult that is not found in any other insects. The fully grown naiad climbs out of the water onto a stem above the surface, where it changes into a sub-imago, greatly resembling the adult and covered with a delicate membranous skin. Only after it has shed this skin is the true adult stage (imago) attained. In some species of mayflies the sub-imago stage lasts only a matter of minutes, in others up to two or three days. The life of the adult is extremely short, usually only a few days.

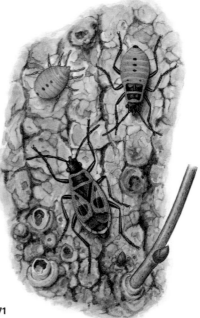

271

Fig. 10. The female Katydid or Green Grasshopper (*Tettigonia viridissima*) has a long, stout ovipositor with which she deposits as many as 100 eggs in the ground.

gether in a mass. The nymphs live for one to four years under stones in streams and rivers. They are more abundant in faster flowing brooks and streams because they require well-aerated water. They are predacious.

Dragonflies (Odonata) are one of the best-known groups of insects. They brighten riversides, ponds and lakeshores but will often fly quite far from water to meadows, fields and forest clearings. These are large insects with an elongated abdomen and long, relatively narrow wings. They are excellent fliers. The eyes are large. The metamorphosis is incomplete. The eggs develop into larvae (nymphs) lacking any resemblance to the adults. These larvae live in water and are very predacious. They hunt small aquatic insects and crustaceans but will also attack small tadpoles and fish fry. Some nymphs develop into adults within three months, others not until a year to four years after hatching.

The nymphs of dragonflies have a well-developed lower and upper lip round the mouth opening. At the sides are mandibles and maxillae. The lower lip is shaped like a mask that aids in seizing prey. At the end of their development the nymphs climb up out of the water onto a plant stem or some other object, where they change into the adult form.

Dragonflies are predacious and hunt various insects, mostly flies but also lepidoptera, on the wing. There are some 4,700 known species in the world; about 100 species are found in Europe. Dragonflies are divided into two suborders: damsel-flies (Zygoptera) and giant dragonflies (Anisoptera). Damsel-flies have both pairs of wings of almost equal size. These are folded vertically when resting. Giant dragonflies have the hind wings broader than the forewings and the wings are held outspread when resting. Whereas damsel-flies fly relatively slowly, giant dragonflies are swift and skilful fliers.

Cockroaches (Blattodea) are moderately large to large flat-bodied insects, although some species measure only a few millimetres. As a rule, however, cockroaches are over 1 cm long, some tropical species being up to 12 cm long. The three-sided head is bent downward and the mouthparts have greatly developed mandibles. The wings are large, the forewings more chitinized, the hind wings broad and membranous and folded beneath the forewings. Both pairs are laid flat against the body. Even though the wings are well developed, cockroaches are poor fliers. In some species the wings are absent or the females may even be wingless. The legs of cockroaches are long and slender, adapted for fast running.

Cockroaches are nocturnal insects, hiding in cracks and crevices during the daytime. They are omnivorous, but generally prefer plant food. Some species form colonies. The metamorphosis is incomplete. The eggs are enclosed in characteristic purse-like cases called oothecae, which the females carry about for several days until they find a place to conceal them. The larvae moult five to nine times; in some species as often as twelve times. The nymphs resemble the adults but are wingless. Cockroaches are distributed primarily in the tropics, where there are more than 3,500 species; some ten species are found in central Europe. Certain species are common pests in mills, bakeries and the like, and are difficult to get rid of.

Mantids (Mantodea) are thermophilous insects distributed mainly in tropical and subtropical regions, where there are some 2,000 species. Only a single species is found in the warm regions of central Europe. Mantids are moderately large to large insects, some being only 1.5 cm long, others as much as 16 cm long. They are distinguished by the unusual form of the front legs which are adapted for seizing and holding prey. The legs are strong, the coxae extremely long, the femora armed with three rows of sharp spines, and the tibia spiny as well. The mantid seizes its prey between the femur and tibia, piercing it with the spines in several places so that its victim cannot escape. The head is three-sided and bent downward, the mandibles large and strong. The predaciousness of mantids is proverbial. Often the much larger female devours her smaller partner. Mantids have large wings, often covering the entire abdomen. Their flight, however, is cumbersome and they fly only short distances. The metamorphosis is incomplete. The females lay their eggs in oothecae which they fasten to plants and the like. They secrete the case together with the eggs. The oothecae rapidly harden, thus providing good protection for the eggs. The larvae hatch after a long time, are predaceous, and feed on small insects.

Straight-winged insects (Orthoptera) are moderately large to large insects with powerful mouthparts adapted for biting. The hind legs are generally very stout and adapted for jumping. The body is compressed from side to side. The head is bent downward and is furnished with large mandibles. The antennae vary in length; in green grasshoppers, for instance, they are very long and thread-like; in field grasshoppers they are short and thicker. Both males and females have wings. Some species are short-winged; in others the wings are ab-

sent in the females or in both sexes. The fore-wings often differ markedly from the hind wings. Whereas the forewings are usually a nondescript colour that blends well with their surroundings, the membranous hind wings are brightly coloured.

The males (very occasionally also the females of certain species) produce shrill sounds by means of a special organ called the stridulatory organ. Each species produces a specific sound by means of which the male tries to attract a mate. Green grasshoppers produce sounds by rubbing the bases of the forewings together; field grasshoppers by rubbing the hind femora against the edges of the upper wings. Crickets have a large 'chirping' apparatus on the fore-wings.

The metamorphosis is incomplete. The larvae that hatch from the eggs moult five to six times and resemble the adults. Some species of straight-winged insects are predacious, others herbivorous. The females of green grasshoppers have a large ovipositor. There are more than 25,000 known Orthoptera species in the world, mostly found in the tropics and subtropics. Only some 120 species are found in central Europe.

Earwigs (Dermaptera) are moderately large insects with a flattened, elongated body that is firm and glossy. The long abdomen of both males and females terminates in two forceps-like appendages that are used for seizing and holding prey, in defence, as well as for attack, and also for pulling out the folded membranous wings or when folding them back again in the case of flying species. The forewings are short and leathery, the hind wings long and membranous and elaborately folded three times under the forewings when resting. The legs of earwigs are relatively short and are used for walking.

Fig. 11. Female Potter Wasps (*Eumenes coarctatus*) build fat-bellied, short-necked nests of clay and saliva for their larvae on walls or stones and often also on heather and the bark of trees. To feed the larvae, they capture a small hairless caterpillar, paralyze it and put it into the nest.

Fig. 12. The Red-bearded Fan Wasp (*Ammophila sabulosa*) takes similar care of its larvae. It drags the paralyzed caterpillar to the nest at the end of an underground burrow, lays the egg on its body, and firmly fills in the entrance to the nest.

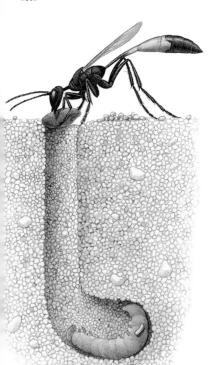

The head projects directly forward and is furnished with thread-like antennae. Earwigs are nocturnal insects. During the daytime they remain concealed in crevices or under bark, emerging to forage for food when dusk falls. They are omnivorous. The metamorphosis is incomplete. The females lay several dozen eggs, covering them with the body until they hatch and protecting them from drying out as well as from fungal attack. They take similar care of the larvae. There are 1,300 known species in the world, about ten species being found in central Europe.

Bird lice or biting lice (Mallophaga) are small, flat-bodied, wingless species, although they had winged ancestors. The head is broader than the thorax and is furnished with well-developed mandibles. The antennae are short, the eyes vestigial or absent. Biting lice are parasites that are found in the feathers of birds or in the fur of mammals. They feed on feathers and hair and often also on dermal scales or occasionally even upon the blood of their host. Their metamorphosis is incomplete. The females lay eggs (nits) that stick to hair or feathers. Nymphs usually take three to four weeks to develop, but sometimes only eight days. There are some 3,500 species in the world; about 130 of these live in central Europe.

Bugs (Heteroptera) form a very large insect order and are to be found in all kinds of environments—in forests, meadows, fields and water, as well as in human dwellings. They are small to

275

Fig. 13. *Cicindela campestris* with prey.

Fig. 14. The Common Sexton or Gravedigger Beetle (*Necrophorus vespillo*) can scrape away the earth under the body of a dead bird until it is completely buried. The female then lays eggs on the body and the larvae feed on the putrefying flesh. *Oeceoptoma thoracica* forages in the immediate vicinity for the dead bodies of the larvae of flies and other insects.

moderately large insects, tropical species usually being larger. The body is greatly flattened dorso-ventrally. The front wings are usually hemelytra, the hind wings are membranous. Some species, however, are wingless. The mouthparts are designed for piercing and sucking. The metamorphosis is incomplete. The larvae resemble the adults but are devoid of wings and are smaller. Some species are troublesome pests of cultivated plants, others are predacious. Some of the predacious species specialize in sucking the blood of warm-blooded animals, including people. Some aquatic species have extremely long hind legs which are used for rowing. There are some 45,000 known species in the world; more than 1,000 are found in central Europe.

Plant-bugs (Homoptera) are usually small insects with two pairs of membranous wings, often folded roof-wise when resting. Some species are wingless. The mouthparts are designed for piercing and sucking. Homoptera usually suck plant juices. The metamorphosis is incomplete. Of the 53,000 known species, more than 2,000 are found in central Europe. Many species, for example aphids (Aphidoidea) or coccids (Coccoidea), are troublesome plant pests.

Bees, wasps and ants (Hymenoptera) are the most perfectly developed group of insects. The head is free, with the mouthparts adapted for chewing. Most species have greatly developed mandibles, only in some are they modified into a licking-sucking apparatus. The two pairs of membranous wings have both longitudinal and transverse venation. The hind wings are usually smaller. Females have an ovipositor. The metamorphosis of hymenopterous insects is complete. The larvae moult a number of times before changing into a pupa from which the adult emerges after a certain period. They vary greatly in size, some species measuring only 1 mm while others may be giants of 6 cm. This is an extremely large order with more than 150,000 known species distributed throughout the world; more than 10,000 are found in central Europe.

Beetles (Coleoptera) include among their number many small as well as extremely large species. In most species membranous wings are folded beneath thick elytra. The mouthparts are adapted for chewing. The metamorphosis is complete. Beetles are one of the largest insect orders, with more than 350,000 known species distributed throughout the world; some 7,000 species are found in central Europe.

Alderflies (Megaloptera) are moderately large insects with a large forward-projecting head. The wings are short and broad and are folded roof-wise above the abdomen when resting. Their flight is rather cumbersome. The head bears long, thread-like antennae and mouthparts that are adapted for chewing. The meta-

Fig. 16. The larvae of the Giant Ichneumon Fly (*Rhyssa persuasoria*) develop inside the bodies of large wood wasp larvae that live in wood. The female pushes her ovipositor into the wood and lays the egg in the wood wasp larva's body.

morphosis is complete. The larvae live for two years in water, climbing out onto the shore before pupating beneath leaves. The adult emerges from the pupa after about two weeks. Of the 250 known species only three are found in central Europe.

Fig. 15. The nest of a bumble-bee (*Bombus*) in an underground hole.

Snakeflies (Raphidioptera) are moderately large insects with a greatly elongated neck-like prothorax. The head is large, with mouthparts that are adapted for chewing. The wings are richly veined; both pairs are about the same size and are folded roof-wise above the abdomen when resting. The female has an ovipositor. Adults, as well as larvae, live under the bark of trees and are predacious. The metamorphosis is complete. There are some 200 species worldwide; approximately ten species are found in central Europe.

Nerve-winged insects (Neuroptera) are small to moderately large insects with two pairs of

Fig. 17. Caddis-flies (Trichoptera) are found near water; the larvae develop in water. The cases in which the larvae conceal themselves are made from small grains of sand, fragments of pine needles, leaves, bits of wood or the shells of small molluscs. The species of caddis-fly can usually be determined by the shape of the case and the material from which it is constructed.

Fig. 18. The Garden Tiger Moth (*Arctia caja*) is one of the loveliest of all moths. Its coloration is extremely variable.

practically identical membranous wings, folded roof-wise when resting. The metamorphosis is complete. Of the 7,000 known species, about 100 are found in central Europe.

Scorpion flies (Mecoptera) are small to moderately large insects with the head prolonged into a deflexed beak, at the end of which are sited mouthparts which are adapted for chewing. The antennae are thread-like. The wings are relatively long. In many species the male has the abdomen curved upward at the tip. The metamorphosis is complete. The eggs are laid in the ground. The larvae have outgrowths on their backs and pupate in the ground. Adults, as well as larvae, feed on small insects. Some 350 known species are distributed throughout the world; about ten species are found in central Europe.

Caddis-flies (Trichoptera) are moderately large insects with translucent wings, the hind wings are usually paler than the fore wings. The antennae are thread-like and very long. Adults are found in the vicinity of water. The metamorphosis is complete. The omnivorous larvae live in water where they build a typical portable case in which the soft hind part of the body is concealed. They also pupate in water. The pupa rises to the water's surface before the adult emerges, which is generally at night. Of the 3,500 known species, approximately 250 are found in central Europe.

Butterflies and moths (Lepidoptera) are perhaps the most familiar of the insect orders. They have four wings, usually covered with fine scales. The jaws are converted into a coiled proboscis. The antennae are long and variously shaped, the legs slender. The larvae (caterpillars) have three pairs of thoracic legs, usually four pairs of prolegs and one pair of anal legs

Fig. 19. The female Ant Lion (*Myrmeleon formicarius*) lays eggs in sand. The larvae trap insects, mainly ants, in funnel-shaped pits. The adults are on the wing on July evenings in sandy locations; during the day they rest on bushes.

Fig. 20. The Crane-fly or Daddy-longlegs (*Tipula oleracea*) often flies indoors but there is no need to fear it as it does not bite or sting.

known as claspers. The metamorphosis is complete. These are very plentiful insects, numbering some 110,000 known species worldwide; approximately 4,000 species are found in central Europe.

Two-winged flies (Diptera) are small insects with a body distinctly divided into a head, thorax and abdomen. The head is very mobile. The mouthparts are adapted for sucking, licking or piercing. The compound eyes, composed of numerous small ocelli, are strikingly large. In many species they have a metallic sheen. There are also usually three simple eyes on top of the head. The antennae are generally rather short. Dipterous insects have only one pair of wings, the second pair are modified into club-shaped organs called halteres that function as sensory flight instruments. The metamorphosis is complete. Of the 130,000 species distributed throughout the world, more than 6,000 are found in central Europe.

Fleas (Aphaniptera) are small wingless insects (although they had winged ancestors) with a flat-sided body. The hind legs are adapted for jumping. The mouthparts are designed for piercing and sucking. Fleas are parasites. The metamorphosis is complete. The larvae feed on organic remnants. The pupa matures inside a cocoon made of feathers and hair. There are some 1,600 species worldwide; central Europe is inhabited by some 100 species of fleas.

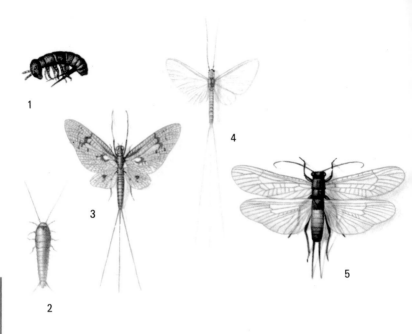

Class: **Insects**—Insecta

Order: **Springtails**—Collembola

1 Black Water Springtail *Podura aquatica.*
Common in Europe. Length 1 mm. Wingless.
Found in vast numbers on aquatic plants or directly on surface of streams, puddles, pools,
etc. Scaly body. Jumps by means of forked
caudal appendage. Female lays over 1,300
eggs. Larvae hatch in 12 days. Several generations a year. Lives on rotting vegetable debris.

Order: **Fish Moths**—Thysanura

2 Silverfish *Lepisma saccharina.* Very common.
Length about 10 mm. Often frequents buildings.
Nocturnal insect. Comes out after dark and
looks for scraps. Found in bathrooms and lavat-
ories, behind wallpaper, etc.

Order: **Mayflies**—Ephemeroptera

3 Common Mayfly *Ephemera vulgata.* Widespread in central Europe. Length 14—22 mm.
Black-spotted wings. Larvae live in slow-flowing
water, bent drainpipes, etc. Development takes
2 years. Swarming time May to August. Attracted by light.

4 White Mayfly *Polymitarcis virgo.* Common in
central Europe. Length 10—18 mm. Snow-white.
Larvae live in large rivers. Develops 2 years.
Swarming time August to September. Mass incidence. Adults live only 1—3 days. Female lays
eggs on surface of water. Larvae resemble adult
insects and live on small animals. Fully developed nymphs leave water and moult (sub-
imago). Next moult produces adult insect capable of further reproduction.

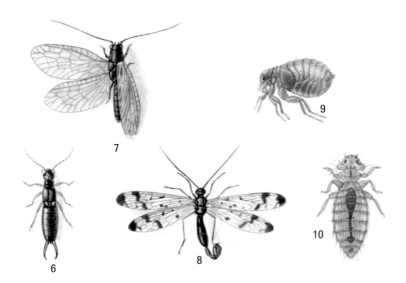

Order: **Stone-flies**—*Plecoptera*

5 *Perla abdominalis.* Common in central Europe. Length 17—28 mm. Found near large ponds and rivers. From April to June, adult insects cling to underside of leaves. Predacious larvae hide under stones on water bed. Mature larvae climb tree trunks, their dorsal skin splits and winged insects emerge. Female lays eggs on surface of water in the evening.

Order: **Earwigs**—Dermaptera

6 Common Earwig *Forficula auricularia.* Distributed all over Europe. Length 9—16 mm. Pincers at tip of abdomen used for defence or for unfolding membranous wings. Appears from April to October. Female lays piles of eggs in spaces under stones and guards both eggs and wingless larvae. Eats eggs of other insects and parts of plants.

Order: **Alderflies**—Megaloptera

7 Luteous Alderfly *Sialis flavilatera.* Lives all over Europe. Length 19—38 mm. Found near water in May and June. Larvae live in water, eat other insects and their larvae. Pupate in damp soil on bank. Adult insects live only few days. Female lays up to 2,000 eggs on rushes, hatched larvae drop into water. Development takes 2 years.

Order: **Snoutflies**—Mecoptera

8 Scorpion-fly *Panorpa communis.* Found all over Europe. Length about 20 mm. Male has tapering abdomen like scorpion's. Female lays up to 75 eggs in hollows in ground. Caterpillar-like larvae live in moss, etc. Eats vegetable and animal matter. Sometimes sucks wounded insects dry.

Order: **Fleas**—Aphaniptera

9 Human Flea *Pulex irritans.* Lives all over the world. Length about 4 mm. Wingless. Adults parasitic on man. After sucking blood, female lays eggs in crevices etc. Legless larvae live on organic debris in which they also pupate. Female lays 4—8 eggs daily for 3 months. Flea-bites turn red and swell.

Order: **Bird Lice** or **Biting Lice**—Mallophaga

10 Fowl-louse *Menopon gallinae.* Very common in Europe. Length 1—1.5 mm. Wingless. Lives in plumage of fowls, eats feathers, bites skin and sucks blood. Female attaches eggs to feathers. Occasionally, but not for long, can live as parasite on man.

Order: **Snakeflies**—Raphidioptera

1 Snakefly *Raphidia notata*. Distributed all over Europe. Length up to 30 mm. Inhabits woods, especially sunny outskirts. Appears during summer, from April. Female has long ovipositor. Catches insects and spiders. Flat larvae live behind bark and catch insects. Female lays up to 50 eggs on wood.

Order: **Nerve-winged Insects**—Neuroptera

2 Owl-fly *Ascalaphus macaronius*. Lives in warm regions, including central Europe. Length up to 30 mm. Found on sunny slopes etc. Appears in June. Catches small animals on wing. Larvae live on ground, in grass, and catch other insects, especially ants. Pupate in soil.

3 Ant Lion *Myrmeleon formicarius*. Abundant in central Europe. Wing span up to 75 mm. Adult insects live only from June to August. Female lays single eggs in sand. Larvae make funnel-shaped pits, in which they mainly trap ants, sucking them dry with their strong hollow jaws. Pupate in soil in sandy cocoon.

4 Green Lacewing *Chrysopa vulgaris*. Very common. Length about 20 mm. Flies mainly in evening. In autumn often seen at windows. Hunts plant lice. Female lays eggs on long stems near plant lice, on which larvae live 10—24 days before pupating. Two generations a year. Adults of second generation hibernate and are brownish, in spring greenish.

Order: **Cockroaches**—Blattodea

5 Croton Bug or **German Cockroach** *Blatella germanica*. Today distributed over whole of the world. Length 11—15 mm. Runs well but flies badly. Hides during day in buildings. Comes out after dark to look for food. Eats vegetable and animal matter, paper, leather, etc. Likes warmth. Reproduces whole year round. Female lays about 30 eggs in special capsule carried on its abdomen. Capsule shed after 14 days. After hibernating, larvae moult 6 times before maturing to adult insects.

6 Black-beetle or **Oriental Cockroach** *Blatta orientalis*. Found all over Europe. Length 19—30 mm. Inhabits old houses, bakeries, etc. Likes warmth. Occurs whole year round. Nocturnal insect. Lives on both vegetable and animal matter. Female lays eggs in capsules (ootheca). Life span up to 6 years.

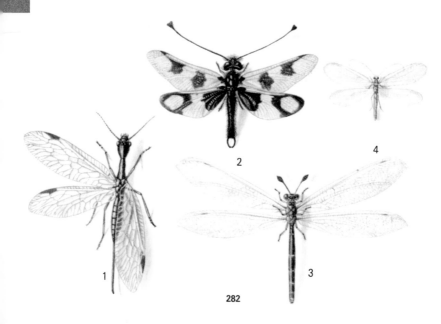

Order: **Mantids**—Mantodea

7 Praying Mantis *Mantis religiosa*. Inhabits only warmest parts of central Europe. Length of male 60 mm, female 75 mm. Lives on bushes. Slow-moving. Appears from June to September. Waits motionless for prey, seizes it with long forelimbs. Lives mainly on insects. In autumn, after pairing, female often devours male. Female lays eggs in capsules attached to twigs. Predacious larvae hatch in spring, mature in August.

Order: **Caddis-flies**—Trichoptera

8 Macro-caddisfly *Phrygaena grandis*. Abundant throughout central Europe. Wing span up to 70 mm. Appears near water from April to August. Female lays piles of eggs on underside of leaves near water surface. Larvae form cases from fragments of plants and pupate in these under water. Imagos emerge en masse, flutter over water and pair.

9 Rhomboid Caddis-fly *Limnophilus rhombicus*. Abundant in central Europe. Length 17 to 44 mm. Appears from May to September. Larvae make case of criss-cross fragments of bark, wood and leaves. Pupates under water. Imago-like pupa bites through cocoon envelope, floats to surface and immediately splits open, releasing adult insect. Adults pair in evening over water. Common fish food.

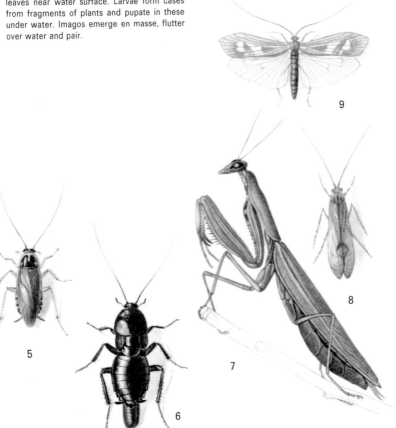

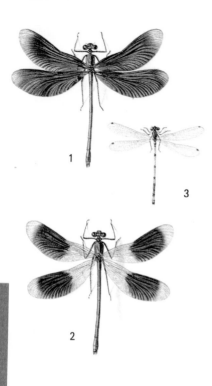

3 *Coenagrion puella.* Found everywhere in central Europe. Length 23—30 mm. Male has slim blue body, female greenish. Appears from May to end of September. Flies among reeds and tall grass beside water. Female lays eggs in plants, often submerging completely. Larvae live in stagnant or slow-flowing water. Develop one year. Mature nymph crawls out of water and after one more moult is transformed to adult insect, whose wings and abdomen soon grow to full length.

Sub-order: **Giant Dragonflies**—Anisoptera

4 Giant Dragonfly *Anax imperator.* Scattered over whole of Europe. Length up to 60 mm. Appears from June to August, often far from water. Swift, skilful flier. Catches insects on wing. Larvae live at bottom of stagnant water, are exceptionally predacious and even hunt small fish. Female lays eggs in plants, but does not submerge completely. Development takes one year.

5 Brown Dragonfly *Aeschna grandis.* Widely distributed in Europe. Length 49—60 mm. Green-blue with black spots. Appears from end of June to end of September. Frequents forest clearings, footpaths near ponds and rivers, etc. Develops 2—3 years. Predacious larvae live among aquatic plants at bottom of stagnant water. Often catch small fish or tadpoles.

6 *Gomplus vulgatissimus.* Abundant everywhere in central Europe. Length 33—37 mm. Appears from May to end of July. Flies quickly, catches insects on wing. Female lays eggs in water while flying. Relatively thick-bodied larvae breathe through intestinal gills. Predacious, catch chiefly insect larvae, small tadpoles and newt larvae. Usually take 3 years to develop.

7 *Libellula quadrimaculata.* Widely distributed in Europe. Length 27—32 mm. Appears from May to middle of August. Rapid, apparently aimless, zigzag flight. Catches insects on wing. Female lays eggs in water while flying. Stout, fat larvae live mainly at bottom of small ponds and pools. Development takes 2 years. Form of migration in large numbers over considerable distances observed.

Order: **Dragonflies**—Odonata

Sub-order: **Damselflies**—Zygoptera

1 Blue Damselfly *Calopteryx virgo.* Abundant all over central Europe. Length 34—39 mm. Male has blue wings, female brownish. Frequents flowing water and ponds. Appears from May to August. Female lays eggs in plants under water, often submerging completely to do so. Slim larvae, which take 2 years to develop, have three leaf-like caudal appendages. When fully developed, they crawl out, grip a reed and wait until dorsal skin splits, releasing adult insect.

2 *Calopteryx splendens.* Very common beside both stagnant and flowing water from May to September. Length 33—40 mm. Male has broad bluish band on wings. Larvae live in water. Develop in same way as preceding species.

8 *Libellula depressa.* Abundant local incidence in Europe. Length 22—28 mm. Flat abdomen, sky-blue in male, brownish in female. Appears from May to beginning of August. Found near ponds and rivers but also far from water. Female lays eggs on surface of stagnant water. Larva short, fat and grey-brown. Development takes 2 years. This species also often migrates in large numbers.

4

5

7

6

8

Order: **Straight-winged Insects**—Orthoptera

Family: **Green Grasshoppers**—Tettigoniidae

1 Katydid or **Green Grasshopper** *Tettigonia viridissima*. Common all over central Europe. Length 28—35 mm. Long antennae. Adult specimens can fly. Female has long ovipositor. Appears from July to October in lowlands and uplands. Males can often be heard chirping loudly in evening from tall trees, but often also during daytime. Female lays 70—100 eggs in soil. Nymphs live in meadows. Last moult before complete maturation end of July. Larvae and adult insects largely predacious. Catch different insects, occasionally also eat plants.

2 *Decticus verrucivorus*. Abundant in places. Length 22—35 mm. Spotted wings. Lives in grass or clover fields. Appears from June to September. Carnivorous. Nymphs often gregarious.

Family: **Crickets**—Gryllidae

3 Old World Field Cricket *Gryllus campestris*. Distributed over most of Europe. Length 20—25 mm. Lives in dry meadows and slopes in lowlands. Appears from May to July. Digs burrows as hideaways. Solitary, except at pairing time, when male chirps loudly to attract female. Female lays up to 300 eggs in ground with ovipositor. Nymphs hibernate, mature following spring. Lives on vegetable and flesh diet.

4 House Cricket *Acheta domestica*. Originally from Mediterranean region, brought to Europe for laboratory purposes. Length 15—25 mm. Frequents warm places, requires at least 10°C. Diverse diet. Female lays eggs in damp soil, etc., up to 4,000 during its 2 months' life span. According to temperature, nymphs are hatched in 8—30 days and moult 9—11 times before turning into adults. Male chirps. Does not fly very well but spreads easily.

Family: **Mole Crickets**—Gryllotalpidae

5 Common Mole Cricket *Gryllotalpa gryllotalpa*. Locally abundant over whole of Europe. Length 35—50 mm. Forelimbs resemble mole's. Flies clumsily. Adults found from May to September. Lives in earth and digs burrows. Male chirps on warm days. Female lays up to 300 eggs in underground chamber lined with saliva. Nymphs hibernate, mature following spring. Lives on vegetable and flesh diet. Garden pest in some places. Tries to get quickly under ground as it is awkward above it.

Family: **Field Grasshoppers**—Acrididae

6 *Stenobothrus lineatus*. Very common in central Europe. Length 16—23 mm. Lives in dry meadows and steppes. Appears from July to September. Males chirp by drawing teeth on inner aspect of femora over ridges on wing case. Female has ovipositor and lays eggs in ground. Eats plants, but does not do much damage.

7 *Omocestus viridulus.* Very common in central Europe. Length 13—24 mm. Particularly abundant in uplands. Found in dry places on hillsides and in meadows from July to September. Female greenish, male grey-brown. Lives on parts of plants, but does little damage. Eggs laid in ground.

8 *Psophus stridulus.* Abundant local incidence. Length 20—34 mm. Red underwings, seen only when it soars into air. Appears from July to October in dry, sunny, often rocky places, in forest clearings and on hillsides. Male flies with creaking sound. Female lays eggs in piles in ground, wrapping them, like other grasshoppers, in frothy secretion. Eggs hibernate. Larvae, hatched in spring, have huge appetite. Adult form attained after 5 moults. Vegetarian.

9 *Oedipoda coerulescens.* Abundant in places. Length 16—24 mm. Bluish underwings. Seen from July to September.

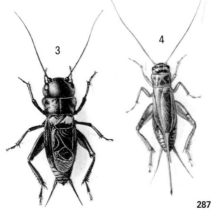

287

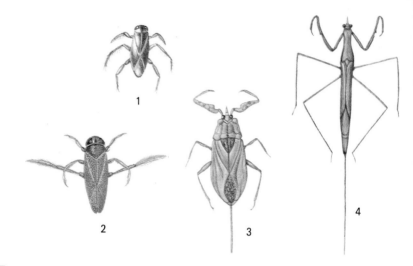

Order: **Bugs**—Heteroptera

Family: **Water-boatmen**—Corixidae

1 Water-boatman *Corixa punctata*. Common all over central Europe. Length about 10 mm. Found in every large pool or pond. Occurs often in winter, below ice. Flies on summer evenings, frequently enters open windows. Produces creaking sounds under water.

Family: **Back-swimmers**—Notonectidae

2 *Notonecta glauca*. Distributed over whole of central Europe. Length about 20 mm, spindle-shaped body. Inhabits stagnant water. Rows with long hindlegs, usually upside down. Predacious. Hunts other insects, stabs them with proboscis and sucks them dry. Its prick can be felt. Flies on summer nights.

Family: **Water-scorpions**—Nepidae

3 Water-scorpion *Nepa cinerea*. Very common in fishpond regions. Length 20—25 mm. Pincer-like forelimbs for catching prey, e.g. insects and fish fry. Long breathing tube at end of body. Lives at bottom of stagnant or slow-flowing water. Sucks prey dry.

4 Water Stick-insect *Ranatra linearis*. Occurs in fishpond regions, at bottom of stagnant water. Long, stick-like body with long legs. Length 30—40 mm. Breathing tube at end of body. Predacious. Catches aquatic insects and larvae with forelimbs and sucks them dry. Stabs painfully.

Family: **Pond Skaters**—Gerridae

5 Common Water-strider *Gerris lacustris*. Common European insect. Length about 20 mm. Found on surface of stagnant water or creeks. End of body and legs covered with non-wetting hairs allowing it to run swiftly over water surface. Predacious, catches insects on surface. Reproduces on land.

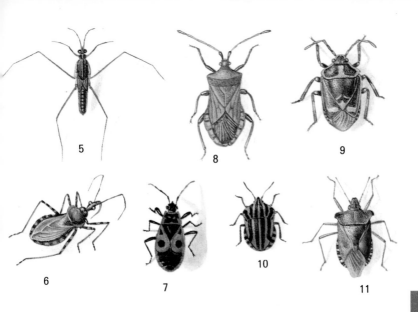

5

8

9

6

7

10

11

Family: **Soldier-bugs**—Reduviidae

6 Red Assassin-bug *Rhynocoris iracundus.* Widespread in central Europe. Length up to 15 mm. Slim body, long legs. Lives on sunny grassy slopes, frequents umbelliferous flowers and other plants. Predacious. Catches insects and sucks their body juices. Lies motionless in wait for prey. Stabs painfully.

Family: **Fire-bugs**—Pyrrhocoridae

7 Common Fire-bug *Pyrrhocoris apterus.* Abundant everywhere in central Europe. Length about 10 mm. Found most often at foot of lime- and chestnut-trees, behind loose bark and on walls. Appears from early spring until late autumn. Occurs in masses, together with nymphs. Lives on juices of dead insects, fruit and seeds.

Family: **Marginated Bugs**—Coreidae

8 Marginated Bug *Coreus marginatus.* Very widely distributed. Length about 15 mm. Has almost square head. Flies on warm days. Lives on bushes and plants. Emits characteristic acrid odour. Vegetarian.

Family: **Stink-bugs**—Pentatomidae

9 Cabbage-bug *Eurydema oleraceum.* Common all over Europe. Length 5.5—7 mm. Metallic lustre, somewhat variable colouring. Occurs on outskirts of fields, etc. Sucks plant juices and in large numbers causes great damage. Mainly attacks brassicaceous plants. Important pest.

10 Striped Bug *Graphosoma lineatum.* Inhabits southern Europe and warm parts of central Europe. Length about 10 mm. Found in gardens on carrot plants, in forests on flowers, raspberry canes, etc. Summer insects. In south does damage to cereals.

11 Red-legged Stink-bug *Pentatoma rufipes.* Very common. Length 13—16 mm. Appears in summer in gardens and woods, especially on oaks and alders. Hunts, stabs and sucks caterpillars, but lives mainly on plant juices. Damages berry-bearing plants, cherry-trees, etc. Nymphs hibernate behind scales of bark.

289

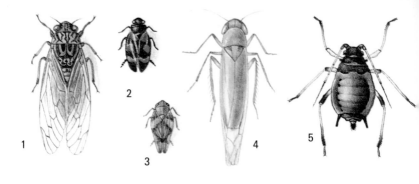

Order: **Plant-bugs**—Homoptera

Sub-order: **Cicadas**—Cicadoidea

1 Mountain Cicada *Cicadetta montana*. Inhabits only warm parts of central Europe, e.g. Danube basin. Length about 25 mm. Males have special chirping apparatus between thorax and abdomen. Punctures bark and twigs. Ground-dwelling larvae suck roots of trees. Development takes several years.

2 Blood-red Spittle-bug *Cercopis sanguinolenta*. Very common in some parts of central Europe. Length about 10 mm. Lives on plants in lowland meadows. Appears from June to August. Female lays eggs in grass. Larvae hatch in spring and suck plant juices. Larvae secrete liquid into which they pump air, turning it into protective froth.

3 Froth-bug *Philaenus spumarius*. Occurs over whole of Europe. Length about 10 mm. Frequents meadows and margins of forests. Female lays eggs chiefly in willow twigs. Hatched larvae suck these twigs. Greenish larva lives in protective froth. Matures after 5 moults. Adult insect can fly and hop well.

4 Green Leaf-hopper *Empoasca decipiens*. Abundant all over Europe. Length about 3 mm. Small and inconspicuous. Appears from June to September in deciduous woods and gardens. In large numbers does damage by sucking trees. Over 200 similar species in Europe, many of which are injurious to cereals and other crops.

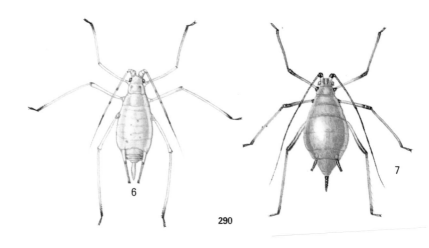

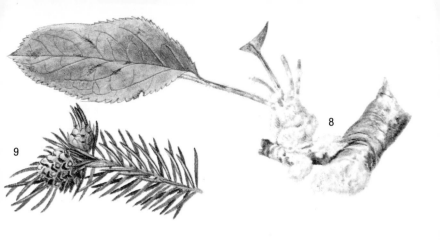

Sub-order: **Plant-lice**—Aphidoidea

5 Black Bean Aphid *Aphis fabae*. Very common in Europe. Small and black. Spends winter on spindle-trees, from which winged females fly to poppies, sugar-beet plants, etc. and suck their juices. In large numbers causes plants to wither and die.

6 *Acyrthosiphon onobrychis*. Abundant in central Europe. Summer insect, occurs mainly on peas but also on other plants. Sucks juice in stems. Like other plant-lice, unfertilized females produce live young (parthenogenesis), fertilized females lay autumn eggs. Males, which are smaller than females, hatch from fertilized eggs. Colony is founded by wingless female hatched from fertilized egg.

7 *Megoura vicia*. Common summer insect, forms colonies on vetches, etc. Biology similar to preceding species.

8 Woolly Aphid *Eriosoma lanigerum*. Widespread over most of Europe, but originally from America. Chiefly attacks apple-trees. Lives in colonies which look like white tufts of cottonwool. Actual body brown, contains blood-red fluid. Larva hibernates behind bark or in ground. During summer reproduces without fertilization. Males and egg-laying females hatch in autumn. One of the most dangerous fruit pests.

9 Yellow Fig Gall-louse *Sacchiphantes abietis*. Widely distributed in Europe. Length about 1.5 mm. Lives permanently on firs. By sucking twigs induces formation of scaly galls. All generations, fertilized and unfertilized, lay only eggs. Fertilized female of last generation lays single egg, larva of which hibernates.

Sub-order: **Scale-insects**—Coccoidea

10 *Eulecanium corni*. Abundant in Europe. Length of female about 5 mm, male 2.5 mm. Lives mainly on plum-trees, ashes, hazels, etc. Wingless female firmly sessile on bark. Lays eggs under its pustulate body. Winged male eats no food. Larvae, after hibernating on roots of trees, suck twigs and females acquire pustulate, sessile form.

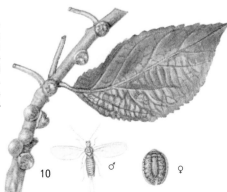

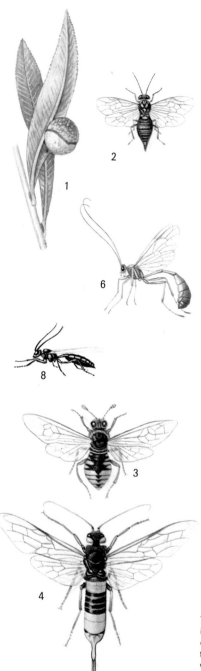

Order: **Wasps, Ants and Bees**—Hymenoptera

Family: **Sawflies**—Tenthredinidae

1 *Pontania viminalis.* Small sawfly, very common round water. Female lays eggs on underside of blade of willow leaves. This induces formation of reddish galls, harmless to trees.

2 Lesser Fir Sawfly *Lygaeonematus abietinus.* Length 4.5—6 mm. Appears at the end of April. Males hatched first. Female lays up to 100 eggs in young fir needles. Greenish larvae, hatched in 4 days, devour needles. In June pupate in mould, in cocoon. Pest.

Family: **Cimbicid Sawflies**—Cimbicidae

3 Cimbicid Sawfly *Cimbex femorata.* Resembles large wasp but has club-tipped antennae. Bright green larva with red-striped back nibbles birch leaves, hibernates on branch in tough, parchment-like brown cocoon and pupates in it following spring. Does no damage.

Family: **Wood Wasps**—Siricidae

4 Horse-tail *Urocerus gigas.* Common, very striking, over 40 mm long, with cylindrical body. Female bores holes up to 1.5 cm deep in healthy fir wood with its long ovipositor. In each hole lays 4 eggs — total up to 350. Appears from June to August. Larvae gnaw tunnels in wood, plug them with debris. Pupate after 2—3 years. Adult insect bites way out, often after wood has been processed. Pest.

Family: **Ichneumon Flies**—Ichneumonidae

5 Giant Ichneumon Fly *Rhyssa persuasoria.* Distributed over large part of Europe and Asia. Length up to over 40 mm. Inhabits large pinewoods. Female looks specifically for wood wasp larvae, pushes ovipositor into tunnel, stabs larva and lays egg in its body. Hatched larva then devours wood wasp larva. Very useful insect.

6 Sickle Wasp *Ophion luteus.* Striking appearance, common in Europe. Length about 30 mm. Curved, flat-sided abdomen. Occurs in clearings, in evening often attracted into houses by light. Parasite of large moth caterpillars. Female stabs caterpillar, lays eggs in its body and larvae devour caterpillar.

Family: **Braconids**—Braconidae

7 Vipionid *Apanteles glomeratus.* Tiny summer insect occurring in woods, gardens and meadows. Female lays eggs en masse in butterfly caterpillars, e.g. whites, fritillaries, etc. Minute larvae first of all live on host's adipose bodies. La-

292

ter bore way out, immediately spin yellow cocoon and pupate. Caterpillar often surrounded
by cluster of cocoons.

Family: **Aphid Wasps**—Aphidiidae

8 Aphid Wasp *Diaeretus rapae*. Very small and
very common. Female lays egg in abdomen of
plant-louse. Hatched larva devours contents of
host's body and pupates inside it. Adult insect
leaves dead host through hole which can often
be seen on shrivelled plant-lice. Very useful
species.

Family: **Gall-wasps**—Cynipidae

9 Oak Gall-fly *Cynips quercusfolii*. Abundant
everywhere. Adult insect inconspicuous, but
eggs give rise to galls, housing larvae, on underside of oak leaves ('oak-apples'). Larva pupates
in autumn and adults often hatch early in winter.
Females emerging at end of February lay unfertilized eggs in buds and these develop into gall-
wasps of both sexes. Males measure only about
2 mm. Fertilized females lay eggs on leaves and
cycle is repeated.

10 Robin's Pin Cushion or **Bedeguar Gall** *Diplo-*
lepis rosae. Most widely distributed gallwasp.
Length 4—5 mm. Adult insect seldom noticed,
but known from moss-like reddish or greenish
galls containing larvae on rose-bushes and dog-
roses. Only one generation known — females
reproducing by parthenogenesis.

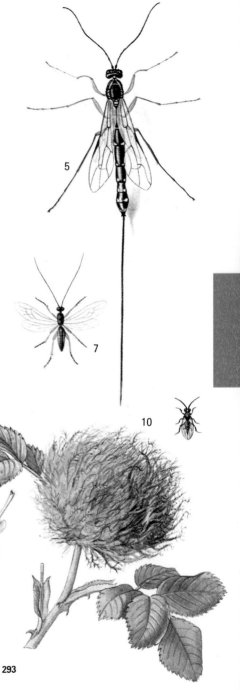

5

7

10

9

Family: **Beetle-wasps**—Scoliidae

1 Yellow-headed Beetle-wasp *Scolia flavifrons*. Huge wasp living in warm parts of Europe — in central Europe in south-east and south. Length about 50 mm. On sunny days can be seen on flowers. Female lays eggs on larvae of rhinoceros beetle. Hatched larva devours host's body from within and pupates beside its remains.

Family: **Mutillids** or **Velvet Ants**—Mutillidae

2 Velvet Ant *Mutilla europaea*. Common in central Europe. Slight resemblance to ant. Brightly coloured. Female wingless. Male visits flowers, female crawls on ground looking for bumble-bee nests. Lays eggs in body of bumble-bee larvae.

Family: **True Wasps**—Vespidae

3 Hornet *Vespa crabro*. Large wasp, abundant in places. Mainly inhabits old forests. Builds large, yellow-brown, papery nest in tree hollows, nesting-boxes, etc. Fertilized female hibernates in hiding-place. In spring lays foundations of nest by scratching away rotting wood and sticking it together with saliva, and sets up first comb. First larvae develop into workers which continue building nest. Males and females hatch in autumn. After females have been fertilized, whole community except females dies. Hornets are predacious, attack other insects. Their sting is dangerous.

4 Pollistes Wasp *Polistes gallica*. Moderately large wasp, abundant in sunny places. Forms simple papery comb with several cells. Nest attached by stalk to base, usually wall, rock, etc., often also bush. Larvae develop into workers which lay eggs giving rise to males — drones. In the Alps and further north often builds nest in enclosed space, holes, nesting-boxes, etc.

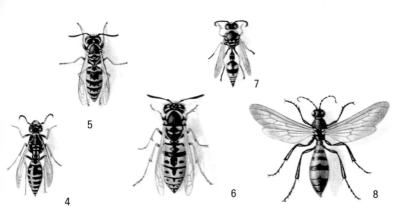

5

4

6

7

8

5 Common Wasp *Paravespula vulgaris*. Commonest ground-dwelling wasp. Lives in large colonies founded by female. Builds first cells on stalk in hole in ground and lays eggs. Feeds hatched larvae for 20 days. Workers hatched 20 days after pupating. They extend nest, add storeys separated by stalk-like supports. Carry away grains of sand, etc., to widen hole. Workers can number up to 2,000. Nest has 5—14 combs. Life in community expires in autumn. Females — queens — hibernate in tree hollows, rooms in houses, etc.

6 German Wasp *Paravespula germanica*. Common all over Europe. Builds underground nests in fields. In south huge nests with about 60,000 members. In September nest contains average of 1,600 workers, 1,600 males and 700 females. Likes warmth, does not fly in cold weather. Diurnal insect. Lives on sweet fruit juice, nectar, etc. Offspring fed mainly on insects. Very aggressive if disturbed, attacks all intruders.

Family: **Potter Wasps**—Eumenidae

7 Potter Wasp *Eumenes coarctatus*. Inhabits whole of Europe. Solitary wasp. Length 11 to 15 mm. Builds fat-bellied, short-necked nest of clay and saliva on forest bushes or heather. Feeds larvae on small, hairless caterpillars, especially of geometers. Larvae frequently parasitized by other wasps (fire wasps).

Family: **Digger Wasps**—Psammocharidae

8 Brown Spider Wasp *Psammocharus fuscus*. Common in warm places all over Europe. Length 10—14 mm. Seen early in spring on flowering sallows. In sandy spots digs holes ending in chamber for larva, for which it brings spiders. Paralyzes even large spiders with sting, when helpless drags them to nest. Though paralyzed, spider sometimes lives over a month and larva feeds on its body.

Family: **Ants**—Formicidae

1 Red Wood Ant *Formica rufa*. Abundant in Europe. Several races with different biology. In one, only one female in nest, in another up to 5,000 females and annual production of up to 2 million individuals. Builds large, domed nest of conifer needles, leaves, etc. Winged males and females hold nuptial flight in summer. Omnivorous. Catch any form of life they can. Useful, destroy all insects within distance of 20 m from nest. Length of workers 4—9 mm, females 9—11 mm.

2—4 Black or **Garden Ant** *Lasius niger*. Very widespread. Worker (4) 3—5 mm., male (2) and female (3) much larger. Underground nest with superstructure above ground. Pairing on warm summer days. After nuptial flight return to ground, females shed wings and males mostly die. Female founds new community and as soon as first workers are hatched confines itself only to egg-laying. After a time new males and females are hatched and cycle is repeated. Omnivorous. Partiality for secretions of plant-lice.

Family: **Thread-waisted Wasps**—Sphegidae

5 Red-bearded Fan Wasp *Ammophila sabulosa*. In Europe abundant in dry, sandy places. Length 18—20 mm. Digs burrows about 3 cm long with chamber at end for larva. On leaving covers hole with small stone. Brings paralyzed pine hawk caterpillars for larva. Sits astride caterpillar and tugs it with jaws. Drags it into nest and attaches egg to its body. Firmly fills in entrance to nest and then builds another.

6 Bee-killer Wasp *Philanthus triangulum*. Inhabits warm parts of Europe. Length 12 to 16 mm. Occurs chiefly on sandy slopes, digs nests. Pounces on bees, falls with them to ground, quickly paralyses them and takes them to larvae. In large numbers damaging to honeybee population.

7 Sand Wasp *Bembex rostrata*. In central Europe common in warm, sandy places. Robust body. Prolongated upper lip. Digs tunnels up to 40 cm long in sandy slopes or moors. Usually lives in colonies. Closes entrance with sand but finds nest unerringly. Catches flies, paralyses them with sting and takes them to larva. Also catches large gadflies and hover-flies. Larvae have huge appetite. Although well concealed, nest is found by scorpion-fly which rakes it open and lays egg on sand wasp larva.

Family: **Cuckoo Wasps**—Chrysididae

8 Fire Wasp *Chrysis ignita*. Very common in southern and central Europe. Length about 5 mm. Has concave abdomen and can curl up if in danger. Female has protrusible ovipositor. Frequents sunny walls, fences, etc. Looks for nests of solitary wasps, especially mason wasps of the genus *Odynerus*. Female forces way into nest, places egg on larva and quickly leaves. Fire Wasp larva has large, hard head and jaws and lives on host's body juices. On maturing it pupates and adult insect emerges in spring. Adult Fire Wasp lives on nectar. Flies during summer.

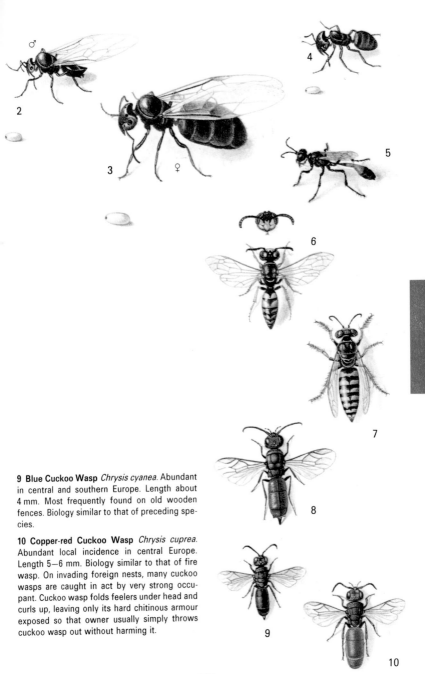

9 Blue Cuckoo Wasp *Chrysis cyanea.* Abundant in central and southern Europe. Length about 4 mm. Most frequently found on old wooden fences. Biology similar to that of preceding species.

10 Copper-red Cuckoo Wasp *Chrysis cuprea.* Abundant local incidence in central Europe. Length 5—6 mm. Biology similar to that of fire wasp. On invading foreign nests, many cuckoo wasps are caught in act by very strong occupant. Cuckoo wasp folds feelers under head and curls up, leaving only its hard chitinous armour exposed so that owner usually simply throws cuckoo wasp out without harming it.

Family: **Bees**—Apidae

1 Blue Carpenter Bee *Xylocopa violacea*. Inhabits southern Europe and warm parts of central Europe. Resembles large bumble-bee. Has black-brown wings with violet sheen. Female bores vertical shafts up to 30 cm deep in old wood, dividing them into chambers with partitions made of wood debris and saliva. Usually 12 chambers in each of which bee places stock of food and lays one egg.

2 Leaf-cutter Bee *Megachile centuncularis*. Distributed over warm parts of Europe. Length 10—12 mm. Female gnaws tunnels in old wood, lines them with fragments of leaves cut from bushes, chiefly dog-roses and garden roses. Places first cell on floor of tunnel, fills it with pollen, lays egg and closes cell with leaf. 'Cylinder' with 8—10 cells formed in tunnel.

3 Potter Bee *Anthidium manicatum*. Lives in warmer parts of Europe. With partly hairless, yellow-striped abdomen resembles wasp. Male has 'notched' abdomen and is larger than female. Lines nest with plant fluff.

4 Horned Bee *Eucera longicornis*. Lives in southern Europe and warm parts of central Europe. Length 10—12 mm. Locally abundant. Male has extremely long antennae. Appears in spring on sunny slopes and hillsides. Favours plants with composite flowers. Has very long mouth parts and can suck nectar from deep flowers.

5 Black Burrowing Bee *Andrena carbonaria*. Abundant all over Europe except for extreme north. Solitary bee. Length 10—12 mm. Appears early in spring. Likes dandelions. Digs nest in ground, often in colonies. Long, slanting passages branch off into several side-chambers, each containing pollen and one egg.

6 Hairy-legged Mining Bee *Dasypoda hirtipes*. Fairly common in central Europe. Collects so much pollen on long hairs on hindlimbs that appears to be wearing trousers. Builds underground nest like preceding species.

7 Mourner Bee or **Armed Melecta** *Melecta armata*. Abundant in central Europe. Length 10—12 mm. Appears early in spring. Female stays near burrowing bees, enters their nests and lays egg before occupant can close chamber. Hatched larva consumes food stocks and burrowing bee larva starves to death.

1

2

3

8 Digger Bumble-bee *Bombus terrestris*. Very common all over Europe. After hibernating female lays foundations of nest in mouse-holes, etc, up to 1.5 m underground. Lines nest with leaves, moss, etc., found in hole. Builds waxy chambers and fills them with pollen and nectar. Larvae also receive additional food. Up to 150 workers and over 100 young females hatch in 20 days. Workers die in autumn, males, old and young females go into hiding and hibernate.

9 Rock Bumble-bee *Bombus lapidarius*. Widely distributed in central Europe. Black with red-tipped abdomen. Nests underground, in piles of stones, rock crevices, etc. Not more than 300 individuals in nest.

10 Honeybee *Apis mellifica*. Universal insect, probably originally from India. Forms permanent community, always with one female — queen. In summer large number of males (drones) and up to 70,000 workers. Only queen lays eggs, in cells in waxy comb. Three types of cells, for workers, males and females. Queen lays up to 1,000 eggs daily in summer — total for one season up to 80,000. If queen is lost, workers rear new one. Development rapid, for workers 20 days. Queen lives 3—4 years. Swarm once or several times a year, after queen has prepared eggs for new queens. Old queen leaves hive and, accompanied by some workers, forms new community.

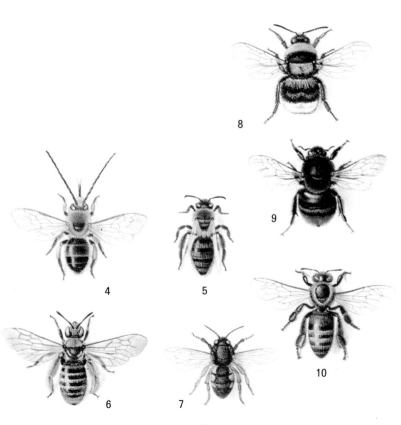

8

9

4

5

6

7

10

Order: **Beetles**—Coleoptera

Family: **Tiger Beetles**—Cicindelidae

1 *Cicindela campestris.* Locally abundant in Europe. Length 12—16 mm. Very large, striking mandibles. Appears from April to June. Frequents sunny, sandy places, paths, deserted quarries, etc. Runs about swiftly looking for prey, spots it reliably at distance of up to 15 cm. Catches mainly insect larvae, spiders and worms. If disturbed, immediately flies away but does not fly in cold weather. Larvae live in burrows up to 2 m deep in clay or sandy soil. Larva has strongly sclerotized head. Waits at entrance to hole for prey (chiefly various insects), seizes it and devours it in burrow. Holds itself fast in passage by means of boss on abdomen. Development of larva takes 2—3 years. Pupates in July, beetles are hatched 4 weeks later and reproduce further following spring.

2 *Cicindela hybrida.* Lives mainly in forested regions. Length 12—14 mm. Beetles found in May and June on sandy forest paths and moors. Biology similar to that of preceding species.

3 *Cicindela silvatica.* Common in places. Length 14—16 mm. Appears in June on forest paths, in clearings, etc., mainly in pine-woods. Biology as for *Cicindela campestris.*

Family: **Ground Beetles**—Carabidae

4 *Carabus hortensis.* Locally abundant in central Europe. Length 24—30 mm. Found in forests and gardens, on bushy slopes, etc. Nocturnal predator. Catches insects, insect larvae, worms and small molluscs. Hides during day behind bark, under stones, etc. Like all ground beetles likes damp environment. In dry, waterless places dies in a few days. Long-bodied, large-jawed larvae also predacious. Catches other insect larvae, worms, etc.

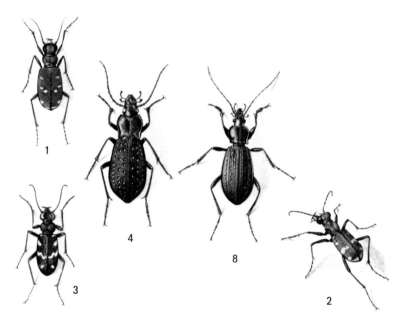

1

4

8

3

2

5 Goldsmith *Carabus auratus*. Abundant in parts of central Europe, particularly Germany, but absent east of Oder. Length 22—26 mm. Seen mainly in May and June, in meadows, fields and gardens. Prefers clayey soil. Also found at higher altitudes. Often hunts in daytime. Eats worms, molluscs and soft parts of insects. Attacks cockchafers when laying eggs. All members of *Carabus* genus spray chewed parts of prey with gastric juice which quickly decomposes connective tissue and organs, making them easy to imbibe. Several beetles may attack a large worm. In spring and summer female lays single eggs in holes in ground — total about 50. Larvae, hatched in 8—10 days, are very predacious. Pupate in chamber in ground. Newly emerged beetles hibernate from end of August, majority of adult beetles die. Development from egg to young beetle takes 78 days.

6 *Carabus coriaceus*. Largest central-European ground beetle. Length up to 40 mm. Occurs in forests mainly in July and August. Nocturnal insect. Hides during day under stones, fallen trees, etc. In rainy weather crawls on to paths. Beetle and larva are both predacious.

7 Violet Ground Beetle *Carabus violaceus*. Very common in central Europe. Length 25—35 mm. Appears mainly in June and July near human dwellings, often found in sheds, cellars, etc. If handled ejects acrid fluid.

8 *Carabus cancellatus*. Very common everywhere in central Europe. Length 17—26 mm. Appears chiefly in May in woods, fields and gardens. Runs very quickly, 1 metre in 5—7 sec. Hides during day under stones, behind bark, etc. Very useful, destroys Colorado Beetles. One specimen devours 9 Colorado Beetle larvae daily, i.e. more than its own weight. Average time of development from egg to beetle takes 71 days under artificial breeding conditions.

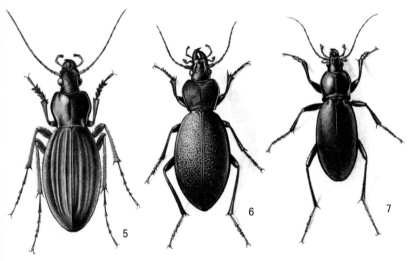

5

6

7

Family: **Ground Beetles**—Carabidae

1 Searcher or **Caterpillar Hunter** *Calosoma sycophanta*. Distributed over practically whole of Europe. Length 24—30 mm. Very handsome beetle. Predacious. Climbs trees in search of prey, chiefly caterpillars. Female after hibernating lays 100—600 eggs. Larvae, hatched in 3—10 days, are likewise highly predacious. In 14 days one beetle (and also one larva) consumes about 40 large caterpillars. In June larva pupates in ground. Adult beetle hatched in September, does not emerge into open until following year in May. Early in July beetles leave trees and again burrow up to depth of 50 cm in ground and hibernate. Beetle lives 2—3 years. Inhabits both deciduous and conifer woods at low and high altitudes.

2 Lesser Searcher *Calosoma inquisitor*. Found everywhere in central Europe. Length 15 to 18 mm. Lives primarily in oak-woods in lowlands. In years with a high incidence of caterpillars appears in great numbers already at end of April or beginning of May. Frequents tree tops, catches mainly caterpillars of geometers and other harmful moths. Retires to burrow in ground at beginning of July and hibernates. Larvae likewise predacious.

3 Bombardier Beetle *Brachynus crepitans*. Common in central Europe. Length 6—9 mm. Several individuals always live in company under stones in warm, sunny spots. When in danger, discharges from anal gland volatile fluid which turns to blue smoke with audible bang. Such 'salvoes' reliably frighten small foes away. The secretion burns and slightly resembles nitric acid.

4 *Pterostichus vulgaris*. Very widely distributed. Length 14—20 mm. Hides during day under flat stones etc. in damp, shady places. Runs quickly. Abundant everywhere, especially in central Europe.

5 *Zabrus gibbus*. Very common everywhere in central Europe. Length 14—16 mm. Adult beetles cling to cereal plants and devour grains. Larvae nibble young spring shoots or grass. In daytime both larvae and beetles hide in holes dug in ground.

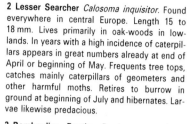

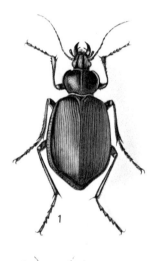

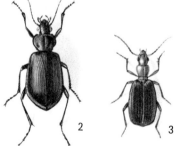

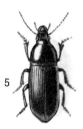

Family: **Water Beetles**—Dytiscidae

6 Tiger Water Beetle *Dytiscus marginalis.* Common all over Europe. Length 30—35 mm. Male has widened tarsi. Inhabits ponds and pools etc. with abundant aquatic vegetation. Female makes slits in plant stems and into each pushes one egg. Larva has three-sided head with powerful, hooked mandibles, used for sucking tadpoles, small fish, etc. Beetles also predacious. Larva pupates beside water. Beetles fly in evening.

7 *Acilius sulcatus.* Distributed over whole of Europe. Length about 18 mm. Inhabits stagnant water with at least a little vegetation. Flies at night and sometimes visits man-made pools. Does damage to fish roes. Larvae, likewise predacious, lie in wait for prey among tangled aquatic plants.

Family: **Whirligig Beetles**—Gyrinidae

8 Common Whirligig Beetle *Gyrinus natator.* Common in places. Length 5—7 mm. Small but conspicuous for its gyrating movements on surface of still water. Dives like lightning when in danger. Predacious, catches small insects. Flies well. Larvae have hollow, hooked mandibles. Beetles usually gregarious.

Family: **Water Scavenger Beetles**—Hydrophilidae

9 Great Black Water Beetle *Hydrous piceus.* Locally common in central Europe. Length 35—45 mm. Inhabits stagnant water with plenty of vegetation. Beetle partly vegetarian but eats also fish roes. Female lays eggs in special capsule made of secretory substance and containing about 50 eggs. Larvae, hatched in 16 days, are predacious.

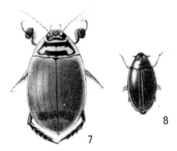

7

8

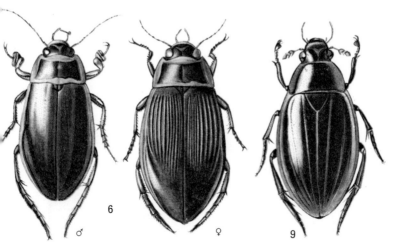

6

♂

♀

9

Family: **Rover Beetles**—Staphylinidae

1 *Staphylinus caesareus.* Widely distributed all over central Europe. Length 15—20 mm. Summer insect. Adult beetles found on putrefying flesh, rotting matter, etc. Beetles and larvae live on decaying matter but also attack insects, worms and molluscs. Larvae resemble adult beetles but have no wings or wing sheaths.

2 *Oxyporus rufus.* Distributed all over central Europe. Length 7—11 mm. Abounds in different mushrooms starting to decompose. Larvae also live in large numbers in mushrooms. One of the causes of 'wormy' mushrooms.

Family: **Sexton and Carrion Beetles**—Silphidae

3 Common Sexton or **Gravedigger Beetle** *Necrophorus vespillo.* Common European beetle. Length 12—22 mm. In evening and at night beetles look for animal carcass and scrape away earth under body until animal is buried. Female then lays eggs on body and larvae live on putrefying flesh. Larvae pupate in chamber in ground. Beetles often infested by mites of *Gamasus* genus.

4 German Gravedigger Beetle *Necrophorus germanicus.* Locally and sporadically found in Europe. Length 20—30 mm. Found under carcasses of larger animals, e.g. hares, rabbits, etc. Very retiring. Flies only at night. One of the largest but rarest members of this family.

5 Black Carrion Beetle *Phosphuga atrata.* Widespread in central Europe. Length 12 to 16 mm. Wing sheaths have three longitudinal ridges. Found from May under stones, paper,

1

2

3

4

etc., in fields and on paths. Often crawls in open. Lives on dead snails and worms but sometimes attacks even live ones. In danger releases malodorous substance.

6 Four-spot Carrion Beetle *Xylodrepa quadripunctata.* Very common in central Europe. Length 12—14 mm. Inhabits oak-woods. Appears in spring. Lives on trees, attacks and eats caterpillars. Beetles disappear in June and are replaced by flat, predacious, caterpillar-eating larvae. At end of summer larvae pupate in ground. Beetles hatch in autumn, hibernate in ground and emerge following spring.

Family: **Steel** or **Hister Beetles**—Histeridae

7 Steel Beetle *Hister unicolor.* Distributed all over central Europe. Length 7—9 mm. Very hard body. Beetles frequently live in cow dung, horse manure, etc. Catch and eat small insects. Many other species in Europe, some with black, red-spotted wing sheaths.

Family: **Carpet Beetles**—Dermestidae

8 Larder Beetle *Dermestes lardarius.* Carried with furs all over world. Length 6—9 mm. Found in stores, households and open country. Larva's back thickly covered with long hairs. In open larvae live on remnants of skin of dead animals, on feathers, etc. Also found in collections of hides, stuffed birds, etc. Development often takes only 6 weeks. Beetles and larvae frequently found on food remnants, e.g. cheese, meat, etc.

9 Tallow Beetle *Anthrenus museorum.* Distributed all over Europe. Length 2—3 mm. Spherical body. Common pest in natural history collections. Damage done by both beetle and larva. Larvae 5 mm long and hairy. Beetles often seen in flowers.

10 Carpet Beetle *Attagenus pellio.* Occurs everywhere. Length 4—7 mm. Very dangerous to furs, stuffed animals, carpets, upholstery, etc. Often found trying to get out of window. Hairy larva about 5 mm long. Adults often seen also on flowers. In the illustration the rare species *A. punctatus* is shown.

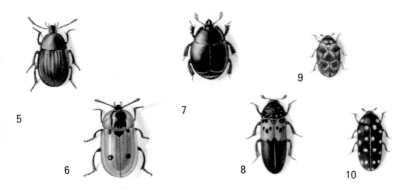

5

6

7

8

9

10

Family: **Stag Beetles**—Lucanidae

1 Common Stag Beetle *Lucanus cervus*. Inhabits whole of central Europe, from south of northern Europe as far west as Portugal. Length of male 37—75 mm, female 30—45 mm. Inhabits oak-woods and mixed forests. Female lays eggs in rotting oak stumps and trunks. Blind larvae develop 3—5 years and attain length of up to 10 cm. Future beetle's sex already discernible in pupa. Beetles hatch in autumn but do not leave hiding place until spring. By day frequent tree trunks with flowing sap. Fly in evening.

2 Balkan Stag Beetle *Dorcus parallelopipedus*. Distributed over large part of Europe. Length 20—32 mm. Abundant in places with sufficient old wood for development of larvae. Beetles rest on branches during day, fly only in late afternoon and evening. Appear at end of April and are still found in September. Larvae develop in rotting wood.

Family: **Chafers**—Scarabaeidae

3 Horned Dung Beetle *Copris lunaris*. Found in warmer parts of central Europe. Length 15—23 mm. Male has pointed horn on head. Mainly frequents cow dung. Makes chamber below dung from which female prepares food stocks for larvae.

4 Dung Beetle *Aphodius fimetarius*. Widely distributed over whole of Europe, Asia and North America. Length 5—8 mm. Female lays eggs in cow or horse dung which provides food for larvae. Some individuals hibernate and can often already be seen on sunny days at beginning of March.

1

5 Great Dor Beetle *Geotrupes stercorosus.* Inhabits whole of Europe. Length 12—19 mm. Exclusively forest-dweller, usually found on carcasses, mushrooms, etc. In May and June digs vertical shaft up to 60 cm deep, with side-arms, below excreta. Female fills passages with dung and lays eggs. Larvae live on dung, hibernate and do not pupate until following year.

6 Common Cockchafer or **May-bug** *Melolontha melolontha.* Native of Europe. Length 20 to 30 mm. From May to June female lays 3 clutches of 15—30 eggs in ground. Larvae (grubs) develop 2—3 years and then pupate. Hatched beetle spends winter in ground and emerges following spring. Grubs eat small roots. Beetles nibble leaves of trees. Fly in evening. Usually swarm in middle of June. Incidence of cockchafers correlated to whether population development takes 3 or 4 years.

7 June-bug *Rhizotrogus solstitialis.* Distributed all over Europe. Length 14—18 mm. Very abundant. Flies after dusk, in some years in large numbers. Appears from June to beginning of August. Female lays eggs in July, in soft soil. Larvae, hatched about one month later, eat grass and cereal roots, etc. Pupate in spring of third year. Adults eat leaves of fruit trees. Important pest.

8 Walker *Polyphylla fullo.* Occurs in central Europe and southern England. Length 25 to 36 mm. Inhabits sandy lowlands. Female lays 25—40 eggs in sandy soil from June to August. Larvae eat grass roots. Pupate after 3 years. Three weeks later, in June, adult beetles fly out after dusk. Larvae sometimes hibernate for fourth year and beetles do not appear until fifth. Larvae sometimes do damage to vines.

9 Garden Chafer *Phyllopertha horticola.* Inhabits most of Europe and extends east as far as Mongolia. Length 8.5—11 mm. Appears from May to July, often in immense numbers. Frequents gardens, orchards, margins of woods, etc. Beetles nibble flowers. Female lays eggs in ground. Larvae, hatched in 2 weeks, gnaw roots. Development takes 2—3 years.

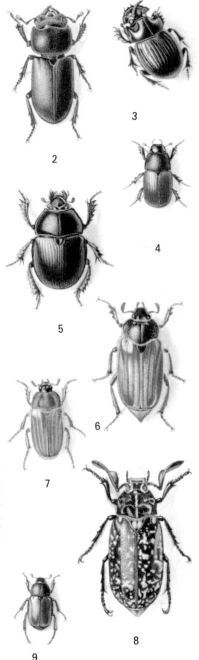

307

Family: **Chafers**—Scarabaeidae

1 European Rhinoceros Beetle *Oryctes nasicornis.* Inhabits practically whole of Europe. Length 25—40 mm. Very variable over vast area of distribution. Larvae develop in rotting stumps and trunks of deciduous trees, mainly oaks and beeches, but also in old compost heaps. Larvae very fat, with dilated abdomen, very hard, large head and huge mandibles. Development of larva takes several years according to conditions. Before pupating larva forms cocoon of soil and sawdust in which mature beetle also remains for up to 2 months. Adult beetle appears from June to August. Nocturnal insect.

2 Goldsmith Beetle *Cetonia aurata.* Inhabits most of Europe. Length 14—20 mm. Beetles found from middle of May well into summer on flowering dog-roses, etc. Female lays eggs in rotting tree stumps, etc. and occasionally in anthills. Development usually takes one year. Mature larva forms cocoon of sawdust and soil, stuck together with special secretion. Larvae moult twice and attain length of 4—5 cm.

3 Hermit Beetle *Osmoderma eremita.* Inhabits practically all Europe but occurs only locally. Not very abundant. Length 24—30 mm. Beetles appear from end of May to July. Fly well. Female lays eggs in hollows in old deciduous trees, e.g. limes, beeches, oaks. Larvae develop several years (not less than 3) and grow to length of up to 10 cm. Before pupating larva forms sawdust cocoon. Beetle gives off curious odour.

4 *Trichius fasciatus.* Occurs over practically whole of Europe. Length 9—12 mm. Wing case designs very variable. Beetles frequent flowers and flowering bushes on warm, sunny days in summer. Female lays eggs in rotting wood of deciduous trees, especially beeches. Larvae develop 2 years. Particularly abundant in wooded uplands.

1

Family: **Metallic** or **Flat-headed Wood-borers**—Buprestidae

5 Pine-borer *Chalcophora mariana.* Found in central Europe, only in warm places. Length 25—30 mm. Copper-coloured back, burnished gold underside. Inhabits pine-woods. Fond of warmth like all members of this family. Beetles appear during hottest hours of sunny days. Found on tree trunks. Larvae develop in pine tree stumps and dry trunks. Bore characteristic flat winding tunnels. Flat larva has segmented body and wide head. Does not do serious damage.

6 Lime-borer *Poecilonota rutilans.* Occurs in warm places in central Europe. Abundant in some regions. Length 10—14 mm. Shows jewel-like metallic-blue back when flying. Appears in June and July in lime tree avenues or on limes on outskirts of forests. Female lays eggs in cracks in bark on sunny side of lime trunk. Larvae, which develop 2 years, devour wood. Repeated attacks of lime-borers cause tree to wither. Dangerous pest in large numbers.

7 Common Wood-borer *Buprestis rustica.* Fairly abundant in parts of central Europe. Length 13—18 mm. Tips of wing sheaths straight-edged. Inhabits conifer woods. Larvae live behind bark or in wood of stumps and freshly felled trees, particularly spruces. Development takes 2 years.

8 Metallic Wood-borer *Anthaxia nitidula.* Inhabits warm places in central Europe. Length 5—7 mm. Beetle appears in June and July. Locally abundant, found on roses, dandelions, ox-eyes, etc. Larvae live on blackthorns.

9 Two-spot Wood-borer *Agrilus biguttatus.* Widely distributed over central Europe. Length 12 mm. Tip of wing sheaths rounded. Appears on sunny days at end of May on tree stumps and flowers. Larvae live in oak stumps.

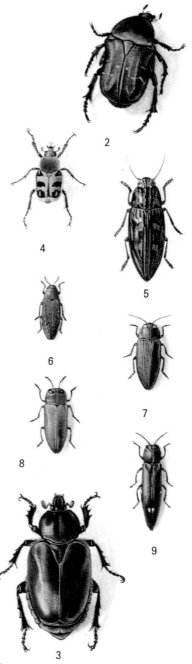

2

4

5

6

7

8

9

3

1   2   3   4

Family: **Click Beetles**—Elateridae

1 Blood-red Click Beetle *Elater sanguineus.* Occurs over practically whole of Europe. Length 13—18 mm. Inhabits foothill forests. Often appears by end of March. Larvae live behind bark or in pine stumps, often gregariously. Larva measures up to 2 cm.

2 Grey Click Beetle *Adelocera murina.* Distributed all over Europe. Length 11—17 mm. Found at both low and high altitudes. Lives in meadows, fields, clearings and gardens. Larva is field and forest pest, gnaws roots and other parts of all crops and young trees. Also carnivorous. Adult beetle appears from spring to autumn and nibbles beech and oak buds. Often found on ears of corn.

3 Wheat Wire-worm *Agriotes lineatus.* Lives in whole palearctic region. Length 8—9 mm. Found at both low and high altitudes. Beetles appear in meadows in May and June. Larvae eat any plants, do damage to tree nurseries and in south to vineyards, etc. Pupate in soil. Development takes 3—4 years.

Family: **Leather-winged Beetles**—Cantharidae

4 Soldier Beetle *Cantharis fusca.* Widely distributed in Europe. Length 12 mm. Appears from spring to summer on plants, bushes and ground. Catches and eats small insects, occasionally eats also young shoots. Hairy larvae have strong mandibles and are predacious. Live under leaves, etc., look for insects and small molluscs. Larvae hibernate in ground but on sunny days often found in snow. Pupate in early spring after hibernating.

5 *Phausis splendidula.* Very common all over central Europe. Length 9—11 mm. Mainly inhabits outskirts of damp deciduous woods. Nocturnal insect. Males fly in large numbers on warm evenings at end of June and in July. Females wingless, with vestigial wing case, crawl on ground. Has brightly luminescent light organ on underside of abdomen. Females and carnivorous larvae also luminescent. Adult beetle lives only briefly. Light organ probably used to attract partner.

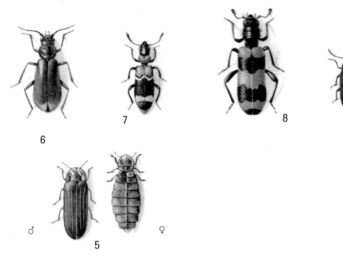

6

7

8

9

♂

5

♀

6 *Malachius aeneus*. Very common everywhere in central Europe. Length 7—8 mm. Soft wing case. Appears in spring on almost all flowers. Larva frequents tunnels of bark beetles and other wood beetles.

Family: **Chequered Beetles**—Cleridae

7 **Ant Beetle** *Thanasimus formicarius*. Abundant all over central Europe. Length 7—10 mm. Female lays up to 30 eggs in groups of 2—4 behind bark scales. Larvae crawl into tunnels of bark beetles and other wood beetles and attack their larvae. Larva seizes prey in first two pairs of legs, turns it on to back, bites through its body at base of abdomen and devours it from within. Larva very active. Both larva and adult beetle can hibernate.

8 **Bee-eating Beetle** *Trichodes apiarius*. Lives in warm places in central Europe. Length 9—15 mm. Adult beetle frequents flowers and eats other insects. Seen from May to July. Larvae mainly develop in nests of solitary bees and eat their larvae or pupae.

Family: **Death Watch Beetles**—Anobiidae

9 **Death Watch** *Anobium pertinax*. Common European beetle. Length 5—7 mm. Lives in wood or in houses in old furniture where it bores tunnels. Bangs head on walls of tunnel to attract members of opposite sex. Knocking superstitiously supposed to portend death. Female lays eggs in opening of tunnel. If repeatedly attacked, old furniture may fall to pieces. Beetle 'plays possum' if handled.

2

3

4

1

Family: **Blister** or **Oil Beetles**—Meloidae

3 Oil Beetle or **May-worm** *Meloe proscara-baeus.* Widely distributed. Length 12—35 mm. Female has large abdomen. Wingless with short wing sheaths. Appears in grass early in spring. Female lays eggs in small pits. Hatched larvae grasp different bees, including honeybees, with claw-like legs and are carried to their nests, get into cells and devour host's egg and food stores. After complicated metamorphosis — firstly pseudopupa, then again larva — they pupate.

4 Spanish Fly *Lytta vesicatoria.* Lives in southern Europe and warmer parts of central Europe. Length 11—22 mm. Winged beetles appear en masse in June, mainly on ash trees. Eat leaves. Beetle produces potent poison, cantharidin. Female lays groups of 40—50 eggs in ground. Larvae attach themselves to bodies of solitary bees of *Osmia* genus and develop in similar way as preceding species.

Family: **Snout Beetles** or **Weevils**—Curculionidae

5 Pine Weevil *Hylobius abietis.* Abundant on all conifers. Length 8—14 mm. Beetle appears from May to September. Female lays 50—100 eggs in roots, bark of fresh pine, fir and larch stumps. Larvae eat bast and sap-wood. Before pupating form 'cradle'. Beetle lives several years.

Family: **Darkling** or **Pineate Beetles**—Tenebrionidae

1 Cellar or **Churchyard Beetle** *Blaps mortisaga.* Widely distributed in central Europe. Length 22—28 mm. Appears from April to autumn. Often lives in houses. Hides during day under floor-boards, in cellars, etc., where larvae also live. Does no damage.

2 Meal-worm *Tenebrio molitor.* Today very common everywhere. Bred artificially. Larvae used to feed birds and lizards. Length 14—17 mm. Beetle often lives in houses, refuse, henhouses and dove-cotes. Larvae also eat flesh, e.g. meat left on bones, dead bodies of small birds and mammals etc., otherwise found in meal stores, etc.

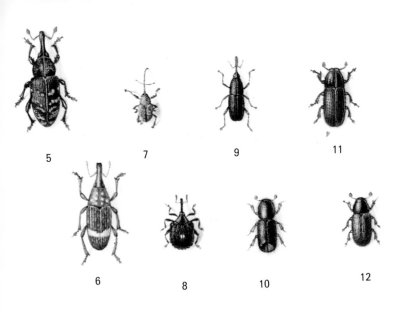

5

7

9

11

6

8

10

12

6 **White Pine Beetle** *Pissodes piceae.* Locally common in central Europe. Length 7—12 mm. Appears on firs and is very serious pest. Sometimes multiplies to such a degree that tree is attacked from roots to crown. Female lays eggs on bark.

7 **Nut Weevil** *Curculio nucum.* Common in central Europe. Length 7—8 mm. Characterized by very long 'snout'. Appears from May to July. Female lays eggs in holes she has made with her 'snout' in young nuts. Larvae eat kernels.

8 *Cionus scrophulariae.* Fairly abundant. Length 4—6 mm. Can fold cylindrical 'snout' on underside of thorax. Lives gregariously on fig-wort and mullein. Legless larvae, wrapped in slimy envelope, nibble leaves and perianths. On pupation mucus hardens and protects pupa.

9 **Granary Weevil** *Calandra granaria.* Original home probably in southern Asia. Carried to all parts of world. Most dreaded grain pest. Length 3—4 mm. Beetle unable to fly and is spread only by carrying. Lives in badly ventilated granaries. Female lays eggs on grains of wheat, rye, etc.

Family: **Bark Beetles**—Scolytidae

10 *Ips typographus.* Inhabits cooler parts of Europe. Length about 4 mm. Dreaded spruce pest. Larvae devour tunnels perpendicular to maternal shaft.

11 *Dendroctonus micans.* Distributed all over central Europe. Length 6—9 mm. Inhabits spruce woods. Larvae form common widening tunnel. Beetles emerge at end of July. Attacks weakened trees.

12 *Myelophilus piniperda.* Widely distributed in Europe. Length 3.5—5 mm. Inhabits large pine-woods. Attacks mainly trunks of felled trees.

Family: **Longicorn Beetles**—Cerambycidae

1 *Prionus coriarius.* Inhabits whole of Europe, extends even to North Africa, Asia Minor and western Siberia. Length 19—45 mm. Male has saw-like antennae with 12 joints, female antennae with smaller teeth and 11 joints. Inhabits old deciduous, mixed and conifer woods. Very abundant in places. Larva develops in rotting trunks and oak, beech, fir, pine stumps, etc., often also in roots. Beetles swarm in July and August, often in daytime.

2 *Ergates faber.* Only locally found in Europe. Length 23—60 mm. Male's antennae longer than body, female's much shorter. Favours old pinewoods. Female lays over 300 single eggs usually on rotting wood which provides firm hold. Larvae often develop in old pine stumps, less often in spruce stumps. Occasionally attacks beams in wooden constructions combined with bricks, which keep wood damp. Also attacks telegraph poles, wooden fences, etc. Larvae measure up to 6.5 cm. Development takes several years. Beetles swarm at night from July to September. Adult beetle lives 3 weeks.

3 *Spondylis buprestoides.* Lives all over Europe and extends as far as Japan. Very plentiful in places. Length 12—22 mm. Larvae develop in old pine and occasionally spruce stumps. Beetles fly after dusk from June to September. Hide during day under logs, etc.

4, 5 *Cerambyx cerdo.* Inhabits Europe. Length 24—53 mm. Male's antennae much longer than body, female's same length as body or slightly shorter. Larvae develop mainly in oaks, occasionally in chestnuts, sycamores, beeches or ash trees. Female lays eggs usually in twos or threes in cracks in bark, preferably in old standing oaks. Larvae, hatched in 12—14 days, start to gnaw bark and hibernate there first year. In spring continue to eat bark and in June—July reach sap-wood and bast where they cause exudation visible as dark patch on trunk. After second hibernation larva bores to depth of 15—50 cm in wood and forms chamber in which it pupates. Adult beetle emerges in same year after 5—6 weeks but does not leave chamber until following year. In living wood beetle's development takes 3 years, in felled trees up to 5 years. Small infestation does no damage but large-scale repeated infestation can cause even large trees to die, while larvae's tunnels depreciate wood. This species has been known to destroy whole oak avenues but is growing steadily rarer because of lack of old oaks. Beetles swarm in June and July, during evening and at night. One of the largest and handsomest European beetles. Can successfully be bred from larvae in captivity.

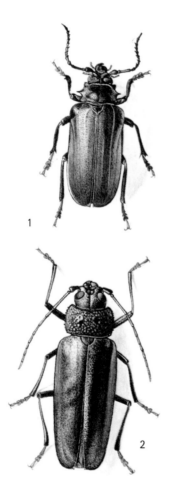

1

2

6 Musk Beetle *Aromia moschata*. Widely distributed in Europe, extends to western Siberia. Length 13—34 mm. Adult beetle found mainly on willows but also on flowers of tall plants. Chiefly attacks old willows and in case of large-scale repeated invasion larvae completely destroy tree in few years. Musk beetle can also develop in poplars or alders. Adult beetle secretes strongly smelling substance. Swarm from June to August. Very beautifully coloured species.

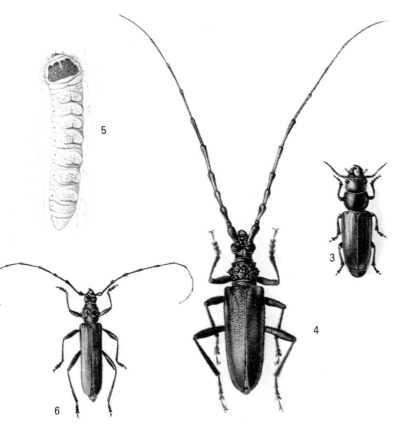

Family: **Longicorn Beetles**—Cerambycidae

1 *Necydalis major.* Distributed over Europe, extends up to Siberia. Length 21—32 mm. Incidence localized but abundant, especially in low-lying country. Very short wing sheaths. Larva develops in deciduous trees (e.g. poplars, limes, birches), fruit-trees and conifers (e.g. firs). Beetles fly in June and July and often sit on tree trunks or stacks of logs.

2 *Rosalia alpina.* Inhabits southern and central Europe, extends north up to south of Sweden. Length 15—38 mm. Colouring very variable. Incidence diminishing because of decreasing number of beeches but still quite abundant in places. Larvae develop in old beeches, occasionally in sycamores. Inhabits mountains above altitude of 600 m, found chiefly on warm slopes. Flies in sunny weather from June to beginning of September. Does practically no damage. Numerous enemies, including woodpeckers, lizards, but especially beetle-collectors attracted by its striking colouring.

3 *Lamia textor.* Abundant in Europe and whole of Asia as far as Japan. Length 15—30 mm. Larvae develop in willows and aspens, mainly in old wood, also in roots. Unimportant pest. In summer adult beetles sit motionless on willow branches and are active only in evening.

4 *Callidium aeneum.* Lives in southern, central and northern Europe, extends east up to Siberia. Length 9—15 mm. Principally mountain-dweller but also often found in lowlands. Very rare in some places. Larvae develop in deciduous trees and conifers, chiefly oaks, beeches and pines. Eat surface of wood. Adult beetles appear from end of May to July.

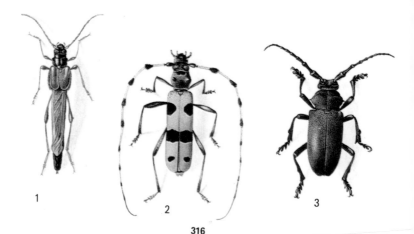

1   2   3

5 *Callidium violaceum.* Inhabits Europe and whole of Asia as far as Japan. Length 8—16 mm. Abundant everywhere in central Europe, especially in conifer woods both at low and high altitudes. Larva lives in dry conifer woods, rarely in beeches, sycamores and fruit-trees. Eats wood from surface, after pupating bores deeper in wood. Female also lays eggs on felled trees, larvae develop even after wood has been processed and can damage rafters if wood is not divested of bark. Adult beetles appear from May to August.

6 *Leptura rubra.* Widely distributed all over Europe. Length 10—19 mm. Somewhat variable colouring, males usually yellowish, females reddish. Larvae live in spruce and pine stumps or trunks, occasionally found on telegraph poles. Adult beetle appears from June to September on flowering plants and bushes. Occurs at both low and high altitudes.

7 *Rhagium bifasciatum.* Distributed over whole of Europe. Length 12—22 mm. Larva develops in wood of old oaks and conifers. Most abundant on pines, spruces and oaks. Found high up in mountains. Adult beetles sit on flowers and flowering bushes, also on tree trunks. Appear from May to August. Relatively common everywhere in central Europe.

8 *Rhagium inquisitor.* Widely distributed in Europe. Occurs at both high and low altitudes. Length 10—21 mm. Very often seen in dwellings, brought on wood from forest. Larva lives behind bark of pines, spruces and firs. Beetles hatch in autumn but hibernate and appear from following April to beginning of September. Often encountered on stacks of logs, also on flowers and bushes.

6

7

4

5

8

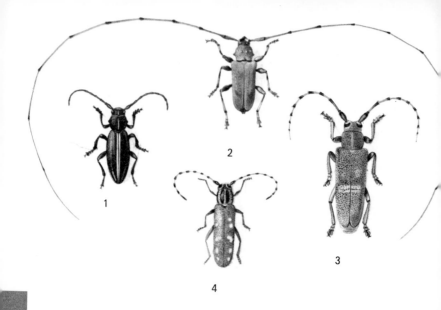

Family: **Longicorn Beetles**—Cerambycidae

1 *Dorcadion pedestre*. Occurs in eastern part of central Europe up to Balkans. Mainly inhabits lowlands but occasionally found at higher altitudes. Length 11—17 mm. Very abundant in spring from April to June. Unlike all other longicorn beetles larva develops underground, on grass roots. In steppe country beetles often found in large numbers on grasses.

2 *Acanthocinus aedilis*. Inhabits Europe and Asia. In central Europe common in pine-woods. Length 12—20 mm. Male has extremely long antennae. Larva develops in pines but is most often found in stumps in which it gnaws winding tunnels behind bark. Less frequently found on felled trees or standing trees weakened by other pests. Pupates in bark. Two generations a year — in March and August. Adult beetle appears from March to September. Beetle also sometimes develops in processed wood, e.g. furniture.

3 *Saperda carcharias*. Extends from Europe up to Siberia. Length 20—30 mm. Larvae develop in poplars or aspens and often do considerable damage. Female lays eggs in bark, preferably of young trees. Larvae bore into wood and form oval tunnels. Development takes 2 years. Beetles fly on warm evenings in June and July, nibble leaves or young bark of twigs. Bite rounded holes in leaves. In large numbers do great damage and can destroy young trees.

4 *Saperda populnea.* Inhabits Europe, North America and Africa. Length 9—15 mm. Abundant everywhere in central Europe. Female lays eggs on shoots or in hole bitten in bark, causing swellings on trunk. Larvae develop in aspens, also in poplars and sallows. Larva first of all lives on swelling and then bores into wood. Pupates at end of tunnel about 5 cm long. Beetles fly from end of May to middle of July. In places does serious damage to young cultures.

5 *Oberea oculata.* Very common in Europe at both low and high altitudes. Length 15 to 21 mm. Larvae found in willows and sallows. Female lays eggs singly in holes bitten in twigs. Larva gnaws tunnel up to 30 cm long. Development takes one year. Hatched beetles bite way out through round opening. Swarm in June and July but still encountered at beginning of September. Dozens of beetles often found sitting on willow twigs making grating sounds.

6 *Stenopterus rufus.* Abundant in southern and central Europe. Length 8—16 mm. Found in warm places. Larvae develop in deciduous trees, most frequently oaks. Adult beetles often encountered on flowers from May to August.

7 *Pachyta quadrimaculata.* Distributed over Europe and Asia as far as Mongolia. In central Europe very common in mountainous regions but rare in lowlands. Length 11—20 mm. Strong, robust body. Larvae develop in wood of spruces but often also in other conifers. Adult beetles appear on various flowers from June to August.

8 *Toxotus cursor.* Distributed over Europe and western Asia. In central Europe common in mountains and foothills. Length 25—32 mm. Several races are known, somewhat variable. Larvae develop in spruce, pine and fir stumps. Adult beetles often sit on stacked logs in forest or frequent forest plants in clearings etc. Beetles found from May to August.

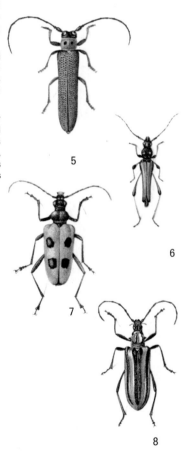

5

6

7

8

1

Family: **Leaf Beetles**—Chrysomelidae

1 *Donacia crassipes*. In central Europe common in places with water-lilies. Length 9—11 mm. Beetles sit on floating water-lily leaves. Female bites holes in leaves and through it lays eggs on underside. Larvae migrate further into depth and make slits in plant's air passages to obtain oxygen. Pupate under water in cocoon, likewise attached to air canal. In summer beetles also sit on other plants.

2 *Clytra quadripunctata*. Very abundant in central Europe. Length 8—11 mm. Adult beetles found in large numbers on willows, alders and limes. Larvae develop in anthills where they form bag-like covering from own excreta in which they hide and later pupate.

3 Poplar Leaf Beetle *Melasoma populi*. Inhabits whole of Europe. Length 6—12 mm. Frequents mainly poplars but also willows. Adult beetles and larvae nibble leaves often leaving only skeleton. If in danger, larvae emit pungent fluid from special warts.

4 Colorado Potato Beetle *Leptinotarsa decemlineata*. Originally from Mexico, has been carried to all parts of Europe. Female hibernates deep in soil, in spring gnaws germinating potatoes. Lays piles of up to 90 eggs on leaves of potato plants. Larvae gnaw leaves. After 20 days larvae pupate in ground, beetle emerges after 2—3 weeks and in 10 more days can again lay eggs. One female lays up to 700 eggs so that third generation can number 80 million. This prolific beetle has caused great damage in many parts of Europe.

5 Alder Leaf Beetle *Agelastica alni*. Very common in central Europe. Length 5—6 mm. Occurs in large numbers. Fertilized female has large abdomen and lays groups of 50 eggs on underside of alder leaves in May and June — total up to 900. Larvae eat leaves and pupate in ground. Beetles emerge in August, eat leaves and hibernate in foliage.

6 *Phyllotreta nemorum*. Widely distributed in central Europe. Minute, only 2 mm long. Gnaws holes in leaves of cruciferous plants. Beetles gregarious. If approached, jump in all directions by means of strong last pair of legs. Larvae have developed legs and warty body. Devour inner portions of leaves often leaving only skeleton, so that plant withers. Most abundant in dry summers.

7 *Cassida viridis*. Widespread in central Europe. Length 7—10 mm. Head covered by plate. Occurs chiefly on labiate plants. Larva flattened with spiny sides and abdominal process on which it carries excreta remnants to disguise itself.

Family: **Ladybirds**—Coccinellidae

8 Seven-spot Ladybird *Coccinella septempunctata.* Very common. Length 5—8 mm. Found in most diverse places. Staple diet plant-lice. Female lays total of up to 700 eggs in piles, near plant-lice. Larvae also eat aphids.

9 Two-spot Ladybird *Adalia bipunctata.* Very common in central Europe. Length 4—6 mm. In April and May female lays groups of 6—20 yellowish eggs near plant-lice. Larvae live on plant-lice or scale-insects. One larva consumes 15 aphids daily. Larva pupates after 20—35 days. Most of hatched beetles hibernate. Adult ladybird consumes 10 plant-lice daily.

10 Eyed Ladybird *Anatis ocellata.* Widely distributed in central Europe. Length 8—9 mm. Usually found in large numbers on conifers. In July female lays eggs on underside of needles and on bark. Larvae mainly eat eggs and larvae of Yellow Fig Gall-louse. Very useful insect.

11 Four-spot Ladybird *Exochomus quadripustulatus.* Common all over central Europe. Length 3—5 mm. Occurs mainly on spruces and pines. Eats scale-insects. Pupates in larval skin.

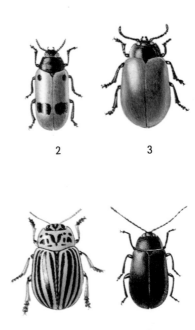

2

3

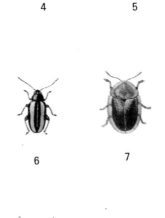

4

5

6

7

8

9

10

11

1

Order: **Moths and Butterflies**—Lepidoptera

Famili: **Ghost Moths**—Hepialidae

1 White-winged Hop Moth *Hepialus humuli.* Common in parts of central Europe. Wing span 45—70 mm. Moth appears from May to August. Flies in evening in low zigzags. Caterpillar yellowish with sparse black hairs. Lives from April to May on hop roots, also on dandelions, sorrel and carrots. Pupates in chambers in ground. Female lays eggs on ground. Development takes 2 years. Male white, female brown-yellow.

Family: **Carpenter Moths**—Cossidae

2 Goat Moth *Cossus cossus.* Widely distributed in Europe. Wing span up to 90 mm. Appears in June and July. Nocturnal. During day sits on tree trunks. Female has ovipositor, lays eggs in cracks of bark. Caterpillar lives in trunks of oaks, willows, poplars and fruit-trees, gnaws long tunnels in wood. Hibernates twice, pupates in cocoon in May of third year. Perfect moth emerges 4—6 weeks later. In large numbers caterpillars completely ruin wood.

3 *Zeuzera pyrina.* Occurs in Europe, not very common. Wing span of males about 50 mm, of females up to 70 mm. Appears from May to beginning of August. Female lays single eggs on tree trunks. Caterpillar tunnels in wood. Lives in deciduous trees, chiefly ashes, elms and horse-chestnuts, also in many fruit-trees. Development takes 2 years. In large numbers damages wood. Caterpillar reddish, up to 5 cm long.

Family: **Bear Moths**—Syntomidae

4 *Syntomis phegea.* Common everywhere in central Europe. Wing span about 40 mm. Appears in June and July. In flight resembles burnet moth. Grey to black hairy caterpillar lives on various herbaceous plants, chiefly dandelions. Hibernates and pupates following year in May.

Family: **Burnet Moths** or **Foresters**—*Zygaenidae*

5 Common Blood-drop Burnet Moth *Zygaena filipendulae.* Common in Europe. Wing span about 35 mm. Appears in large numbers in meadows from beginning of June to end of August. Flies by day, ungainly and clumsily. Sits in sun on thistles etc. Caterpillar fat and yellowish with sparse hairs. Found mainly on birdfoot-trefoil but also on other plants. Pupates in brimstone-yellow, parchment-like cocoon. Moth releases repellent liquid if caught.

6 *Zygaena carniolica.* Very common in warm spots in central Europe. Wing span about 30 mm. Flies in June and July, slowly and clumsily. Caterpillar light green with white stripes and row of black spots. Lives in sainfoin and birdfoot-trefoil. Pupates in cocoon.

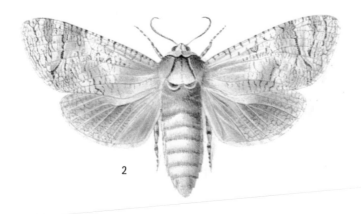

2

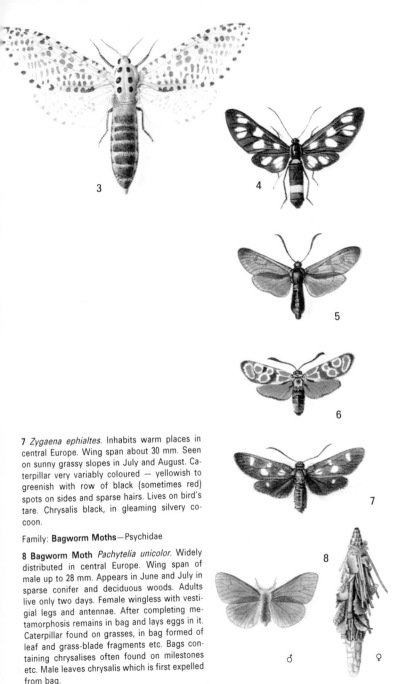

3

4

5

6

7 *Zygaena ephialtes.* Inhabits warm places in central Europe. Wing span about 30 mm. Seen on sunny grassy slopes in July and August. Caterpillar very variably coloured — yellowish to greenish with row of black (sometimes red) spots on sides and sparse hairs. Lives on bird's tare. Chrysalis black, in gleaming silvery cocoon.

7

Family: **Bagworm Moths**—Psychidae

8 Bagworm Moth *Pachytelia unicolor.* Widely distributed in central Europe. Wing span of male up to 28 mm. Appears in June and July in sparse conifer and deciduous woods. Adults live only two days. Female wingless with vestigial legs and antennae. After completing metamorphosis remains in bag and lays eggs in it. Caterpillar found on grasses, in bag formed of leaf and grass-blade fragments etc. Bags containing chrysalises often found on milestones etc. Male leaves chrysalis which is first expelled from bag.

8

♂   ♀

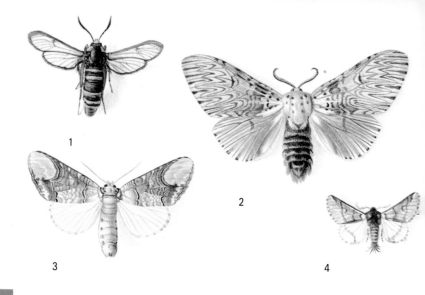

1

2

3

4

Family: **Clearwings**—Sesiidae

1 Hornet Clearwing *Sesia apiformis.* Fairly common in central Europe. Wing span about 40 mm. Closely resembles hornet. Wings transparent. Appears from June to end of July. Sits on poplar trunks. Flies swiftly with humming sound. Female lays eggs singly, mainly on poplars, but also on birches, willows and limes (over 1,000 eggs altogether). Caterpillars bore through bark, hibernate, following year tunnel into wood and hibernate again. Pupate in sawdust cocoon. Before moth emerges chrysalis is expelled from opening.

Family: **Puss Moths**—Notodontidae

2 Puss Moth *Cerura vinula.* Widely distributed in Europe. Wing span up to about 70 mm. Flies after dusk from May to beginning of July. Striking, humped caterpillar with typical 'prongs' at tip of abdomen. Found on willows and poplars from July to September. Prongs are claspers converted to tubular appendages from which caterpillar extrudes pink filaments to scare foes. Caterpillar pupates in crack in bark, in cocoon made of wood debris and fragments of bark. Can do serious damage to tree nurseries.

3 Buff Tip Moth *Phalera bucephala.* Very common in Europe. Wing span about 50 mm. Appears in May and June. Flies in evening, prefers lime and poplar avenues. Fine-haired, black-brown, yellow-striped caterpillar found from June to October on willows, limes, poplars and birches. Large number often crowd on single twig. Disperse when older. Pupate in ground. Dark, glossy chrysalis capable of motion.

Family: **Procession Moths**—Thaumetopoeidae

4 Oak Procession Moth *Thaumetopoea processionea.* Very common in central Europe, especially in southern parts. Wing span about 30 mm. Moths frequent only tops of oaks. Fly in August and September. Easily attracted by light. Female lays piles of 200—300 eggs and covers them with hairs from own body. Caterpillars, hatched in May, remain in common nests. Search for food at night crawling in head-to-tail procession. Pupate in July in cocoons, again in common nest.

Family: **Silk Moths** or **Saturnids**—Saturniidae

5 *Saturnia pyri.* Abundant in south of central Europe. Largest European moth. Wing span to over 120 mm. Appears in May, flies on warm evenings in orchards, at margins of woods, etc. Caterpillar found from end of May to August on pear- and other fruit-trees. Has striking light blue tubercles with stiff bristles. Pupates in brown cocoon on bark between branches. Caterpillar makes squeaking sounds.

6 Emperor Moth *Eudia pavonia.* Occurs over large part of Europe. Wing span of male about 60 mm, female up to 75 mm. Flies in May and June. Seen in sparse deciduous woods and at margins of forests. Mature caterpillar bright green with black cross-stripes and yellow tubercles. Found from May to August on decidous trees or shrubs, e.g. brambles. Chrysalis black-brown in whitish or yellowish-brown, very strong, pear-shaped cocoon.

7 *Aglia tau.* Very common in parts of central Europe. Wing span about 65 mm. Appears in April and May, chiefly in open beech-woods. Male flies in abrupt zigzags, female usually sits on tree trunk close to ground. Caterpillar greenish with white-yellow cross-stripes and one longitudinal stripe on sides. Found mainly on beeches from May to July. Pupates in loose coccon.

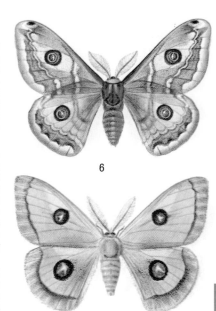

6

7

5

1

2

pears in July. Female lays 150—250 large eggs, in piles on pine twigs or needles. Caterpillars, hatched in 3 weeks, eat needles, moult 3 times, descend to ground at end of October and hibernate in loose top-soil. Crawl back to top of trees in spring, grow to 7—10 cm and pupate in June. Some caterpillars hibernate once more. Chrysalis in cocoon attached to nibbled pine shoots or fixed in cracks in bark. Caterpillar brownish and hairy with light stripe on side.

4 Bramble Moth *Macrothylacia rubi.* Widely distributed in Europe. Wing span about 50 mm. Flies on summer evenings, often appears also during day, flies swiftly and jerkily. Female lays eggs mainly on brambles but also on roses and young oaks. Caterpillar velvety black and hairy with narrow orange cross-stripes. Found chiefly in autumn on grassy slopes and in meadows, parks, etc., crawling on ground. Often still seen in November looking for hideout in ground to hibernate. Pupates in spring of following year in soft, greyish cocoon. Many hibernating caterpillars die in ground.

5 Lappet Moth *Gastropacha quercifolia.* Abundant in practically whole of Europe. Wing span up to about 80 mm. Edge of wings indented. Flies from June to August. Caterpillar greyish brown, sparsely haired, with reddish tubercles on sides of back; grows up to 10 cm. Lives on fruit-trees, other deciduous trees and blackthorns. Pupates in soft hairy cocoon. In large numbers damages fruit-tree nurseries.

Family: **Meadow Moths**—Lemoniidae

1 *Lemonia dumi.* Distributed all over central Europe. Wing span up to 20 mm. Flies in evening from September to October, sometimes to November. Caterpillar found from May to July on marsh-marigold, lung-wort, garden lettuce and dandelions. Pupates in ground.

Family: **Birch Moths**—Endromiidae

2 Kentish Glory *Endromis versicolor.* Common in central Europe. Wing span about 50 mm. Moth often appears as soon as end of February, flies until May. Caterpillar lives on birches, sometimes on sycamores, seldom on other trees. Young caterpillars gregarious. Caterpillar green with whitish back and cross-stripes on sides. Chrysalis red, in cocoon.

Family: **Tent Caterpillar Moths**—Lasiocampidae

3 Pine Moth *Dendrolimus pini.* Abundant over whole of central Europe. Wing span of male about 55 mm, female up to 80 mm. Moth ap-

3

326

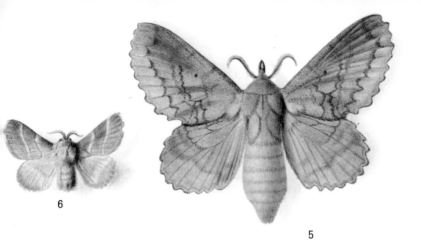

6

5

6 Lackey Moth *Malacosoma neustrium.* Widely distributed over practically whole of Europe. Wing span up to 40 mm. Flies from end of June to August. Female lays eggs ring-wise round young fruit-tree, blackthorn, poplar, oak and birch twigs — 200—400 eggs in one ring. Caterpillars not hatched until following May, after eggs have hibernated. Caterpillar thinly haired, with blue head and often blue, white and red stripes down body. Caterpillars gregarious. Weave whitish nests, crawl out in search of food. Disperse after third moult and in second half of June pupate in white or yellowish cocoon on bark or between leaves of trees.

7 *Lasiocampa quercus.* Abundant in temperate zone of Europe. Wing span up to 70 mm. Moth appears in woods and avenues from June to August. Caterpillar mainly brownish yellow with yellowish hairs, grows to 7 cm. Lives on various deciduous trees, also conifers. Hibernates and pupates following May in firm, brown cocoon. In mountains and northerly regions hibernates second time as chrysalis. Does little damage.

4

7

327

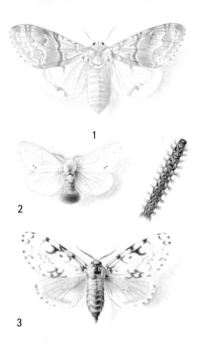

3 Nun or **Black Archer** *Lymantria monacha*. Very common in Europe. Wing span of male up to 45 mm; female up to 55 mm. Colouring very variable, including black aberrations. Appears in July and August. Female lays eggs behind scales of bark on conifers, occasionally also deciduous trees. Caterpillars do not hatch until following year, usually in April. Disperse into tree crowns and eat needles or leaves. Pupate in cracks in bark after about 9 weeks. Very variably coloured. Have few hairs.

4 Gypsy Moth *Lymantria dispar*. Distributed over almost whole of Europe. Wing span of male 35—40 mm, female 55—70 mm. Flies from end of July to September, lives only 7—8 days. Female lays eggs in piles. Caterpillars do not hatch until following April or May; found on deciduous trees, mainly oaks, limes, etc. Caterpillar brownish and hairy, with blue and red tubercles. Pupates in loose cocoon on south side of tree trunks, often in groups.

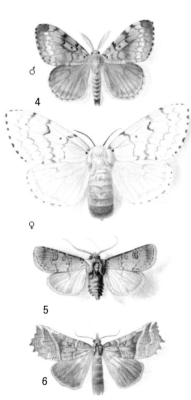

Family: **Tussock Moths**—Lymantriidae

1 Pale Tussock Moth *Dasychira pudibunda*. Abundant in whole of central Europe. Wing span about 45 mm. Appears in May and June, sometimes second generation in October. Inhabits sparse woods, orchards, etc. Caterpillar very variably coloured — yellow, pink or reddish, with hairs of same colour and with yellow or orange bristles on back. Lives on deciduous trees and pupates in yellow, extremely hairy cocoon.

2 Gold-tipped Tussock Moth *Euproctis phaeorrhoea*. Widely distributed in central Europe. Wing span about 35 mm. Flies from end of June to end of July. Female lays piles of eggs on underside of oak leaves and covers them with hairs. Caterpillars hatch in August. Gregarious, hibernate in nests and disperse in spring. Pupate at end of June in cocoon which is hidden in rolled leaf. Do damage in large numbers.

7

8

9

Family: **Owlet Moths**—Phalaenidae

5 *Agrotis segetum.* Common European moth. Wing span about 40 mm. Moth appears in May—June and August—September in fields, meadows and gardens. Caterpillars eat turnips, cereals, grass, etc. Caterpillar smooth and greyish with light lines down back and sides and black spots. Hides during day, comes out to feed at night.

6 *Scoliopteryx libatrix.* Very common in Europe. Wing span about 40 mm. Forewings indented. Moth appears in August and September, hibernates in holes, cellars, etc., and flies again in March and April. Caterpillars found on poplars and willows from May to September. Caterpillar green with yellow band on sides. Chrysalis black.

7 Blue Underwing *Catocala fraxini.* Distributed over all central Europe. Wing span up to about 90 mm. Appears from end of July to September. Sits on tree trunks during day, flies in evening and at night. Caterpillar up to 10 cm long; greyish or greenish, black-speckled, on back with light spot in black band on 8th segment. Found on ashes, poplars and elms.

8 Red Poplar Underwing *Catocala elocata.* Distributed over most of Europe. Wing span about 75 mm. Occurs from July to October. Clings to tree trunks during day. If disturbed, abruptly unfolds forewings, displaying red hindwings to frighten enemy. Caterpillar grey with dark dorsal and lateral stripes. Found mainly on poplars, also on willows, from May to June. Chrysalis reddish brown, dusted with blue.

9 Red Willow Underwing *Catocala electa.* Widely distributed in central Europe. Wing span about 70 mm. Flies in July and August. Caterpillar yellowish grey to brown with small black dots; over 7 cm long. Found on willows in May and June.

Family: **Tiger Moths**—Arctiidae

1 White Tiger Moth *Spilosoma menthastri.*
Widely distributed in central Europe. Wing span
about 40 mm. Flies in evening in May and June.
During day can be seen sitting on plants in forest clearings and in gardens. Caterpillar hairy,
dark brown with orange-yellow line down back.
Found through summer on various plants, chiefly stinging-nettles and mint. Pupates on ground.
Chrysalis black in grey cocoon.

2 *Utetheisa pulchella.* Lives in southern part of
central Europe but often strays far north. Wing
span about 40 mm. Flies in June and September—October in damp meadows near woods, in
clearings, etc. Caterpillar white and soft-haired,
with black dots and red spots. Found on forget-
me-not, viper's bugloss, rib-wort and other herbaceous plants in May—June and September—
October.

3 *Phragmatobia fuliginosa.* Common over practically whole of Europe. Wing span 30—35 mm.
Many colour varieties. Moth in April and May,
second generation in August. Flies after dark,
often enters open windows. Caterpillar grey to
reddish brown, with tubercles surmounted by
tufts of hairs. Found on forget-me-not, sorrel,
bedstraw, wild lettuce, etc. Pupates in greyish
white felty cocoon.

4 *Rhyparia purpurata.* Abundant in central
Europe. Wing span about 45 mm. Several colour
varieties. Flies after dark, in June and July. Caterpillar somewhat variable; usually black with
dark red hairs and yellow lateral hairs. Has yellow, red and black spots on sides. Found on mil-
foil, rib-wort, bedstraw, etc. from autumn to
spring.

5 Garden Tiger Moth *Arctia caja.* Distributed
over most of Europe. Wing span up to 70 mm.
Often very variably coloured. Moth abundant
everywhere during summer. In daytime hides
under leaves of plants or bushes. Caterpillar
long-haired with black and white tubercles; dorsal hairs black, lateral hairs russet. Found on
various plants from August to September and,
after hibernating, from May to June.

6 *Panaxia quadripunctaria.* Fairly common in
central Europe on sunny, and especially limestone, slopes. Wing span about 55 mm. Several
colour varieties. Moth appears on grassy slopes
in July. Caterpillar found on rib-wort, clover and
willowherb, also beeches and oaks in April and
May. Grey-brown to black with yellow dorsal
and lateral stripes and orange-spotted sides.
Pupates in loose cocoon.

7 *Panaxia dominula.* Fairly abundant in central
and northern Europe. Wing span about 55 mm.
Several colour varieties. Moth seen in June and
July among bushes, on outskirts of woods, in
avenues, etc. Caterpillar found in autumn and
again in spring on stinging-nettle, deadnettle,
wild strawberry, forget-me-not and willow, poplar and other trees.

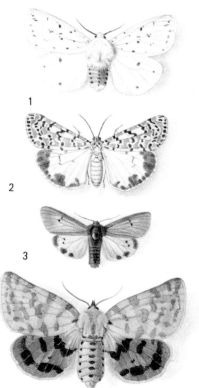

1

2

3

4

5

6

7

Family: **Geometers** or **Emeralds**—Geometridae

8 Emerald *Geometra papilionaria*. Occurs in central and northern Europe. Wing span about 45 mm. Flies from June to August in sparse woods. Sits on tree trunks. Caterpillar green with yellow stripe along sides and five protuberances on back. Found on birch, alder, beech and hazel in May. Chrysalis yellow-green with reddish brown back.

9 Magpie Moth *Abraxas grossulariata*. Distributed over whole of Europe. Wing span up to 40 mm. Moth appears from June to August; common in gardens and in woods with wild gooseberry bushes. Caterpillar whitish with wide black spots on back and orange stripe along sides. Found on gooseberry bushes.

8

9

1

Family: **Hawk Moths**—Sphingidae

1 Death's Head Moth *Acherontia atropos*. Inhabits southern Europe, regularly flies to central and northern Europe. Wing span up to about 110 mm. Flies late in evening and at night. Excellent flier; comes in summer from Mediterranean region. In central Europe female usually lays eggs on potato plants, also on henbane. Caterpillars, which by end of summer measure 10 cm, are yellow-green with black, blue and yellow stripes and spots; large spine at tip of abdomen. Pupate in ground in hard clay capsule. In colder parts of central Europe chrysalis dies.

2 Convolvulus or **Morning Glory Hawk** *Herse convolvuli*. Abundant from Atlantic coast as far as Australia. Wing span about 105 mm. Flies after dark in May and June, second generation in August and September. Flies from south to extreme north of Europe. Female lays eggs on bindweed. Mature caterpillar, which measures 9 cm, is usually light brown or greenish with light oblique stripes on sides and dark stripe down back. Caterpillar found mainly on bindweed from June until autumn. Hides during day, often in holes in ground; comes out to feed towards evening. Chrysalis has curved proboscis sheath.

3 Privet Hawk *Sphinx ligustri*. Common in central Europe. Wing span about 90 mm. Appears in May and June, sometimes until August. Flies after dark; often attracted indoors by light. Caterpillar light green with oblique violet stripes, bordered with white on underside, on sides; yellow tip of abdomen. Found on elder, privet and other shrubs from end of June to September. Chrysalis reddish-brown.

4 Pine Hawk *Sphinx pinastri*. Common all over central Europe. Wing span up to about 80 mm. Moth appears in conifer forests from April to September. Sits on tree trunks, blends with surroundings. Female lays eggs on pines and spruces. Caterpillars eat needles. Because of numerous parasites has never multiplied dangerously in central Europe. Caterpillar light green with brownish line on back, narrow white and yellow stripes on sides and red spots. Found on conifers from June to October. Chrysalis hibernates, sometimes twice.

2

5 Willow Hawk *Smerinthus ocellatus.* Common in central Europe. Wing span about 85 mm. Moth appears from May to August, mainly near water with groups of willows or poplars. Caterpillar green with blue cross-stripes on sides, whitish spots and a blue spine. Found from June to September on willow, poplar and young fruit-trees. Moth often attracted indoors by light.

6 Oak Hawk *Marumba quercus.* Inhabits southern Europe, rarely visits central Europe. Wing span up to about 100 mm. Appears in southern Europe from May to August, in central Europe usually in July. Inhabits oak-woods. Caterpillar green with oblique yellow stripes and orange spots on sides. Found from June to October chiefly on young oaks. Chrysalis brown with metallic lustre.

7 Poplar Hawk *Laothoe populi.* Locally abundant in central Europe. Wing span up to about 75 mm. Moth appears in May and June and sometimes in August and early September. Sits on poplar trunks. Caterpillar yellow-green with yellow spots and with oblique yellow stripes on sides. Found from June to September mainly on poplars, but also on willows. Pupates in ground. Chrysalis dark brown.

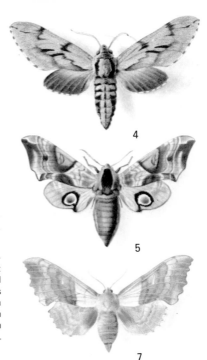

4

5

7

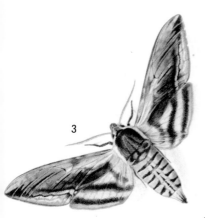

3

6

Family: **Hawk Moths**—*Sphingidae*

1 Spurge Hawk *Celerio euphorbiae*. Very common in central Europe. Wing span about 70 mm. Moth appears from May to September in clearings and pastures, by rivers and anywhere where spurge grows. Flies after dusk, visits flowers, sucks nectar with long proboscis. Caterpillar found on spurge in July and August. Strikingly coloured; basic colour black, red stripe down back and yellow spots and stripes on sides. Pupates in ground. Moth sometimes does not emerge for several years after several hibernating stages of pupa.

2 Bedstraw Hawk *Celerio gallii*. Common in central Europe. Wing span about 70 mm. Moth appears from May to July, sometimes to September. Flies swiftly after dark. Caterpillar usually dark green with yellow dorsal line and large, yellow, black-ringed spots on sides. Found from July to August on bedstraw, willowherb and spurge. Mainly frequents open sunny places. Chrysalis yellow-brown with dark lines.

3 Elephant Hawk *Deilephila elpenor*. Very common in central Europe. Wing span about 65 mm. Moth appears mostly in May and June, rarely from July to September. Fast flier. Mainly frequents places with willows, e.g. streams, clearings, etc. Caterpillar found from June to end of August on willowherb, bedstraw, vines and other plants. Up to 8 cm long. Three colour types — green, brown and blackish. Brown and white eye-spots on fourth and fifth segment. Chrysalis yellowish-brown with black spots. Moth often attracted indoors by light.

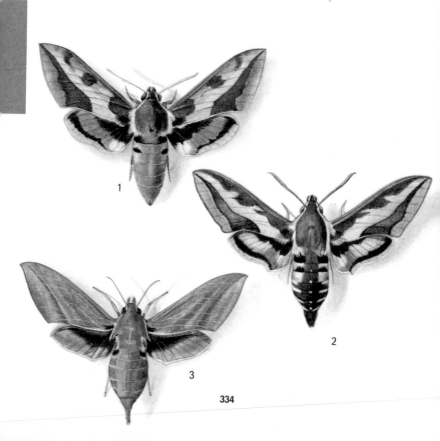

1

2

3

4

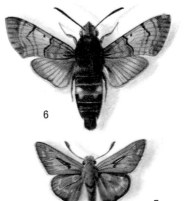

5

6

7

4 Oleander Hawk *Daphnis nerii.* Inhabits North Africa and southern Europe. Wing span about 100 mm. In summer visits central Europe where female sometimes lays eggs and caterpillars can be found. Caterpillar up to over 9 cm long; bright green with white lateral stripe from fourth segment and two white, blue-ringed eye-spots on either side of third segment. Found on oleanders and occasionally on winter-green from April to June, second generation in August and September. Chrysalis slim, brown-yellow, marked with black dots.

5 *Proserpinis proserpina.* Distributed over central and southern Europe. Wing span about 40 mm. Ragged-edged wings. Moth appears in May, flies after dusk. Caterpillar green or brownish with black marbling and with yellow, blue-rimmed spots on sides. Found in July and August on willowherb and evening primrose. Chrysalis reddish-brown.

6 *Macroglossum stellatarum.* Common in central Europe. Wing span about 45 mm. Moth flies from June to October, mainly during day, in clearings, forest meadows, etc. Has very long proboscis, sucks nectar from trumpet flowers. Flies very abruptly, hovers like hummingbird when sucking nectar. Caterpillar green with white stripe along sides. First generation of caterpillars appears in June and July, second in August to September. Found on bedstraw and woodruff. Caterpillar hides by day, comes out in search of food at night. Chrysalis grey-brown or blue-green.

Family: **Skipper Butterflies**—Hesperiidae

7 Silver-spotted Skipper *Hesperia comma.* Widely distributed all over Europe. Wing span about 30 mm. Flies very quickly during daytime. Seen from June to August in clearings, on hillsides and in meadows, also in mountainous regions. Caterpillar dark grey with double black line on sides. Found in autumn on various meadow grasses, hibernates and reappears following spring. Makes itself tube from grass leaves. Chrysalis brownish, dusted with blue.

Family: **Meadow Browns** or **Satyrs**—Satyridae

1 Marbled White *Melanargia galathea*. Occurs in central and southern Europe. Wing span about 50 mm. Butterfly abundant from June to August in forest meadows and clearings, on slopes, etc., also at high altitudes. Flies during daytime. Caterpillar yellowish with dark dorsal and reddish lateral line. Hides by day, eats various grasses at night.

2 *Hipparchia circe*. Distributed over whole of central and southern Europe. Wing span up to about 80 mm. Flies from June to August in open woods. Caterpillar has dark brown, white-lined back and yellow-brown sides with russet, white and black lines. Found on different grasses from May to June.

3 *Hipparchia briseis*. Widespread in central Europe. Wing span about 55 mm. Flies from July to September. Frequents sunny rocky slopes, likes to settle on warm rocks or stones. Caterpillar yellowish grey. Dark line on back; one dark and two light lines along sides. Found mainly on sesleria but also on other grasses in autumn and, after hibernating, again until June.

4 *Pararge achine*. Occurs in central and northern Europe. Wing span about 50 mm. Flies in shady woods in June and July. Caterpillar light green with one black and two white lines on back. Found in August and September and, after hibernating, again in May on rye-grass and other grasses, also on wheat. Pupates in May. Chrysalis green with white stripes.

Family: **Fritillaries**—Nymphalidae

5 Peacock Butterfly *Nymphalis io*. Common all over Europe. Wing span up to about 60 mm. Butterfly occurs from March until autumn, sometimes in three generations. Hibernates often inside windows, in cellars and caves, etc. Caterpillar black with white dots and black spines. Caterpillars gregarious, live mainly on stinging-nettle, also on hops and brambles from April to September. Chrysalis light brown with golden spots, hangs head downwards. Butterfly emerges in 1—2 weeks but third generation pupa hibernates.

6 Camberwell Beauty *Nymphalis antiopa.* Common in central Europe. Wing span up to over 70 mm. Flies from June until autumn, hibernates and reappears from end of April. Mainly frequents birch groves. Sits on trunk and sucks sap from injured wood, also drinks nectar. Caterpillar black with striking, red-spotted back and black spines all over body. Gregarious, lives from May to June on birches, also on poplars, willows and elms.

7 Small Tortoiseshell *Aglais urticae.* Common European butterfly. Wing span about 50 mm. Two or three generations of butterflies appear from end of June until October. Hibernating males and females appear early in spring.

Several varieties. Frequents hillsides, clearings, fields and gardens. Often found inside windows, in cellars, etc. Caterpillar black with yellow-green stripes down body and spines. Found from May until autumn on great and small nettle and occasionally on hops.

8 Comma Butterfly *Polygonia c-album.* Abundant in central Europe. Wing span about 50 mm. Several colour varieties. Butterfly in 2—3 generations from May to October, hibernates and reappears in early spring. Flies on outskirts of forests, in glades and in gardens. First third of caterpillar's body russet, remainder white, underside reddish. Armed with spines. Caterpillar found on nettle, gooseberry, hop, elm and hazel leaves. Chrysalis hangs head downwards.

6

7

5

8

1

2

3

4

5

Family: **Fritillaries**—Nymphalidae

1 Red Admiral *Vanessa atalanta*. Common in central Europe. Wing span about 60 mm. Butterfly in two generations, from June until autumn. Found almost anywhere in open places. Second generation butterflies hibernate and appear early in spring. Caterpillars variably coloured, most often black with yellow line on sides and with spines. Found in May—June and August—September in rolled leaves, chiefly of stinging-nettle.

2 Painted Lady *Vanessa cardui*. Distributed over practically whole of world. Very common in central Europe. Wing span about 55 mm. Butterfly appears in sunny places from end of May until autumn, in 2—3 generations. Likes to settle on flowers. Caterpillar brownish and spiny, with yellow stripes and dots. Found from May to September on leaves of stinging-nettle, colt's foot, burdock and other plants. Chrysalis grey with golden spots.

3 *Araschnia levana*. Abundant in central Europe. Wing span about 35—40 mm. Butterfly has spring and summer generation. Spring generation (March—April) yellowish-red with black spots, summer generation (July—August) blackish-brown with yellow spots. Caterpillars, gregarious when young, found in June and August—September on stinging-nettle. Resemble peacock butterfly caterpillars but have two long spines on head.

4 Purple Emperor *Apatura iris*. Occurs all over central Europe. Wing span about 60 mm. Upper surface of wings metallic-opalescent. Butterfly from June to August in sparse deciduous woods. Flies low, early in morning, sucks dung, carrion, etc. Caterpillar green with yellow stripes and dots and two long blue horns on head. Found from August on sallow, aspen and willow, hibernates and again eats leaves from April to June.

6

7

then gnaw young violet roots, mainly at night. Pupate at end of June. Caterpillar brownish with yellow dorsal stripe, dark lateral stripes and long yellow spines. Chrysalis found on tree trunks.

5 White Admiral *Limenitis camilla.* Occurs in central, southern and south-western Europe. Wing span about 50—55 mm. Butterfly seen from May to July in open deciduous woods. Favours damp places. Settles on blackberry flowers. Green, red-spined caterpillar found on honeysuckle. Hibernates.

6 Great White Admiral *Limenitis populi.* Locally abundant in central Europe. Wing span up to about 80 mm. Butterfly in July and August. Female has broad white bands on wings. Settles on damp ground, excreta, etc. Gliding flight. Caterpillar green with hairy excrescences. Hibernates in curled leaf and in spring, up to May, eats poplar leaves, mainly that of young trees. Also found on aspens. Butterfly leaves chrysalis in 3—4 weeks.

7 European Sailer *Neptis hylasaceris.* Occurs in warm parts of central Europe. Wing span up to about 55 mm. First generation of butterflies appears in May and June, second in July to August, in open deciduous woods. Local incidence only. Caterpillar yellow-brown with small tubercles. Found on lady's finger.

8 Silver-washed Fritillary *Argynnis paphia.* Very abundant in central Europe. Wing span up to about 70 mm. Butterfly seen from beginning of July to middle of September. Appears mainly in damp forest meadows, clearings, etc. Settles on thistles and sucks nectar. Female lays eggs on violets usually in August. Caterpillars, hatched in 14 days, hibernate until May and

9 Queen of Spain Fritillary *Issoria lathonia.* Very common in central Europe. Wing span 40—45 mm. Butterfly in 2—3 generations from early spring until autumn. Flies in meadows and fields, on hillsides, etc. Caterpillars live on violets and sainfoin and hibernate. Caterpillar brownish with whitish back, brown-yellow lines on sides and short reddish spines.

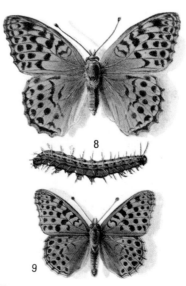

8

9

Family: **Blues, Coppers** or **Hairstreaks** — *Lycaenidae*

1 *Lycaena virgaureae.* Abundant in central Europe. Wing span up to about 35 mm. Male has golden orange wings, female brown-spotted wings. Frequents clearings, meadows, etc. in open woods. Caterpillar dark green with yellowish stripes on back and bosses on body. Lives on sorrel from April to June. Pupates on stem or in ground.

2 Adonis Blue *Polyommatus bellargus.* Occurs in central and southern Europe. Wing span about 33 mm. Butterfly in two generations, May—June and July—September. Flies in fields, on hillsides, etc. Sucks nectar from clover and lucerne flowers etc. Caterpillar blue-green with dark dorsal stripes and often reddish yellow spots. Found from April to July on clover and other papilionaceous plants. Usually pupates in the ground. Chrysalis greenish in colour.

3 Large Blue *Maculinea arion.* Occurs in central Europe in several forms. Wing span about 25 mm. Butterfly appears from June to August on sunny slopes and meadows. Likes to settle on betony flowers. Caterpillar blue-green with dark dorsal line. Found on betony from autumn.

Hibernates and pupates in anthills. Before pupating lives on ant larvae and pupae. Ants like its secretion.

Family: **Swallowtails** — Papilionidae

4 Swallowtail *Papilio machaon.* Distributed over whole of Europe. In central Europe generally two generations, April—May and July—August, in south up to October. Wing span up to about 80 mm. Good, enduring flier. Prefers dry hilly regions. Likes to settle on flowers and sucks nectar. Female lays eggs singly on umbelliferous plants, e.g. pimpernel, cummin, carrots, etc. Young caterpillar blackish, mature caterpillar light green with black cross-stripes and bright red spots. Chrysalis fixed to stems by fibres, head upwards. Some chrysalises hibernate twice.

5 Scarce Swallowtail *Papilio podalirius.* Very common in central Europe. Wing span up to about 75 mm. Spring and summer generation. Occurs mainly on sunny slopes. Female lays eggs singly on fruit-trees or blackthorn. Caterpillars hatch in 10 days. Caterpillar green with yellow dorsal stripe branching into oblique yellow cross-bands on sides. Pupates head upwards, held by fibrous loop round chrysalis. Surface of chrysalis uneven.

♂ 1

♀

2 3

6 *Zerynthia hypsipyle*. Inhabits southern Europe and southern parts of central Europe. Wing span about 50 mm. Butterfly appears in April and May, abundant in places. Flies in open sunny spots where birthwort grows. Caterpillar found on birthwort from June to August. Caterpillar russet, reddish or grey with red excrescences. Chrysalis yellow-grey.

7 Black Apollo Butterfly *Parnassius mnemosyne*. Abundant in places in central Europe. Wing span up to about 60 mm. Butterfly appears in June mainly in mountainous regions, but also at lower altitudes. Caterpillar black with rows of red spots. Hides by day, comes out to eat late in evening. Found on fumitory in April and May. Chrysalis fat and yellowish, dusted with white.

8 Red Apollo Butterfly *Parnassius apollo*. Locally common in mountainous regions of central Europe. Wing span up to about 70 mm. Dark form known in the Alps. Butterfly from June to August on sunny slopes. Likes to settle on thistle flowers. Caterpillar black with two rows of large red spots and bluish tubercles. Found in May and June on stone-crop. Pupates in ground in loose cocoon. Chrysalis bluish.

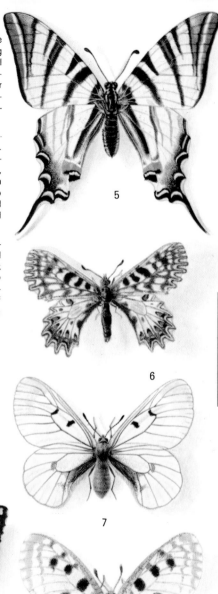

5

6

7

4

8

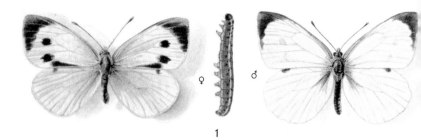

1

2

to June and from August to September. Caterpillar yellow-green with black dots and yellow stripes on back and sides. Before pupating climbs on to higher object, e.g. wall or tree. Chrysalis yellow-green with black blotches and spots. Important pest. Caterpillars often attacked by ichneumon flies.

Family: **Whites**—Pieridae

1 Large White *Pieris brassicae.* Common all over Europe. Wing span about 55 mm. Butterfly occurs from April until autumn in 2—3 generations. Flies practically everywhere. Female lays small piles of yellow eggs on underside of cabbage leaves and similar plants. Caterpillars devour leaves right down to stalk. Found from May

2 Small White, Cabbage or **Turnip Butterfly** *Pieris rapae.* Abundant all over Europe. Wing span about 45 mm. First generation of butterflies appear in April—May, second in July, sometimes third in autumn. Appears in fields, meadows and gardens. Caterpillar greenish with yellow stripes on back and sides. Found in June and again in August and September on cruciferous plants, mainly turnip leaves.

4

3

3 Black-veined White *Aporia crataegi.* Distributed over whole of Europe. Once important pest, now plentiful only in places. Wing span about 60 mm. Butterfly flies in June and July. Female lays eggs on underside of fruit-tree leaves (mainly apple-trees). Caterpillars appear from September, wrap themselves in leaves and hibernate. Early in spring form large nests round buds and eat them. Pupate at end of May on tree trunks etc. Caterpillar blue-grey with black and rusty brown stripes.

4 Orange-tip *Anthocharis cardamines.* Abundant in central Europe. Wing span about 40 mm. Male's forewings tipped with orange. Butterfly appears from beginning of April to June. Male very striking in flight. Flies close to ground in gardens, sunken lanes and forest paths. Caterpillar blue-green with white-striped sides. Found mainly on cress from June to August.

5 Pale Clouded Yellow *Colias hyale.* Very common in central Europe. Wing span about 40 mm. Butterfly appears from May to June and again from August to September. Flies on sunny, grassy slopes and over clover fields, stubble fields, etc. Caterpillar dark green with four yellow stripes down body. Found on vetches and clover in June—July and August—September. Chrysalis grey-green with yellow stripes.

6 Alpine Clouded Yellow *Colias palaenoeuropomene.* Found in central Europe in peat-bogs. Wing span about 50 mm. Butterfly seen from June to July or August over peat-bogs with plenty of crowberry plants on which caterpillars live. Caterpillar green with yellow stripe, edged below with black, along sides. Chrysalis yellow-green.

5

6

7

7 *Colias edusa.* Inhabits practically whole of Europe. Wing span about 50 mm. Basic colouring of male orange to yellowish-red, female whitish to orange and yellow. Two butterfly generations, May—June and July—August. Seen on sunny slopes and in fields and clearings, etc. Caterpillar green with white, yellow-spotted stripe along sides. Found on papilionaceous plants.

8 Brimstone Yellow or **Yellow-bird** *Gonopteryx rhamni.* Common everywhere in central Europe. Wing span about 55 mm. Butterfly seen from July to autumn. Hibernates and reappears on sunny days at end of March. Flies in gardens, fields and meadows, etc. Caterpillar dark green with white stripe on sides. Found from July mainly on buckthorn, in mountainous regions also on bilberries. Chrysalis green with two white stripes on sides.

8

Order: **Two-winged Flies**—Diptera

Family: **Crane-flies**—Tipulidae

1 Crane-fly or **Daddy-longlegs** *Tipula oleracea*.
Plentiful everywhere from April to June. Female
lays up to 500 black eggs in ground. Larvae
hatch in 2—3 weeks. Live on humus, later nibble
roots of crops. Adult insect measures 15—
23 mm. Often attracted indoors by light.

Family: **Gall-gnats**—Cecidomyidae

2 Hessian-fly *Mayetiola destructor*. Common
over whole of Europe. Length 2.5—4 mm. Flies
from April to May and again in September. Female lays eggs singly or in twos on underside of
rye, wheat or barley leaves. Larvae, hatched in 8
days, suck blades. Second larval generation
penetrates to roots of winter seedlings and
causes swellings on plants which usually die.

3 Beech Gall-gnat *Mikiola fagi*. Abundant in
beech-woods. Small and inconspicuous. Female
lays eggs singly on upperside of beech leaves.
Larvae form striking red galls, sometimes several on one leaf. Larvae of related species form
similar galls on leaves of other trees.

344

Family: **Hair-gnats**—Bibionidae

4 March-fly or **St. Mark's Fly** *Bibio marci*. Very common in woods from March to May. Length 10—13 mm. Black, with extremely long legs. Flies slowly. Larvae found in humus, live on vegetable matter. In large numbers does damage to tree nurseries.

Family: **Gadflies**—Tabanidae

5 Gadfly *Tabanus bovinus*. Distributed over practically whole of Europe, mainly near ponds, lakes and rivers. Length 20—24 mm. Flies during summer. Female attacks warm-blooded animals and man and sucks their blood, needed for development of its eggs. Bite smarts and swells. Female lays eggs on aquatic plants. Larvae crawl down into water and live predaciously in mud. Development slow. After 7—8 moults larva transformed to immobile pupa. Gadflies have numerous enemies, e.g. birds and spiders.

6 Horse-fly or **Cleg** *Haematopoda pluvialis*. Abundant near rivers and ponds. Length 10 mm. Male's eyes hairy; female's are hairless and beautifully green. Flies in summer. Bites viciously, especially before storms. Predacious larvae live in mud.

7 Greenhead *Chrysops caecutiens*. Very common near water. Length 8—9 mm. Female has golden green eyes. Appears from May to September. Female attacks large mammals and man and sucks their blood. Lays glossy black eggs on aquatic plants. Round-bodied, predacious larvae live in mud. Pupate in sand and soil.

Family: **Bee-flies**—Bombyliidae

8 *Hemipenthes morio*. Striking fly frequenting dry clearings. Length 5—12 mm. Found in summer. Female flies over bare ground looking for caterpillars attacked by caterpillar-fly or ichneumon fly larvae. Lays eggs on these and larvae parasitize parasites. Adult insects fly swiftly about in sunny parts of woods, settle on flowers and drink nectar.

Family: **Soldier-flies**—Stratiomyidae

9 Soldier-fly *Stratiomys chamaeleon*. Common, striking fly with flat abdomen. Length 12 to 14 mm. Appears mainly in summer. Flutters on flowers and bushes near water and drinks nectar. Not shy. Female lays eggs on leaves above water. Hatched larvae slip into water and live in tangled aquatic plants in shallows. Have long breathing tube. Predacious. Before pupating crawl out of water. Pupate in ground.

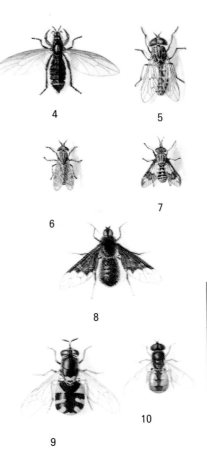

4   5

6   7

8

9   10

10 Green Soldier-fly *Eulalia viridula*. Abundant on leaves of bushes near water. Length 6—7 mm. On rainy days hides on underside of leaves.

Family: **Hover-flies**—Syrphidae

1 Currant-fly *Syrphus ribesii.* Occurs in central Europe. Length 10—11 mm. In summer and autumn appears on flowers and sucks nectar. Darting flight. In sunny spots often flies in circles. Female lays eggs on leaves. Greenish larvae catch aphids, mainly on currant bushes but also on vegetables. One larva consumes about 300 plant-lice during development.

2 *Eristalis arbustorum.* Common in central Europe. Found mainly in clearings from summer until late autumn. Length 10—12 mm. Larva lives in mud, cesspools and manure. Larva cylindrical and whitish with tail-like breathing tube. Pupates on tree trunks etc.

Family: **Fruit-flies**—Drosophilidae

3 *Drosophila melanogaster.* Abundant in summer and autumn. Length only 3.5—4 mm. Appears in flocks on soft windfall fruit, in houses and on any fermenting material. Develops very quickly. In some places nuisance as carrier of undesirable yeast cells.

Family: **Horse-ticks** or **Forest-flies**—Hippoboscidae

4 Forest-fly *Ornithomyia avicularia.* Very common, especially in woods. Length 5—6 mm. Wings permanent. Parasite of various birds, lives in plumage and sucks blood. Females produce developed larvae which immediately pupate and drop to ground. Perfect insect capable of reproduction in 3 days. Normal life span 4—6 months.

Family: **True Flies**—Muscidae

5 Common House-fly *Musca domestica.* Occurs in human dwellings all over world. Length 7—8 mm. Female lays eggs in dung, manure and rotting refuse. Development takes only 14 days, several generations may occur in a year. Hibernates as larva or as pupa. Since fly alights on excrement and then on food and human skin, can transmit many dangerous infections.

1   2

6 Common Stable-fly *Stomoxys calcitrans.* Very common in cattle country. Length 6 to 7 mm. Female lays eggs in cow dung. Adult insect also flies into homes and bites man. Bites itch. Can transmit different diseases, e.g. anthrax and in south cholera, etc.

Family: **Blow-flies**—Calliphoridae

7 Gold Blow-fly *Lucilia caesar.* Very common everywhere. Settles on tall plants and leaves of bushes. Length 7—10 mm. Brightly gleaming body. Looks for putrefying animal carcasses and human excreta in which female lays eggs and maggots develop.

8 Bluebottle *Calliphora vicina.* Very common in dwellings. Robust body 8—12 mm long. Appears from spring until autumn, betrayed by loud buzz. Female lays eggs in animal carcasses, excrement, cheese and meat. Maggots

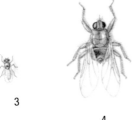

3

4

6

5

7

hatch in 24 hours, develop in 4 weeks and pupate in ground.

9 Common Flesh-fly *Sarcophaga carnaria.* Very common everywhere. Length 10—16 mm. Found on flowers, walls, tree trunks and in dwellings. Female lays live, legless maggots on fresh vertebrate carcasses or meat in which maggots develop. Maggots pupate as brown, barrel-shaped pupae. Contaminate food.

Family: **Caterpillar-flies**—Larvaevoridae

10 Caterpillar-fly *Exorista larvarum.* Occurs everywhere in sunny grassy places. Length 6—15 mm. Female lays eggs on caterpillars. Larva penetrates caterpillar's body and devours it from within. Burnet moth caterpillars most frequent hosts but other species also. Mature larvae leave host's body and pupate in ground. Very useful insect as not more than 5 per cent of attacked caterpillars develop into moths.

8

9

10

347

Cyclostomes, Cartilaginous Fishes and Bony Fishes

Cyclostomes (Cyclostomata) belong to the superclass Agnatha, comprising jawless vertebrates with only a primitive cartilaginous skull and no jaws. Best known of this group are the lampreys (Petromyzoniformes). They do not possess true bone tissue and their skeleton is cartilaginous. The body is long, snake-like and bare, but is bordered by a continuous dorsal fin on the hind part and has a hint of a caudal fin.

Lampreys do not possess paired fins. The circular mouths are without jaws but are furnished with horny teeth. There is only one nostril and that is closed. On either side of the body, behind the eyes there are seven gill slits. The eggs laid by lampreys develop into larvae with eyes covered by skin. The larval stage lasts two to four years. Some species live both in the sea and in fresh water.

Fig. 1. The Salmon (*Salmo salar*) can leap over barriers up to 3 m high.

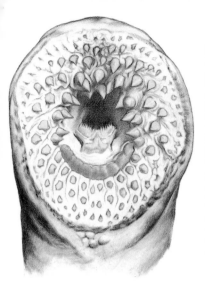

Fig. 2. The funnel-shaped mouth of the Sea Lamprey (*Petromyzon marinus*) is furnished with horny teeth. The tongue, likewise furnished with teeth, functions like a bore or a piston.

Fig. 3. The Stone Loach (*Noemacheilus barbatulus*) lives on the bed of flowing rivers. It feeds on the larvae of midges (Chironomidae).

Most commonly found in the fresh waters of Europe are two species: the Lampern (*Lampetra fluviatilis*) and the Brook Lamprey (*Lampetra planeri*). However, one might also find the Sea Lamprey (*Petromyzon marinus*), which reaches a length of 100 cm and a weight of 2—3 kg. The Sea Lamprey inhabits the northernmost parts of the Atlantic, off both the North American and European coasts, but in the spring it swims up rivers and larger streams to spawn. It usually breeds on the stony bed in flowing water, where the female lays up to 250,000 eggs. Lampreys that travel to the upper reaches of rivers die after spawning, but those that remain near the sea coast may spawn a number of times. The Sea Lamprey feeds mostly on the blood of fish, but it has also been known to attach itself to a shark or a small invertebrate on the sea floor. The Sea Lamprey is often caught in fish-traps, in Europe mostly off the coast of France, Germany and Britain.

The Lampern also lives in the sea off the coasts of northern Europe. Spring populations swim up rivers and spawn right away; autumn populations overwinter in the river and spawn the following year. Lamperns feed only in the sea. They are of little importance in commerce and are caught mostly in the Gulf of Finland.

Cartilaginous fish are the most primitive stage in the evolution of jawed vertebrates (Gnathostomata) with a skull that has jaws, of which the lower one is free and mobile. They also have paired fins; higher groups have paired limbs.

Cartilaginous fishes (Chondrichthyes) have a cartilaginous skeleton and a typical transverse mouth on the underside of the body. The mouth has jaws furnished with numerous sharp-pointed teeth. When the teeth are worn, they

Fig. 4. The Northern Pike (*Esox lucius*) has a typical dorsal fin, located far back near the tail.

Fig. 5. The predacious pike always seizes its prey crosswise at first, only afterwards turning it lengthwise so that it can swallow it.

bend forward and new teeth grow in behind them. The teeth are of dermal origin. Best known of the cartilaginous fishes are the sharks (Selachiformes) which have an elongated body covered with spiny, placoid scales whose tips are directed backward, making the skin extremely rough to the touch. On each side of the body there are five to seven gill slits.

The skeleton of sharks is still cartilaginous, but calcareous salts are deposited inside it. Their digestive tract is relatively short, leading from the mouth cavity to the pharynx and via a short gullet to the stomach. Sharks have a large liver, containing a large amount of liver fat, for which sharks are often hunted. Shark fins are also considered a delicacy, particularly in China.

Most sharks bear live young. A smaller number lay eggs that are usually square-shaped with long tendrils at each corner, by means of which they attach themselves to various plants.

Many sharks reach a length of only 1 m, but others may be up to 20 m long. Some species will even attack humans. More than 250 species inhabit the seas throughout the world except for the Caspian Sea. Only one species lives in fresh water.

The related rays (Rajiformes) have a dorsally flattened body with greatly broadened pectoral fins. The gill slits, numbering five pairs, are on the underside of the body. The tail is often whip-like.

Bony fishes (Osteichthyes) are a higher evolutionary group of jawed vertebrates. Their skeleton is either cartilaginous or bony, the body usually covered with scales, less often bare. In some species the scales have fused to form armour consisting of bony plates. In practically all instances, the fish have well-developed fins. The paired pectoral and pelvic fins correspond to the fore and hind limbs. The remaining fins are unpaired and consist of one or more dorsal fins, a caudal fin and one or more anal fins. The jaws are armed with teeth or are toothless. Practically all fish have a lateral line along the sides of the body, in which sensory cells are located, enabling them to perceive vibrations produced in the water like a kind of radar apparatus. Fish breathe by means of gills that are protected by a bony covering called the operculum.

Of the soft-boned fishes belonging to the super-order Chondrostei, which have rows of large bony plates down the length of the body and a cartilaginous skeleton, best known are the sturgeons (Acipenseriformes). Sturgeons have a head prolonged into a snout and a toothless mouth in the adult fish. On the underside of the mouth there are tactile appendages (barbels).

True bony fishes of the super-order Teleostei have a bony skeleton. The body is generally covered with dermal scales and the skin contains glands that secrete mucus. The skull is formed of flat, bony plates. Many species occur in shoals numbering millions of fish, for example herrings (Clupeidae). This family includes some 160 species of fish classed in 50 genera. They inhabit tropical and subtropical seas but are also found in the temperate zone, and even in arctic waters. They may also be found in fresh waters. Herrings generally stay far from the coast for most of their lives. During the spawning period they form huge shoals of more than 1 km long and 50 m wide. The annual haul of herrings comprises nearly 40 per cent of all worldwide commercial fishing, which indicates how important these fish are in our diet. Also well known are the salmonids (Salmonidae), which include freshwater as well as marine species, distinguished by having a small rayless adipose fin between the dorsal and caudal fins.

Of the freshwater fish, the best known are the pike (Esocidae) and the commercially important carp and minnow (Cyprinidae) which are bred artificially in ponds. Cyprinids are freshwater fish with toothless jaws but with oesophageal teeth on the last gill arch. Popular game fish are the catfish (Siluridae) which inhabit deeper bodies of fresh water. They have a naked scaleless skin and six long barbels around the mouth. The flesh of eels (Anguillidae) is very tasty. They are distinguished by having an extremely long snake-like body. Perch and their relatives (Perciformes) have hard fin rays in the forward portion of the double dorsal fin. Their number includes both marine and freshwater species. Often fished are mackerel (Scombridae), predacious marine fish with a spindle-shaped body, which occur in huge shoals. Cod and their relatives (Gadiformes) include many commercially important, mostly marine fish, for example Gadidae, which have a single barbel on the lower lip.

Fig. 6. With its long ovipositor, the female European Bitterling (*Rhodeus sericeus*) deposits eggs in the mantle cavity of live freshwater clams or mussels.

Class: **Lamprey and Hag Fishes**—Cyclostomata

Order: **Lampreys**—Petromyzoniformes

1 Brook Lamprey *Lampetra planeri*. Distributed over whole of Europe. Lives permanently in rivers and streams. Length up to 16 cm. In spring female lays 500—2,000 eggs. Larvae transform to adult individuals after 2—4 years. In spring, after completing metamorphosis, lampreys spawn in upper reaches where larvae also live. Adults die after spawning.

2 River Lamprey *Lampetra fluviatilis*. Lives in sea off coasts of northern Europe. Length up to 50 cm. In autumn migrates up rivers and in April or May spawns near source in places with sandy bed. Male builds nest — depression up to 50 cm in diameter — in which female lays 5,000—40,000 eggs. Male and female then die of exhaustion. Larvae, hatched in 14—21 days, live on small organisms. Grow to 18 cm, undergo metamorphosis at end of summer of third year. Toothless mouth acquires teeth and eyes emerge onto surface of head. On completing metamorphosis which takes 6—8 weeks, young lampreys migrate to sea where they live predaciously on different fishes. Tear food to pieces with teeth and suck it in. Grow quickly. When adult, return to spawning sites in rivers and streams. Swim 15—25 km daily against current. Lamprey has savoury flesh.

Class: **Cartilaginous Fishes**—Chondrichthyes

Order: **Sharks and Allies**—Selachiformes

3 Lesser Spotted Dog-fish *Scyliorhinus caniculus*. Lives off European coasts, including Mediterranean. Common round England. Length 1 m. Not dangerous to man. Hunts food (molluscs and crustaceans) on sea bed. Nocturnal animal. Female lays up to 20 eggs in hard capsules, with tendrils or corners for attachment to plants. Embryo takes about 6—7 months to develop. Fish's flesh edible but liver supposed to be poisonous.

Order: **Rays and Allies**—Rajiformes

4 Thorn-back Ray *Raja clavata*. Commonest European ray, also found in North Sea. Male attains 70 cm, female up to 125 cm in length. Wide pectoral fins give body rhomboid form. Dorsal skin covered with sharp spines. Ray mainly frequents ooze in shallows. Lives on crabs, shrimps, plaice, etc. Hard egg capsules have process at each of four corners. Eggs laid individually in sand. Embryo takes 4.5—5.5 months to develop. Ray's flesh very tasty.

1

2

3

Class: **Bony Fishes**—Osteichthyes

Subclass: **Ray-finned Fishes**—Actinopterygii

Order: **Sturgeons and Allies** — Acipenseriformes

5 Common Sturgeon *Acipenser sturio*. Abundant off coast of northern parts of Atlantic and in North Sea, Baltic, Mediterranean and Black Sea. Length about 2 m (maximum given as 3 m). Migrates in spring to large rivers to spawn and then returns to sea. Eggs, which resemble frogspawn, are laid on stony bed. One female lays 800,000—2,500,000 eggs. Fry hatch in a few days. Young migrate to sea within 2 years. Sturgeon looks mainly on sea bed for food (molluscs, crustaceans, worms, small fish) using tactile barbels, seizes it in protrusible mouth. Has now practically vanished from European rivers.

6 Sterlet *Acipenser ruthenus*. Lives in rivers emptying into Black and Caspian Seas. In central Europe occasionally appears in Danube as far as Linz. Long snout. Length 50 cm. Spawning season May—June. Catches food in same manner as preceding species. Has excellent flesh. Caviare is eggs or roe of female.

Order: **Herrings and Allies**—Clupeiformes

Family: **Herrings**—Clupeidae

7 European Shad *Alosa alosa*. Inhabits North Sea. Length up to 70 cm. In spring swims upstream to spawn. Female lays up to 200,000 eggs on river bed. Feeds on small animals. Likes clear water.

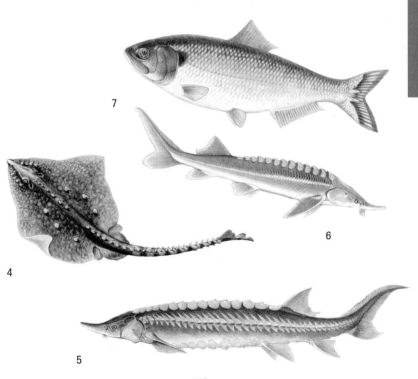

7

4

6

5

Family: **Salmonids**—Salmonidae

1 Salmon *Salmo salar.* Lives in sea off coasts of Europe, Asia and America. In autumn migrates en masse to source of rivers where it spawns in winter. The young (parrs) remain in river 3—5 years and then migrate to sea. Attain adulthood several years later. At spawning site, in cold water about 1 m deep, female makes depression by slapping tail, lays eggs in it and covers them with sand. Unlike other migratory fishes, salmon spawn several times, although many die of exhaustion or are killed by predators. One female lays up to 40,000 eggs. Survivors return to sea in early spring. Adult salmon measures up to 1.5 m and weighs 50 kg. Belongs to disappearing fauna of European rivers, although until fairly recent times hundreds of thousands still migrated inland to spawn every year. In time of migration and spawning does not eat. In sea lives on herrings, sprats, crustaceans, etc. Young salmon eat insect larvae and later small fish.

2 Trout *Salmo trutta.* Several species formerly differentiated, now races. Sea Trout (*S.t. trutta*) lives off coasts from France as far as Baltic. Length 1.3 m. Migrates up rivers only at spawning time. Lake Trout (*S.t. morpha lacustris*) inhabits Alpine and near-Alpine lakes and spawns in their inflowing streams. Female measures up to 80 cm, lays about 30,000 eggs. Most familiar form, Brown Trout (*S.t. morpha fario*) inhabits 'trout zone' of fast mountain streams. Distributed over whole of western, central and northern Europe as far as Finland and south to Italy and Morocco. Length up to 30 cm. Spawns in winter at age of 2—3 years, female lays up to 1,500 eggs. Likes clear water. Lives on insects, molluscs, worms, etc. One of the most popular fishes. Often bred artificially by collecting eggs and separating and cultivating viable ones. Rainbow Trout (*Salmo gairdneri irideus*), originally from North America, also bred in many parts of Europe. Tolerates warmer water, spawns in spring.

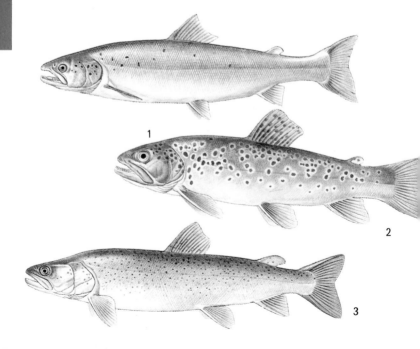

1

2

3

3 Huchen *Hucho hucho*. Lives in clean tributaries of Danube. Never migrates to sea. Measures up to 150 cm, weighs 15 kg (occasionally up to 30 kg). Highly predacious, catches fish and other aquatic vertebrates. In March—April swims short distances upstream and spawns on stony beds. Fully grown female lays up to 25,000 eggs. Sometimes bred artificially. Flesh excellent.

4 Alpine Charr *Salvelinus salvelinus*. Resembles trout. Inhabits cold Alpine lakes. Variable colouring and size (in lakes with poor food supply only up to 40 cm). Dark, normal and large form measuring up to 80 cm and weighing up to 10 kg distinguished. First two live on plankton, third on fish. Spawns from November to January near shore or in July on bed, at depth of 20—80 m.

5 Freshwater Houting *Coregonus lavaretus*. Inhabits cold lower reaches of rivers, brackish water and deep lakes in northern part of central and northern Europe. Very variable. Four basic forms, each with own local variability, distinguished. Lives on plankton. Some forms successfully bred in ponds.

6 Grayling *Thymallus thymallus*. Distributed over most of Europe. High dorsal fin. Length up to 48 cm, weight about 1 kg. Inhabits clean rivers and larger streams but likes warmer water than trout. Males larger than females, brightly coloured in spawning season (March—April). Lives on insect larvae, small animals, etc. Valued by anglers for its tasty flesh.

4

5

6

Order: **Pikes and Allies**—Esociformes

Family: **Pikes**—Esocidae

1 Pike *Esox lucius.* Inhabits rivers and stagnant water over whole northern hemisphere. Length up to 1.5 m., weight 40 kg. and more. In Europe spawns in March and April. Female lays up to 1,000,000 eggs in shallow water. Fry sink to bottom. After 2—3 hours attach themselves to aquatic plants or stones by means of special gland at end of head. Mouth and gills do not open for 8 days. Young pike then surface to fill bladder with air. Pike lives on fish, amphibians, etc.

Order: **Carps and Allies**—Cypriniformes

Family: **Carps and Minnows**—Cyprinidae

2 Carp *Cyprinus carpio.* Originally from southeastern European and Asian rivers (China, Japan), has now been introduced into all European rivers. Bred artificially in ponds. Occasionally can measure up to 1.5 m and weigh 35 kg. River carp (wild form) has low body. Carp have been bred in Europe since 13th century. Many local breeds exist. Fully grown in 3—4 years. Spawning time May—June, at temperature of 15° to 20°C. Female lays 100,000—1,000,000 eggs, fry hatch in 3—6 days. In winter carp retires to deeper, muddy spots and hibernates. Lives on small animals and aquatic plants. Life span up to 50 years.

3 Crucian Carp *Carassius carassius.* Inhabits central and eastern Europe, also distributed in Asia and North America. Lives in stagnant and slow-flowing water. High body, no barbels. Length only 20—30 cm, weight about 1 kg. Spawns in May and June. Female lays up to 300,000 eggs on aquatic plants. Feeds on in-

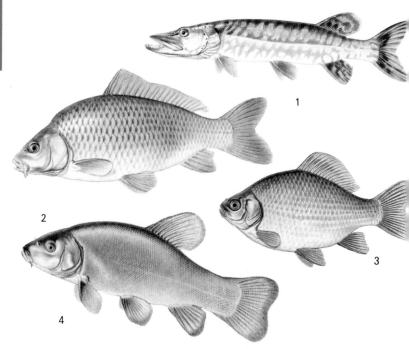

sects, molluscs and small crustaceans. Golden form also distinguished.

4 Tench *Tinca tinca*. Inhabits stagnant and slow-flowing water in Europe and western Siberia. Also occurs in brackish water of Baltic Sea. Length up to 50 cm, weight about 5 kg. Minute scales, slimy skin. Life span 20 years. Large specimens found only in deep lakes. Spawning time May—July. Female lays about 300,000 sticky eggs which adhere to aquatic plants. Nocturnal fish. Tasty flesh.

5 Roach *Rutilus rutilus*. Occurs in all rivers and in stagnant water in central and northern Europe. Also found in brackish water. Abundant everywhere. Length 15—35 cm, weight sometimes over 1 kg. Spawns near bank in April and May. Female lays 100,000 eggs. Important as food for predacious species, e.g. pike. Valueless in fishponds, in rivers popular with anglers.

Lives on river plants, small molluscs, crustaceans and insects.

6 Bream *Abramis brama*. One of largest European freshwater fishes. Length up to 70 cm, weight over 7 kg. High-backed, flat-sided body. Distributed from Urals to west of France and Britain. Inhabits stagnant and slow-flowing water with muddy bed. Spawns in May—July. Female lays 20,000—300,000 eggs at night. Young remain near banks in large shoals. Looks for food (small animals) mainly on bed, surfaces only at night.

7 Silver Bream *Blicca bjoerkna*. High-backed, short, very flat-sided body. Inhabits European rivers and ponds. Usually measures only 30 cm and weighs less than 1 kg. Spawns in May—June. Female lays about 100,000 eggs among aquatic plants. Of no economic importance. Lives on small animals and aquatic plants.

5

6

7

Family: **Carps and Minnows**—Cyprinidae

1 Orfe *Leuciscus idus.* Inhabits rivers and river-fed lakes all over Europe. Length 30—45 cm, occasionally up to 70 cm, weight 1—4 kg. Spawns in large shoals near banks from April to June. Female lays 40,000—100,000 eggs on stones and aquatic plants. Lives on insects, worms, small molluscs and crustaceans. Large specimens also eat small fish but Orfe not counted as predator. Has very tasty flesh but is comparatively rare.

2 Chub *Leuciscus cephalus.* Commonest fish in slow-flowing European rivers and streams. Length 30 cm (occasionally up to 70 cm), weight 0.25—5 kg. Spawning time April and May. Female lays up to 200,000 eggs on aquatic plants. Omnivorous. Eats water plants and small animals, often destructive to young trout populations. Flesh quite tasty.

3 Dace *Leuciscus leuciscus.* Distributed over whole of central and northern Europe. Inhabits fast rivers and streams, also stream-fed ponds. Length 15—20 cm, weight not more than 1 kg. Spawning season March—May. Rival of grayling and trout. Lives on small animals and some plants. Not very popular as food.

4 Asp *Aspius aspius.* Only truly predacious member of carp family. Found near surface of large rivers. Distributed over central and eastern Europe, also found in brackish waters of Baltic Sea. Robust but elongate body. Length 40 to 60 cm, weight 2—4 kg (in rare cases up to 1.2 m and 10 kg). Spawns from March to beginning of June. Female lays 80,000 to 100,000 eggs on sandy bed. Catches fish, amphibians and occasionally young birds, especially of aquatic species. Very retiring. Has tasty flesh so popular with anglers.

5 *Leucaspius delineatus.* Inhabits central and eastern Europe. Occurs in stagnant and slow-flowing water, also in small ponds and pools. Usually found in shoals. Characterized by silvery sheen and shortened lateral line. Length only 5—6 cm, in exceptional cases up to 12 cm. Spawning time April—May. Female lays about 150 eggs in spirals or rings round stems of aquatic plants. Male guards fry and fans oxygenated water towards them with pectoral fins. Young capable of further reproduction in one year. Lives on algae and small organisms. Important as food for predacious species.

6 *Alburnoides bipunctatus.* Inhabits central Europe. Common in southern and western Germany, elsewhere rare. Lives in shoals in fast, clean rivers, but not at altitudes of over 700 m. Length 9—11 cm. Spawns in April—June. Female lays eggs on sandy bed in flowing water. Fish used by anglers as bait.

7 Bleak *Alburnus alburnus.* Distributed over whole of Europe from Alps as far as Volga. Also found in brackish waters of Baltic Sea, but not in Scotland and Ireland. Inhabits lowland rivers or large river-fed lakes and ponds. Stays near surface. Length 10—15 cm. Spawns from March to June in shallow water near bank, to accompaniment of loud splashing. Female lays eggs at roots of trees extending into water, on aquatic plants, etc. Very abundant fish, important component of diet of predacious fishes. Also significant for destruction of large quantities of mosquito larvae. In addition eats plankton on surface of water. Often employed by anglers as bait in catching predatory fish. In places with very high incidence sometimes used for feeding pigs.

4

5

6

7

Family: **Carps and Minnows**—Cyprinidae

1 *Pelecus cultratus.* East-European fish. Formerly also inhabited bays of Baltic Sea. Often migrates from Black Sea up Danube. Length up to 60 cm. Lives in shoals. Spawns in May and June in salt and fresh water, some individuals in upper reaches of rivers. Female lays about 100,000 eggs on aquatic plants. Lives mainly on plankton.

2 Minnow *Phoxinus phoxinus.* Inhabits fast-flowing streams all over Europe, including mountains. Length 7—14 cm. Males don bright colours in spring. Spawning season May—July. Spawns in daytime, in shoals, in shallow water with sandy bed. Female lays 100—200 large yellow eggs. Fry grow very quickly. Life span 3—4 years. Lives on insect larvae and worms. Found in shoals near surface.

3 Bitterling *Rhodeus sericeus.* Inhabits central Europe north of Alps. Found in stagnant and slow-flowing water. Length 4—10 cm. Male brightly coloured at spawning time, female grows ovipositor. Fish collect in groups in sandy places with bivalves living on bed. Male releases cloud of milt in immediate vicinity of bivalve, which imbibes it together with water. Female inserts ovipositor into shell and lays egg which is fertilized inside shell. Process repeated until all eggs — usually about 40 — have been 'planted'. Shell protects both eggs and fry, which leave shelter after yolk has been consumed. Bitterling largely vegetarian but also eats small crustaceans and worms. Sometimes bred in aquariums.

4 Nase *Chondrostoma nasus.* Once plentiful in most European rivers, especially Oder and Elbe. Still abundant in Danube, Rhine and tributaries. Head produced to snout. Bottom-dweller. Spawning time March—May. Migrates upstream to stony places and spawns in shoals. Female lays up to 100,000 eggs. Adult fish attains up to 50 cm of length and weighs 2 kg. Lives on water plants and small animals. Flesh not very popular.

5 Barbel *Barbus barbus.* Inhabits whole of central Europe north of Alps, but rare west of Elbe. Lives at bottom of clear flowing water and pools. Length up to 70 cm, weight up to 5 kg. Gathers in shoals. Swims upstream in spawning season (April—June). Female lays 5,000—30,000 golden yellow eggs on sandy bed. Eats small animals, e.g. mayfly larvae and eggs and fry of other fishes. Its own roe is regarded as poisonous.

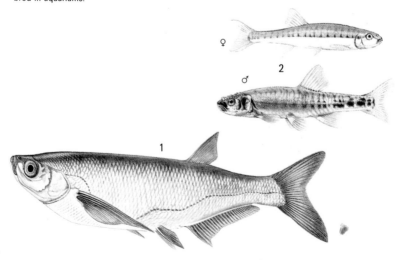

6 Rudd *Scardinius erythrophthalmus.* Inhabits stagnant and slow-flowing waters in Europe, in Alps up to altitude of 2,000 m. Adult fish has bright red abdominal, anal and caudal fins. Length up to 30 cm, weight 1 kg. Spawns in April and May. Female lays up to 100,000 reddish eggs on plants. Feeds on greenstuff and small animals. Has tasty flesh.

7 Gudgeon *Gobio gobio.* Distributed from west of France as far east as central Siberia. Absent in Spain and northern Sweden and Norway. Several subspecies. Single barbel on either side of mouth. Strikingly large fins. Lives at bottom of streams and rivers, also in stagnant water with stony and sandy bottoms. Occurs in brackish water in western part of Baltic. Often found in very large numbers in stream-fed ponds. Length 10—20 cm. Spawns from May to June. Female lays 1,000—3,000 eggs in small clumps on stones and aquatic plants. Young hatch in 10—20 days, according to temperature. Lives on small animals and vegetable debris. Gathers in large shoals, often in company of other fishes.

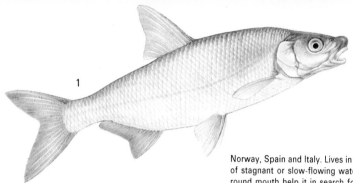

Family: **Carps and Minnows**—Cyprinidae

1 Eastern European Bream *Vimba vimba*. Common in central and eastern Europe. Lives near bed. Protruding upper jaw. Length 20—30 cm, weight up to 2 kg. Back often turns black at spawning time. Spawning season April—June. Thousands of fish frequently throng spawning site. Female lays 100,000—200,000 eggs. Lives on small bottom-dwelling animals. Flesh of no great value as food.

Family: **Loaches**—Cobitidae

2 Weatherfish *Misgurnus fossilis*. Inhabits greater part of Europe, but absent in England, Norway, Spain and Italy. Lives in mud at bottom of stagnant or slow-flowing water. Ten barbels round mouth help it in search for food. Length 20—30 cm. Spawning season April—June. Female lays up to 10,000 eggs on aquatic plants. Weatherfish has accessory intestinal respiration allowing it to live in oxygen-defficient water. Weatherfish has accessory intestinal respiration allowing it to live in oxygen-deficient water. Surfaces, swallows air, forces it down highly vascularized intestine and releases used air through anus. Eats small molluscs and other bottom-dwelling animals, also vegetable debris. Has savoury flesh.

3 Spined Loach *Cobitis taenia*. Inhabits whole of Europe except Norway, Scotland and Ireland. Lives at bottom of clean, slow-flowing or stagnant water with sandy bed. Has 6 short barbels on upper lip and 12—20 round spots on sides. Small, high-set eyes with yellow iris. Length 8—12 cm. Likes to burrow in sand with only head showing. Spawns April—June. Lives on small bottom-dwelling animals. Has accessory intestinal respiration. Below eyes has erectile spine raised when in danger. Hisses if handled.

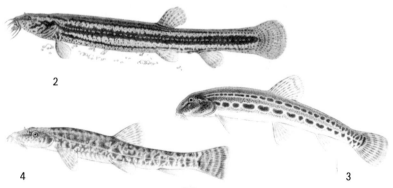

4 Stone Loach *Noemacheilus barbatulus.* Distributed over whole of Europe except Norway and Sweden. Also abundant in Baltic bays. Lives at bottom of clean, flowing water in lakes and ponds. Smooth snake-like body with scales on sides only. Colouring very variable, but belly always white or bluish. Length 10 to 15 cm. Spawns from April to June. Female lays about 6,000 eggs on aquatic plants. Eats small bottom-dwelling animals. Once regarded as great delicacy.

Family: **Catfishes**—Siluridae

5 European Catfish *Silurus glanis.* Distributed from Rhine as far east as western Asia. Large head with wide snout. Scaleless body. Inhabits deep, slow-flowing rivers, dams and lakes. In deep water may measure up to 3 m and weigh 250 kg. Solitary fish, occurs in pairs only at spawning time. Spawns from May to June near thickly overgrown banks. Female lays up to 200,000 eggs in shallow water at 18° to 20°C. Stays mainly near bottom, but likes to surface at night. Ungainly in appearance, but swift in action. Predacious. Hunts fish, aquatic birds up to size of goose, small mammals. Young specimens eat insects, molluscs and amphibians. Flesh has excellent flavour.

Family: **North American Catfishes**—Ictaluridae

6 Horned Pout *Ictalurus nebulosus.* Originally from USA Introduced into Europe in 1885 and now bred in rivers and ponds. Length up to 45 cm., weight 1 kg. As distinct from European catfish, has 8 barbels (i.e. 2 more) and adipose fin behind dorsal fin. Stays near bottom, active at night. Spawns in early spring, when found in pairs. Female forms nest-pit between roots, male guards eggs and young fry. Lives on small animals, e.g. fish, etc.

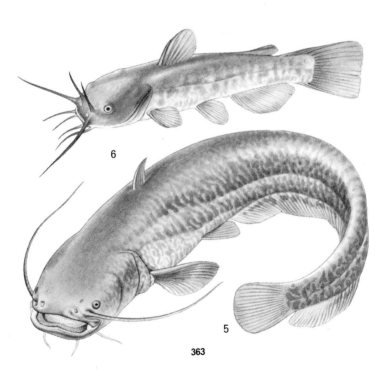

6

5

Order: **Eels and Allies**—Anguilliformes

Family: **Eels**—Anguillidae

1 European Eel *Anguilla anguilla.* Inhabits European coastal waters and rivers. Length over 1 m. (male only 50 cm), weight up to 5 kg. Eels migrate to western part of Atlantic (Sargasso Sea, east of West Indies), spawn in early spring at depth of 400 m and temperature of 17°C and then die. Larvae, formerly described as separate species, travel to European coasts with Gulf Stream. At two years measure about 7.5 cm and reach Europe. At three years acquire typical form and are known as 'elvers'. Invade rivers, develop slowly. Females develop in rivers, males at river mouth. On attaining sexual maturity migrate back to spawning site in sea, taking no food during journey. Male matures at 9, female at 12 years. Predacious fish, lives on different animals. Young bred in ponds.

Order: **Gar Pikes and Allies**—Beloniformes

Family: **Gar Pikes**—Belonidae

2 Gar Pike *Belone belone.* Lives in shoals in north-eastern part of Atlantic, also in Baltic, Mediterranean and Black Seas. Predacious fish. Lives on swimming crabs, fish, insects. Spawns in shallow water. Female lays eggs from May to June, among aquatic plants. Bones turn green when boiled.

Order: **Lophobranchiate Fishes**—Syngnathiformes

Family: **Pipe Fishes**—Syngnathidae

3 Narrow-nosed Fish *Syngnathus typhle.* Common in Baltic and North Sea. Length up to 30 cm. Variable colouring. Inhabits shallow water with dense vegetation. Spawns from April to August. Male carries fry in special abdominal brood pouch, later deposits fry in sea. Eats small crustaceans and fish fry. Suctorial mouth, imbibes prey together with water.

Order: **Perches and Allies**—Perciformes

Family: **Sea Basses**—Serranidae

4 Sea Bass *Morone labrax.* Inhabits coastal waters of Europe and Africa. Often invades rivers, e.g. Elbe. Length up to 1 m. Spawns at river mouths, also in rivers, from May to July. Sea eggs float, river eggs lie on bed. Fry hatched in 6 days. Predacious fish, pursues pilchard shoals. Has savoury flesh.

Family: **Perches**—Percidae

5 Perch *Perca fluviatilis.* Inhabits rivers, lakes and ponds all over Europe. Common fish. Length up to 40 cm, weight 4 kg. For growth over 30 cm requires 15 years. Consorts in small

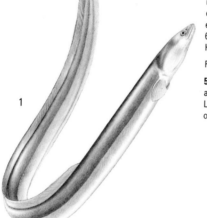

1

2

3

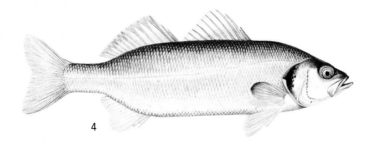

4

shoals. Spawning season April to beginning of June. Female lays strings of eggs (total up to 250,000) on aquatic plants etc. Fry hatched in 18 days, take no food up to age of 14 days. Predacious fish, often hunts in shoals. Tasty flesh.

6 Pikeperch *Stizostedion lucioperca*. Distributed over central and north-eastern Europe. Occurs in clean rivers, ponds and brackish water. Length up to 1.3 m, weight 10 kg. Spawns from April to June at depths of 3—5 m. Female lays up to 300,000 eggs in clumps. Predacious fish. When young catches small animals, later different fishes. Flesh has excellent flavour.

7 Pope or **Ruffe** *Acerina cernua*. Inhabits rivers of central and northern Europe. Abundant. Length up to 20 cm. Has preference for deep, clear water and for Baltic bays. Spawning season March—May. Female lays 50,000—100,000 eggs. Predacious fish. Eats insects, worms, crustaceans and eggs and fry of other fishes. Sometimes does serious damage.

8 Streber *Aspro streber*. Occurs only in Danube and tributaries. Lives in flowing water with stony bed. Length only 14—18 cm. Spawns from March to May. Predacious. Lives on worms, insects, small crustaceans and small fish.

5

6

8

7

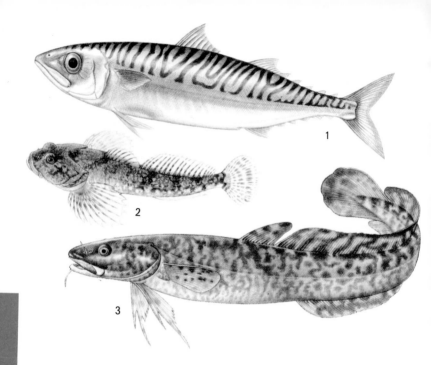

Family: **Mackerels**—Scombridae

1 Common Mackerel *Scomber scombrus.* Inhabits Atlantic, Baltic, North Sea, Mediterranean and Black Sea. Length up to 50 cm. In summer frequents shallow coastal water, in winter deep water. Forms huge shoals. Spawns from May to August near coast. Female lays up to 400,000 eggs. At 3 years young mackerel measures 30 cm and is capable of reproduction. Lives first of all on small crustaceans, later on small herrings, sprats and molluscs. Has excellent flesh. Popular food all over Europe. Caught with nets while migrating.

Family: **Sculpins**—Cottidae

2 Miller's Thumb *Cottus gobio.* Inhabits practically whole of Europe. Found in swift-flowing rivers and streams, also in lakes. Stays near bottom and often hides under stones. Length 10—18 cm. Spawning season March—April. Female lays piles of eggs (total 100 to 300) in pits. Eggs guarded by male. Lives on small animals, including trout fry.

Order: **Cods and Allies**—Gadiformes

Family: **Cods**—Gadidae

3 Burbot *Lota lota.* Distributed over whole of northern hemisphere. Southern limit in Europe northern Italy. Lives in deep, flowing water or river-fed lakes and ponds. Found at quite high altitudes. Length 40—80 cm, weight up to 3 kg. In spawning season (November to beginning of February) swims short distances upstream and looks for sandy site. Female lays up to 1,000,000 eggs in shallow pits or on aquatic plants. Fry hatched in 4 weeks. Nocturnal fish. Predacious, catches smaller fishes and other animals. Flesh regarded as delicacy.

Order: **Flounders**—Pleuronectiformes

Family: **Soles**—Soleidae

4 Sole *Solea solea.* Found along European coasts of Atlantic, North Sea and part of Baltic. Length up to 50 cm. Colouring adapted to environment. Adults live on sandy bed at depths of not more than 50 m. Active at night. In North Sea spawns from April to August. Young specimens, still symmetrically built, remain near shore up to 2 years and even invade rivers. Eats worms, molluscs, crustaceans and small fishes. Great delicacy. Caught mainly in North Sea.

Order: **Anglers and Allies**—Lophiiformes

Family: **Anglers** or **Fishing Frogs**—Lophiidae

5 Common Angler Fish *Lophius piscatorius*. Occurs in North Sea, off coast of western Europe and in northern part of Mediterranean. Length up to 2 m. Has isolated, free fin rays on head and anterior part of body. Foremost ray carries leaf-like appendage. Several rows of sharp teeth in mouth. Frequents sea bed, usually found in mud. Spawns in March and April at depths of 1—2 km. Eggs rise to surface. Fry very bizarre in shape. Predacious fish. Lies in wait for prey, 'angling' with long dorsal spines. Lives on fishes, including small sharks and rays. Has very good flesh.

Order: **Sticklebacks and Allies**—*Gasterosteiformes*

Family: **Sticklebacks**—*Gasterosteidae*

6 Three-spined Stickleback *Gasterosteus aculeatus*. Distributed all over Europe, but introduced artificially in many places. Also plentiful along coast. Length 4—7 cm. Care of offspring interesting. At spawning time (April—June) brightly coloured male builds spherical nest from plant fragments and defends surrounding area. Female lays 80—100 eggs in nest and male guards eggs and fry. Several females may lay in one nest and one female may lay 5—6 times in one season. At end of spawning season sticklebacks combine in large shoals. Life span 2—3 years. Very predacious fish. Eats eggs and often fry of other fishes and sometimes does considerable damage. Can be kept in large aquariums with cold water.

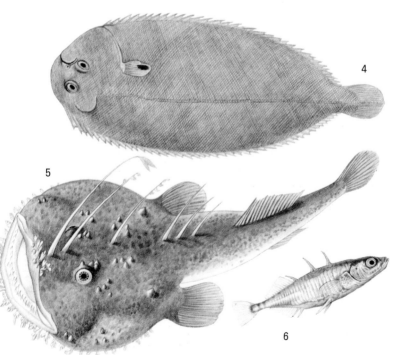

4

5

6

Amphibians and Reptiles

Amphibians (Amphibia) are four-footed vertebrates that develop by metamorphosis. The larva lives in water and breathes by means of gills, while the adult animal possesses lungs and can live on dry land. Some species, however, are ovoviviparous, that is the female gives birth to live young that have developed and hatched from eggs within her body. The skin of amphibians is scaleless and glandulous. It produces secretions that are often poisonous.

Tailed amphibians (Caudata) have four limbs that are well developed, although relatively puny, in adults and are used for crawling. The long, flat-sided tail is retained throughout the animal's lifetime and, together with movements of the body, enables it to swim. Tailed amphibians have a high regenerative capacity. This means that they are able to grow replacements for lost body parts, including bones. They are very plentiful animals that live on dry land but in rather moist places. In spring they make their way to water, usually to still bodies of water, where the females lay their eggs. During this period the males of many species develop a conspicuous crest on the back and tail. Very occasionally, as in the Alpine Salamander (*Salamandra atra*), the female does not bear aquatic larvae but gives birth directly to fully developed young that cast off their gills while still inside the female's body.

The jaws and inside of the mouth cavity are furnished with small simple teeth serving only to seize food. The tongue has little mobility and is usually attached along the whole of the underside. The eyes have eyelids. In species living in the dark waters of caves, the eyes are atrophied; in other species they are large and keen-sighted. The hearing apparatus lacks a middle ear and eardrum, and therefore tailed amphibians have imperfect hearing. In the larval stage they breathe by means of gills, in the adult stage by means of lungs and often also through the skin or through the lining of the mouth. It is interesting to note that some species can reproduce in the larval stage; this is called neoteny. Some species remain in the larval stage their whole life, breathe only by means of gills and never leave the water.

One of the European species that spends its entire life in water as a larva and does not change into a terrestrial form, is *Proteus sanguinus*, found in the karst region of Yugoslavia, in Dalmatia and Herzegovina and also in neighbouring regions of Italy. It lives in the waters of caves in almost constant darkness and has reduced eyes covered with skin. It will reproduce by means of eggs, but when the temperature reaches 15°C, as is usually the case in these caves, the embryos in the eggs develop inside the female's body and she then bears live young.

Most tailed amphibians live on dry land in the adult stage but still require considerable moisture. For this reason they seek places of concealment in damp places on warm dry days — in moss, under stones, under fallen tree trunks, or in rock crevices and holes. Most species do not emerge until dusk, when the air is cooler and moister, or during the daytime mainly after a rainfall.

The largest family of this order are the salamanders and newts (Salamandridae). Best known in Europe is the Fire Salamander (*Salamandra salamandra*). It is very plentiful in some places, mainly in forests around clear streams. It emerges from its hiding place mostly in the evening or early morning, but also regularly during the daytime after a rainfall. Its skin secretion is poisonous and may cause an unpleasant burning sensation in the mucous membrane of humans and predators.

Newts (*Triturus*) may be found in almost any still water, including flooded ditches, small pools in sand quarries and the like, primarily in spring. Newts have a very flat-sided tail, which indicates that they spend a great part of the year in water, where they swim primarily with the aid of their tails. During the breeding season the males differ markedly from the females. They develop a tall crest on the back and tail and also become extraordinarily brightly coloured. At the end of this period the crests and bright coloration disappear and the males again resemble the females.

Frogs and toads (Salientia) are tailless amphibians, usually with strong, muscular hind legs and webbed feet. Their larvae (tadpoles) have a tail that is absorbed following metamorphosis, as are the gills. The skin is bare and slimy. In many species, for example toads (*Bufo*), the fluid secreted through the skin is poisonous. The eardrums are located on the top of the head and are clearly visible. The eggs are laid in clusters or strings, usually in water, although in some tropical, as well as European, species the females lay their eggs on dry land. The tadpoles live in water, breathe by means of gills and undergo metamorphosis. The adult individuals that emerge from the water after metamorphosis breathe with fully developed lungs.

Frogs and toads have a very well-developed sense of territory and direction and this knowledge is, to a certain degree, permanently imprinted. Many species travel several kilometres every year on their return to pools, ponds or other bodies of water where they first developed as tadpoles. Early in spring they may often be seen moving in hordes in the direction of their natal pond. On the way they must overcome numerous obstacles, especially dangerous highways. At regular crossings of this kind, conservationists often erect bands of cloth or plastic alongside the highway, thus forcing the frogs to halt before this insurmountable barrier. They then catch the frogs and carry them to the other side of the road where the frogs can continue, unharmed, on their way across fields and meadows to their goal.

During the breeding season, vocal communication plays an important role and the sounds uttered by the males of many species are very distinctive. Some species remain in water only during the breeding period, for example toads. Others always live near water and still others live in water for most of the year, for example *Bombina*.

Fig. 1. The Moor Frog (*Rana arvalis*) usually inhabits pools on moors, but also occurs in ponds, particularly in spring.

Many frogs and toads have special protective equipment that serves to frighten or ward off attackers, for example the brightly coloured bellies of *Bombina* toads. When danger threatens and the toad cannot escape into water, it lifts its head and places its front legs on its curved back, thereby suddenly showing the warning coloration of its belly. If, in spite of this, a predator seizes the toad in its mouth, it immediately feels the effect of poisonous fluid secreted by the skin, which causes a sharp burning sensation in the mouth. Usually the attacker learns its lesson and the next time it sees the warning coloration it leaves the toad alone.

Fig. 2. Male Crested Newts (*Triturus cristatus*) grow a high, toothed crest down the length of the back during the mating season.

Fig. 3. The Yellow-bellied Toad (*Bombina variegata*) buries itself in mud when danger threatens. When there is not time to do this, it shows the warning coloration of its belly to frighten off the enemy.

Reptiles (Reptilia) are higher vertebrates that no longer require an aquatic environment for their development. The eggs with their embryonic membranes show a marked adaptation to development in a terrestrial environment. The skin of reptiles has a horny epidermis and is covered with horny scales to prevent the body from becoming too dry. Turtles have bony plates fused with certain bones to form a shell.

Reptiles breathe only by means of lungs. They cannot regulate their body temperature; their blood, and thereby their body, gains heat only from the environment around them. When that becomes hotter, they warm up; conversely, their body loses heat as the environment becomes colder. They are then less active or even practically immobile and during the cold season they hibernate. They wait out periods of drought in summer in a similar torpid state, particularly in the case of aquatic reptiles when the body of water they live in dries out.

Sight is a very important sense in many species of reptiles. The eyes are fitted with eyelids that are variously shaped in the different groups, for example fused concentrically in chameleons or completely fused and transparent in snakes (Serpentes) or geckos. The hearing apparatus of reptiles lacks earlobes, the eardrum being protected only by skin or scales. Snakes have no eardrum whatsoever, nor do they have a Eustachian tube, therefore they are deaf to airborne sounds.

The senses of taste and smell are imperfectly developed in most reptiles but in many they are replaced by the so-called Jacobson's organ. Snakes and certain lizards (Sauria) have a broadly forked tongue which they extend, flick from one side to the other, and then retract. With the tip of this tongue they 'collect' molecules of volatile substances from the air, which they then place inside a special paired depression on the upper roof of the mouth for

371

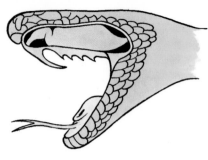

Fig. 4. The poison apparatus of the Common Viper (*Vipera berus*). Venom is produced in a paired gland located in the upperpart of the head far behind the eye. The gland is encircled by constrictors, muscles that contract violently to push the venom, via a small channel, into the fangs.

analysis. This depression contains very sensitive cells, similar to the cells in the human nose. The reptile is thus immediately informed either of prey within reach or of imminent danger. Some reptiles, for example lizards, are also furnished with a sense of smell that is independent of the Jacobson's organ.

Some reptiles are toothed, for example snakes and lizards; others, such as turtles, are toothless and only have jaws that are similar to the beaks of birds of prey. Teeth are usually adapted only for seizing and holding prey. In some species the salivary glands are transformed into poison glands that secrete venom. Venomous reptiles have special grooved or hollow teeth through which the venom can flow into the body of the snake's victim when it is bitten.

Many reptiles have four well-developed limbs; others have variously reduced limbs or none whatsoever.

Reptiles usually reproduce by laying eggs, which have either a hard, calcareous shell or only a leathery or parchment-like cover. Some species are ovoviviparous; that is, the eggs develop within the body of the female. The female then bears live young, or else the young hatch immediately after the eggs are laid.

Turtles (Testudinae) are a distinctive group of reptiles that possess an unusual organ of passive defence—a hard, bony body cover. This is composed of two parts: an upper, dorsal shell called the carapace, and an undershell called the plastron. In some species of turtles, however, the shell is atrophied and sometimes it is covered with a thick, leathery layer. The two pieces are joined at the sides, either firmly or by ligaments, with an opening in front for the head and forelegs and one at the back for the tail and hind legs. The dorsal shell is usually convex, the undershell flat. The surface is covered with horny plates. Some species can conceal the head, tail and legs completely inside the two shells.

The turtle's jaws are toothless and covered by a horny skin, like the beak of a bird. On the edges of the jaws the horny layer is sharp, especially in carnivorous species. The tongue is fleshy and attached along much of its length so that it cannot be extended. Turtles have a good sense of sight; the eye has two eyelids and a nictitating membrane. The legs usually have five digits and are adapted either for burrowing in terrestrial species or for swimming in aquatic species. Some species have fewer than five digits. All turtles reproduce by means of eggs which have a hard, but relatively elastic, shell. The females bury these in sand or loose soil. Turtles can go without food for a long time; some species may fast for over a year.

Fig. 5. Like all snakes, the Grass Snake (*Natrix natrix*) gets its bearings by means of its forked tongue.

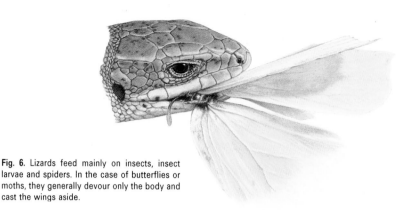

Fig. 6. Lizards feed mainly on insects, insect larvae and spiders. In the case of butterflies or moths, they generally devour only the body and cast the wings aside.

Lizards and snakes together comprise the order Squamata. The distinguishing features they have in common are a body covered with scales and a slit-like cloaca.

Lizards (Sauria) are the largest group of reptiles. They usually have well-developed legs but in some species the legs are atrophied or absent altogether. Their most important sense is sight. The eyes are furnished with eyelids which, in geckos, for example, are fused together and transparent. Many species of lizards have a cartilaginous disc in the tail vertebrae, at which point the tail readily snaps off. This is an important means of defence when danger threatens. The lizard casts off its tail, the enemy generally goes after the moving tail, and the lizard makes its escape. The broken-off tail usually grows in again; the new one can be distinguished by the different shape of the scales. The skeletal parts of the tail do not grow in again, however, and the tail is now stiffened by a band of tough ligaments. This group of lizards includes the European lizards (*Lacerta*) and geckos. Most lizards reproduce by laying eggs, usually enclosed in a membranous cover. Some species are ovoviviparous. Lizards feed on both animals and plants.

Snakes (Serpentes) are a specialized group of reptiles adapted for seizing and swallowing large victims. They are without limbs. The eyelids are fused together and transparent. Snakes shed their skins regularly and every time they do so the skin of the fused eyelids also peels off. Snakes reproduce either by laying eggs which have a soft outer covering, or else they are ovoviviparous. Snakes are carnivores, feeding exclusively on living prey. Some species suffocate their victims first and then swallow them whole, others kill them by injecting venom with their fangs before swallowing their prey.

Fig. 7. The young of the Grass Snake hatch from eggs enclosed in a soft, leathery covering.

Class: **Amphibians**—Amphibia

Order: **Tailed Amphibians**—Caudata

Family: **Salamanders and Newts**—Salamandridae

1 Fire Salamander *Salamandra salamandra.* Inhabits whole of central Europe and extends as far as North Africa. Lives in damp moss, among stones near streams and in small rodent holes. Found at altitudes of over 1,200 m. Hibernates deep underground or in caves, often gregariously. Reappears at end of March. In April—May female deposits up to 70 well developed larvae with gills and 4 limbs and measuring about 3 cm, at source of brook. Metamorphosis (transformation to terrestrial form) takes place after 3—4 months. In rare cases larvae spend winter in water. After completing metamorphosis young leave water. Fully grown after 5 years. Length 20 cm. Lives on spiders, worms, gastropods and insects. Skin secretes poisonous substance lethal for small animals. Life span 18 years. Can sometimes be heard squeaking. Most often encountered on forest paths after rain.

2 Alpine Salamander *Salamandra atra.* Glossy black all over. Inhabits Alpine regions (at altitudes of 700—3,000 m) and certain Balkan ranges. Length about 15 cm. Hides under stones and moss and in bushes. Not dependent on water. Female produces two fully developed young which before birth grow to 5 cm and lose gills. Larvae in female's body live on yolk of eggs which fail to develop. Salamander's diet consists of small insects, spiders, worms and small molluscs. Fully grown after 3—5 years.

3, 4 Crested Newt *Triturus cristatus.* Inhabits whole of central Europe and extends to Urals. Length 14—18 cm. Rarely found at altitudes of over 1,000 m. At pairing time male grows high, doubled crest which starts on forehead and stretches up to tip of tail. Males court females in striking nuptial ceremonies. Crestless female lays over 100 eggs on aquatic plants in stagnant water in April or May. Larvae hatch in 2—3 weeks. Metamorphosis after 3 months when larva measures 4.5—9 cm. Adults remain in water long after egg-laying, often until late summer. Newt fully grown at 4 years. Hibernates under leaves and in holes, occasionally under water in mud. Predacious. Catches small crustaceans, insects and molluscs, also eats frog's eggs and tadpoles and larvae of own species.

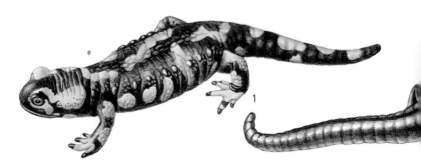

5 Smooth or **Common Newt** *Triturus vulgaris*. Distributed over whole of Europe. Length 8—11 cm. Very plentiful. Dorsal crest at pairing time less dentated than in Crested Newt and continuous at tail base. Female lays 100—250 eggs singly on aquatic plants, usually from beginning of May until June. Larvae hatch in 2 weeks. Metamorphosis after 3 months. Adults visit water only at pairing time. Lives on insects, worms, gastropods and, in water, on tadpoles, etc.

6 Alpine Newt *Triturus alpestris*. Mainly central-European animal, but also extends further west. Length 8—12 cm. At pairing time male wears low dorsal crest and its orange underside turns red. Found at altitudes of up to 3,000 m. Inhabits clear lakes, mountain pools and slow-flowing water. Female lays eggs from March to June. Larvae, hatched in 2—3 weeks, measure about 7 mm. Metamorphosis after 3—4 months when larvae attain 3 cm of length. Cases of reproduction in larval stage known.

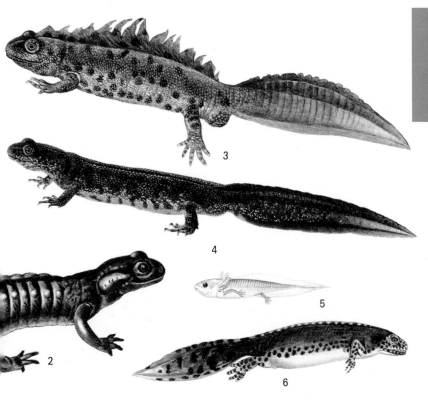

Order: **Tailless Amphibians**—Salientia

Family: **Discoglossids**—Discoglossidae

1 Red-bellied Toad *Bombina bombina*. Inhabits central and eastern Europe. Occurs mainly in lowlands. Length about 4.5 cm. Lives in ponds, pools, etc. Female lays eggs several times a year but chiefly in May and June. Deposits them in groups on aquatic plants or on bottom. Tadpoles very large. Metamorphosis in September—October. Hibernates in holes, under leaves, etc. Reappears in spring and spends whole of summer in water. Eats small aquatic animals. When in danger, burrows in mud.

2 Yellow-bellied Toad *Bombina variegata*. Inhabits whole of Europe except north and Britain. Eggs laid in June, sometimes later. Tadpoles hatch in 7—9 days. Metamorphosis after 4 months. Hibernates on dry land. From spring, for whole of summer, lives in water. Staple diet mosquito larvae.

3 Midwife Toad *Alytes obstetricans*. Inhabits west of central Europe and south-western Europe. Found in uplands and mountains. Length 5.5 cm. Pairing season early spring to summer. Pairs on dry land. Male winds strings of 20—100 large eggs round legs and carries them until tadpoles are hatched (3—6 weeks). Hatched tadpoles remain in water, undergo metamorphosis in late autumn or following spring. Nocturnal animal. Bell-like call. Lives on insects, worms, spiders, etc.

Family: **Spade-footed Toads**—Pelobatidae

4 Spade-footed Toad *Pelobates fuscus*. Distributed over whole of central Europe, extends east to western Siberia. Length up to 8 cm. Nocturnal animal, seldom seen in daytime. From March to May female lays 1,000 eggs in strings 15—50 cm long, in pools etc. Tadpoles black, measure over 10 cm. After metamorphosis toads measure 3 cm. Crawl out on to dry land. Adults also live on land and leave water after eggs are laid. Hibernate in holes up to 2 m. deep. Eat small animals. Toad emits garlicky odour.

Family: **True Toads**—Bufonidae

5 Common Toad *Bufo bufo*. Distributed over whole of Europe and Asia. Length 12 cm, in south up to 20 cm. Abundant everywhere. Occurs in woods, fields, gardens, etc.; often found in cellars. Nocturnal animal. Eats insects, molluscs, worms, occasionally small amphibians. Hibernates in dry holes, etc. Female lays 2 strings of 1,200—6,000 eggs which both parents twine round aquatic plants. Tadpoles, hatched in 12 days, live gregariously. Metamorphosis after 77—91 days; young then leave water. Grow slowly, attain adulthood at 5 years. Life span up to 40 years. Male utters snorting barks.

6 Green Toad *Bufo viridis*. Distributed through western and central Europe as far as Mongolia. Occurs even in dry habitats, in mountains up to altitude of 3,000 m. Digs burrows about 30 cm deep. Nocturnal animal. Lives on insects, spiders, worms, etc. Hibernates on dry land. In spring female lays two strings of 10,000—12,000 eggs, 3—4 m long, on aquatic plants in shallow water. Male's pairing call in spring is pleasant trill. Metamorphosis after 60—91 days. Fully grown at 4 years.

7 Natterjack Toad *Bufo calamita*. Distributed over western and central Europe. Length 6—8 cm. Crawls, does not jump. Good swimmer, climber and burrower (in winter to depth of 3 m). In May female lays 3,000—4,000 eggs on aquatic plants. Metamorphosis after only 42—49 days. Young (1 cm) climb into trees. Nocturnal animal. Loud, croaking call. Eats insects, worms, etc.

5

6

7

377

Family: **Tree Frogs**—Hylidae

1 Common Tree Frog *Hyla arborea*. Found all over Europe. Length 3.5—4.5 cm. Takes to water at pairing time. In May female lays up to 1,000 eggs in clumps. Metamorphosis after 90 days. Young frogs crawl out on to land. After egg-laying adults return to bushes and trees. Colouring adapted to environment. Lives on insects and spiders. In autumn frogs retire under stones, into holes, etc. Many hibernate in mud. Males have clear tinkling call.

Family: **True Frogs**—Ranidae

2 Edible Frog *Rana esculenta*. Inhabits whole of Europe, Asia and North Africa. Occurs at both low and high altitudes. Found only near water. Male attains 7.5 cm of length, female up to 13 cm. In May or June female lays 2,000—3,000 eggs in clumps. Tadpoles hatch in 5—6 days. Metamorphosis after 130 days. Tadpoles sometimes hibernate in water. Lives on insects, worms, spiders and small fish. Adults hibernate at water bed in mud, young on dry land. Fond of taking sun-baths. Males have typical croak (crax-crax).

3 Marsh Frog *Rana ridibunda*. Distributed over central and southern Europe, also occurs in south-eastern England, Holland and on Baltic coast. Found near water in warm places in lowlands. Length 15—17 cm. Pairing time April—May. Female lays 5,000—10,000 eggs. Metamorphosis after 83—125 days. Catches insects, worms, small fish and young of small mammals and birds. Very loud call (cray-cray-cray-cray). Hibernates at water bed. Old individuals often hibernate in slow-flowing water.

4 Common Frog *Rana temporaria*. Distributed over most of Europe, extends to eastern Asia. Can be found beyond Arctic Circle. Abundant everywhere. Frequents parks, gardens, woods, etc. In Alps found up to altitude of 3,000 m. Length 10 cm. Often pairs in March, in mountains and north in May and June. Heard only during pairing season. Female lays 1,000—4,000 eggs. Tadpoles hatch in 3—4 weeks. Metamorphosis after 2—3 months but tadpoles sometimes hibernate in water. After egg-laying frog lives on dry land, but in mountains may also remain in water during summer. Nocturnal animal. At end of October returns to water to hibernate but young individuals (up to 3 years) mostly hibernate on land. Eats insects, slugs, spiders and worms.

5 Field Frog *Rana arvalis*. Extends from Belgium across central and northern Europe to Arctic Circle and east to Siberia. Occurs mainly in boggy meadows. Pairs in March and April. Female lays up to 2,000 eggs in 1 or 2 spherical clumps. Spends summer on land, in autumn returns to water to hibernate. Metamorphosis after 2—3

months. Fully grown at 3 years. Nocturnal animal but young also active during day. Lives on insects, molluscs, worms, etc. Deep, muted call. Male turns bluish at pairing time.

6 Dalmatian Frog *Rana dalmatina*. Inhabits central and south-eastern Europe. In north extends to south of Sweden. Lives in damp riverside woods in lowlands. Male attains 6 cm of length, female 9 cm. Very long hind legs (up to 12.5 cm). Jumps 1 m high at distance of 2 m. Pairs at night at end of March and in April. Female lays 600—1,500 eggs in pools, etc. Metamorphosis after 2—3 months. Young frogs crawl out on to dry land. In summer often found far from water. Eats mainly insects. Hibernates chiefly in water. Call barely audible.

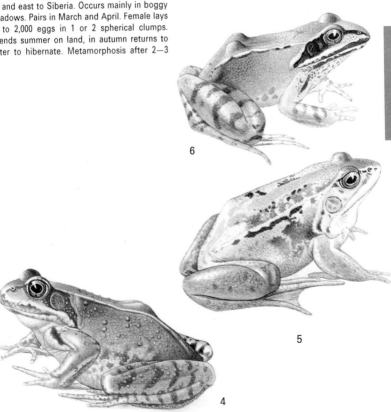

6

5

4

Class: **Reptiles**—Reptilia

Order: **Testudinates**—Testudines

Family: **Freshwater** or **Pond Turtles**—Emydidae

1 European Pond Turtle *Emys orbicularis*. Distributed over central and southern Europe, south-western Asia and north-western Africa. Formerly also inhabited England and Rhineland. Length up to 35 cm. Mainly frequents stagnant water, creeks or slow-flowing water with muddy bed and plenty of vegetation. Eats insects, worms, molluscs, small fish and some greenstuffs. Fond of sunning itself beside water. In May or June female lays 3—15 eggs about 3 cm long in small pit in bank and covers them. Young, hatched in 8—10 weeks, measure 2.5 cm. In October turtle retires to mud to hibernate.

Order: **Scaly Reptiles**—Squamata

Suborder: **Lizards**—Sauria

Family: **Skinks**—Scincidae

2 Snake-eyed Skink *Ablepharus kitaibelii*. Distributed over south-eastern Europe, extends to Hungary and Czechoslovakia in central Europe. Length about 10 cm. Inhabits rocky wooded steppes, deserted vineyards and outskirts of dry, open woods. Lives mainly on small insects. Very quick and agile. Female lays 3—8 eggs.

Family: **True Lizards**—Lacertidae

3 Wall Lizard *Lacerta muralis*. Distributed round Mediterranean, extends to western and central Europe. Length up to 20 cm. Expert climber of rocks and trees. Diet consists of insects, spiders and worms. In May or June female lays 2—8 eggs in small pit. Young hatch in 6—8 weeks. Hibernates in holes, crevices, etc. Each animal has own 'preserve'.

4 Sand Lizard *Lacerta agilis*. Very common in Europe north of Alps. Extends west to England and east to central Asia. Length up to 20 cm and over. Male's back predominantly green, female's grey. Frequents warm, sunny slopes, clearings, etc. Found at altitudes of up to 2,000 m. In May or June female lays 3—15 eggs in shallow pit. Young hatch in 7—12 weeks. Hibernates in holes, under piles of leaves, etc. Each animal has own 'preserve'. Eats insects, spiders and centipedes.

5 Green Lizard *Lacerta viridis*. Inhabits southern and central Europe. Length up to 50 cm in south, about 30 cm in central Europe. Frequents warm, rocky places. Expert climber. In spring males fight. In May or June female lays 5—13 (in south up to 21) eggs. Young hatch in 6—8 weeks. Lives on insects, molluscs, small lizards and snakes. Digs burrows up to 1 m deep. Retires to hibernate in October, reappears in April.

1

2

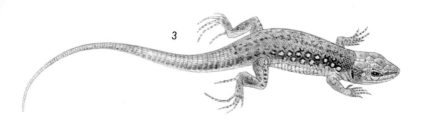

6 Common or **Viviparous Lizard** *Lacerta vivipara*. Distributed over central and northern Europe, occasionally found beyond Arctic Circle. Occurs mainly in mountainous regions but also in plains. Female lays 2—12 eggs at short intervals. Young hatched immediately, measure about 3 cm. In north young hatched in female's body but in Pyrenees from laid eggs. Lives on insects, spiders, etc. Young also eat plant-lice.

Family: **Slow-worms**—Anguidae

7 Slow-worm or **Blind-worm** *Anguis fragilis*. Distributed from England to south of Sweden and across whole of Europe to Algeria. Length up to about 50 cm. Variable colouring. Very abundant in places. Occurs at altitudes of up to 2,200 m. Found mainly under leaves, stones, etc. in deciduous woods with damp soil. Hibernates in holes from end of October, usually gregariously. Ovoviviparous (young hatched from eggs immmediately); one female produces 5—26 young. Eats molluscs, worms and insects. Tail easily snapped off but grows again.

Suborder: **Snakes**—Serpentes

Family: **Colubrid Snakes**—Colubridae

1 Tessellated Snake *Natrix tessellata*. Extends from south-west of France across Germany to central Asia and to eastern part of North Africa. Length up to 1 m, usually less. Spends greater part of life in water. Found at altitudes of up to 2,700 m. Staple diet small fish, occasionally eats amphibians. In some places wreaks havoc among fish fry. Female lays 4—12 eggs at end of June or in July. Disappears in October, often hibernates in rodent burrows near water.

2 Grass Snake *Natrix natrix*. Common all over Europe, extends east as far as Aral Sea. Found mainly near water. Occurs at altitudes of up to 2,000 m. Has distinctive spots on sides of head. In autumn retires to hibernate in crevices, holes, etc., often gregariously. Eats amphibians, occasionally small fish and mammals. Young also eat insects. In July—August female lays 6—30 (in rare cases up to 70) eggs under leaves, in waterside soil or in moss. Young, hatched in 2 months (in south sooner), measure 11—18 cm.

3 Aesculapian Snake *Elaphe longissima*. Inhabits warm parts of Europe and south-western Asia. Length up to 2 m. Largest European snake. Lives in deciduous woods or areas with plenty of bushes. Found in Alps at altitudes of up to 2,000 m. Climbs trees extremely well, plunders birds' nests and devours young. Main diet, however, small rodents and lizards. At end of June or beginning of July female lays 5—8 tough eggs 5.5 cm long and 3.5 cm wide in holes, hollow trees and stumps. Young hatch in 6—8 weeks. Snake starts to hibernate in autumn. Uses hollow tree stumps, mammals' burrows, rock crevices, etc.

4 Smooth Snake *Coronella austriaca*. Inhabits practically whole of Europe except Ireland and Mediterranean islands. Extends eastwards into western Asia. Length not more than 75 cm. Very abundant in places. Preference for woods and thickets. Found at altitudes of up to 2,200 m. Lives mainly on lizards, occasionally eats small rodents or birds and sometimes other snakes. Young also eat insects. Ovoviviparous. Female lays 2—15 eggs at end of August or beginning of October and young are hatched immediately. Often mistaken for viper.

Family: **Vipers**—Viperidae

5 Common Viper *Vipera berus*. Inhabits central Europe, parts of southern Europe, northern Europe to beyond Arctic Circle and large part of Asia as far as Japan. Length about 80 cm. Variable colouring, typical zigzag line invisible in black specimens. Usually found in mixed forests. Occurs at altitudes of up to 2,700 m. Largely nocturnal, hunts also by day at very high altitudes only. Staple diet small rodents. Potent venom. Does not actively attack man. At end of August or beginning of September female either gives birth to live young or lays 6—20 eggs from which young are hatched immediately. In spring males fight, each attempting to 'flatten' rival but without injuring it. Retires in October. Hibernates gregariously, often together with other snakes, in holes in ground, crevices in rocks, etc.

6 Asp Viper *Vipera aspis*. Distributed over south-western Europe, extends to southern part of Black Forest (Germany). Occurs in rocky places in uplands and on lower slopes of mountains. Nocturnal animal. Lives on small rodents and occasionally small birds. Young catch small lizards. Female gives birth to young in August. Venom very potent, bite fatal in 2—4% of cases. Length not more than 75 cm.

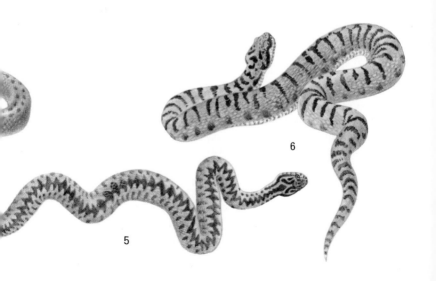

6

5

Birds

Birds (Aves) are higher vertebrates than reptiles, with a constant and relatively high body temperature, ranging from 38—44 °C. Birds have two pairs of limbs, the front pair being in the form of wings, which are normally used for flying. Some species of birds, however, have frail wings that are incapable of flight or are adapted only for swimming. Of the European birds, one such flightless bird was the Great Auk, now extinct. All present-day European birds belong to the group of fliers (Carinata).

The sense organs of birds have developed in different degrees. For instance, birds have little sense of taste because taste buds are usually located quite deep inside an animal's mouth on the soft upper palate and on the mucous membrane underneath the tongue. Also, birds do not

Fig. 1. The Sand Martin or Bank Swallow (*Riparia riparia*) flies swiftly above the surface of rivers, ponds and lakes, capturing insects on the wing.

chew their food but swallow it whole or in chunks and thus are unable to taste it as mammals do. The sense of smell is likewise very poorly developed in birds.

The sense of touch is developed in varying degrees. Birds generally have sensory organs inside the bill and on the tongue, but some also have them at the base of certain feathers and on the legs. Birds that obtain their food from the ground where they cannot see what they are picking up even have these organs at the tip of the bill, for example the woodcock (*Scolopax*). Special organs for perceiving heat are usually located on the unfeathered parts of the body.

A bird's most perfect and important sensory organ is the eye. Birds see far better than other animals. The eye is large and focuses not only by means of muscles squeezing the lens, as in the case of mammals, but also by flattening or bulging. The eyes can be moved independently and thus each can look at a different object at the same time. The eyes are usually located on either side of the head and thus each has its own field of vision. Some birds, however, such as owls, have both eyes facing forward. Colour vision in birds is about the same as in people. In addition to an upper and lower eyelid, birds have another special lid, called a nictitating membrane, which extends from the inner corner and can cover the entire eye. The retina has a greater density of sensory cells than the eye of a human; this is up to five times greater in raptors which can thus spot their prey from a great height.

Fig. 2. The Kingfisher (*Alcedo atthis*) feeds chiefly on small fish, plunging abruptly beneath the water's surface to capture its prey. It then carries this to a branch before swallowing it so that it can savour its meal in peace.

385

Fig. 3. The Eagle Owl (*Bubo bubo*) has large eyes at the front of the head, as do all owls.

Fig. 4. The Barn Owl (*Tyto alba*) has a very keen sense of hearing. The flight of owls is silent. As they fly they can hear even the slightest squeaking of rodents or rustling of leaves on the ground and thus readily capture their prey.

Another important sensory organ is the ear, even though it is less perfect in structure than the eye and still resembles the ear of the reptiles. There is only one earbone, corresponding to the stirrup in the human ear, and the external ear channel is relatively short. Despite this, a bird's hearing is very good and some species, such as the owls, use it to hunt their prey in the dark.

The vocal organs, located at the lower end of the trachea, also play an important role in the life of birds. This organ, called the syrinx, is exceptionally well developed in songbirds. In other groups of birds the vocal organs are simpler and these birds usually have a monotonous call or may only produce raucous sounds. And then there are some birds, such as the White Stork (*Ciconia ciconia*), that have no vocal organs at all and communicate by clapping their beaks.

The bird skeleton is not only strong, it is also light because most of the bones are hollow and filled with air. The long bones, in particular, are tubular. The low weight of the skeleton is an important factor in flight. Birds' feathers are also very light and are arranged to form an impermeable surface that traps pockets of air. The simplest form of flight is passive gliding flight in

Fig. 5. The White Stork (*Ciconia ciconia*) is a mute bird, producing only hissing sounds. Breeding pairs communicate by clapping their beaks. They usually lay their heads along their backs in greeting.

which the bird travels only by means of its outspread wings, supported by the resistance of the air. Another similar form of flight is when the bird takes advantage of rising air currents to soar upward. The chief form of flight, however, is active flight achieved by flapping the wings, which, of course, consumes large amounts of energy. The speed of active flight of various species differs and the wings are adapted ac-

cordingly. Birds with long narrow wings are better fliers than birds with short, broad wings.

The bill, covered by a thick and horny sheath, is another important part of the bird's body. The bill shows marked variation in shape in different species of birds, depending on the kind of food they eat. In the bill of raptors, the upper mandible is downcurved and very sharp on the edge, which enables the birds not only to rip and tear the flesh of their victim but also to cut off pieces. Ducks have a flat bill with a serrated edge, which serves to sieve food. Seed-eating birds have a stout, hard, conical bill that enables them to break hard seed coverings. The bill of insectivorous birds is narrow and pointed at the tip to help them to extricate insects from crevices. Herons (Ardidae) have a long, pointed bill which they often use as a spear when hunting. Some birds have an upcurved bill; in others it curves downward, while some specialists, such

Fig. 6. Raptors have a stout, hooked beak that is used to kill and tear prey as well as to pluck it.

Underneath the contour feathers the body is usually covered with fine down feathers with a short, fine quill but without a shaft and with barbules that do not possess hooklets. In many birds, such as ducks, the down feathers play an important role in nesting, for the birds use them to line the edges of their nests. Down feathers provide good heat insulation and prevent the eggs from getting cold during the temporary absence of the female, who covers them before her departure from the nest. Another type of feather is the filament feather which is thin, almost hair-like, with a brush-like tip. These feathers usually grow immediately next to the contour feathers. Growing at the gape of the beak of certain birds are bristle feathers, which serve mainly as tactile organs when catching prey.

Feathers may be variously coloured. Such coloration is of two kinds. One is caused by colouring matter (pigments), the other by the

Fig. 7. The long beak of the Curlew (*Numenius arquata*) is adapted for hunting molluscs and insect larvae in mud, or earthworms in soft soil.

as the crossbills (*Loxia*) have bills with overlapping tips to facilitate the extraction of seeds from the cones of conifers. Other birds have a bill that is adapted for catching fish; some have a bill that is adapted for cracking the hard shells of bivalves.

The body of a bird is covered with feathers. These do not grow over the entire surface, however, but are arranged in definite tracts called the pterylae. The bare spaces between the feathered tracts are called apteria. Because these are masked by the surrounding feathers, they are not apparent at first glance. The feathers that give the body its typical shape are called contour feathers, for example the flight feathers. Such a feather has a long, firm, but flexible, shaft bordered on both sides by a web composed of separate individual barbs which, in turn, carry rows of smaller barbules supplied with hooklets. If the web is damaged in any way, the bird strokes it with its bill or claws, causing the hooklets to catch and restore the web again. The oar feathers, or tail feathers, are also usually long, with strong barbs. In some birds, such as woodpeckers, the tail feathers are remarkably strong and flexible. They serve the bird as a prop while it chisels holes and when climbing. The part of the feather embedded in the skin is called the quill.

refraction of light which gives the feather a metallic sheen. If there is a deficiency in pigment, the feathers will be white; this is known as albinism. On the contrary, when there is an excess of dark pigment and the bird is nearly black, this condition is known as melanism. These deviations may also be partial and then the bird's plumage will be variously streaked.

The feathers of all birds are replaced regularly by the process called moulting. Old feathers are shed, pushed out by the new ones growing in. Some birds moult once a year, but most songbirds and many other groups moult twice a year. The contour feathers are usually shed successively so that the bird does not lose the power of flight. However, in many species of water birds, such as ducks, the flight feathers are shed all at once so that the birds are incapable of flight for a certain period until new feathers grow in. Many species of birds have

Fig. 8. Pigeons have a rather small beak that is soft at the base — only the tip is hard and slightly curved and it is with this that they peck up hard seeds and fruits.

Fig. 9. The Hoopoe (*Upupa epops*) has a slender, pointed beak with which it readily extracts beetle larvae from the soft ground in meadows and pastures as well as from the rotting wood of old stumps.

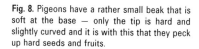

two differently coloured sets of plumage a year. One is the brightly coloured breeding plumage worn mostly by the male, the other the drabber, non-breeding winter plumage. Some birds acquire different winter plumage following a complete moult in the autumn, and this later changes into the breeding plumage after the partial spring moult. These species include the Brambling (*Fringilla montifringilla*), shorebirds and gulls (Laridae). Sometimes there is a marked difference in the coloration of the male and female; this is known as sexual dimorphism. Good examples are the European Blackbird (*Turdus merula*), Red-backed Shrike (*Lanius collurio*) and the Pheasant (*Phasianus colchicus*). In other species the male and female

have the same coloration and cannot be distinguished at first glance, for example the Jackdaw (*Corvus monedula*), Rook (*Corvus frugilegus*) and White Stork (*Ciconia ciconia*).

Birds are not such free souls as some people think. During the breeding season each pair of birds inhabits a given nesting ground or territory. This is a specifically delimited area, with an imaginary boundary, that could be compared to the garden or plot on which a human family builds a house, and its boundaries are generally respected by other birds of the same species.

Some birds, even songbirds, nest in colonies in which the nests cluster close together, sometimes practically on top of each other, as in the case of the House Martin (*Delichon urbica*). Here the nesting ground is so small that it is limited only to the nest and its immediate surroundings. These birds do not quarrel among themselves over territory for they are usually expert fliers and capture food either in the air or fly far from the nest in search of it. Living in colonies has its advantages, primarily that of greater safety.

How can birds tell if a certain territory is already occupied? Songbirds advertise their ownership by song. The male often sings from an elevated spot even before he starts to build the nest, thus notifying other males of the same species that the place is taken. In the case of songbirds, it is usually the males that seek a nesting place, the males of many species arriving from their winter quarters several days ahead of the females. Sometimes the song, especially in young, unpaired males, has another purpose — that of attracting a mate. At the same time it is also intended to serve the purpose of frightening off other males in the vicinity. A strong, healthy bird has a loud, rich song, thus demonstrating its superiority over the weaker individuals of its kind. It is interesting to note that a weaker bird often falls silent as soon as it hears such a loud song nearby.

Fig. 10. Woodpeckers have extraordinarily strong, but flexible, tail feathers, which serve as a prop on tree trunks while they hack holes in the wood or extract wood beetle larvae.

Fig. 11. Stables, barns and passageways are where the Swallow (*Hirundo rustica*) builds its basin-like nest of grass blades and lumps of clay mixed with saliva.

Besides song, most birds also produce other sounds that are typical for the given species. Most important of these is the call note, used by both sexes to communicate among themselves even out of the nesting season, when, as a rule, the males do not sing. In addition to this, other sounds express fright or warning. All of these various sounds are innate to the given species and will be produced even by young birds reared in captivity, which have never heard the voices of their parents. Some birds, such as the Red-backed Shrike (*Lanius collurio*), do not have a song of their own but mimic the various melodies of other songbirds.

Before nesting, birds must build a nest where the eggs will be incubated and the young nestlings reared. Many birds, mostly songbirds, build very solid, complex, truly artistic structures, others make only simple nests and still others simply lay their eggs in a shallow depression in the ground. Special nests are built by birds that nest in cavities, such as woodpeckers (Picidae). These species hollow out cavities in the trunks or thick branches of trees, inside which the eggs are laid freely on the bottom. Other birds seek out ready-made, abandoned cavities or various crevices in which they then build their own nest. Very occasionally, birds do not build a nest at all, but lay their eggs in the nests of other birds; this is done, for example, by the Cuckoo (*Cuculus canorus*). In some species the nest is built by the female, in others both partners share the task of construction, and in still others the nest is built by the male and is then lined by the female.

Some birds build nests that are ingeniously suspended from the branches of a tree; others create a covered nest on the ground. The nest is generally constructed of plant material and lined with feathers and hair. Some birds also use other inorganic material. The Song Thrush (*Turdus philomelos*), for instance, lines the interior of its nest with mud and rotting wood. Other species build the entire nest of mud, for example house martins.

The construction of a nest of a given type is innate to the given species. The nest built by young birds for the first time in spring is identical to that of an older bird that is experienced in this task. The location of the nest is also innate. Most birds build their nests in the same place. For example the Chaffinch (*Fringilla coelebs*) always builds its nest on a branch, the woodpecker in a cavity. Construction of the nest is quite rapid as a rule, usually taking only a few days.

Some birds nest only once a year; others regularly do so twice, and in the case of the

Fig. 12. The Black-throated Diver (*Gavia arctica*) sites its nest right on the water's edge so that it can slip straight in. The reason for this is that its legs are located at the very rear of the body and thus the bird is unable to take to the air from dry land.

House Sparrow (*Passer domesticus*) even four times a year. Birds that have become associates of, and live in the neighbourhood of, people where feeding opportunities are much more promising, often have more broods a year than woodland birds of the same species.

Fig. 13. A cuckoo nestling has taken over the cup-like nest of the Reed Warbler (*Acrocephalus scirpaceus*), woven around several reed stems.

The colouring of the eggs is likewise characteristic for the given species and the eggs can be identified accordingly. The eggs of some species may show diversity of colour but always within a certain range and certain colour types. As a rule, the coloration of the eggs corresponds to the surroundings of the nest. The eggs of birds that nest in cavities are white because they are well concealed and do not need to have cryptic colours like those of birds that lay their eggs more or less in the open and leave them uncovered, for example, on a sandy shore. The speckled eggs of such birds some-

intervals, while in other species the male relieves the female only now and then. In several other species only the male incubates the eggs. The incubation period is characteristic and constant for each individual species. The young peck their way out of the egg with the aid of an 'egg tooth', a special projection on the upper mandible. This is used to cut a small, round opening in the egg shell. This lid then falls off and the way out is open.

Birds are divided into two groups, according to whether they feed their nestlings or whether the young feed themselves: the first are termed nidicolous birds, and the second nidifugous birds. Examples of nidicolous birds are song-

Fig. 14. A Tree Creeper (*Certhia familiaris*) beside its nest, located under a piece of loose bark.

Fig. 15. A Red-backed Shrike (*Lanius collurio*) establishing a larder of spare food against the time when insects remain in hiding because of bad weather. This bird impales its prey on thorns.

times seem to merge completely with their surroundings. However, some birds, even though they nest in cavities, still have speckled eggs. One such bird is the Kestrel (*Falco tinnunculus*). This species originally nested on rock ledges and it is to this background that the coloration of the eggs still corresponds. Only later did this bird begin to seek out cavities.

Many birds begin incubating after the last egg has been laid and the young then hatch all at the same time. Other birds begin incubating as soon as the first egg is laid and the young then hatch successively. In a clutch of five eggs laid at 48-hour intervals, the difference in age between the first and last nestling is a full ten days. In the case of a larger clutch, the nestlings that hatch last simply cannot compete with their older and larger siblings and they will die.

As a rule, only the female incubates the eggs, while the male brings her food. In some species both parents take turns in incubating at regular

birds, woodpeckers and pigeons; examples of nidifugous birds are ducks and gallinaceous birds. In the case of certain species, during the first few days the adult birds bring food to the young in their beaks but the young take it themselves. One such example is the rails (Rallidae) in whom this instinct of bringing food is so innate that even older, independent fledglings of the first brood will bring food to the younger nestlings of the second brood.

The young of many nidicolous birds, particularly songbirds, generally lack feathers on hatching, being covered here and there with patches of thin down. Their eyes are shut tight. In other species of nidicolous birds, however, for instance owls and raptors, the young hatch wearing a thick coat of down. The young of gulls also hatch with a thick coat of down but, in addition, they are able to run about and swim from the very first day.

The young of nidifugous birds are well developed at birth and feed themselves immediately, but the parents still watch over and protect them.

In Australia and certain Pacific islands there lives an unusual family of birds, the Megapodidae, that bury their eggs in mounds of decaying leaves and lava sand. Inside this artificial hatchery heat is produced by the decaying process

and the eggs are thus incubated. The newly hatched young are fully independent at birth, needing no parental care whatsoever.

The young of most nidicolous birds are usually cared for by both parents and are also fed by both. In the case of raptors, food is brought by the male, but it is portioned and fed to the young by the female. In many other species, however, larger nestlings are fed directly by the male.

Adult birds usually remain faithful to their nesting site, returning to the same spot every year. Young adult birds establish their own territories during their first year, unless they are colony nesters.

Birds are divided into three basic groups, depending on whether they remain in their breeding grounds or leave for the winter. Resident birds do not leave their breeding grounds even

Fig. 16. A Goldfinch (*Carduelis carduelis*) feeding its offspring.

Fig. 17. The Jay (*Garrulus glandarius*) stores acorns or beechnuts in the autumn. Generally, however, it fails to locate most of these stores when the need arises and they become welcome finds for other animals.

in winter but remain in the general neighbourhood. Migratory birds leave their nesting grounds every autumn and fly, often for thousands of kilometres, to warmer quarters for the winter. Transient migrants, or dispersive birds, roam far afield, often hundreds of kilometres from their nesting grounds, after the breeding season.

However, there are not always sharp distinctions among these three groups. In some species some members are migratory and others resident. In other species the females are migratory and the males resident. And sometimes among species that were once definitely migratory there occur populations that now remain in the nesting grounds. Blackbirds, for example, were previously migratory, but in the vicinity of people they have become resident and now only some females will depart for the winter.

European birds migrate in roughly three main directions: south-west from northern and north-eastern Europe across western Europe and the Iberian peninsula; straight south from the north across Italy and Sicily; south-east across the Balkan peninsula and Asia Minor. Various populations of the same species may fly in different directions. The migration paths of birds encompass a broad front, although in some places this narrows so that the flock becomes denser, for instance where there is a barrier such as a range of high mountains, when the birds must seek out mountain passes. Many European birds winter no further away than southern or south-western Europe; others journey as far as tropical or even southern Africa.

Such a journey cannot be made non-stop, without a break. Some birds cover 100 km a day, others more. Then they must stop to rest and, more important, obtain food. Some will rest for several days before continuing on their way, and thus the journey to tropical Africa may take as long as several weeks. The birds stay in their winter quarters for only a few weeks, after which they set out again on the return trip to their nesting grounds. The return trip is usually much faster because the birds are urged on by the breeding instinct.

In the vicinity of the nest, birds find their way about mainly by sight, apparently using their memory of the nest's location and various landmarks in the neighbourhood where they normally fly when looking for food. Many birds move in regular circuits, somewhat like the trails of mammals, and these are firmly fixed in their memory.

Some species of birds are declining in number every year, partly due to the lack of nesting sites. Special consideration should be given to birds that nest in cavities. Natural cavities in old trees are few and far between and the birds must often seek alternative sites, nesting, for instance, in a pile of stones on the ground. Here, however, they are exposed to greater danger and become easier prey for their enemies. Such birds can best be helped by people through putting up nest boxes, not only in parks and gardens but in the wild as well. Make sure the boxes cannot be reached by cats.

Fig. 18. The Rook (*Corvus frugilegus*) is not a colourful bird. Its plumage is entirely glossy blue-black and is the same in both sexes, there being no difference between the male and female.

Class: **Birds**—Aves

Superorder: **Carinate Birds**—Carinatae

Order: **Passerine** or **Perching Birds**—Passeriformes

Family: **Crows**—Corvidae

1 Raven *Corvus corax*. Distributed in Europe, Asia and North Africa. In eastern Europe also lives in villages together with jackdaws, on church towers, etc. In central Europe occurs in vast wooded regions. Builds nest on tall trees or on rocks. Uses and adds to it many years. Building done by female, male fetches material (twigs, moss, hairs, etc.). Female lays 5—6 green-spotted and speckled eggs, often at end of February. Young hatched in 21 days, nest-bound about 40 days. Eggs hatched mainly by female with occasional help from male. Diet consists of small vertebrates, insects, debris of animal origin.

2 Carrion Crow *Corvus corone corone*. Distributed over western and central Europe. Completely black. Inhabits wooded areas interspersed with fields and meadows. Often seen looking for food near water. Builds nest in tall trees, usually in March. Nest made of twigs, moss and diverse materials. At end of March or beginning of April female lays 5—6 greenish, dark spotted eggs. Incubates them 17—20 days, fed by male. Young nest-bound for about one month. In winter families combine in large flocks. Both vegetable and animal diet. Collects seeds and berries etc., catches insects and small vertebrates and also eats carrion.

3 Hooded Crow *Corvus corone cornix*. Distributed in eastern and central Europe. Crossing of two subspecies normal along dividing line, which follows Elbe and Vltava to Vienna and crosses Alps into northern Italy. Biology same as for Carrion Crow but often also nests in large town parks. Very suspicious and wary. Frequently plunders partridge and pheasant nests and is consequently shot on sight by gamekeepers and also by farmers.

1

3

2

4 Rook *Corvus frugilegus*. Distributed over practically whole of Europe from middle of France and northern Italy, extends east into Asia north of Himalayas. Forms flocks and nests in colonies (often huge). Likes open country, looks for food in meadows and fields. Sometimes nests in towns, e.g. in cemeteries etc. Builds nests on tall trees; large number of nests on one tree quite common. Female lays 3–5 greenish, dark spotted eggs, usually at beginning of April. Young hatch in 17 days and remain about 5 weeks in nest. In winter migrates southwards in flocks and in central Europe is replaced by more northerly population. Mixed diet. Collects seeds, acorns, etc., also feasts on carrion.

5 Jackdaw *Corvus monedula*. Inhabits whole of Europe, northern Asia and north-western Africa. Lives in colonies. Nests on rocky ledges, in towers, hollow trees, etc. Often found in towns. In March builds nest from twigs, straw, moss, feathers, etc. At end of April female lays

4–6 blue-green, grey-speckled eggs. Eggs incubated 17–18 days, mainly by female. Young remain one month in nest and then roam neighbourhood with parents. In autumn Jackdaws join flocks of rooks. Lives on insects, spiders, molluscs, worms, only occasionally young of small vertebrates; also seeds, berries, etc. Often calls while flying. Easily tamed.

6 Magpie *Pica pica*. Distributed over whole of Europe, large part of Asia, north-western Africa and North America. Characteristic black and white colouring, long tail. Length about 45 cm. Prefers flat country with small copses and shrubs. Builds nest from twigs, turf, blades of grass, leaves, etc. in trees and small bushes. In April female lays 3–10 greenish, thickly speckled eggs. Young hatch in 17–18 days. Fledged after 26 days and remain with parents through winter. Lives on insects, molluscs, small vertebrates, seeds and berries.

Family: **Crows**—Corvidae

1 Nutcracker *Nucifraga caryocatactes.* Distribution area extends from Scandinavia to eastern Asia. In central Europe and Alps inhabits conifer woods, only in mountainous regions. Absent in western Europe. Length over 30 cm. At end of February, in densest branches of tall firs, up to 15 m from ground, builds nest from broken twigs, moss, lichen, hairs, grass, etc. At end of March female lays 3—4 light green, brown- and grey-speckled eggs. Incubates them alone 16 days, fed by male. Young fledged in 21—25 days, but still remain with parents. Eats insects, occasionally young birds, seeds, acorns, nuts, etc.

2 Jay *Garrulus glandarius.* Distributed over whole of Europe, Asia as far as China and north-western Africa. Lives mainly in deciduous or mixed woods. At beginning of April, in tall trees, sometimes only 2 m from ground, builds nest of twigs, grass, moss, etc. At end of April or beginning of May female lays 5—7 grey-green, brown-spotted eggs. Incubated by both parents in turn 16—17 days. Jay is very wary at nesting time. Can imitate call of different forest birds. Jays often fly long distances, not in flocks, but singly, with long intervals. Do not call when flying. Raucously announce approach of humans. Live on mixed diet, make stocks of acorns beside tree stumps, etc.

3 Alpine Chough *Pyrrhocorax graculus.* Distributed mainly in Alps, Pyrenees and some parts of central Asia. Length about 37 cm. Occurs at altitudes of over 2,000 m. Seen in lowlands only in winter. Lives in flocks. Builds nest from twigs, hairs, rootlets, etc. in rock crevices. At end of April female lays only 2 green, brown-spotted eggs. Agile mountaineer. Lives on insects, molluscs, small vertebrates and seeds.

1

2

3

Family: **Starlings**—Sturnidae

4 European Starling *Sturnus vulgaris.* Distributed over whole of Europe, east into central Asia, also in North Africa. Length 16.5—18.5 cm. Speckled at mating time, otherwise black. In autumn (usually September) migrates to southern Europe and North Africa. Before departing congregates in huge flocks and spends night in sedge. Returns in March. Occasionally resident. Originally nested in hollow trees in deciduous woods, today in orchards, parks and gardens with nesting-boxes. Female builds nest from dry grass, feathers, etc.; male sometimes also fetches material. At end of April female lays 5—6 green-blue eggs, incubated 14 days by both parents. Young fed by parents. After leaving nest form flocks. Lives on insects, worms, cherries and other fruits.

5 Rose-coloured Starling *Sturnus roseus.* Inhabits southern Europe and central Asia. Visits central Europe in flocks and occasionally nests there. Spends winter in northern India. Length about 23 cm. Builds nest in hollows, in piles of stones, in ground or even in open. Lives mainly on locusts, follows them into steppes in huge flocks. Also eats other insects and fruit, in winter rice. Female lays 3—8 pale blue eggs. Young fed by both parents which bring them food at short intervals.

Family: **Orioles**—Oriolidae

6 Golden Oriole *Oriolus oriolus.* Widely distributed in Europe, North Africa and western, central and southern Asia. European population migrates to Africa in winter. Length 21—23 cm. Males have high-pitched, fluting call. Inhabits deciduous woods, large parks and gardens. Nest woven from long grass blades, built by female in fork of branch. Female lays 3—5 whitish eggs with small red-brown and mauve spots. Young hatch in 14—15 days. Lives chiefly on insects and insect larvae, spiders and small molluscs, sometimes fruit, e.g. cherries. Migrates from Europe in August.

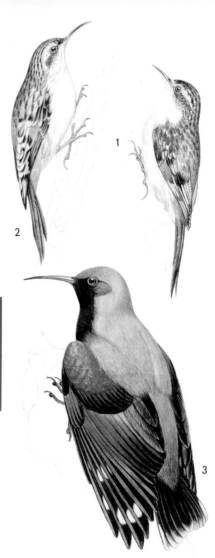

Family: **Tree-creepers**—Certhiidae

1 Common Tree-creeper *Certhia familiaris.* Distributed over most of Europe, central and eastern Asia and North America. Length 11—15.5 cm. Mainly frequents conifer and mixed forests. Usually builds nest behind peeling bark or in stacked timber. Nest made of twigs, grass, moss and feathers. Female lays 6—7 white, red-spotted eggs in April or May. Incubated by both parents in turn 13—15 days. Sometimes nests twice. Climbs tree spiral-wise. Eats small insects and their eggs.

2 Short-toed Tree-creeper *Certhia brachydactyla.* Distributed in central, western (except England) and southern Europe, also Tunisia. Length about 13 cm. Inhabits old deciduous woods, large parks and gardens. Nesting biology as for preceding species. Tree-creepers are resident, i.e. non-migratory birds.

3 Wall-creeper *Tichodroma muraria.* Distributed in mountains of southern and central Europe, e.g. Alps, Pyrenees, Carpathians, and east across Balkans to Himalayas. Length 16—17.5 cm. Mountain-dweller, occurs in lowlands only in winter. At nesting time in couples, otherwise solitary bird. Skilled at climbing rock faces. Builds nest from grass, moss, etc. in crevices. At end of May female lays 3—5 white eggs with red-brown spots and dots. Incubates them unaided. Eats insects, insect larvae and eggs, spiders, etc.

Family: **Nuthatches**—Sittidae

4 Nuthatch *Sitta europaea.* Distributed over whole of Europe and Asia (except southern Asia). Body length 13—16 cm. Resident bird. Lives in forests, parks, etc., also in towns. Nests in tree hollows, nesting-boxes, etc., to which it brings scales of pine bark or fragments of dry leaves. If opening too large, fills it with mixture of mud and saliva. Female lays 6—8 white, red-speckled eggs in May, incubates them 15—18 days. Both parents feed young. Diet insects, insect larvae, spiders and seeds stored in cracks.

Family: **Finches**—Fringillidae

5 Hawfinch *Coccothraustes coccothraustes.* Distributed over whole of Europe, temperate part of Asia, North Africa. Length 16.5—17.5 cm. Thick beak most characteristic feature. Inhabits deciduous woods, large parks and orchards. Resident bird. Builds nest in April, usually beside trunk, 2—10 m from ground. Nest made of rootlets, grass, hairs, etc., on foundation of thick twigs. At beginning of May female lays 4—6 bluish eggs with grey and mauve spots and streaks. Young hatch in 12—14 days. Eats different seeds and nuts, plus insects at nesting time.

6 Greenfinch *Carduelis chloris*. Distributed over whole of Europe, extends to central Asia and north-western Africa. Length 15—17 cm. Abundant in woods, parks and gardens. In April builds nest from rootlets, dry grass, twigs, etc. in dense branches (chiefly of conifers), 1—20 m from ground. At beginning of May female lays 5—6 whitish eggs with red-brown spots and blotches. Incubates them 12—14 days, fed by male. Both parents feed young. Diet mainly seeds. Some Greenfinches migrate to Italy for winter, others remain behind and live in flocks, together with other birds.

7 Goldfinch *Carduelis carduelis*. Distributed over whole of Europe, Asia Minor, central Asia and North Africa. Length 13—15.5 cm. Inhabits small, open, mixed and deciduous woods, parks, gardens, cemeteries, etc. At end of April builds nest at tip of branch (usually of deciduous tree), 3—10 m from ground. Nest made of moss, lichen, fluff, horsehair, etc. Nests 2—3 times a year. Lays 4—6 white eggs with violet and reddish speckles and dots. Female incubates eggs 12—14 days. Lives mainly on seeds, in summer also eats insects and insect larvae.

4

5

6

7

1

Family: **Finches**—Fringillidae

1 Siskin *Carduelis spinus*. Distributed over most of Europe, in east to central Asia. Length 11—13.5 cm. Primarily mountain-dweller but also lives in lowlands. Female builds nest unaided, usually at tip of branch of tall conifer. Nest made of twigs, moss, etc., lined with cocoon silk, hairs, etc. In April female lays 4—6 white eggs with red-brown speckles. Incubates them 12—14 days. Sometimes nests twice. Lives mainly on seeds, in summer also insects. In winter lives in flocks.

2 Linnet *Carduelis cannabina*. Distributed over whole of Europe, in east to western part of central Asia, also in North Africa. Length 13—15.5 cm. Inhabits copses, cemeteries, gardens, etc. Partly migratory. In April builds nest 1.5—2.5 m from ground in dense bushes, junipers, etc. Nest made of twigs, grass-blades and rootlets, lined with hairs, plant fluff, etc. In April female lays 4—6 whitish eggs thickly speckled with red. Incubates them 12—14 days. Diet seeds and insects.

3 Redpoll *Carduelis flammea*. Distributed in northern Europe, Asia and America, also England. Occasionally nests in central Europe. Length 12—14.5 cm. Seen in central Europe in winter, in large flocks. Builds nest from thin twigs, grass, moss, etc. in bushes or dwarf trees. Lays 4—6 bluish, brown-spotted eggs, incubates them 10—12 days. Lives on seeds, occasionally insects.

4 Serin *Serinus serinus*. Distributed over most of Europe except England and Scandinavia. Length about 11.5 cm. Lives near human communities, in gardens, parks, etc. Migratory bird. Returns at end of March. Male sings from telegraph wires, tall trees, etc. Nest built by female in branches 2—4 m from ground, from rootlets and grass; lined with feathers, horsehair, etc. Female incubates whitish rusty-speckled eggs 11—13 days. Both parents feed young. After nesting time consort in small groups. Occasionally resident.

2

3

4

5 Bullfinch *Pyrrhula pyrrhula.* Distributed over whole of Europe and temperate parts of Asia. Length 15—19 cm. In central Europe nests mainly in mountains, occasionally in lowlands. Inhabits conifer and mixed forests, also parks and gardens with dense trees and bushes. In April builds nest from twigs, moss, leaves, hairs, etc., relatively close to ground (about 2 m). Female lays 4—6 pale blue eggs with reddish and violet blotches and black dots. Incubates them 13 days. Lives on seeds, shoots, berries, insects and larvae. In winter frequents lowlands in small troupes.

6 Crossbill *Loxia curvirostra.* Distributed over whole of Europe, temperate parts of Asia, North America. Length 17—18.5 cm. Inhabits conifer forests. Nests at different times of year according to supply of pine and fir cones, seeds of which are food for young. Nest built beside trunk or on forked branch. Winter nests have thick walls and deep basin. Female lays 3—4 greyish-white eggs with scattered violet and red-brown spots. Incubates them unaided 14—16 days, fed by male. Newly hatched young have straight mandibles, which begin to acquire typical curved shape after 3 weeks.

7 Chaffinch *Fringilla coelebs.* Distributed over whole of Europe, western Asia, North Africa. Body length 14—18 cm. One of most numerous birds. Lives in woods, gardens and parks. Occurs at altitudes of up to 1,500 m. Many Chaffinches resident, joined by others from north. Nest built in trees and bushes 2—10 m from ground. Rounded woven structure made of rootlets, moss and lichen, thickly lined with hairs, etc. Female lays 6—8 light brown or blue-white eggs marked with red-brown and rusty spots and streaks. Young hatch in 13—14 days. Diet seeds, berries, insects.

7

5

6

Family: **Finches**—Fringillidae

1 Brambling *Fringilla montifringilla.* Inhabits northern Europe and Asia. Length 15 to 18 cm. Nests in birch-woods or mixed woods. Nest usually situated low on tree. Made of birch twigs, moss, feathers, etc. Female lays 5—7 eggs like chaffinch's. Seen in central Europe every year from October in flocks. Often visits feeding troughs.

Family: **Weavers**—Ploceidae

2 House Sparrow *Passer domesticus.* Distributed over whole of Europe, Asia and North Africa, also carried to America and Australia. Body length 14—18 cm. Commonest European bird. Lives near human communities. Builds loose nest from straw, fibres, hairs, feathers, etc. on branches or in hollows. Nests up to 4 times a year. Female lays 3—8 blotched and speckled eggs of somewhat variable colouring. Incubates them 13—14 days. Lives on different seeds, buds and, in summer, insects.

3 Tree Sparrow *Passer montanus.* Distributed over whole of Europe and Asia except India. Length 14—16.5 cm. Lives chiefly in open country, gardens, orchards, outskirts of towns and deciduous woods, etc. Builds nest from straw, wool, feathers, etc. in hollow trees, walls or other birds' nests. Nests up to 3 times a year. Female lays 5—6 grey-green, dark spotted eggs, which are incubated by both parents in turn 13—14 days. Eats insects and different seeds. Young fed mainly on insects. Resident bird.

Family: **Buntings**—Emberizidae

4 Corn Bunting *Emberiza calandra.* Distributed in Europe from southern Scandinavia, south to North Africa, east to Asia Minor. Length 18—20 cm. Usually inhabits large meadows with shrubs. Builds nest in shrubs on ground, or between tufts of grass. Lines it with grass, leaves, wool, hairs, etc. Female lays 3—6 usually reddish-yellow eggs with dark surface spots, deep spots and streaks. Incubates them unaided 12—14 days. Diet seeds, in summer insects.

5 Yellowhammer *Emberiza citrinella.* Distributed over whole of Europe, east to western Siberia. Length 16—20 cm. Abundant in open country or on outskirts of forests. Female builds nest unaided, usually on ground, from blades of grass, horsehairs, etc. At end of April lays 2—5 whitish eggs with numerous dark blotches, spots and streaks. Eggs incubated by both parents 12—14 days. Often nests 3 times. Lives on different seeds, in summer insects, spiders and centipedes. In winter consorts in flocks, often together with other birds.

6 Ortolan Bunting *Emberiza hortulana.* Distributed over whole of Europe and Near East. Length 15—17.5 cm. Inhabits lowlands and uplands, regularly found in orchards. Migratory bird. Winters in southern Europe, returns in middle of April. Ground-nester. Female lays 4—6 whitish-grey eggs with dark brown blotches, spots and scrolls. Incubates them 12—14 days. Some couples nest twice. Eats different seeds and, in summer, insects, spiders, etc.

7 Reed Bunting *Emberiza schoeniclus.* Distributed over whole of Europe and temperate parts of Asia. Length 15—17.5 cm. Found in lowlands near ponds, lakes, etc., thickly overgrown with reeds and willows. Nests on or just above ground in grass or bushes. Female lays 4—6 usually brownish eggs with brown-black spots and streaks. Incubates them 12—14 days. Nests twice. Staple diet different seeds. Winters in southern Europe.

8 Snow Bunting *Plectrophenax nivalis.* Nests in most northerly parts of Europe, Asia and North America. Length 15—19 cm. In winter spreads over whole of Europe. Builds feather- and hair-lined nest between stones. In June lays 5—6 bluish-white eggs with rusty spots and streaks. Incubates them 14 days. In summer lives on insects, in winter on different seeds. Found in central Europe in winter, in company of Bramblings.

Family: **Larks**—Alaudidae

1 Crested Lark *Galerida cristata*. Distributed over practically whole of Europe, temperate and southern Asia, south extends up to tropical Africa. Length 18.5—20.5 cm. Found near towns and villages in open, deserted country, fields, etc. Resident bird. Builds nest from grass blades, rootlets, hairs and feathers in depression in ground. Lays 3—5 whitish, dark-spotted eggs, incubates them 13 days. Young fed on insects. Diet seeds and often horse manure remains.

2 Wood Lark *Lullula arborea*. Distributed over whole of Europe, Near East, North Africa. Length 14.5—17.5 cm. Common in pine-woods, also found near towns. Often sings at night. Migratory bird, winters in Mediterranean region, returns in March. Ground-nester. Nest made of grass blades, moss, etc. Female lays 3—5 usually whitish, finely spotted eggs. Incubation period 13—15 days. Diet mainly insects.

3 Sky Lark *Alauda arvensis*. Distributed over whole of Europe, greater part of Asia, North Africa. Length 15—20.5 cm. Always found in fields. Male flutters high in air, singing. Nest lies in depression in ground; lined with fibres, grass blades, hairs, etc. Female lays 3—5 blotched and speckled eggs of greatly variable colouring, incubates them 12—14 days. Lives on insects, spiders, worms, seeds. In autumn migrates in flocks, returns in February. Occasionally found to be resident.

Family: **Wagtails and Pipits**—Motacillidae

4 Tree Pipit *Anthus trivialis*. Distributed over whole of Europe, in east extends up to Siberia. Winters in central Africa, returns to nesting area in April. Length 15.5—18 cm. Inhabits conifer, mixed and deciduous woods. Common everywhere, often occurs in mountains. Male sits singing on tall trees or telegraph poles. Ground-nester. Nest woven from grass and moss and lined with hairs, hidden in grass. Female lays 5—6 variably coloured eggs marked with spots and streaks. Incubates them 12—13 days. Diet insects and seeds.

5 Meadow Pipit *Anthus pratensis*. Inhabits practically whole of Europe. Winters in southern Europe and North Africa. Length 15—17 cm. Frequents damp meadows and mountain sides, but also found in lowlands. Male sings while flying. Nest built on ground, from moss, sedge, hairs, etc. Female lays 4—5 light-coloured eggs with dark blotches and streaks. Incubates them 13 days. Lives mainly on insects and spiders, in autumn also seeds. In autumn and spring gathers in flocks in fields. Seldom resident.

6 Yellow Wagtail *Motacilla flava.* Distributed over whole of Europe, in Asia north of Himalayas, North Africa. Winters in Africa. Length 16—19 cm. Inhabits damp lowland meadows. Female builds nest on ground, from grass blades, feathers, hairs, etc. Lays 4—6 whitish to reddish eggs thickly marked with grey-brown speckles. Incubation period 13 days. Eats insects, spiders, worms and small molluscs. Migrates in September, after first forming flocks which spend night in rushes.

7 Grey Wagtail *Motacilla cinerea.* Distributed in Europe, large part of Asia, Africa. European birds winter in Africa. Length 17—20 cm. Occurs in both mountains and lowlands. Found near streams and ponds. Usually builds nest in rocky bank, wall, etc. Lays 4—6 yellowish eggs with reddish and brownish spots and streaks. Incubation period 12—14 days. Sometimes nests twice. Main diet aquatic insects and larvae and water-fleas caught in shallows. Migrates in September.

8 White Wagtail *Motacilla alba.* Distributed over whole of Europe, Asia and Africa. Length 18—20.5 cm. Affinity for water, often found in towns. Builds nest from grass blades, rootlets, moss, etc., lined with feathers and hairs, between stones, in hole in wall, etc. In April or May female lays 5—6 whitish eggs thickly marked with dark spots and streaks. Young hatch in 12—14 days. Lives on various insects and larvae, spiders and worms. In autumn gather in flocks, migrate in September—November. Occasionally resident.

Family: **Tits**—Paridae

1 Great Tit *Parus major*. Distributed over whole of Europe except north, Asia and part of North Africa. Length 14—16.5 cm. Inhabits forests, gardens and parks. In winter gathers in troupes in company of other tits. Often found at feeding troughs. Nest built in various hollows, from moss, lichen, hairs, feathers, etc. Female lays 6—14 whitish eggs with red-brown spots. Young hatch in 13—14 days. Nests twice. Parents feed young 15—20 days. Lives mainly on insects and, in winter, seeds. Tempted by lumps of suet on string.

2 Blue Tit *Parus caeruleus*. Distributed over whole of Europe except north, North Africa, in east to Caucasus. Length 11.5—13.5 cm. Inhabits woods, in towns also parks. Nests in hollows, tree stumps, crevices, pipes, etc. Female lays 7—16 whitish eggs thickly sprinkled with rusty blotches and dots. Sits on them 13—15 days. Diet mainly insects and their larvae and in winter seeds. Couples stay together even in winter, often in company of other tits.

3 Coal Tit *Parus ater*. Distributed over whole of Europe, in east to Japan, in south to North Africa. Length 11—12 cm. Resident in central Europe. Inhabits mixed forests, but mainly frequents conifers. Builds nest in tree hollows, from moss and hairs. At end of April lays 7—11 whitish, red-speckled eggs. Young hatched in 14—16 days, fledged at 15 days. Lives mainly on insects, in winter conifer seeds.

4 Crested Tit *Parus cristatus.* Inhabits whole of Europe, in east to Urals. Length 12—13 cm. Found mainly in conifer forests. Builds nest in holes and cracks. Female lays 5—11 whitish eggs with red-brown spots. Young hatched in 15—17 days, fledged at 20 days. Eat insects in all developmental stages. In winter join and lead flocks of other tits.

5 Marsh Tit *Parus palustris.* Distributed in Europe and south of eastern Asia. Length 12 to 14 cm. Inhabits deciduous and mixed woods, parks and gardens. Hole-nester, builds nest from straw, grass, moss, hairs, etc. Female lays 6—10 whitish, red-spotted eggs. Young hatched in 14—15 days, fed by parents 17—19 days. Couples remain together even in winter, but form small troupes. Lives on insects, spiders, in winter also minute seeds.

Family: Aegithalidae

6 Long-tailed Tit *Aegithalos caudatus.* Distributed over whole of Europe, in east as far as Japan. Length about 15 cm. Very long tail. Inhabits deciduous woods, parks, etc. When not nesting consorts in small flocks. Nests in trees and bushes, preferably on forked branch. Nest ovoid and closed, with side entrance. Made of moss, lichen, cobwebs, etc. Thickly lined with small feathers. Female lays 7—12 whitish eggs with red blotches and dots, incubates them 13 days. Diet insects.

Family: Remizidae

7 Penduline Tit *Remiz pendulinus.* Distributed in southern Europe, south part of central Europe, in east to Japan. Length 10.5—11.5 cm. Found near water, especially ponds. Builds closed spherical nest suspended from tips of terminal willow twigs by fibres made from poplar fluff, etc. Nest has tunnel-like entrance. Female lays 6—8 white eggs, sits on them 12—15 days. Male meanwhile builds new nest. Eats mainly insects and spiders.

Family: **Goldcrests**—Regulidae

8 Goldcrest *Regulus regulus.* Distributed over whole of Europe, Asia, North America. Length 8.5—10.5 cm. Smallest European bird, weighs 5—6 g. Inhabits conifer forests. Builds nest from twigs, grass blades, hairs, cobwebs, etc. on dense fir or pine branches. Female lays 8—11 yellowish eggs marked with dark scrolls. Incubation period 16—17 days. Diet small insects and spiders. In winter moves about in tree-tops in small groups, twittering.

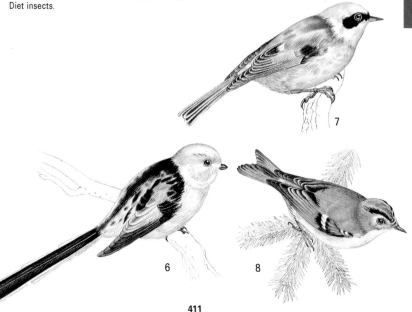

7

6

8

411

Family: **Shrikes**—Laniidae

1 Great Grey Shrike *Lanius excubitor.* Distributed in Europe, Asia, North America, North Africa. Length 24—27.5 cm. Inhabits open country, especially with thorny shrubs. Sometimes impales prey (insects and small vertebrates) on thorns. Builds nest from dry twigs, straw, moss, etc. on tall bushes. In May female lays 5—7 whitish, grey- and brown-spotted eggs. Young hatched in 15 days, fed by parents 20 days.

2 Red-backed Shrike *Lanius collurio.* Distributed over practically whole of Europe and Asia. Winters in Africa and southern Asia, returns to Europe in middle of May. Length 18—20.5 cm. Frequents areas with thorny shrubs. Nest hidden in thicket, 1—2 m from ground, from twigs, straw, rootlets and moss, lined with hairs. Female lays 3—7 pink, red- and brown-spotted eggs. Young hatch in 14—15 days. Leave nest after 2 weeks but remain in bushes. Lives mainly on insects, also young of small birds and rodents. Impales prey on thorns. Imitates call of other birds.

3 Woodchat Shrike *Lanius senator.* Distributed over whole of Europe except England, in east to Poland, in south to North Africa. Winters in Central Africa. Arrives in Europe at beginning of May, leaves in August. Length 19.5—20 cm. Nests on sunny places. Builds nest in bushes like that of red-backed shrike. Lays 5—6 yellowish or greenish, grey- and olive-spotted eggs. Young hatched in 14—15 days, fed by parents 20 days. Eats mainly insects.

Family: **Waxwings**—Bombycillidae

4 Waxwing *Bombycilla garrulus.* Distributed in most northerly parts of Europe, Asia and North America. Length 19—23 cm. Visits central Europe only in winter, often in large flocks. Most often seen on rowans or berry-bearing bushes, eating berries. In north nests in conifer and mixed forests. Tree-nester, builds nest from twigs or moss. Female lays 4—6 bluish, black- and violet-spotted eggs, incubates them 14 days. Also eats insects.

Family: **Accentors**—Prunellidae

5 Dunnock *Prunella modularis*. Distributed over whole of Europe and north-western Asia. Length 14.5—16.5 cm. Common in central Europe, but very retiring. Inhabits dense conifer woods. In dense branches builds relatively large mossy nest lined with hairs. Lays 4—7 plain blue-green eggs in May. Often nests twice. Young hatch in 12—14 days. Eats mainly insects, in autumn small seeds. In October migrates to Mediterranean region.

Family: **Wrens**—Troglodytidae

6 Wren *Troglodytes troglodytes*. Distributed over whole of Europe, temperate parts of Asia, North America, north-eastern Africa. Length 9.5—11.5 cm, weight about 9 g. Resident in cen-

tral Europe. Solitary bird except at nesting time. Builds spherical nest with side entrance from twigs and moss, lined with hairs and feathers. Lays 5—7 whitish, red-spotted eggs. Young hatch in 14—16 days. Diet insects.

Family: **Dippers**—Cinclidae

7 Dipper *Cinclus cinclus*. Distributed over whole of Europe, extends east to central Asia, Himalayas and north-western Africa. Length 17.5—20 cm. Frequents mountain streams and rivers. Resident bird. Hunts for food (insects and insect larvae) under water, on bed. Also collects material for nest under water. Nests in spaces between stones, often at foot of waterfall. Female lays 4—6 white eggs. Young hatch in 15—17 days, leave nest in 3 weeks.

Family: **Flycatchers**—Muscicapidae

1 Spotted Flycatcher *Muscicapa striata*. Distributed over whole of Europe, in east to Mongolia, in south to north-western Africa. Winters in tropical and southern Africa. Leaves in September, returns at beginning of May. Length 14—17 cm. Lives on outskirts of forests or in parks. Builds relatively large nest from grass blades and rootlets, lined with hairs and feathers, usually on horizontal branch or overgrown wall, etc. Lays 4—6 bluish white, grey- and russet-spotted eggs. Eggs incubated 13 days by both parents. Eats insects, catches prey on wing.

2 Pied Flycatcher *Ficedula hypoleuca*. Inhabits whole of Europe, western Asia, north-western Africa. Winters in Africa. Length 12.5—14.5 cm. In some regions abundant. Lives in open deciduous woods and parks. Builds nest from moss, fibres, cobwebs, etc. in hollow trees and stumps. Lays 4—8 bright blue-green eggs. Young hatched in 13 days, fed by parents 18 days. Migrates at end of October. Diet insects.

Family: **Warblers**—Sylviidae

3 Lesser Whitethroat *Sylvia curruca*. Distributed over most of Europe, in east up to Siberia. European birds winter in central Africa. Leave in August or September, return in second half of April. Length 12.5—13.5 cm. Frequents bushes in woods, gardens and parks. Weaves very loose nest from grass blades and rootlets in tall nettles, shrubs, etc. Female lays 4—6 whitish or yellowish eggs with violet-grey and yellow-brown speckles and black streaks. Young hatch in 11—13 days. Eats insects and spiders.

4 Blackcap *Sylvia atricapilla*. Distributed over whole of Europe, in east to river Ob and in north-western Africa. Winters in Central Africa. Leaves in September, returns at end of April. Length 14—15 cm. Inhabits deciduous woods and parks and gardens with plenty of shrubs. Builds nest from grass blades and cobwebs, in brambles, bushes, etc., usually about 75 cm from ground. Female lays 4—6 yellowish or greenish, grey or red-spotted eggs. Young hatch in 13—14 days. Diet chiefly insects, supplemented in autumn by raspberries or bilberries.

5 Garden Warbler *Sylvia borin*. Distributed over most of Europe, in east to western Siberia. Winters in Central Africa. Leaves at end of September, returns in middle of May. Length about 14 cm. Frequents places with shrubs. Weaves nest from stalks among raspberry canes, in brambles, etc., 0.5—3 m. from ground. Lays 4—6 yellowish or greenish eggs with grey and olive spots or marbling. Young hatch in 12 days. Often rears young cuckoos. Eats various insects and their larvae.

1

2

6 Barred Warbler *Sylvia nisoria*. Distributed in central Europe, in east to western Siberia. Winters in eastern half of Africa. Leaves in August, returns at end of April. Length 16 to 18 cm. Inhabits large parks, overgrown gardens and margins of forests. Builds nest from grasses, blades, horsehair, etc. in dense bushes, 1—2 m from ground. Female lays 4—5 yellowish or greenish, grey-speckled eggs. Young hatched in 14—15 days, fed by parents 16 days. Lives mainly on insects, at end of summer also berries.

7 Icterine Warbler *Hippolais icterina*. Distributed in Europe from central France to upper reaches of Ob river. Winters in Africa. Leaves in August, returns early in May. Length 13—16 cm. Inhabits open deciduous woods and large parks. Builds nest from stalks, leaves, rootlets, etc. in deciduous trees or bushes. Masks it with birch bark. Usually lays 5 pink eggs sprinkled with black dots and blotches. Young hatch in 13 days. Eats mainly different insects.

Family: **Warblers**—Sylviidae

1 Chiffchaff *Phylloscopus collybita*. Distributed over whole of Europe, in east to Lake Baikal, and north-western Africa. Winters in north-eastern Africa. Leaves in October, male's monotonous song heard soon after return at end of March. Length 12—14 cm. Inhabits deciduous or mixed woods and parks. Female builds closed spherical nest from grass blades and moss in clump of grass on ground. Lays 5—6 white eggs with reddish brown dots. Incubates them unaided 13—14 days. Young fed 2 weeks. Eats only small insects.

2 Wood Warbler *Phylloscopus sibilatrix*. Distributed over whole of Europe except north, and in western Asia. Winters in Central Africa. Leaves in September, returns in middle of April. Male chirps. Length 12—14 cm. Inhabits large woods and parks. Ground-nester. Builds closed, hair-lined nest with side entrance. Female lays 6—8 white eggs with dark brown spots and streaks, incubates them 13 days. Young fledged at 12—15 days. Eats mainly insects.

3 Grasshopper Warbler *Locustella naevia*. Distributed over whole of Europe except north and south, in east up to Mongolia. European birds winter in North Africa. Leaves in August, returns at end of April. Length 13—15 cm. Lives hidden in thick shrubs beside ponds and rivers. Builds deep grass nest on ground under bush. Lays 5—7 pink eggs with rusty blotches and dots. Eggs incubated 13—15 days by both parents in turn. Young leave nest at 10 days, before fully capable of flight. Diet mainly insects.

4 Great Reed Warbler *Acrocephalus arundinaceus*. Distributed over whole of Europe except England and Scandinavia, in east up to Australia, also North Africa. European birds winter in equatorial Africa. Leave in August and September, return in first half of May. Length about 20 cm. High-pitched, screechy song. Inhabits rushes beside ponds, lakes and rivers. Builds basket-like nest between rush stems. Female lays 4—6 bluish eggs with olive green and brown spots. Incubated 14—15 days by both parents in turn. Eats mainly insects.

5 Reed Warbler *Acrocephalus scirpaceus*. Distributed from central Europe to southern England and central Asia. Winters in northern and equatorial Africa. Leaves at end of September, returns in middle of April. Length 15—16 cm. Lives beside water among reeds. Weaves nest from long stalks. Lays 4—5 whitish eggs with olive-coloured surface spots and deep spots. Young hatch in 11—12 days. Male has sweeter song than Great Reed Warbler. Lives on insects and spiders.

416

Family: **Thrushes**—Turdidae

6 Fieldfare *Turdus pilaris*. Distributed in central and northern Europe, in east to Lake Baikal. Length 24.5—28 cm. Migratory bird, northern population comes to central Europe in winter. Weaves nest from grass, twigs, moss, etc., usually reinforced with mud. Often nests in colonies (several nests on one tree) in open conifer woods, also in junipers, sometimes quite low down. Female lays 5—7 greenish-white eggs thickly marked with rusty brown spots and streaks. Young hatch in 13—14 days. Eats mainly insects, in winter berries.

7 Mistle Thrush *Turdus viscivorus*. Distributed over whole of Europe, in east to Lake Baikal, in south to north-western Africa. Northern birds migrate south. Length 26—29.5 cm. Prefers conifer woods, occasionally found in large parks. Nest usually situated on pines, about 10 m from ground, woven from rootlets, grass blades and moss, reinforced with mud. Female builds nest, male fetches material. In April female lays 4—5 blue-green eggs with violet, grey and brown spots, incubates them unaided 13—14 days. Eats mainly insects caught on ground. From autumn onwards roams countryside in small troupes.

Family: **Thrushes**—Turdidae

1 Song Thrush *Turdus philomelos.* Distributed over whole of Europe, Asia Minor, in east to Lake Baikal. Winters in southern Europe and North Africa. Leaves in October, returns in March or early April. Length 22—24.5 cm. Inhabits woods, gardens and parks. Builds nest from stalks, twigs, etc., inner side reinforced and faced with mixture of mud and saliva. Nests on bushes, trees and walls. Female lays 4—6 green-blue eggs sprinkled with black dots, incubates them unaided 12—13 days. Young leave nest before fully fledged. Eats insects, worms, molluscs, and in autumn berries.

2 Ring Ouzel *Turdus torquatus.* Distributed in England, Scandinavia, Alps, Pyrenees, Giant Mountains, Caucasus. Winters in North Africa. Leaves in October, returns in April. Length about 27 cm. Inhabits mountain sides. Nests in dense branches of dwarf pines. Lays 4—5 greenish, thickly marbled and streaked eggs. Incubated 14 days by both parents in turn.

3 Blackbird *Turdus merula.* Distributed in whole of Europe, east over narrow zone to China. Part of population resident, part migrates to Mediterranean region. Length 23.5—28 cm. Inhabits forests, parks and gardens near human dwellings. Makes nest from grass blades, rootlets, etc. on trees, bushes and wooden beams, etc. Female lays 4—6 blue-green eggs thickly marked with grey and brown blotches, dots and streaks, incubates them 13—14 days. Young fed by both parents. Sometimes nests three times a year. Lives on insects, worms, molluscs, berries, fruit, etc.

4 Wheatear *Oenanthe oenanthe.* Distributed over whole of Europe, Asia, North America and Greenland. Winters mainly in tropical Africa. Leaves in August or September, returns in April. Length 15—17 cm. Inhabits stony, unwooded slopes, rocky planes or quarries. Builds nest from grass blades, hairs and feathers among stones, in abandoned holes, etc. In May female lays 5—7 greenish eggs, incubates them 14 days. Young leave nest before fully fledged. Diet mainly insects.

5 Whinchat *Saxicola rubetra*. Distributed over most of Europe, in east to western Siberia. Winters in equatorial Africa. Leaves in August or September, in small flocks, returns in April. Length 13—15.5 cm. Frequents uplands with large shrub-strewn meadows. Likes to sit on hummocks. Ground-nester. Nest made of grass blades, moss, etc., lined with grass and plant fluff. In June female lays 5—6 bluish-grey eggs, often marked with rusty spots, incubates them 13—14 days. Young leave nest early. Diet mainly insects.

6 Redstart *Phoenicurus phoenicurus*. Distributed over whole of Europe, Asia Minor, in east to western Siberia; also North Africa. Winters mainly in equatorial Africa. Leaves in August or September, returns in first half of April. Length 13.5—17 cm. Lives almost everywhere, in woods, gardens, near human communities. Builds nest from grass blades, rootlets, leaves hairs, etc. in all sorts of hollows, in walls, between wooden beams, etc. Female lays 5—t green-blue eggs, incubates them 13—15 days Nests twice. Eats mainly insects skilfully caught on wing.

7 Black Redstart *Phoenicurus ochruros*. Distributed in central and southern Europe, in west to England, in east up to northern China. European birds winter in North Africa. Leave in October, return at end of March. Length about 15 cm. Originally rock-dweller, now lives in vicinity of man. Builds nest from rootlets, grass blades, hairs, etc. under shed roofs, in barns, on cornices. Female lays 5—6 white eggs, incubates them 14 days. Young leave nest before fully fledged and go into hiding. Diet mainly insects.

Family: **Thrushes**—Turdidae

1 Nightingale *Luscinia megarhynchos*. Distributed in western, central and southern Europe, in east to central Asia, in south to North Africa. Winters chiefly in equatorial Africa. Leaves in August, returns at end of April. Migrates only at night. Length 18—20 cm. Inhabits margins of deciduous or mixed woods, thickets beside rivers and ponds, etc. Male sings during day as well as at night. Song carries long distances. Builds nest from grass blades, rootlets, moss, rush stems, etc., lined with hair, in branches of impenetrable bushes. Female lays 4—6 olive brown, sometimes thickly speckled, eggs, incubates them unaided 13 days. Young leave nest early. Diet mainly insects and worms.

2 Bluethroat *Luscinia svecica*. Distributed over whole of Europe except England and Mediterranean region, in east as far as Mongolia. Winters in North Africa. Length about 15 cm. Seldom nests in central Europe, but often found in large numbers in riverside shrubs during migration. Builds nest from dry grass blades on or near ground, in bushes near stretches of reeds. Female lays 5—6 bluish eggs sprinkled with brown spots. Young hatch in 13 days, leave nest after 2 weeks. Eats small insects and their larvae.

3 Robin *Erithacus rubecula*. Distributed over whole of Europe, Asia Minor, in east to western Siberia. Most birds migrate to North Africa in October, but old males often remain behind. Length 13—16 cm. Frequents thickets in woods, parks and gardens. Ground-nester, hides nest under clump of grass, between stones, in holes, etc. Nest made of moss, rootlets, grass blades, hairs, etc. Female lays 5—7 yellowish eggs marked with red blotches and dots, incubates them unaided 13—14 days. Young fed by both parents. Some birds nest twice. Lives mainly on insects, in autumn and winter supplemented by berries and forest fruits.

Family: **Swallows**—Hirundinidae

4 Swallow *Hirundo rustica.* Distributed over whole of Europe, most of Asia, North America, North Africa. European birds winter in Africa south of Sahara. Leave in September, return in first half of April. Length 18—23 cm. Basin-like nest built by both partners from small lumps of clay mixed with saliva and from grass blades lined with hairs and feathers. Female lays 4—6 whitish, red- and violet-spotted eggs. Incubates them 14—16 days, fed by male. Young fed 3 weeks by both parents. When young are fledged, birds spend night in flocks in sedge beside ponds. Eats mainly insects caught on wing.

5 House Martin *Delichon urbica.* Distributed over whole of Europe, most of Asia, North Africa. European birds winter in Africa south of Sahara. Leave in September, return in second half of April. Length 15—16.5 cm. Builds clay nest on vertical wall, under eaves or cornices. Nest completely closed except for side entrance on top. Birds often form large colonies. Female lays 4—5 pure white eggs. Incubated 12—13 days by both parents in turn. Young fed 20—23 days. Some birds nest again in July. Eats mainly insects caught in air.

6 Sand Martin *Riparia riparia.* Distributed over whole of Europe, large part of Asia, North America, north-western and north-eastern Africa. European birds winter in equatorial and southern Africa. Leave in August, return in second half of April. Length 12.5—14.5 cm. Lives preferably near rivers, lakes and ponds, also in sand-pits with sheer walls, in which it makes burrows 1.5 m long. Nest chamber lined with feathers and grass blades. Nests in colonies. Female lays 5—7 pure white eggs in middle of May. Eggs incubated 15 days by both parents in turn. Young fed in nest 23 days. Lives on insects caught in air.

4

5

6

Order: **Woodpeckers and Allies**—Piciformes

Family: **Woodpeckers**—Picidae

1 Green Woodpecker *Picus viridis.* Distributed over whole of Europe except most northerly parts, in east to Ukraine. Length 33—37 cm. Resident, but after nesting season roams long distances. Has predilection for open woods, parks and orchards. Both partners hack hole in rotting tree trunks, finished in 14 days. Line hole only with splinters. Female lays 6—8 white eggs, incubated 15—17 days by both parents in turn. Young leave nest after 17—20 days. Birds live mainly on larvae of different wood-beetles, also rake open anthills and collect pupae and adult ants on their long, sticky, protrusible tongue. Occasionally visit beehives, especially in winter.

2 Great Spotted Woodpecker *Dendrocopos major.* Distributed over whole of Europe, extends east in narrow zone to Japan, in south to North Africa. Length 22.5—26.5 cm. Inhabits woods, parks and large orchards. Resident bird, but in winter roams countryside round birthplace. Hacks hole in deciduous trees and conifers 2—10 m from ground, lines it with small splinters. Female lays 4—8 glossy white eggs in April or May. Young hatch in 13—15 days. Lives on beetle larvae (e.g. on bark beetles), wedges hazelnuts in crevice, cracks shell and eats kernel, also eats seeds of conifers. In winter often consorts with nuthatches or tits.

3 Black Woodpecker *Dryocopus martius.* Distributed over whole of Europe except England and southern parts, in east extends as far as Japan. Length 42—48.5 cm. Mainly inhabits large conifer forests in lowlands and mountains, but also encountered in deciduous woods where it nests in strong beeches or birches. Like other woodpeckers, in spring drums on dry branch stumps. Usually nests over 4 m above ground. Both partners hack hole about 50 cm deep in 2 weeks, making pile of splinters at foot of tree. Female lays 4—5 white eggs. Young hatch in 12—14 days, leave nest after 24—28 days. Eats mainly wood beetle larvae and ants and their nymphs.

4 Wryneck *Jynx torquilla.* Distributed over whole of Europe, in east to Japan. Migratory bird. Winters in northern and eastern Africa. Usually leaves in August, returns in second half of April, immediately utters typical plaintive call. Length 18.5—19.5 cm. Inhabits outskirts of deciduous woods, parks, orchards and large gardens. Does not make own nesting hole, often content with crack in wall. Does not line nest. In May—June female lays 7—10 white eggs. Parents incubate eggs 13—14 days, feed young 24—26 days. Feeds on caterpillars, ant pupae, etc. Wryneck can turn long, flexible neck by up to 180 degrees.

Order: **Swifts and Allies**—Apodiformes

Family: **Swifts**—Apodidae

5 Common Swift *Apus apus.* Distributed over whole of Europe, in east to China, in south to north-western Africa. Migratory bird. Leaves at beginning of August (sometimes end of July), winters in Africa south of Sahara, returns at end of April or beginning of May. Length 18—21 cm. Builds nest under eaves of tall houses, on steples, towers, etc., using pile of plant debris and feathers snapped up during flight and stuck together with saliva. Female lays 2—3 white eggs, incubates them 18 days, fed by male. Young leave nest at 6 weeks, immediately able to fly. Eats insects caught on wing. Swifts like to consort in darting, screeching flocks. Rapid fliers, cover about 900 km a day.

5

4

Order: **Rollers and Allies**—Coraciiformes

Family: **Rollers**—Coraciidae

1 Roller *Coracias garrulus*. Distributed in Europe except England and north, in east to India, in south to north-western Africa. Migratory bird. Leaves at end of August, winters in Africa south of Sahara, returns at beginning of May. Length 30—34 cm. Nests in tree hollows. Female lays 3—5 pure white eggs. Eggs incubated by both parents in turn, young leave nest at 28 days. Keeps look-out for prey, catches it mainly on wing. Lives on insects, small vertebrates, in Africa mainly locusts.

Family: **Bee-eaters**—Meropidae

2 Bee-eater *Merops apiaster*. Distributed in southern Europe, Asia as far as India, north-western Africa. Nests in central Europe in Slovakia, Moravia and Hungary, in recent years also in Sweden, Denmark and Holland. Migratory bird, winters in Africa south of Sahara. Frequents places with sandy or clay banks, in which it makes burrow with beak (in about 3 weeks). Lives in small colonies. Lays 5—6 white eggs, incubated 22 days by both parents in turn. Eats mainly hymenoptera, especially bees and wasps.

Family: **Kingfishers**—Alcedinidae

3 Kingfisher *Alcedo atthis*. Distributed over whole of Europe except north, in east to Asia, and north-western Africa. Resident bird, but northerly population shifts somewhat south. Nomadic during winter. Length 16.5—18.5 cm. Inhabits places with clean water and sheer banks. Makes burrow about 1 m long above waterline, lines nest-chamber with fish scales and bones. Female lays 6—8 white eggs. Young hatch in 21 days. Kingfishers catch prey — small fish — by swooping into water.

Family: **Hoopoes**—Upupidae

4 Hoopoe *Upupa epops*. Distributed over whole of Europe and Asia except northern parts, and practically whole of Africa. Migratory bird. European population leaves in August or September, winters in equatorial Africa, returns in April. Length 28—32.5 cm. Prefers open country with meadows and pastures, also found in old avenues near ponds, or in open deciduous woods. Nests in tree hollows or piles of stones. In May female lays 4—8 greyish or brownish white eggs, incubates them unaided 16 days, fed by male. Eats chiefly beetle larvae. Name describes typical call.

Order: **Nightjars**—Caprimulgiformes

5 Nightjar or **Goatsucker** *Caprimulgus europaeus*. Distributed over most of Europe, in east to central Siberia, also in north-western Africa. Migratory bird. Leaves in September, winters mainly in Africa south of Sahara, returns in first half of May. Length 26—28 cm. Nests in bare depression in ground. Female lays 2 whitish, grey-speckled eggs indistinguishable from background. Eggs incubated 16—19 days by both parents in turn. Young fed only at night. By day, Nightjar perches lengthwise on branch. Goes hunting after sundown. Lives on insects — mostly moths and beetles — caught on wing.

Order: **Owls**—Strigiformes

6 Snowy Owl *Nyctea scandiaca*. Distributed in European, Asian and North American tundra. Flies south in winter and occasionally appears in central and southern Europe. Length 56—65 cm. Mainly diurnal bird. Likes high perches. Skilful flier. Nests on ground or in cleft rocks. Lays 3—8 white eggs with staggered hatching. Catches mainly rodents, sometimes small birds, occasionally fish.

2

3

Order: **Owls**—Strigiformes

1 Eagle Owl *Bubo bubo.* Distributed over whole of Europe except England, whole of Asia except southern and northern parts, North Africa. Resident bird, not nomadic during winter. Length 62—72.5 cm, female slightly larger. Inhabits extensive forests, wooded rocks and ravines. Occurs at both low and high altitudes. Nests in tree hollows, in ruins and on ground. Female lays 2—5 white eggs at end of March, incubates them unaided 35 days. Hides during day, flies only at night, fairly close to ground. Hunting radius 15 km. Catches mammals up to size of hare, birds, occasionally fish.

1

2 Long-eared Owl *Asio otus.* Distributed over most of Europe, in east as far as Japan, North America, North Africa. Resident bird in Europe, sometimes migratory. Length 35—39 cm. Abundant in forests, preserves and parks. Nests in old nests of other birds or squirrels. Female lays 4—6 white eggs, usually in April, incubates them unaided 27—28 days, fed by male. Eats mainly voles, also maybugs and other beetles caught after dark. During day hides in dense branches. In winter often roams countryside in troupes, looking for rodents.

3 Little Owl *Athene noctua.* Distributed over whole of Europe except north, in east as far as Korea, North Africa. Resident bird. Length 23.5—27.5 cm. Inhabits outskirts of woods, ruins, parks, avenues; likes to perch on roofs, behind chimneys. Nocturnal bird, but also hunts in afternoon of dull days. Plaintive call often heard at night near human dwellings. During day hides in holes and hollows. Nests in similar places. Female lays 4—7 white eggs, incubates them 28 days. Catches small rodents, occasionally small birds, especially sparrows, often also insects, chiefly beetles.

4 Tawny Owl *Strix aluco.* Distributed over whole of Europe except north, parts of Asia, North Africa. Resident bird. Length 41—46 cm. Goes hunting after dark. During day hides in dense branches, usually in same place, piles of ejected pellets to be found under tree. Inhabits forests, parks, large gardens and avenues, at both low and high altitudes. Nests in tree hollows, under wooden beams, etc. Female lays 2—5 white eggs, incubates them 28 days. Young fully fledged after 3 months. Catches mainly small rodents, also small birds, amphibians and insects.

4

5

5 Barn Owl *Tyto alba*. Distributed over whole of Europe, southern Asia, Australia, Africa and America. Resident bird. Length 33—39 cm. Originally rock-dweller, in Europe now lives in vicinity of man. Nests in attics, below eaves, in ruins, towers or dovecots. Female lays 4—6 white eggs on bare base, incubates them 30—34 days, fed by male. Young fledged after 50 days. In years of vole plagues nests several times. In addition to voles and mice catches moles, shrews, sparrows and insects. Young birds often fly far afield.

Order: **Cuckoos and Allies**—Cuculiformes

Family: **Cuckoos**—Cuculidae

6 Common Cuckoo *Cuculus canorus*. Distributed over whole of Europe, most of Asia, Africa. European birds migrate in August or September, winter in Africa south of Sahara, return at end of April when male immediately makes himself heard. Length 31—39 cm. Has preference for open woods with undergrowth. Female lays eggs (average 18) one by one in nests of small birds. Young hatch in only 12 days, after 10 hours throw all other occupants (eggs or young) out of nest. Young cuckoo remains in nest 23 days and is fed by foster-parents 3 more weeks. Eats mainly caterpillars (even hairy ones), spiders, etc.

6

Order: **Birds of Prey**—Falconiformes

Family: **Falcons**—Falconidae

1 Peregrine Falcon *Falco peregrinus.* Distributed in Europe, Asia, Africa, North America, Australia. Length 41—50 cm. Wings long and pointed at flight. Nests in cleft rocks, towers, or nests abandoned by other birds of prey. In April lays 3—4 eggs with red-brown spots. Young hatch in 28—29 days. Male hunts for young, female feeds them. Hunts primarily in air. Swoops on prey at velocity of up to 200 km an hour. Catches mainly birds — pigeons, crows, starlings, gulls, etc. Formerly trained for hunting. Young birds migratory, old birds sometimes resident.

2 Hobby *Falco subbuteo.* Distributed over whole of Europe, temperate parts of Asia, North Africa. Migratory bird. Winters in southern Africa, returns to nesting places in April. Length 32—36 cm. Nests in deserted nests of crows or other birds. Frequents small woods. Female lays 2—4 eggs with red-brown spots. Young hatch in 28 days. Male brings prey for young, female feeds them. Catches small birds or insects in air. Can even catch swifts and swallows. Devours prey on tree. Protected.

3 Kestrel *Falco tinnunculus.* Distributed over whole of Europe, Asia and Africa. Length 31—38 cm. Nests on jutting rocks, in abandoned nests of other birds, in towers and hollows. Sometimes nests in colonies. In May female lays 3—8 eggs with red-brown spots. Young hatch in 28 days. Prefers to hunt in open country, fields and meadows. Hovers in air, swoops on prey, mainly small rodents and insects. Migrates in autumn to North Africa, but some birds remain behind.

Family: **Eagles and Allies**—Accipitridae

4 Golden Eagle *Aquila chrysaetos.* Distributed in Europe, Asia, North America, North Africa; in Europe mainly Alps, Pyrenees and Scotland. Length 82—92 cm., wing span about 2 m. Long tail spread during flight. Nuptial flights held in March. Builds nest on rocks, using sticks, clumps of grass, hairs, etc. Female lays 1—3 brown-spotted eggs, incubated 45 days by both parents in turn. Male mostly fetches prey for young, female prepares it for them. Catches mammals and birds up to size of small chamois or goat.

5 Lesser Spotted Eagle *Aquila pomarina.* Distributed in central Europe, in east to southern Asia. Length 61—65 cm., wing span about 150

cm. Nuptial flights in spring. Builds nest in trees, from twigs, grass, etc. Female usually lays 2 spotted eggs, occasionally relieved by male while incubating them. Parents generally rear only one young. Catches rodents, reptiles, birds and insects. Migrates in winter to southern Africa. Locally abundant in Europe.

6 Marsh-harrier *Circus aeruginosus.* Distributed over whole of Europe, across Asia to Far East, Africa, Australian region. Length 49—60 cm. Frequents large ponds and lakes. Locally abundant. Builds nest from piled rush stems in large reed beds. Female lays 3—6 greenish white eggs in May. Young hatch in 32—33 days. Both parents hunt for food, only female feeds young. Catches young gulls, voles, frogs, etc. Winters in tropical Africa, returns in March.

7 Buzzard *Buteo buteo.* Distributed over most of Europe, extends east as far as Japan. Length 46—55 cm. Very variable colouring, from black-brown to pure white. Nests in trees in small woods near hunting ground in open country. Builds nest from small sticks 8—15 m. from ground. Female lays 2—5 eggs with brown and violet spots. Eggs incubated 30 days by both parents, but more by female. Catches voles, mice, occasionally birds. Likes to sit on high perches. Resident bird, nomadic in winter. Some individuals fly to North Africa.

Family: **Eagles and Allies**—Accipitridae

1 Rough-legged Hawk *Buteo lagopus*. Distributed in north-European, Asian and American tundra. Always winters in central and southern Europe. Length 53—60.5 cm. Wears feather 'trousers'. Arrives in central Europe in October and remains until March. Often forms large flocks. Catches voles and, in times of shortage, partridges. In native habitat nests in trees, lays 2—7 eggs and lives mainly on lemmings.

2 Black Kite *Milvus migrans*. Distributed in Europe, Asia, Africa and Australia. Length about 56 cm. Inhabits regions with rivers, lakes or ponds. Also frequents human communities in role of scavenger. Builds nest in tree top or uses nests of other birds. Female lays 2—3 eggs, incubates them 30 days, occasionally relieved by male. Lives on small vertebrates, but likes to collect scraps on ground or water surface. Winters in Africa.

3 White-tailed Eagle *Haliaeetus albicilla*. Distributed in central and northern Europe, whole of Asia except southern parts. Also nests in Scotland. Length 75—98 cm, wing span up to 230 cm. Inhabits coast, lakes or large ponds and rivers. Makes nest from branches, usually in tall trees, occasionally on rocks. Uses same nest for years, adds to it. Female lays 2—3 whitish eggs, incubated 6 weeks by both parents in turn. Catches mainly fish, also birds up to size of heron, but chiefly weak individuals.

4 Goshawk *Accipiter gentilis*. Distributed over whole of Europe, Asia except southern parts, and most of North America. Length of male 52—56 cm, female 60—64.5 cm. Colouring often variable. Inhabits small woods, often settles near villages. Radius of nesting area about 5 km. Builds nest from twigs and green sprays on tall trees, adds to it every year. Female lays 3—5 grey-green eggs, often with brown spots, incubates them 38 days, mainly unaided. Catches squirrels, rabbits, birds (mainly jays, pigeons, crows, etc.). Useful bird in falconry.

5 Sparrow-hawk *Accipiter nisus*. Distributed over whole of Europe, most of Asia except north, north-western Africa. Length of male 31—34 cm, female 37—41 cm. Resident and nomadic, some birds migratory. Forest-dweller with preference for conifer woods. Builds nest from dry twigs, preferably in tall spruces, beside trunk. In May female lays 4—6 bluish-green eggs with brown-red spots, incubates them unaided 31—36 days, fed by male. Male fetches food for young, female feeds them. Catches mainly small birds, especially sparrows, but also blackbirds, finches, etc.

6 Honey Buzzard *Pernis apivorus*. Distributed in Europe except north and south, in east as far as Urals. Migratory. Leaves in October, winters in western and central Africa, returns in April. Length 50—57 cm. Prefers deciduous and mixed lowland woods. Frequents chiefly places inhabited by wasps which are its staple diet. Nests in abandoned nests of other birds of prey near clearings or margins of forests. Female usually lays only 2 whitish eggs with red-brown spots. Young hatch in 30—35 days. Digs out wasps' broods, but also eats soft fruits.

430

Family: **Ospreys**—Pandionidae

7 Osprey *Pandion haliaetus.* Distributed in central, northern and southern Europe, Asia, Australia and America. Migratory bird. European population leaves in September, winters in Africa, returns in April. Length 56—61.5 cm. Inhabits basins of large rivers, area round ponds and lakes or coastal regions. Builds nest from twigs, clumps of grass, turf, etc. in tall trees, especially pines and oaks. Female lays 2—3 bluish eggs with red-brown spots. Young hatch in 29 days. Lives mainly on fish. Hovers above water, then dives after prey.

431

Order: **Cursory Birds**—Ciconiiformes

Family: **Herons**—Ardeidae

1 Heron *Ardea cinerea*. Distributed over most of Europe, Asia as far as Japan, Africa. European birds winter in Africa, return at beginning of April. Length about 90 cm. Inhabits regions with ponds and lakes. Builds nest from dry twigs in tall trees. Lives in colonies. Female lays 4—5 blue-green eggs, incubated 25—28 days by both parents in turn. Young hatch in same order as eggs were laid. Catches small fish, amphibians, molluscs, insects, small rodents and birds. Flocks of northern herons often seen in central Europe in winter.

2 Purple Heron *Ardea purpurea*. Distributed in southern, eastern and occasionally central Europe, southern Asia, Africa. European birds winter in Africa, leave at end of September. Length about 80 cm. Inhabits large reed beds round ponds and lakes. Builds nest from grass blades and twigs on flattened rushes. Usually nests in colonies. Female lays 7—8 bluish-green eggs, incubated 24—28 days by both parents in turn. Lives mainly on fish, frogs and insects.

3 Night Heron *Nycticorax nycticorax*. Distributed in southern Europe, southern parts of central Europe, south-eastern Asia, whole of Africa, America. European birds winter in Africa, leave at end of August or in September. Length about 55 cm. Inhabits regions with ponds, swamps, etc. Builds nest from small sticks in trees or bushes. Lives in colonies. Female usually lays 4 green-blue eggs, incubated 21—23 days by both parents in turn. Lives mainly on valueless fishes, hunts over wide area.

4 Little Bittern *Ixobrychus minutus*. Distributed in Europe except England, in east to Siberia, most of Africa, Australia. European birds migrate in August, winter in Africa, return at end of April. Length about 35 cm. Inhabits sedge round ponds, pools, creeks, etc. Builds nest on flattened reeds near water level. Female lays 5—6 whitish eggs, incubated 16—19 days by both parents in turn. Young climb rushes at one week. Eats small fish, frogs and insects.

5 Bittern *Botaurus stellaris*. Distributed over whole of Europe to south of Sweden, in east to Japan, also in Africa. European birds migrate in October to equatorial Africa, return in March.

Occasionally resident. Length about 70 cm. Lives secretively in large reed beds round ponds and lakes. Booming call. Builds nest on flattened rushes. Lays 4—6 green-grey eggs in April or May. Young hatch in 25—26 days. Catches frogs, small fish, insects, etc. Freezes with beak held to sky if disturbed.

Family: **Storks**—Ciconiidae

6 White Stork *Ciconia ciconia.* Distributed in Europe, central and eastern Asia including Japan, North Africa. European birds migrate to Africa at end of August, return in first half of April. Length about 1 m. Builds large nest on tall trees, roofs and chimneys. Female lays 2—6 white eggs, incubated 30—34 days by both parents in turn. Parents fetch food for young, regurgitate it on to nest. Catches insects, amphibians, small mammals and birds. Voiceless, clatters beak.

7 Black Stork *Ciconia nigra.* Distributed in central and eastern Europe, south of Sweden, Iberian peninsula, in east across China to Sakhalin. European birds migrate in September, winter in Africa south of Sahara, return at beginning of April. Length about 1 m. Inhabits wooded regions at both low and high altitudes. Has large nesting area. Builds nest on tall tree close to trunk. Female lays 2—5 bluish-white eggs, incubated by both parents 28—32 days. Lives mainly on fish, but also catches amphibians or small vertebrates and insects. Flies far afield. Does not clatter beak, but utters hoarse hissing sounds.

433

Order: **Pelicans and Allies**—Pelecaniformes

Family: **Cormorants**—Phalacrocoracidae

1 Great Cormorant *Phalacrocorax carbo*. Distributed in Europe, Asia, Africa, Australia, North America. Central-European birds migrate in September to Mediterranean region, return at beginning of March. Length 80—90 cm. Nests in colonies. Builds nest in trees, from small sticks. Female lays 3—4 blue-green eggs. Young hatch in 28—30 days, remain 8 weeks in nest. Lives mainly on fish, hunts under water. Often hunts together with pelicans, which do not dive.

Order: **Ducks, Geese and Swans**—Anseriformes

2 Whooper Swan *Cygnus cygnus*. Distributed mainly in northern parts of Europe and Asia. In winter often seen on rivers or ice-free lakes in central and southern Europe. Length 155—170 cm, wing span up to 2.5 m, weight about 10 kg. In native habitat lives beside lakes or bays surrounded by rushes, in which it builds large nest. Female lays 4—6 eggs, incubates them mainly unaided 35—40 days. Lives on small aquatic animals and greenstuff. In severe winters migrates southwards in large flocks.

3 Mute Swan *Cygnus olor*. Distributed in northern Europe and central Asia; in recent years lives in halfwild state on many lakes and ponds in central Europe. Length about 160 cm. Builds nest from twigs, reeds, etc. in reed beds or on ground. Female lays 5—9 white, green-tinged eggs. Incubates them mainly unaided. Male keeps watch but occasionally relieves female. Young hatch in 35 days, on second day take to water with female. Swan with young aggressive. Mainly vegetarian but also eats insects etc.

4 Greylag Goose *Anser anser*. Distributed in Scotland, Scandinavia, in central and eastern Europe, across Asia to Far East. Migrates south at end of October (northern birds winter in England), returns to nesting areas at end of February or beginning of March. Length 78—92 cm. Builds nest using rush stalks and other material, usually in reed beds, but sometimes in small willows. Lines nest with down. Female lays 4—7 whitish eggs, incubates them unaided 28 days. Eats seeds, grass, shoots, etc.

1

2

3

5 Bean Goose *Anser fabalis*. Distributed in northern parts of Europe and Asia, coast of Greenland. Length 73—90 cm. Winters from September in central, western and southern Europe. Frequents ice-free water. In some years appears in huge flocks. Very wary bird. Looks for food in meadows and fields. Returns to nesting area in May. Builds nest from grass blades etc. Female lays 3—6 eggs, incubates them about 26 days. Vegetarian.

6 Brent Goose *Branta bernicla*. Distributed over coasts of northern Asia and North America. Length 58—88 cm. In winter migrates along west coast of Europe to Spain and Morocco. Some flocks stray far inland, into central Europe. Builds nest from grass blades in dry parts of tundra. Female lays 3—6 eggs, incubates them about 25 days. Lives on grass, seeds, lichen.

7 Shelduck *Tadorna tadorna*. Distributed over coasts of northern and western Europe, round Black Sea, in east as far as Mongolia. Length about 65 cm. In winter (sometimes in spring) appears on rivers and ponds in central Europe. Nests in holes and hollows, also uses deserted foxes' earths. Sometimes nests in rocks. Female lays 6—16 plain yellowish eggs, incubates them unaided. Young hatch in 28 days. Lives on greenstuff, insects, worms, small crustaceans, etc.

4

5

6

7

Order: **Ducks, Geese and Swans**—Anseriformes

1 Mallard *Anas platyrhynchos*. Distributed in Europe, Asia and North America, in winter also North Africa and India. Length 49—63 cm. Inhabits overgrown pools, ponds, lakes and rivers. Often nests on small ornamental ponds in town parks. Nest usually built on ground, in clump of grass or under bush, occasionally in tree. Female lays 8—14, generally green-grey eggs, incubates them unaided 26 days. When dry, young follow female to water. Young promptly dive if in danger. Mixed diet. Like all ducks, males have same colouring as females during summer.

2 Widgeon *Anas strepera*. Distributed in southern England, central Europe, in east as far as Amur, and North America. Length about 48 cm. European birds migrate in October to Mediterranean region, return in March. Mainly inhabits overgrown ponds. Nest hidden in reed-grass, nettles, etc. In May or June female lays 8—14 creamy eggs, incubates them unaided 26 days. Mixed diet.

3 European Teal *Anas crecca*. Distributed over whole of Europe except Spain, temperate and northern Asia, large parts of North America. Length 30.5—38 cm, weight about 0.3 kg. European birds migrate in August, winter in southern Europe and North Africa, return in April. Inhabits thickly overgrown ponds. Nests on ground in meadows etc., often far from water. In May female lays 8—10 eggs. Mixed diet. Form flocks in autumn. Swift flier.

4 Garganey *Anas querquedula*. Distributed in Europe, extends east as far as Japan. Length 34—40 cm. In September European birds migrate in flocks to North and Central Africa. Inhabits places with thickly overgrown water. Nests in dense clumps of grass or under bushes. At end of April female lays 8—12 eggs, incubates them about 23 days. Mixed diet.

436

5 Shoveller *Anas clypeata.* Distributed in western, central and northern Europe, in east across Asia to North America. In September migrates to Mediterranean region, returns in second half of March. Length about 45 cm. Inhabits regions with ponds and meadows. Nests in grass in meadows and fields. Lines nest with dry reedgrass and down. Female incubates 9—12 greyish eggs 23—24 days. Catches mainly small animals in shallows. Wide bill acts as sieve.

6 Red-crested Pochard *Netta rufina.* Distributed in parts of central Europe, western and central Asia. In recent years has spread to many places in central Europe. Migrates in September to southern Europe, returns in April. Length about 60 cm. Nests on small islands or right beside water. Female incubates 7—10 grey-yellow eggs 27 days. Gathers food on surface of open water.

7 Pochard *Aythya ferina.* Distributed mainly in central Europe, in east to western Siberia, North America. Both migratory and resident. Length about 40 cm. Very common. Inhabits large ponds and lakes surrounded by reed beds. Lives mostly on water. Builds nest near water, on clumps of reed-grass or small islands. Female incubates 8—14 relatively large, yellow-green eggs about 24 days. Seeks food — aquatic animals and plant shoots — mainly under water.

8 Tufted Duck *Aythya fuligula.* Inhabited originally northern Europe, Asia and Iceland, but has begun to move south. Today common in England and central Europe. European birds winter on coasts of western Europe and Mediterranean. Leave in October. Length about 38 cm. At end of May builds nest in clump of reed-grass or on ground, close to water. Female incubates 6—9 green-grey eggs 25—26 days. Young completely black. Mixed diet, gathered mainly under water. Excellent diver.

Order: **Ducks, Geese and Swans**—Anseriformes

1 Golden-eye *Bucephala clangula.* Distributed in northern parts of Europe, Asia and North America, recently parts of central Europe. Migrates in October to coasts of western and southern Europe, returns to central Europe at end of March. Length about 40 cm. Builds down-lined nest in tree hollows or nesting-boxes, often at great height. Female incubates 8—18 greenish eggs about 30 days. Mixed diet, gathered mainly in water.

2 Eider Duck *Somateria mollissima.* Distributed in most northerly arctic regions of Europe, Iceland, Greenland, North America and north-eastern Siberia. Length about 58 cm. In autumn and winter regularly appears on ice-free rivers in central Europe. Builds nest near sea, in grass, among stones, etc. Female lays 4—5 greenish eggs, packed in finest down, incubates them 24—27 days. Lives mainly on small animals but also eats some plants.

3 Goosander *Mergus merganser.* Distributed in northern parts of Europe, Asia and North America. Regularly appears on ice-free rivers in central Europe, frequently in large flocks, from November to April. Length about 65 cm. Nests inland, often far from water, usually in tree hollows. Female incubates 7—12 dull green eggs 35 days. Young hop out of nest unaided. Lives on small fish, water snails, aquatic insects, etc.

Order: **Divers and Allies**—Gaviiformes

Family: **Divers**—Gaviidae

4 Black-throated Diver *Gavia arctica.* Distributed in northern parts of Europe, Asia and North America. Also nests in Scotland and north of Poland. Occasionally appears on central European rivers from October to April. Length 70—74 cm. Inhabits lakes, mainly in tundra and taiga belt. Nests beside water. Each couple has own nesting 'preserve'. Both parents incubate 1—3 spotted eggs about 25 days. Lives on fish, supplemented by molluscs, large insects, small crustaceans, etc.

1

2

3

Order: **Grebes and Allies**—Podicipediformes

Family: **Grebes**—Podicipedidae

5 Great Crested Grebe *Podiceps cristatus.*
Widely distributed over whole of Europe and
Asia except most northerly parts, whole of Africa and Australia. Winters in western and southern Europe and often on rivers in central
Europe. Migrates by night. Length 54—61 cm.
Inhabits lakes and large ponds thickly overgrown with rushes. Builds nest from aquatic
plants among reeds. Nest sometimes floats. Female usually lays 3—4 dingy greenish eggs, incubated by both parents 25 days. Parents often
carry dark-striped young on back and push food
down their beaks. Catches small fish and insects.

6 Black-necked Grebe *Podiceps nigricollis.* Distributed over whole of Europe except Scandinavia, in east to western Siberia, west to North
America, eastern Africa. Migrates in October or
November to western and southern Europe, returns in April. Length 31—33.5 cm. Inhabits
thickly overgrown ponds and lakes. Often nests
in colonies of up to several hundred couples.
Builds nest in rushes. Female incubates 3—4
(occasionally up to 6) dull white or greenish
eggs 20—21 days. Lives mainly on insects.

7 Little Grebe or **Dabchick** *Podiceps ruficollis.*
Distributed over whole of Europe, southern and
south-eastern Asia, Australia, whole of Africa.
Length about 23 cm. Very common, but shy and
secretive. Inhabits small ponds, pools, creeks,
etc., overgrown with reeds. Arrives in April.
From fragments of aquatic plants builds floating
nest among rushes, close to open water. Female
lays 4—9 white, green-tinged eggs, incubated
20 days by both parents in turn. Eats mainly
aquatic insects. Often resident on ice-free parts
of rivers.

Order: **Doves, Pigeons and Allies**—Columbiformes

Family: **Doves and Pigeons**—Columbidae

1 Wood Pigeon *Columba palumbus.* Distributed over whole of Europe except most northerly part, Asia Minor, north-western Africa, in east to central Asia and Himalayas. European birds migrate in September or October to southern Europe and north-western Africa, return in middle of March. Length about 40 cm. Mostly inhabits conifer and mixed woods, but also encountered in large parks. Builds loose, untidy nest from dry twigs, usually 5—30 m from ground, on spreading branch. Female lays 2 white eggs in April, sometimes second clutch in June. Young hatch in 16—18 days. Lives on seeds of forest plants, but also raids crops.

2 Stock Dove *Columba oenas.* Distributed over whole of Europe except Scandinavia, in east to central Asia, in south to north-western Africa. European birds migrate in September or October to southern Europe and North Africa, return in middle of March. Length about 34 cm. Chiefly inhabits deciduous woods with old beeches and oaks, in hollows of which it builds nest. Also uses nesting-boxes. Female lays 2 white eggs in April and again in June. Young hatch in 17—20 days. Lives mainly on seeds.

3 Turtle Dove *Streptopelia turtur.* Distributed over whole of Europe, in east to central Asia, whole of North Africa. In September—October migrates to Africa north of equator, returns in April. Length about 30 cm. Inhabits young woods and overgrown hillsides with fields and meadows in vicinity. Builds nest in thick undergrowth, in tall, dense bushes, etc., 1—7 m above ground. Female lays 2 white eggs. Young hatch in 14—17 days. Lives on seeds (especially of weeds), small molluscs, etc.

4 Collared Turtle Dove *Streptopelia decaocto.* Inhabited originally southern Asia, Asia Minor and southern part of Balkans. A few decades ago started to spread west, now inhabits whole of Europe and is one of commonest birds. Resident bird. Frequents human communities, lives in town parks, gardens, orchards, etc. and accepts titbits left outside window. Nests several times a year, from early spring to autumn. Winter nesting and laying also known. Builds nest from sticks and grass blades in dense tree tops or tall bushes. Has preference for spruces and ornamental trees in parks. Lays 2 white eggs.

Lives on various seeds, molluscs and insects, in winter will eat scraps and chopped meat. Has loud call.

Order: **Waders and Allies**—Charadriiformes

Family: **Auks, Razorbills and Puffins**—Alcidae

5 Guillemot *Uria aalge.* Distributed over coasts of northern Europe, England, north-eastern Asia, north-western part of North America. Length about 45 cm. In winter frequents coasts of western Europe and Mediterranean countries. Rock-dweller. On ledge of rock female lays single large, spotted egg, incubated 35 days by both parents in turn. Lives on small fish, crustaceans, etc., caught in sea.

6 Puffin *Fratercula arctica.* Distributed mainly over coasts of Scandinavia and northern islands, west coast of England, Iceland, Greenland. Length 30—36 cm. In winter appears along coasts of western Europe and Mediterranean countries. Builds nest in burrow up to 3 m long. Female lays single egg, incubated 35 days by both parents in turn. Catches mainly small fish.

5

6

Family: **Gulls and Terns**—Laridae

1 Black-headed Gull *Larus ridibundus*. Distributed in Europe, extends to Far East. Length 33.5—43 cm. In nesting season has black-brown head, in winter white. European birds winter mainly in western and southern Europe, but many remain behind on ice-free rivers in central Europe. Arrives in nesting area in second half of March. Nests in large colonies on small islands in ponds. Nest made of grass blades, twigs, leaves, etc. Female usually lays 3 spotted eggs of very variable colouring. Young hatch in 22—24 days. Lives on insects, small fish, fruit, e.g. cherries, etc. Follows plough and snaps up grubs and worms.

2 Common Gull *Larus canus*. Distributed in England, northern Europe, northern Asia, north-western part of North America. Winters along coasts of western Europe, often flies inland to rivers of central Europe. Returns to nesting areas in April. Length 38—48 cm. Nests in grass on small islands, etc. Female lays 3 spotted eggs. Young hatch in 25—26 days. Fed by parents 35 days. Eats insects, molluscs, other birds' eggs, fruits and seeds.

3 Herring Gull *Larus argentatus*. Distributed over coasts of northern and southern Europe, northern Asia and North America. Length 55—69 cm. Nests on ground on shore, in Balkans also on roofs of houses. Female lays 2—3 spotted eggs. Young hatch in 26 days, fully fledged after 8—9 weeks. Lives on small animals, scraps, etc. In autumn also roams inlands to rivers, particularly Danube.

4 Great Black-backed Gull *Larus marinus*. Distributed over coasts of Scandinavia, Iceland, England and North America. Length 61—76 cm. In winter lives nomadically along coasts of northern and western Europe. Often accompanies ocean-going liners out to sea, hoping for scraps. Otherwise eats fish, crustaceans and birds' eggs and young. Nests on cliffs. Usually lays 3 spotted eggs. Both parents incubate eggs 29—30 days and then feed young.

5 Arctic Skua *Stercorarius parasiticus*. Inhabits Arctic waters and coasts of northern Europe, Asia and North America. Length about 46 cm. In winter comes to African coast. Common on coast but strays to rivers in central Europe. Nests in colonies. Female lays 2 spotted eggs on bare ground, between clumps of grass. Young hatch in 25—26 days. Lives on different animals caught in sea, also hunts lemmings and eats berries. Chases gulls, forces them to drop food, snaps it up in air.

6 Common Tern *Sterna hirundo*. Distributed over whole of Europe, temperate parts of Asia, North America. Length 34—40 cm. Migrates in August to southern Africa, returns at beginning of May. Nests in colonies. Makes nest on ground, from a few sticks, roots, shells, etc. Female lays 2—4 spotted eggs of somewhat variable colouring. Young hatch in 20—22 days. Diet small fish. Hovers in air looking for prey, dives after it at high speed.

7 Black Tern *Chlidonias niger*. Distributed over large part of Europe, in east to central Asia, part of North America. Length 24—27 cm. European birds migrate at end of July to equatorial Africa, return in May. Lives in small colonies. Builds nest on floating aquatic plants. Female lays 2—3 spotted eggs. Young hatch in 14—17 days. Lives mainly on aquatic insects, small crustaceans and fish, but also often travels several miles to look for insects in fields.

Families: Charadriidae, Scolopacidae

1 Lapwing *Vanellus vanellus*. Distributed over whole of Europe, in east to temperate parts of Asia as far as Korea. Length about 30 cm. Very common. Skilful flier. Winters in western and southern Europe and North Africa, often returns at end of February. Inhabits damp meadows and fields near ponds and lakes. Builds nest on small hummock, lines it with blades of grass. Female lays 4 olive-brown speckled eggs, incubated by both parents 24 days. After 2 days, young disperse and hide in surrounding grass. In autumn forms flocks round ponds. Eats insects, worms, molluscs, seeds.

2 Golden Plover *Pluvialis apricaria*. Inhabits northern Europe, England, Iceland, east coast of Greenland. Winters in west and south-west of Europe and in North Africa. In September to October always migrates across central Europe, can be seen there mainly in fields, usually in small flocks. Length 25—30 cm. Inhabits swampy areas in north. Builds nest like lapwing's on ground. Lays 4 eggs, young hatch in 20 days. Catches insects, worms, etc.

3 Little Ringed Plover *Charadrius dubius*. Distributed over whole of Europe except England and Scandinavia, most of Asia, North Africa. European birds migrate in September—November to equatorial Africa, return in middle of April. Length 16—19 cm. Likes sandy ground beside lakes, ponds and rivers. Nests in small depression in pebbles. Female lays 4 yellowish, dark-spotted eggs, incubated by both parents 22—24 days. Eats insects, insect larvae and worms.

4 Sea Plover *Charadrius alexandrinus*. Distributed along all European coasts except most northerly regions, whole of temperate and southern Asia, whole of Africa, Australia, southern U.S.A. and west of South America. European birds winter on African coast south of equator. Length 16—18.5 cm. Prefers sandy shores beside sea or salt lakes. Female lays 4 spotted eggs in depression in stones, incubates them 24 days. Catches insects, small crustaceans, worms and molluscs. Migrating birds often seen in central Europe.

5 Dunlin *Calidris alpina*. Distributed in England, north coast of Germany, Scandinavia and northern parts of Asia and North America. Winters on coasts of western Europe, Mediterranean region and Africa. Migrating birds seen in large numbers beside ponds from end of August. Length 19—22.5 cm. Nests mainly in tundra belt, builds nest in peat moors. Female lays 4 eggs, incubated by both parents. Lives on insects, worms and molluscs.

6 Ruff (female **Reeve**) *Philomachus pugnax*. Distributed over northern parts of Europe and Asia, but also nests in central Europe, e.g. Poland, Holland and Belgium. Winters in Africa. Appears in flocks beside ponds over whole of central Europe during migration. Length 23—33 cm. Male's colouring very variable. During nesting season males wear 'ruff' and fight duels. Female builds nest lined with grass blades and leaves in small pit. Lays 4 eggs, incubates them unaided 20—21 days. Eats mainly insects, worms and molluscs.

3

4

5

7 Redshank *Tringa totanus.* Distributed over whole of Europe and across temperate belt of Asia to Far East. Migrates in August—October, return at end of March. Length 27—31 cm. Inhabits flat ground beside large ponds and lakes. Builds grass-lined nest in depression in ground. Female lays 4 grey, dark-speckled eggs, incubated 22—25 days by both parents in turn. Young fledged at 25 days. If enemy approaches nest or young, parent birds fly up, screeching. Lives on insects, worms, molluscs, crustaceans and small fish.

6

7

Families: Scolopacidae, Recurvirostridae

1 Black-tailed Godwit *Limosa limosa.* Distributed in northern part of western Europe except England, Iceland, northern Germany, central and eastern Europe, across Asia to Far East. European birds migrate in August or September to northern and equatorial Africa, return in first half of April. Length 39.5—49.5 cm; female always much larger. Inhabits water-logged meadows beside ponds and lakes. Makes nest in shallow depression in thick grass or on clod, lines it with a little grass. Female lays 4 dark-spotted eggs, incubated 24 days by both parents in turn. If enemy approaches, flies up into air, uttering piercing, piping cries. Eats insects, insect larvae, worms, small molluscs.

2 Avocet *Recurvirostra avosetta.* Distributed in southern Spain, coast of Germany, occasionally swampy ground round lakes and ponds in central Europe, in east to Mongolia. European birds winter in southern Africa. Length 42—47.5 cm. Builds nest among plants in depression in mud of drained ponds, etc., lines it with a few plants. Female lays 4 olive-green eggs with grey-brown spots. Eggs incubated 24—25 days by both parents in turn. Lives on insects, insect larvae, crustaceans and molluscs found in shallow water and mud.

3 Curlew *Numenius arquata.* Distributed in Europe except south, Iceland, in east to western Siberia. European birds winter in eastern Africa, return at end of March. Length 54—69 cm. Inhabits large, wet meadows or steppe country in vicinity of water. Builds nest in small depression in ground, among grass. Female lays 4 spotted eggs, often strewn with dark dots and streaks. Eggs incubated 26—28 days by both parents in turn. Female responsible for care of young. Lives on insects, insect larvae, seeds of aquatic plants, etc.

4 Woodcock *Scolopax rusticola.* Distributed over whole of Europe except most northerly parts, in east forms belt across Asia to Japan, also found on Azores and Canaries. European birds winter in southern Europe and North Africa, return at end of March. Migrate by night. Length 34—38 cm. Inhabits deciduous or mixed woods where it frequents large, damp, grassy spaces, streams, etc. Nests in a small leaf- or moss-lined depression under a bush. Female lays 4 spotted eggs of somewhat variable colouring, incubates them unaided 22 days. Eats insects, worms and molluscs.

5 Common Snipe *Gallinago gallinago*. Distributed over whole of Europe except south, in east across temperate parts of Asia to Japan. European birds winter mainly in Africa, return in March. Occasionally resident. Length 24.5—31 cm. Inhabits swamps, damp meadows and peat-bogs. Nests in deep depression in dense grass. Female lays 4 eggs with olive and green spots, incubates them unaided 19—21 days. Lives on insects, spiders and worms. In autumn congregates in flocks. At mating time male flies high into air and dives with spread tail feathers, vibrations of which produce bleating sound.

Order: **Cranes, Rails and Allies**—Gruiformes

Family: **Cranes**—Gruidae

6 Crane *Crus grus*. Distributed in northern Europe and Asia. Occasionally nests in north and east of central Europe. European birds winter in North Africa and along Nile, return in April or May. Length 105—120 cm. Inhabits extensive swamps and marshes. Flies in typical V-formation. Couples remain together. Female builds large nest in swamp, from reeds and aquatic plants. Usually lays 2 grey-green, dark-spotted eggs. Young hatch in 29—30 days. Eats mainly greenstuffs, but also insects, molluscs and occasionally small vertebrates.

3

5

4

6

447

Family: **Rails, Moorhens and Coots**—Rallidae

1 Water Rail *Rallus aquaticus*. Distributed over whole of Europe, in east across temperate Asia to Japan, also North Africa. Winters in southern Europe and North Africa, returns in middle of April. Length about 28.5 cm. Mainly nocturnal bird. Inhabits fishpond regions. Nests on swampy ground under bush etc. Nest made of grass, reed-grass, leaves, etc. Female lays 6—12 yellowish, rusty-spotted eggs, incubated 20 days by both parents. Newly hatched chicks are black. Parents push food into their beaks. Lives on insects, worms and small leaves.

2 Spotted Crake *Porzana porzana*. Distributed over most of Europe, in east to central Asia, north-western Africa. Migrates to southern Europe and North Africa in October, returns in middle of April. Length 21—25 cm. Leads secretive existence. Builds nest from grass and leaves on clump of reed-grass in swamp. Female lays 6—8 spotted eggs. Young hatch in 18—21 days. Eats insects, spiders, molluscs, seeds and parts of aquatic plants.

3 Moorhen *Gallinula chloropus*. Distributed over most of Europe, central and eastern Asia, America, Africa. European birds occasionally resident, but mostly winter in North Africa. Length about 32 cm. Inhabits overgrown lakes, ponds and pools. Makes deep-basined nest from reeds and aquatic plants on surface of water among rushes. Female lays 6—8 yellowish eggs with rusty brown spots. Young hatch in 19—22 days. Lives on insects, worms, seeds and parts of plants.

4 Coot *Fulica atra*. Distributed over whole of Europe, across temperate parts of Asia to Japan, Australia, north-western Africa. European birds winter in western and southern Europe, but often occur in flocks on rivers of central Europe. Return to nesting places in March. Length 38—45 cm. Inhabits any type of overgrown stagnant water. Builds nest on surface of water, at margin of vegetation, from rush stems, sedge, etc., often with a connecting 'bridge'. Female lays 5—15 mauvish, black-spotted eggs. Young, hatched in 22 days, have orange-coloured head. Lives on small aquatic animals, seeds and parts of plants.

Family: **Bustards**—Otididae

5 Great Bustard *Otis tarda*. Distributed in southern and central Europe, in east to China, north-western Africa. Length of male about 100 cm, female about 80 cm. Inhabits steppes and vast fields. Female lays 2—3 brownish spotted eggs in depression in ground, incubates them about 30 days. Large nesting sites near Berlin and in southern Slovakia. Lives on insects, worms, small vertebrates, seeds and parts of plants.

Order: **Game Birds**—Galliformes

Family: **Pheasants, Partridges and Quails**—Phasianidae

6 Partridge *Perdix perdix*. Distributed over most of Europe except northern Scandinavia, in east to central Asia. Length about 26 cm. Inhabits steppes, in Europe mainly fields. Usually at beginning of May female lays about 15 olive-

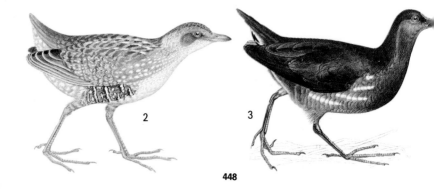

2   3

brown eggs in pit in ground, incubates them unaided 23—25 days, but male also cares for young. Eats mainly plants, supplemented in summer by insects, spiders and molluscs. In autumn gathers together in small flocks. Highly prized game bird in Europe.

7 Quail *Coturnix coturnix.* Distributed over most of Europe, temperate parts of Asia as far as Japan, North and South Africa. European birds winter mainly in Africa. Leave in October, return at end of April. Length about 18 cm. Inhabits steppes, meadows and fields. Male polygamous. Female digs small pit, lays 6—18 eggs, usually marked with dark brown blotches and dots, incubates them unaided 18—20 days. Lives on seeds, shoots, small molluscs, worms and insects.

4

6

5

7

1

Family: **Pheasants, Partridges and Quails**—
Phasianidae

1 Common Pheasant *Phasianus colchicus.* Originally distributed in a few races in central and eastern Asia, but introduced into many parts of Europe and North America. Known in central Europe since 14th century. European races now thoroughly crossed. Length of cock about 80 cm, hen about 60 cm. Inhabits copses, wooded slopes, etc. in lowlands and uplands. Female lines depression in ground with leaves and grass, lays 8—15 plain brownish eggs, incubates them unaided 23—27 days. Cock polygamous. Lives on plants, shoots, seeds and various small animals. Important game bird.

2 Rock Partridge *Alectoris graeca.* Distributed in mountainous regions from southern Europe east to China. Abundant in Balkans and on southern slopes of Alps. Introduction attempted in many places in central Europe. Length about 35 cm. Inhabits rocky slopes. In summer ascends to dwarf timber belt, in winter descends into valleys. In May or June female lays 10—15 light brown, often thickly spotted eggs in depression in rock or in clump of grass. Lives on seeds, grass, insects, etc.

Family: **Grouse and Ptarmigans**—*Tetraonidae*

3 Ptarmigan *Lagopus mutus.* Distributed in tundras in northern Europe, Asia and North America, also England, Spain and Alps. Length about 35 cm. In summer brownish with white wings, in winter completely white except for black tail. White colouring makes it blend with snow. Female usually lays 7—10 russet-speckled eggs in depression among stones or in clump of grass, etc. Eats shoots, buds (e.g. of willows, birches, etc.), seeds and, in summer, insects, spiders and small molluscs. In winter spends night in holes in snow.

4 Black Grouse *Lyrurus tetrix.* Distributed over whole of Europe except south, whole of temperate Asia, but mainly more northerly regions, primarily taiga. Length of cock about 65 cm, hen about 45 cm. Cock weighs about 1.5 kg. Likes deciduous and mixed woods with damp meadows in vicinity. Early in spring birds congregate on special 'parade grounds', in clearing, on moor, in meadow, etc., where cocks fight duels. Cock polygamous. Hen lays 6—10 yellowish, dark-spotted eggs in moss- and grass-lined pit, incubates them unaided about 26 days. Lives on seeds, berries, shoots, insects, worms, etc.

4

6

5

5 Capercaillie *Tetrao urogallus.* Distributed in northern England, central and northern Europe, eastwards to Sakhalin. Length of cock about 100 cm, hen 70 cm. Cock can weigh up to 6 kg. Inhabits large forests. Males perform interesting nuptial rites. 'Song' divided into three parts: knocking, trilling and slurring. Hen lays 5—12 yellowish, brown-spotted eggs in shallow depression lined with leaves, conifer needles, etc., incubates them unaided 24—27 days. Lives on shoots, conifer needles, whole tips of conifer branches, insects, molluscs, etc. Most highly prized game bird.

6 Hazel Hen *Tetrastes bonasia.* Distributed over whole of central and northern Europe, extends east to eastern Siberia and south-eastern China. Now scarce in mountains of central Europe, but still abundant in Scandinavia. Length about 38 cm. Inhabits mixed forests, especially with birches and dense undergrowth including bushes, cranberries and bilberries. Female lays 8—12 yellowish, dark-spotted eggs in shallow depression at foot of tree, incubates them 25 days. Lives on seeds, shoots, berries, insects, small molluscs, etc. Flesh very savoury.

Mammals

On the evolutionary scale mammals (Mammalia) are the highest group of vertebrates with a constant body temperature. The only exceptions are certain mammals that hibernate, for example bats, whose temperature drops as low as 0° C in winter.

Mammals' bodies vary in shape and are adapted to the animals' mode of life. The typical body is usually elongated, with two pairs of limbs. In some groups of mammals the limbs have been transformed, for example into wings in bats and fins in cetaceans (the hind limbs of cetaceans are atrophied). The skin is thick and covered with hairs; a few species lack hair, for example dolphins. In other species, such as hedgehogs, the hairs have been converted into spines. Hairs are a product of the skin and are a typical characteristic of mammals.

In some mammals the skin is covered with horny scales, which in scaly anteaters (Pholidota), for example, form a hard armour. Mice and rats have a tail covered with horny scales. Scales are also a product of the skin.

Many mammals have tactile organs on various parts of the body. Beasts of prey have whiskers on the sides of the face. In other mammals tactile hairs are found on the feet or flanks — always on parts that come into contact with the animal's surroundings. The hairs that form the coat or fur of animals are shed regularly and replaced by new ones. This is called moulting and usually takes place in spring when the animals acquire a thinner, shorter coat, and in autumn, when they acquire a long, dense winter coat.

A characteristic feature of mammals is their great number of skin glands. Oil glands keep the skin oily and supple; sweat glands cool the surface of the body through the evaporation of water and also excrete salts and waste substances in the sweat. Some mammals do not have sweat glands, their sweat or oil glands being transformed into scent glands that are located by the anus, on the belly, between the hooves (as in red deer and sheep), on the cheeks, etc. Scent glands in mammals whose activities are governed mainly by the sense of smell are extremely important. Some animals mark out the boundaries of their territories with a secretion from these glands, and scent also plays a vital role in finding a mate. Some mammals, such as skunks (*Mephitis mephitis*) and European polecats (*Mustela putorius*), eject an intensely malodorous secretion when startled,

thus defending themselves against an enemy. Mammary glands have also developed from skin glands. These secrete milk to feed the young. This milk contains 90 per cent water, proteins, fats, sugars and mineral substances. With the exception of monotremes, mammals secrete milk through nipples, of which there are one, to fourteen pairs, depending primarily on the usual size of the litter in the given species.

Mammals have characteristic dentition, growing several types of teeth: the incisors are adapted for cutting; the conical, pointed canines are used for holding or killing prey; the premolars and molars are adapted for grinding food. The dentition is adapted to the kind of food the animals eat. The number and shape of the teeth is characteristic for each individual group or species of animal. Very occasionally, some species of mammals lack teeth altogether, for example anteaters (Myrmecophagidae).

Some mammals have developed secondary sex characteristics influenced by the hormones produced by the sex glands. For instance, the male lion has a huge mane, the male roe-deer large antlers, bulls (in cattle) are much larger than cows, male elephants have large tusks, etc. In many species, however, the male and female cannot be distinguished at first glance.

The attainment of sexual maturity differs in the various species and depends, among other things, on the animal's size. A male elephant, for example, attains sexual maturity after eighteen years, the males of small rodents within only a few months.

During the breeding season males come together with females. In some species, however, the partners remain together throughout the year, or even throughout their whole lifetime. Some males are polygamous and have a greater number of female partners. Males usually mate only once a year; some species only once in two to four years, whereas small rodents may have as many as six broods a year. The size of the litter depends on the size of the animal. The largest females generally bear only a single offspring, larger carnivores usually two or three,

Fig. 1. The male Red Deer (*Cervus elaphus*) has huge antlers.

smaller carnivores may bear more than ten. One exception among the small mammals is the bat; the female produces only a single offspring because she must carry it on her nightly flights. The young of some mammals are naked and blind at birth, for example mice. The young of carnivores are also blind at birth, but are covered with hair. Ungulates, on the other hand, give birth to fully developed young that are able to follow their mother within a few hours of birth.

Fig. 2. The Long-eared Bat (*Plecotus auritus*) in flight.

Fig. 3. The young of the House Mouse (*Mus musculus*) are born naked and blind, but become mature at six to seven weeks old.

Mammals are primarily terrestrial animals, but they also include freshwater as well as marine species. They are distributed throughout the whole world. Some 90 species of wild mammals are found in central Europe.

Plentiful in Europe are the insectivores (Insectivora), which hunt invertebrates as well as small vertebrates. Hedgehogs (Erinaceidae) form a large family. European species are distinguished by having the back and sides covered with spines. Underneath their skin hedgehogs have a special muscle by means of which they can curl up into a ball, thereby protecting their vulnerable belly. Hedgehogs are nocturnal creatures and do not set out to hunt until darkness falls. They spend the winter season in hibernation under piles of leaves or in holes. Their body temperature may drop as low as 5 °C at this

Fig. 4. The Common Mole (*Talpa europaea*) is superbly adapted to life underground. It has unusually large, shovel-like forefeet for digging underground tunnels. It often lays in stocks of earthworms, paralyzing them by biting through their nerve centre so that they are unable to move and cannot escape.

time. On awakening from their winter sleep in spring, they begin moving about only after their body temperature has risen to at least 20 °C.

Shrews (Soricidae) are another large family of insectivores. They are small mammals with a mobile, fleshy snout and a short, silky coat. The tail is relatively long. The legs are short and for that reason shrews do not move very fast. They are nocturnal creatures. Some species have become associates of people and roam around in gardens and parks.

Bats (Chiroptera) are a distinctive group of mammals. The members of this order are generally small animals that are covered with silky fur. Unlike other mammals, they are able to fly and capture their prey on the wing. Stretched between the long digits of the forelimbs, trunk and hind limbs is a richly veined membrane which makes flight possible. The digits of the hind limbs are clawed to enable the bat to hang upside down. Extending from the heel is a special projection that serves to stretch the membrane between the hind limbs and the tail. Bats are nocturnal animals, usually setting out in search of prey only after dusk, and passing the day in tree hollows, attics, galleries, etc. Their eyes are small but bats do not really need them when flying at night for they are equipped with a special radar-like system. During flight they emit supersonic sounds, inaudible to the human ear, which rebound from objects and are perceived by the bat's sensitive ear and then analysed. In colder regions bats hibernate, during which time their body temperature drops nearly as low as 0° C.

Hares and rabbits (Lagomorpha) are distinguished by having a second pair of small, narrow incisors behind the upper incisors which grow continuously as they are worn down. When chewing food, the lower jaw moves from

Fig. 5. The colouring of the Red Squirrel (*Sciurus vulgaris*) is extremely diverse. Besides rust-coloured squirrels one may often encounter squirrels that are brown or black. In Britain Red Squirrels are almost extinct, having been usurped by the Grey Squirrel (*S. carolinensis*).

left to right, whereas in rodents it moves from front to back. Hares and rabbits are all plant feeders. Many species live gregariously.

Rodents (Rodentia) have two incisors in both the upper and lower jaws. These are sharp-tipped, chisel-edged cutting teeth that continue to grow as they are worn down. Rodents are the largest group of mammals, not only in terms of number of species but numerically as well. Sometimes they overmultiply, reaching plague proportions and causing much damage. Some rodents yield precious fur, for example, the Beaver (*Castor fiber*) and the Coypu (*Myocastor coypus*), which is bred on a large scale on farms. Rodents live on land, under the ground, on trees and in water.

Beasts of prey (Carnivora) are superbly adapted for seizing and killing live quarry. They are of great importance in the food chain be-

Fig. 6. The Common or European Hare (*Lepus europaeus*) is an important small game animal. What few people know is that it can swim fairly well.

Fig. 7. The Northern Lynx (*Lynx lynx*) — a beast of prey with very keen sight and hearing — is distinguished by having long tufts of hairs on its earlobes.

cause they help to preserve the ecological balance among herbivorous animals, which would otherwise multiply excessively and destroy all the vegetation. Carnivores have powerfully deduveloped teeth which they use as an excellent means of attack or defence. They kill prey with their long, pointed canines. The last premolar on each side of the upper jaw, and the first molar on each side of the lower jaw, called the carnassials, serve to tear meat. Some beasts of prey are exclusively flesh-eaters, others are omnivorous.

The most perfectly adapted beasts of prey are the cats (Felidae), which have powerful, sharp-pointed claws that can be retracted, except in the Cheetah (*Acinonyx jubatus*). Cats have keener eyesight than other carnivores and they also have colour vision.

Dogs (Canidae) are distinguished by their long snouts and long legs. The toes are generally furnished with strong, blunt, non-retractile claws. Dog-like carnivores run swiftly and tirelessly. Their sight is not as keen as that of the cats and they cannot distinguish colours. When dogs are hot and excited, they extend their tongues and pant. This is their way of cooling off, because they do not have sweat glands with openings through which sweat could leave the body. Dogs often roam in packs or troops.

The mustelids (Mustelidae) are a large family of animals that are distinguished by having a long, cylindrical body and short legs. They are very dextrous carnivores. Most species secrete a pungent substance. Some are terrestrial, others arboreal, and still others aquatic, for example the Common Otter (*Lutra lutra*).

Bears (Ursidae) are the largest of the carnivores, with a robust body, wide head, tapering jaws and short tail. The toes are furnished with strong, blunt claws. Bears walk on the whole sole of the foot. Most are omnivorous. Only one species — the Brown Bear (*Ursus arctos*) — lives in central Europe.

Pinnipeds (Pinipedia) are mammals that are adapted to life in water, as evidenced by their torpedo-shaped body. They are relatively large animals. The limbs are paddle-like, the digits webbed and with rudimentary claws. The tail is also rudimentary. The teeth are sharp-pointed and conical. Even the molars are sharp-edged, so that there is little difference between them and the other teeth. The teeth serve only for grasping the slippery bodies of fish.

The European seas are also the home of mammals known as cetaceans (Cetacea), which include the whales, dolphins and porpoises. They are large to huge animals, completely adapted to a marine environment. Their jaws are generally long. Only toothed whales have teeth, all of the same shape.

Of the even-toed ungulates (Artiodactyla), several species are found in central Europe. The weight of the even-toed ungulates is borne on two central toes — the third and fourth toes, which are usually the most developed and are the same shape and size. The other toes are rudimentary or absent. Even-toed ungulates often form herds and are divided into several groups.

Non-ruminants (Nonruminantia) are omnivorous and have complete dentition and one stomach; included in this group are the pigs (Suidae). Ruminants (Ruminantia) have a stomach divided into three, or more often four, compartments. Ruminants have no incisors in the upper jaw and usually have no canines. Deer are ruminants that are characterized by their antlers. In most species only the male deer carry antlers, the exceptions are female reindeer and caribou which also carry antlers, but weaker ones than the males. Musk Deer (*Moschus moschiferus*) lack antlers. Antlers are shed and regrown each year.

Horned ruminants have horns, which are usually carried by both males and females. However, those of the males are usually much larger. Horns are a permanent fixture and grow continually.

Fig. 8. The omnivorous Wild Boar (*Sus scrofa*) is occasionally a pest, particularly in fields which are sometimes visited by whole herds that have come to feed on potatoes and beets, as well as on earthworms and insect larvae.

Class: **Mammals**—Mammalia

Order: **Insectivores**—Insectivora

Family: **Hedgehogs**—*Erinaceidae*

1, 2 European Hedgehog *Erinaceus europaeus.* Two races — western (*E.e. europaeus*) with brown underside and dark bands round eyes, and eastern (*E.e. roumanicus*) with white underside. Dividing line from Oder along upper reaches of Elbe and Vltava. Hedgehog inhabits deciduous and mixed woods with dense undergrowth and town parks. Likes dry places. In Alps up to 2,000 m. Makes nest in hole, under pile of leaves, etc., usually with two entrances. Female gives birth to 3—8 (in rare cases up to 10) young with soft white spines. Young open eyes at 14 days. Nocturnal animal. Hibernates from end of October to March under pile of leaves, in burrow, etc. Lives on worms, insects, small vertebrates, birds' eggs. Also kills venomous snakes without getting bitten and eats them. Almost immune to snake venom. Length up to 30 cm, weight over 1 kg. Newborn young weigh 12—25 g. Life span 8—10 years.

Family: **Moles**—Talpidae

3 Common Mole *Talpa europaea.* Abundant in whole of central Europe and western Asia. In Alps up to 2,400 m. Lives underground in damp places with loose soil. Digs burrows with chambers and passages. Length 13—17 cm, weight 70—120 g. Twice a year female gives birth to 3—9 tiny young which grow very quickly. Open eyes at 3 weeks, suckled 4—6 weeks, independent at 2 months. Life span 2—3 years. Non-hibernator.

Family: **Shrews**—Soricidae

4 Common Shrew *Sorex araneus.* Abundant in whole of Europe except Mediterranean region and Ireland. Frequents damp places with undergrowth. In Alps up to 2,000 m. Occurs mainly in damp woods and peat-bogs, also in ditches. Inhabits vole and mole burrows, but sometimes digs own. In winter found in houses and outbuildings. Length 6.2—8.5 cm, weight 7—15 g. Newborn young weigh only 0.4—0.5 g. Between April and September female produces up to 4 litters of 5—7 hairless, blind young. Coat

grows from 6th day, opens eyes at 18—25 days. Active mainly after sundown and before sunrise. Non-hibernator.

5 European Water Shrew *Neomys fodiens.* Inhabits whole of central Europe. In Alps up to 2,500 m. Frequents rivers, streams, ponds and pools. Inhabits rodent burrows and makes own burrow beside water. Likewise found in flooded cellars. Also nests in tree hollows, up to 0.75 m above ground, but always near water. Swims well. Catches insects, worms and small fish. Length 7—11 cm, weight 10—20 g. Female gives birth 2—3 times yearly to 4—10 hairless, blind young, which are suckled 5—6 weeks and reach adulthood at 3—4 months. Nocturnal animal, active mainly in early morning. Life span not more than 1.5 years. Non-hibernator.

6 Common European White-toothed Shrew *Crocidura russula.* Inhabits western, southern and parts of central Europe. Occurs up to altitudes of 1,600 m. Lives in open country, less often on margins of forests, but chiefly in gardens and parks. In winter often frequents human dwellings, cowsheds, cellars, etc. In wild surroundings lives in mouse-holes or digs own burrow. Length 6—8.5 cm, weight 6—7.5 g. Female gives birth to 3—10 young 2—3 times a year. Young open eyes at 13 days, suckled about 20 days, are adult at 4 months. Life span usually about 1.5 years, in rare cases up to 4 years. Non-hibernator. Lives on insects and worms. Nocturnal animal.

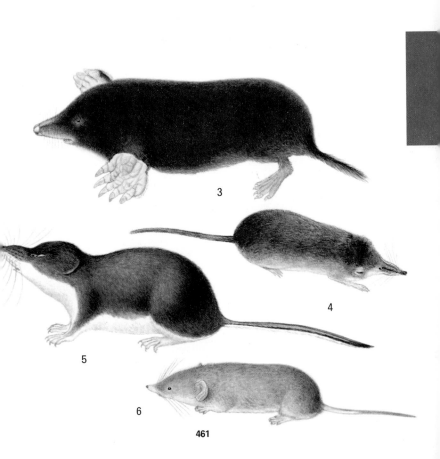

3

4

5

6

Order: **Bats**—Chiroptera

Family: **Horseshoe Bats**—Rhinolophidae

1 Lesser Horseshoe Bat *Rhinolophus hipposideros*. Inhabits south of central Europe. In Alps up to 2,000 m. During day shelters in attics, steeples, caves, etc. Slow and ungainly in flight. Comes out well after dark and only in warm, calm weather. Hibernates in deep caves, mines, etc. Hangs from roof in groups of up to 100, in long rows. One litter of 1—2 young annually. Young open eyes at one week, are adult at one year. Born in colonies of females. Hibernates from October to April. Life span 14—15 years.

Family: **Typical Bats**—Vespertilionidae

2 Brown Bat *Myotis myotis*. One of commonest European bats. Shelters during day in attics, towers or cellars. Hibernates in caves, mines, etc., often in vast numbers. Goes hunting after dark. Flies slowly and clumsily, at height of 5—8 m, over gardens, parks, etc., at 15 km an hour. Known to migrate distances of over 200 km in spring and autumn. Has one young yearly, in May or June, born in colonies of 100—2,000 females. Young grows quickly, can fly at 5—6 weeks. Hibernates from October to April. Maximum life span 14.5 years.

3 Fringed Bat *Myotis nattereri*. Inhabits most of Europe. Lives in small colonies of up to 30 individuals, males singly. During day shelters in tree hollows, nesting-boxes, etc. Hibernates in mines, caves and cellars. Circles low and slowly round trees. Catches insects sitting on branches. Hunts from dusk to dawn, but not in windy weather. Female gives birth to single young. Long hibernation period. Life span up to 15 years.

4 Noctule Bat *Nyctalus noctula*. Distributed over whole of Europe. During day shelters in small groups in tree hollows. Hunts in woods, parks, over water, etc. Starts early in evening and flies until dawn. In autumn appears in afternoon. Migrates 750—1,500 km south or southwest to hibernate, but sometimes remains in hollows, cowsheds, etc. Female gives birth to 1—2 young, which open eyes at 6—7 days and can fly at 45 days. Flies quickly, 50 km an hour. Hibernates from October to April.

5 Long-eared Bat *Plecotus auritus*. Distributed in Europe, Asia and North Africa. Strikingly large ears. Abundant near human communities. Appears after dark. Flies low, frequently veering. Hunts on outskirts of forests, in parks and also within woods. In June female gives birth to 1—2 young which are independent at 6 weeks. Hibernates in caves, cellars, etc. from October to end of March, alone or in groups of 2—3 individuals.

462

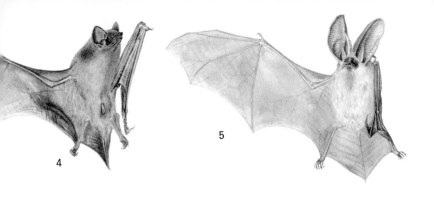

4

5

Order: **Hares and Rabbits**—*Lagomorpha*

6 Snow Hare *Lepus timidus*. Inhabits Ireland, Scotland, northern Europe, Asia, North America. One subspecies also in Alps. In summer ascends to 3,400 m, in winter comes down below 600 m. In winter shelters in snow, marmot burrows, etc. Weighs up to 3.5 kg. In summer grey-brown, in winter pure white. Between May and August female gives birth to 2—5 young with open eyes, suckles them about 3 weeks. Life span 8—13 years. In Europe protected.

7 Common or **European Hare** *Lepus europaeus*. In Europe distributed over cultivated grasslands, other races inhabit large areas of Asia and Africa. In Alps up to 3,000 m. Also lives in forests. Weighs up to 8 kg. Between February or March and September female produces 3—5 litters of 2—7 young with open eyes. Suckles them only 2—3 weeks. Active after dusk and at night. Hides in bushes during day. Herbivorous. In some regions important as game.

6

7

Order: **Hares and Rabbits**—Lagomorpha

1 European Wild Rabbit *Oryctolagus cuniculus.*
Originally from west of Mediterranean region.
Since Middle Ages introduced into other parts
of Europe; now relatively abundant everywhere.
In mountains seldom found above 600 m. Inhabits open woods, parks, etc. Weighs up to 2 kg.
(rarely 3 kg). Digs burrows. Between March and
September female produces 3—6 litters of
5—12 or even 15 blind young which open eyes
at 10 days, are suckled 4 weeks and attain adulthood at 6—8 months. Life span 10 years. Forms
colonies (warrens). Hunted for flesh. Can become pest. Ancestor of domestic rabbits.

Order: **Rodents**—Rodentia

Family: **Squirrels**—Sciuridae

2 Red Squirrel *Sciurus vulgaris.* Distributed
over whole of Europe, extends across Asia as
far as Japan. Forest-dweller, occurs in mountains up to limit of tree belt. Builds large spherical nest from twigs, leaves, moss and hairs, in
trees; also uses deserted birds' nests and tree
hollows. From January to August female produces 2—5 litters of 3—7 blind young. Lives on
tree seeds, fruits, mushrooms, insects, birds'
eggs and young; also gnaws shoots. In August
lays in stocks of food under moss. It does not
hibernate.

3 European Ground Squirrel *Citellus citellus*. Inhabits eastern part of central Europe as far as China. Does not live in western Europe. Steppe-dweller. Occurs on grassy slopes up to altitude of 700 m. Digs burrow 1—4 m deep and up to 7 m long. Female gives birth to 6—11 young which open eyes at about 4 weeks. Lives on grass, fruit and insects. Hibernates in burrow from October to April. Does not lay in food stocks.

4 European Alpine Marmot *Marmota marmota*. Inhabits Alps, Carpathians and mountains in Asia. Frequents rocky slopes at 800—3,000 m. Digs burrows 1.5—3 m deep and up to 10 m long, with several entrances. Lives in colonies. For winter digs special burrow and blocks entrances. Hibernates from end of September until April. Builds up body fat deposits in autumn. Female gives birth to 2—6 blind young which open eyes at 20 days. Active both during day and at night. Very cautious, utters warning whistles. Lives on grass, seeds, berries, insects. Does not store food. Life span up to 18 years.

Family: **Dormice** —*Gliridae*

5 Fat Dormouse *Glis glis*. Distributed from north of Spain across central Europe to Asia Minor. Inhabits deciduous woods at altitudes of up to 1,500 m. Common in orchards and parks, frequents also buildings. Length up to 19 cm. Between June and August female gives birth to 2—9 blind young which open eyes at 20 days. Nocturnal animal, lives on buds, shoots, seeds, fruit, insects and occasionally young birds. Hibernates from end of August until May. Makes moss-lined nest in hollows or nesting-boxes.

6 Garden Dormouse *Eliomys quercinus*. Distributed from Portugal across central Europe to Urals, in south to North Africa. Mainly inhabits conifer woods with undergrowth, but also parks. Builds spherical nest in rock crevices, tree hollows, etc. Litter comprises 2—8 young which open eyes at 18 days. Nocturnal animal, excellent climber. Lives on shoots, berries, fruit and insects. In autumn enters human dwellings. Hibernates in hollows, nesting-boxes, squirrels' nests and attics, from September to April.

7 Common Dormouse *Muscardinus avellanarius*. Distributed in Europe as far as central Sweden, part of England, in south to Italy. Absent in Spain. In mountains up to 2,000 m. Inhabits dense thickets, especially young undergrowth. Sometimes found in gardens. In summer builds spherical nest up to 12 cm across with side entrance, usually 1—1.5 m, but sometimes 20 m, above ground. Lives on seeds, berries, buds and insects. Hibernates from October to end of March in tree hollows, cleft rocks or under pile of leaves. Body temperature drops to 1°C. Litter comprises 3—9 young which open eyes at 16 days.

6

5

7

Family: **Old World Rats and Mice**—Muridae

1 House Mouse *Mus musculus*. Distributed over whole of Europe, originally from Asian, North-African and Mediterranean steppes. In Alps at up to 2,700 m. Lives in dwellings, outbuildings, woodpiles, etc. Good climber. Makes nest in holes, skirting-boards, walls, etc. Female produces litters of 4—8 (occasionally up to 12) blind, hairless young several times a year. Young open eyes at 12—14 days, become mature at 6—7 weeks. Life span about 1.5 years, in captivity up to 4 years. Does not hibernate. Lives on waste matter, seeds, etc. In large numbers does damage to food stocks.

2 Harvest Mouse *Micromys minutus*. Distributed in Europe, in east to south-eastern Asia, but not very abundant. Lives on margins of forests, in reed beds beside ponds, in oat- and other fields. Builds spherical nest with side entrance between stalks, 40—80 cm above ground. Female produces 2—3 litters of 3—12 blind young a year. Young open eyes at 7 days. Also builds sleeping nest with two entrances. In winter visits barns, outbuildings, etc. Climbs and swims very well. Active mainly at night. Lives on seeds and insects. Non-hibernator. Life span 4 years.

3 Long-tailed Field Mouse *Apodemus sylvaticus*. Distributed over whole of Europe, in north to Iceland, in south to Crete. Very abundant. In Alps up to 2,500 m. Inhabits dry conifer and mixed woods, thickets and fields, in winter ap-pears in houses, but only on ground floor. Nesting burrow has 2—3 entrances. Female produces up to 4 litters of 2—9 young a year. Young open eyes at 12 days. Climbs well and can jump distances of up to 80 cm. Can also swim. Nocturnal animal. Non-hibernator. Lives on seeds, roots, shoots, insects. Maximum life span 6 years, average 1.5 years.

4 Black Rat *Rattus rattus*. Originally from tropical belt of Old World, spread by ships all over globe. European incidence now localized (usually near large rivers, in harbours and towns). Frequents attics and storehouses. Climbs and jumps well. Female produces up to 6 litters of 4—15 (rarely 20) naked and blind young a year. Grow coat in 7 days, open eyes at 13—16 days. Lives mainly on vegetable matter and household scraps. Non-hibernator. Life span up to 7 years.

5 Brown or **Norway Rat** *Rattus norvegicus*. Originally from north-eastern Asia, has been carried all over globe. Very common in whole of Europe. Important pest, carrier of many diseases. In mountains up to 1,600 m. Frequents places with water, canals, sewers, rubbish dumps, etc. Via waste pipes enters cowsheds, cellars and buildings, mainly in winter. Lives in groups. Builds nest in burrows. Digs well and can swim and dive. Female produces 2—7 litters of 6—9 (or even 22) young a year. Young open eyes at 13—17 days. Non-hibernator. Omnivorous. Also attacks small vertebrates. Life span 4 years.

Family: **Hamsters**—Cricetidae

6 Common Hamster *Cricetus cricetus*. Distributed from France across central Europe as far as Yenisei river. Inhabits cultivated lowland steppes. Digs burrows (30—60 cm deep in summer, over 2 m in winter) with several exits, nest chamber and storeroom. Female produces 2—3 litters of 6—18 young a year. Young open eyes at 14 days. Nocturnal animal. Hibernates from October to March, body temperature falls to 4°C. Wakes every 5 days and eats from stocks, which can weigh up to 15 kg. Omnivorous. Eats plants, seeds, invertebrates and small vertebrates. Carries food to burrow in facial pouches.

Family: **Voles**—Microtidae

1 Musk Rat *Ondatra zibethica*. Originally from North America. Introduced into Europe near Prague in 1905, has spread over whole of Europe, advancing 25 km a year. Lives in lakes, ponds, pools and rivers, in mountains up to 1,000 m. Digs burrow about 1 m deep in bank with one or more entrances. In large numbers can do considerable damage to earthworks. Builds winter structures 1 m high and 2 m in diameter over water, from rushes and sedge. Female produces up to 4 litters of 5—14 young a year. Young open eyes at 11 days and leave nest at 3 weeks. Good swimmer and diver. Active mainly at night and in morning. Non-hibernator. Lives on aquatic plants, molluscs, occasionally fish. Life span about 5 years.

2 Bank Vole *Clethrionomys glareolus*. Distributed over whole of Europe except south, Asia as far as Yenisei river. Similar form in North America. In Alps up to 2,200 m. Abundant. Lives on outskirts of forests, in bushes, etc. Ground-dweller. Builds spherical nest from grass, moss, etc. in bushes, up to 1 m above ground, otherwise underground. Female produces 3—4 litters of 3—8 young a year. Young open eyes at 9 days. Climbs well and can jump. Non-hibernator. Lays in food stocks, e.g. seeds, covers them with leaves. Lives mainly on vegetable matter, occasionally insects. Life span 1.5—2.5 years.

3 Common Vole *Microtus arvalis*. Distributed in Europe except England and Scandinavia, in east as far as China. Inhabits cultivated steppes, fields, dry meadows and open woods. Often occurs in large colonies. Digs branching passages in surface soil and nest chamber at depth of about 0.5 m. In winter tunnels under snow. Female produces up to 12 litters of 3—13 young a year. Young open eyes at 8—10 days. Active mainly at night. Non-hibernator. Lives on grass, shoots and field crops. Life span 1.5—4 years. Important pest.

Family: **Beavers**—Castoridae

4 European Beaver *Castor fiber*. Once inhabited whole of Europe, now almost completely exterminated. Today found in only a few parts of Europe, mainly in north and east. Extends east as far as Mongolia. Lives beside stagnant and slow-flowing water. Digs burrows in bank, with shaft leading below water level. Also builds 'lodges' 2—3 m high on water. Lodges are made of branches and small trunks which beaver fells by gnawing and drags to building site. Builds dams across flowing water, from branches, grass, etc. Couples live in colonies. Very good swimmer and diver. At end of April female gives birth to 2—7 fur-coated young with open eyes, suckles them about 8 weeks. Nocturnal animal. Not true hibernator. Lives on plants and tree shoots. Lays in winter stocks, e.g. willow branches, etc., under water. Life span up to over 30 years. Very valuable fur.

Family: **Nutrias**—Myocastoridae

5 Nutria or **Swamp Beaver** *Myocastor coypus.* Comes from South America. Bred in Europe on farms. Now also found wild there (descendants of escapees). Weighs up to 8 kg, sometimes more. Spends much time in water. Digs burrows in bank, 6 m long and 3 m deep. Also builds nest in waterside shrubs. Excellent swimmer but poor diver. Female produces 2—3 litters of 4—7 open-eyed young a year, suckles them 8 weeks, but young start to take solids after only 10 days. Lives on grass and aquatic plants. Active after dusk and during day. Non-hibernator.

Order: **Beasts of Prey**—Carnivora

Family: **Cats**—Felidae

1 Common Wild Cat *Felis silvestris.* Distributed in Europe, Near East, central Asia, North Africa. Lives only in deep forests, chiefly in mountains. Shelters in tree hollows, old badger sets, etc. Female gives birth in shelter to 3—7 blind young, which open eyes at 9—11 days. Suckles them 4 months, but at 6 weeks young can already take hunted food. Cat has clearly demarcated 'preserve', but in mating season or times of food-shortage roams up to 100 km. afield. Except for mating season lives singly. Does not hibernate. Active at night. Catches small vertebrates and insects. One of its subspecies may be ancestor of domestic tabby cat.

2 Northern Lynx *Lynx lynx.* Distributed over eastern and northern Europe and Balkan mountains. In central Europe still abundant in Czechoslovakia. Also occurs in French Alps. Inhabits wooded, mountainous country up to 2,500 m. Solitary animal except at mating time. Nocturnal. Hides during day in cleft rocks, hollows, etc. Weighs up to 30 kg, occasionally 45 kg. Excellent vision and hearing. Climbs well, runs swiftly. In May female gives birth to 2—3 (rarely up to 5) spotted young which open eyes at 16 days and are suckled 2 months. Life span up to 17 years. At night catches mammals up to size of roe deer and birds (chiefly game birds). Lies in wait for prey and pounces on it.

Family: **Dog Tribe**—Canidae

3 Wolf *Canis lupus.* Once inhabited whole of Europe, but was practically exterminated. Still to be seen in north-eastern Europe. In central Europe quite common in Czechoslovakia and Poland. Occurs at altitudes of up to 2,500 m. Lives in large forests and shrub-grown steppes. In spring and summer lives in families, in autumn forms large packs. Weighs up to 50 kg (in rare cases 70 kg). Gestation period 60—65 days. In April or May female gives birth to 4—8 blind young which open eyes at 10 days. Nocturnal animal. Travels long distances (up to 70 km) in search of prey, catches it by 'round-up' system.

Can run up to 160 km during night. Pack takes on large domestic animals, gives man wide berth. Eats different vertebrates, insects, molluscs and even fruit. Perhaps only ancestor of domesticated dogs.

4 Red Fox *Vulpes vulpes*. Commonest European member of this family, also occurs in Asia and North America. In Alps up to 3,000 m. Inhabits forests, game preserves, large parks, etc. 'Snoops' round human communities and steals small livestock. Digs 'earth' with several exits. Sometimes occupies it together with badger. Gestation period 51—54 days. Between February and May female gives birth to 4—12 blind young which open eyes at 12—15 days. Eats voles, other small mammals, birds, insects and molluscs, but also forest fruits. Life span 10—12 years. Useful animal rather than nuisance, unless too numerous.

Family: **Mustelids**—Mustelidae

5 Common Otter *Lutra lutra*. Originally common in whole of Europe, Asia and North Africa, but exterminated in many parts of central Europe. Inhabits stagnant and flowing water with unregulated banks. Adapted for aquatic existence. Excavates lair in banks, or uses various types of hollows. Lair has entrance 50 cm below surface and 1 or 2 ventilation shafts. Swims and dives extremely well, can stay under water 6—8 minutes. Gestation period 61—63 days. Female gives birth to 2—6 young which do not open eyes for 4 weeks. Eats mainly fish, also crustaceans, amphibians, etc. Life span 10—18 years. Valuable for fur. In central Europe protected.

Family: **Mustelids**—Mustelidae

1 Pine Marten *Martes martes*. Distributed over practically whole of Europe, in east as far as Asia Minor. Forest-dweller. Climbs trees extremely well and leaps from tree to tree over distances of up to 3.5 m. Makes lair in tree hollows, deserted birds' and squirrels' nests and sometimes owls' nests. Female gives birth to 2—7 young which do not open eyes for 34 days. Catches small mammals (especially squirrels), birds and insects; in autumn also eats fruits and berries. Life span 8—14 years.

2 Stone or **Beech Marten** *Martes foina*. Distributed over whole of Europe except British Isles and Scandinavia, in east across Asia to Himalayas and Mongolia. In Alps up to 2,000 m. Fairly common. Frequents vicinity of human dwellings and often settles in attics, even in towns. Makes grass lair under roofs, in ruins, in cleft rocks and often in hole in ground. In spring female gives birth to 3—7 young which open eyes at 34 days. Suckles them 3 months, but young can already take solids at 6 weeks. Active at night. Catches birds, steals poultry and eggs, also likes fruit, e.g. plums.

3 Common Stoat or **Ermine** *Mustela erminea*. Distributed in Europe; southern limits Pyrenees, Alps and Carpathians. In Alps up to 3,000 m. Found in both dry and damp environments, in steppes and woods or in gardens near dwellings. Mostly red-brown in summer, white with black-tipped tail in winter. Makes lair in holes in ground, in walls, under outbuilding floors, etc. In April or May female gives birth to 3—7 young which do not open eyes for 40 days. Climbs well and can swim. Lives on small rodents and birds, occasionally eats invertebrates and fruit. Life span 5—10 years.

4 Weasel *Mustela nivalis*. Distributed over whole of Europe except Ireland, North Africa, northern and temperate parts of Asia. In Alps up to 2,700 m. Commonest member of this family. Very slim, can slip through narrow holes, e.g. of ground squirrels and rats, etc. Inhabits forests, hedges, parks and gardens. In winter approaches dwellings and shelters in cowsheds, barns, haystacks, cellars, etc. Female gives birth to 3—7 (rarely up to 12) young which open eyes at 21—25 days. Suckles them 6—7 weeks. Very useful animal; catches mice, voles, young rats and ground squirrels. Occasionally also eats invertebrates. Life span 4—7 years.

5 European Polecat *Mustela putorius*. Distributed over practically whole of Europe, temperate parts of Asia, Morocco. Lives in woods and fields, but also frequents dwellings. In winter shelters in barns, sheds, etc. Makes lair in rabbit burrows, tree hollows or pipes. Locally abundant. Mainly terrestrial; does not like climbing, but swims well and can dive. In April or May female gives birth to 3—11 white-coated young which open eyes at 30—37 days. Nocturnal animal. Eats small mammals, birds and their eggs, invades chicken-roosts, steals eggs and bites hens.

6 Ferret *Mustela furo.* Domesticated form of polecat, used for catching wild rabbits. Can be crossed with polecat. Has similar colouring, from pure white to dark. When ferret is placed in rabbit burrow, rabbits rush out and are snared in nets. Easily tamed if caught young.

7 Common Badger *Meles meles.* Distributed in Europe and temperate parts of Asia. In Alps up to 2,000 m. Mainly inhabits woods, also shrub-strewn hillsides and sometimes town parks. Digs 'set' composed of chamber, several passages and ventilating shafts. Likes warm, dry places. Female gives birth to 2—6 blind young which open eyes at 3—4 weeks. Nocturnal animal. Not genuine hibernator, wakes up every few days. Omnivorous, eats anything from insects to small vertebrates and forest fruits. Life span 10—15 years.

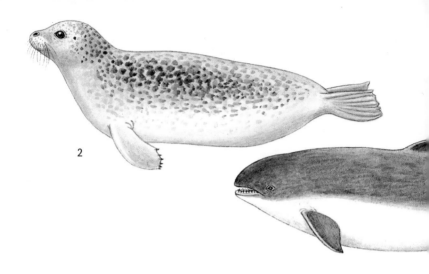

2

Family: **Bears**—Ursidae

1 Brown Bear *Ursus arctos.* Several races, from Europe to Asia and North America. Rare in central Europe. In recent years has multiplied in Czechoslovakia and neighbouring Poland. Inhabits wooded, mountainous regions. Found at altitudes of up to 2,600 m. Makes lair in hole in ground, under uprooted tree or in cave. Males larger than females; in Europe weigh up to 350 kg. Female gives birth to 2—5 very small, blind young which open eyes at 4—5 weeks. Littering period December to February. During this time female lies in den, not eating, and warms young by holding them close to body with paws. In spring, at 4 months, young follow mother and remain with her 2 years. Long winter sleep (November to March), but not true hibernation as body temperature does not fall. Life span 35—60 years. Omnivorous, eats practically anything — insects, worms, reptiles, birds, mammals up to size of deer. In times of shortage attacks sheep or even cows. Catches fish and has weakness for honey. In autumn eats forest fruits, berries, etc.

Order: **Pinnipeds**—Pinnipedia

2 Harbour or **Hair Seal** *Phoca vitulina.* Distributed in coastal waters of North Atlantic and North Pacific. Strays up rivers, e.g. up to 700 km inland up Elbe. Occasionally seen in western Baltic. Gregarious, lives in herds. Diurnal animal. Males weigh up to 150 kg. Gestation period about 340 days. At beginning of June or in July female gives birth to 1—2 young weighing 10—15 kg and measuring 90 cm. Suckles them 4—6 weeks. When weaned, young live 6 weeks on shrimps. Can dive as soon as they are born. Adult at 3—4 years. Can stay under water 5—6 minutes, in exceptional cases up to 15 minutes. Sleeps under water, floats up to surface with closed eyes for air. Swims at about 17 km an hour (at 35 km when hunting). Lives mainly on fish. Life span up to 30 years.

Order: **Whales**—Cetacea

3 Common Porpoise *Phocaena phocaena.* Distributed in North Sea, Baltic, Mediterranean, Black Sea, Atlantic and North Pacific. Still fairly common off coasts of Europe, especially Germany. Often swims inland up rivers, e.g. Rhine, Elbe, Thames, etc. Consorts in small groups. Gestation period 10—11 months. Female gives birth to one young weighing 6—8 kg. Adult weighs up to 80 kg. Huge appetite. Lives on fish such as herrings, mackerels and salmon. Unpopular with fishermen as often tears nets when caught in them. Its flesh is edible.

3

4 Bottlenose Dolphin *Tursiops truncatus*. Distributed in Baltic, North Sea, Mediterranean, Black Sea and Atlantic. Length 2.5—3 m. Has long jaws. Gregarious, communities often large. Female gives birth to single young late in summer, suckles it very long. Swims extremely well, up to 35 km an hour. Predacious animal. Both jaws armed with strong teeth. Lives mainly on fish frequenting upper layers of sea. Also eats octopus, squid, sea snails and other marine animals. In places where there are few fish often does great damage and is mercilessly destroyed by fishermen. Males fight each other at mating time. Bottlenose likes to leap out of water while swimming.

1

Order: **Even-toed Ungulates**—Artiodactyla

Family: **Pigs**—Suidae

1 Wild Boar *Sus scrofa.* Widespread in Europe, Asia and North Africa. Inhabits forests with undergrowth. Lives in families and herds, but old boars are solitary. Hides in thickets during day, comes out to feed at night. Gestation period 16—20 weeks. Sow gives birth to 3—12 striped young in bed of moss and grass. Young attain adulthood at 5—6 years. Life span 10—12 years. Omnivorous, but prefers berries, fruit, roots, grass, etc. Roots in soil for worms, insects and small vertebrates. In large numbers can severely damage potato and sugar beet crops, etc. Boar weighs up to over 200 kg. Game animal. Excellent flesh. Ancestor of domesticated pigs.

Family: **Deer**—Cervidae

2 Common Fallow Deer *Dama dama.* Originally inhabited Mediterranean region and Asia Minor. Brought to Europe in 10th and 11th century and bred for hunting. Later escaped from preserves and today, in some parts of Europe, is found in large forests. Lives in small herds or singly. Occurs chiefly in lowlands, but also in uplands. Males have palmated antlers. Weight of male up to 125 kg, female 50 kg. Rutting (mating) season from middle of October to November. Gestation period about 230 days. In June or July doe gives birth to one (occasionally 2—3) young. Nocturnal animal. Lives on grass, field crops, acorns, bark, shoots, etc. Game animal. Life span 20—25 years.

3 Red Deer *Cervus elaphus.* Several subspecies distributed in Europe, Asia, North Africa and North America. Inhabits both plains and mountains. Found in Alps at altitudes of up to 2,000 m. Forms herds of about 6—12 animals (rarely up to 80) led by old female (hind). These herds contain hinds and calves. Except at rutting time, old males (harts) live alone or combine in small herds led by strongest. Hide during day, come out at night to feed in clearings, at forest margins, in meadows and fields. Keep within fixed limits and use regular tracks. In rutting season (September—October) males separate and strongest wage battles for herd of hinds. Gestation period 231—238 days. Hind gives birth to one (occasionally 2) young which joins herd with mother on 8th day. Hart weighs up to 225 kg, hind 120 kg. Game animal. Antlers are prized trophy.

4 Sika Deer *Cervus nippon.* Originally native of nothern China and Japan. Imported and bred in Europe in preserves, now found there even wild. European animals mostly outcome of crossing of several races. Lives in plains and hills. Spotted during summer. Male weighs up to 55 kg, female 45 kg. Few tines on antlers. Rutting season October—November. One or two young born in June. Life span about 20 years. Same diet as other deer; grass, field crops, shoots, acorns, bark, twigs, etc.

5 Roe Deer *Capreolus capreolus.* Distributed over most of Europe and large part of Asia. In Alps up to 2,400 m. Inhabits forests with undergrowth, copses, meadows with bushes, etc. Lives within specific limits. In summer occurs singly or in small groups, in winter in large herds led by old dams. Except for rutting time, males lead solitary existence, however. Weight 15—30 kg. Primary rutting season July to beginning of September, secondary season November and December. Longer gestation period after summer fertilization. Female gives birth to 1—3 young in May or June. Lives on grass, shoots, forest fruits, etc. Life span 10—17 years. Important game animal.

Family: **Deer**—Cervidae

1 Elk *Alces alces*. Distributed in northern Europe, Asia and North America. Not resident in central Europe, but seen there many times in recent years (from Poland). Lives in large, dank forests, swampy scrublands, beside lakes and pools, etc. In summer lives alone or in families. In winter forms herds of 10—15 animals, but without old males. One of largest European animals. Weighs up to 600 kg. Male has huge, palmated antlers. Rutting season end August to October. Gestation period 35—38 weeks. At end of April or beginning of May female gives birth to 1—2 (seldom 3) young which accompany her after 3—4 days. Grazes towards evening and early in morning. Lives on shoots, aquatic plants (gathered standing in water), twigs, etc. Life span 20—25 years. Game animal, but protected in central Europe.

Family: **Hollow-horned Ruminants**—Bovidae

2 Chamois *Rupicapra rupicapra*. Inhabits high European mountains, extends east to Caucasus. In some places brought down to lower altitudes. Found in Alps up to 3,000 m. In summer ascends to snowline, in winter comes down to lower altitudes. Lives on steep, rocky slopes with little vegetation. Climbs nimbly and can leap 8 m. Except for old males lives in herds, usually led by female. If startled, utters warning whistle. Male weighs up to 60 kg, female 40 kg. Horns curved at tip, thicker in males than in females. In rutting season (October—December) males wage fierce duels. In April or June female gives birth to one (rarely 2 or 3) young which remains with mother 2 years. Diurnal animal. Grazes on grass, leaves, shoots, etc. Life span 15—20 years.

3 Ibex *Capra ibex*. Distributed in high parts of Pyrenees, Alps, Caucasus and central Asia. In Alps above forest belt. Even in winter usually remains at altitude of 2,300—3,200 m. Herd consists of females, young and young males. Except at rutting time, adult males live in separate communities of up to 30 animals, old males singly. Males weigh up to 110 kg, females 50 kg. Rutting season from middle of December to beginning of January. Gestation period 22—23 weeks. At end of May or beginning of June female gives birth to one (rarely 2) young which follows her only a few hours after birth. Ibex leaps and climbs extremely well. Lives on mountain plants, leaves, lichen, etc. Life span up to 30 years.

4 Mouflon *Ovis musimon*. Originally native of Sardinia, Corsica and Cyprus. Introduced into many parts of central Europe. Inhabits dry, rocky places in wooded uplands and hills. Lives in herds of usually 10—20 animals, in winter over 30. Found mainly in deciduous and mixed woods. Old rams in separate troupes, very old rams solitary. Male weighs up to 50 kg. Rutting season October—December. Gestation period 21—22 weeks. Between end of March and beginning of May ewe gives birth to one (seldom 2) young. Primarily nocturnal animal, rarely ac-

1

tive in daytime. Lives on various grass, leaves, shoots, etc. Life span 20 years.

5 European Bison or **Wisent** *Bison bonasus.* Wild European stock exterminated at end of 18th century. Now bred in a few national parks and zoos. Caucasian race completely extinct. Frequents mixed forests with dense undergrowth. In summer prefers damp localities, forest meadows and peat-bogs, in winter drier places. Lives in herds of 6—40 animals led by old cows. Only very old bulls are solitary. Male weighs up to 1,800 kg. Rutting season August and September. Gestation period 40—41 weeks. In May or June cow gives birth to usually one calf (occasionally 2). Both diurnal and nocturnal animal. Grazes mainly in evening and morning. Lives on leaves of bushes and trees, twigs, grass, bark, etc. Life span 30—40 years.

INDEX OF ILLUSTRATED SPECIES
Plants

485

Animals